THE MYSTERIOUS WARNING

Frontispiece to the 1796 edition

Gothic Classics

THE
MYSTERIOUS WARNING,

A GERMAN TALE.

FOUR VOLUMES IN ONE.

Eliza Parsons

Edited with a new introduction and notes by
Karen Morton

"Thus conscience
Can make cowards of us all."

Kansas City:
VALANCOURT BOOKS
2008

The *Mysterious Warning* by Eliza Parsons
First published by William Lane in 1796
First Valancourt Books edition, February 2008

Library of Congress Cataloging-in-Publication Data

Parsons, Mrs. (Eliza), d. 1811.
The mysterious warning : a German tale: four volumes in one /
Eliza Parsons ; edited with a new introduction and notes by Karen
Morton. – 1st Valancourt Books ed.
p. cm. – (Gothic Classics)
Originally published: London : William Lane, 1796.
ISBN 1-934555-34-7 (alk. paper)
I. Title. II. Morton, Karen, 1958-
PR5127.P15 M97 2008
823'.6–dc22
2007048490

Published by Valancourt Books
Kansas City, Missouri
http://www.valancourtbooks.com

Composition by James D. Jenkins
Set in Dante MT

10 9 8 7 6 5 4 3 2 1

CONTENTS

For my father and in memory of my mother

INTRODUCTION

WHEN Isabella Thorpe, in Jane Austen's *Northanger Abbey*, informs her friend Catherine Morland that she really must read "horrid" novels, seven of whose titles she lists, she gives no authors' names, and indeed for decades afterwards, scholars assumed Austen had invented them, until one by one they were rediscovered. Their writers are largely forgotten, so it is intriguing for modern readers to learn that two of the novels were written by the same hand, suggesting a popularity long gone. Eliza Parsons is represented in the list by her 1793 text, *Castle of Wolfenbach*, and by this one, *The Mysterious Warning*, first published in 1796.

That Austen allocates two of the seven places on the list to Eliza Parsons is notable, not only for the assumed successful status of a writer we no longer remember, but also because she would seem from this choice to have been the creator of particularly "horrid" works. In fact, the truth may be much simpler:—both the novels are subtitled "German" tales, and this, of course, would render them extremely horrid to the sensation-hungry Isabella—and, perhaps, to Jane Austen, searching for titles suggestive of particularly excessive content.

Eliza Parsons's nineteen novels are all to some extent Gothic-tinged, but none so explicitly as the two *Northanger* texts. The style of her other writing differs from them in a number of significant ways: perhaps the most important of which is that the remainder of her works lack the explained supernatural so expertly manipulated in these two novels. The quality of playfulness is always present in her works, however, as though she recognises that she must follow the trend if she wants her books to sell, whilst disapproving rather of the genre in which she has elected to write. She therefore twists, reviews, and ultimately deconstructs various elements of the Gothic mode in a number of her novels.

The 1790s, when both these titles were published, was the heyday of the Gothic. It was represented in novels, plays, poetry, and art, and many writers clamoured to get on the bandwagon, publishing formulaic works of ever increasing excess. The characteristics of the mode generally included tyrant lords, crumbling castles, terrorised heroines, subterranean chases and heroic saviours. The German form featured the abduction of young women by bandits into sublime scenery. Morals were tested, ruin was threatened to maidens' virtue and fortune, and the emotions of young female readers were stimulated by the notion of so much running around in dark tunnels and mountainous landscapes. Readers who craved sensation were well satisfied; sensibility was interrogated and challenged, with depictions of fainting, shrieking heroines driven practically senseless by threats and displays of masculine passion.

Into such a highly-charged milieu came Eliza Parsons, driven at 50 years of age by the death of her husband and the consequent necessity to feed and clothe eight children alone, to find a means of making money which would accord with her status as a well-connected, well-educated and previously wealthy member of society, whose position, despite her sudden widowhood, would hardly have allowed her to take in washing. She had already, with the support of the wife of the Lord Chamberlain, taken up a position as seamstress in St. James's Palace in 1795 due to the failure of Mr. Parsons's business. She retained this position until her death: it was not, after all, her decision, but the king's, that she should continue in the post, but it brought in only £40 per year, and even this paltry sum was paid nearly two years in arrears. Her husband had been given a place as clerk in the same palace, but had the first of two strokes not long after. He died as a result of the second one in 1789. Now Eliza Parsons needed a secure source of income, which writing would provide, so long as she chose a popular form. The novel fit the bill effectively, and she began by publishing by subscription a novel of contemporary wit, *The History of Miss Meredith*, in 1790 with Thomas Hookham. The list of subscribers' names was almost five hundred strong, and included those of the Prince of Wales and Horace Walpole. She wrote more examples of this style of novel throughout her seventeen-year career, as well as a play of manners, but as the 1790s progressed, she must, like everyone else, have been struck by the eruption of Gothic texts with which the circulating libraries were bulging, and her next target became the publication of a popular Gothic novel. In 1793, she succeeded markedly with *Castle of Wolfenbach*, and after the publication of a number of other novels between, *The Mysterious Warning* followed in 1796.

This novel is prefaced by a "Card," addressed to readers who might be concerned about the moral pitfalls of reading a frivolous, perhaps scandalous, Gothic text. In particular, Eliza Parsons directs her comments to parents. She, too, she informs them, is a parent, and she understands their concerns about the dubious morality of reading a Gothic novel. They need not fear, however, since she has

> never dictated one page, or suggested one idea inimical to the precepts of virtue, or that should suffuse the cheek of innocence with a blush.

She concludes that her merit resides in this factor alone. It is her only claim, and she ends by throwing herself "on the mercy of liberal and candid minds."

While this sentiment has a charmingly virtuous air, more lurks in the preface than her frequent protestations of "deficiency in talents." Hidden among the pleas for indulgence is a critique of the form in which she is writing. She tells us she has been accused of dwelling on horror and admits that her own melancholy may colour her writing, claiming an incapacity to divert her readers, but she goes on to defend her supposed lack of sparkle.

> Dulness [sic] is a defect of the head, and is pardonable.—Wit, and spirited talents, are too often apt to run riot; their redundancy may sometimes draw vicious characters, and describe profligacy of manners in such seducing glowing colours, as to affect the imagination, to catch the attention of young people, into whose hands works of this kind frequently fall, and may have the dangerous tendency to lessen the horror they ought to feel at vice, and the detestation such characters should inspire.

A number of layers are present here. First of all, she is distancing herself from hack writers of the Gothic who serve up the mixture-as-before to readers of little discernment, and at first sight it appears as though she is sabotaging her own attempt to sell the novel, but this is a clever piece of psychology. Worried parents will be reassured that she, like them, is concerned about the danger of reading Gothic literature, particularly its capacity to blur the moral boundaries in young minds, and will doubtless approve her endeavour to redress the balance. However, there is another layer of information. Readers of the Gothic have not chosen the book for its cheerfulness. Horror is what they seek, and this preface seems to be promising an abundance of it. She subliminally implies that young people will want to read this book and makes it clear that she is one of the writers of "works of this kind." Young thrill-seekers see the words "seducing," "horror," and "vice" and cannot wait to delve inside the covers. Their parents read about "virtue," "innocence," and "common sense" and are reassured. Both parties are satisfied and Eliza Parsons has achieved another publishing success.

Another element facilitating her aim to achieve both respectability and notoriety at one and the same time is her dedication of the novel to Caroline of Brunswick, Princess of Wales. She displays her pride at being permitted to dedicate—not all novelists did so with the knowledge and consent of their dedicatee—stating that she acknowledges

> with equal pride and gratitude, the lively sense I entertain of the distinguished honour conferred upon me, in being permitted to inscribe the following Work to your Royal Highness

though not daring to hope the princess will derive much amusement from it. Once again, a skilled writer hides her ability to influence her reader under a declaration of humility. The only capitalised words within this dedication are concerned with the princess's Charm, Station and High Birth, and later the same treatment is accorded the Readers. What stands out in particular is the capitalisation of Work. Clearly, the writer has a strong sense of her achievement and worth, whatever protestations she may make to the contrary.

The choice of the Princess of Wales is a shrewd one for the Gothic novelist. The "German" story is dedicated to a German princess, who might be presumed to know what to expect from a novel so subtitled. The fact that she has given permission for the dedication suggests to Eliza Parsons's readers that the writer knows what she is about and they can expect a thoroughly "horrid" read. The name of the princess between the pages of the novel conveys an implication of high status for its author, but it also adds a frisson of scandal, given the circumstances of the marriage. The Prince of Wales had met his future wife only three days before their wedding in April 1795, and had been pressured into marrying her. They separated almost immediately after the nuptials, their only child evidently conceived on the night of, or night after, the wedding. Though championed by the masses, the princess was reviled by the palace, and was frequently denounced for her adultery and indelicacy of conduct. Thus Eliza Parsons's choice of her as dedicatee for this text lends it a perfect blend of society glitter and sensational spice.

In the dedication, once again the insistent claim to respectability of the text is repeated:—

> [t]he few presumptions I have to merit are merely negative ones: I have
> never written a line tending to corrupt the heart, sully the imagination,
> or mislead the judgment of my young Readers.

She may be reassuring the wrong person here, since Caroline's daughter, Princess Charlotte Augusta, born in January 1796, had been removed from her care and given into the indifferent and negligent hands of her father. Contemporary readers were doubtless aware of this, and, as we shall see, the respectability of the text and, by association, its author, are at times wafer thin.

Eliza Parsons made her name through her respectability. Many of her reviewers repeat her own words, taken from the preface to her first novel, *The History of Miss Meredith*: that she was born to affluence but had been driven to a writing career through necessity. They often mention her strict morality, at times suggesting there is no danger in giving such a text to young readers, as it is so dull. Yet a number of circumstances in her life, some of them after the publication of this text, show her edging danger-ously close to scandal. She knew Matthew Gregory Lewis, author of the scandalous 1796 text, *The Monk*, and had dedicated her novel *The Valley of St. Gothard* (1799) to him, besides having given publishing advice to his mother, who had also been touched by disgrace after eloping from her marriage with her son's music master. She is known to have visited Mary Robinson, actress and mistress of the Prince of Wales, among many other things, on Robinson's deathbed. Eliza Parsons had herself been threatened with the King's Bench prison for non-payment of debts and had been under house arrest for two years. She had appeared before the magistrate, accused of tax misdemeanours, and had once had to abandon her home to escape debt-collectors. This inconsistency of moral integrity arises on numerous occa-sions in Eliza Parsons's life and work and complicates our reading of her. The remainder of this introduction will discuss elements of the plot of the novel, and since it will reveal a number of details, you may wish to read it afterwards.

The intriguing mix of respectability and scandal mentioned above is manifest in the text to a high degree. The hero, Ferdinand, is a man of hon-our and rectitude, who acts with kindness and displays a keen understand-ing and empathy in his dealing with others, especially those less fortunate than himself. He is heartlessly defamed by his elder brother Rhodophil, whose evil machinations have caused their father to reject Ferdinand, who had made a hasty and unsuitable marriage. Rhodophil has told their bedrid-den father, Count Renaud, that Ferdinand never visits, though in fact he does, but is always informed that Renaud does not wish to see him. In this way, Rhodophil ensures that he will be the Count's only heir. Renaud also has another child, though Eliza Parsons conceals this fact from us for some time. He had an illegitimate daughter, Charlotte, brought up by her nurse to hate Renaud, who had seduced her mother. The nurse, Dupree, is also the aunt of Ferdinand's wife Claudina. This brings in a complicated case of a rather technical form of incest. Claudina is the daughter of Charlotte's mother after her affair with Renaud was over. Thus, Ferdinand's half sister is also the half sister of his wife, and this circumstance is the reason Renaud did not want his son to marry Claudina, though Ferdinand does not dis-cover this until he has been married for some time. When he does realise, he is concerned and anxious about it. Eliza Parsons's strict moral code will not permit the marriage to continue, but since Ferdinand's close relation-ship to Claudina had been unknown to him at the time of the wedding, his happiness will ultimately prevail.

Another doomed marriage is that of Count M*** and his wife Eugenia. Her father had forced her to marry a cruel man despite her love for the Count. She had spoken the vows automatically but had not meant them. Later that night the Count had rescued her from her bridegroom and they had gone through a private marriage and had been happy together till fate caught up with them. Eugenia's response to the dreadful consequences is to blame herself for having been unfaithful to the vows she made, no matter how enforced. The critic who reviewed the novel for *The Critical Review* considers that here Eliza Parsons has been too assiduous in her moralising.

> ...Eugenia's early errors were of the most pardonable kind; and her only *real vice*, the sacrificing of her own happiness and activity, and wounding the peace of her husband, by a foolish and romantic monastic notion of heroism. (*Critical Review* 16 [1796]: 474)

Interestingly, though the reviewer deems Eugenia's retreat to a convent excessive, Eliza Parsons herself appears to find it the only acceptable way out for her. This is because, as in so many of her novels, she wants to show us what happens when a parent is unfeeling or irresponsible in the choice of marriage partner for a daughter. Whilst she rarely allows the young woman to escape entirely from a headstrong decision to rebel, she makes clear her view that a father must not impose his choice on his daughter for his own reasons. Her stern father characters are often chided for their condescension and hauteur, and though their daughters will be made to suffer for disobedience to parental will, it is clear where her sympathies lie. Just so here, when Eugenia needs to make her peace with God for disobeying her father's wishes and even the reviewer feels she is too hard on herself. All this makes for an air of reputable, ethical decency. Into such honourable company suddenly steps Charlotte. This character is one of the most remarkable of the age, worthy company for Lewis's Ambrosio and Dacre's Victoria. She is a wicked lady *par excellence*, who changes her name to Fatima and leaves her country, Austria, and her religion to live outside marriage with a Muslim in Turkey. When Heli, her paramour, takes her to live in Vienna, she quickly becomes bored and flees from the house with the thieves who have come to rob him. She plots with a male servant to commit further robberies and cross-dresses to carry them out. She bursts in and harangues Ferdinand to give up their father's fortune in her favour. Finally, she stabs her accomplice and commits suicide. Eliza Parsons is so little read now that when she is mentioned at all, it is only to say that she was poor and respectable. Yet here we have the astonishing and innovative creation of a wicked female character who predates Victoria in Charlotte Dacre's 1806 text, *Zofloya*, by ten years. She appears in the same year that Matthew Lewis publishes *The Monk*. She is a wild woman, who receives her just deserts, but there is more to her than the mere figurehead of a cautionary tale.

First of all, she allows women readers to enjoy the possibilities of rash actions. They know the rules of the popular novel: Fatima/Charlotte is bound to die, but in the meantime they can at least experience the thrill of such bad, and seemingly, such enjoyable behaviour. Charlotte has a wild time whilst she can, and possibly considers the game worth the candle. Next, Eliza Parsons makes it clear that, whilst her approach is unacceptable, something of Charlotte's application to her half brother is just. She is her father's daughter and, as such, ought properly to be entitled to a share of his estate. She ruins the effect by violently demanding all of it. Ferdinand says later that he would not have been averse to sharing it with her, had her submission to him been undertaken in a more fitting manner. That she behaves so atrociously is not Eliza Parsons failing womankind by her creation of such a negative character. Rather, it is a recognition that the law would not automatically support an illegitimate daughter's claim on her father's estate, and seems to me to be a political comment:—since no satisfaction in law can result from her request, Charlotte instead goes down fighting.

It is significant that Charlotte bears the same name as the daughter of the novel's dedicatee. Princess Charlotte Augusta was only months old by the time this novel was published, but it is tempting to suppose she is so named to serve as an example of a child from a broken family whose parents have subsequently indulged in numerous affairs and might stand as a warning of what such a child might become. Once more Eliza Parsons displays considerable dexterity in her endeavour to please everyone:—the Princess of Wales will surely recognise the character as one who has not been allowed a mother's love, whilst it was unlikely to irk her father, who had once again taken up with Mrs. Fitzherbert, whom he had privately married before his wedding with Caroline. As a past patron of Eliza Parsons, and the son of her employer at the palace, the Prince of Wales was to be placated, and she treads the line skilfully whilst still delivering a plot of no mean excitement and a satisfyingly wicked anti-heroine.

Eliza Parsons makes use of the Gothic mode in a variety of ways, reshaping it where necessary and thus becoming one of the architects of the form. One notable use she makes is of the trope of the explained supernatural. The mysterious warning of the title is uttered to Rhodophil upon his father's death, warning him not to strive for the disinheritance of his brother. At the same time, Ferdinand, whilst praying by his father's deathbed, had heard the ghostly words, "Pardon and peace," satisfying him that his father had forgiven him and was seeking reconciliation from beyond the grave. Each brother goes forward into the plot with his own supernatural message to the forefront of his mind. Rhodophil, whilst ignoring it for most of the novel, nonetheless is influenced by it when he finally renounces evil. Ferdinand is heartened by it. What is of note is the provenance of the phantom pronouncements. Rather than being the words of the deceased Count Renaud, they are those of the steward, Ernest. It is significant that Eliza Parsons finds it easier to suggest that counsel issues from a ghost than from a servant. Ferdinand, though a decent man, might not have expected a subordinate to proffer advice of his own volition, and Rhodophil would have dismissed him for his impertinence. In an act of political import, Eliza Parsons allows a servant to run the plot. His words influence the actions of the brothers, his nephew will be presented to Ferdinand as tutor to his son and he is the only recipient of secrets unknown to the rest of the characters, and to us, until the end of the novel. This is characteristic of Eliza Parsons's sense of equality, and her servants and middle-class characters are all usually more interesting than the nobility.

The arrogance and violence of Charlotte, the organisational qualities of Ernest, the evil deeds of Rhodophil, and the wilful selfishness of Claudina all serve to feminise the character of Ferdinand. He occupies the space where we normally find the Gothic heroine. He asks Ernest's advice, he cries, faints, and believes in ghosts. He is emasculated by cuckoldry, acts as carer and displays feminine sensibility. He shares a number of characteristics with Mackenzie's Man of Feeling. In a number of such ways does Eliza Parsons toy with the machinery of the Gothic, rendering her a writer of considerable importance for us.

The only modern edition of this text was as part of *The Northanger Set of Horrid Novels*, published by the Folio Press in London in 1968, edited by Devendra Varma. Basically a faulty reprint, this edition was prefaced by an introduction including a biography containing a number of errors, such, for example, as the statement that Eliza Parsons died at the age of 62. In fact, she was 71, a circumstance which strikes me of immense importance when a search of critical material usually turns up only an infrequent mention of her name followed by a reiteration of her poverty-stricken situation. Whilst it is true that she was in dire financial straits, I feel it is more to the purpose to recognise her as a successful woman, forced by circumstances to learn and become employably proficient in a new skill, reaching an advanced age for her era and having brought up, educated and found employment for a large family by means of her own labour. There are many like her whom scholars are recovering and disentangling from their accepted lowly status to be acknowledged by us as communicators of significant disclosures about the philosophies, hopes and anxieties which animated women of the late eighteenth and early nineteenth centuries.

Karen Morton
Sheffield

October 12, 2007

ABOUT THE EDITOR

Dr. Karen Morton teaches on English, History, and Education modules at Sheffield Hallam University and on various English Literature topics at the University of Sheffield's Institute for Lifelong Learning. Her special interest is in lost Gothic writers and her monograph, entitled *A Life Marketed as Fiction: An Analysis of the Life and Work of Eliza Parsons*, is forthcoming from Valancourt Books in 2008.

A NOTE ON THE TEXT

THE Valancourt Books edition follows as closely as possible the text of the first edition of 1796. Every effort has been made to be faithful to the original text in terms of spelling, punctuation, grammar, and formatting.

The original edition often employs variant spellings (e.g., "favor" and "favour") or spellings that today are archaic, but were common at the time (*e.g.*, "mattrass" or "chesnut"). The vast majority of these have been retained, as it is unlikely that twenty-first century readers will have much difficulty with such spellings as "cloyster," "negociation," "stopt," "risque," etc. Only in cases of obvious errors—that is to say, spellings that were neither acceptable in 1796 nor today—have silent corrections been made. Thus "shuned," "gaged," and "setts" have been emended to "shunned," "gagged," and "sets." Parsons (or her printer) also uses "where" in three instances where "were" is clearly intended; these too have been corrected.

Although variant spellings of words have been left untouched, spellings of names have been regularised. For example, Parsons refers to the same character at different points as "Baron S******," "Baron S***," "Baron S****—," and "Baron S——"; these have all been emended to "Baron S***" for clarity's sake. The same has been done for D'Alenberg (*alias* D'Allenberg, d'Allenberg, and d'Allemberg), Sultsbach (*alias* Sultzbach), Dunloff (also Denloff), Dupree (Dupreé), Reiberg (Rieberg), and Count M*** (Count M****).

Parsons's grammar is often problematic as well. She frequently employs run-on sentences as well as fragments, and very often has trouble with subject/verb agreement. However, although these errors may seem strange to modern readers, they pose no difficulty in comprehending the text and thus have been retained as part of the original's flavour. Similarly, where Parsons uses "run" instead of "ran" or "eat" instead of "ate" (both common usages in the eighteenth century), these usages are preserved in this edition.

Parsons's superabundance of punctuation, including parentheses, dashes, commas, colons, and semi-colons, has been preserved as in the original. However, the first edition's use of quotation marks is very slapdash and has required some emendation. Frequently the printer of the 1796 edition will include a quotation mark at the beginning or end of a paragraph where no one has been speaking; these extraneous marks have been removed. There is also a pervasive difficulty with inset quotation marks—when one character is relating what happened in the past and quotes another character.

Sometimes these are rendered with double quotation marks, and sometimes with single. Editorial restraint has been exercised wherever possible in this edition, but in some cases it was necessary to add quotation marks, or to change double quotation marks to single in order to make the text comprehensible. It should be noted that in many instances in the novel, Parsons does use quotation marks in a way that would be considered gramattical by modern standards; thus I have chosen to presume that the instances of erroneous usage are her printer's errors, not hers, and have silently corrected them accordingly.

Two more substantial corrections deserve to be singled out. In the exchange between Ferdinand and Rhodophil which occurs on page 19 of this edition, the 1796 edition runs in the paragraph that begins "I hope my dear brother..." with the preceding paragraph (Ferdinand's speech), while it is clear from the context that these lines are actually spoken by Rhodophil; thus, a paragraph break has been inserted here to remove this ambiguity. Similarly, in the paragraph that begins "At that moment dinner was announced" (on page 389 in this edition), the first edition reads:

> At this moment dinner was announced. Ernest arose: "Stop, my friend (said he) this day ends all other distinctions between us...

For this edition, "Ferdinand" has been substituted for "he" to make it clear that these lines are spoken by Ferdinand, rather than Ernest, as it reads in the original edition.

Finally, in Volume II, the first edition misnumbered Chapter VI as Chapter V; this has been corrected and the subsequent chapters renumbered accordingly.

A NOTE ON THE PUBLICATION HISTORY OF
THE MYSTERIOUS WARNING

The Mysterious Warning: A German Tale was first published at William Lane's Minerva Press in 1796, in four volumes. It was reprinted in 1824 by Simon Fisher of London, retitled *The Mysterious Warning: Including the Memoirs of the Solitary Man of the Desolated Mansion*, sold in nine sixpenny numbers (or in a bound one-volume edition for five shillings) and illustrated with ten plates. In the twentieth century, Montague Summers prepared an edition of the novel, which was to have been part of a series of limited edition reprints of the *Northanger* novels. The first two books in the series, *Horrid Mysteries* and *The Necromancer*, were issued in 1927, published by Robert Holden of London. *The Mysterious Warning* was advertised as the third in the series, but never appeared. In his *A Gothic Bibliography* (1940), Summers lists his edition as appearing in 1928, in a "limited edition"; Timothy d'Arch Smith, in his *Montague Summers: A Bibliography* (1983) states that, "The book was never published, although it reached the page proofs . . . [which] were destroyed when the publisher's flat was blitzed in World War II." In fact—and this should tell us something about Summers, in his bald-faced assertion that the book appeared in a "limited" edition—the book survives in precisely one copy, in the Special Collections of the University of Kansas Libraries. This copy bears the bookplate of Alphonsus Montague Summers and is bound without the biographical sketch of the author mentioned by Summers in *A Gothic Bibliography*; instead, a printer's proof of the introduction, on four oversized pages, is folded and tucked into a pocket inside the front board of the first volume. Both volumes are bound in green cloth, but internally are uniform with the other two *Northanger* books published by Holden. Summers's edition is titled *The Mysterious Warning: Including Memoirs of the Solitary Man of the Deserted Mansion*, and its imprint is London: Robert Holden and Co. Ltd., 1928. In addition to this rare edition, a 1968 reprint appeared, published by the Folio Press with an introduction by Devendra Varma. Varma's edition unfortunately contains a number of factual errors in its introduction and numerous textual errors, including a persistent difficulty in deciphering the long "s" in the 1796 original in such words as "fought"/"sought."

Readers will therefore rejoice at Karen Morton's excellent new edition, which corrects the errors of previous editors and makes this exciting and scarce Gothic text available again for the first time in forty years.

James D. Jenkins

THE

MYSTERIOUS WARNING,

A GERMAN TALE.

IN FOUR VOLUMES.

BY MRS. PARSONS,

AUTHOR OF

VOLUNTARY EXILE, &c.

----------- " Thus confcience
Can make cowards of us all."

VOL. II.

LONDON:

PRINTED FOR WILLIAM LANE,
AT THE
Minerva Prefs,
LEADENHALL-STREET.

M.DCC.XCVI.

Title page of the first edition (1796)

On hearing a deep & heavy groan Ferdinand
started up and eagerly gazed on the lifeless
body of his Father.

Page 12

Frontispiece to the 1824 edition

The Mysterious Warning

Volume I

TO

HER ROYAL HIGHNESS

THE PRINCESS OF WALES.

MADAM,

THAT respect, which High Birth, exalted Station, and personal Charms, exacts, is generally paid without discrimination, because they are adventitious circumstances from whence no merit can be derived to the possessor: But when added to these, we see the most brilliant accomplishments, a graciousness of manners, a condescending sweetness, that implies a wish to be distinguished more by goodness than greatness; then, indeed, we cheerfully tender the homage of our *hearts*, and feel the highest gratification when uniting admiration with respect, we love and reverence the same object.

To this voluntary homage your Royal Highness is more peculiarly entitled; the dignified features in your character are affability, and that condescension, which, from the pre-eminence of your situation, have irresistible claims upon the mind, confirms the fascination of the eye, and has insured to you, Madam, the affection of a grateful and admiring people.

The suffrage or praise of an obscure individual can be no ways interesting to your Royal Highness; happily your virtues and graces speak for themselves, and require no officious herald to blazon them to the world.

Under this conviction I repress my own feelings, and have only to acknowledge, with equal pride and gratitude, the lively sense I entertain of the distinguished honour conferred on me, in being permitted to inscribe the following Work to your Royal Highness; though I have not the presumption to hope you can derive much amusement from the perusal. The few pretensions I have to merit are merely negative ones: I have never written a line tending to corrupt the heart, sully the imagination, or mislead the judgment of my young Readers.

With the most profound respect, and every sentiment that admiration and gratitude can inspire, I have the honour to remain,

Madam,

Your Royal Highness's

Most obliged,

And most devoted,

Humble servant,

ELIZA PARSONS.

Leicester-Square, No. 22,
Nov. 15, 1795.

A CARD.

THE Author of the following Work feels herself under the necessity of apologizing to her numerous Friends, for the too frequent demands she makes on their indulgence.—Conscious of her deficiency in talents, inclination has no share in her feeble attempts to entertain the Public: She obtrudes neither from vanity or confidence, and shrinks from the severity of criticism, in the hope that her insignificance may protect her from the pointed darts of ridicule.—To wit and humour, the effervescence of a lively imagination and a happy turn of mind, she can make no pretensions; her former works have been thought to dwell too much on scenes of horror, and melancholy events; she cannot refute the charge: Perhaps her writings take their colouring from her mind;—when the heart is not at ease, it is incapable of communicating cheerful ideas to the descriptive pen; therefore she wisely declines an attempt she is unequal to, of *diverting* her Readers.

Dulness is a defect of the head, and is pardonable.—Wit, and spirited talents, are too often apt to run riot; their redundancy may sometimes draw vicious characters, and describe profligacy of manners in such seducing glowing colours, as to affect the imagination, to catch the attention of young people, into whose hands works of this kind frequently fall, and may have the dangerous tendency to lessen the horror they ought to feel at vice, and the detestation such characters should inspire.

The Author of this Work is a *Parent*; as such, she has been strictly observant that her writings should never offend against delicacy or common sense.—She has never dictated one page, or suggested one idea inimical to the precepts of virtue, or that should suffuse the cheek of innocence with a blush.—Here rests her merit; she has no other claims, and throws herself on the mercy of liberal and candid minds.

MYSTERIOUS WARNING.

CHAPTER I.

NO sooner had the struggling soul escaped from the clay-cold body of Count Renaud, than his eldest son, Count Rhodophil, hastened to the library, and opening the secret cabinet, where his late father usually deposited his papers of consequence, after a strict examination of the contents, returned to the anti-chamber, on the floor of which lay extended his brother, the deeply-afflicted Ferdinand, just recovering from a fainting fit, and overwhelmed with inexpressible anguish.

"Brother!" said Rhodophil, in an accent of grief and tenderness, "Brother! here is *my* father's will, and I have little doubt but that you will find he was your father also, and that, however severely his resentment was expressed in his life-time, he has not extended it beyond the grave, nor forgotten, in the disposal of his effects, that he had a younger son, and a grandchild."

Ferdinand, who had been lifted from the floor, turning his eyes on his brother with a look of fixed sorrow, exclaimed, "His will! Alas! what have I to do with that? He expired without seeing me, without granting me, all I ever wished for, or expected, his pardon, and his blessing! O, Rhodophil! my friend—my brother—why, why did you not urge him to pronounce me forgiven in his last moments, to revoke that curse, which now weighs me down to the earth with sorrow and remorse!"

"Did I *not* urge him," replied the Count, "Did I not supplicate him on my knees in your behalf? Did I not beseech him to consider your situation and his own? Unjust Ferdinand to reproach me—me, who have for three years wearied my father with tears, supplications and entreaties, to forgive and receive you to his paternal arms! What have I left *unsaid*, or *undone*, to convince you of my brotherly affection?"

"Pardon me," cried Ferdinand, extending his hand: "Forgive me, my dear brother, I know my inexpressible obligations to you; but grief, despair, and heart-rending retrospections, deprive me of my reason. O, my father!

to the grave, even beyond this world, hast thou carried thy hatred and reprobation of thy wretched son! How great, how good, how benevolent, how forgiving to *all*, was Count Renaud! What then must my crimes have been, in what magnitude must they have appeared to him, thus to draw down *everlasting resentment!*"

He covered his face with his hands, and throwing his head upon the bosom of his brother, wept aloud; his whole frame was convulsed, and Rhodophil was obliged to call for assistance, that he might be conveyed to a bed, where it was some hours before the extreme violence of his feelings subsided into a melancholy silent sorrow. His brother and the steward of the late Count remained with him, and when they found the turbulence of grief had a little abated, the Count again mentioned the will.

"As it may be possible some particular orders may be given respecting the funeral, and more than probable that the contents of this packet may speak peace to your wounded mind, it is necessary, my dear brother (continued he) that we break the seals."——Ferdinand bowed an assent; speech was denied him at that moment, the principal domestics being summoned to the apartment, Rhodophil broke the seals, and delivered the packet to the steward.

"Do you read it," said he; "neither my eyes or my heart will permit me to do it."—The steward obeyed. There was a schedule of his estate and effects, which in a few words Count Renaud gave to the entire possession of his dear and dutiful son Rhodophil, "a few legacies only excepted to his servants."

"How!" cried the Count, "*all*, what *all* to me! Impossible! Is there no mention made of my brother?"

"No, my Lord," replied the old man, delivering the papers with a look of sorrow; "no, I have too truly read all the contents."

Not a word escaped from the lips of Ferdinand; at that moment riches or poverty was indifferent to him, nor could the wealth of nations have given him peace or comfort, when unaccompanied with the forgiveness of a parent.

"How cruel, how unjust!" cried Rhodophil; "but he knew my heart. Yes, my dear brother," added he, embracing Ferdinand, "our father well knew that in giving *all to me*, he had procured to me the inexpressible delight of voluntarily sharing it with my brother. Henceforth (looking round on the servants) know you have *two* masters; my brother is equal with me in fortune, power, and command."

The servants bowed and withdrew, all but the faithful and affectionate Ernest, who had been upwards of twenty years steward to the late Lord, and had ever fondly loved the unhappy, reprobated, Ferdinand.—Rhodophil reiterated his caresses, and tender expressions: "We will no longer be separated (said he;) your Claudina, your little Charles, shall be equally dear to me, as to yourself."

Ferdinand started up:—"Claudina! my Claudina!" repeated he, "Well, have you reminded me, I left her oppressed with sickness and sorrow."

"Hasten to her, then," said the Count; "let her be removed to the Castle immediately; accommodated here, she will soon be restored to health."

Rhodophil withdrew; his brother taking Ernest by the hand, "My worthy old man, your looks bespeak a sympathizing soul.—You read my heart: Oh! Ernest, it is not the loss of riches I deplore, my brother's kindness will relieve me there; but a father's curse, carried beyond the grave! there, there's the wound that never can be healed. My wife, poor, poor Claudina! how shall I return to tell her the sad event, already sinking under sorrows she thinks she has deserved—in her situation too!"

"Dear master, dear Sir," cried Ernest, "I beg you to take comfort, the worst is now past, I am sure, I know my late good master forgave you in his heart, his mind never, never, harboured eternal displeasure and resentment. Things are contrary to my expectation; but—I dare not say all I think, nor will it avail now; but I beseech you, Sir, to hasten home to your poor dwelling, from whence you shall quickly return with all that is dear to you; I will prepare every thing, and then follow you."—With a heavy sigh that seemed to burst his heart-strings, a look of inexpressible grief, Ferdinand wrung his hand, and with slow and trembling steps repaired to his humble habitation in the suburbs of Baden, about a mile from the Castle of Renaud.

When his footsteps reached the threshold, he stopped, and paused: "The truth will kill her (cried he:) Sure, if ever deception was pardonable, it may be now; yet how dearly have I already paid for the violation of truth! Heaven pardon me, for I must deceive her. Alas! one deviation from rectitude is productive of innumerable errors which spring from each other, and plunge us rapidly into guilt!" He entered the house at the very moment when his unfortunate wife had given birth to a daughter. The intelligence pierced his heart: "Another burthen on the bounty of a brother!" exclaimed he, softly as he passed to the room where his Claudina lay. The sight of her instantly banished every idea, but anxiety for her safety.

He flew to her, "My love! my wife!" She fixed her feeble eyes upon him: "I am become a mother to another poor unfortunate. Ah! Ferdinand, have *you* found a *father?*" What a dagger to the heart of her husband was this question!

"*All* is well, my love," answered he, struggling to repress his emotions:

"Compose your mind, and expect happier days; the moment you can be removed without danger, we shall reside at the Castle."—She uttered a faint exclamation of joy, and fainted. Ferdinand was terrified, and blamed himself for his abrupt communication; but happily she was soon restored, and capable of rejoicing at such unhoped-for intelligence.

"You are no longer reprobated then," said she, tenderly kissing his hand, "no longer consigned to misery, and our dear infants will not endure the pinching gripe of poverty. Blessed, blessed Count! you have at length relented, and I may think existence a blessing." This apostrophe was more than the unhappy Ferdinand could bear. Unable to speak, he hastily left the room; his poor deceived wife judging what he must feel from such a (supposed) revolution in his circumstances, imagined he had withdrawn, that their mutual transports might not too much agitate her spirits; a thousand pleasing visions floated in her brain, and to have her husband restored to a father's love, to have her dear children rescued from want and misery, were such delightful considerations, that she was not sorry she could indulge them freely, and repressed her curiosity for particulars, satisfied that the event was certain.

Mean time Ferdinand sat lost in thought, and overwhelmed in wretchedness, the kindness of his brother afforded no compensation for the unalterable displeasure of his father, nor could he reconcile to himself, that determined hatred which one error (in his eyes a venial one, and not deserving such everlasting resentment) had drawn upon him, as at all consistent with the benevolence which had always formed a distinguished feature in the character of the late Count Renaud. Tormented by these painful conjectures he was found by Ernest, who came to acquaint him, that he had given orders for apartments to be instantly prepared for him and his family, and was come to wait on his Lady to the Castle.

Ferdinand, roused by the entrance of his good old friend, soon informed him of the impossibility of their immediate removal, from his wife's situation, and also of the deception he had been compelled to give into.—"She does not as yet know of my father's death (continued he;) her too susceptible heart would sink under the knowledge of what *my* sufferings must be in such circumstances; by degrees, as her strength returns, I must reveal the dreadful truth:—But, oh! my friend, I cannot live a burthen on the bounty of a brother, something I must resolve on, and if his kindness protects my wife and children, I will endeavour to support a separation from all that is dear to me, and carve out my own fortune by my sword."

Ernest had nothing to answer against this resolution but affectionate regrets, he had but too much cause to think the intention would be as necessary as it was becoming in a young man of spirit and honour; therefore he only hoped, "that his dear young master would do nothing rashly, but wait until his wife and children could have some *certain* independence secured to them."

"How! (replied Ferdinand) would you have me limit my brother's bounty, or seem to doubt his generosity and kindness? How contemptible should I appear in his eyes by a bare suggestion, by the remotest hint, that I wished for any *certainty* more than what I may rely on from his affection and generosity, so recently proved on an occasion, where not one out of a million would have conducted themselves with that nobleness of spirit, that true fraternal affection Count Rhodophil has manifested."

"I presume not, Sir," answered Ernest, respectfully, "to dictate, or even to advise *you*; but, nevertheless, as we are all mortal, subject every hour to be suddenly deprived of health and life, as we can no more answer for our own hearts than for our own lives, as it is possible Count Rhodophil may marry, and new engagements may give birth to new sentiments; all these natural occurrences *may* happen, and both for your children's sake, and for his honour, it would be better to place a circumstance, of so much consequence to your family, beyond the power of chance to injure them."

"I own (said Ferdinand, after pausing a few minutes) I own what you say is both wise and prudent; but such a proposition as relates to any settlement must originate with my brother.—No selfish proposals, no narrowness of heart, shall mark my conduct, or render me less generous than himself."

Ernest sighed, but was silent.—The other observing his dejection, added: "You know, my old friend, that Rhodophil's mother was a woman of very superior birth, with a much larger fortune than my mother could boast, who, though by no means despicable, yet owed her elevation to my father's rank, more to her beauty than hereditary claims, therefore my brother's generosity is the more estimable."

"You, Sir, are the best judge (replied the steward) and I hope you will forgive my presumption, which is directed by true affection to your interest."

"I know it well (answered Ferdinand) but now, my good Ernest, return, and acquaint my kind brother of the event, which must preclude us from removing for some time. In the evening, or to-morrow morning, you may expect me, for I have a melancholy duty to perform, from which nothing shall divert me."

The steward bowed, and was about to retire, but stepped a few paces very reluctantly; then suddenly turned—"Sir (said he) I hope you will not be offended if I presume to leave this purse; when you are settled at the Castle, you may return it." He laid the purse upon a chair, and hastened out of the house.

"Good creature! (exclaimed Ferdinand) I will not *now* mortify thee by a refusal of proffered kindness, because *now* I know I shall have it in my power to repay the money, and reward thee tenfold in thy estimation, by my attentions and marks of gratitude."—He strove to stifle his painful reflections by procuring several little necessaries and indulgencies for his Claudina, which in her situation were wanted, and which the fear of not being able to supply had tormented him for many preceding days. She received and enjoyed them with delight, as the proofs of a parent's returning affection.—In the evening, when Ferdinand was sitting by her bedside, and she observed the deep gloom that every now and then pervaded his features, in spite of all his efforts to *appear* happy. She looked at him several moments in silence, then pressing his hand: "My dearest husband (said she) from whence proceeds that sorrow which clouds your features, and seems to fill your eyes with tears? Tell me, have you deceived me into hope, or is your father's forgiveness fettered with conditions that distress your feelings? Your looks correspond not with the joyful intelligence you communicated this morning.—Tell me, I beseech you, what there is behind which is a drawback upon such an event as I thought must have insured your happiness."

Ferdinand endeavoured to recover himself, and by a little evasion prepare her for future communications.—"Your penetration, my dear Claudina, cannot be eluded; know then that the state of my father is such as inclines me to think it is almost past a doubt, that *you* will see him no more. I see you are affected (added he) but you know he has long been ill, and therefore such an event may be expected; compose *yourself*, however, and do not let me be doubly afflicted; to-morrow I shall see him again; perhaps, at my return I shall be in better spirits."—

"Heaven grant it (returned she, sighing.) Ah! what a world is this, so chequered, that seldom any good arises without its concomitant share of evil!"

"True, my love (answered Ferdinand;) but then reverse the picture, and thank our bounteous Father that almost every evil to our imperfect view, brings with it some alleviating circumstances we cannot always foresee."

"Yes (returned she) perhaps we are indebted to his increased weakness, and expectancy of death, the very pardon, and favour he has accorded to us. Would to Heaven, however, that I may once more see, and thank him on my knees for his goodness to you and my dear infants!"

Ferdinand could not stand this, tears gushed from his eyes, and, throwing his arms round her, he freely indulged them. She also wept, but not with that poignancy of sorrow to injure her health, the mutual indulgence relieved, and after a time, afforded them a melancholy composure.

CHAPTER II.

THE next morning, Claudina having past a tolerable night, and her spirits being much better, Ferdinand left her avowedly to *visit his father.* On his arrival at the Castle, he saw the solemn preparations for an event that filled him with horror. Sending for the steward, "My dear Ernest (said he) I must see my father, he shall not be committed to the earth without my tears bedewing his clay-cold form, without supplicating his hovering spirit to speak peace and pardon to his most wretched son! Let me not be interrupted in my last duties; I will not be long, but I must be alone."

Ernest bowed in silence, and conducted him to the chamber of death, calling from thence those whose duty it was to watch the sacred remains. All departed; Ferdinand shuddered involuntarily at the scene before him, day-light was excluded, the glimmering tapers, the solemn stillness, the black pall thrown over the bed which concealed a lifeless form, once so beloved and revered, accustomed to smile upon a then darling son, and hold him to his heart with unutterable fondness.

"Oh! (cried Ferdinand, agonized by the painful recollection) oh! just Heaven, how severe has been my punishment for one act of disobedience!"—He advanced hastily to the bed, withdrew the pall, and saw a face from which death had excluded no trait of mild benevolence; the features were placid and serene, yet Ferdinand thought, on a near investigation, that an air of sorrow was diffused over the countenance, and that the very serenity wore more the face of pious resignation than perfect content. He gazed with inexpressible sensations, threw himself on his knees in an agony of grief:—"O, father, ever revered and beloved! forgive your unhappy son, let not my offence be remembered against me in the land of spirits; for, oh! severe has been my punishment, misery has followed hard upon my disobedience!"

His head fell upon the bed, and he wept aloud; but his almost stagnated senses were instantly recalled by a deep and heavy groan that vibrated to his heart: He started up, and eagerly gazed on the lifeless body, all was still as death; he looked fearfully round the room, the gloom seemed increased, the tapers burnt more dimly, horror took possession of his soul; the groan was not a chimera, not the illusion of fancy; but from whence could it proceed, for it seemed very near to him? Again he turned his eyes to the bed, busy imagination, agitated spirits, and unsteady eyes, made him conceive the lips moved; overcome with every sensation that terror, panting expectation, and trembling apprehension, could inspire, he sunk again on his knees, attempted to speak, to look, but the words died on his lips, and involuntarily he hid his face by the side of the pall. Almost instantly a low and hollow voice pronounced the words *"Pardon and peace!"* He heard the words distinctly, attempted to rise, but with a faint shriek fell senseless on the floor!

On his recovery, he found himself supported in the anti-chamber by Ernest and a maid-servant; the voice still seemed to vibrate in his ears; he looked earnestly from one to the other: "How came I in this apartment?" demanded he.

"We heard a sudden scream," answered Ernest, "and entering the next room found you on the floor; we brought you here, and, thank Heaven, you are recovered."

"Recovered!" repeated Ferdinand,—"Good God! what have I——."

"You may leave the room," said Ernest to the girl.—She obeyed.— "Dear master," continued he, "compose yourself, why, would you wound your heart by a sight?"—

"A sight!" repeated he again: "Ernest, dear Ernest, deem me not visionary or mad; but credit me, when I declare to you I have heard my father's voice pronouncing the blessed words *'Pardon and peace.'*—Yes, such were the words; it was not the effect of fancy but a reality; the voice still hangs upon my ear, and I will now believe, that the spirit of the *good* and *just* man may be permitted to convey *happiness sometimes* to the wretched. My bosom seems lightened, my heart beats more freely, and I *already* feel returning peace."

"Thank Heaven!" cried Ernest, "I have no doubt, Sir, of your veracity, for you were never given to indulge visionary or superstitious notions. Extraordinary things do happen sometimes to be sure, but, if what you have heard was to be related, it might injure weak and credulous minds, and cause many ridiculous stories; it will be best therefore, my dear master, to conceal the whole affair, and submit with resignation to the stroke that now afflicts you, comforting yourself with the remembrance of those words which were spoken to console your mind, and relieve you from the oppression of that imprecation which has so long and so cruelly disturbed you."

"I *am* relieved," answered Ferdinand, "that painful stroke *is removed*, at least, I hope so: Alas! happy I can never be; yet, my good Ernest, had my lamented father sanctioned my marriage by *his forgiveness*, had I been considered as a child, few men would have known more true felicity, for my Claudina justifies my choice; she is the best of women, and of wives."

"Then, Sir, you have more happiness than falls to the lot of thousands, and therefore should be content; but pray walk down, your brother, my Lord, the Count, is expecting you." With a look of awful veneration and sorrow, Ferdinand threw his eyes on the opposite room, and without speaking descended to the saloon.

Rhodophil rose and embraced him, and, without reverting to the melancholy visit he had been paying, congratulated him on the safety of his wife, and the birth of his daughter. "I trust (said he) she will soon be in a state of health to be removed hither, and will consider this house as her own:—Mean time, I hope, I shall be admitted to pay my respects to her."

Ferdinand, whose mind was in a state of agitation, equally susceptible to joy, or grief, was painfully affected by his brother's kindness, his heart overflowed at his eyes; but a little abashed at such womanish weakness, which the other seemed superior to, he hastily dispersed the drops that forced their way down his cheeks, and, in a faltering voice, thanked the Count for his attention to his wife, and assured him she would rejoice to behold him. One thing, however, he must promise to him, previous to the visit.

He then explained to him the necessity he had been under to disguise the truth of the late events. "She believes (said he) my father has forgiven me; that he still exists, and that I may probably be included in his will. I dare not yet acquaint her with the extent of our obligations to you; the death of my father I shall announce to her, the rest must follow some time hence: I know so well her sensibility, and the delicacy of her affection for me, that, was she now informed I was unpardoned, portionless and dependent, she would accuse herself as the cause of my misfortunes, and her constitution, which has been impaired already by her regrets on this head, would be unable to sustain the shock. Will you then, my dear brother, vouchsafe to countenance the deceit, and excuse the omission of those grateful effusions you are so justly entitled to?"

"Mention it not (cried the Count) you owe me no obligations, I have merely performed a duty, and a sacred trust; I beg therefore neither you nor your wife will ever pain me by acknowledgments I am no ways entitled to; for had our situation been reversed, would *you* have done less for *me?*"

"No, by Heavens! (exclaimed Ferdinand, with fervor) that wealth would have been worthless to me without the participation of my beloved Rhodophil."

"I believe you (said the other) therefore here ends the chapter of obligations and thanks, for we are friends as well as brothers."

They then entered upon some consultations on domestic affairs, after which Ferdinand retired to break the death of his father to his wife; but not before the Count had pressed upon him a sum of money, that made Ernest's grateful service useless for the present, and which he repaid before he left the house.—On his way home, the recollection of the scene in his late father's apartment, a scene which, however strange and improbable it would appear on relation, he was perfectly convinced was not the illusion of his senses, and which seemed to him the voice of the dead speaking peace to his wounded mind.

The more he reflected on the circumstance, the more extraordinary it appeared. The refusal of Count Renaud to admit him to his presence in his last moments, to bestow one consoling word, nor yet even to recall the heavy curse that he had laid upon him when his union with Claudina was declared. Such stern, such unrelenting anger, seemed as inconsistent with his natural goodness of heart, as a pardon pronounced *after* death.—"All supernatural interpositions (thought he) I have ever discredited, but I cannot resist conviction; possibly my father did not think his dissolution so *very* near, strong resentments cling to the heart, and *he thought* I deserved to suffer. Perhaps, at the very moment when he felt the awful separation between the soul and body, he might *wish* to pronounce my pardon; and *how* that wish has been granted is a mystery incomprehensible to me, and possibly improper for me to desire a solution of." The agitation of his spirits was visible in his countenance, and when he entered his wife's humble apartment, the disorder of his air caught her attention.

"Ah! (cried she) my dear Ferdinand, I fear to ask.—Your father——!"

"You already anticipate the event (said he, throwing himself into a chair) your conjectures are but too just."

"Alas! (returned she, softening into tears) how painful the reflection, that we cannot now have the power to shew our love and gratitude, and that the pardon he has accorded to us, was more, perhaps, an act of piety than the result of filial affection."

"We must not be too nice (answered he) in our search after the motives of our best actions, but be content to judge of them by their effects: If he condescended, in his own good time, to reconcile us to ourselves, and to forgive us in his last moments, it is our duty to be thankful, and to examine no farther."—Claudina, who saw his mind was disturbed, and knew how to allow for it, made no reply; but after she had indulged those tears she found it impossible to repress, held up her sweet infant to his view, and exulted in the resemblance she traced between its unformed features and himself. Melted by her tenderness, and gazing on the lovely child, he embraced both with ardour, and, in grateful acknowledgments for the blessings before him, forgot, for a short time, both recent afflictions, and puzzling conjectures.

The funeral obsequies of Count Renaud, being over, Claudina able to leave her bed, and her husband more composed, though far from being tranquillized as his brother seemed to be, they began to think of a removal to the Castle, where in truth Claudina was very anxious to reside; nor is it to be wondered at when she contrasted her miserable apartment with the noble and splendid rooms at the Castle. Her humble dwelling was in the suburbs of the city, a lowly roof, small circumference, and meanly furnished; there she had known the extreme of wretchedness; now she was invited to partake of grandeur, to consider herself as the mistress of that superb mansion, and to see her dear children cloathed, and attended suitable to their father's birth: 'Tis not surprising therefore that she exerted unusual strength to bear the removal, nor that, when she was settled at the Castle, the satisfaction of her mind should communicate itself to her body, and render her recovery equally rapid and perfect.

Rhodophil treated them with the highest degree of tenderness and consideration; every wish was anticipated, and he doated on the children. Near a month was passed in a most delightful manner on the part of Claudina, but a deep and increased melancholy clouded the mind of Ferdinand; to live idle and inactive, dependent on the bounty of a brother, even the small allowance which his late father had afforded him, he could no longer call his own. The Count, indeed, was profuse in his presents of money and valuables to his wife; but was there not something mean and selfish in the acceptance? Could they last for ever? Might not his brother marry, and, if so, what then might be their fate? He recollected the advice of Ernest, but could he condescend to *ask*, what, if agreeable to his brother's inclinations, he would voluntarily offer—a settlement? No, he would die first. He was resolved to enter into the Emperor's service; but what could be done for his wife and children during his absence, and before he had the power to assist them?

Under these, and a thousand other painful reflections, he used to escape from the observation of his brother and his wife, and range from the gardens to the wilderness, and from thence into an adjoining forest, where he commonly spent hours every day, forming a thousand schemes, and rejecting them as quickly from their uselessness or impracticability. One morning, as he was taking his customary ramble, at the entrance of the forest he met Ernest. He started, "Pardon me, my dear master (said he) if I have broken upon you abruptly; I have long observed your solitary walks."

"You have watched me then (cried Ferdinand, rather haughtily) it is an unbecoming liberty."

"Pardon me, Sir (returned Ernest, in a tremulous voice, and with a look of humble sorrow) pardon your poor servant, if duty and affection———."

"My good old friend (exclaimed the other, instantly recollecting himself, and ashamed of his petulance) my faithful Ernest, pardon *me*; I know your attachment, and truly love *you*; but indeed I am altered, vexation and perplexity sour my disposition, I grow hateful to myself and to others." The old man, overcome by this condescension, could have humbled himself at his feet, but being pressed for time, and anxious to know if his "poor endeavours" could in any shape be useful, he earnestly besought Ferdinand to explain the cause of his melancholy.

He very readily acknowledged to him every feeling of his heart, and added, "that he was come to a determination to quit the Castle, but was distracted on account of his wife and children."

"As you resolve not to speak to your brother about any partition of my late master's effects, or any settlement for your children, I beseech you, Sir, to suspend your resolution for a few days, and, perhaps, I may obtain some information that may be of consequence. Fear not, Sir (added he, seeing Ferdinand was going to speak) do not be apprehensive I mean to say any thing to the Count; I am not honoured with his notice sufficiently to authorise any freedom of speech on my part; but I have other designs, and the result you shall know in a day or two."

With a low bow the good man departed, leaving Ferdinand penetrated with gratitude for the affectionate concern this faithful follower of his broken fortunes had ever manifested towards him and his family.

CHAPTER III.

WHEN the over-charged heart vents itself in a friendly communication, it lightens the oppressive load, and admits a ray of hope to illumine the prospect of future hours. Ferdinand returned to the Castle with quicker steps, and a countenance less overcast than for many preceding days; in the garden he met his wife under the supporting arm of his brother; he joined them, and was composed enough to converse freely on several subjects. Among other things, the war with Prussia was mentioned, and he dropped a hint that he should like the service. Rhodophil applauded his spirit, and observed, "that a young man, with his brother's address and vivacity, would be a great acquisition to the army."

"*Vivacity!* (repeated Claudina) alas! it is long since that any traces of pleasure or vivacity have been visible in my poor Ferdinand."

"Then (returned the Count) he must be the most insensible of men; with such a wife, and such lovely children, I think him uncommonly fortunate."—At that instant the nurse appeared with the infant; Claudina quitted them, and retired into the house with her child.

"I think, brother (said Rhodophil) you seemed to express yourself *feelingly* on the subject of the war; have you any wish to offer your services?"

"*I have* (replied Ferdinand, rejoiced at this opening) nor would I hesitate a moment but on account of my family."

"I hope my dear brother can have no doubts or fears concerning *their* happiness; I take upon me to ensure you every thing that affection or fortune can procure for their pleasure and comfort; and *you* may *command* whatever is necessary or proper for your appearance, with honour to yourself, and credit to your family. Surely we have no separate interests."

"I think not (replied Ferdinand) at least I know *my* heart participates in every enjoyment of yours, and if I feel any distress it is all my own."

"But why should you feel any (asked Rhodophil) when you have only to speak your wishes, and they will be gratified."

"Generous friend! (exclaimed the other) will you then endeavour to reconcile Claudina to my departure? Will you employ your interest to procure for me a commission and introduction to the Emperor?"

"I will do every thing you wish for (returned the Count) and this very day shall witness my affection for yourself and family."

This conversation restored Ferdinand to some degree of composure, and bid him look forward to a situation where *he* might at least be independent, and he still hoped his brother would make some fixed establishment for his family previous to his departure.—That evening the Count told him he had written to Vienna, "and as I entertain no doubts respecting the success of my applications, we will lose no time in procuring the necessary equipments for your campaign."

Ferdinand thanked his brother warmly at the moment; but after he had retired to rest, and began to reflect on every occurrence, there appeared, he thought, an indecent eagerness in Rhodophil to hasten his departure: At first he told me I should possess an equal share of my late father's fortune; the servants were told they had *two* masters, and equal power was to be lodged in my hands. 'Tis true I had no right to expect it, yet why make such liberal offers, when the tenor of *his* conduct, and the behaviour of the servants are contradictory, when every thing he does carries the air of a favour, and every attendance in the servants is ushered in with "my master ordered

me to do this, or that?" yet, perhaps, I am capricious, my situation is delicate, and my mind, from a long habitude of discontent, may see things with
a jaundiced eye, which in themselves bear a very different interpretation:
Let me not be unjust in my surmises, for surely the Count has been ever
warmly my friend, nor is it his fault that I am cut off from a participation of
my father's fortune. How few half brothers would have acted like Rhodophil!—Ashamed of his first uneasy doubts, Ferdinand turned eagerly to the
bright side of his brother's character, and did him *more* than justice from an
apprehension that he had done him *less*.

The next morning, taking his accustomed walk, he met Ernest, anxious to ease the heart of his old friend, and do credit to his brother, he
repeated the conversation on the preceding evening. Ernest heard him
with attention, and made the following reply:—"You will, I am sure, Sir,
do justice to my heart, and believe that I am neither prejudiced against my
master, the Count, nor naturally suspicious. I speak from the best grounds,
and it is with pain I destroy the opinion you entertain of his affection and
honour; but I must develope the seeming generosity that captivates your
mind. Count Rhodophil has learned the courtly art of professing much and
meaning little, which gives consequence to himself, and sends the poor deluded expectant away to indulge visionary hopes, and be again deceived by
smooth words that mean nothing.

"That well remembered day, which cut you off from all legal claims on
your father's fortune, never shall I forget the consequential air, the parade
with which the domestics were informed that they had *two* masters."—
"Stop, Ernest (cried Ferdinand) do not sully the generosity of my brother,
by imputing to him such despicable motives as pride and self-consequence;
it ill becomes me to hear one of his family rob him of the merit due to so
much frankness and brotherly love: I cannot suffer you to proceed in this
strain."

"Were I base enough to be unjust, or speak from the prejudices of my
own opinion, I should be deserving of your displeasure, Sir, but I entreat
you to hear me without interruption, and then I will submit to your judgment."

"Well, well (returned he, rather a *little* displeased) you may go on."

"That day, Sir (proceeded Ernest) after you had received such proofs
of his affection, and returned to your miserable abode with an intention to
fetch your Lady, I withdrew to an apartment, which I gave orders to have
fitted up for you. The good old house-keeper, Madam Lambert was with
me:—You know, Sir, it adjoins to the old library, and was, I believe, the cause
why the books have been since removed; but, however, not to be tedious

(*here* Ferdinand smiled) *there* we were, when presently the Count entered
the library with Peter; they were speaking as they shut the door; we heard
your name mentioned, and I put my finger to my mouth; we were silent
and listened. I see, Sir, you look displeased; it was a liberty and a meanness
if I could not justify it to my own heart, but I had my reasons.

"Well, Sir, we heard Count Rhodophil say, "the world has in general
thought my father very cruel in his treatment of Ferdinand, his whole fortune being given to me, they would be apt to censure and suspect me of
taking an advantage of his resentments; it is therefore to avoid any unpleasant reflections, to do away any prejudices that might be conceived against
me, and to humble Ferdinand's spirit into a sense of obligation, added to
another view I look forward to still more gratifying, that I have made him
and his family an offer of my house, which perhaps he will presume from
what I said just now, to think is to be his also; but I was before determined
how to act: I shall, by degrees, change every servant but yourself; Ernest I
shall be obliged to keep until all his accounts are made up, but no longer;
then the succeeding domestics, ignorant of my present declaration, and
taught to believe highly of my generosity in supporting a brother's family,
will learn to estimate us properly, and treat him accordingly."

"This, Sir, was verbatim your brother's speech, which Peter applauded
in very free words I thought for a servant, and we stole softly out of the
room lest we should be discovered. You must have observed, Sir, the servants *are all changed*, on one pretence or other, and being done without
consulting you, proves how little equality of power *you* have in the house.
Madame Lambert went two days ago; my turn will soon come; in truth
but for you I care not how soon; but I believe your intention of going into
the army has greatly rejoiced him, as it procures your absence without any
reflection being thrown on him. Peter has of late paid much court to me,
but as I look upon him to be in the plot against you, I have taken very little
notice of him. Two or three times he has remarked, "how very melancholy
Mr. Ferdinand looked!"—I thought something might be gathered from him
of his master's intentions towards your family, so yesterday I threw myself
in his way after I had left you; and your Lady passing into the garden, I
observed how handsome she was, and what beautiful children Master and
Miss were; adding, 'that it was a pity but some settlement was made for
them, lest the Count should marry, and his Lady not happen to like his
brother's family.'—'As to marriage (said he) I believe my master don't think
of that, and I dare say he will always be kind to Madame Claudina, if she is
civil to him, so it must be her own fault if she loses his favour. As to settlement, Mr. Ernest, master knows better than that, make folks independent,

and you make them saucy and ungrateful, whilst they are obliged to you they will be humble, tho' I fancy my master would have no objection to put forth a little to send his brother in some place abroad, for to be sure it is a shame to see a young man idling at home, who has nothing of his own, and hanging upon a generous Gentleman, who is but a half-brother after all, and not *obliged to maintain him.*' I was so provoked at his impudence that I could have throttled the rascal; but I curbed my passion, and saying, 'Very true, Peter,' I turned short from him, and retired to my room. Now, Sir, putting all this together, what must you think of the Count?"

Ferdinand, who was walking rather before Ernest, and his head hanging on his breast, turned round suddenly, with a look that expressed a thousand contending passions, twice he opened his lips to speak, but the conflict in his mind precluded all powers of articulation, and he gladly availed himself of a seat which just then appeared in view, though only the root of a tree, to sit down, for his trembling limbs could no longer support him. Poor Ernest saw, with infinite concern, the effects of his intelligence; tears stood glistening in his aged eyes.—"My dear master (said he) resume your courage; let not the machinations of the wicked have power to wring your noble heart with sorrow, to shake your fortitude, which has already struggled through the bitterest troubles."

"Ernest (said Ferdinand, after a long pause) you have bereft me of my last and only hope; all the consolation I could look forward to in life must derive its source from my brother. My brother did I say? alas! if what you tell me is true, and surely you would not deceive me, I have no longer a *brother.* Count Rhodophil is my father's heir, and I am cast off for ever. O, what a blessing is ignorance! Yesterday I thought myself wretched, but it was a state of bliss to what I now feel; my head burns like fire. Oh! my old, and now my *only* friend, tell me where, where shall I fly to, now that all my visionary hopes of this morning are vanished into bubbles! My wife! my children! merciful Heaven! who will provide for them?"

"*That Heaven* you invoke (answered the steward;) fear not, Sir, Providence never deserts the virtuous man." "But what, what is now to become of my intended expedition to the army?"

"If I may be so bold as to offer my advice (replied Ernest) I would act as if I was still unacquainted with the Count's real character; I only wished, Sir, to put you on your guard against duplicity, and not to have you weighed down with an idea of obligations which proceed only from selfish considerations. Whatever advantages you receive from the Count, is your undoubted right, as children of the same father you have an equal claim to his property; nor could resentment be justifiable carried to such lengths, as to consign one child to misery, that the other might riot in luxury."

"Surely, Ernest (cried Ferdinand) my father had a right to make what distinctions he pleased."

"I cannot think so, Sir (returned the other) in sudden anger was that will made, and I am confident it was intended to be altered, unhappily it was delayed until too late. Think of the words '*Pardon and peace!*' Believe me, Sir, my blessed master never died with hatred in his heart: Be not scrupulous therefore, but take, without hesitation, what the Count offers you, and boldly ask for some certain income for your Lady; he cannot, I think, refuse; if he does, he unmasks himself at once."

"What! (exclaimed Ferdinand) receive, nay, even ask favours from a man whom I suspect of the vilest duplicity; owe pecuniary obligations, the existence of my family to."

"Softly, Sir (said Ernest) it is a share of *your father's* property, *as such* receive it freely. I beseech you, Sir, to keep what I have told you in your mind; but do not let it influence your actions to the disadvantage of yourself and family."

The appearance of Rhodophil and Claudina at a distance interrupted their conversation. Ferdinand arose, and walked hastily into the forest, unable to meet them in the present perturbed state of his mind. He revolved every thing Ernest had told him; he recollected a thousand little inattentions he had received; the air of protection his brother often assumed, the change in the household, his readiness to lay hold of the little inclination he had shewn for the army: In short, the more he reflected, the more he was convinced no real brotherly affection existed in the bosom of Rhodophil: "Yet, (exclaimed he) did he not shew us a thousand acts of kindness, when sinking under the displeasure of my father? Did he not often relieve us from want, and labour incessantly to bring about a reconciliation? And is it possible that a sudden change of fortune, being possessed of *all*, should make such a revolution in his principles? If so, alas! how dangerous is prosperity? What a contractor of the heart is wealth!"

Distracted with the various conjectures that occupied his mind, he walked on regardless of time or distance, until faint and weary, he stopped, and looked round, that he might trace his way back; but he had bewildered himself among the trees, and observed no particular path, he therefore was at a loss how to regain the direct road; to complete his difficulties, the air grew dark, the clouds heavy, and in a short time it began to rain violently. Scarcely sensible of the torrents that poured upon him, Ferdinand sought to explore his way to the Castle, though he dreaded to encounter the looks of its master. It was some hours, however, before he saw the turrets rising above the trees, and when arrived at the garden, he was so exhausted with fatigue, so drenched with the rain, that it was with much difficulty he reached the saloon door before his senses fled, and he fell extended on the floor. Happily a servant was passing the room, and hearing a noise, opened the door, and beheld the lifeless body.

His exclamations soon brought every one to know the cause, and poor Claudina was nearly distracted with terror and anxiety.—He was soon restored to his senses, and immediately put into a warm bed, and through the attention of his wife and old Ernest (who was terrified to death at an accident, of which he thought himself in a great measure the cause) after some hours he grew better, and able to account for his indisposition, by mentioning the length of his walk through the rain. He endeavoured to assume a composure in his behaviour to his brother that surprised even Ernest, and having taken his resolution, he stifled his feelings, and conducted himself as usual. A violent cold and fever were the consequences of his ramble, and for several days he was quite an invalid, and in some danger; during this time Rhodophil behaved with the utmost tenderness, which made him doubt the communications of Ernest, and to suspect the justice of his own observations.

The first day that he left his bed, the Count came to him in a transport of joy:—"My dear Ferdinand, we are successful, I have this moment received an express, your commission is granted, and the Emperor wishes to see you without delay. I am happy, my dear brother, in being the messenger of such agreeable and wished-for intelligence."

The agitations of Ferdinand were inexpressible; he hesitated whether he should accept or refuse the commission procured for him. The Count seemed surprised: "You are silent, my dear brother, have your sentiments undergone any change that I am unacquainted with?"

"They have indeed, (answered Ferdinand, with a deep sigh;) the danger I was in a few days since has alarmed me for the future welfare of my family. I know well (added he, fixing his eyes steadily on Rhodophil, whose own fell under the penetrating glance) how much I may depend upon your *brotherly kindness*; but you may marry, little occurrences may arise at present unforeseen to interrupt the harmony that exists in your family, and the idea of a precarious and accidental provision, must ever give pain to a feeling heart."

"What is it you mean or expect?" asked the Count, in a quick tone.

"A small settlement on my wife, that I may depart with a certainty that, whether I live or die, she will not want the common necessaries of life; superfluities, such as she now enjoys, I neither expect or wish for."

"What then (cried Rhodophil) you will not trust to my honour, or affection for your family?"

"Be not offended (answered Ferdinand, calmly) and I will be explicit; for my own provision, my sword shall carve it out, and for my family I expect only a mediocrity of fortune. The grandeur and elegance that reigns here they are not entitled to, nor can they expect a continuance of; a more humble situation is most proper for them: If therefore you will settle a *very moderate* pension upon my wife and children, I will place them in some decent cottage suitable to their fortunes, and *then* I shall depart in peace."

The countenance of Rhodophil underwent many changes whilst his brother was speaking, nor was his answer quite ready when he stopped. At last, "I know not (replied he) whether I should be most grieved or offended at your unaccountable proposition. Is not Claudina my sister? Are not your children my heirs? I never intend to marry; but supposing I should, would not my honour and fraternal affection compel me to make a handsome provision for you and your family?"

"A handsome provision I neither expect nor am entitled to (answered Ferdinand.) In this commission, you have procured for me, lies the extent of my wishes for myself. My wife has no right to splendid expectations, and my children shall be taught by industry to provide for themselves. The greatest misery of life is to be accustomed in early youth to indulgences which enervate both the mind and body, and lead to hopes which may be blighted by a thousand accidents.—My children shall indulge no hopes independent of their own exertions, and that I am convinced is the surest road to competency and happiness."

"What, then (said the Count) you would bring them up to trade, to disgrace their family?"

"No (replied Ferdinand, warmly) I will, if I live, prevent them from *disgracing* their family, by teaching them a spirit of independence, and a mediocrity of expectations; their minds shall be noble, though their fortunes may be humble; they shall be superior to base actions from an integrity of heart; and capable of providing for their own maintenance, they never can disgrace their connexions, though they may mortify pride."

"Your language and sentiments are very strange (replied Rhodophil, in a tone of pique and vexation;) but methinks you promise too much for your children, whose ideas may not happen to coincide with your's."——

"At least," said Ferdinand, "I will endeavour to inculcate my sentiments, and form their young minds agreeable to my wishes; there is no dependance upon the human heart it is true: I may fail of success, but I will not abate of my endeavours; the rest I must leave to Providence."

"Well," returned Rhodophil, "since you have no reliance on me, and insist upon an independence, be so good to name your terms." The spirit of

Ferdinand revolted against this demand, and he was on the point of refusing every assistance; but the recollection of his family timely interposed, and with evident reluctance he named four hundred crowns yearly.

"Four hundred crowns!" repeated the Count, with surprise, "why, such a sum will scarcely find them bread!" "It is double, however, to any advantages I have had for them for those last two years, and I should despise myself if I considered your fortune more than their real wants."

"You are much too moderate," said the Count; "but I will enter into a compromise with you; I will settle that sum upon them during their residence in this Castle, and double it should I marry; but then I expect that you will permit them to remain here in your absence, during your first campaign. Deprive me not of all my comforts at once; let me sooth the sorrows of my sister on your first separation; your children are too young to imbibe any prejudices against your intended frugal system, and I expect, as a proof of your brotherly affection, that those sweet pledges of your dearest love may be confided to me."

Ferdinand hesitated a little, but at length said, equivocally, "Your kindness is truly painful to me, but Claudina shall decide on this point; and now my wish, as to a small provision for them being generously acceded to, I have only to hasten preparations for my departure."

"A small provision, indeed!" repeated the Count, "however, it will be always in my power to augment it, for I shall ever consider *we have equal claims* to the fortune of our ancestors."

He now withdrew at Ferdinand's request to reveal every particular to Claudina, and left him variously affected by the preceding conversation. "If I have wronged him by giving credit to erroneous reports, or suspicious observations, I must appear as an ungrateful and most unworthy character; and ought I to believe the perhaps mistaken representation of Ernest against a series of kind actions, particularly within those last two years, when interest could have no share in directing them to me, then under my father's malediction? Good Heavens! if I have wronged him, how shall I detest myself!" For some time Ferdinand dwelt on every favourable side of his brother's character with self-indignation, but soon other ideas obtruded. If he really had been sincere in the equality he talked of, would he not have seized the first moment to ensure it to me? Would he not have hastened to relieve me from a sense of obligations by nobly making me independent, and rendering my separation from my family unnecessary?—Could he not have resigned over one of his estates to me as a residence I might have called *my own?* Does he seem to have a feeling heart, or regret the loss of a parent ever good and bountiful to him? Has he not discharged the old servants, grown grey in the service of the family, with only the small legacies (much less, indeed, than I expected the munificent spirit of my father would have bequeathed to them) so insufficient for the support of their old age? Are not these many proofs of a heart deficient in generosity, and a right way of thinking? Tormented by these and many other doubts, he exclaimed, "Would to Heaven I could read his heart, that I might do him justice!" A deep and hollow voice cried, "It is a corrupt one!!!"

Ferdinand sprung from his seat, looked wildly round the room: "Astonishing! (he cried) again that voice, sure it is, it *must be*, more than human!" He opened the door that led into the next apartment; the room was empty, and universal silence reigned:—Again he reseated himself, in trembling expectation of the same sounds, but he heard no more. Extremely agitated, though he endeavoured to assume a composed air, he feebly crept to the dressing room of Claudina, where he found the Count. His blood grew chill at the sight; both started, and exclaimed at his appearance; with difficulty he supported himself till assisted by his wife to a chair; she blamed him for attempting to leave his apartment: "You are too weak (said she) to walk as yet; I was coming to you."

"I shall soon recover (replied he) and gain strength by the change of air; I already feel better."

Indeed, the first shock being over, though the voice still vibrated on his ear, he viewed Rhodophil with a scrutinizing eye, and traced, as he thought, duplicity in every line of his countenance, so governed are our ideas by accidental circumstances! His love, his reverence for his brother, shrunk into nothing, and he believed the voice of the dead against all those superficial appearances which had hitherto lulled him into an unsuspecting confidence. After a short pause, "I have been complying with your wishes, my dear brother," said the Count, "and had just opened the business to your wife as you appeared."

"Ah! Ferdinand," cried Claudina, "can you think of leaving me, of exposing your life to the uncertain chance of war?"

"The hand of Providence is there, is here, and every where," answered Ferdinand. "Fear not for me, my dear Claudina, divest yourself of prejudice, consider my situation dispassionately, and you will be reconciled to an inevitable necessity."—"I leave you," said the Count, "to discuss the subject between yourselves; my prayers and wishes have been unsuccessful; you, Madam, may have more influence." He bowed, and left the room.

CHAPTER IV.

FOR a few moments they were silent; at length Ferdinand explained to her his motives without entering into any strictures on his brother's conduct; and by the arguments he adduced in support of his plan, brought her to be convinced, or at least to appear convinced, that he was perfectly right. He mentioned his intention to take a small cottage for her and his children, at the same time that he told her of the Count's wishes that she would remain at the Castle.—"On this head, my dear Claudina, your inclinations shall decide, for I wish to leave you perfectly contented with your situation in my absence, determine therefore as you feel most inclined."

"I own, then," answered she, "that I prefer staying here; to remove into a strange house, among strange people, unaccustomed to manage for myself, would be altogether unpleasant. Here, as our good brother solicits our stay, I can at least be as comfortable as it is possible I can be in your absence, and make myself useful enough to do away any sense of obligation."

"As you please, so let it be," returned Ferdinand, rather hurt at her choice, but determined not to controul her, "and I hope a few days will finish all our preparations, and give me strength to repair to Vienna." A further conversation took place relative to domestic matters; but he cautiously concealed the two extraordinary occurrences that had befallen him, because he had never yet undeceived her, with respect to the pardon which, she believed, the late Count had accorded to him before his death.

In the course of the evening Ferdinand saw Ernest, and related to him, not only what had past between his brother and himself, but the words which he had a second time heard in his apartment. "It was the same voice that I heard before in the room where my father's body lay. You, Ernest, will believe me, to no one else would I mention the circumstance, for from no one else should I gain credit; but it is wonderous strange!"

"True, Sir," answered the steward; "but nothing is impossible, and now forewarned, you may guard against any evil practices."—"Would to Heaven my wife had otherwise decided," cried Ferdinand.

"Do not be uneasy, Sir," replied Ernest, "whilst I have life and limbs I will be faithful to your family, nothing shall escape my observation." "But if you should be discharged?"

"I have some cause to think that cannot well take place, and should I quit the house, I have an infallible method of knowing what passes here; whilst I live, therefore, you need not fear."

This cheerful assurance calmed the tumult of Ferdinand's mind, and enabled him with alacrity to prepare for his journey. The following day Ernest waited on him by the Count's order with a handsome sum of money for his necessary expences; the colour mounted to Ferdinand's cheeks, he hesitated, paced about the room, and seemed in violent agitations.—"Pray, dear Sir," cried Ernest, "take the money, think of it less as your brother's present, than as a small part of your father's property, to which you have unquestionably a right."

"Not so," replied Ferdinand, "I can have no right to what he has bequeathed from me, and to receive pecuniary favours from a man I think capable of duplicity, lowers me in my own esteem."

"Be not so scrupulous, Sir, I beseech you," returned Ernest; "take it, fortune may enable you to return it, and I'll pledge my life you will not hereafter regret accepting the money, or think much of the obligation as you call it."

"You persuade me," said Ferdinand, "and against my inclinations I comply; (then seeing the largeness of the sum,) good Heavens! can this man have a bad heart? Is there not munificence in this present? O, Rhodophil, if concurrent circumstances have led me into an error, if I injure you by doubt and suspicion, how severe will be my repentance!"—Ernest was silent, indeed he could not view the necessary arrangement for the departure of a man he loved and revered, without feeling the deepest sorrow; yet he thought the plan he had adopted was most suitable to his birth, his age and situation, and therefore only regretted the necessity for its execution, whilst Ferdinand painfully looking forward to the hour of separation from a wife and children that he doated on, sought, in the bustle of preparation, to blunt the severity of his feelings.

The day of parting at length arrived, and as such scenes can afford no gratification to minds of sensibility, we shall not dwell upon them: Sorrow was reciprocal on all sides, at least to appearance, and we cannot penetrate into the remotest corner of the heart, therefore give those appearances due credit. To follow Ferdinand would be unnecessary, we shall then take this opportunity to look back into the family history of his father, the late Count Renaud.

CHAPTER V.

DESCENDED from a noble and an opulent family, Count Renaud succeeded to the estates of his ancestors at the age of five-and-twenty: Two years previous to which he had, to please his family, married a Lady of noble birth and great riches, her only recommendations. Proud, fastidious, and violent, she sought, by the haughtiness of her demeanour, to exact that respect and servility as substitutes for veneration and esteem, to which her manners and conduct laid no claims. The Count, who had another attachment, conscious that he was deficient in tenderness to her, and afraid of irritating a spirit so ungovernable by any opposition to her plans, quietly permitted her to conduct his household as she pleased, nor ever interfered with her pursuits or expences. Nearly at the same period, when he came into the possession of his father's fortune, his wife presented him with an heir in the person of Rhodophil. The birth of a son made him for some time more attentive to his Lady, but his affection for a dearer object soon drew him into his customary distant civilities. Happily the Countess had no violent susceptibilities, her heart had never been softened by love, and though she was often provoked at the neglect of her Lord, yet her feelings arose more from disappointed pride, than from any warmth of affection, consequently, though displeased, she was not grieved, and offended pride found a relief in the imperiousness of her manners to all those who were subjected to her caprice.

When her son was about a twelvemonth old, a young Lady, who was a near relation to the Countess, and had just been liberated from a convent where she had resided from childhood for education, came to pay them a visit: She was received with kindness by the Countess, with politeness by the Count; but in less than a fortnight the sentiments of both parties underwent a total alteration.

Caroline, the name of this young Lady, had one of the finest forms imagination could paint; her face was handsome, her air and manners captivating, from a certain kind of bashful naïvete which joined to a natural elegance, was extremely fascinating. At first sight you admired her, on an acquaintance an unprejudiced mind must love her. By imperceptible degrees, even to himself, the Count grew enchanted with the charms of Caroline, he delighted in her society; she was sensible, gentle, and unassuming; she was to him a new character; his Lady proud of her birth and riches, with a natural violence of temper, and devoid of personal attractions, was more than indifferent; she was disgusting to him: His mistress, vain of her charms, conscious of the power she had long held over his affections, and which had received additional strength from the birth of a daughter, had for some time past relaxed in her endeavours to please, and by her little solicitude to amuse him in those hours which he devoted to her, had insensibly weakened her powers of attraction, and rendered the visits he paid her rather a retreat from the more disagreeable society at the Castle, than the effects of that violent passion he had once and for a long while felt for her, and which, perhaps, only her own folly and caprice caused an abatement of.

His passions were therefore in that dormant state which of all others is the most dangerous in a susceptible mind, because, if once roused into action, they blaze with more uncontrolled fury than when kept in constant agitation. Such was the Count's situation when first Caroline became an inmate in his house; nor did her person at first sight appear particularly charming; he sought her company and conversation more as a pleasing variety than from any expectation of delight; but a short time convinced him how dangerous an indulgence was the society of a young and beautiful girl, who, new to the world, was grateful for the attentions he paid her, pleased with his conversation, and desirous of profiting by the information his understanding daily unfolded to her. Every hour her attractions gained upon his heart, and he was sensible that he had conceived a passion more delicate and violent than any he had ever before admitted to his bosom.

Unhappily the young and inexperienced Caroline caught the infection, the contagion spread itself through her innocent mind, and she grew melancholy and unhappy; for a long time insensible of the nature of her disease, until one morning that some unguarded expressions, and too tender looks of the Count, too fully explained his sentiments, and taught her to develop the secret of her own. Extremely shocked at the discovery, when she withdrew to her apartment she took herself severely to task for her involuntary crime, and directly determined to quit the house, and fly the dangerous society of its master. Whilst she was forming this prudent resolution the Countess entered her apartment, her features deformed by passion, her eyes flashing fire: "Insolent, depraved, ungrateful girl!" exclaimed she, "so, you have formed a vile intrigue with my husband; under a pretence of visiting me you carry on your shameless connexion in my very house. Abandoned wretch! I have seen, I have heard enough; you shall quit it this day, base as you are, I will expose you to my servants, to your friends, and to the world."

She was stopped in the midst of her threats by seeing the unhappy girl fall senseless at her feet. She rang the bell for assistance, but on the entrance of the servants continued her exclamations and upbraidings. "Recover the infamous creature who has so basely injured me; pack up her rags, and the moment her senses return, turn her out of the house to her base paramour my husband, whom she has seduced from me. I have discovered their intrigue, nor shall she sleep again under this roof. Disobey me at *your peril*," said she to the servants, who stood aghast at her fury; "let her be thrust out from my house within this hour." She flew out of the room at the moment when returning life visited the cheeks of the much-injured Caroline.

She opened her eyes and beheld the servants; she looked with terror round the room, her ears still holding the dreadful words which had deprived her of her senses. Seeing only the two women who looked on her with compassion, though believing her guilty: "Am I a base, infamous wretch?" said she: "Is my character lost, my innocence blasted, by vile suspicions? O, Heavens! what is to become of me, injured and undone, whither can I fly? But no, I will not go, I will see the Countess, she must, she shall hear me. I am *innocent, indeed* I am," added she, bursting into a torrent of tears that greatly affected the women, who endeavoured to sooth her into a composure impossible to be obtained. One of them, more courageous than the other, offered to go in search of her Lady, and entreat an audience for the poor afflicted.—"No," said she, rising hastily from the bed, "I will not *entreat*, I will demand to be heard, and you shall accompany me." She rather flew than walked towards the Countess's dressing room, who was at that moment abusing her in the vilest terms to her own woman. Caroline burst into the room, surprise chained the Countess to her chair, and stopped her tongue.

"Hear me, Madam," said she; "it is a justice I demand; you have accused, condemned, and insulted me with the charge of crimes my soul abhors: You seek to murder my future happiness by destroying my reputation. You are deceived and abused. Neither my conduct or sentiments ever injured you, and the infamous accusation of an intrigue with your husband is as false as Heaven is true; to that Heaven I appeal for my innocence and integrity. I will leave your house, but not as a guilty wretch, nor until my uncle arrives to take me hence; confine me to this room if you please, I will only see the Count once more, and that shall be in your presence: He will do me justice; but you *shall not* drive me from hence until you have recalled your accusations, and that I can depart with a character unspotted, as my heart is unstained, with guilt."

That the Countess heard her so long without interruption proceeded not from patience, or a desire of hearing her in her own defence: On the contrary, surprise and increasing rage precluded speech for a few moments; but just as Caroline pronounced the last words, she sprang forwards, and struck her so violent a blow as laid her on the floor, and would have trampled upon her, had not the women with-held her by violence. The noise of the fall, her rage, and the screams of the servants, alarmed the whole household, and the Count, who had just entered from the garden, hearing and seeing the confusion, ran up stairs with them to learn the occasion.—

What were his emotions on entering his wife's dressing-room, to behold Caroline on the floor weltering in her blood, and the Countess foaming, stamping with rage, and struggling with her servants.

He flew to the senseless Caroline: "My God! what—how is this? Is she *killed?*" he was going to say; but overpowered, he sunk into a chair, whilst those that had followed him raised the poor girl from the floor, and said, the blood proceeded from her nose.—The women, who held the Countess, now gave way to her ungovernable rage, and carried off the poor victim of it to another room. The shock actually suspended all powers in the Count, and he looked on his wife with an air of stupid wildness. She, mistaking the cause of his silence, vented her passion in such language, and spoke of Caroline in such infamous, opprobrious terms, that he was no longer at a loss to account for the scene he had witnessed. He started up like a mad-man, seizing her hands, he forced her into a chair: "Sit there, Madam," he cried, in a voice choked with rage and horror; "Stir not for your life till I have seen that angel you have so basely injured: Yes, she is an angel, in-nocent and spotless; dare not to quit this apartment. When I have seen the injured Caroline I shall know what *treatment you* deserve." He quitted the room, and on entering the apartment where the unhappy girl was carried, found her restored to her senses, and the blood stopped; but she had a vio-lent bruise on the side of her head, and another on her shoulder; she was incapable of speaking, and whilst she was conveyed to bed, and a surgeon was sent for, the Count was nearly distracted. One of the women gave him complete information of the preceding scenes, which threw him into par-oxisms of rage little short of madness.—He a thousand times protested the innocence of Caroline, and execrated her malicious accusers. Not a servant in the house but believed him, for her gentle, unoffending manners had gained her as much love and respect amongst them, as the Countess was beheld with hatred and dread.

But little respect or attachment can be expected from domestics, when their principals degrade themselves by the exercise of insolence and passion over those whose humble situation in life is perhaps the only circumstance in which they are inferior to their employers; for goodness of heart, and nobleness of principle, are by no means confined to the rich and titled, who derive their boasted superiority too often more from hereditary claims than from their own personal rights.

The Countess had *servants,* but she had no friends, and her ill humour and insolence was borne by them, because from habitude they had learned to despise it. Their master they loved, and a simple asseveration from him gained more credit than oaths, or the most plausible testimony could obtain for their Lady: No wonder, therefore, that every one was attentive to the unfortunate young Lady, and anxious for the arrival of the surgeon; he at length appeared, and to their great joy declared no material injury had been received, the bruises he hoped soon to remove, but the great loss of blood, and a tremor which he supposed was owing to the fall, rendered it necessary that the patient should be kept exceeding quiet. A little more composed by this report, the Count returned to his wife, whose rage had been succeeded by a fit of sullenness and reflections not very pleasant.

With very little ceremony he reproached her warmly for her inhuman treatment of Caroline, vindicated her innocence with energy and truth; insisted that she should publicly ask her pardon for the insults she had given her, or be assured that he would instantly separate himself from her for ever, and do justice to the character of a young Lady she had so wantonly injured, without the least provocation. Not deigning to make any reply, she drew from her pocket a letter, and gave it into his hand. How great was his astonishment to see, in spite of an endeavour to disguise it, the hand-writing of his mistress, who, as a friend to the Countess, accused her husband and Caroline of an intrigue, and repeated a number of bitter expressions, which had sometimes been drawn from him relative to his wife's person and disposition, as if spoken by him to Caroline, and by her repeated to her.—The whole information was calculated to inspire every diabolical idea that jealousy, personal resentment, and a sense of vile ingratitude, could animate a naturally irritable temper to indulge.

He put the paper into his pocket:—"I know your wicked informant," said he, "and she shall dearly repent the baseness of this attempt, to injure a character superior to the machinations of persons who hate the virtue they cannot copy. This letter, Madam, in a small degree, might excuse your suspicions; but nothing can atone for your improper and cruel treatment of a young woman, who, as a relation and a guest, had a claim to your hospitality."

"What!" interrupted the Countess, indignantly, "when I was informed *she* had violated the rights you talk of, and injured me irreparably?"

"At least," answered the Count, "you ought to have shewn this letter to her or to me, to have judged, from your own conviction, before you took the liberty of being your own avenger, and not blindly have permitted your passions to be guided by a vile incendiary, and proceed to such outrages as the lowest of your sex should be ashamed of: However, Madam, you have still the power to atone for your aspersions on the young Lady's fame before your servants by a public recantation. The personal injury, the degrading blow, *it is possible she* may forgive; but if you have any feeling, *you* can never forgive *yourself.*"

Ending those words he left her, and went to the house of his mistress, where he had not been for several days: To his astonishment he found it shut up, and on inquiry learned, that the Lady, with her child and nurse, had gone from thence two days before; that the furniture had been privately disposed of, and that a Gentleman came in a carriage and took them from the house without any one's knowing to what place they were gone. This information hurt the Count much, not on account of the Lady, who had been some time indifferent to him, but he was fond of the infant, and to have it taken away, solely in the power of a woman whose principles were not virtuous, distressed him greatly; and he painfully felt that the errors he had committed might too probably be retaliated on his own child, and that he had given existence to a being who might fall a victim to the vices of another, with passions as ungovernable as his own!

The conviction struck him with shame and remorse; he returned to the Castle overwhelmed with dejection, and more than ever anxious that the character of Caroline should be justified, that *she* might not be a sufferer through his attachment, which, however carefully concealed, it was evident, the jealous curiosity of his mistress had penetrated into, and possibly others might have made the same observations, though not impelled by the same motives. In consequence of these reflections, he sought a conversation with his Lady; to her he confessed the nature of his long attachment to his late mistress, the birth of a daughter, his growing indifference, and little attention to her for some time past, which he supposed had induced her from pique and revenge, to give her the information contained in that letter she had delivered to him, in the hope of creating jealousies and disturbances to embitter their future days.

"You tell me nothing, Sir," answered she haughtily, "but what I have long since been informed of, except who was the writer of the letter; the conjecture is not wholly improbable, nor the motives which gave rise to it, at all unlikely. My passions carried me beyond the bounds of decency when I struck Caroline; but she intruded at an improper time, and was the sufferer. I have no objection to accede to your proposition, and declare her innocence as far as *my own* belief goes; but I expect *that letter* shall be produced as *my* justification. You see, Sir, to what meannesses you subject me by your attachments; I expect *this* to be the last folly of the kind; if you chuse to make yourself ridiculous, I desire to be left out of the business."

She left the room with an air of disdain and superiority, that convinced him concessions on his part only served to make her more arrogant. In a few days Caroline was perfectly recovered; she sent for the Count and Countess to her apartment, the first time she had admitted either from the day of the quarrel.

"I expect my uncle," said she, "tomorrow to take me from this house, which I hourly regret I ever visited! Your unjust suspicions and cruel accusations have wounded my character, have injured my health; but I take God to witness, that I would not be the guilty, ungrateful creature you supposed me for all the enjoyments this world can offer. From you, Madam, I have a right to expect more than an apology, an acknowledgment that you have wronged me: Your women heard me accused; it is fit also that they should hear me justified."

"I own it," replied the Countess, a little affected, and much confused, "I have used you ill, my dear Caroline, I entreat your forgiveness, and request you will hear the information which threw me into passions so injurious to you, and unbecoming in myself."—She drew the letter from her pocket; Caroline rejected it: "No, Madam, I am perfectly satisfied; if you believe yourself imposed upon, if you are convinced that I am incapable of being the wretched creature you supposed me to be; I am restored to *your* good opinion, and justified in the sight of others; self-approbation, thank Heaven, I have never forfeited."

The Countess withdrew soon after, the scene was disagreeable to her on many accounts; she had injured Caroline, and therefore could not love her, and it likewise gave her a conscious superiority which the Countess could not admit of in any other than herself. The Count was in a situation most deplorable, his love for Caroline exceeded all bounds, yet *respecting* her with equal fervor, he determined to confine his passion within his own bosom, and never to see her more after she had quitted his house. On the next day, this amiable and unfortunate young woman took leave of the family, carrying with her a barbed arrow which pierced her heart, and wrung it with sorrow, when the last adieus were pronounced between the Count and herself. She returned home, but for a long time her days were melancholy, and her nights restless.

The Count and his Lady were little less unhappy; there was nothing respectable or estimable in the Lady's character to conciliate esteem, nor any endeavours to render herself pleasing. No longer a favourite mistress to engross his hours, his reflections on the past were painful, and in prospect no less disagreeable: He grew reserved, solitary and unhappy; yet behaved with more attention and complacency to his Lady, and was extremely fond of his infant son. Nine months passed in a dull uniformity, when an accident happened that gave a new turn to his thoughts.

The Countess was again in the family way, and generally went out in the mornings to ride on horseback. One day, when attended only by two servants, she was riding through the forest not far from the Castle, by the sudden discharge of a gun her horse took fright, and flying between the trees, she was thrown off with great violence, and when the attendants came up, lay to all appearance dead. On a nearer inspection they found she still breathed; between them she was conveyed to the Castle, a surgeon was sent for, and the Count seemed greatly affected. She remained speechless, though sensible, and the surgeon apprehended some very dreadful inward bruises from the fall, which was really the case, for in spite of every medical assistance she expired before the next morning.

Having already described the Count's feelings, it is needless to say, that after the first shock was over, a thousand pleasing images floated on his brain, and every thought was full of Caroline. When decency authorised him to make known the situation of his heart, he applied to that young Lady's uncle for permission to address her; an offer so very advantageous could not be refused, and he was permitted to visit her; but, alas! how severely was he wounded when he first saw her, pale, emaciated, and dejected; she was no longer the blooming Caroline, whose animated charms had first inspired him with a real passion; but she was an object a thousand times more interesting, for all her sufferings were on his account, and that idea rendered her inexpressibly dear to him.

Conscious of the alteration in her person, the generous girl decided against her own wishes, and refused to marry him; but the Count was not so easily induced to give up a favourite point so essential to his happiness; her uncle seconded his wishes, and wearied out by his continued perseverance, and yielding as well to the tenderness of her own heart, she at length consented; they were united, and the happy Count thought his felicity was now complete.

Poor simple mortals as we are! that see not by every day's experience how often the accomplishment of our eager wishes proves the source of future misery!

The amiable Caroline was indeed the most desirable of women, the most engaging of wives; but unhappily her constitution had been too delicate to support her under a fatal passion which preyed upon her heart, and for which she had incessantly reproached herself; a slow but gentle decay imperceptibly weakened her lovely frame. She was sensible of her own situation before she gave her hand to the Count, but was persuaded by her friends that a happy union might restore her health. For a few weeks she appeared better, and being in the way of becoming a mother, a relapse into weakness, debility and languor, was attributed to that circumstance. She knew better, but she suffered them to mislead themselves, because she could not bear to see her friends unhappy. She struggled with her complaints until the hour arrived when nature made its last efforts, the same moment that gave birth to a son deprived the unhappy Count of its angelic mother, and the spirit of the amiable and too tender Caroline fled to Heaven!

It is impossible to paint the distraction of her miserable husband, who for many days was in that dreadful state, to give great cause for apprehension that he would quickly follow his beloved wife to the grave; but at length it pleased Heaven to restore his health, but his vivacity and cheerfulness were fled for ever. He devoted the remainder of his days to the education of his two sons, and the image of his lost Caroline was never absent from his thoughts. Sensible that his eldest boy, Rhodophil, would inherit his paternal estates, he determined to save a handsome fortune for his young Ferdinand, who was the perfect resemblance of his unfortunate mother. The Count retrenched every useless expence, and though he was benevolent and liberal to others, he denied himself every thing superfluous that he might benefit his darling son, who, as he grew up, discovered every trait of a good heart, and an excellent constitution.

Rhodophil was the counterpart of his mother, both in person and disposition.—Stern, haughty, insolent and unfeeling, no tenderness could move, no remonstrances avail, to make him unbend his temper, and grow more tractable in his juvenile days; but when advanced to manhood, he became all at once fond of and submissive to his father, and almost servilly attentive to his brother, who, open, generous and unsuspecting, really loved Rhodophil, and rejoiced at the alteration that appeared to have taken place in his disposition.

CHAPTER VI.

RHODOPHIL was about one-and-twenty, and Ferdinand in his eighteenth year, when walking one evening in the suburbs of Baden, they met an elderly woman, plainly but cleanly dressed, with a young one by her side, whose uncommon beauty instantly attracted the eyes of both the brothers. By mutual consent they turned and followed her; they observed them enter a mean-looking house correspondent to their appearance:—Both were eager to make inquiries, and were informed by a neighbour that the woman's name was Dupree, and the young girl, who was her niece, was called Claudina; they had only resided a few months in the town, and appeared to have but a very slender income. With this intelligence they returned home, both thoughtful, and each suspecting the sentiments of the other, which was, a desire of seeing and knowing a little more of this lovely Claudina.

When they met next morning, Rhodophil began to talk of the "pretty girl" they had seen; but in a lively manner, and in a tone of indifference that surprised Ferdinand, whose young heart had received a first impression, and who could not mention her but in terms of rapture that drew upon him the pleasantry of his brother. Ferdinand, incapable of art or dissimulation, openly avowed his intention of going in search of another view of his charmer; his brother laughed at his folly, and said he should take a different route.

Not to dwell too long on this part of the story, we shall only say, that Ferdinand found means to get acquainted with this young woman, and very soon engaged *his* heart to her, and acquired no small share of her's.—Mean time overtures were made to the woman by a friend of her's to *sell* her niece, or in other words, she was offered a handsome sum for herself, and a settlement on Claudina by a young Nobleman. Dupree, mercenary and poor, could not withstand the temptation; she endeavoured, to the utmost of her skill, to seduce the mind of her niece, by a display of all the advantages such an attachment would secure to her; but Claudina had the best security for the preservation of her honor, which was her love for Ferdinand, and the hope that, though not an elder brother, he would have a handsome fortune, and that his affection for her was an honourable one.—Those splendid overtures were therefore firmly rejected, though often renewed, and her lover felt himself under additional ties of love and obligation to a young woman, whose affection and good principles had stood the test of every temptation.

Mean time his mind could not be easy; he had every reason to imagine his father never would approve of a connexion so mean and unsuitable to the future views he had for his establishment; he dared not mention his attachment, and hourly dreaded the discovery and its consequences. His brother often rallied him upon his passion, and at first persuaded him greatly against the indulgence of a love so improper; but finding Ferdinand inflexibly determined to persevere, he had for some time ceased to speak on the subject. This young man grew daily more enamoured, and every moment more vexed and mortified at her humble situation, and the dangers to which she was exposed by her residence with an unprincipled woman. He had her taught privately several branches of education, and was charmed with her docility and the progress she made in her studies; every hour his love increased, and he determined to marry her privately.

One day walking in the garden, in a very pensive mood, Rhodophil joined him, and affectionately inquired into the cause of his melancholy.— Ferdinand, whose love for Claudina had by no means lessened his affections towards his brother, after a little hesitation, confessed the cause of his embarrassment, his resolution to wed Claudina, and the dread he entertained of displeasing so good a father, whom he dearly loved and honoured.

"If your resolution is taken," replied Rhodophil, "it would be a waste of time to enter into any arguments with you on the subject; the disadvantages attending it must be as obvious to yourself as to me. Your father never will give his consent, and if you *do* marry her, you must keep the affair secret; *your father cannot live for ever.*"

This last observation shocked Ferdinand extremely.—"Good God!" exclaimed he, "shall I enter into an union where my only chance of happiness must arise from the death of a parent so tender and respectable? Perish the thought! No, let me be miserable from the disappointment of my wishes, but never let me be criminal, detestable in my own eyes." Rhodophil observed, that he was more hurt than was necessary at the hint he had dropped, which meant nothing more than a natural conclusion: "However," added he, "to prove the sincerity of my fraternal affection, marry Claudina; I will add to your allowance by a portion of mine; you will then be enabled to maintain her, and by removing her to a different quarter of the town may elude all suspicion and observation."

How unequal was the prudence and resolution of eighteen to withstand the incitements of passion, or decline the indulgence of it when sanctioned by a brother! Ferdinand embraced his generous brother with transport, and, blind to all the ill effects that might be dreaded from an union so rash and unsuitable, he no longer hesitated, but the following day he informed Claudina and her aunt of his resolution, and for the first time asked, "Who, and what were her parents?" The aunt answered, "That her father, in early life, had been in the army, an officer; but dying soon after her birth, her mother had only a small pension to live on, which poorly supported her for about three years, when she also died, leaving Claudina to her care; that she (Dupree) having only a hundred crowns a year to live on, had remained in the country until this last year, when she thought it best to remove near the city, in the hope that her niece's beauty would get her a good husband." With this account Ferdinand was satisfied, and not a little pleased to find his mistress owed her birth to an officer, though she was poor and friendless. In a very few days he was united to his Claudina, and removed her to another quarter in the suburbs, where she lived decently, if not elegantly, and having an affectionate heart, and a good understanding, she was grateful for the advantages Ferdinand's love procured for her, without extending her wishes beyond them.

He had been married about six months; his wife promised an increase to their family, when one morning his father, who had appeared uncommonly grave at breakfast, ordered Ferdinand to attend him to the library. He obeyed; the *manner*, more than the words, struck him, and with an agitated heart he appeared before him.

"Ferdinand," said the Count, in a tone of solemnity, "I ardently wish to see you settled in life, an opportunity now offers not to be rejected. Count Benhorff has offered to give you his daughter, the Lady Amelia, whose large fortune and personal charms render the alliance most truly desirable, and entirely unobjectionable." He stopped, Ferdinand was thunderstruck; this was an occurrence that he had never once dreamt of. He hesitated, faltered, at length muttered out something about "the impropriety of being married before his brother."

"That is not your business, Sir," resumed the Count; "your brother has other views; Count Benhorff and his daughter have done you the honour of a distinguished preference, and it only remains for you to receive my orders, and I should suppose, to comply with them immediately with gratitude and transport, suitable to an offer so splendid, and so much superior to my expectations of settling you in life; as you well know you have only a share of my *personal* fortune to expect." "With whatever share you have the goodness to appropriate for me, Sir, I hope I shall be content and thankful, nor meanly wish to aggrandize myself by marriage without I could love and honour the Lady. Pardon me, Sir," added he, gathering a little more courage, "pardon me, therefore, if I do not so readily accord to your wishes as you may expect, but never will I marry a woman I cannot love."

"And what, Sir," said the Count, kindling into a rage, "should prevent you from loving the Lady Amelia, who has a hundred adorers, though she has condescended to single you out, undeserving as I fear you are of the distinction. Tell me, Sir, what are the obstacles to your being attached to so charming a young woman?" Never did Ferdinand experience equal perplexity to that moment; he trembled, and his emotions scarcely permitted him to speak.

"I have no knowledge of her temper; her——."

"Say no more," cried the Count, interrupting him; "no more equivocation, I see I have not been misinformed, you have formed another attachment; say, tell me, is it not so?"

"I am above uttering a falsehood," answered Ferdinand; "I own it, Sir, there is a young woman——."

"Foolish, imprudent boy!" exclaimed the Count, in a violent rage; "your youth hath been seduced into an intrigue with an artful wanton."

"By Heavens! No," cried Ferdinand, "I have *not* been seduced, nor is she a wanton."

"Hold, insolent!" returned the Count, "and *hear me*; if you have formed an imprudent connexion, break it off, I will enable you to give a handsome sum, and have done with it. Prepare to carry your addresses to the Lady Amelia; these are my absolute commands, which I expect you to obey, or you are no longer a son of mine."

"Oh! my father," cried Ferdinand,—"reverse that cruel sentence, command not impossibilities."

"I *do not*," answered the Count, a little softened; "an affair of gallantry has nothing to do with an engagement of honour, an union for life. You are young, and have been drawn away by your passions; but decency forbids you to continue your attachment whilst you are soliciting the Lady Amelia's hand: I therefore *request* you, Ferdinand, I will not command, I *desire* you to dissolve your present connexion, and let me have the happiness of seeing you established in my life-time. You are the only pledge left me of a too tender affection: Your angel mother *died* in giving *you life*; let not that life so dearly purchased render my latter days unhappy; let me meet her in the realms above with the conscious delight of having completed the happiness of her child."

The Count's voice faltered as he pronounced the last words. Ferdinand was in agonies; he threw himself at his father's feet:—"Spare me, spare your wretched son; oh! Sir, happiness and Lady Amelia cannot be joined with me; happiness consists not in titles, grandeur, or riches: I am moderate in my wishes; my brother will aggrandize your house."

"And *you*," said the Count, interrupting him with fury, "*you* resolve to disgrace it. Just Heaven! how am I punished for *my* errors in the person of my darling son! *Yes, you are* my punisher; you have chosen to be the instrument of vengeance, to retaliate upon your father, and hasten the few short days that are allotted to me, full of sorrow and despair: But hear me, once more I command you to promise me that you will give up your present infatuation, that you will quit the society of that woman who has seduced you from your duty. Speak, say you will obey me."

"I dare not deceive my father," replied Ferdinand, with grief and horror in his countenance; "I dare not forfeit my integrity."

"You persist then in your folly, in your crimes," exclaimed the other, in a rage little short of madness; "then mark my words: The allowance I have given you, I shall resume as long as you resist my will; the creature who has bewitched you I will punish, and if you dare to form any legal sacred connexion with her, my everlasting curses attend you both!"

"Stop, oh! stop," cried the frantic Ferdinand, "*she is my wife!*" The Count dropped into a chair.

"Wretch! unnatural wretch! what hast thou done?" said he, in a tone of horror, "thou art now an alien to my blood. I recall not what I have denounced; my curses are registered above; go, leave me, see me no more; dare not to enter any mansion where I reside, for I solemnly protest this is the last time I will behold thee!"—He rose from his chair, withdrew to a closet, and rang the bell. Orders were given to carry every thing belonging to Ferdinand out of the Castle that instant, and never to admit him more within its gates.

CHAPTER VII.

MEAN time the unhappy youth had fainted on the floor, where he was found by his brother, who recovered and tried to sooth him into composure; but the dreadful curse still vibrated in his ears, distraction was in his looks, and his tongue refused utterance to the emotions of his heart. He was conveyed to Rhodophil's apartment, who assured him he would leave nothing undone to soften his father's displeasure.—"Comfort yourself, my brother," said he, "all violences must subside, time must be allowed, fear not, I will be your friend and advocate, and for means of subsistence you may rely on me."—Ferdinand could make no reply; he pressed his brother's hand, and, attended by the faithful Ernest, left the Castle, and returned to his wife. The moment she saw him she screamed. Never was a man so altered in so short a time. Ernest was obliged to explain to her the discovery which had been made, and she no longer wondered at the grief and despair visible in her husband; she blamed and execrated herself as the cause; and in the height of her agitations absolutely proposed to him to give her up, to renounce her society, and permit her to spend her days in sorrow and obscurity. But Ferdinand would not be outdone in affection and generosity.—"You are my wife," said he; "you have not offended, and it is both my inclination and my duty to protect *you*, my dearest consolation, under every affliction." Ernest endeavoured to calm the grief and agitations of both; he promised to assist the entreaties of Rhodophil, by every representation that could soften the Count towards Ferdinand, and induce him to think favourably of Claudina.

But in vain was every effort to mitigate the Count's resentment, until one day, long after Claudina had been brought to bed of a boy, (whom Ferdinand named Charles Rhodophil, after his father and brother) when she was walking with her child in her arms, in the skirts of the forest for air, the Count and Rhodophil, who had been on a hunting party, met her; the latter dropped back to speak to her; the Count eyed her attentively, and when his son came up, inquired who she was; with some hesitation he acknowledged she was the wife of Ferdinand. He started, and was silent for several minutes; at length, sighing deeply, "I own," said he, "she is extremely beautiful; she has a child too!—Ill-fated Ferdinand! thou hast undone thyself, and rendered me culpable and wretched; but the infant is at least innocent; I did not curse, not reprobate *that*, therefore I will allow something to keep it from want."—On his return Ernest was called, and directed to pay them quarterly twenty crowns. The old man was overjoyed, and tried to obtain a larger allowance, but his master was immovable: "To keep them from want is sufficient, it is the charity I would bestow on a stranger, *they* have no claims upon me."

Glad even to have gained this point, Ernest hastened to them with the intelligence, with a quarter's advance, and bid them look on it as a lucky omen of future reconciliation. Ferdinand was transported; he wrote to his father a letter full of acknowledgments, deep contrition for having offended him, and every possible submission his situation would allow of; but his letter was returned unopened, and Ernest forbidden to mention his name.——Rhodophil frequently visited them, and often made Claudina little presents, which were very acceptable, for they experienced a loss which made their little income very confined. One morning, on coming down stairs, there seemed a disorder in the room very unusual; no fire was made, no preparation for breakfast, and the door of the house left on the latch. Their aunt, who had always performed all the offices of a servant, assisted by Claudina whilst Ferdinand nursed his little boy. This aunt it was plain was gone out, but for what, or where to, they could form no conjecture; however, they exerted themselves to do the necessary offices, but when they came to prepare their breakfast, they could find no spoons, and in a short time after discovered the drawers in the room had been opened, and all Claudina's linen was taken away; they likewise missed Ferdinand's watch, which hung in the room.

Strangely alarmed, they made every possible search, which only served to discover more losses, and to convince them they had been robbed, and by this aunt. Their consternation cannot be expressed; but the cruel truth was unquestionable, and with the very little money they had, they were obliged to purchase necessaries for use, which was a heavy drawback. What could have induced this woman to injure and desert them they could not imagine; but the fact was certain, and the loss and inconvenience great. Claudina was again with child, and this event added to the continued displeasure of the Count, which affected her husband with a deep melancholy, threw her into a low nervous disorder, which rendered her but little capable of domestic business, and but for the kindness of Rhodophil and Ernest, they must have perished. Mean time it was very visible that a heavy dejection overwhelmed the Count, his constitution grew weak, his spirits sunk, his appetite lost.—Every one was alarmed; the physician gave it as his opinion that it was a constitution breaking up, but no immediate danger; at length he confined himself solely to his apartment, and saw only Rhodophil, the physician, and his valet.

Ferdinand was informed of his father's situation, and was nearly distracted. He entreated Rhodophil to intercede for him, "that he might once more throw himself at the feet of his justly offended parent, and receive a last blessing." His entreaties were rejected—his presence forbidden. He then wrote a few lines, imploring his beloved father to revoke the heavy curse he had laid upon him and his wife.—His brother returned the letter, his father had refused it, and commanded him to mention his name no more. The truly wretched Ferdinand used to walk before the Castle gates for days together, imploring admittance, but all was fruitless; no servant dared to disobey orders, so positively given to the contrary.

One morning, whilst leaning his arms on the outside gate, Ernest came to him: "*I will* run the risque, follow me to my chamber, Sir, no time is to be lost." More dead than alive, he attended Ernest without speaking, when, at the very entrance of the house, they met his brother. He started back with amazement: "Good God! Ferdinand! how came you here?"

"Pardon me, Sir," said Ernest, much confused; "but from what I hear, my noble master is at the point of death; now, and now only, when he must solicit mercy from his heavenly father, is the time to try if he will extend that mercy, on his part, which he must supplicate from the Almighty."

"You are right," replied Rhodophil;—"Come with me to the anti-chamber, my dear brother, and I will procure you admittance, though *all others* are forbidden."—Ernest bowed and withdrew; with a beating heart and trembling limbs Ferdinand entered the anti-chamber, where Rhodophil's valet sat, who also started at seeing the unexpected guest his master brought in.

"Wait without," said Rhodophil, "nor at your peril permit any one to enter."—The servant quitted the room.

"Now," said the former, "I will go in and see the state our father is in, and administer a cordial to support his spirits."—Scarcely daring to breathe, Ferdinand waited near a quarter of an hour in all the agonies of suspense and terror.

Rhodophil at length appeared:—"He sleeps," said he, "every thing de-

pends on rest, we must not disturb him, wait a little." Ferdinand bowed his
head, he could not trust to his voice, his heart beat with increasing violence.
Near half an hour elapsed, when his attention was suddenly roused by two
or three deep groans. He started, and flew to the door; a short gallery communicated to the bed chamber of the Count, there he listened, a kind of
bustle seemed to be in the room, but the groans were not repeated; his
hand was on the lock, hardly sensible whether he intended to open it or
not, when it was suddenly opened on the other side. The Count's valet
appeared: "Be so good to return!" said he, "all is over, my master is no
more!"

Ferdinand tottered back into the other room, and fell lifeless on the
floor, where his brother found him on his return to the library, at which
period this history began.

The subsequent circumstances have been fully related, and having sent
Ferdinand to Vienna, we shall attend to Claudina and her children, who
were for several days inconsolable for the departure of her husband.

CHAPTER VIII.

EVERY attention that affection, and the duties of hospitality enjoined, was
paid by Rhodophil to his sister-in-law, and no longer restrained by the prudence and pride of Ferdinand, he made her a number of considerable presents, increased the finery of her wardrobe, was assiduous to amuse her, and
in short gained so highly on the esteem and gratitude of Claudina, that she
insensibly felt her regret lessened for the loss of her husband, and although
she sometimes felt and expressed a concern for his safety, yet the well-timed
amusements Rhodophil prepared for her, left that occasional anxiety but
as a passing cloud upon her memory, that was followed by brighter ideas.
Ernest, who had engaged to pay every attention to his mistress, as he called
her, found nothing was wanting from him to comfort her, and so captious is
the human mind, that, though he would have been grieved to have seen her
unhappy, yet he was very much displeased to see her so *cheerful*.

She commanded the house entirely, every servant was at her disposal,
and the master of it seemed to have no will but her's, no laws but of her
making. If we look back, and see the very humble state in which Claudina had lived before she knew Ferdinand, and even the humble mediocrity which she enjoyed with him before the death of Count Renaud; if we
consider that, though Ferdinand had procured masters to teach her accomplishments before she married, and of course with the advantages of his

conversation her mind must have been enlightened, and her understanding improved, yet still a number of improper ideas, habitual from early life, would at times recur, and render both her sentiments and behaviour very unequal. She had been always taught to expect that her beauty would make her fortune, therefore of course she thought highly of her charms, and when she sometimes listened to the extravagant praises of Rhodophil, she was ready to blame herself for so quickly accepting the offer of a younger, portionless brother, when, in all probability, had she waited, she might have been a Countess.

A too frequent repetition of those thoughts by degrees undermined the warmth of her affection for her husband, and one day, when walking in the garden with Rhodophil, that he was lavish in his encomiums on her person, she interrupted by asking, with a look of naïvete, "How it happened, that, if he thought so well of her, he had not loved her like Ferdinand?"

"And did I not love you?—Yes, Claudina," replied he, "from the first moment I adored you; but could I see my brother wretched?—Or could I hope you would reserve the blessing of your hand for me until my father's death? Neither dared I think of marrying you to involve you in wretchedness. Had you suffered for me, what I have known you to bear with Ferdinand, I should have been distracted. No, Claudina, such was the delicacy of *my* passion, that I chose to be miserable *myself*, rather than make the woman I adored unhappy; to lay her under the interdiction of a father, the weight of a curse would have sunk me to the grave."

Not a word of this was lost on Claudina; every syllable sunk into her soul; she began to reflect on what she had forfeited by marrying Ferdinand, and blamed the ardour of that love which had sought its own gratification at *her* expence. Rhodophil saw the workings of her mind, and pursued his insidious tale.

"When my brother married you, how great was my misery—what sleepless nights, what days of anguish! yet how did I labour for your happiness? Now I may tell you:—Know then, my father never allowed you one shilling; I invented that tale to spare your delicacy, that you might not feel yourself too much obliged to me; but *could* I do *too much* for the woman I adored? During my father's illness I laboured with uncommon zeal to procure a settlement for you, to procure a pardon for my brother. I ventured to brave his utmost resentment by taking him into the next room (not thinking his death so very near) in the hope of having him revoke that dreadful curse he had laid upon him; but, alas! he died, and all my endeavours were fruitless."

"How!" exclaimed she, "Did he not see his father? Did he not forgive him on his death-bed?"

"No," he replied, "he never saw the Count after the day your marriage was discovered."

"Good Heavens!" said she, "what imposition, what falsities did Ferdinand tell me!" She then repeated to him what has been already mentioned, and the very circumstances which he had invented to calm her mind, and restore her peace, were now turned against him, as a piece of base duplicity, and the inference drawn was, "that if he was capable of so much deceit in one thing, he *might* in another, and therefore she could have no confidence where there was room for doubts."—Rhodophil, who was perfectly acquainted with his brother's motives for the deception, pretended to be entirely ignorant of them, and, by the most artful finesse, gave a colouring to an action dictated by tenderness alone, that stamped an indelible impression on the mind of Claudina, to the injury of that love and truth she owed to the most affectionate of husbands.

Letters very soon arrived from the much injured Ferdinand, acquainting them of his arrival at Vienna, his introduction to the Emperor, and the desirable situation in which he found himself placed. His expressions to Claudina were replete with tenderness, and all his anxiety arose from a separation that he *knew* must be equally painful to her. The only consolation he could promise to himself were her letters, and he besought her to indulge him with hearing of herself and children by every opportunity. To his brother he was grateful and affectionate; to Ernest kind and friendly, requesting him to watch over the health and peace of his beloved wife, whose tender sensibility he was apprehensive would injure her constitution.

Poor Ferdinand! little did he conceive that his little bark of happiness was wrecked upon a fatal shore that blasted all his hopes for ever; much less could he have an idea to what hand he was indebted for conducting her to the port of destruction. Ernest, when he had perused his letter, sighed heavily:—"Alas!" said he, "how one fatal action has destroyed the peace of a whole family for ever! The mole that has long laboured to undermine the happiness of Ferdinand has now succeeded; his own rash hand first pointed the weapon that must wound his bosom beyond all possibility of a cure, for I too plainly see his wife is grown indifferent to him, and attached to the pleasures of the world!"

Days and weeks passed away, and saw Claudina gay and happy; they heard often from Ferdinand, who had been twice in an engagement, and had been promoted.—When the campaign was over he hoped to return and embrace all the treasures he possessed in one circle, a tender wife, a generous and affectionate brother, and his darling children.—This hope, so flattering to him, was little capable of giving pleasure to the inhabitants of the Castle; and Ernest observed all at once a deep thoughtfulness take possession of the Count, and a pensive melancholy steal over the features of Claudina, for neither of which was there apparently any cause.

One day, being in the room which had formerly been the library, and adjoining to Claudina's bed chamber, sitting at the window indulging his own reflections, he thought he heard the Count's voice in a whispering tone; there was nothing extraordinary or reprehensible in his being in her apartment, yet some how Ernest found his curiosity excited to know why the conversation should be in a whisper; he therefore listened, and though he could only make out indirect sentences and half words, he understood but too much, and retired overwhelmed with astonishment and horror; a scheme replete with the most unpardonable wickedness seemed to be in agitation, which it was his duty, if possible, to prevent.

The following day Ernest sought out the Count's valet, who had been always more civil to him than ever his master had, since the old Count's death, and which indeed arose from a circumstance Ernest had long since forgotten. In the juvenile days of Rhodophil and Ferdinand, when they were riding out one day, accompanied by Peter (then also a lad) and Ernest, the horse of Peter took fright: Ernest, who had an excellent one, as quickly followed, overtook the other, and by a dexterous manœuvre stopped the horse in the very moment when he must have plunged over a precipice. This signal service Peter never had forgotten, and though he could boast but of little principle or integrity in any one point, yet he always looked up to Ernest as the preserver of his life; when the old man scarcely remembered a single circumstance of it, and had sometimes been at a loss to account for Peter's particular civilities to him. These attentions, however, encouraged Ernest to address him, and to endeavour, if possible, to gain his confidence, being well assured that his master's secrets were in his possession.

Meeting by chance in the gallery, the old steward invited him to his apartment in the evening, an honour Peter was proud of, and took care not to neglect: He found a good bottle of wine prepared for him, and a very friendly reception; both warmed his heart. After a little preparatory conversation the old Gentleman remarked, "that he was fearful the Count, or his sister-in-law, was ill, as they appeared to be very dull and melancholy."

"As to illness, Mr. Ernest," answered Peter, "there is not much of that I believe; but they have enough to make them melancholy, when it is likely Mr. Ferdinand may soon come home."

"How!" cried the other, "that is strange indeed! I should rather think they would be overjoyed at that, though to be sure he won't stay long."

"Ah! bless you, Mr. Ernest, you know nothing of the business, and yet it is as plain as the nose in your face."

"Why, you know, Peter, I never pry into secrets, and am no tatler of other people's affairs."

"No, I'll be sworn, you ar'n't; you are a good man, Sir, and don't know what wickedness goes forward here."—"Why don't you drink, Peter?"

"I do, I do, thank your love." Two or three glasses opened his heart still more freely. "To tell you the truth, Mr. Ernest, my master, the Count, is but a bad man, for seeing he has got all the fortune, he might have let his brother keep his wife to himself."

"How! why, sure! why, you do not think he wants to separate them, do you?"

"Bless your soul, why they be leagued together, and to my mind Madame Claudina loves him more than ever she did her husband."

"Astonishing!" cried Ernest.

"Yes, 'tis astonishing to be sure, because Mr. Ferdinand is a much handsomer man; but I'll let you know the whole if you'll be secret."

"You know I am no talker, Peter."

"Nor more you ar'n't, for you never made mischief on any poor servant, so I'll tell you, then, as sure as you be alive, Madame is a breeding."

"Impossible!" exclaimed the other.

"No, no, 'tis not unpossible, the truth is out, and master wants to persuade her to go away to some place in Hungary, as if she runned away, and then they think Mr. Ferdinand will kill himself, or break his heart, or something, and then they two are to be married. This was one scheme; then another was, to have Mr. Ferdinand way-laid and killed, for if he comes home all will come out, and then 'twill for a certainty be murder among them."

"Good Heavens! what treachery and infamy! How did you learn all this, Peter?"

"Why, because I am in master's secrets; he can't do without me."

"Then I conjure you, Peter, to let me know all your proceedings; I will amply reward you, and God will bless you if you serve the innocent."

"Why, as to that, Sir, I know I am not very innocent to be sure; but I love you, for you saved my life you know, when the horse was going to caper over the mountain with me, and so I think it my duty to serve you, and if you desire me I will tell you all, only don't speak a word of it to master or any body." This Ernest faithfully promised, and Peter engaged to step into his room, whenever he could gain any intelligence to communicate.

This information of Peter's corroborating the conversation he had overheard in the library, left Ernest no room for doubt of a connexion terrible to think of, yet what steps to take, whether to acquaint Ferdinand with the dreadful secret, or to let him still remain ignorant and happy, were measures he thought must depend on the result of *their* determinations, and for the knowledge of them he depended on Peter. Nothing particular transpired for two days. Claudina's dejection increased, and she seemed very ill, her appetite was lost, and frequent faintings alarmed the family; but she refused to have medical advice, and said it was only weakness from a violent cold. On the third night, however, she was seized with convulsions, only her maid and Rhodophil attended her, and for hours her life was in great danger; but towards the morning she grew better. Rhodophil seemed transported that the convulsions had left her, and observed among the servants that his sister-in-law had for many years been subject to those fits at times, and the approach of the disorder had occasioned the weakness and dejection of her spirits for some days before, he was glad the *crisis* was over.

This tale passed current with the servants; but Ernest had his suspicions, which a short time confirmed, for she soon recovered, and was as gay and as happy as usual. The arrival of Ferdinand, in about three weeks after, seemed to give general joy in the family.—Ernest alone was unhappy, because he knew too much, yet he resolved to be silent, rather than destroy the peace of his beloved master, (as he *always* called him) and render his future days miserable.

CHAPTER IX.

FERDINAND had a month's leave of absence; he had been promoted to a higher rank than he could have hoped for, his prospects in the army were such as to inspire a hope of being in a short time able to provide for his family. He returned to them enlivened by expectation, and transported to embrace a darling wife, and a generous brother. In the evening, when retired to the apartment of his Claudina, when expressing his raptures at seeing her so well and happy, a deep and hollow groan made him start from his chair, and threw his wife into a trembling fit.—"What, or where does that groan come from?" cried she. He was about to answer, when a second, still more alarming, was followed by those words from the same voice Ferdinand had twice before heard:—"*Fly, fly from her arms, as you would avoid sin and death!*"—Claudina shrieked and fainted. Her husband rang the bell for assistance. She relapsed from one fit into another for several hours; all was fright and confusion, for he did not chuse to account for her disorder among the servants: One, however, observed these were worse fits than she had lately, because they lasted longer.

"What then," asked Ferdinand, "has she before now had such seizures as this?"

"Yes, Sir," answered the servant, "a short time ago, and my master told us, as to be sure you know, that Madame was often troubled with them."

This information surprised him, the conclusion in his own mind was, that she had before now been alarmed in a similar manner; but the words dwelt upon his memory:—What could be their import—"As you would avoid sin and death!" Good God! how shocking! He had not time, however for much reflection, the state his wife lay in chiefly engrossed his attention; he insisted upon medical advice, and a physician was sent for. Before he could make his appearance distraction had seized her brain; she talked wild and incoherent, of death, murder, Rhodophil and Ferdinand! When the Doctor came he declared her in a frenzy fever, and methods were taken to lower it so effectually, that in a few hours she lay quite in a torpid state, insensible to every thing round her.—Poor Ferdinand withdrew for a few moments at the request of Rhodophil.

"Alas!" cried he, "is this my welcome! Have I returned home with the dear delight of being happy in the bosom of my family, and must this dreadful prohibition cause me consummate wretchedness!"

"What prohibition?" asked Rhodophil, eagerly. Ferdinand was sensible that he had said too much, that he had excited a curiosity he knew not how to elude. After a little pause and consideration, he acquainted Rhodophil with the preceding circumstance, adding, "that the voice seemed to be his father's." The other sunk back in his chair, pale and trembling, unable to utter a syllable, his eyes fixed on his brother with a wild inquiring look.—"I see," said Ferdinand, "you are extremely shocked; had not Claudina been present with me, I should hardly have ventured to relate to you so strange and improbable a circumstance, fearful lest you should have ridiculed my visionary ideas; but I am too well assured of the reality."

"Of what?" cried the Count, falteringly: "What did you hear else?"

"No more than the words I have repeated, words sufficient to harrow up my soul, to fill me with dreadful apprehensions, and terrifying images. What they mean, Heaven only knows, for I am not conscious of any crimes, and after having so long lived with my wife, why this alarming caution now? Why, I am forbidden to return to her arms by supernatural powers, is beyond my comprehension to define; I see only that there is, there must be, some dreadful cause, and that I am marked out for misery. O, Rhodophil!

wretched are the days of those who fail in their first duties, obedience to a parent; and sure destruction follows a father's curse." No longer able to repress his emotions Ferdinand wept aloud.

Rhodophil, who was by this time a little recovered (though his eye was still wandering with an affrighted glance, and his limbs no longer boasted their usual steadiness) sought to speak comfort to his brother: "I will not (said he) tell you that it is possible your senses might be deceived; I am neither credulous, nor superstitious, yet I think you would do right to pay some observance to a warning from the dead, and all that we can infer is, that the union between you and your wife is displeasing to Heaven."— "Wherefore," cried Ferdinand, "the want of birth and riches is no *crime* in the sight of God; I married unknown to my father, that was a sin against his authority; but can it be a crime of that magnitude to draw down the displeasure of Heaven?

"Oh! yes, if it provoked a father's malediction, it rendered both criminal, and *I* am the wretched victim; *I* am singled out from hundreds who have committed the same error, the same unpardonable act of disobedience, to be held up as a pharos to warn unthinking youth of the miseries attending a too hasty connexion unsanctioned by a parent's approbation. Oh! my father, I am indeed severely punished!"

This apostrophe drove Rhodophil from the room; he could not support the sight of his brother's distress. Ernest immediately entered; the afflicted heart clings for consolation to the first sympathizing friend; the old man was shocked to see him; he rested his head on the shoulder of Ernest, whilst he repeated what had happened in Claudina's apartment. "Dear unhappy creature!"—added he, "I have destroyed *her* peace, my fatal love has undone her; in humble obscurity she might have been happy, and *I* have dragged her into wretchedness."

"My dear master (said Ernest) do not reproach yourself on *her* account; your wife *cannot*, ought not to blame *you*, whatever the circumstances may be that renders your union improper; to *her you* have always done your duty. If she is unhappy, you are not to blame; the offence against your father was designed to promote *her* happiness as well as your own, *why* it has failed, we are not to inquire; but remember this, that the same voice which bid you '*fly*' from your wife, pronounced the words '*Pardon and peace;*' if there is credibility in one, there is in the other."

Ferdinand raised his head, and looking earnestly in his face, "There is an implication in your words that shock me, that would fill me with the most torturing apprehensions, but that I know the impossibility of there being any grounds for them. The 'pardon and peace' has never been one day absent from my memory, strange if it should, when it is the ground-work, the only hold I have to reconcile me to myself: But, alas! if I lay hold on *that* for consolation, if I look on those words as a sacred command, what must I now sacrifice to the same mandate? My wife, my dear innocent wife, the mother of my children, the sweet comforter under all my misfortunes, must I give up her society, fly her arms? Oh! stern and cruel!"

"Stop, Sir (said Ernest, interrupting him) reflect, who you are accusing, remember that, to us short-sighted mortals, the events which often appear most distressing, are intended for our greatest blessings."

"Ernest," replied Ferdinand, "you are a *natural* philosopher, you know not the difficulty of being a practical one, and at your age the passions have lost their turbulence. O, that I also was old, or laid peaceably in my grave! But I forget Claudina," (added he, rising briskly, and rushing to her apartment.) She had just began to shew some signs of recollection, but the moment he appeared she shrieked and turned from him. His little boy Charles was in the room; he ran to his father: "My mamma will not speak to me, will not kiss me; indeed, papa, I have not been naughty."—The artless voice of innocence overcame Ferdinand; he struggled to repress his emotions, but the big drops rolled down his face. He embraced his child, then turning to her, "Claudina! my dear Claudina, will you not speak to us?" She turned her head, her eyes met his, she groaned, and averted them to the child. "My poor boy!" exclaimed she. He ran to her arms. She embraced him: "Go, go, my child, to your father." Ferdinand was deeply affected. He ordered the attendants to withdraw, then seating himself by her: "My best, my only love (said he) take comfort, you have been terrified, recover yourself, my Claudina." He would have taken her hand; she withdrew it. "Revere the voice of Heaven," cried she, greatly agitated, "obey its decrees, pollution is in my touch, and unless you wish me mad indeed approach me not. Poor unhappy man! well may you curse the hour you first saw me."

"Who, I!" cried he, "*I* curse; alas! too well I know the horrors of that rash impetuosity of the mind. No, but for *your* sake I have no regrets; *I* have drawn down the wrath of Heaven and you, innocent as you are, must suffer the sad effects."

"Innocent!" repeated she, "leave me, Ferdinand, I beseech you to leave me; once more, if you would preserve us both from everlasting perdition, reverence that sacred command, fly me as you would do a scorpion that might sting you to death." Inexpressibly shocked, and apprehensive that her senses were again wandering, he rang the bell, and on the entrance of the servants withdrew: Regardless of what constructions might be put on the orders she gave, she insisted that neither her husband or Rhodophil should be again admitted to her apartment.

The house was melancholy, for every one in it was gloomy and un-happy; they shunned each other; the two brothers met at meals, but those meals were short and unsociable; each feared to inquire into particulars they had reason to dread; yet they heard Claudina was better. The third day, when torturing suspense, and disappointed love, had worn Ferdinand al-most to a shadow, Ernest entered the room: "I am come, Sir, from Madame Claudina."

"What (cried the other) have you been admitted?"

"I was sent for, Sir, and have had a long conversation."

"O, tell me, quickly tell, the result, my mind is in tumults."

"I know it, Sir, and therefore am I come. Pray, Heaven, that what I have to relate may compose it. I received an order to attend on your Lady; I obeyed, and my old heart ached to see the ravages grief had made. She ordered every one from the room; she was sitting on the side of the bed: Ernest (said she, with much solemnity) you are the faithful servant and friend of the family; on your fidelity I rely, and your assistance I solicit."

"Assistance! (repeated Ferdinand) of what nature, pray?"

"Have the goodness to hear me, Sir, without interruption," resumed Ernest: "I assured *the Lady* she might depend upon my readiness to serve her in every thing consistent with my duty." This was her answer.

"Some circumstances have arisen that render it absolutely necessary I should quit this house, and be separated from my husband; I wish to go away equally unknown to him or his brother: I am not destitute of money, and for this purpose shall use it without scruple. I intend to retire into a con-vent, will you assist me privately?" I assured her I would, and immediately took an oath never to reveal the place of her abode without her consent."

"How! (cried Ferdinand) is this your affection for me? And do you think I will permit her to quit this house, leave me and her children, my generous brother, bury herself in a convent, *she* to be the sacrifice for my errors? Do you think I will ever suffer this?"

"*I do*, Sir (answered he, calmly) I think you respect the will of Heaven, that you will consider, you *must* separate *to be happy.*—I shall this day set about an inquiry for a proper residence for her, and when I have found it, neither force nor persuasions shall oblige me to reveal the secret without her permission. What I say to you is in confidence which she allows of; but it is her earnest request you do not mention it to your brother."

Ernest withdrew, leaving Ferdinand overwhelmed with grief, astonish-ment, and irresolution. He resolved, however, to watch her apartment and Ernest also, that they might not elude his observation, and that he might at least have the satisfaction of knowing her place of residence.

The next day the old man was absent, and Ferdinand rightly conjectured he was about making preparations for her departure. He kept his eye on her apartment, his heart was in great agitations, he found the "awful voice" had effectually terrified Claudina, and that her resolution was taken; he could not but applaud her fortitude, though he was overwhelmed with anguish. Sometimes it occurred to him as very extraordinary, that having resided several months together after his father's death in that house, in that same apartment, without the least disturbance; why *now*, after so much time had elapsed, a supernatural being should command him to '*fly from her arms*, as he would *avoid sin and death.*' The more he reflected, the more he was puzzled, the whole was so very wonderful, so much exceeding credibility, that he was sometimes tempted to think it was all illusion; but then the proofs returned, Claudina heard the last fatal command as well as himself, there could be no doubt of it: If then he admitted the one, he could not be mistaken in the other: Had his brother then a 'corrupt heart?' His brother, who had ever been his friend, the protector of his wife and children, whose conduct had ever *appeared* so fair, so open? Then he recollected his information from Ernest, and other circumstances, as a counterbalance to those acts of generosity. Puzzled, lost in conjecture, and miserably unhappy, Ferdinand passed that day and night, having inquired, previous to his retiring, how his wife did, and heard that she was much better, but desired to be undisturbed; they will then proceed on their plan, thought he, in a day or two, and it behoves me to be attentive to their motions.

The morning came, weak and unrefreshed, he threw on his clothes, and proceeded to the gallery, which communicated with Claudina's apartment, there he met Ernest:—"Return, Sir (said he) if you please, to your apartment, I wish to speak to you."—Ferdinand complied; they entered, and shut the door. "Now, my dear master, collect your fortitude, be governed by reason; Claudina is gone."

"Gone!" exclaimed the other, "how—where—when?"

"She went from hence last night, and is already in a place of safety."

"Then she cannot be far off," cried Ferdinand.

"Pardon me, Sir, when I said she was in a place of safety; it did not imply that she was at the end of her journey; but, however, here, Sir, is a letter, which she ordered me to deliver to you."—He hastily tore it open, and read the following lines:

"Adieu, my amiable and too tender husband:—Husband! O Heavens! my tears blot out the name; adieu then best, and most injured of men— warned by a miraculous event, *I fly from you*, from guilt and misery. Forget me and be happy: I am dead to you and the world; on the verge of the grave, the prospect was dreadful: I devote the rest of my days to penitence and prayer. My infant I take with me; she may one day emerge into the world if she lives; should she die, her happiness is secured.

"You shall from time to time hear *of me*, but you will never *see* me more. I have darkened all your prospects of felicity; I have returned the tenderest attachment with ingratitude. I am now no more. You have my full and entire consent to marry again under more fortunate auspices, for I again repeat that I am dead to you, solemnly devoted to a solitary life. May you live and be happy. Let not my dear boy detest the memory of his mother, he is young, and may believe I am dead; I wish not to be remembered. Return to the army, let glory be your mistress; she will amuse your mind, and lead you in the road to happiness, by teaching you to forget Claudina. Heavens bless you, and my dear, dear boy, for ever. I have written to the Count; the letter is of little consequence. May my name never more pass your lips. Hasten from hence; confide in the faithful Ernest; forgive and forget the unworthy Claudina."

Ferdinand perused this letter with all the marks of the wildest astonishment. "What fatal mystery lurks beneath the expressions in this paper!" cried he, "Of what crimes has she been guilty, but her attachment to me, and wherefore does she accuse herself of ingratitude? Marry again! Oh! Claudina, you little know my heart. There is, there must be some secret with which I am unacquainted, every line in her letter discovers it, why else call me injured? Oh! Ernest, declare this secret, whatever it is, the knowledge cannot make me so miserable as this dreadful uncertainty, this painful imagination."

"From me, Sir," answered Ernest, "you can learn nothing, for I have nothing to reveal; reconcile your mind to this event, which must be for the advantage of both.—Nothing on earth shall make me betray my trust, nor, whilst I live, discover the place of her abode. Should I die, when you are from me, I will take care you shall then, through a particular channel, still hear from, or of her, if you desire it; but I hope time will have its usual effects to restore your tranquillity, and forget the object that now causes your distress."

"Impossible!" exclaimed Ferdinand,—"impossible that I should ever forget my wife, the mother of my children, the choice of my heart! O, why, wherefore am I marked out to be the veriest wretch that crawls the earth, cut off from every endearing tie, and from some fatal unknown cause interdicted from enjoying the only blessing my misfortunes had left me!"

"My dear master," answered the old man, tears in his eyes, "recollect you have still one tie, one blessing, your son; to the dispensations of Providence it is our duty to submit, it avails nothing to inquire into the causes of things beyond our comprehension."

"Had she died, I trust, I should have borne my sorrows like a man; but this strange, incomprehensible mystery——. My child too! a blessing! O, Ernest, may he not live to wring a father's heart with grief, to retaliate upon me! He may, and I deserve it should be so, but, he may make *me* wretched, he may shorten *my days by disobedience and affliction*; but never, never shall he experience *a father's curse*, nor struggle under a malediction registered in Heaven, and never to be expunged!" "Do not indulge that idea, Sir, Heaven hears not, confirms not, man's rash imprecations, uttered in a moment of frenzy; their confirmation must depend upon circumstances; Heaven heeds not the curses of disappointed ambition."

"I have no longer any business here," cried Ferdinand, starting from a reverie, and hardly attending to the words of Ernest;—"nor will I return to the army, I care not what becomes of me, but I will see my brother."—He flew out of the room to Rhodophil's apartment, which entering without ceremony, he found him gazing on a letter that he held in his hand, fixed like a statue. The entrance of Ferdinand startled him; he rose, crushed the paper into his pocket,—"Well, Sir!" was all he could say.—"O, my brother! O, Rhodophil! Claudina's gone, fled, I know not whither."

This address occasioned an alteration in the looks of the other, from a haughty fierceness, they softened into an appearance of compassion and curiosity. "Is it possible (asked he) that she has not acquainted you with her motives for withdrawing, nor where she intends to reside?"

"Neither (replied he;) she bids me adieu for ever, will never see me more, and desires me to forget her as unworthy of my affection; for Heaven's sake tell me if you can divine the cause of this cruel, unaccountable conduct."

"Indeed I cannot (answered Rhodophil.) Some weeks ago she was low spirited and melancholy, then she had fits one night, but in two or three days got better, and seemed more tranquil; it is certain her disposition has been very unequal, the cause of which I could never rightly comprehend."

"Good God! (exclaimed the other) it is very strange, her letter seems to imply as if she had behaved imprudently, yet surely it is impossible."

"Something certainly lay heavy upon her mind (said the Count;) women are inexplicable beings; *she may* have deceived you; I do not say she has, because I know nothing; but some cause there must be, and all that I can advise you is, to forget her."

"How easy to advise where the heart is not interested! To forget is a hard lesson, memory given to us for a blessing, but too often proves the source of the bitterest sorrow; and my hopes of happiness are clouded for ever. One only request I have now to make."

"What is it?" asked Rhodophil, with some emotion. "As the unfortunate Claudina has entirely secluded herself, tell me, has she the means for her support?" The other hesitated a moment, then taking the paper from his pocket, which he had been gazing on, he gave it into his hands, "*that* will satisfy you," said he. These were the contents:

TO COUNT RHODOPHIL.

"When this reaches you, I shall have bid the world adieu for ever; my much injured husband never will incur the wrath of Heaven for his attachment to a worthless woman after this day—I shall see him no more.

"The settlement you made on me is in the hands of Ernest; half of that sum I shall send for quarterly, but no clue will be found by that means to trace me; I have taken my measures too securely for any possibility of a discovery: The other half of that settlement I have made over in trust to Ernest for the education of my son. May he never hear that he has a mother existing! *Two* persons only know the place of my retreat, *they know all!* They are sworn to secrecy, and never will be *bribed* to betray their trust; if *provoked* they may say *too much*.

"May Heaven comfort, bless, and preserve Ferdinand and my child! I would extend my blessings, but they may prove curses; from a wretch like me all good wishes may be reversed; yet Heaven will distinguish between the innocent and the guilty; the 'awful voice' convinced me of that truth, and bids *me* fly from the world for ever! May the *warning* be extended to others guilty as myself.

CLAUDINA."

"Strange mystery!" cried Ferdinand; "those two persons that '*know all!*' What is that dreadful *all*? O, how torturing is this doubt! Ernest is one (he has confessed it) that enjoys her confidence; but he has declared no force on earth shall induce him to betray her. Who the other is I know not; but no doubt she was well advised in her choice of confidants. Her own words pronounce her 'guilty,' but of what? What guilt can *she* have committed? Where had she the opportunity?"

"It is in vain to puzzle ourselves with conjectures," answered Rhodophil; "time only can develop the mystery, and we must endeavour to be content until that period arrives; some unexpected incident may bring all things to light. You see she will not be without a support, which I shall regularly pay. As for your son Charles, I take upon *me* the care of *his* fortune, and will send him to a school at my own expence; the moiety of his mother's settlement shall be paid to Ernest, and be left to accumulate for his expences hereafter.

"This has been a melancholy visit to you, my dear Ferdinand; but I entreat you to endeavour, if possible, to overcome this shock, to think of Claudina as dead, and as one whom you ought not, from her own confession, to lament."

With a deep sigh Ferdinand replied, *"I will endeavour;* but the more I think, the more the mystery increases, and the more wretched I am. I thank you for my poor Charles; the little Claudina, I trust, her mother will not neglect. Within three days I shall leave you."

"How! (cried the Count) in three days? Surely my brother will not desert me: Let us comfort each other, resign your commission, partake an equal share with me, and let me have the satisfaction of contributing to your returning peace. We will take a tour into Hungary; I have an estate there I have never seen. You will be amused. Pray oblige me."

"I thank you most sincerely (answered Ferdinand;) but my resolution is taken, and I intend to *ramble,* I neither know nor care where, chance shall be my guide."

"That is a ridiculous, romantic idea (said the Count;) you may encounter a thousand accidents by such a scheme, with scarce a possibility of being amused without a companion, or any plan in view." Ferdinand made but a slight answer, yet sufficient to convey his determination, and the entrance of company drove him from the room.

Ernest only was admitted into his confidence, and with him he consulted about the disposal of his son Charles. As there was an excellent academy at Baden, they thought it best he should be there, because Ernest would have him under his eye.—"My years are great (said the good old man) between sixty and seventy, and my days may be few, but whilst I live, never will I remit my attention to him. I have a nephew, a young man of integrity, who is the third master in that very academy: I can depend upon his care there, and *here* I will watch over his interests. I am *certain* the Count will not discharge me *now."*

"Why *now,* more than before?" asked Ferdinand.

"Because, because (said he, a little confused, conscious that he had said too much) he does justice to my fidelity, and is certain of my attachment to his family." Satisfied with this answer, the other consulted with him on his projected ramble, and as Ernest found him determined, he made no efforts to oppose him in a pursuit that he thought would amuse him for a time, and, like all other novelties, soon subside; and what made him the more readily come into it was, that an account arrived of a truce being agreed upon between the Emperor and his opponent, and that the troops were ordered into winter quarters, consequently there was no necessity for resigning his commission, as he might have leave of absence for a few months.

Rhodophil appeared to regret his design, yet nevertheless furnished him with a handsome sum for his expences, and requested he would draw freely upon him whenever it was necessary. Charles was informed his mother was gone a journey (and after a time Ernest was to acquaint him that she was dead.)—The same information was circulated in the family, though not as readily believed, for every one concluded she was run away from her husband unknown to them all: But Charles, who was only three years old, gave easy credit to any thing he was told, and in his new situation, where Mr. Dunloff, the nephew of Ernest, paid him the attention of a father, and he had a variety of young companions (a thing quite new to him) he soon ceased to lament the loss of his real parents, and was delighted with the change of residence.

CHAPTER X.

Ferdinand was impatient to be gone from the Castle, and within ten days after Claudina had disappeared he saw his son fixed, heard from Ernest that his mother and the *little* Claudina were well, and having taken leave of his brother, who requested to hear often from him, one fine morning, equipped only with a change or two of linen, which he contrived to put in his pockets, a stout stick, and a small pair of pocket pistols, he set off on his intended pedestrian tour.—Ernest accompanied him to the entrance of the forest, and when Ferdinand embraced the good old man, tears rolled down his aged cheeks: "May Heaven preserve you, my dearest master, when there is only a *choice of evils*, we must endeavour to bear with that which appears the lightest; I therefore trust you to Providence rather than to the wicked and malignant. Take care of yourself, and depend upon my love and fidelity." His increasing emotions precluded farther words on either side. Ferdinand wrung his hand affectionately, and unable to repress his own tears, they, as if by mutual consent, turned and walked hastily from each other, the one to the Castle, the other pursued his way through the forest.

He walked leisurely on for some hours without feeling fatigue, for his mind was wholly occupied with revolving on all the extraordinary occurrences that had happened since the death of the late Count, and although he had never given credit to the improbable stories of ghosts, or believed in the old legends handed down to posterity by the slaves of fear and monkish superstition; yet there was such a conviction in his mind, that he could not be deceived in the voice which three times had startled him; and the last time was not only heard by Claudina, but appeared from her own letters to have struck her with a sense of conscious guilt, (though of what nature he could not divine) that it was impossible there could be any misapprehension, where there was no fear, or expectation of terror. All was strange and inexplicable, and he found himself involved in a labyrinth of perplexity, without any clue to guide him through it.

He at length came to a side of the forest which had a very steep hill, or rather mountain, rising from a narrow valley, which was watered by a small stream that seemed to meander slowly round the sides of the hill beyond the view; here Ferdinand stopped, and for the first moment recollected that he was tired and faint for want of refreshment, which, though a very natural occurrence, he had never apprehended; and Ferdinand concluded, without inquiring, that he would take the right-hand side of the forest, where two or three little hamlets lay dispersed, and would afford him some accommodation.—He viewed the mountain with a wearied eye, beyond the little valley the forest was very thick, nor did he know its termination; the other side he was acquainted with, but here he was entirely at a loss: Whilst he deliberated, he seated himself on a piece of the rock, where he had rested but a few moments before he heard the tinkling of a bell, and presently several sheep came to the opposite side of the rivulet; they stopped, looking at him, as if afraid of a stranger:—"Poor, simple animals! (exclaimed he) fear not a wretched, powerless man! Alas! thy very looks claim pity, so void of guile, hard and callous must that heart be grown, whose profession leads him to put the murderous knife to a throat so unoffending!"

He had scarcely finished those words, when he saw a young shepherdess descending from the mountain to attend the watering of her flocks. He marked her as she came nearer; plain and humble was her attire, simple and unfashioned her air; a good height, and a clear brown skin, with a ruddy complexion, were all her attractions. "Behold the child of nature! (thought he;) innocence of heart, simplicity of manners!" She came down to her sheep, the small rivulet only parted them. He saluted her. She returned a rustic bow, looking earnestly on him: "I have lost my way, shepherdess, and am faint and tired."

"Go round the hill (said she, pointing with her finger) there is a little bridge, cross it, follow the path way, it will bring you up to our cottage, my father is there, and you may rest yourself."

"And you (said he) where do you dwell?"

"There also (answered she.) When I have watered and housed my sheep, I shall come there too."

Ferdinand did not hesitate; he walked slowly to the bridge, and with difficulty began to climb the winding ascent. After much fatigue he reached a kind of platform in the middle of the hill, where he saw a small cottage, a deep hanging brow of the mountain seemed suspended over it, and appeared as if every moment it would fall, and crush the humble dwelling into dust. He shuddered as he beheld it; but advancing to the cottage, saw a venerable looking man sitting to enjoy the breezes that played over the hills.

The old man viewed him with evident surprise; Ferdinand related the direction he had obtained from the shepherdess, and appeared so very much spent with toil, that the shepherd desired he would walk in, gave him his own stool as being the best, brought him some milk, and a cake, he said, of his Maria's baking. Never was repast more delicious than this milk, when almost choaked with thirst; Ferdinand drank the wholesome beverage, looked at the simple shepherd, and his humble dwelling clean and comfortable, though unadorned, with delight. "My good father (said he) I thank your hospitality, you have revived my fainting spirits."

"You are truly welcome (replied the shepherd;) but may I inquire, son, where you are going to on foot, and alone, for it is too late to reach Baden now before the close of night?"

"I came *from Baden* (said Ferdinand) and am going I know not whither; going to travel."

"To travel?"

"Yes."

"What on foot—alone?"

"And why not, father? I go to see the country, to amuse myself, a horse would be sometimes inconvenient, for instance, a horse could not have brought me here."

"No (replied the old man;) but was there a necessity that you *should come here?*"

"Not a necessity to come here particularly; but I am on a tour of curiosity, and therefore the lowly valley, or the towering mountain, will equally attract me; I can never be out of my way."

"Strange (said the shepherd, eying him attentively) strange, that a young man, who seems formed for the world, should take a fancy to roam the forests on foot, without a companion or necessaries to refresh him!"

"The first I want not (said Ferdinand) and for the last I trust to benevolence and hospitality, such as I now experience."

"But suppose you *had not* met my daughter, your trust would have been a very feeble one, for I know not another hut for a great way off, and you would have been benighted in the forest. Think of your danger in that case."

"Could we always foresee (observed Ferdinand) we might possibly avoid many disagreeable accidents, many melancholy circumstances; but no such prescience is allowed to man, and if it was, and the evils of life unavoidable, we should be still more wretched than we are."

"True (answered the old man;) but *had I* guessed you was coming here, I might have been better prepared, for we eat up our eggs at dinner; bread and milk is all your fare."

"I desire no better, and if you will permit me to lay on that bench till the morning dawns, I shall be still more obliged to you."

"Thank Heaven (said the shepherd) I can treat you better; to lay on the floor, wrapped up in warm skins, is nothing new, nor uncomfortable to me, and my poor bed is at your service; it is clean, though homely." Ferdinand was going to refuse, when the shepherdess entered.——After some con-versation on their simple way of life, which he found they had always been accustomed to, they overpowered all his refusals, and obliged him to take the old man's bed, which was in one corner of the room; the other room was the young woman's and those two rooms were all they had.

He asked "if they were not apprehensive of the rock breaking over their cottage?" They said, "Sometimes, when sudden thunderstorms broke over them they were alarmed; but they trusted in Heaven for protection." "I have only one fear, one care (said the shepherd;) it is some years now since I lost my wife; should I be taken suddenly too, what must become of my poor child?"

"Whenever that day arrives, father, which I hope is yet far off, I will sell my sheep, and go to service; all my fear is, lest I should be sick, and not able to help you; but then I hope good Mr. Ernest, our Lord's steward, will consider you."

"What! (cried Ferdinand) do you know Ernest? Are you tenants to Count Rhodophil?"

"To be sure, Sir (answered the girl;) we know Mr. Ernest, for he buys our sheep.—As to tenants, Sir, we pay no rent, because the mountain is free to live in; but we are vassals to the Count, his estate lies round the forest."

"Do you ever go to the Castle?" asked he again.

"I never did but once (replied the shepherdess) and the walk is too long for my father; but Mr. Ernest sends to us sometimes, and we meet him in the valley, and agree about our sheep. He is a good man, and never drives a hard bargain with the poor."

"Well (said Ferdinand) I know him too, and will take care that both you and your father shall be more safely provided for in future." Each looked at the other with wonder, but spoke not. They soon after retired to rest, contented and happy; not so their guest, he flung himself on the bed, a prey to the most melancholy reflections; and it was near morning when nature exhausted, gave him a temporary repose for about three hours, which seemed to refresh him, and after breakfasting on milk, he prepared to renew his ramble.

He was but very little acquainted with that side of the country which being rocky and mountainous, was unfavourable to excursions on horseback, and therefore had not fallen under his observation; but just as he was taking leave of his hospitable entertainers, he remembered to have heard there was a convent situated somewhere beyond this mountain; that certainly (thought he) is the retreat of Claudina: I will go to it, perhaps she will not see me, but it will be a satisfaction to know where she is. He inquired of the shepherdess if his conjecture was right respecting the convent? She told him it was, that about seven miles off there was a convent so remote and dreary, that it seemed shut out from the world, and was almost as much unknown as if in a desert.

"I have never been near it (said she) for, indeed, what I have heard about it is enough for me, and I have something else to do than to ramble into such places, where one may get nothing but a great fright for one's pains." "Ah! (concluded Ferdinand) this is the very place which seems to be designed for an entire seclusion from the world, there I will direct my steps." Having bid adieu to the good girl and her father, and taking a direction towards the convent, he began to descend the hill. The morning was fine, the dew drops still hung upon the under-wood, sparkling as the rising sun glittered among the trees, the birds were singing on the lofty branches, and the whole scene was calculated to inspire pleasure and serenity; even Ferdinand felt the enthusiasm of the moment; he looked round with delight:—"Ah! (said he) the face of nature shines on all its children; happy is the mind that can enjoy the pure pleasures that it so freely offers, free from corroding care, or guilty self-upbraidings! How much happier is the lowly peasant than his proud guilty Lord, who riots in unlawful pleasures, forgetful of the sting that follows in the voice of conscience; whilst the humble shepherd rises blith and innocent, pursues his daily occupation, blessed with content, he gathers in his flock at night, thankfully partakes the healthful food his family provides, and sinks to rest undisturbed and happy!"

Full of these thoughts he pursued his way until he reached the foot of the mountain, and descended into a narrow, wild and obscure glen, where nothing relieved the eye but high and lofty hills covered with trees, which threw a dark shade beneath, and entirely obscured the sun from penetrating through; he heard the sound of distant waters, but knew not from whence they came. He walked on a considerable way, until by a sudden turning he found himself at the foot of another mountain, from whence issued the most beautiful water-fall he had ever seen, descending into two or three natural basons, which fell from one to the other until they came to the bottom, and formed the lake, which winding itself around the mountain on the opposite side, divided into smaller streams of which the rivulet he had first seen was one. Here he sat down to rest, and to admire the course of the water. He had another hill to mount, and he observed there was something like a path-way in a gradual ascent round the side of it; he could see it was not much trodden upon by the weeds, but they were not so high as to impede his steps, and therefore, after resting about half an hour, he followed the direction, made his way through the weeds and under-wood, and, with infinite labour, arrived at the summit.

Here he stopped to look round him, another valley was beneath, which seemed to terminate in a thick wood on the right, and more hills to the left. Heartily tired of ascending and descending, he resolved to go into the woods from the vale beneath, rather than climb another mountain: Descending, however, to the valley, his attention was arrested by the beauty of the vines, which entirely covered the southern side of the hill; and several small streams, which had forced their way from the cascade on the other side, here crossed each other in the valley, and divided it into many parts like a cluster of small vales, which had a beautiful effect upon the eye, and agreeably amused Ferdinand till he came to the entrance of the wood, which he found uncommonly thick, and seemingly difficult to penetrate. He hesitated a moment, supposing that it might be the retreat of a troop of banditti, which had for some time past committed many outrages in the neighbourhood of Baden: "But what have I to fear? (exclaimed he) my life is not worth the taking; from a single man they can expect no booty, and the basest of cowards only would attack a defenceless being that cannot injure them."

Fortified by these considerations, he proceeded through the wood, in which there was no path-way, and in many places so difficult to pervade, that he more than once repented of his attempt, which he was fearful would at last prove fruitless; persevering, however, with infinite difficulty, he walked on. The trees were very lofty, and it appeared as if he descended gradually all the way. For three hours he kept on, till quite exhausted, he was obliged to rest himself at the foot of a tree, and eat a small cake the shepherdess had given him. "I have no doubt (thought he) but that I must be near the convent, as it certainly lies in this direction, though most probably there may be a less troublesome road to it. They informed me at the cottage it was about seven miles from the hill, surely I must have walked over more ground than that:" But he considered not how much time he had lost in forcing his way through the wood, which impeded his steps, and made him advance but very slowly.

Having a little refreshed himself he went on, and at length the wood opened into a deep and narrow valley, with lofty thick pines on each side, which threw a gloom over it sufficient to create horror in the mind of the boldest traveller.

Ferdinand felt its influence, but he was not easily intimidated, nor, indeed, could he now well retreat. Walking forward, he saw at the bottom another thick cluster of trees, which, when he came up to them, seemed to terminate the valley, and to be impervious to any human being. These were chesnut-trees, so interwoven with each other, that he looked round in vain for an opening, for the under-wood formed a thick fence that was impassable.—Extremely disconcerted, and apprehensive lest he should have the same road through the valley to retrace, he turned a little to the left, forcing his way down by the side of the trees, and after persevering near a quarter of a mile with infinite difficulty, to his great joy he discovered a small stream of water, over which was an old wooden bridge that led the way to a narrow path made through the wood. This track he followed, and, after walking near an hour, came to another dark avenue, at the end of which stood an old building encompassed with very high walls.

"At last (thought he) I have reached the convent;" and exhausted as he was with toil and want of refreshment, the appearance of those mouldering walls, gave him more pleasure than he might at another time have received from a view of the most superb palace. A pair of iron gates, which seemed rusted on their hinges, with a bell on one side, flattered him with the hopes of obtaining an entrance: He rang the bell with some force, and heard its sound, though at some distance. After waiting a considerable time, he was about to repeat the pull, when a very small wicket was opened (for the inside of the gates were lined with wood) and the meagre face of an old man appeared, who demanded, in a deep, feeble voice, "Who was there?"

"A wearied and unfortunate traveller, (replied Ferdinand) who entreats rest and refreshment."

"I fear (replied the man) neither can be obtained here."

"Is not this a convent?" asked Ferdinand.

"No (answered the other) *there is* a convent about five miles to the right of the valley you have passed."

"What then is this place?"

"Once a castle, now a heap of ruins!"

"Yet it is inhabited it seems, and I am really so overcome with fatigue, that if you can procure me entrance, I shall be most truly thankful to rest an hour."

"I will inquire," said the man, and withdrew.

Ferdinand was extremely mortified to find he had taken a wrong direction, *from* the convent as it appeared, by keeping to the left; yet he was so very languid and tired, that he found it hardly possible to measure his steps back without some rest or sustenance; for, however grief may fill up the mind, or weaken the appetite, nature will assert her rights, and remind the woe-begone traveller that something is necessary for her support. He waited some minutes, not with the patience of a Socrates, when at length the same face appeared through the hole: "I will let you in for a short time to the huntsman's room, but no farther." He proceeded to unbar the gate, which from its screeking noise, and the difficulty attending its opening, gave evident proofs that the practice of hospitality was not customary in that ruinous building.

When the gate was opened Ferdinand absolutely started at the figure of his conductor; he even hesitated whether he should follow him; haggard, emaciated and tottering, was the man before him. A large court, overgrown with weeds, led to another wall, with a pair of gates similar to those he had passed, and discovered no more of the building than the lofty battlements and high turrets he had discerned on his first approach. On one side of the court was an old low building, to which the man conducted him. They entered a hall lined with the huntsman's trophies, covered with dust; through that they went into a smaller room, where a table, some benches, and a fire place, had the appearance of having been *once* inhabited.——"You may rest *here* (said the man) and I will bring you some food; but if you stir one step beyond, your *death* will be the consequence."

Ferdinand, instead of being intimidated found his curiosity greatly excited, and though he quietly acquiesced with the prohibition, yet his thoughts were employed in considering on means to obtain further knowledge of these ruins and its inhabitants. Some time elapsed before the man returned with bread, wine, and grapes, which, whilst Ferdinand gladly devoured, he was observed, with the most scrutinizing attention, by his entertainer; nor were the other's eyes unemployed.—When he put the flask of wine to his mouth, for no cup had been thought necessary, he drank to the other's health, which was returned with a bow of the head; but no persuasions could induce him to return the compliment. "I drink no wine," said he, in a mournful voice.

"Indeed, my good friend, I think you need it," said Ferdinand, "weak and feeble as you are, wine seems absolutely necessary for you."

"I have sworn to the contrary," replied the other, with an increased dejection.

"It appears to me," returned Ferdinand, "to have been a very cruel injunction, if *forced* upon you, and a very unwise one, if voluntarily made, for the good things of this life were given to us by a bounteous Creator to be our support and comfort; the *abuse* of them is only improper, and when advanced in age, as you appear to be, such things as nourish the body and enliven the spirits, are highly requisite."

"To some persons," answered the man, "it may be so; but not to a man to whom the hours that he drags here are a weary pilgrimage, such a one seeks not by stimulatives to prolong a life long since grown hateful to him."

"Alas!" cried Ferdinand, "few men can be more wretched than myself; recent afflictions have driven me from my home, and from my friends; yet do I hold it cowardly to desert my post, I have no power over that life I could not give myself; and to neglect the means of its preservation, is little less sinful than to destroy it at once.—But, pardon me one question, are you the owner of this Castle?"

"I am not," returned the other; "but do not be curious in matters that cannot concern you, nor by an idle curiosity which can receive no gratification, oblige me to repent of my charity."

"You must at least," said Ferdinand, "forgive me one observation; your first appearance, and manner of bringing me here, led me to suppose you a domestic; your language convinces me I was mistaken: Whoever, or whatever you are, if you are unfortunate, as your words seem to imply, I most sincerely pity you; unhappy myself, I can feel for every child of sorrow." The tone, in which those words were uttered, with the look that accompanied them, had a powerful effect upon his auditor. He turned from him, clasped his hands, tears ran in torrents down his furrowed cheeks, and, with a heartbreaking sigh, he flung himself upon a bench almost suffocated with the excess of his emotions.

Ferdinand approached him:—"If *I* have been, though involuntarily, the cause of exciting those tears, and of recalling ideas that perhaps were faded on the memory, I entreat you to forgive me; indebted to your hospitality and kindness, I am exceedingly concerned to have made a return so unworthy as to create pain in the bosom of my benefactor."

"You stand acquitted in my opinion," answered he, endeavouring to recover from his first transports; "sympathy, perhaps, led you to observations you could not foresee would plunge me into sorrow. It is now twelve years since I have seen a human being to interest me; twice only during that period have those gates, by which you entered, been opened to admit any one within them: Society is hateful to me, and I thought this place sufficiently hidden from the world to preclude all possibility of intrusion; the sound of a bell is but seldom heard, and only at stated times: I was therefore alarmed at the circumstance, and when I opened the wicket had no thoughts of admitting you; but the expression of your countenance struck me, the mournful accents of your supplication vibrated to my heart, and in one moment overturned the scrupulous caution of twelve years."

"I feel (replied Ferdinand) that my obligations to you are infinite, nor will I abuse them by an expression of curiosity which is improper to be gratified; not one step beyond the boundaries of your injunctions will I attempt to stray.

"May Heaven give you comfort, and sooth your mind to ease and tranquillity. I am rambling to forget myself, and those most dear to me. I have incurred the heaviest maledictions, and am a victim to the severity of them. A cruel mystery hangs over me, and has driven me from every prospect of happiness."

"Poor youth!" exclaimed the old man, "how many are the unfortunate beings compelled to exist in this world of cares, either from their own misconduct, or through the crimes of others? I can afford you no comfort, for within these walls misery, oppression, and despair, have fixed their seat for ever!"

"Then," cried Ferdinand, "*I* should be an inmate; for equally wretched and hopeless is the being before you: I know not why it is, but methinks I am driven by an irresistible impulse to open my heart to you, if you can allow me to intrude so long upon your patience."

"The communication of sorrow, it is said, relieves the mind; if such may be the effect, I will readily listen to you; but must premise before-hand that of whatsoever nature your sorrows may be, it is impossible that *I* can either comfort, or serve you."

"They will at least prove to you," answered Ferdinand, "that *you* are not alone unhappy, and though you cannot, indeed it is impossible *you* should, serve me, you may at least give me the benefit of your advice."

The old man shook his head, but with a deep sigh requested he would proceed. The other obeyed, and took up his story from the first time he had seen Claudina, as the epoch from which originated all his subsequent troubles, and from which he dated her misfortunes and his own. He related every event without palliation or exaggeration, and complained heavily of the mystery which hung over the interview with his wife on his return from the army, and the self-accusation contained in her letters, her flight, and his ignorance of her situation.

CHAPTER XI.

THE stranger heard him with much attention, and when the narrative was concluded made the following reply. "Your imprudent marriage with a stranger, unknown to your father, was the source from whence flowed all your misfortunes, consequently from that wrong step you may trace every ill in progression. I do not however exculpate him from blame in being so rash and unadvised, as to draw upon you the evils of life by a father's curses; the idea is horrible, it is usurping the power of the Most High, to whom *only* curses belongeth; yet I have rarely observed through life, that an union, contracted contrary to a parent's approbation, has been fortunate or happy; to a mind of sensibility there must ever be a drawback from felicity, when conscious of giving pain, and disappointing the best hopes of those so nearly interested for our happiness, and who have a right to more than a negative obedience, if I may so express myself, when a marriage is contracted without consulting the parents; but when completed, contrary to their wishes and commands, few, I am convinced, are the instances of matrimonial happiness: But I see I oppress you, therefore, to drop that point, permit me to observe, you did wrong in not seeking opportunities to soften your father. Was your brother a *warm* advocate, think you? I fear not; much less can I believe that a good man could have left the world without being in charity with it, and revoking, as far as he could, the imprecation his passion had dictated.

"As to the other circumstances, the voice at different times, so applicable to your situations, I shall only observe, that they were very extraordinary, but not impossible.—Respecting your wife, I fear much black treachery remains concealed, beyond your penetration; her flight, after hearing the prohibition of the voice, confirms my conjectures. O, you know not (said he, starting from his seat) you know not to what excesses a corrupted heart may be driven!"

He paced about the room for two or three minutes, then suddenly stopping:—"The leading features towards explaining the particular circumstances of your story are wanting; it is impossible I can give any advice that ought to influence you in your future conduct or sentiments. Your wife *may be* in the neighbouring convent, but I see not what you can promise yourself from the discovery, because it is not at all probable that she will see you: I sincerely wish you returning happiness, and am sorry I must remind you that your departure from hence is necessary before the day is too far advanced; you must return through the valley, and take the opposite direction towards the convent, which is nearly as much retired as this melancholy place."

Ferdinand arose: "I beg your pardon," said he, "for obliging you to remind me that I have trespassed too long on your kindness: I feel regret at leaving you in this solitary desolated mansion, and yet, such is the complexion of my mind, I could be contented to remain in it myself with such a companion."

"Leave me (replied the other) add not to the horrors of my situation by permitting me to taste the solace of a companion from which I am for ever excluded."

"How! (said Ferdinand) are you then here alone? Did you not say that you was not master here?"

"I told you that I was not the *owner* of this castle: I spoke truth; inquire no farther." As his brow grew contracted, his eyes wild, and his whole figure agitated, Ferdinand repressed his curiosity, and prepared to depart. The other attended him to the gate with a sort of sullen civility, and opened it without speaking. Ferdinand took his hand, "Heavens bless you," said he, "I thank your charity. Must we never meet again?" The supplicating tone melted the hardened heart of the stranger, his features relaxed:—"Why should you wish it?"

"Not from an unwarrantable curiosity," returned the other, "not from a wish to penetrate farther into your secrets, or your habitation, than you would choose to allow of; but from sympathy, from a desire of participating in sorrow, and a wish to render *your* situation less deplorable by the converse of a fellow sufferer."

The man paused, viewed Ferdinand from head to foot with a searching eye, opened his mouth to speak, again paused, and turned from him. The other seeing *his* emotions, was also affected: "I have afflicted you undesignedly; pardon me (added he) I will not be intrusive, I submit to your restrictions." He was turning from the gate, the stranger caught his hand: "You have overcome (said he) my hitherto invincible resolutions; you have awakened sensations long, very long strangers to my bosom: I will consider, I must have time to reflect, and to determine, I can promise nothing; go to the convent, satisfy your anxiety respecting your wife.—Return to this gate to-morrow, I shall by that time decide on your wishes, and either wholly repress my own rising inclination, or gratify it without reserve; but expect nothing, for I make no promises." He hastily shut the gate without waiting for an answer, and left Ferdinand under a great perturbation of spirits.

He had now to retrace his steps, through the gloomy valley, and force his way through the woodlands. The various conjectures that occupied his mind relative to the old man, and his ruinous solitary mansion, lessened the apparent difficulties, and tedious length of the road. He regained the foot of the mountain, and turned to the right, where he met with a chain of small rocky hills both painful and dangerous to climb, and to descend from, and which so far impeded his haste, that he saw the twilight drawing on fast, and the appearance of the heavy clouds portending rain or snow. He redoubled his speed, and on coming over a pretty high hill discovered a grove of chesnut trees before him, in the midst of which he saw something rising above them like a turret. "At last (cried he, almost exhausted with fatigue) at last I have found the convent." The object in view seemed to diminish the distance, and he walked for some time through the grove before he arrived at a large moat, which extended round the walls of the building.—He took a circular walk, in the hope, which was not disappointed, of finding a bridge.—On one side was a narrow stone causeway made on piles, but more resembling a path-way than a bridge; this he crossed to the gate that appeared in the wall, and rung the bell.

The door was almost instantly opened by the porteress, and to his great joy he found himself at the desired port. She seemed extremely surprised at seeing him, and demanded his business. "Was there not a young Lady brought here within this fortnight?" said he.

"There was (she replied) and what then?"

"I beseech you (said he) to tell her, her nearest relation wishes to speak with her."

"'Tis very improbable a *relation* should come *here* to see her. Young man, you have not spoken the truth; nor will you, whoever you are, be permitted to see her."

"Oh! (cried Ferdinand, off his guard, and agonized by vexation and fatigue) oh! tell her it is her husband, it is the father of her child; she has no right to withdraw herself from me, nor can *you* answer it, to detain a wife from her husband without his knowledge or consent."

The porteress seemed staggered. "What you assert (replied she) seems very strange and improbable; I will, however, report it to the Abbess, which is all *I can* do in the business."

She shut the grate, and left him overwhelmed with vexation. He was now convinced that Claudina was here, and could he see her, and obtain from her satisfaction relative to her self-accusation, and a confession of the real motives which had induced her to leave the Castle under such an appearance of mystery, he concluded that he should be much easier in his mind, and submit patiently to a separation which seemed to have been *commanded*, though *why* at *that particular period* he could not conceive, and was what he supposed a conversation with her would clear up. During the absence of the porteress, his mind dwelt on these circumstances; the grate was at length opened, and the old woman appeared.

"The young Lady refuses to see you; she denies that you have any authority over her; bids you remember the *dreadful circumstances lately passed*, and never presume to trouble her more. The *letter* she left for you sufficiently explained her sentiments: *Her child* is with her, but it has *no longer a father*, nor after this day will any messages from you be received or delivered here."

"Barbarous woman!" exclaimed Ferdinand, "ungrateful and unjust! Would she but explain herself with openness and candour, I could submit to the *'dreadful circumstances'* she alludes to; but this silence, this mystery, and my child too! 'It has no longer a father!' Just Heaven, how am I punished!"

"I am sorry for you," said the porteress; "but *I* cannot help you. Night is drawing on; a short distance to the left is a convent of Friars, there you may be accommodated for the night; but return no more here, for it avails nothing to complain where you cannot be heard." She shut the grate, and left Ferdinand standing in an attitude of fixed despair.

He stood for some moments insensible to every thing around him, when the sound of a distant bell roused him from the torpor that had seized him, and instantly recollecting the convent mentioned by the old Nun, with reluctant steps, and an oppressed mind, he walked through the wood, keeping to the left as she had directed him; but overwhelmed by a thousand doubts and painful conjectures, he proceeded so slowly that night overtook him, and it was with much difficulty he espied through the trees a rising hill before him which terminated the wood, and on reaching to the foot of it, he perceived an old building on one side of the declivity, with large pieces of rock suspended over it, which seemed to threaten hourly danger: He recollected the shepherd's cottage; "strange (thought he) that people should chuse such dangerous situations to erect dwellings on! It appears to me a daring presumption, or a total insensibility." He rang the bell, a small gate was opened by a Friar, Ferdinand announced himself as an unfortunate and wearied traveller seeking shelter from the inclemencies of the night.

"Enter, my son, and welcome," said the father. "Seldom does the traveller find his way to our solitary mansion, so remote and distant from any great road; enter therefore freely, and partake of our homely fare, and humble lodging." Ferdinand followed his conductor to a large room, where several of the Fathers were assembled just returned from their evening vespers. All but one saluted him, and withdrew, that one advanced, and requested he would be seated. Some bread, sallad, milk and fruit, were brought in, of which Ferdinand partook very sparingly, for the uneasiness of his mind had destroyed his appetite.

"You look fatigued, my son," said the Friar, "and I suppose must have wandered considerably out of your way to have arrived at this dwelling, seldom in the habit of receiving strangers."

"I have indeed been wandering about," replied the other, "and with very little satisfaction to myself. To this house I was directed from a neighbouring convent; both houses are so remote, so impervious, even to the eye of curiosity, from the woods and deep vallies, that only a wretched fugitive, like myself, could possibly have found it."

"If you are unhappy, my son, I am sorry for you, but yield not to despair; *hope* is implanted in the mind of man by our great Creator as the sweetener of life, and only one set of beings are excluded from that cordial drop in earthly pursuits."

"And who are those?" asked Ferdinand.

"Men and women devoted to a monastic life," answered the Father; "cut off from every worldly expectation, their hopes are founded in heavenly promises which can receive *no* disappointment but from *themselves*; they depend not on others; no earthly views can distract their attention from the one great object of their wishes: Happiness *unalloyed* by fears or doubts must inhabit the bosom of a religious man."

"Most true," replied Ferdinand; "but that man must be detached from worldly cares, must have no dear connexions that twine about the heart; no wife, no children; no agonizing apprehensions for those he loves; no distracting doubts he cannot comprehend. The man who secludes himself from society, who can devote his days to religious duties only, must have a heart and mind at ease, ere he can embrace such a life as you have chosen."

"Alas! my son, and does not religion hold out comfort to the afflicted?"

"Undoubtedly, *that* is the rock on which we must erect the foundation of all our hopes and expectations both here and hereafter; but a monastic life I still aver, should be sought for only by those free from the ties that nature binds about the heart, and who have ceased to be solicitous for worldly objects."

This conversation was interrupted by the entrance of another Friar, not so old as the one before him, in whose countenance Ferdinand discerned traits of benevolence and sensibility, his heart sprung to meet him, and involuntarily he arose as if to do him homage.

"Father Joseph," said the former one, with a supercilious air, "you will see this traveller comfortably lodged, and then attend your duty." Turning to Ferdinand, "Son, I shall see you to-morrow, and hold some further conversation with you." He withdrew.

"You will follow me, my good brother," said Father Joseph, with an air of mildness, taking up the lamp. The other obeyed; he was conducted through an outer court into a very small chamber, about eight feet square, with a bed made in a niche of the wall, a table, on which stood a crucifix, and one stool. "May you rest in peace under the protection of Heaven!" said the Father, and was going to leave him.

"Ah!" exclaimed Ferdinand, "and *must* you go? I feel a rising wish to be indulged with your company; must I repress it?"—"For the present I am obliged to leave you; but if sleep is not more desirable than conversation, I will return to you in half an hour. Go to bed, rest if you can, for I see you are overcome with fatigue." He retired, and left his companion with the pleasing hope of seeing him again. The countenance of this man beamed with mild complacence, and Ferdinand hoped from him to gather full information respecting the other convent, and possibly of the ruinous building where he had been so oddly received. Not to offend the Friar, he got into the bed, which was pretty hard, and very unlikely to lull him presently to sleep, he therefore anxiously watched for the approach of Father Joseph, who came when he had began to despair of seeing him.

"I have complied with your wishes, son, and now tell me how I may serve you; I have one hour to spare." Ferdinand then briefly repeated the latter part of his story from the time his wife had left him, his reception at the old Castle, and his treatment at the convent. He concluded with saying, that all he wished for from his wife was, "an explanation of her letter, and a candid confession of her motives for withdrawing herself from the protection of her friends."

"If (said he) as I suppose, you have communication with the convent, I beseech you to see my wife, tell her I will not *force* myself into her presence, let her but write to free me from my present doubts and inquietude, and I will obey her orders, and never intrude myself into any place she inhabits without her permission."

"Your story is very strange (observed Father Joseph) and I fear you will obtain no satisfaction; *I* have no power to serve you: Our Superior, whom you have been with, is the only one that visits the convent; the order is one of the severest in all Germany: Ours is much more relaxed, yet we can derive little advantage from the indulgence allowed us, because our situation precludes all chance of society, and Father Ambrose only admitted to visit the convent, to which he is confessor. As your wife is in that retirement, be assured she is dead to you. Those that enter that house seldom return again to the world."

"Distraction!" cried Ferdinand; "but my child, they cannot keep my child from me!"—"At a certain age she may make her own election: Mean time you may represent the case to the Bishop, that is all you can do, having taken sanctuary in the bosom of the church, and the child being at this age more immediately under the care of its mother; at present, you cannot oblige her to resign it." Observing that Ferdinand appeared overwhelmed with vexation, he went on.

"The building you have mentioned, so buried from all observation, was once, I have heard, a most superb mansion, inhabited by one of the Bavarian family, who marrying an heiress of a Suabian Baron, came into the possession of that estate which has long fallen into decay, nor did I ever hear that it had been inhabited these twenty years. On the other side it joins with the black forest, and has been always understood, from its being desolated in one of the late wars, and never repaired, uninhabitable ever since; the house must be in ruins, and the grounds round it barren and uncultivated. Who the person or persons can be that reside there I have no idea, and indeed I should suppose it can afford no accommodations for any other than banditti."

"Or the sons of misery," cried Ferdinand, "such are neither delicate in their accommodations, nor fastidious in their choice of situations; all places are alike to the wretched, and I hope to-morrow I shall be admitted as an inmate."

"And *I hope not*," returned Father Joseph. "My son, you are very young, let not the first disappointment in your calculations of happiness induce you to renounce the world. You have been wrong, perhaps, in your first selection of the means to attain it. Man has but little prescience, and that little is often ill-directed. Consider your present troubles as a chastisement for some misconduct, some rash actions resulting from the impetuosity of youth; receive the correction with humility, but give not way to despair. *Believe me*, there is no merit in retiring from the world; society has its claims not incompatible with your sacred duties; on the contrary, duty towards God, and duty towards your brethren, is equally commanded and inculcated. A young man may have a thousand opportunities of doing active service to his fellow creatures, and of promoting the cause of religion and virtue. Retirement suits not with the ardour of youth; let me advise you therefore to resume your situation in life, whatever it may be, to scan over your past actions with discrimination and impartiality; you will then discover the errors that have impeded your expectations of happiness; you will chalk out for yourself a new path, and the end will be mental tranquillity, and the never-fading satisfaction of having been beneficial to the extent of your abilities towards the less fortunate and happy."

"And is *this*," cried Ferdinand, "the language of a man detached from the world, *this* the advice of a holy Father, to expose a fluctuating disappointed heart to the allurements and dissipations that tempt, in a hundred pleasurable shapes, the mind of youth, and lead him into vice?"

"It is the language of truth and reason," answered Father Joseph, with energy, "it is the advice of dear-bought wisdom and experience. Man was not intended for a solitary being, and a *young* man, who flies from the world because he has indulged delusive hopes, and formed expectations that in the nature of them must at one time or other receive a severe check, who neglects the duties he has it in his power to perform, and by a rash and ill-judged misanthropy, shuns mankind to give up his mind to despair; believe me, such a man is a pusillanimous wretch, who deserts his post, and by his cowardice and impatient spirit, lays up for himself bitter repentance, and never-ending regret, that will mix itself in his most earnest devotions, render those acts of religion, which should communicate joy and cheerfulness to the mind, cold, gloomy, and mechanical; whilst the good, the active, the benevolent mind, performs his sacred duties with delight, from conviction and choice diffuses blessings to all around him, and by precept and *example* animates others to the practice of religion and virtue, which his conduct renders both easy and pleasant."

"If I may judge from the expression of your countenance," said Ferdinand, "your advice is not the declamation of an unimpassioned man, who has forsaken the world from choice, but the warnings of a feeling heart, desirous of saving others from equal regret and misery with himself."

"You have observed justly, I will not deny," answered the Father: "Many are the victims in this house to pride, impatience, and avarice, sacrificed by their friends, or driven by the impetuosity of their own passions. Some there are doubtless from choice and the purest motives, but these last are comparatively few; a monastery therefore I do not recommend, nor a residence with that solitary being, whoever he may be, that inhabits those stately ruins; even this desultory mode of gratifying your curiosity, rambling among uninhabited and almost impassable hills and vallies, can benefit neither yourself, nor others, may subject you to much inconvenience, perhaps to certain dangerous situations, you do not apprehend: Once more then I recommend you to seek an active life, and an occupation that may diversify your thoughts, and engage your attention. Good night, reflect on what I have said, and may Heaven direct you for the best; I will see you again after morning service."

The good father having withdrawn, left Ferdinand overwhelmed with a variety of contending emotions, whether to profit by, or disregard the advice he had received:—whether he should yield to the dictates of prudence and experience, or follow the lead of his own inclinations. Sleep at length overtook him before he had settled the point, and, hard as his bed was, fatigue threw him into a profound repose, from which he started on the entrance of Father Joseph. "I come only to inform you," said he, "that you are expected by Father Ambrose, breakfast is prepared for you, hasten therefore to attend him."

"How!" cried Ferdinand, "do you leave me? I thought to have had a further conversation with you."

"I am forbidden to indulge it, and have received a reprimand for being so long in your room last night: I may just whisper you, that the passions of mankind are the same in all places, and in all situations; jealousy, envy, and avarice, prevail as much in monasteries as in palaces, they pervade in the most profound retirements, and lead to the most despicable actions and sentiments. Adieu, may Heaven preserve you." Ending those words, he darted from the room, and left Ferdinand to follow.

On entering the apartment he had quitted the preceding evening, he found Father Ambrose alone, refreshments before him, and having inquired of the other his name and rank in life, he began to launch forth in the praise of a monastic life, as the only asylum from trouble and pain; that abstracted from the world, its hopes and fears, the holy Fathers fixed their thoughts on things above, where no cares or disappointments could attend their hopes or desires. He harangued so long, and so eloquently on the subject, that, had not the advice of Father Joseph guarded his mind from the fascination of the picture of contentment held to his view, it is more than probable that Ferdinand, under the impression of his present vexations, might have been induced to end his travels, and have fixed himself for life in that solitary mansion; but already pre-possessed, the avenues to his heart were closed, and the eloquence of the Superior was exerted in vain: He heard him, however, with complaisance, but alledged *absolute necessity* for his departure, as an excuse for not embracing that plan of life so calculated to insure happiness. He added, "that it was by no means improbable, but that he should return, and have the pleasure of visiting the community for a longer time, if he might hope for admission."

The zealous Father, eager to make a proselyte of a young Nobleman, greatly approved of his design, and assured him of a hearty welcome. Ferdinand felt half inclined to have mentioned Claudina, but not much prepossessed in his favour, nor desirous of being then detained from visiting the solitary, who had permitted his return, he repressed the sentiment of confidence half rising to his lips, and rose to take leave, with grateful thanks for his hospitality. When conducted to the grate, he saw Father Joseph in company with some others; a general salute only passed between them, but their eyes spoke much cordiality towards each other.

CHAPTER XII.

FERDINAND now hastened to the Castle in the wood, and knowing the way, he pierced through its intricacies that to a stranger seemed impassable, and in much less time than he expected was at the gates. He hastily pulled the bell, which, to his infinite vexation, broke off in his hand; for having been so long useless, it had been eaten out with rust, moved with difficulty the preceding day, and now, by a second pull, snapped to pieces. Exceedingly disconcerted, he began to apprehend that he should gain no entrance; fortunately the solitary man, who had expected him, being walking in the court, heard the faint sound, which the jarring of the wires occasioned, and instantly appeared at the little wicket. Ferdinand was agreeably surprised at his sudden appearance. "You see me returned (said he) anxious to cultivate your acquaintance, and in your conversation blunt the keen edge of my own calamities."

"Enter (said the solitary) I have expected you, curiosity is so strongly implanted in the mind of man that I scarcely doubted of your return." They passed through the first court, and walked round the wall of the second to a small postern door; on advancing towards it, he added, "Having once permitted you a free entrance, my confidence shall not be a partial one." He then opened the door which led to a handsome colonade fronting the great gates that were boarded up, and excluded it from being seen in the outer court. They entered a large hall, round which run a gallery supported by pillars that led to the apartments above stairs; but the painting was almost effaced by the damp, the pillars entirely discoloured, some of them decayed and crumbling to pieces, threatening the destruction of the gallery they supported, and indeed the whole bore the appearance of total neglect. The solitary opened a door at the farther end of the hall, and conducted his guest into what he called his library, for as such it seemed to have been intended; but the glasses in many places were broken, the books all tumbling in disorder, and so covered with dust, that they were scarcely discernable. A few old-fashioned velvet chairs, once of crimson, but changed by the damps, two tables, with a writing desk of a very particular old-fashioned construction; a large dog that lay before a great wood fire, and seemed by age rendered almost incapable of moving, though he growled at the stranger; a sword, and a pair of pistols, that hung against the wall, comprised the whole furniture of this room.

Being seated, the solitary inquired of his success at the Convent. Ferdinand related his reception there, and at the Friar's monastery; adding, "You see my wife will afford me no sort of satisfaction, and her message is as extraordinary and inexplicable as her whole conduct."

The old man sighed deeply: "I pity you (said he) not for your present disappointment, but because you are *young*, and must feel, poignantly feel, the stings of ingratitude, and the destruction of those sanguine hopes of happiness you had figured to yourself in an union with the object of your choice, and who, I have little doubt of pronouncing, has proved unworthy of your attachment."

"How! (exclaimed Ferdinand) do you believe my wife is criminal?"

"Hath she not confessed as much?" replied the other.

"Impossible!" said Ferdinand, "she had no acquaintance, no man visited her, in my absence she resided with my brother, who lived very retired; impossible she could wrong me."

"Cease to torment yourself with conjectures that cannot be elucidated; one day or other be assured every thing will be explained.—Yes (continued he, raising his voice) time and accident develops the darkest schemes, the machinations of the wicked will be detected, and, if to know the worst, your imagination can form, will afford any degree of ease, doubt not but that you will one day be satisfied; 'till then, try to repress your anxiety, and revere that command so extraordinarily delivered; try to forget that you have a wife existing, for she has declared 'she is dead to you.'"

Ending these words he stamped on the floor, and presently a man, old and feeble, entered the room.—"Bring some bread and wine."

"Strange! (thought Ferdinand) this man said he was not the master, yet he seems to command; he drinks no wine himself, yet keeps it here, for whom then, when he lives thus solitary? Or is there another person here who is the master?"

The old servant returned with bread and wine and a cup; he looked

very attentively on Ferdinand, and then withdrew. The Recluse, who penetrated through the silence of his guest, said, "I read your surprise, and guess
at the doubts which occupy your mind: I will satisfy them in part. I am not
the *owner* of this once magnificent seat, yet I am the master here, and have
resided in it above twelve years. In a clear moon-light night I walk, sometimes to the skirts of the Black Forest, but at other times I never exceed the
courts of the Castle, for the gardens are now a wilderness of weeds. Once a
week the provisions I want are brought from a village about five miles off,
on the edge of the forest. Wine is sometimes drawn here, though not by
me, I have that within me which supports my strength and spirits; my old
attendant requires more substantial food. Bread, fruits and water, is all that
my table affords, and as much as nature requires. I am not so old as you may
suppose from my appearance, only fifty-two, twelve of which I have past in
the manner I tell you."

"It would ill become me (said Ferdinand) to express a wish to penetrate
into the cause which has led you to this extraordinary seclusion from the
world, though you must allow that it sufficiently warrants the most curious
conjectures; but I will deserve the favour you have bestowed on me by my
discretion."

"You are wise and prudent (replied the other) qualities not often attached to youth, and perhaps acquired by sorrow and experience; on such
terms you are welcome to remain here as long as you please."

"May I be permitted to make one observation?" asked Ferdinand.

"Certainly, *speak* freely, the *answer* depends upon myself."

"When I first came to your gate, you expressed it necessary to *inquire*
if I could be admitted, now you confess yourself the master, and without
society."

"Your curiosity in this point is so very natural that I will satisfy it without reserve. The discovery of this mansion through the *impenetrable*, as I
thought, woods, hills and vallies, so out of the common road, and even
an object of terror to the few inhabitants that dwell on the other side, the
sound of a bell, which had been silent for above nine years, and your appearance when I opened the wicket, altogether astonished me! Callous, as I
thought my heart was grown, it softened at the view of sorrow and weakness in so young a frame. To your request of admittance I said, "I would
inquire." I came back, and consulted Francis; it was possible you might be
what you seemed, then there was no danger in permitting you to enter the
outer court, but to guard against surprise, Francis secured the gate of the
inner court, and was planted in a small room, within the huntsman's, where
I led you, armed with *that* brace of pistols, which had you attacked me, or

strove to force your way beyond the bounds I allowed, he had orders to discharge, and instantly to dispatch you."

Ferdinand heard him with some degree of terror, and "Who, or what can this man be?" darted naturally into his mind, and having taken some refreshment, he began to consider whether it would be prudent to remain in a place that seemed to be the abode of wretchedness, fear and distrust. Curiosity however predominated, and as *he also* was armed with a brace of pistols, he thought himself at least a match for two old men, should they harbour any sinister designs against him. Having thus made up his mind, he began to remark on the conversations between Father Joseph and himself, and the different language of Father Ambrose, the Superior. "I much fear (said he) that the former has been an unhappy victim, and feels no satisfaction in his situation; for I can conceive that even a good mind well disposed towards religion and moral rectitude, if *compelled* to forsake the world, and lead an inactive life, contrary to the natural disposition, will grow languid in the performance of those duties, which free-will might have performed with pleasure and alacrity: For my own part, all my prospects of happiness for ever clouded, oppressed with the weight of a much-loved father's denunciation, and which seems to be so literally fulfilled in this life—a brother, a husband, a father; yet separated from every endearing tie; what can *I* promise myself in this world, that can counter-balance that tranquil, that serene life which pervades in a convent, and which my misfortunes seem to point out as my only place of rest; and if I can assure to myself such a companion, such a friend, as Father Joseph, what can I desire more?"

"Revenge!" cried the Solitary, with an eye darting fire through his emaciated countenance: "Yes, revenge!" repeated he, with a violence that startled Ferdinand; "Live to detect the artful villany of those that have wronged you, and to punish them!"

"But I know no such persons," said Ferdinand; "I know of no wrongs that I have met with that require revenge. If my wife has been guilty, she is already punished; and for her accomplice, if such there be, he will not escape with impunity; and to drag on a wretched life, with the diabolical intention of destroying another, would be only redoubling my own miseries here, and assuring to myself punishment hereafter."

"So young a stoic!" exclaimed the old man, with a look of contempt, "either you are a hypocrite, or you were born without passions."

"The detestable character of *the first*," replied the other, "I utterly disclaim, and had I been created without passions, all the misfortunes of my life would have been avoided: No, *I am not* without passions, but adversity has taught me wisdom, has moderated the impetuosity of youth, and suffering as I do under the violence of momentary rage, which in an instant may be guilty of excesses never to be repaired, I have learned to *bear* and to *forbear* in points that are doubtful, and where my courage and honour are not questioned."

"You are a philosopher, Sir," answered the Solitary, apparently much agitated, "and fitter for the convent, perhaps, than the world, since you can so easily, so tamely, wait for time to elucidate your injuries; but I beg pardon, it cannot concern me; persons born with different sentiments will act differently, and as in this point we do not agree, we will change the subject."

He did so, and Ferdinand found him learned, intelligent, and communicative, yet on every subject he discoursed with a vehemence so little to be expected from the feebleness of his looks and manner when he first appeared at the wicket, discovered a temper so violent and so decided, that his manners rather repulsed than conciliated any growing esteem, and seemed to promise that little pleasure could be derived from cultivating his acquaintance. After some hours conversation the Solitary took him up to the gallery, which was extensive, and had once been magnificent. He opened the doors of several apartments that overlooked the gardens, and an extent of country; but the former was a confused mass of trees, shrubs and weeds, and the country beyond appeared an immense forest.

This was certainly an unpleasant situation to build a superb house on, observed Ferdinand. Our Castle is on a rocky ground, and adjoining to hills and mountains; but they are cultivated and inhabited: Here every thing has the appearance of a desert. Is there no town or village near, for I profess myself entirely unacquainted with this part of the country, from always thinking the woods both dangerous and impenetrable?—"There is a village a few miles distant, but I know not its name," was all the answer.—He then carried him across the gallery to another wing of the building, and opening a door, "Here you may sleep if you please; Francis can find linen for the bed, and shall light a fire, though possibly the chimney may not draw." This room had been handsomely furnished, but it was in a very decayed state, and the whole appearance was so cold and comfortless, that Ferdinand hesitated a moment whether he should accept the offer, and sleep there or not; but the day was shutting in, and he might even lose his way to the monastery, he thought he could be in no hazard of danger, and therefore it would be most prudent to pass that night there, tho' he felt no inclination to *prolong* his stay, especially as he could hope for no gratification to his curiosity, for the Solitary's heart seemed locked up and carefully guarded. Returning to the lower room they spent the evening together in conversation on various subjects. Ferdinand was pleased with the strong understanding and knowledge of the world which the other displayed; but he observed, on several occasions, that he was decided and peremptory in his opinions, and that he evaded every thing tending to his own situation, and gave not a single instance of that confidence he had at first led his guest to hope for.

At ten o'clock Francis appeared with a lamp, the Gentlemen wished each other a good night, Francis was ordered to attend the stranger to the *door* of his apartment, and then return to his master. Ferdinand judged this order was to preclude any conversation between him and the old man, and therefore he was silent; but as they parted at the door he thought Francis suppressed a rising sigh, and looking at him saw his face was clouded by a heavy expression of grief. He bowed, retired, and pulled the door after him. A cheerful fire was blazing in the chimney, and examining the door of his apartment, he perceived there was a lock and two strong bolts; these he secured, and having placed the lamp on the table, he threw off his clothes, and got into bed.

Here he lay some time revolving all past circumstances, and considering which road he should pursue in the morning, when suddenly he conceived that he heard some faint shrieks as if at a great distance, he sprung up in the bed and listened; he heard no more, all was a dead silence; yet still he could not be persuaded but that he heard the cries:—He lay some hours in a kind of fearful expectation of, he knew not what. No sort of noise however invaded his ears, and at length he dropped asleep, from which he was awakened by a voice at the door, telling him breakfast was ready. He was soon dressed, and found the Solitary waiting for him, coffee on the table:—"Did you sleep well?" demanded he.

"Perfectly well," replied Ferdinand, suddenly determined not to mention the cries; "indeed my bed was so very superior to what I have had those last two nights, that no wonder I indulged myself so long this morning."

"You are welcome to use the bed as long as you like," was all the reply. The day became gloomy, and in a short time the snow fell in great quantities; this the Gentleman of the house observed, saying, "you are now weather-bound, and must amuse yourself as well as you can."

Ferdinand found among the books the works of many excellent authors, and therefore was at no loss to beguile the time, and indeed had reason to be thankful for his situation, as before night the snow was at least two feet deep on the ground. About the time of retiring the snow ceased, the moon broke through the clouds, and a cold, sharp wind arose denoting a severe frost. When he came into his apartment, the reflection of that resplendent orb induced him to go to the window, and he sat down by it for some time admiring the appearance of the trees and under-wood, which being covered with the snow, exhibited a hundred fantastic shapes to engage the attention.

Lost in the recollection of past events, he sat a long time without thinking of the hour, until suddenly the same faint shrieks broke upon his ear, that he had heard the preceding night. He started up, and opened the window, the voice ceased; he listened attentively a long time, it was no more repeated. Convinced, however, that it was no illusion of a disordered imagination, he began to consider from whom, or from whence it could proceed. The sounds both nights were exactly similar, and he concluded must issue from some person distressed and confined. "There is some unaccountable mystery hangs about this forlorn place, and the Solitary who inhabits it dares not trust me with the secret: I will avail myself of his permission, and stay here a few days to see if I can penetrate through it."

Thus thought Ferdinand when he retired to bed; he slept undisturbed, and when he appeared below, the first question asked him was, "If he slept quiet?"

"Entirely so," answered he; "this place is remote from all disturbance, and is calculated for the Court of Somnus by its stillness."

The Solitary seemed pleased, and observed, "That the depth of the snow must preclude him from an attempt at travelling in that obscure and unfrequented part of the country." The other raised no objections to remaining another day, and both were much entertained by a mutual communication of observations that seemed greatly to relax the unbending features of the solitary man; but yet he preserved a profound silence relative to his own concerns. Fruit, eggs and sallad, were their only refreshments, with which Ferdinand was perfectly content.

When night came, and Ferdinand retired to his apartment, he met Francis on the stairs. The old man stopped; "Are you going to live here, Sir?" asked he.

"For a few days only," replied the other.

"I am sorry for it," said the old man.—"God knows we want company."

"I think so," answered Ferdinand, "for your master must have a horrid time of it here."

"Horrid indeed! You know all then, Sir."

"No, indeed, I know nothing; your master keeps his own secrets, and I do not presume to be inquisitive, though certainly every circumstance about this mansion and its master must raise strange conjectures, and inspire curiosity." The voice of the Solitary calling Francis, obliged the old man to hasten away, though by his earnest look and the motion of his lips he appeared about to say something interesting. Ferdinand was vexed at the interruption, and retired to his apartment, not to sleep, but fixed himself again to the window, that he might more distinctly hear the cries, should they be again repeated.

The more he reflected on this man's conversation and behaviour, the more extraordinary and inconsistent it appeared. On their first interview there seemed more of melancholy than ferocity in his manners, and he had *blamed* the late Count for *his* rashness. He had given traits of sensibility and humanity; yet in a late conversation he had advised *revenge*, and seemed animated by rage to a degree of fury in his looks. He had said, on his entering the Castle a second time, "that his confidence should not be a partial one;" yet his secrets were more guarded than ever, nor was there any probability that he would be more communicative.

"I thought," said Ferdinand, mentally, "that if admitted to this house I could be content to remain here and spend my days in solitude, I supposed this mansion might be an asylum for the unfortunate, or the abode of undeserved misery, driven from a faithless world; but I fear there is more of guilt than suffering in this man; for affliction makes people plaintive, and if the mind is *free* from *guilt*, it naturally expands and grows communicative to a fellow sufferer. I know not what to conclude upon, more than a resolution not to make *this* my resting-place, should I be invited to do so, which seems not very likely to happen; yet I should be loth to depart without being better informed of the mystery that pervades here."

He sat ruminating on the occurrences that had befallen him some time, when again his ears were assailed by the same cries, though rather fainter, and being on the watch to catch the sound, he was convinced that it proceeded from the other side of the building, and from some place where the sound was suppressed. Excessively agitated, he began to consider in what manner there was a possibility of being satisfied, or of obtaining a solution of this unaccountable business.—He had every evil to apprehend from the resentment of the Solitary, should he be discovered in *prying* into his secrets, and yet to know some person was *regularly ill-treated*, which seemed to be the case, and to be incapable of assisting that person, or to leave the Castle without receiving any explanation, was what both his humanity and curiosity revolted against.

In the day he was never alone, or if alone, always in view of the Solitary; nor had he ever an opportunity of speaking to Francis, his master carefully watched him; it appeared impossible therefore to penetrate into this mystery, unless he could by any finesse elude his vigilance, and have an opportunity to ramble about the mansion alone.

CHAPTER XIII.

IN forming and rejecting a thousand plans to gratify his curiosity Ferdinand passed the night, and obtained but a very few hours sleep in the morning, though they were none of them early risers. His looks unrefreshed, were observed by his entertainer, who asked him, "If he had not rested well?"

"No," replied Ferdinand, "I did not."

"Did any thing particular disturb you?"

"No, only my own uneasy thoughts; you will allow I have sufficient vexations, which, if reflected on, must sometimes preclude rest."

"At your time of life," answered the other, "the activity of the mind cannot be confined by particular circumstances, or local situations. Retirement will not do for *you*; travelling will amuse the eye, and give a diversity to your ideas; variety is absolutely necessary to keep the mind alive, and prevent it from dwelling on such circumstances as might, if indulged, overwhelm it with despair, and stagnate the senses: The snow growing firm will be no impediment to your travelling, and for the cold, a soldier should be accustomed to bear it."

"I am not apprehensive of fatigue, or incapable of bearing cold," answered Ferdinand; "but perfectly a stranger to this side of the country, there would be some danger of losing my way, as there are no tracts in the snow to guide me: I think, however, that if the weather continues fair, I will pursue my ramble to-morrow, if you will allow me to partake of your hospitality another day?"

"Certainly," returned the other; "but I think your scheme a very desultory and unsatisfactory one. As you are now acquainted with the residence of your wife, and her determination to see you no more, what is it you pursue? Why not return, and pass your winter at the Castle, look after your son, *if you think him such*, and prepare yourself for returning in the spring to the army?"

"The mansion of my brother is hateful to me on many accounts," replied Ferdinand, "it would continually remind me of every misfortune: No, *there* I cannot reside; and to live near my boy, for *mine I am sure* he is, could be no benefit to him, and having placed him in the hands of integrity, I am entirely easy on that head. I once thought that retirement would make me at least resigned; but I am now of your opinion, that a diversity of objects is more likely to amuse my mind, and that, where peace and contentment are for ever fled to procure a chance of temporary ease, variety of places and objects are absolutely necessary; yet will you pardon me for observing, that either your advice proceeds from a conviction that you have yourself chosen wrong in devoting yourself to solitude, or that you are weary of my company."

"You conclude wrong in the first instance," answered he: "I have never repented my residence here, on the contrary, it is the only circumstance that enables me to support the burthen of existence; on the other point I will not deceive you; I long since thought every passion, every feeling, but one, was annihilated in my bosom.—Your appearance, your voice and manner, was unexpected, was touching; a few dormant embers of sensibility procured you entrance at first, and a particular consideration, in which I have been disappointed, induced me to receive you a second time. I now feel that I have been too long secluded from the world to find any satisfaction in a companion, and therefore I frankly confess I do not solicit your stay here. In the advice I have given you I am governed rather by what I think more agreeable to *your own* feelings than *mine*, for we differ on particular subjects, and I, in your case, should act otherwise than you do: But—I have no more to say. You may stay a week, or depart to-morrow; consult your own convenience, and do as you please." He left the room as he ended these words, without waiting for an answer.

Ferdinand stood some moments in astonishment; he would have given the world to have known who this extraordinary man was, and to have penetrated into the mystery that enveloped him; but he saw no prospect of gaining the smallest intelligence to gratify his curiosity by remaining there, and after the civil dismission he had received, he could feel no inclination to a longer residence—being left alone, a thing not usual since he had been in the house; he went into the next apartment, which had a door opening into, what had once been a very spacious garden, though now entirely overgrown with weeds; a very narrow path-way, where they seemed to be trodden down but not cleared, went by the side of the building, close under the windows, and here he walked on, observing the dreadful ruinous state the rooms were in, the glass broken, the floors had been long entirely exposed to the weather, and bore every mark of decay and desolation.

He proceeded till he came to the other wing, and immediately recollected that the feeble cries he had heard seemed to have issued from thence. He walked slowly round, and elevating his voice, "What cruel neglect has this once noble mansion endured: Surely whoever is, or was the master of it, must have met with uncommon misfortunes; and to what a wretched state must that mind be brought that can support existence in this desolated place." He had scarcely pronounced those last words, when he heard a heavy groan and an articulate voice, which appeared to be at no great distance from him. He stopped: "Did I not hear a voice?" said he aloud.

"The voice of misery!" was the answer, in a feeble voice, that sounded as if underneath him.

"Whoever you are, speak; I am a friend, can I come to you?"

"I fear not," was the reply, and at the same moment Ferdinand observed Francis at the steps of the glass doors, as if looking for him. "I am called," said he, softly, "what hour of the night is safe?"

"Not till after twelve," repeated the same voice, with a kind of groan.— Ferdinand turned short round, and met Francis advancing as quick as his feeble frame would permit.

"Oh! Sir, make haste, pray make haste."

"What is the matter?" demanded the other.

"My master, Sir, O! pray make haste." He turned back quickly, Ferdinand following him, and being more nimble got before, and run mechanically to the library, where lay extended on the floor the Solitary, apparently insensible. On advancing towards him, he perceived one side of his face distorted; he fixed his eyes on Ferdinand, and attempted to speak, but his words were inarticulate, and gave evident marks of a paralytic affection. On the entrance of Francis they attempted to raise him; but succeeded with infinite difficulty, as he had received a partial stroke which entirely disabled one side; with much trouble they got him upon the bed, and not knowing what else to do, they poured some wine down his throat, though he strove with one hand to prevent it.

"What can be done?" cried Ferdinand; "Is there any help to be procured?"

"I know of none," answered Francis: "I am unable to get to the village." Before the other could reply, a sort of convulsive motion seized on the unhappy man, and in a few moments he was no more!

"O, good Lord!" exclaimed Francis, "he is gone, he is dead, and all his cruelties unrepented of!"

"He is indeed no more!" said Ferdinand, struck with horror at the sudden event, "and may Heaven have mercy on him, whatever may have been his errors. Follow me down stairs," added he to the old man, who appeared to be planet struck, "I wish to talk with you." They each took a glass of wine, and then looking stedfastly on Francis, "Tell me," said he, "who is confined in this Castle, whose cries are those I have nightly heard?"

"How, Sir!" cried the other, "have *you* heard their cries? Who, or what they are, I know not, nor their place of confinement; but that there are some poor souls some where underground is sure enough."

"What," said Ferdinand, "were not you in your master's secrets? Have you not resided with him many years?"

"I have lived with him nine years; Sir; but I never knew his secrets, for he never conversed with me more than to ask for what he wanted, nor ever sent me out of the Castle. Whenever the man, who brings things from the village twice a week, rings at the bell, he always went himself, and so, Sir, I could speak to nobody."

"How came you to be with him?" asked Ferdinand.

"Why, Sir, it is now better than nine years ago since I had been reduced by sickness and the rheumatism, to be unable to work for my bread, and lived by the charity of the village, which was little enough; so one day a farmer, who now and then gave me milk, said to me, Francis, if you would like to have a good bed, plenty of milk and eggs, and neither labour or trouble, I can get it for you; so, Sir, my heart leaped for joy, for many a day I had nothing, because my rheumatism would not let me walk; so I said, I should be heartily obliged to him. He then told me the Gentleman in the Castle, whom we had often heard of, and all the village was afeared to come near the place; so he said, this Gentleman wanted an old man to be with him, whom he would treat kindly, if he could bear confinement. At first, Sir, I was dashed, and much afeared; but the farmer said he was a very quiet good sort of a Gentleman, and I might live very comfortable; so I thought again he could mean no harm to such a poor fellow as me, and besides, if I didn't like him, I could come away with the farmer again—but there I was out of my reckoning; so, Sir, persuaded, at last I ventured to come to the gates on the other side the house towards the village; so when the farmer told him, he opened the gate and let me in: God help me, I little thought I should not go out again; and so, Sir, to be sure he always behaved kindly to me, but it was so lonesome that I grew tired; but what could I do? every time the farmer came he went with me to the wicket. Once I did venture to say, I would rather go back; so says he, what have you to complain of? So I said 'twas so cruel dull. O, said the farmer, if that's all, Francis, an old man (like you) may be glad to be quiet, you can want nothing with the world; and so, Sir, I saw plain enough he was glad to be rid of me, and, as I thought I might not live long, and to be sure had good usage, I rested quiet, and have been here ever since."

"Well," said Ferdinand, a little impatiently, "but what do you know of the persons confined?"

"Nothing, Sir, but this: One day, after I had been here about a month, I walked down where you was this morning, and I thought I heard some groans, so deadly affrighted I hasted back, and told my master.—Ah! (said

he) don't go that way again, Francis, I have heared the same noise sometimes; but 'tis no where else to be heard, so don't go again.

"I said no, I would take care of that; but I was terribly scared, because
I believed it was ghosts, and I could not sleep all night, and in the middle of
the night I thought I heared some cries, so, Lord help me, I was in a terrible
fright; but taking courage I got out of bed to go towards master's room,
t'other side of the gallery, when, just as I opened the door very softly, I saw
master go into his room, with a lamp in his hand, and a little whip and a
basket, which I had always seen on a shelf, in t'other hand; so he went in
and shut the door without seeing me, being in the dark: I thought it was
cruel strange, so next day I looks in the basket, and seed crumbs of bread,
so then I looked at the loaf, and some of it was gone. Well, Sir, I said nothing, but I made a hole on one side of my chamber door, and when I went to
bed I marked the loaf; so instead of going in to bed I watched at the hole,
and at midnight I saw him come out with the same things in his hands, and
go down stairs, and after a little time I heared the same cries.—Lord! how I
was afrightened; so after a time back he came, and next morning I looked
at the loaf—a good piece was gone; so when I carried it in to breakfast, I
said I believes the fairies or ghosts eat our bread, for I am sure it goes faster
than we eat it. That's nothing to you, said he, with such a terrible look as
made me shake again; you don't pay for it, and no matter which way it goes;
so, Sir, from that day I said no more. I was for a good while always afeared,
but at last, as I may say, I grew used to it, and so I was content as well as I
could.

"When he camed and told me your honour was at t'other wicket, and
made me fasten the outer gate, and ordered me into t'other room to shoot
you, if you forced your way farther. Dear me, what a fright I was in, the
pistol was of no use to me, and when you came again my heart rejoiced, in
the hope that you was going to live with us; but after the first day master
told me you must go again, which made me cruel sorrowful, and this, Sir,
is all I know."

Ferdinand, heartily tired of this prolix account began to consider how
he could find the way to this unhappy person, or persons, who were confined. He returned to the room where the deceased lay, and searching his
pockets found only one crown and a key, which key Francis said belonged
to the library bookcase, where he kept all the keys of the Castle; they again
descended to the library, and opening the desk saw a bunch of keys, which
for the present was all he sought for. They went towards the other wing
through a long gallery, which terminated with a large door; here they tried
their keys, and at length found the right; on opening it a dark staircase was

before them; they now concluded a light would be necessary, and Francis was sent back to procure one.

On his return with a lamp, they descended the stairs into a long vaulted passage. On one side were three rooms that had once been inhabited as domestic offices; they proceeded until their progress was impeded by an iron door: Here also they tried their keys, and opened it, there was another descent of a few steps, and the bottom seemed a damp, cold dungeon.—Ferdinand stopped, and speaking aloud, "Is there any person confined in this place?"

A faint voice replied, "Yes, two wretched beings!" The sound appeared to be near them, but still deeper; they moved a little onward, and perceived another door, with two strong bolts drawn across; these were easily removed, and another descent of three steps brought them to a vaulted room, but cautious in advancing, for their lamp emitted but a very faint glimmer.—"Is this your prison, are we right?" asked Ferdinand.

"Yes," answered a voice, so close to him that he started, and extending the light perceived a figure that made him shudder, and Francis scream with terror.

It had the appearance of a man, from an immense long beard that reached almost to his knees as he sat upon a bench, with a small table before him, on which was a wooden plate, and a little wooden bason: He had a blanket wrapped round him, and his hair covered his shoulders down to the bottom of his back; his features they could make nothing of, but his eyes, from the meagre countenance, looked sunk, yet wild; they now perceived a glimmering lamp was fastened against the wall on one side.

"Gracious Heaven!" exclaimed Ferdinand, "can a human being have existed here?"

"Yes," replied the poor wretch; "many years I have struggled with life, but wonder not at me, look yonder;" he pointed to the other side, where on advancing they perceived another iron door, and a little on one side a small opening in it, through which another human face was visible, but more emaciated than the other.—"Have we a key for this door?" cried Ferdinand, inexpressibly shocked.

"That door," answered the man, "is seldom opened," in fact none of their keys were large enough.

"O," said Francis, "I recollect a large heavy key hangs on one side of the chimney piece."

"Will you venture to fetch it, or will you remain here whilst I go back?" asked Ferdinand.

"O Lord, Sir, I'll fetch it; stay here!" repeated he, looking fearfully round the place, and at the shocking figure before him, "No, no, I'll make what haste I can." He took the lamp and hastened off. The faint one that glimmered against the wall served only to make "darkness visible," and to throw additional horrors on the place.

"Good Heaven!" cried Ferdinand, "is it possible human nature could support a long confinement in this place!"

"Ah! Sir," replied the man, feebly, "we know not till put to the test what very severe trials nature *can* sustain. Death is not so ready to relieve the wretched. Our cruel persecutor found out a way to make us support, nay even wish for life. That dear, unhappy woman! think what must have been her sufferings; upwards of twelve years, as the avenging monster told us a few days since, have we been here. Long, long ago, *we* lost all power of computing time. O, Eugenia, shall I live to see you free!"—"To be spared the misery of seeing *you die*," answered a faint but sweet voice, "is all the boon I ask of Heaven!"

Mutual sighs succeeded this tender expression, and Ferdinand, overcome with emotions at a scene so replete with horror, could not suppress audible proofs of his sensibility.—"O!" cried the wretched man, "how piercing, how inexpressibly sweet, to the heart, is the voice of compassion! Heaven only knows how you obtained entrance here; but should that cruel monster discover you?——"

"Fear not," said Ferdinand, hastily, "he is no more; death has stopped his career of wickedness at last."

The man was about to reply, when Francis entered with the key, for so strongly was his mind impressed with terror, that, though he dared not stay in the vault, he was almost equally afraid to go back, and return alone. Much quicker than he had attempted to move for many years did he exert himself on his errand, and heartily rejoiced to find he was once more safe by the side of Ferdinand, who eagerly snatching the key unlocked the other iron door, and entered a dungeon still more frightful, with only a few rays of light that served not even to distinguish objects, and proceeded from a small iron grating at the very top of the vault, which grating was almost covered by rust and weeds.

His own lamp guided him to the woman, for such he found she was, her hair almost covering her whole figure: She was also seated on a bench with a table, plate and bason, similar to the man's, a blanket round her also.—"For Heaven's sake!" exclaimed he, "let us remove you from this wretched place."

"I know not," said she, feebly, "how it can be done—we are chained."

"Chained!"

"Yes, each hand and foot is chained together, so as not to prevent our moving; but the Count will shew you."

"The Count!" cried Ferdinand, returning again to the man, who opening the blanket, the other saw a stout chain was fastened to each leg, which went round the opposite arm, not preventing the movement, but yet confined them so as to preclude any exertions, by pulling them cross ways when they attempted to walk.

"Is there no way of getting off those chains?" said Ferdinand.

"Only by a key or a file," answered the man.

"Have patience, my good friends," returned Ferdinand; "I will return, and seek for something that may answer the purpose."

"Yes," added Francis, darting out first, lest he should be asked to stay there, "we will find something I warrant you."

Notwithstanding the extreme agitation of Ferdinand's mind, he could not choose, but observe the great alacrity with which Francis hastened his steps. When they had reached the library, they searched about for a file; nothing of that kind was to be seen, but they found two odd constructed keys, which they supposed might belong to the chains; having recruited the fire with wood, taking a bottle of wine, their keys, and two or three old knives, they soon returned to the wretched prisoners, and to their great joy found they could relieve them from their chains. Ferdinand supported the woman into the next dungeon, they rushed into each other's arms, and fell to the ground. With the assistance of Francis they were lifted up: Ferdinand prevailed on them to take some wine.

"We are not strangers to this liquor," said the man, gratefully pressing the hand of his preserver; "once a week we have had a half-pint each of us, not as a favour, but with a degree of refined cruelty, to support and enable us to bear the miseries inflicted on us."

Without shoes, only coarse flannel stockings, a kind of petticoat of the same, and the blanket round their shoulders, they had only been accustomed to struggle rather than walk to the end of their dungeons, where a small partition was contrived to afford a proper separation from the place they were to sit and lye on, for beds they had none. With infinite difficulty Ferdinand and Francis got them out of the dungeon, and up the steps into the vaulted passage: Here they rested for some time, and at length reached its termination; but no sooner did the light and air dart upon them, than the woman fainted, and the man was almost blinded. By proper applications they recovered the Lady, and Francis, by shutting some of the windows, rendered the light less offensive; yet so extremely feeble were the unhappy prisoners, that it was a considerable time before their deliverers could get them into the library, where placed in two old easy chairs at some distance from the fire, that it might not operate too powerfully upon them, and being refreshed with a little bread and wine, their spirits began to return, and the Lady burst into a torrent of tears, that flowed for some time with such violence as frightened Ferdinand; but the man thanked Heaven for the relief. "Be not uneasy, Sir," said he, "not one tear has fallen from those eyes for years; I thought those sources of relief to the overcharged mind were entirely dried up; the indulgence will, I trust, be attended with happy effects."

Indeed it proved so, for after the first turbulence was abated, she recovered sufficiently to thank her deliverer in the warmest terms. Ferdinand proposed her retiring to bed, the one he had slept in Francis had prepared for her; he lamented the impossibility of procuring her linen and necessaries for the present.

"It is not impossible," said the Gentleman suddenly, "but that our trunks and clothes are still here, though perhaps decayed by time."

"I'll be hanged," cried Francis, "if those trunks, in a room next to this Gentleman's, ben't the very ones, for there they have been locked up ever since I camed here."

On this hint Ferdinand sallied forth with his bunch of keys to the room mentioned, where the trunks were deposited, and after trying several keys to no purpose, Francis was dispatched for an instrument of some kind to break them open, which with much difficulty they at last effected, and found them full of clothes and linen for both sexes; also some childrens necessaries, which last rather surprised Ferdinand; they however selected some for both persons, which seemed less injured by time than might have been expected; these were carried down, and when aired, the Lady was helped to her apartment, and linen left for her, which, from the stiffness of her arms and general debility of her limbs, she was a considerable time before she could put on; and when covered, and she was laid down, the sudden transition from such extreme misery to hope and comfort, affected her so forcibly as to preclude sleep for many hours: At length, however, she fell into a refreshing slumber; such as she had very long been a stranger to.

Mean time Francis had prepared *his* bed for the Gentleman, for though there were many other beds in the house, it was thought improper to put him into a room without first airing it. Being accommodated with comfortable linen, he very readily accepted their assistance to retire; and, after having seen him into bed, Ferdinand and Francis returned to the library to talk over this extraordinary affair, which afforded much room for observation and conjecture.

"Lord have mercy on us!" cried Francis, "how could they two poor souls live so for twelve years, naked and starving? O, dear me, I used to think *my* lot hard, but to be sure, Sir, it was Paradise to what they had. What a shame for me to think of trouble!"

"True, Francis," replied Ferdinand, "if we could, when afflicted, but examine into many circumstances that tend to lighten our own calamities, and compare them with the more painful disadvantages which others labour under, we should learn patience and resignation under the evils we suffer; but the human mind is too apt to view their *own* situation, and that of *others* under the medium of error, make partial comparisons, and draw unjust conclusions to increase their own misery.

"It appears to me that the Gentleman and Lady are the owners of this Castle, and had their persecutor died before I came here, doubtless they must have been starved in that horrid dungeon, for it is not likely you would have discovered them."

"*Me*, Sir! O, no, I should have crept out of the Castle as fast as I could if he had died when I was alone with him, though the Lord knows how I should have managed, for I could not walk to the village I am sure, and he might have died many days before our market man came, and I should never have been able to stay in this place with a dead corpse by myself.—So Providence sent you here, Sir, to save them poor souls from starvation, and me from dying of fear or fatigue." During this time Ferdinand had opened the bookcase to replace the keys, and curiosity induced him to search if there were any papers or memorandums relative to the deceased. Opening one drawer he met with a manuscript, the pages being open as if lately written, his eye caught the words: 'The stranger, who calls himself Ferdinand.'—"Ah!" exclaimed he, "this is doubtless a kind of journal, and may develop the whole mystery." Turning to the back, he saw it was entitled, 'Memoirs of the Baron S***.' The writing was extremely bad, and many pages seemed hardly legible, evidently written with a weak and trembling hand. He ordered Francis to make a fire in another apartment, air more linen, and get refreshments for the Lady and Gentleman against they should awake; then kindling a fresh blaze for himself, he prepared with eager curiosity to peruse the manuscript before him, which contained the following Narrative.

CHAPTER XIV.

MEMOIRS OF BARON S***.

SHOULD these memoirs ever fall into the hands of an intelligent being, let him mark the instability of expected happiness; let him learn to detest the fascinating charms of false, deceitful woman, and to beware of the insidious arts, the treacherous designs of base, perfidious man; let suspicion mark his eye, and caution guide his judgment; let him shun the syren *woman*, turn his ears from the delusive voice of pleasure, and lock his bosom close from professions of friendship, which tend only to deceive, and under a specious covering envelop the most treacherous designs. Should those cautions be read too late to preserve him from the machinations of the deceitful heart, then let him learn from me the triumph of *Revenge!!!*

My father was a Bavarian Baron, but supporting his rank with that splendour necessary to keep his vassals in awe, and give consequence to his dignity at Court, he diminished the value of those estates bequeathed to him by his ancestors, and left me possessed of equal pride, ambition, and desire of grandeur and magnificence, without a capability of gratifying either. Unable to appear at Court with the consequence attached to my title, I retired to my estate, and sought, in the submissive obedience of my vassals, and in the authorative and sullen grandeur I assumed over them, a consolation for that retirement disappointed ambition had driven me to choose, as a smaller evil than supporting the arrogance of riches, where there could be no superiority of birth to my own. Five years I dragged on an inactive life without enjoying any advantages from my seclusion, but what arose from lording it over my tenantry, without knowing the blessings of society, for there were none I deigned to converse with. In a kind of gloomy magnificence that was confined to my own estate, which inspired awe, but which repressed love or reverence, I passed my *days* in riding over the same track of ground which had no variety, and my *nights* in constant regrets for the loss of that consequence I was born to assume, but which the prodigality of my ancestors had compelled me to resign.

One day, attended by several of my vassals, I was riding round the skirts of a wood which bounded my estate, when I was suddenly alarmed by quick and repeated shrieks that seemed to issue from the wood: I instantly rode to the side from whence the voice proceeded, and in a few moments perceived a carriage surrounded by four or five banditti, and two horsemen laying dead in the road. The appearance of myself and servants, who speeded towards them, caused the villains to desist, and provide for their own safety. It was in vain to attempt pursuing them, as through the closeness of the wood they might elude our observation, I therefore hastened to the carriage where a young Lady sat, who had thrown herself upon the bosom of a man to all appearance dead or dying. When she raised her head, never shall I forget the moment that decided my future destiny, and ruined my peace for ever! When she turned her eyes upon me, Heavens! what were my sensations! until that luckless hour a stranger to the captivating charms of beauty, a blaze of charms dressed in the fascination of tears and sorrow, and which conveyed a thousand tender ideas to a susceptible heart: She held out one of her lovely hands, "Save him, O, save my father!" she cried in a voice of softest melody, "or pierce *my* bosom also!"—O, the remembrance of that moment of delight, pregnant with years of ceaseless misery! O, beautiful, false, enchanting, destructive charmer! Woman, vile abandoned woman! but I will be calm, am I not *revenged?* Yes, and that exquisite satisfaction shall attend me to my grave!

Let me proceed: Under a delirium of sudden rapture I exerted myself with uncommon alacrity, having prevailed on her to quit the chaise, I entered it, and found the Gentleman had received a wound in his breast, whether dangerous or not I could not know, I perceived he still lived, and having sent off a servant to procure the attendance of a surgeon, I entreated the Lady to go on to my Castle in the carriage, whilst my vassals formed a kind of litter, to carry the wounded man much easier than the motion of the wheels would admit of. She acquiesced in every request with the warmest expressions of gratitude for my attention to her parent; every tender look, every gentle word, twined itself about my heart, and confirmed me a wretch for ever!

We arrived at my Castle, the surgeon soon made his appearance, and, after examining the wound, gave us hopes that it would not prove mortal. The Gentleman did not recover his senses until the pain, which the probing of the wound occasioned, roused him from the insensibility that had overpowered his faculties, and enabled him to discover his daughter kneeling at the side of the bed, and bathing his hand with her tears. "My child!" he exclaimed—"Gracious Heaven, I thank thee, my child is safe!"—He was desired not to speak, and after some inarticulate blessings on his deliverer, weakness compelled him to give over the attempt.

The two servants that lay in the wood when I first discovered the carriage, we found to be entirely deprived of life, and the post-boy had fled thro' the trees: I knew not therefore the names or quality of my guests, but every thing in their appearance and manners seemed to denote that they were of no contemptible rank. During three days, I saw the young Lady only at the bed-side of her father; but in that time the subtle poison stole into my heart, and love, the most ardent and most impetuous, took possession of my whole soul, and engrossed every faculty of my mind. On the fourth day, the old Gentleman was declared to be out of danger, and allowed the privilege of speaking. He desired to see me; when I attended him his gratitude was boundless; he called me the preserver of his life, and the guardian-angel of his Eugenia.

He told me that he was a Nobleman of Suabia, his name Count Zimchaw. Having been on a visit to a relation at Munich, he was returning to Suabia through Mindelhiem, that he might call on another friend. Coming thro' the wood, which he took as the nearest route, he was attacked by four men. His servants, as well as himself, having fire arms, prepared to resist them; but his faithful attendants were shot dead, and the carriage surrounded. Finding then that resistance could have no avail, he was in the act of resigning his pistol, after having, in the beginning of the attack, discharged it without effect, when, as he reached his arm to deliver it, a cowardly assassin stabbed him in the breast, and he fell back senseless: The shrieks of his daughter on that event he supposed reached my ears, and providentially brought me to their assistance. This little account of himself was accompanied by the warmest sentiments of gratitude, in which the too lovely Eugenia joined.

He recovered fast, and had more than once mentioned his desire of renewing his journey, from an apprehension of intruding upon me: But far gone in a fatal passion that was to mark my future days with sorrow, I earnestly besought him to remain some time with me, and endeavoured, by every act of attention and complaisance, to gain the esteem of the father, and the heart of his daughter. My sentiments could not long be unnoticed by either. The Count viewed me with kindness and complacency; but Eugenia grew more reserved, and though always grateful and polite, there was a respectful coldness in her manners, repulsive to the warmth with which I always involuntarily addressed her.

Unaccustomed to meet with any opposition to my will, I was not prepared to expect a denial to my wishes, when I should think it a proper time to disclose them, and being one day alone with the Count, I seized a favourable opportunity, and without reserve opened my heart to him, solicited the hand of his daughter, and made the most liberal offers my circumstances would admit of.—The Count's character was propitious to my views; he was naturally proud and avaricious, the want of a male heir had disappointed the first passion, and increased the second. A nephew was to enjoy his estates by the marriage settlements after his death, and what he could save from his income was all he could dispose of in favour of his daughter. He had been desirous of uniting her with his nephew, but that Gentleman travelling into England, had there married a young Lady of rank and fortune, an account of which had reached Count Zimchaw a very few weeks previous to my meeting with them in the wood. Disappointed in his wishes, he felt a good deal of anxiety for the settlement of his child; when therefore I declared my love, and made my proposals, he could not disguise his satisfaction:—"To bestow my daughter on the preserver of *my life* and *her honour* (cried he) is the highest gratification I could picture to myself, and confers on me additional obligations. Yes, my dear Baron, Eugenia is your's, I pledge you my word, and answer for my child, that she will with joy ratify the gift I make you of her hand, and reward our deliverer from death and dishonour."

Mistaken man! he knew not the heart of his degenerate daughter. Transported with the prospect of my expected happiness, yet wounded by the recollection of her coldness, I entreated the Count to be my friend, and speak his approbation of my wishes, before I ventured to disclose them to her.

"We will lose no time," answered he, "and it is sufficient for me to declare my pleasure, and for her to obey. After we retire from dinner, your desires shall be confirmed." I left him under perturbations difficult to describe; joy, hope and fear, assailed me at once. I had no doubt of her compliance with the commands of her father, but I feared her *heart* would have no share in her obedience.

After dinner we retired to the saloon, my mind was so extremely agitated, that my emotions attracted the observation of Eugenia, nor did the uncommon spirits of the Count pass unnoticed: She viewed us alternately with a mixture of concern, and curiosity depicted in her countenance, which I well understood, and when we entered the saloon, as I led her to a seat, I felt her hand tremble in mine. The Count scarcely permitted us to be seated, and the servant to shut the door, before rising briskly, and taking his daughter's hand, "My dear Eugenia, (said he, abruptly) our worthy friend and preserver Baron S***, has done us the honour to solicit an alliance with us; yes, my child, he offers his hand to your acceptance. *I* have with joy accorded to his wishes, and here, my Lord, I ratify the gift," putting her hand into mine, as I bowed profoundly before her. She started up, trembled, and strove to disengage her hand as I pressed it to my lips: "My Father! my Lord!" cried she, extremely agitated, "spare me, O, spare me, I cannot, *indeed I cannot!*"——

"Cannot *what?*" exclaimed the Count, with a wrathful countenance: "Dare you resist *my* will? Can you refuse the hand of your benefactor, the hand that saved your father's life? Ungrateful girl! cold and insensible to the honour you ought to receive with transports! Teach your tongue a different language, learn to be grateful, and obey my commands." He had scarcely pronounced those last words, when she fell lifeless before us.

The Count was excessively enraged: I was wounded to my very soul, yet called for that assistance he would have denied to her. She was carried to her apartment. "Pardon a foolish wayward girl (said he;) perhaps the idea of marrying out of her own country has occasioned this *apparent* reluctance; a foolish local prejudice has got hold of her, which argument and reason will subdue. Be not disconcerted, my dear Baron (added he, embracing me) I swear to you that Eugenia shall be your wife." He left me at those words, and I remained overwhelmed with a thousand turbulent passions, disappointed love, wounded pride, jealousy and despair, by turns agitated me almost to madness. Her coldness, her repugnance, augmented my love and inflamed my pride; passion and resentment were raised to their utmost pitch; I accused her of ingratitude and insensibility, and in the workings of my rage, swore she should be mine, whatever might be the consequences!

I walked into the gardens to calm, if possible, the agitations of my spirits, but after strolling about two hours returned as restless as before. I met a servant, who said the Lady Eugenia wished to see me in her apartment. I flew thither with undescribable emotions. She was sitting on a sofa, looking pale as death, but more beautiful, more interesting than ever. Trembling I advanced, and would have flung myself at her feet.—"Hold, my Lord (said she, in a faint but serious voice) this humiliation neither becomes you nor me; have the goodness to be seated, and hear me with compassion, and without displeasure." I took my seat. "My Lord (continued she, in a firmer voice) think me not ungrateful, or insensible to *your* merits, or my great obligations to your generosity and humanity; I feel, I acknowledge all: You have claims I never can reward, and to give you my hand, circumstanced as I am, would be a base return for favours so unbounded.—My Lord, I have *no heart* to give! *that* has long been in the possession of another; my father knows it well, but as his consent could not be obtained to an union he thought unworthy of his approbation, *I have sworn* never to marry without it—I never will; but neither can I, will I, ever give my hand to another; deign then, my Lord, to withdraw your generous intentions in my favour, save me from the displeasure of my father, and let me be still further indebted to your nobleness of mind; the favour I solicit is no common one; but you have a soul superior to self-consideration, and on that I rest my confidence."

She might have proceeded for some time without interruption from me, so astonished and mortified did I feel at her address; but when she had ceased speaking, I endeavoured to recover my spirits, and told her, "that had there remained a possibility of her being united to the object of her attachment, I would have imposed silence upon my wishes for ever; but as it was evident such a connexion never could take place, as I flattered myself that my tenderness, and earnest endeavours to gain her heart, and promote her happiness, would in time have the desired effect; she must forgive me if I could not comply with her request, or forego a blessing her father had so kindly promised me."

"Blessing!" cried she, indignantly; "can you call a reluctant hand, a heart devoted to another, and a lifeless form that will shrink with horror from an union imposed upon her by a stern parent, who to an unjust prejudice would sacrifice his daughter; can you call such a sacrifice a blessing? See, see me at your feet (added she, endeavouring to prostrate herself, which I prevented:) I beseech, I implore you, not to persist in your addresses; respect your own happiness, if you cannot feel for mine, misery must follow a compulsion so repugnant to my soul."

At this moment her father entered the room: She threw herself at his feet in an agony, "Father, my dear father! by that tender name I conjure you to hear me! To your commands I have given up the dearest wishes of my heart; I have sworn never to marry the Count without your approbation; do not compel me to be miserable with another; never, never can I love the Baron as a husband: I esteem, I honour him as your preserver; I would lay down *my life* to prove my gratitude, but I have *no heart* to give."

The Count sternly bid her rise. "I have heard *you* with patience (said he) and now do you *hear me*; and not only *hear* but *obey* me. You have dared to single out my greatest enemy as the object of your love, and even yet avow your affection for him to my face: I ought not therefore to be surprised that this Nobleman, who has preserved *my life* and your honour, should be the object of your aversion! Your conduct sufficiently explains itself, and I know how to set a just value on your love and duty so much boasted of: *Now* I put it to the *proof*; this instant I command you to give your hand to the Baron, or my everlasting curses shall follow you to the grave!" She started up, in a kind of wild horror: "Hold! O hold! behold your devoted daughter, though distraction and death must be the consequence, take, take my hand, *you* may bestow, *I* can never *give* it!" He snatched her offered hand, and put in into mine; "receive her, my Lord, as a pledge of gratitude from a father, who dares to boast the gift is worthy of your love; duty and obedience will make her all you can wish for. And you, Eugenia, remember what you owe for *me*, and for yourself, happiness is in your own power." She answered not a word, her tears had ceased to flow, I lifted her hand to my lips, she withdrew it not, but appeared senseless and inanimate, looked alternately at her father and myself, a wildness in her aspect, that seemed unconscious of the objects before her. I tried to recover her from this torpid state by the tenderest expressions: She heard me unmoved, and the Count having called her attendant, advised me to withdraw; I did so, and left them together.

END OF THE FIRST VOLUME.

The Mysterious Warning

Volume II

MYSTERIOUS WARNING.

CHAPTER I.

I RETIRED to my own apartment overwhelmed with vexation and resentment. What, could I submit to marry a woman who avowed her
love for another, who detested me, and in whose eyes my very perseverance
must appear meanness? Where was my pride, my feeling, to accept a reluctant hand? Yet when her beauteous form swam before me, her fascinating
charms, could I coldly resign her to another? Was she not ungrateful and
disdainful, and must I be the sufferer for saving her father's life? No, I would
teach her to love, or if not to love, to obey and please me; I would consult
my own gratification, nor bear the insult of rejection from a preference to
another! Thus determined, love, pride, and resentment, took full possession
of my soul, and I resolved to urge a quick completion of the nuptial rites.

The Count joined me soon after, and congratulated himself and me
on our success.—"Bear with her coldness, my dear Baron (said he) I know
her principles, her integrity. In a very short time she will be sensible of
her duties, and become every thing you can wish for; the sooner the marriage takes place the better." This met my wishes, and we settled it that the
ceremony should be performed in three days. At supper, when sent for,
she directly followed the servant; she spoke not, but tried to eat; it was an
attempt only, for she could not swallow. The Count and myself addressed
her with the kindest expressions. She only bowed; but being warmly urged
by her father, she drank a glass of wine, and instantly burst into a torrent
of tears, so violent that I was quite terrified.—For upwards of an hour she
wept incessantly, till quite exhausted she was conveyed to her apartment,
and in all probability the tears she shed preserved her intellects, as, after
they had ceased to flow, she grew more composed, spoke to her attendant,
but passed the night without rest, and sighed continually.—The next day
the Count passed above two hours with her alone, and then led her into
the saloon to me. Pale, trembling and dejected, she received my ardent addresses without manifesting any reluctance, yet, without the least mark of

complacency, tortured to death by her cold disdain, I ventured to complain, to remonstrate. She turned her eyes full upon me:—"Of what, Sir, can you complain? I hear you, I obey my father, *you know* I can do no more, I cannot play the hypocrite; if I become your wife I shall do my duty, but love or affection I can never promise, and"—she paused, then fixing her penetrating eye on mine—"and, to a mind so little delicate as your's, the tender feelings of the soul can be but of trifling estimation:—Urge me then no more, you may deserve my esteem, but never can possess my heart."

"Eugenia!" cried the Count, in an angry tone, "is this treatment for *you* to offer, or my benefactor to endure?"

"Your pardon, Sir, (returned she;) I simply speak the dictates of truth, and the Baron has no cause to be offended; I know my duties, and will perform them."—Provoked as I was, and vowing vengeance in my heart, I thought it best to diversify our subjects of conversation, and appear submissive to her will: I endeavoured to repress my feelings, and by silent assiduities obtain her attention; but a chilling reserve, and a studied politeness, was all the return I met with. I freely confess, rage and resentful pride had an equal share with love in my desire to obtain her hand. Unaccustomed to have my will disputed, I was hurt and mortified to see all my complaisance thrown away, and to feel humbled before the woman I considered as under obligations to me:—Stimulated therefore by every turbulent passion, I determined she should be mine, be the consequences what they might.

Preparations were made for the marriage; she heard, she saw all, without a single observation; and the day previous to that on which we were to be united, her father informed her, that at twelve the following morning the ceremony was to be performed.

"I shall obey your pleasure, Sir," was all her reply.

The day came, ten thousand curses on it, and the false, dissembling, artful wretch! But I am *revenged*. Let me then proceed: At the appointed hour we assembled in the Chapel adjoining to my Castle, there I received the perjured creature's hand in the moment when she was planning to deceive and destroy my peace for ever! After the ceremony was performed, and we retired to the saloon, she turned to me with an air of solemnity: "I have obeyed my father, Sir, and complied with your wishes, permit me to solicit a favour in my turn."

"Name it, my angel," cried I, in a foolish transport, kissing her hand.

"Suffer me to pass the remainder of this day alone, in my own apartment."

"How!" said the Count, "not dine with us, Eugenia? Impossible, you cannot expect your husband will accede to such an absurd request."

"*You*, Sir," answered she, with an expressive look, "have this day re-signed over all *your* authority to this Gentleman, it is to him therefore I ap-ply. A few hours to myself is no great boon; I again repeat my request not to be broken in upon till the supper hour."

Fool! blockhead as I was! fearful of irritating her, and in the hope I should please her by my compliance, "Dearest Eugenia! (I cried) be mistress of your own time, I submit to any mortification that can oblige you, and let me trust to your generosity to reward my self-denial." I kissed her hand, and led her to the door. She turned her eyes upon her father, tears gushed from them, which she strove to hide, and, bowing to me, hastily withdrew.

"You are wrong, my dear Baron," said the Count, "to indulge her."

"Pardon me," answered I, "reflection will be favourable to my wishes, her vows are now given and a consideration of the duties she has taken upon herself to perform, will probably operate in my favour, and produce a desirable change in her behaviour."

"You may possibly be right," replied he, "but some how I am neither pleased nor satisfied."—Ah! he had his reasons for distrusting the perfidious wretch, whilst I was lulled into a blind security! The woman that attend-ed her had orders to carry some wine and biscuits to her apartment. The Count and myself eat our dinner, and the day being wet, seated ourselves quietly to piquet, though my emotions did not permit me to pay much at-tention to the game; I felt more than once inclined to have asked particulars respecting the man who had possessed the heart of my wife; but delicacy repressed my curiosity, as the Count had always evaded any explanation on that head.

The hours passed tardily until the time arrived, when she had permit-ted an interruption. The moment the supper was prepared I flew to her apartment, and gently knocked at the door: No answer was made, when I repeated it louder: I looked through the key-hole, and saw the key was on the inside; yet no noise or the least bustle was made.—Extremely alarmed I called for her servant; she was no where to be found, nor had she been visible for some hours. The Count by this time had joined me, and ordered the door to be forced. The apartment was empty!

Never, never shall I forget the anguish of that moment! The window which looked into the garden was open: "She is gone—she is lost! (I cried) and I am undone!"

"My dear son," exclaimed the enraged Baron, "lose no time in fruitless grief, let us pursue her through different roads, we soon shall hear of the faithless wretch, whom I blush to call daughter." The servants were instant-ly summoned; it was a dark, stormy night, but I ordered them to prepare horses for me and for themselves; it was impossible in such weather they could travel fast. On examining we found her clothes were gone. Agnes, who had waited on her, said, "that when she carried the biscuits the Lady ordered her to retire." The Count, with some of my vassals, were to search all the neighbouring cottages, whilst we scoured the roads. Heedless of the weather, myself and four servants took one direction; two more, with some of the tenantry I had caused to be called together, took another, and large rewards were promised to the successful pursuer.

Two days and nights were spent in a vain pursuit round the country and through the woods, without obtaining the least intelligence to guide our search, and I began to be well convinced that she must be concealed somewhere in my own neighbourhood. I returned to the Castle, and found the Count had not been more successful than myself.—Rage, vexation and fatigue, threw me into a fever, which confined me to my bed for eight days; but though incapable of acting myself, I still sent persons to watch the roads night and day. The fourth day of my confinement, a woman servant entered the room with two letters; "having that morning been to Eugenia's apartment to clean the room, and take the linen from the bed, under the pillow she had found those papers." I hastily snatched them from her hand, and saw one was addressed to me, the other to the Count, the writing Eugenia's. I tore it open, and read the following words:

"All endeavours to discover my retreat will prove fruitless, nor will you ever see me more. Had not the prospect of a deliverance from your power been held out to me, my own hand would have terminated my life. To avoid the completion of a father's malediction, I obeyed and gave you *my hand*, but I secretly repeated other vows.—May Heaven forgive me, for I had no alternative. Had they been given to you I must have been perjured. Love, such as I have an idea of, had no share in your bosom, for you sought your own gratification at the expence of my happiness: On your account therefore I feel no regret; you have preserved the life of my parent to deprive me of his love and protection. You have made *me* miserable, may you render *his* future days happy! Adieu for ever!

EUGENIA."

THE LETTER TO THE COUNT WAS AS FOLLOWS:

"Humbly on her knees the lost, unhappy Eugenia implores a father's pardon, and invokes from Heaven every blessing on his head! Had any thing but her everlasting happiness been at stake, she would have sacrificed herself with transport. To a father's wishes she gave up an attachment founded on merit, truth and honour, she resigned her fondest hopes of felicity.—Ah! my Lord, was she not then entitled to a negative voice? Must she be compelled to violate every feeling of her heart, and devote herself to misery? Impossible! the most rigid duty cannot require such a sacrifice.—You commanded your wretched daughter under the penalty of your 'everlasting curses,' dreadful denounciation! to give '*her hand*' to Baron S***. He cruelly availed himself of the dread command, and she obeyed:—But there your power ends. The Supreme Being never will sanction constrained or perjured vows, and in the very act of giving her hand, she mentally pronounced others than those dictated by force to her trembling lips: No ties therefore subsist between the Baron and Eugenia; may he make another and a more fortunate choice. For *you*, dear and ever honoured parent, whilst your unfortunate daughter exists, for *you*, her prayers will be offered to the Throne of Grace, that every blessing that Heaven can bestow may be yours, and that you may grant that forgiveness she solicits on her knees with a bleeding heart, for the pain and disappointment she is compelled to give you. Grant, Gracious Heaven, that Eugenia may one day kneel and obtain a father's blessing! The pangs of death can scarcely exceed those she feels when she resolves to fly from your paternal arms, and bury herself in solitude, *perhaps* for ever!

EUGENIA."

Such were the contents of two letters indelibly imprinted on my memory. The Count's rage was little inferior to mine; from him I learned that she had, almost from infancy, formed an attachment to the young Count M***, son to a man he had once esteemed, but now detested, from a discovery that his principles were inimical to the good of his country: He had therefore broken off the intended marriage. The grief and disappointment attending that event had driven the lover to quit his country in search of returning peace, far from the object of his wishes. This affair had preyed greatly on Eugenia's spirits, and it was to relieve her disquietudes, and by a diversity of objects engage her attention from dwelling on one set of painful ideas, that the Count undertook a journey to Munich, and by a cruel fatality was thrown in my way to complete my misery; we had little doubt but that her lover had been instrumental in her flight, and that a secret correspondence had been carried on between them, but how or which way they could have conducted her escape, so as to baffle all intelligence, has ever remained a mystery to this hour.

I had scarcely attained a state of convalescence, before the old Count fell ill; indignation had for a time supported him, whilst there remained any hopes of discovering her; but when all our different messengers returned unsuccessful, he began to droop, and in proportion as grief and reflection on the loss of an only child, took possession of his mind, his bodily strength decayed. After staying with me near three months, heavily oppressed both in mind and body, hopeless and languishing, he took leave of me to return into Suabia; at the moment of his departure, however, he solemnly protested, that should his daughter ever be recovered, he should consider her as my wife, honour, gratitude, and the rights of an injured parent confirmed her such, unless I chose to break the ties between us. "My dear Baron (said he, as he entered the carriage that was to convey him from me:) My dear Baron, depend upon my integrity, *you* are free, but *I* and my *daughter* are bound; whether she ever returns to her duty or not, *you* are the heir to all I can dispose of from my nephew, and I trust that I shall shortly see you in Suabia."

We parted to meet no more. I had refused to accompany him, in the faint hope that time might bring me some information respecting the fugitive; and he was desirous of returning that he might make an inquiry respecting Count M***. Some time past before I heard from Count Zimchaw, and of course I concluded he was as far as myself from obtaining the least degree of satisfaction. For my part, neither time nor disappointment had abated my passion; I still loved to a degree of fury; for rage, and a desire of revenge on her and her paramour, went hand in hand with my inclination for her person; and being at length convinced they could not remain so long undiscovered in my neighbourhood, I was on the point of setting off for Suabia when I received a letter from the Count. He informed me that a severe fit of illness had prevented him from writing, tho' he did not neglect every necessary inquiry that might tend to procure a development of the dark plot against our happiness. To his astonishment he learned that the young Count M***, having been recalled by the death of his father, had resided for some time past at his estate, still overwhelmed with a deep melancholy, which had appeared lately to be greatly increased, arising, as he supposed, from the report he had given out on his arrival to his own Castle, "That the Lady Eugenia was married to Baron S***, still desirous (added the Count) of preserving the reputation of an ungrateful wretch, whom I can never again acknowledge as a daughter, unless *she is* your wife."—He added, "that from every circumstance he had investigated, it was certain that Count M*** held no correspondence with her, and that in his opinion the most certain conclusion was, that she had escaped to some Convent. He earnestly pressed me to come and reside with him, leaving a trusty person on my own estate, who might still continue every proper inquiry, and that should it be possible for her to lie concealed in my neighbourhood, my absence would throw her off her guard, and when we least expected it, she might be discovered."

This letter at once determined me, and in a very few days after I set off on my journey to Suabia. The Count's Castle lay between Stutgard, the capital of Suabia, and Baden, and, after a fatiguing journey, I arrived on the very day on which he had expired, of the gout in his stomach. I found his domestics expected my arrival, in consequence of my answer to their master's letter, and was presently informed he had declared me his heir, and from me they were to take every direction. I was touched with this proof of the Count's gratitude and affection, and more than ever desirous of recovering his daughter, that she might share in that fortune her worthy father had bequeathed to me. Not entirely divested of hope, I accounted for her absence by saying, "that she was likely to produce an heir, and being in a delicate state of health, the physicians had forbidden her to undertake the journey." This passed with every body. I took upon me the management of the household, saw the remains of Count Zimchaw deposited in the family vault, and as his nephew was to have possession of the Castle and estate, I disposed of the furniture, dismissed the servants, and took a lodging at a farmer's for a few days previous to my return home.

The truth was, I had an invincible desire to see Count M***, whose residence was only a very few miles distance. Every day I rode round his grounds, and grew quite desperate that chance did not befriend me.—One morning, riding through a narrow valley, accompanied by one servant only, I met a Gentleman with a gun, and an English pointer running by his side. As he advanced I saw a young man, of a noble air, and an engaging countenance; struck with a presentiment that this must be the Count, I accosted him, and inquired to whom that mansion, whose turrets we saw through the trees, and the neighbouring grounds, belonged?

"To Count M***, Sir (replied he, eying me with a scrutinizing look:) Are you a stranger in this country that you ask the question?"

"I am (answered I) having resided in these parts only a fortnight."

"A fortnight! (repeated he, with some emotion) you are on a visit then I suppose?"

"No; I came here for that purpose, but found my good friend dead, the late Count Zimchaw."

"Count Zimchaw! (he exclaimed.) Great God! perhaps I see Baron S***?"

"You are right, Sir, that is my name."

In a moment he turned pale, trembled, and convinced me by his emotions that my conjectures were just, and that in him I beheld a detested

rival. To an indifferent by-stander our appearance must have excited astonishment; we viewed each other for some moments in silent rage, but fortunately prudence predominated over passion, and I recollected that it was
necessary to dissemble. I immediately added, as soon as I could speak. "And
I have the happiness of being the husband of his daughter, the Lady Eugenia." He leaned against a tree unable to support himself. "O name for ever
dear! (cried he) sacred be *your* peace, whatever becomes of *mine!*"—"Leave
me, Sir, leave me to retrospections more painful than you can wish to your
bitterest enemy." For a moment the thought crossed me to put a period to
his existence; but whilst I deliberated, two of his servants appeared with
dogs and guns. Looking at him with the most pointed contempt I could
assume, I departed in silence; but with more heart-felt ease than I had experienced a long while, convinced now that Eugenia was not with him, nor
of course in that part of the country. Having in a short time settled every
thing with Count Zimchaw's heir, who was also led to believe his relation
was my wife, and at my Castle; I left Suabia to return home, richer, but
more wretched, than before I had known the Count and his daughter. On
my arrival I learned that every search had been fruitless respecting the ungrateful woman, who had so shamefully and suddenly deserted us, I sought
to amuse my mind by embellishing my Castle; but in vain I endeavoured
to root out my ill-fated passion from my heart.—Eugenia, beautiful and
engaging, was ever before my eyes, and threw me into a gloomy dejection,
from whence nothing could rouse me. The little society that I had sometimes indulged in, grew hateful to me, love, and a desire of revenge, wholly
occupied my mind, and the only idea that could communicate the least
degree of satisfaction to my soul, was, that Count M*** was apparently as
wretched as myself.

Four years I passed without a friend or a companion to harmonize my
feelings, or without the least intelligence of the object that had caused all
my misery: During that time I had changed my servants two or three times,
for nothing pleased me, and the men preferred serving in the army rather
than to support the capriciousness of my temper. One faithful fellow only
remained, who had been invariably attached to me for some years, who had
the command over the others, and had been generally hated by them for
that reason. This man, Peter, who was in my confidence, I had twice dispatched into Suabia, to make private inquiries relative to Count M***, and
was informed, that within three months after my departure he had quitted
his palace overwhelmed with a deep melancholy, and was gone to travel for
the recovery of his health.

The last inquiry afforded no other information than that he was

abroad. I had also set on foot a diligent search through all the neighbouring convents to procure intelligence of my wife, curse on the name! but all
proved abortive; yet neither time, nor despair, caused any revolution in my
sentiments; I loved and hated to excess.

CHAPTER II.

FOUR years had just been completed when one night I was suddenly awakened by Peter, who conjured me to rise and save myself, for the Castle was
in flames. Greatly alarmed, I threw myself out of bed, and found his information but too true, and the principal part of the building was consumed,
and my furniture destroyed before assistance could be procured. This event
gave a new turn to my thoughts, I resolved to dispose of the remainder
of my effects, to leave my ruined Castle without rebuilding of it, and to
travel from one principality to another, that by change of place and objects
I might amuse my mind. I settled every thing with my vassals, and, accompanied only by Peter, quitted Bavaria. I passed through Italy, France, the
Netherlands, Switzerland, and at length came into Suabia, on my return to
Bavaria, without deriving much benefit from my tour, either to my mind
or body, for I carried in my heart a barbed arrow, which no local circumstances could extract; insensible to pleasure, my eye wandered over every
new object with indifference, and Eugenia, the *faithless*, ungrateful Eugenia, occupied every thought and desire.—Passing through this country, my
good genius prompted me to pay some attention to its romantic and picturesque views. Riding about, I had not attended to the sun's decline, and the
approach of a heavy storm, which came on suddenly, accompanied with
thunder and hail. We were on the skirts of the Black Forest, and distant,
as we thought, from any village; finding the storm grew more violent, I
sought to get some shelter from the thickest part of a wood at the extremity
of the road: I rode with great swiftness towards it, and soon forced my way
through the trees, and obtained from their thick foliage a defence against
the fury of the storm. In a short time the weather changed, the clouds dispersed, and the moon rose with additional splendour from the contrast of
the black clouds rolling off behind the mountains.

Turning our horses to leave the wood, I observed, at some distance,
the turrets of a Castle, which, had not the moon shone full upon them,
might never have attracted the notice of any traveller, being enveloped in
the thickest of the trees, and far from any public road: Curiosity, or a powerful presentiment, urged me to explore this dwelling; Peter sought to dis-

suade me, he conceived it to be some ruinous place, the residence of a banditti, which was known to infest the Black Forest and its environs. I allowed
the probability of his suggestions, yet could not be persuaded to relinquish
my design: It was with much reluctance that he followed me; we pushed
through the wood, until we found it so close on every side as to impede the
horses from advancing. Peter again urged me to return, as the night was
far advanced, and the neighbourhood dangerous, still, an unaccountable
propensity to see this retired dwelling made me disregard his solicitations,
and despise the apprehension of danger. I dismounted, and fastened my
horse to a tree, obliging him to do the same, though he declared we should
never see them again, and I firmly believe, had he not been afraid to go back
alone, unknowing of the road, that he would have left me; but he run an
equal risk, and therefore attended me through almost impassable places,
when all at once we came to a declivity, at the bottom of which was a small
vale, from whence we saw two towers very plain among some trees at a
small distance.

We soon arrived through those trees to a large old building moated
all round. After going by the side of the moat, about a hundred yards, we
saw a small bridge, which led across to a pair of iron gates, which looked
into an outer court, within which was another high wall. Peter I observed
trembled with apprehension, but I boldly pulled the bell: In a little time a
boy appeared, and demanded "who and what we were?"

I replied, "A Gentleman and his servant, who travelling had lost their
way, and begged shelter for the night."

The boy replied, "That his master having been ill, was retired to rest,
his Lady also; that the servants were likewise going to bed, and he could
not disturb them, or admit strangers into the house: If we returned through
the wood, and kept to the right-hand of the Forest, we should reach a small
village." Ending these words he disappeared abruptly, and, though I repeatedly called to him, did not return.

Peter rejoiced that we were not to enter this Castle, pressed our immediate return lest our horses should be stolen. Vexed and reluctant I found
myself obliged to comply, as I saw no probability of getting entrance there.
The next step was to find the village, from whence I hoped to gratify my
curiosity respecting this obscure habitation. We soon recovered our horses,
and by the light of the moon explored our way from this difficult and dangerous place. After a good deal of trouble and fatigue we reached a few
scattered cottages just as the morning dawned, and the poor industrious
peasants were coming forth to their daily labour (how did my soul sicken at
the sight!) whose ruddy, cheerful countenances bespoke happiness and con-

tent; whilst I, possessed of wealth, titles, and what the world might judge perfect felicity, was a prey to every torment, that disappointed love, and a hopeless desire of revenge, could inspire!

We alighted at a miserable public-house, for this being an unfrequent-ed road, no decent accommodation could be expected; we got, however, rest for ourselves, and food and shelter for our poor tired beasts. Peter went to bed, but I had no inclination for sleep, and after eating a couple of eggs, and drinking some small wine, I inquired of the mistress of the house the name of the dwelling I had seen, and the quality of its owner?—She said its name was "The Solitary Castle," because of its situation; that it belonged to a great Count, she did not know what he was called, and that for these three years past some great folks lived in it; but nobody in the village knew who they were, they were never seen, and only one man servant came now and then for things they wanted.

This unsatisfactory account, in which there appeared to be a mystery, only augmented my curiosity and desire of penetrating into the secret; im-pelled by an irresistible impulse, I resolved to stay a few days in that wretch-ed place for the purpose of obtaining further information. Soon, too soon for my peace, was the mystery developed.

About the middle of the day I lay down for a few hours, during which time Peter had risen. When I returned to the room, he entered it after me, and shut the door:——"Sir (said he) as I was standing near the window, a man entered the house, whose face was very familiar to me; I was on the point of going out when I heard him bargaining with the woman for ducks; they agreed about the price, and he said he would fetch them to-morrow. He left the house, and again passed before the window, when seeing him again I instantly recollected who he was; then I asked the landlady where he lived?" She answered, "He was servant to the gentry that live in the Solitary Castle."

"Ah! (cried I, interrupting Peter) and who is this man?"

"One of your vassals, Sir, who courted our housekeeper Agnes; his father was a substantial man, and we all thought it would be a match; but you know, Sir, after you returned from Count Zimchaw's, Agnes left you to go home to her mother, and I heard the young man went soon after to Vienna to live with an uncle. What has happened since I don't know; but I'll take my oath, this man I have seen is Mr. Arnulph, though they say he is a servant."

"I hope you are right, Peter, then to-morrow I shall have my curiosity gratified."

The to-morrow came, and I was constantly on the watch for the arrival of Arnulph. At length we saw him, and Peter darting out upon him:—"Your servant, Mr. Arnulph, who should have thought of seeing you?" The fellow started, looked wild and motionless:—"Bless me, Peter (said he, falteringly) how, how came you here?"

"Why, I have been travelling round the country, and came here only a day or two ago; but pray do you live in this neighbourhood?"—The fellow, without making a reply, turned to the woman: "I must leave the ducks with you two or three days longer." I had been observing his motions, surprise, confusion, and fear, were marked in his features, and I saw he was retreating to the door as he spoke, a sudden emotion I could not account for, impelled me to spring forward, and seize him by the arm. The moment he saw me he shrieked, and fell on his knees speechless. Peter raised him: "Follow me instantly" (exclaimed I, in an agony of suspense, doubt, and hardly knowing what I had to fear or expect:) I led the way to my room. Terror had so evidently overcome his courage that he quietly obeyed. When the door was fastened, I demanded where he lived, and with whom?

After much irresolution, and many subterfuges, he said, he was married to Agnes; that she lived housekeeper, and himself steward, to a Gentleman a few miles off; there was nothing improbable, or likely to interest me in this account, and I was growing very calm, and about to ask some particulars relative to his master; when taking notice of his extreme agitation, the wildness of his looks, and the terror with which he surveyed me and Peter, it naturally engaged me to believe there was some secret which he was fearful of being discovered, and which he was desirous of concealing from me. Possessed with this idea I laid hold of his arm, and in a commanding tone of voice: "Hear me, Mr. Arnulph, I am not to be imposed upon, I am no stranger to the Solitary Castle; hide nothing from me therefore as you value your life."

"Ah! Good God! (cried he) and is all discovered?" Then falling again at my feet, "Forgive me, my Lord, I had no hand in the business, I knew nothing of the matter till Agnes sent for me after she had left your service; I had never seen the Gentleman or *your Lady* till I came to this Castle in the wood."

Struck with astonishment, unable to articulate a single word, I stood gazing upon him with such an air of wildness, as added to the poor fellow's terror. Embracing my knees, he again supplicated mercy and forgiveness. Recovering at length my disordered senses, I bid him rise, assured him I could not blame him; but to deserve the pardon he solicited, he must acquaint me with every particular that had happened, and how long he had lived with Count M***, for I doubted not but that he was the companion of my faithless wife. His information was without reserve: "He knew not the name of the Gentleman but as a Count; he received a letter from Agnes about three years and half ago, saying, that if his love for her continued, and he had no objection to quit his residence and be united to her, she could insure him the place of a steward where she was housekeeper, and in case he liked the proposal he must be at this village on such a particular day, where she would meet him. His father being dead (he said) all places were alike to him, and having a great love for Agnes he joyfully complied, and was here at the appointed time. She told him her residence was retired and lonely, but that she had the best master and mistress in the world, who, on account of some cruel relations, were obliged to live in obscurity and unknown. If he could resolve to live retired she would marry him, and they might live happy with a good and generous pair."

To this proposal he consented with joy, remained two days in the village, on the third they were married at the village church six miles off, and, without returning here, he accompanied her across the skirts of the Forest to the wood, where they sent back their horses, and he followed her into the Castle. He said, he did not half like such a dismal remote place, but it was too late to retreat, especially as he loved Agnes. When introduced, he was thunderstruck to see the Lady, whom he had frequently seen at my Castle, and who he had been told I was married to, but who had afterwards gone into a Convent (for such was the report I circulated, and indeed believed); the Gentleman he had never seen before. Agnes told him they had been privately married some years ago, before Count Zimchaw came to my Castle, but dared not to own it, therefore when she was obliged to marry me she had fled to avoid the consequences; that apprehensive of my revenge they lived retired from the world, and that he must take an oath never to let any one know who or where she was. This he readily promised, and from that day they have all lived very happy, and the Lady lay-in of a little girl about two years and half ago.

This was the substance of Arnulph's information, which inspired me with the most eager desire of revenge; my soul was in tumults: I inquired what domestics were with them? He said, only a poor ignorant peasant lad, whom they had hired some miles off, and from the parish, who had no parents living, and who never went out of the Castle. I observed, from Arnulph's manner of telling his story, and words that dropped from him, that he was tired of a life so solitary, and that it would not be difficult to bribe him to my purpose. Giving him some pieces of gold, I assured him I would make his fortune if he would follow my orders, otherwise I would certainly put him to death: The alternative admitted of no consideration, for cowardice was his predominant feeling, and to that I was indebted for the relation he had made; I therefore soon arranged my plan, and kept him with me until towards night, when we set off together for the wood, walking my horses as far as it was passable, and then alighting fastened them as before.—On leaving the poor alehouse I told the people I had found the gentry at the Castle were my relations, and that I was going to visit them; ignorant and inattentive they heard and were silent.—Peter and myself were armed with pistols, and I had my sword.—Neither him nor Arnulph were acquainted with my purpose, and I privately resolved they should never witness against me. I declared to them I would not injure the lives of the Count or my wife; that my sole intention was to bind them, oblige the former to renounce all right to the Lady, and carry her with me into Bavaria.

The simple fellows either did, or affected to believe all I asserted; every circumstance was favourable to my design: The Count had been indisposed, and was still weak and incapable of any exertions; the child had been ill in the meazles, and Agnes confined herself with her, the mother divided between the two had suffered an anxiety very detrimental to her health and spirits. When we arrived at the gate, I turned to Arnulph with a sternness that terrified him: "Now mark me well, if you, by word or look, give the least alarm, that moment you are a dead man; you know your master cannot help you, therefore beware how you offend me." He assured me of his obedience, and rang the bell, the boy appeared, we stood on one side, hearing Arnulph's voice, he unbarred the gate, and we rushed in. I instantly seized him, and pulling him into a kind of lodge, I gagged and bound him. From thence, by Arnulph's direction, I proceeded to the Count's apartment, we listened at the door; and I heard Eugenia's voice, as if speaking to her child. Fury, almost to madness, seized me, and I burst in upon them with a pistol in each hand. He started from his bed, she shrieked, and looking at me, sunk on the floor.

The Count attempted to throw himself out of bed, he uttered some words I do not now recollect, and called upon his servant. I advanced furiously towards him: You call in vain for help, I am master of your destiny. I ordered Peter to throw himself upon him, and hold him down. In vain he struggled, for the efforts being too much for his strength, he was the more easily overpowered. With the pistol to his breast, whilst Peter secured his arms, I obliged Arnulph to cut the cords from the bed, and in spite of every resistance securely confined the Count, who now condescended to implore mercy for Eugenia; his first execrations were changed into supplications, and I enjoyed them.

Arnulph had been endeavouring to restore to life the deceitful Eugenia; her child was crying over her, and by its lamentations brought in Agnes. On seeing us, her first intention seemed to be flight, for she screamed and run to the door; but looking at her mistress she flew back to assist her, as she appeared returning to life; she besought me to spare her Lady.

"You have no cause for apprehension," I replied, exquisitely gratified at seeing them all in my power: "I swear to you that I will not destroy your Lady, or your Lord, I do not mean to murder them."

"What then is your intention?" asked the Count. "Why break in upon us like a midnight robber?"

"I have no leisure to answer questions," said I, interrupting him, "therefore you may as well be silent; for *you*, ungrateful, perjured creature," added I, addressing Eugenia, who by this time was restored to a sense of her situation, and hid her face in the arms of Agnes, both violently agitated, "*you*, who at the altar gave *me* your hand and faith, and now live as an adultress with the man you swore never to be joined with without your father's consent; know you are still *my* wife, and I will prove my right by my power of punishing you."

She uttered not a word, terror had deprived her of speech. I ordered the two men to carry her into the next apartment. She made no resistance: I drove Agnes and the child after her; there I had recourse to the same means, cut the cords from the bed, and bound both mistress and maid, telling Arnulph aside I would release his wife the following morning: I saw by his countenance that he repented of his confidence, and was much moved by the situation of the women, and the cries of the child, which I silenced by threats that drove her to the feet of her mother. I was convinced it would be necessary to get rid of him speedily; having therefore secured my prisoners, and locked them in separate rooms, I bid Arnulph conduct me over the Castle. I followed him through the apartments, and found one wing of it had been neglected, and was more out of repair than the rest, looking only towards a thick wood from the tower.

I examined carefully, and at the end of a gallery went down a staircase, which had a vaulted passage. Opening one of the apartments, which received a glimmering light from the top of a broken window shutter, I bid the man see if he could pull it down.—He tremblingly obeyed me, and as he was making the trial I stabbed him in the back: He fell; I repeated the stroke in his heart; he ceased to live, and I hastened from the place. The ferocity that had taken possession of my soul precluded every sense of fear, and drove every humane feeling from my heart for ever: I could now revenge my injuries, and I felt a gloomy triumph that inspired more pleasing sensations than I had for four years enjoyed.

Leaving the wretched victim, I explored the passage until I came into two horrible dungeons, and by the staples in the walls, and chains hanging from them, was convinced those dungeons had been formerly used as prisons by the owners of the Castle. This place answered my purpose exactly. I returned to the Count's apartment, told Peter Arnulph was employed at the other part of the house, and bid him assist me in carrying the Count to a place I had provided for him. He obeyed, incapable of resistance he submitted in silence.

When we descended into the dungeon I observed Peter trembled, and threw a melancholy glance on the prisoner; he was obliged, however, to help me in fastening the chain in a secure manner round the Count's legs and arms: I then unbound him.

"Use *me* as you please (said he) but spare the unfortunate Eugenia, and an innocent child."—His voice faltered.

"I mean not to divide you (I replied.)—You shall have your family party here to share your felicity." Ordering Peter to accompany me, I went back to the women, and obliged him to drag Agnes to the same vault. Eugenia made not the least resistance, when told she was to have her child and the Count with her.

"Conduct me where you will (said she) with the dear objects of my heart, and I shall not complain:" But when she entered the dismal abode, and saw him chained, she sent forth a piercing shriek, and then descended to implore mercy and supplicate forgiveness. I felt a sensation of pity at the moment, but I had gone too far to recede. Agnes and the child uttered loud and dismal cries; Peter's tears ran down his cheeks, but I shut my ears and my eyes against being moved by their distress. We carried Eugenia into the inner dungeon, and chained her in a similar manner with the Count. Having thus secured them, I demanded of the faithless woman by what means she had escaped from me, who assisted her, and where she had been concealed?

"Those are particulars you shall never know (said she;) I have nothing now to fear, for death would be a relief; your savage nature may be gratified by *my* miseries, but never shall you learn from me the names of those who were my friends and deliverers."

"It is well (cried I, enraged at her perverseness) here is one however," seizing Agnes, "who has been an accomplice, and whom I will oblige to speak: Say, wretch, where didst thou hide that infamous perjured woman? Who were thy assistants? Instantly confess the whole, or certain death attends thee."

"I had no assistants (answered she, firmly) nor do I fear to die; be assured, my Lord, that whilst I am confined in this horrid place, whilst those unfortunate ——." I interrupted her, with my poniard at her breast, and at her peril bid her conceal any thing from me.

"I will follow the example of my beloved mistress (said she;) from me you will learn nothing."

"Die then, audacious wretch," I exclaimed, and plunged the poniard into her breast!

"Hold! O hold! (cried Eugenia) and I will tell you all:" But seeing the woman fall expiring on the ground:—"Inhuman monster! (added she) to murder the innocent and helpless, well dost thou justify the aversion my soul conceived against thee, stern, cruel barbarian! O, my father! my dear father! thy peace and happiness sacrificed to gratitude, and thy daughter a miserable victim to an unjust prejudice! Fatal, fatal prepossessions!" "'Tis *you*, unjust and cruel woman, 'tis *you* (cried I) who are the cause of all those murders, of that ferocity and cruelty thou upbraidest; 'tis love, 'tis hatred, that teaches me revenge; *one* passion shall at least be gratified."

I turned from her, heedless of her lamentations, or the cries of her child. On entering the other dungeon I saw the Count trembling, and speechless from the violence of his emotions, I left him with the triumphant satisfaction that he was now as wretched as myself. On my return to the habitable part of the house, I examined the looks of Peter, pale and agitated, I saw he was but half a villain, and enjoyed not the glorious revenge of his master. He asked for Arnulph, in a tone of voice that conveyed his suspicion that *he also* was no more.—Plunged so far into guilt, murder was familiar to my thoughts, and to secure myself, it was necessary I should permit no witnesses to exist against me.

Could I have confided in his secrecy, he would have been most useful to me, but I dared not risk the hazard; therefore, after a moment's recollection, I bid him follow me, and he would see what Arnulph was employed about. With a doubtful look and a trembling step, he descended with me to the offices below, and passing the kitchens at the end of a long colonade, I opened a door which led into a room that appeared to have been a laundry, and being detached some way from the other offices (the thing I sought for) was designed to rid me of all apprehensions from Peter.—"Arnulph is not here," said he, in a tremulous voice. Seeing that I stopped:—"No, but *you* are," and in a moment I buried the poniard in his bosom.—He fell dead without uttering a word, only one dismal groan, which made me start.— Looking round, and then on the bleeding object before me, whose services had ever been faithful, and who I had sacrificed to *fear only*, a transitory re- morse smote me to the heart: I flew hastily from the dreadful scene without recovering my weapon. I regained the chamber where I found the Count, and throwing myself upon the bed which lay on the floor, gave way to the most terrible reflections I had ever experienced; the horrors in which I spent that night will ever live in my remembrance.

I had committed three murders: The fury that had possessed me on my first entrance, now subsided into gloomy retrospections, and unsettled designs. If I destroyed the Count and Eugenia I had nothing to fear; but my revenge in that case would be incomplete; I wished to see them miserable, to endure a living death. Some times different ideas struck me, which my still violent passion suggested as a greater triumph over Eugenia, to assert my claim as a husband, and force her to submit to me even in preference of the object she had preferred to me. In short, the morning dawned before I had resolved on any plan, or without having rested a single hour.

When the day-light advanced I descended to the kitchens, there I found bread, butter and cheese, with a cold fowl; a wine cellar well stored, and a yard full of poultry; plenty of wood, and an outhouse full of old hay and stray, that was musty from age. I opened the windows to give it air; and going from thence to the gardens, saw one part was well cultivated with vegetables, and another with flowers and fruits.—"It will not be difficult to live here," I exclaimed, and from that moment determined on my plan, and from which I have never varied in the treatment of my prisoners: Every day to carry to them a certain portion of bread and water; once a week a half pint of wine, and once a month clean straw to rest upon. I resolved to pre-serve their lives that I might prolong their sufferings, and the gratification of my revenge was a much superior pleasure to any that I could promise myself from society, or an acquaintance with a world I had long since been disgusted with; for altho' the bequests of Count Zimchaw had done away my first objections, by enabling me to appear with more consequence, and more suitable to my rank, yet habit had so accustomed me to retirement, that I felt no inclination to mix with mankind, and to retaliate my wrongs upon an ungrateful woman, and a successful rival, afforded me the most pleasing contemplation, and a supreme delight.

CHAPTER III.

I passed the morning in examining every part of the Castle, which was a good deal out of repair, except in the wing where they had taken up their residence. About noon I visited my prisoners, and carried to them the por-tion I had allotted for them.—They appeared to be differently affected, the

Count was very weak, his pride, his spirits seemed subdued by the consideration of the distress his child and Eugenia had suffered. He condescended to supplicate for them; the child screamed on my approach, and flew to her mother, who with a look, and in a tone of mingled grief and haughtiness, thus addressed me:

"Whatever evils you have resolved to overwhelm *me* with, I can bear. *You* think I have deserved to suffer; but who, Sir, made you a judge in your own cause? I never deceived you, I told you I had no heart to give; you persisted, ungenerously laid a tax on the gratitude my dear father felt, and insisted that the hand of his daughter should be your reward for services, which common humanity would have dictated to the poorest peasant, had his power been equal to your's. Your claims, added to an unhappy, and I will say unjust, prejudice my father had conceived against the man I loved, proved destruction to my peace and happiness; commands which I had never disputed, and the impending horrors of a parent's curse drew from me an equivocal promise that I would give you my hand. Heaven has punished me for a duplicity I could not, according to my own feelings, avoid or evade. At the altar, neither my heart nor lips ratified the gift of my hand, for my vows were given to another. The consequence you know.

"You now, Sir, usurp an unjust power over us; but do not deceive yourself, neither peace nor pleasure can follow such unjustifiable, such cruel deeds; murder has many tongues, and your own conscience will avenge our wrongs."

Here she ceased; I had listened to her with pain and impatience; the music of her voice thrilled to my very soul, but her words drove every soft idea from my heart as instantly as they were conceived.—"There is bread and water (exclaimed I, my passions roused to a degree of frenzy) *that*, and a bed of straw is what you may expect from me." I returned to the offices, I brought two small tables and benches; I fixed a faint and glimmering lamp against the wall, which served only to throw a gloomy light, and additional horror, on the dismal dungeons. A small opening was between them, and the length of their chains permitted their approach near to each other; I fetched straw and a blanket for each; they observed all these preparations in sullen silence, I was as little disposed to talk. When I had completed the business, and was about to leave them, "You now see that I am in earnest (said I;) once a day I shall visit you, and gratify my feelings by a view of your miseries."

"O, my child! my dear child!" exclaimed Eugenia, passionately.—I made no reply, but a look of scornful exultation, and returned to the apartments I had fixed on for my residence.

I was now alone, condemned to solitude without a friend, or even an attendant: I regretted the loss of Peter; he had served me some years with fidelity, why then did I distrust him? Why suffer my cowardly apprehensions to deprive me of a companion so necessary? These were my reflections as I looked round on the gloomy woods which appeared from every window, and heard the hollow winds whistling through the trees.—Surely, thought I again, this Castle was built for deeds of darkness; murder has been familiar within these walls, and the Count's ancestors, perhaps, were not less criminal than myself.

A violent storm of hail and thunder confined me to the apartment for the remainder of the day. I employed myself in arranging matters for my own accommodation, when towards the evening, as I was musing over the recent events, it darted into my mind that the poor boy whom I had confined in the lodge, if not dead, might be useful to me; the situation of this boy had never occurred to me till that moment: I hastened to the place, and found him in a most pitiable state, almost without life. I released and assisted him into the house; I told him, the Count and his family had been obliged to fly to avoid being imprisoned by the Emperor, whose orders had been issued for that purpose; that being related to the Count's Lady, I remained in the Castle, at their request, to keep possession for *them*, and would be kind to him if he behaved well.

Young, extremely ignorant, and overjoyed to escape from the apprehensions of death, he implicitly believed every thing I asserted, and when, by a little bread and wine being cautiously administered, I had brought him to a small return of strength and courage, he bestowed a thousand blessings on me for preserving his life; so strangely had the sudden fright and terror overcome his senses when he was seized upon, that he described five or six great tall men armed breaking into the Castle, and swearing to murder every one in it. He rejoiced to hear that his master and Lady escaped from them, and never once expressed any surprise at my being there, or asked by what means I came to know of his confinement. From that day he served me faithfully; I was obliged to trust him once into the village for necessaries, but after that time I engaged a farmer to come himself once or twice a week, and as I paid him handsomely, he never expressed any curiosity, or a wish to penetrate into my motives for this recluse way of life, and having slightly hinted the same tale I had fabricated to the boy, he as readily believed it.

Three months passed away without the least alteration in the plan I had laid down and regularly pursued, only that I visited my prisoners at night, after the boy was retired to rest, and had nailed up the doors of those rooms where the wretches lay whom I had sacrificed to my own safety. I am apt to believe the Count and Eugenia sometimes flattered themselves that time would subdue my resentment, or that I should grow tired of living in that solitary mansion; but if such ideas occurred to them, they were mistaken; solitude nursed the ferocity of my disposition, and the patience and resignation they evinced in their horrid situation only increased my desire of continuing their punishment till despair and sorrow should more completely gratify my revenge. 'Tis true, I sometimes looked back with regret on the few weeks I had spent with the Count and his daughter at my own mansion, far the happiest days of my life, and for which I have dearly paid by subsequent miseries!

I some times felt a degree of envy rise in my bosom when I read of the pleasures enjoyed by a social converse with our fellow creatures; and there were moments when I was tormented with the idea, that even my prisoners experienced some satisfaction in being able to communicate their feelings to each other. It is certain that had there been a possibility of placing them separately I should have done it, but I was incapable of making a new arrangement myself, and dared not confide in the boy. A circumstance, however, soon took place, which rendered them as completely wretched as my vindictive heart could desire.

On one of my nocturnal visits, I found the Count overwhelmed with an unusual gloom, and the mother supporting her child on her bed of straw, almost drowned in tears.—When I approached her, "See, barbarian! (cried she) the work of thy cruel hands;—behold this dear innocent victim devoured by a fever occasioned by the damps of the dungeon, and want of proper food. O, if thy heart is not more callous than the fiercest beasts of prey, compassionate my child, save, oh! save its life, or be merciful and destroy us all at once!"

My heart fluttered at this address, and a something like pity rose for a moment to my soul; but instantly recollecting that she had pledged her vows to me at the altar with an intention to deceive, that the child was the offspring of a detested rival, and that *now* was my turn to triumph; those ideas in a moment chased the weakness from my heart, and gave place to very different sensations. Before I could reply, the Count addressed me, in a tremulous voice:

"I never thought to supplicate pity, or sue for any favours, but nature, all-powerful, subdues both pride and hatred. My child! Baron, save my child, spare its wretched mother this bitter climax of sorrow." He was interrupted, the child called for drink, the small portion I had brought was quickly gone. Again Eugenia exerted her eloquence, her tears. I heard her unmoved, and turning from them, *"Now* then, wretches, you can feel, *now* you know what it is to mourn as I have done; may the loss of *your* dearest hopes revenge *my* injuries."

I returned to my apartment exquisitely gratified. The following night I repeated my visit; there, on her bed of straw, lay the once captivating Eugenia, pale, dishevelled, her voice choaked with sighs and tears, her late beautiful child consuming by a fever, and gasping for life, the Count stretched on the bare ground in silent agony, incapable of assisting those objects so dear to him! O, what a luxury of revenge!

When I drew near, before the mother could speak, the child extended its feeble hand, "Water, water, mamma!" Eugenia started, hastily reached to take the jug; her weak and tremulous hand, too eager to grasp the prize, dropped it between us! She shrieked, "O misery! O, Baron! Water, for the love of Heaven some water!"

"You have had your allowance, you must suffer for your own heedlessness."

With an air of distraction she crawled to my feet: "If you wish that Heaven should pity you in your last moments, *now*, now shew mercy to the wretch before you; save my child, procure me instant relief, see life quivering on its parched lips! Oh! God, for me it suffers! Baron, Baron, save the innocent!"

She sunk back on the damp ground; the Count groaned with anguish, and dashed his chains with rage. The child again feebly called for drink; she sprung up, "O, inhuman, merciless monster, worse than a savage beast! Thou wearest a human form, cannot *our* misery content thee? This agonizing sight!" She turned her eyes on the child, it was that moment seized with convulsions; its struggles, and the wild screams of the mother, made me shudder. I quickly hastened from the scene, which however gratifying to my wished-for vengeance, gave a temporary shock to my soul, that I was obliged to shake off by recalling to my memory the wrongs I had endured from a faithless, ungrateful woman.

That night and the following day I passed in steeling my heart against all supplications, and acquiring fortitude to bear the wild reproaches of a frantic mother, I doubted not but that the child was dead, and I anticipated the pleasure I should feel in seeing her wretchedness complete.

At the accustomed hour I entered the dungeon. The Count fixed his stern and haggard eye upon me with a look that penetrated me with horror: He spoke not a word. I advanced, and beheld Eugenia seated by her child, which lay, as I expected, dead. She spoke not, nor raised her head at my approach. "There is your allowance, (said I) and I will remove this object from your view." She seized the body, and turning up her face with a significance of woe inexpressible, a wildness in her eye, though sunk deep in her head by sorrow.

"Prepare the bed (said she) and I will follow; but *my arms* only shall convey my child, it sleeps sweetly now. Yes, yes, my love, your grand sire now relents; your birth-day shall be kept with splendour. Pray let us have a soft pillow, let us have music, the soft notes shall waft us to Heaven;—come, give me some food, I can eat now under this glorious canopy."—I saw her reason was disturbed, that grief had distracted her. She took the bread, and eat with eagerness; it was the day on which I gave them an allowance of wine; she drank it freely, talking wildly all the time, yet not with any violence.

My heart smote me, I went back to the Count: "Barbarian! (exclaimed he) now triumph, my child! the poor lost Eugenia!" His voice faltered, large drops fell upon his face. He dried them up, then looking steadily on me: "Whilst that dear unfortunate angel lives, *I* must exist; I receive this wretched sustenance for her sake; in its own good time Heaven will release us from thee, cruel, merciless wretch!"—But why should I repeat the ravings of a man in *his* situation? It is sufficient to say, that his insults, his impotent threats, roused me from that lethargy of soul, into which the incoherent language of Eugenia had plunged me, and turned my momentary remorse into fury: In the bitterness of passion I swore, that if Eugenia died, I would inflict unheard of tortures on *him*; and should *he* escape my power, then *his mistress* should feel the severest vengeance that I could devise. Worked up to madness by the agitations of my mind, I scarce remember what passed between us, nor did I ever pass a night so replete with horror as the succeeding one.

The following night I found Eugenia still the same, cheerful and melancholy by turns, but all recollection of her situation entirely lost. Sometimes she talked of her father, her child, her dear Count, as if all were present with her; then looking on me she would scream, and call for help, "a ruffian was going to murder her!" But, as during those paroxisms she walked swiftly backward and forward to the extent of her chain, I seized a moment, when her back was turned to drag the dead object of her sorrows from the dungeon to an outer hole, where I had left the corpse of Agnes. She soon missed her child, and uttered the most piercing cries, cries which froze me with terror, and which I saw no way to silence but by rough measures: I seized her by the arm, and drawing a dagger, which I always carried by my side:

"Woman! (I exclaimed, in a voice and with an action equally menacing) woman, cease these screams, be composed and silent, or this weapon shall be buried in your bosom." She shrunk and trembled; she, who had heretofore braved death, and defied my power, now shuddered with affright, and threw her eyes wildly round, as if imploring succour. Having succeeded in terrifying her, I placed her on the bench, again threatening her with death if she repeated her cries.—She sat still as death, her eyes fixed, her limbs trembling. I turned from her to quit the dungeon: "Stop, miscreant (said the Count) stay and end our miseries, give us the death you threaten, destroy both, and I will thank you!"

"Death! (I replied) No, that would rob me of my vengeance; you shall *live* to curse the hour you ever saw *my* wife; *now* revel in her company, *now* enjoy a teté à teté at my expense, and boast your triumph over Baron S***."

Without waiting a reply I left him. It is now eight years since this event took place. Eugenia continues in the same hopeless state, yet blessed in some degree that she is very seldom sensible of her miserable situation, except when I appear before her, she then utters the wildest lamentations; but on threatening her with a whip or stick she shrinks down and is silent. The Count evidently struggles to preserve his life for her sake, for hope I think must long since have forsaken him; he perseveres in a sullen silence, and my treatment of them has been uniformly the same. Time has not extinguished my hatred, nor glutted my vengeance; my death must forerun theirs; then, and not till then, will their sufferings end. How strong is the passion of love, but how much stronger the desire of Revenge!!

Memorandum,

I have lost my boy in a consumption: I have, through the kindness of the farmer, procured an elderly man, whose poverty renders solitude preferable to want. I envy *his* happiness, for *he* has peace of mind!!

A stranger, calling himself Ferdinand, has discovered this place; his society may be useful and comfortable.—No! he is a poor humane, pusillanimous wretch; he is fit for the world, he shall go.

The End of the Memoir.

CHAPTER IV.

FERDINAND perused the manuscript with eagerness, and an increasing curiosity that would not admit of an interruption until he had gone through the whole.—When the memoir was concluded, he sat for some time motionless, overcome with astonishment, and scarcely believing there could have existed a man who had for years cherished in his bosom such a diabolical passion for revenge, and such a persevering cruelty. He shuddered with horror when he reflected on the situation of those unhappy victims, and the fate they must have experienced, had not Providence conducted him to the Castle previous to the old Baron's death.—His own misfortunes appeared light in the balance, when weighed against the uncommon miseries the Count and his Eugenia had sustained; and the heart-felt delight at being the instrument to deliver *them*, at that moment seemed to overpay all the sorrows which had conducted him to that wretched habitation.

Francis, whose youth appeared to be renovated by the enjoyment of society, exerted himself to make all the accommodations in his power to afford ease and pleasure to Ferdinand and his guests, not having the least idea that they were the owners of the Castle; fortunately it was the day on which the farmer regularly came for orders, and to his great surprise he had a demand for such luxuries as had long been unasked for there. Francis mentioned the death of his old master, and that his heir was now arrived, and desired to see him.

It was not without some reluctance that the man ventured inside the gates, for a thousand ridiculous stories had been promulgated in the village sufficiently strange to terrify a weak and ignorant mind; but Francis, who knew the stimulative to a selfish disposition, held out such hopes of advantages to himself in being serviceable to his *young master*, that self-interest predominated over fear, and the man was at length persuaded to appear before Ferdinand. He was then informed that the old Gentleman being dead, it was necessary to have proper measures taken for his funeral, and the farmer was requested to send such persons as would be useful on the occasion. This he promised to do, and also to bring a young woman to attend the sick Lady.

After the farmer's departure, Ferdinand more closely examined the papers in the cabinet where he had found the manuscript, to see if the deceased had held any correspondence, or to find by what means he had acquired money for his support during the twelve years he had resided in that solitary mansion; but his search was attended with no gratification to his curiosity, farther than the discovery of near three hundred crowns in a private drawer, and the deeds and papers belonging to the estate Count Zimchaw had bequeathed to him, which appeared very extraordinary, and unlikely to be found there: The more he reflected on the memoir, and conduct of the Baron, the greater was his astonishment that any mind could indulge the horrid passion of revenge to such a degree, as to render him indifferent to every pleasure and convenience in life, to undergo the most painful of all situations, an outcast from society, dead to the world, to family, fortune, and friends, solely to inflict punishments upon others, which from habit must, he thought, have long since ceased to afford the smallest degree of gratification to his vindictive and cruel disposition. His sudden death, under such a frame of mind, made Ferdinand shudder, and was, he thought, a severe retribution for his uncommon cruelties.

Anxious to hear the story of the Count and Eugenia, he flattered himself sleep would restore them to a comparative degree of strength, and enable them to relate their "eventful history."

Frequently, during the course of the evening, Ferdinand went to the doors of their apartments to listen if they were awake, and at length he heard the Count moving, upon which he entered the room. The Count extending his hand, pressed his deliverer's to his lips: "The voluptuary in his highest enjoyments," said he, "never experienced the luxury I have felt this day. O, Sir! to conceive the misery I have endured is impossible, nor can language describe it. To the goodness of Heaven (who strengthened me to bear, what must appear almost incredible for a human creature to suffer) I owe the preservation of my senses, and the enjoyment, the exquisite delight of this blessed hour. To you——."

"Not a word to me, my dear Sir," cried Ferdinand, interrupting him; "I have simply performed a duty the poorest and most ignorant of mankind would have done as well had they been in my place. I rejoice to see you thus refreshed, and I hope the Lady will feel equal benefit from a few hours sleep."

"The poor Eugenia!" exclaimed the Count, with a deep sigh, "great and unparalleled have been her woes; for years, Sir, she lost her reason, and all sense of her miseries, and to that state I doubtless owe her life, which must otherwise have sunk under the oppressive recollection of past scenes, and continued miseries. 'Tis not many months since that her dreadful malady took a sudden turn, and that was occasioned by an accident which I feared would have been her death.

"Walking one day pretty quick, the sudden check of the chain threw her down with such force, that she struck her mouth and nose violently, and bled to an alarming degree. Unable to afford her any assistance, judge what were my feelings to behold her in that situation! She rolled towards the straw, and at length fainted; that temporary death, which I thought a conclusive stroke, by stagnating the powers of life, I believe caused the bleeding to stop, and in a short time, to my infinite surprise, for I could scarcely be said to feel joy, she shewed signs of returning life, and what was still more unexpected, the first words she faintly uttered convinced me that her senses and reason were also wonderfully restored. She continued very weak, and now and then rambled a little for several days, and even to the day of our deliverance she never saw our tormentor enter the dungeon without a temporary deprivation of her reason, by shrieking most violently as he approached to lay down our food; nor do I believe the inhuman wretch ever had an idea of her being at all recovered from the melancholy situation she had fallen into through his barbarity.

"I hope her present refreshing rest will be of equal service to tranquillize her mind, and restore her to some degree of strength."

"I hope the same," replied Ferdinand, "and have already spoken to a person to procure an attendant for her; mean time you must be content with our services."

The Count made the warmest acknowledgments, and entreated the assistance of Francis to dress him: "My arms," said he, "have so long been confined, that the muscles are stiffened, and will be some time, I fear, before they are relaxed so as to enable me to help myself."—Ferdinand withdrew to send Francis, who was but an awkward valet de chambre; however, he helped on his clothes, and assisted him to the parlour, which they were obliged to darken, the Count's eyes not being able to support the glare of light after having been so many years in a visible darkness.

The Gentlemen partaking of some refreshment, and having stationed Francis at the door of the Lady's apartment, the Count addressing Ferdinand, "Doubtless, Sir," said he, "your curiosity must be sufficiently excited to know our extraordinary story, and if you'll pardon the frequent pauses which weakness may oblige me to make, I will endeavour to gratify you."

Ferdinand then mentioned the manuscript, which, he said, "had already acquainted him with every thing subsequent to Count Zimchaw's arrival at the house of the late Baron, except the Lady Eugenia's escape from him, and her story until the Baron discovered them in the Castle."

"What a mind of determined cruelty must that man have possessed," exclaimed the Count, "who could sit calmly down and commit his diabolical deeds to paper! I hope, for the sake of human nature, there exists not such another monster; but I have always observed, that it is dangerous to let a single passion engross the mind, it generally tends to the most violent excesses; the love of such a man as Baron S*** must be *furious*, and meeting with a disappointment which equally wounded his pride, produced that implacable hatred which settled in a stern and cruel revenge, the gratification of which, like Aaron's rod, swallowed up every sentiment of humanity. Poor wretch! I can pity him, for his death, in such a frame of mind, disarms resentment."

CHAPTER V.

"I WILL briefly relate to you those events with which you are unacquainted. My father and the late Count Zimchaw were neighbours, and once good friends. Eugenia and myself, at an early period in life, felt a mutual attachment, which death only can dissolve. There was nothing to impede the progress of our affections; age, circumstances, and the approbation of our parents, gave a sanction to our love, and we arrived at an age, when it was determined upon, that in a very few months our marriage should take place. Alas! what revolutions may occur in a short space of time to overthrow the best formed plans for happiness! One evening the two Gentlemen entered into a conversation on the war, on the conduct of the Ministers in the Imperial Court, and such other topics as frequently produce disputation from different opinions. My father had retired from Court in disgust; he thought himself ill-treated, and his services neglected; he spoke therefore with some acrimony, and much warmth against the measures adopted for carrying on the war; Count Zimchaw, formerly a moderate man, having, by his interest not long before, procured a handsome establishment for his nephew, felt himself called upon to be the champion in defence of his friends: Their dispute was carried on for some time without personal resentment; but unhappily growing animated on both sides, they forgot the ground of their first argument, and turned every thing into intended insults on each other; they lost sight of friendship, and even good manners, and had not some company unexpectedly entered the room, it is more than probable the sword would have terminated the dispute. Every effort was used by their mutual friends to bring about a reconciliation, but they had gone too far on both sides to make any concessions; they parted with an avowed hatred to each other, and in the same hour Eugenia and myself were commanded to avoid all future intercourse with the respective families, and never to converse or see the object of our dearest affections more.

"Eugenia, who held the commands of a parent in the utmost veneration, promised implicit obedience, though her heart and spirits sunk under
the effort, and she fell dangerously ill. Almost distracted with her situation
and my own, I exhausted myself in fruitless endeavours to restore harmony
between our fathers: I left nothing unsaid or undone to soften their resentments; but the remembrance of their long friendship only served to increase
their animosity to each other, and the asperity with which both the one and
the other accused his opponent, could neither be forgiven or forgotten. I
wrote to my dear Eugenia; I conjured her 'not to give me up a sacrifice to
her father's resentments, to consider that we were not amenable for their
unjust quarrels, nor could compulsatory obedience be any virtue, where
the commands were cruel and unjustifiable.' In short, I omitted no arguments I could adduce to over-rule the resolution she had taken to obey her
father. Her answer was short but decisive: 'She never would marry, much
less encourage a clandestine correspondence, contrary to the commands
of her father; and as there existed no hope that his consent would coincide
with her wishes, she conjured me, if her peace was dear to me, from that
hour to cease all further desire of an intercourse between us, which could
only be productive of misery to both; that her promise was already given,
and her fixed resolution taken at the same time, that if not permitted to be
my wife, I might assure myself she would never be the wife of another.'

"This answer was conclusive, for I knew her too well to hope for any
change in a plan she had once decided upon: As soon as I heard therefore
she was in a convalescent state, I resolved to quit my father's mansion, and
by travelling give some diversity to that load of anguish seated at my heart.
My father did not oppose my design, conscious of the misery his intemper-
ate conduct had produced, I believe it grew painful to him to see me, and
that a separation was little less desired by him than by myself.

"My journies were by no means interesting, for I sought not pleasure,
and received but little amusement: I preserved that respect due to a parent,
of sometimes writing to my father, who concealed the increasing weakness
of a broken constitution from me, until the faculty had given up all hopes
of his life. This intelligence, quite unexpected, recalled all that dormant affection and respect I had once so warmly entertained. I hastened my return,
but came too late; the night preceding my arrival my father expired. I was
deeply affected, and still more so when the steward, and an intimate friend
of our family, informed me, that a day or two previous to my return, he accused himself as the destroyer of *my* happiness, and entreated his friend to
exert his best endeavours to procure a reconciliation between Count Zimchaw and myself; acquainting the former, that *he* lamented the part he had

acted, and besought him to spare himself a similar regret in *his* last stage of life, by consenting to the union so long projected by both families, and so hastily and unwarrantably broken off by passion and prejudice.

"But, alas! in the same moment that I had this pleasing acknowledgment on the part of my father, I was told Count Zimchaw had taken his daughter into Bavaria, and that a report was current in the country that she was married to Baron S***. Distracted at this intelligence, I sent to the Count's mansion to know the exact truth, and was shocked by a confirmation of the report. My hopes of happiness were now annihilated: I sunk into a gloomy despondency for a long time, from which no endeavours of my friends could rouse me.—I was dragged about a lifeless body without a soul, from one friend to another, till at length, tired with exerting unsuccessful kindness, they left me to myself.

"About this time Count Zimchaw returned into Suabia, and his daughter's marriage was beyond a doubt. No longer desirous of his returning friendship, I avoided all intercourse with himself or his friends.—He was soon afterwards taken ill, and I was informed his son-in-law was sent for, to whom he had secured all his personal fortune. This intelligence gave me undescribable sensations, I doubted not but that Eugenia would accompany her husband, and I had not resolution enough to leave the country, though sure of suffering extreme torture by seeing her in the arms of another. The Baron, however, arrived too late to see the Count, and came without Eugenia, whose particular situation was mentioned as an apology for her absence."

"Will you pardon me, Sir, for interrupting you?" said Ferdinand; "but in the Baron's memoirs your meeting is mentioned, and every circumstance until his return to Bavaria."

"I thank you," replied the Count.—"Well, then, the Baron had left Suabia, I believe, a fortnight, when one day I received a note in an unknown hand, 'requesting me to be at the end of my Park, next the village, about twilight, when I should meet an old friend.' I hesitated for some time whether I ought to comply with this singular request; but at length determined to go, and grew quite impatient for the hour.

"At the appointed time I hastened to the spot, and descried through the gloom two young men, in an ordinary garb, approaching towards me: Not being entirely devoid of suspicions, I had a pair of pocket pistols, one of which I held in my hand, and as they drew near, and their features were not distinguishable, I cried out, 'stop, and announce yourselves, whoever you are.'

" 'Ah!' exclaimed a sweet but tremulous voice, 'does not your heart inform you it is Eugenia?' I heard no more, but flew, and caught the trembling fugitive to my breast. Neither could speak, for words were inadequate to our feelings. O, the rapture of that moment never to be forgotten! 'Lead the way to your house (said she) and every thing shall be explained.' In an instant I recollected that I had embraced the wife of Baron S***: I withdrew my arms, but she retained one as her support, and with hasty steps, and mutual silence, we proceeded through the Park.

"When we entered the saloon she sunk into a chair, and bursting into tears, 'I see,' exclaimed she, 'that I am no longer the object of your love or esteem!'

" 'Not love you,' I cried, dropping at her feet, 'not love you, Eugenia!' I could say no more, for I was overpowered by a variety of emotions difficult to describe, and dared to entertain suspicions unfavourable to the purity of an angel. She saw the tumults the disorder of my soul: 'Rise, Count,' said she, assuming an air of dignity, 'I forgot, that in your eyes I must appear as a runaway wife, as a degraded character; compose yourself, and listen to me without interruption.'

"She then entered into a detail of all the circumstances attending her meeting with the Baron to the conclusion of her marriage; with all which particulars I find you are acquainted, I shall therefore confine myself to a relation of the subsequent events. Soon after her arrival at the Baron's, she perceived that Agnes was warmly attached to her, and she did not conceal the strong aversion she had to an union with her master. The good woman attempted not to lessen the prejudice she had conceived against him, on the contrary she ingenuously confessed, that the severity of his manners, and harshness of his temper, were but little calculated to render a marriage life happy. Thus strengthened in her dislike, which grew more confirmed every day, she concerted with Agnes the plan of her elopement, which was first intended to have been previous to the ceremony; but her father having been in the act of denouncing his malediction against her, if she did not give *her hand* to Baron S***; she was so extremely shocked as to promise unreserved obedience, and in that moment determined to become a sacrifice to her duty.

"She retired to her apartment overwhelmed with sorrow, and meeting Agnes, told her, 'She now gave up all idea of quitting that *house*, which henceforth she considered as the tomb of her happiness.' This faithful creature (whose untimely death we have never ceased to lament) heard with surprise a resolution, which gave her equal pain; in her zeal to serve Eugenia, she disclosed some particular circumstances relative to her master, displayed his odious character, and cruel disposition, in such strong colours, as again staggered the fortitude the former had endeavoured to acquire; and at length she was persuaded by Agnes to adhere to her former design, and, by a kind of sophistry, not perhaps altogether defensible, she was induced to keep the promise made to her father of giving her hand to the Baron, and afterwards to effect her escape. This plan you know was executed, and it only remains to mention the manner in which she was so effectually secreted from all discovery.

"The Castle in which the Baron resided was large, and some parts of it entirely out of repair. At the back of the building were some ruinous apartments on the ground floor, which served for no other purpose than as a temporary shelter for the poultry, and a depository for their grain. The farthest of those apartments had a door, which opened to a descent down a flight of steps to a long passage which led underneath to an old Chapel, long before shut up, and entirely disused.—Here it was resolved upon that Eugenia should reside, until the search naturally expected to be made for her should subside, that she might be enabled to get undiscovered to a convent; and to this place, in this passage, Agnes had already conveyed several necessaries. She had procured, from a long-neglected wardrobe of her master's, a complete suit of man's apparel, with several other precautions taken from time to time previous to that day they were now obliged to decide upon for the execution of their design.

"After the marriage ceremony, when Eugenia retired to her room, she lost no time in escaping to this passage. The window of her apartment was opened that it might be supposed she had escaped from thence into the wood adjoining the garden, and the door, which led through an antichamber to a gallery on the other side, was locked on the outside. Agnes accompanied her to the dark passage, where a lamp, a stool, and a piece of matting for her feet, were previously prepared. Eugenia has often mentioned the horror that took possession of her whole frame when she was left alone in this dismal place, she foresaw not how many tedious years she was to exist in one still more horrid! When the discovery of her flight took place, when the house and out-houses had undergone a strict search, and the Baron, with his servants, were sat off, Agnes stole to her with refreshments, and conducted her to the little room assigned for the priest's use, in the Chapel where she passed the night, and indeed both day and night when the Baron was not at home; but as he employed many persons to scour the roads, she was obliged to remain in this painful situation, particularly as he had set a watch on all the neighbouring convents. At length the Baron set off on his journey to Suabia (Agnes concealed from Eugenia the illness of her father) and when he had been gone about three days, disguised in her masculine dress, her eye-brows blacked, and, with a pretended lameness in her gait, she repaired to the house of a peasant in the neighbouring village, where she hired a miserable apartment, giving out that ill-health had driven her to that situation for change of air; this account, which her pale countenance and lameness confirmed, evaded all curiousity among those ignorant people:—Agnes never came *to* her, but they used to meet in the wood frequently; the good creature being busy in finding out some asylum, some convent, where she had not been described, and where she might hope to rest concealed.

"The sudden return of the Baron, with an account of the Count's death, his succession to his fortune, with the circumstance of his meeting me, which he related to Agnes when he questioned her if any intelligence had been gained relative to her mistress.—Those occurrences determined Agnes to be ingenuous with Eugenia respecting her father, and persuade her to accept of an asylum with me. Hitherto my father's death, and my return, were unknown to Eugenia, and therefore she had no idea of my being in Suabia, though possibly if she had, whilst Count Zimchaw had lived, her vows would have been a barrier to our meeting. The information of Agnes caused her much sorrow, nor could she for a long time be persuaded to adopt the plan of Agnes, and repair to my estate. At length, however, when her grief for the death of her father was a little subsided, she accorded with the wishes of the other. Agnes pretended to be sent for by her parents, and applied for her discharge from the Baron, which was granted. Among her own clothes she conveyed Eugenia's, which had remained in the dark passage till that time, and having procured another suit of mens cloaths, after she had left the Baron, she disguised herself, and came as the brother of the lame man to fetch him home.

"So thoroughly was Eugenia altered by her dress, and the precautions she had taken, that there was little room for apprehension that she would be discovered, and the Baron having relaxed in his inquiries since his return from Suabia, they contrived to have their clothes sent by a waggon to Stutgard, only nine miles from my house, and then quitted the village together on horseback, until they came to the next town, where they took a chaise to the small Hamlet adjoining to my Park, from whence they dispatched the note to me that I have already mentioned. Thus, Sir, I have briefly repeated what Eugenia related to me.

"You may judge of my transports in thus unexpectedly recovering the woman I adored, and to find she was not more than a nominal wife to the man I had detested. My raptures soon removed every doubt she had expressed of my affection, and brought her to confess, that the death of

her father having released her from those vows, passion and prejudice had
compelled her to make, she no longer scrupled to become my wife, as she
could in no light think the ceremony binding which had passed between
the Baron and herself.—All that now remained to be decided upon, was
our future residence, for although I would not have hesitated a moment to
have asserted and defended my rights in the face of the world, yet her timid
mind shrunk from the idea of being the public theme, or of hazarding any
revengeful machinations naturally dreaded from the Baron.

"I proposed going to France or England to reside, unhappily she ob-
jected, unacquainted with the language, and dreading the eye of observation, knowing that the Baron talked of travelling, she was fearful some unlucky chance might throw him in our way, she therefore wished to reside
for some time in a profound retirement. Although I was still of an opinion
that we should be much safer in a foreign country, yet finding her repugnance to that plan was not easily to be overcome, and being naturally of a
studious disposition myself, and fond of domestic comforts, certain that in
the society of my loved Eugenia, I could feel no wish for the amusements
and trifling conversations which engage the frivolous part of mankind, I
consented without reluctance to her desire of retirement. In our solitude
I determined to make her acquainted with the English language, as I perfectly understood it, and hoped, by effecting that, to obviate her objections
in time to a residence in that country.

"This estate had belonged to my mother's family, but being in a situation so remote from either pleasure or comfort, so little capable of cultiva-
tion; it had been entirely neglected by my father, and the Castle suffered
gradually to decay. What grounds were tenantable had been let off on long
leases, and an old man and his family were permitted to reside in the house
without expence. Some little time before the death of my father, he received an account of the old man's death, and that the widow and family
were going to live in Bohemia with her friends; from that time no one had
lived in the house. My steward had mentioned it to me, but from inattention, or other thoughts, I had neglected to concern myself about it.

"The anxiety Eugenia expressed to live, secluded from observation, recalled this Castle to my mind, and I resolved to send over a trusty person
to see what state it was in.—This step was perfectly agreeable to her; she
and Agnes were to retain their masculine dress, and remain as visitors with
me until the affair was settled, which, as I was impatient to be united to
Eugenia, you may suppose I lost no time in forwarding it. I was very soon
informed, that part of the Castle was habitable, and that some of the furniture, though old and faded, was tolerable.—On this intelligence I told my

steward I had bestowed it on an unfortunate couple of my acquaintance, who were so far reduced in circumstances as to think it a comfortable asylum, and that they were to take immediate possession. This account precluded him from any farther care or inquiry about the place.

"I restrained my impatience more than a fortnight after this, for as I was not sure but the Baron might have spies upon me, I was resolved to be very circumspect. I gave out that I intended returning to England: I collected together a good deal of money, and also made remittances to England, from whence I could draw at any time. When every thing was completed, the trunks of Agnes were removed from Stutgard to the neighbouring village under a disguised name, and they took leave of me three days previous to my intended departure, as if going back to Bohemia, but were to wait for me at the village. After those precautions for their safety, I settled every thing with my steward, whose integrity I could rely on, and telling him that I might possibly travel a year or two before he would hear from me, bid him not be uneasy, but act with unlimited authority for my interest during my absence; that I should take no servant with me, as a German, unacquainted with the language would be useless, but intended to hire servants in England.

"Having thus eluded both curiosity and discovery, I soon joined my beloved Eugenia, and we proceeded to the Castle. I believe we both felt similar emotions on entering this solitary mansion. We threw our eyes round, and then looked at each other, but both were silent: Agnes, however, made her observations without ceremony, at the same time qualifying her first exclamations by saying, that 'when she had been a few days in the place she would give things another sort of countenance.' I shall not trouble you with our proceedings, to render it a little comfortable, we all exerted our endeavours, and the fourth day after our arrival, I had the happiness of being united to my loved Eugenia in the village church, she dressed in the plainest garb belonging to Agnes, and myself in a great coat. I then ventured to the village, and procured a boy to assist Agnes in the domestic business, and she proposed sending for Arnulph: It was doubtless a presentiment that made me shudder when she mentioned it; but we were too much obliged to her, and indeed too much in her power to refuse her request, and had really a strong affection for her that would not admit of an objection to her being equally happy with ourselves; we therefore consented: Arnulph came, and we enjoyed so perfect a contentment, made our rooms so commodious, and our garden and poultry-yard so pleasant and profitable, that I grew entirely reconciled to a seclusion from the world.

"Eugenia in due time brought to the world a little cherub, the image of herself; (here the Count's voice faltered at the recollection of its untimely and miserable death, but soon recovering himself, he went on) and as she advanced in infantine knowledge, we had a source of entertainment that engaged many of our hours, and enlivened our solitude.—We agreed that when this little darling should arrive at the age of five years, we would go to England, under the belief that before that period the Baron would cease to concern himself about Eugenia, and perhaps form another connexion. Thus in a deceitful calm, in the midst of future happy prospects, that dreadful storm burst upon us, so unexpected and terrible, as to overwhelm us with complete misery.

"As it appears you are perfectly well informed, Sir," said the Count, addressing Ferdinand, "of every step that revengeful monster took to gratify his malice, I shall not trouble you with a repetition, and as to our feelings and sufferings, they will not admit of a description, for the horrors of our situation were beyond all conception or credibility. I shall only observe, that whilst our dear child existed, we endeavoured to support our own strength for her sake; nor indeed did we imagine our persecutor would long submit to a situation so painful to himself merely to punish us. The cruel death of Agnes was a severe stroke; but when we saw our dear infant began to droop, a slow fever consuming her, from the close and humid air, which we received only through a few iron bars on the top of our prison, from whence fell all the inclemencies of the winter season, and so small a quantity of air and light, as only rendered our abode the more terrible. When we saw our beauteous babe in danger of sinking a victim to the malice of our cruel gaoler; we then forgot our wrongs and our pride. What supplications, what entreaties, did we not use! but all was vain, not a drop of water to wet its parched lips in the hour of death.

"O, my God! never, never shall I forget that hour, and the calamity which followed! Its wretched mother lost her reason for years, yet at times seemed sensible of our miserable fate, and always knew me when she heard my voice. In this situation she never refused her poor pittance of bread and water, but rather took it eagerly; and I, Sir, I strove to repress my feelings, strove to live for her sake, for to die and leave her was a distracting thought that harrowed up my soul. Thus the monster had found the means to prolong our misery, and make me dread that death which otherwise I should have devoutly prayed for.

"Such a refinement of cruelty could only have been practised by himself, who, far from being tired out, or satiated, appeared to receive fresh gratification every day. It was very remarkable, that from the hour in which Eugenia's intellects were deranged, and even after the accident which I mentioned to you had restored her, from the night of the child's death, she never saw him enter without screaming, until silenced by fear. Often have I dreaded that the villain would have been provoked to strike her; many times has he threatened it, but yet never could subdue the terror that vented itself in shrieks whenever he appeared. Thus, Sir, I have related to you this strange story, which almost exceeds probability; for never, I believe, was the diabolical passion of revenge carried to such extremes before, for a man to resign every comfort in life, and be a wretch himself to punish others."

Just as the Count had concluded his relation, and before Ferdinand could make any observations, Francis came in, and said the Lady was awake, and wished to see the Count. Ferdinand assisted him to ascend the stairs (his legs being too stiff to accomplish it alone) and then returned to enjoy his own reflections on the extraordinary occurrences of the day, and the story he had heard.—The Count and Eugenia being now restored to life and liberty by the death of their tormentor, the Castle their own, and free to enjoy their fortune in whatever situation they liked, were now likely to feel the happiness that awaited them to a much greater extent than if they had known more tranquil days, and had been exempt from their former sufferings.

In this perfect content, thought Ferdinand, I shall leave them, for their felicity will throw a comparative wretchedness upon me, by reminding me of what I have enjoyed, and what I have for ever lost. Overwhelmed by a retrospection on his misfortunes, he sat for some time lost in thought, until the return of the Count and Francis; the latter withdrew.

"I have seen Eugenia in such a state of comfort," said the former, "that it has given transports to my heart, long, very long, a stranger there. I have persuaded her to continue in bed, the warmth of which must be of service to her limbs, and I trust by to-morrow she will be a new creature. O, Sir! next to Heaven, you are entitled to our warmest gratitude. May you never know sorrow, or, if such an exemption is not the lot of mortals, may you always meet with minds good and sympathetic like your own, ready to communicate happiness, and restore you to peace!"

"I thank you, Sir," replied Ferdinand, "for your good wishes, which, in my case, must, I fear, prove fruitless; however, let me not sadden his hour of pleasure: I rejoice to hear your Lady is so much recovered, and we must endeavour to procure for her some refreshment."

"Wine and toast," said the Count, "will be sufficient this night, and to-morrow we shall have assistance."—After taking proper refreshments, the Count was helped to his apartment, and Francis having made good fires in two other rooms, and aired some necessaries, he and his master, as he called Ferdinand, retired to rest, after the fatigues of this eventful day.

CHAPTER VI.

THE next morning the farmer arrived with a young woman, and necessary people to attend the dead: The Count was with Ferdinand, and appeared as the heir of the deceased, who from a long and habitual melancholy had secluded himself, until finding his end approaching he had sent for his relations, who on their arrival found he had expired that very morning. This account was given and believed, because Francis had been previously prepared to corroborate it. The Lady's weakness was accounted for from fatigue, and a very violent rheumatic cold; the young woman was to attend her, and another was ordered to officiate as a cook.—In short, in the course of the morning, every proper arrangement was made. Francis was informed that the Count was the owner of the Castle from the late Baron's memoirs, and he heartily rejoiced that he had made such a desirable change in the person he was to serve.

At noon the Lady Eugenia, assisted by her female attendant, made her appearance below: She appeared like a fine statue that had long been exposed to the injuries of time, and lost the beautiful polish that first adorned it; a most elegant form reduced to that delicate thinness which the slightest blast of air might dissolve;—a face, the contour of which was inexpressibly beautiful; but the roses and lilies that once adorned it were all fled; the eyes hollow and sunk in the head, a sickly hue over the countenance, and a solemnity in every feature, altogether gave her whole appearance such an image of a woe-worn mind, that it was impossible to behold her without being deeply affected.

She returned the civilities which Ferdinand involuntarily paid her with some hesitation, but much sweetness. "Pardon me, Sir," said she, "if I am deficient in expressing my obligations to you for liberty and life; I have almost forgotten the use of language, but to utter words of misery and despair."

"Words," cried the Count, kissing her hand, "words which, I trust, my dear Eugenia, will never have cause to utter again: We have no longer cause for sorrow, no longer an enemy to fear, we may emerge into the world, return to our country like long-absent friends, and elude curiosity by saying we have resided in a foreign state."—"But your estate," said she, "by this time may have passed into other hands, your steward may be dead, and much trouble and perplexity may still await you to prove, and to enjoy your rights."

"Fear nothing, my dear Eugenia," replied the Count, "*all* my friends cannot be dead; I shall find no difficulty in proving my identity, and in being acknowledged."—She sighed, but made no reply.

Ferdinand then mentioned having seen in the cabinet the will and papers relative to the estate of the late Count Zimchaw, which, said he, "I was surprised to find there."

"It is rather singular," answered the Count; "but I suppose he had them with him when he set off on his travels; with those, however, we have nothing to do. If he has any heirs, they may have possessed themselves of his fortune by this time, and in justice to them and ourselves I think a paper should be drawn up, briefly mentioning his residence here, your arrival, and his sudden death, which, with the testimony of Francis, will be sufficient, and preclude any necessity for our names being mentioned at all."

"I agree with you," said Ferdinand, "that such a paper is absolutely proper; it is an awkward affair, and I think an express should be sent to the Baron's estate immediately of his demise."

In this opinion Eugenia coincided, and it was a matter concluded upon: Ferdinand resolved also to procure a messenger on his own account, to carry letters from him to his brother and his faithful Ernest. He was anxious to know what had passed in the Castle since his departure, and to hear of his little son; but how great was his surprise when questioning the farmer (who was now their oracle) of the distance to Baden on horseback, he was informed that it was five days journey.—"Five days!" repeated he, "impossible! Why, I came here in two days over the hills and through the woods."

"It may be so," replied the farmer;—"but I believe, Sir, no man but yourself would have made the attempt: I am sure I have never heard of any body that has penetrated the woods, or crossed those rugged hills, nor indeed did I think it could be done; but horses, Sir, can go no such places, and the road is a very troublesome one, because great part of the way, by the skirts of the Forest, has never yet been levelled."

"Well," cried Ferdinand, "be the distance what it may, I must have a messenger." This was promised him the next morning, and as he conceived the Count and his Lady would gladly be alone together, he retired into another apartment to write. Having given Ernest a brief recital of his travels through the woods and vallies until his arrival at the Castle, he mentioned nothing of his adventures there, though he confessed his visit to the convent, and the strange and unsatisfactory answer he had received from Claudina. He besought Ernest to be unreserved, to develop the mystery that hung over him, let the consequence be what it would, for that the most painful truths could not give him greater misery than the suspense he now endured. He recommended the old shepherd and his daughter to his care, and desired he would, if possible, procure for them a safer habitation than among those impending rocks, which seemed to threaten them with hourly destruction.

Having finished his letters he returned to the other apartment, and was surprised at his entrance to mark an increased air of trouble about the Count, and deep sorrow trembling in the eyes of Eugenia; he was too delicate to make any observations; they sat down to a slight repast, of which the others partook but very sparingly, and exchanged but a very few words.

Some time after, when they were alone, the Count addressing Ferdinand, "Your penetrating eye, my good friend, must observe the gloom that pervades my countenance, it is a transcript of my mind; from you I ought not to have any reserve, you are impartial, you shall judge fairly between us:—Now, when the heavy cloud that has so long involved us in night and wretchedness, seems to be withdrawn, and the prospects brighten to our view. Will you believe it possible that Eugenia, she who has a thousand times told me that I was dearer to her than life, who in a horrid prison felt her own woes but lightly, when she considered what her husband suffered—can you, will you believe, that this wife ever adored, and a million times dearer to me than ever from her unparallel'd sufferings, can, *now* that happiness is in our power, tell me, 'that on the most mature deliberation this past day and night, she has determined to retire to a convent for the remainder of her days; beseeches me to make no opposition to her choice, but rather strengthen a resolution founded on the purest principles of religion and virtue.'

"I will not tell you what were my feelings, nor repeat to you the arguments I have used; as a husband I can command, and I can prevent the accomplishment of her strange unkind intention; but I disclaim all *power*, if her heart no longer acknowledges me, if the years of misery we have suffered together has worn out all traces of her former affection, I submit to be the victim; but let an unprejudiced person judge between us, and say whether I have *deserved* to lose the affection of my wife."

"Oh! Count," cried Eugenia, the tears no longer restrained from dropping on her face, "ever beloved of my heart, spare the unkind reproach: *Hear me*, Sir," added she to Ferdinand, "you have candour, you will judge me fairly. You know our story, you know I had vowed *never* to marry the Count without my father's consent: I did more, at his command I accompanied the Baron to the altar. Ah! was I not guilty of sacrilege, of profanation, when I uttered with my lips vows I rejected in my heart? Say they were compelled, could that excuse my subsequent conduct? Passion blinded me to the impropriety of my intentions; I ought never to have approached the altar, or when I had done so, I should have fulfilled my vows; my father's prejudice, or cruelty, could be no excuse for my depravity:—Heaven approved not of my broken vows, and Heaven was pleased to punish me; but was *I* the only sufferer? O, no! When I look back, how many innocent victims bled for my crimes! Arnulph, the faithful Agnes, Peter, and, O misery, my child! my dear innocent babe! let me not dwell on that;—even the wretch who was ordained to be my punisher, he lived, he died, miserable! And can I return to the world, can I talk of happiness, and trample on the memory of those unfortunates who suffered for me? No, it is impossible: Great have been my miseries, but great have been my faults; let me then expiate them as I ought; let me retire to peace, penitence and prayer; let me pray for the souls of those who fell by an untimely death on my account, and let me make my peace with Heaven by devoting my future days to retirement. *You,* who are, who ever will be dear to my heart, who will be a principal object in my oraisons, you must strengthen my resolutions; *you* must approve of my conduct, and though the heart murmurs, the reason *must* be convinced. And now, Sir," concluded she, addressing Ferdinand, "now I have explained my motives, speak with candour; tell me, does not your judgment approve my determination? Do you not see that in the world my life would be embittered, by painful retrospections that must preclude happiness, and that in devoting myself to retirement, I pursue the only path that points to peace and tranquillity?"

Ferdinand was for a few moments silent, astonished at such a revolution, so little expected, from that plan of felicity he had so lately thought them possessed of, and which to him seemed an enviable situation. He paused a little, but seeing they both impatiently expected his reply:—"Forgive me, my dear Sir," said he to the Count, "if thus called upon, I confess that my esteem, my admiration for the Lady Eugenia, rises in equal proportion with my compassion for you; for the more I approve her exalted resolution, and admire her virtues, the more I feel must be your distress at the idea of being separated from an object so truly deserving your esteem; but I must be free to confess, that this Lady's reasons are unanswerable, and that however innocent she may be of any actual guilt, yet as the death of so many persons was in consequence of her flight from the Baron, a feeling mind like her's would constantly revert to the primary cause, and never cease to accuse herself;—therefore under such circumstances, her intention of retiring from a busy deceitful world, to devote her days to the duties of religion, is surely praise-worthy, and commands our approbation."

"It is well, Eugenia," said the Count, in a mournful tone, "you have found a champion to support *your* opinions, and I have no more to do than to acquiesce; but since you have chosen *your* path towards happiness, I may be allowed to chalk out one for myself. I shall take this night to consider of it, and to-morrow will acquaint you with my final resolution." "May Heaven, who knows the fervency of my affection, inspire you to choose that which may conduce both to your present and future happiness." Ending these words Eugenia desired to retire, for the weakness of her body, and the agitations of her mind, overpowered her fragile form, which could hardly support the transitions she had experienced, and was unequal to the sight of that melancholy, but too visible, in the Count's pale face, that seemed silently to reproach her of cruelty.

When she had left the room, Ferdinand observing the sorrow that seemed fixed in the features of the Count, strove to change the current of his thoughts by speaking more freely of his own affairs than he had yet done, and at length, encouraged by the interest the Count appeared to take in his concerns, he made an unreserved communication of his whole story.

"Indeed, my young friend," observed the Count, when Ferdinand had concluded his relation, "indeed, there are some very extraordinary and unaccountable circumstances in your story, that one cannot elucidate by any conjectures on the subject. I do not blame you for seeking to amuse your mind by travelling, but you are wrong in chusing this mode of doing it; wandering through woods, and over almost impassable hills, may be attended with more danger than you are aware of, and in an evil moment you may fall a sacrifice to some concealed ruffian, or a troop of banditti; besides the natural inconvenience of suffering both cold and hunger."

"What you observe is very just doubtless," answered the other; "but you should remember I am not a man of fortune, an independent man, and that it behoves me to avoid all unnecessary expences in my rambles, for travelling, in the general sense of the word, is beyond my abilities to undertake; I wish to forget myself at present, and when the campaign opens, may possibly resume my station in the army, yet, that must depend upon circumstances.—With your leave I will remain here until my messenger returns, and then the world will be once more before me."

"This conversation," said the Count, "has given a different turn to my thoughts from what I entertained an hour ago; I already feel that interest and affection for you, that it shall not be my fault if we are separated; but more of that to-morrow."—Having sent off their different expresses, one to Baron S***'s estate, another to Count M***, and a third to Count Rhodophil's Castle, it was thought most advisable to delay the funeral of the Baron until the return of the messenger.

The following day, when they all assembled at table, the Lady Eugenia appeared less feeble, and with a more placid countenance, than on the pre-ceeding day. When the servants were withdrawn Ferdinand congratulated her on the visible amendment.

"I do indeed feel better both in mind and body," said she, "the one is generally dependent on the other. Since I have determined on my plan, and my dear Count has given up his objections to it, I find a composure in my soul to which it has very long been a stranger. The dreadful malady which I laboured under for years, has certainly weakened my intellects, as I frequently experience a confusion in my ideas, and very odd sensations in my head; the world therefore would be a very unfit place for me, and the sooner I can find a retirement, such as I wish for, the better; the pang of separation must be felt, and I am anxious to have it over."

It instantly darted into Ferdinand's mind, that if Eugenia entered the Convent where Claudina resided, it might afford them mutual consolation, and possibly might, by mutual confidence, put it in the power of the former to develop to him that mystery so carefully and cruelly concealed from him by Ernest and Claudina. He hastily mentioned the adjoining Convent, as having been well spoken of by Father Joseph, and offered his services to make all the necessary inquiries. This offer was joyfully accepted by Euge-nia, nor opposed by the Count. She said, "that, to avoid impertinent ques-tions, it was her intention to pass for a widow, who wished to retire into the bosom of the church for the remainder of her days. I must be a boarder, (said she) but I shall conform to all their rules, and subject myself to all their severities and self-denials. In calling myself a widow I am guilty of no de-ception, for from the moment I enter the gates of the Convent I am parted from the object of my affections for ever!"

The Count rose greatly agitated—"Eugenia," cried he, "you either de-ceive yourself when you talk of your affection for me, or you have *more* than *female* fortitude."

"Neither the one nor the other," answered she: "I know my own heart, and I feel that, in this separation, it must endure pangs worse than the stroke of death; but conscience, that all-powerful monitor, has spoken incontro-vertible truths; her voice has taught me my duty, and pointed out the only way by which I can atone for my errors, and procure pardon for the death of those innocent persons that were sacrificed for me."

"I have no more to urge," replied the Count; "it is fit that I also should be a victim."

"By no means," exclaimed Eugenia;—"you have nothing to blame your-self for, you have committed no errors but pardonable ones, and I trust, my dear Count, that many, very many, happy years are in store for you: *My* tranquillity must, in some degree, be dependent on your's; return to the world, and to society, they have claims upon you: I hope you have here acquired a friend that may succeed in composing your mind; forget Eugenia, or if you remember her, think only that she is set off on a long, long journey, where you may at some distant period arrive also, and remember, that it is only her duty to *Heaven*, that she prefers to *you*."

Overpowered with her emotions, she rose, and with feeble steps she retired to another room.

"Exalted creature!" cried the Count,—"from this hour I will no more add to thy distress by my reflections, nor wound thee even by my looks; I will try to *assume* a composure, though my heart is torn with anguish." Ferdinand then mentioned his intention of going the following day to the Monastery adjoining to the Convent, and through Father Joseph get the Lady proposed as a boarder, desirous of conforming to all the rules of the house. This being agreeable to all parties, early on the next morning he went to visit Father Joseph; the Count pressed him to take a man with him through the gloomy and solitary road he had to pass; but Ferdinand chose to go alone, and after more than four hours tedious travel over the hills, and through the deep and woody vallies, he arrived in view of the Monastery. Having pulled the bell, and inquired for Father Joseph, the good man soon appeared. He uttered an exclamation of joy on seeing Ferdinand: "Heaven bless you, my young friend, this is an unexpected pleasure."

"It is a pleasure to me, my good Father, to see you in health; I have undertaken business of consequence to serve another, chiefly that I might once more behold you."

"Enter freely, my son, I will conduct you to Father Ambrose; he only is privileged to talk of worldly concerns, or transact business."

With hasty step he led the way to a private room: "Rest here," said the good Father, "and I will acquaint Father Ambrose of your visit to him; he is before this apprised of your entrance." He withdrew in a quick way, that reminded Ferdinand of his former observation relative to the envy and jealousy which pervaded through a Monastery. The Superior soon appeared, with a look so gracious, and so unbending from the natural haughtiness of his demeanour, that Ferdinand, whose soul knew no disguise, advanced to salute him with equal complacency.—"You are welcome, my son, I rejoice to see you; I trust that Heaven has directed you here as to the mansion of peace."

Ferdinand, without entering into any particular discussions, opened the business which brought him there: "A widow Lady, of family and independence, having lost all the ties which had bound her to the world, was desirous of retiring to the neighbouring Convent for the remainder of her days; but a stranger to the modes necessary to procure admittance, he had waited on Father Ambrose as the Confessor of the Convent, to acquire information on that head."

"Is the Lady related to you?" asked the Father.

"No," replied Ferdinand; "but she is nearly related to a dear friend of mine, and at their joint request I undertook this commission."

"Well, son," said the Father, with a more reserved air, "if the Lady is a woman of character, she need not fear admission: I will speak to the Abbess on the subject, and if she wishes it, and will apply to me, I will introduce her. She has no doubt sufficient to pay handsomely; the Convent admits none but such, as the expences of the house are great, so many poor, sick and disabled, to maintain, their charity consumes a large revenue."

"The Lady will have no cause to fear a rejection on that head," answered the other; "she will readily contribute her share to enlarge their charitable beneficence."—"And you, my good son, what is your plan of life? May we hope for your society?"

"Not at present," replied Ferdinand; "I have yet some duties to perform which call me into the world; I know not how long indeed, but my mind is not now disposed to enjoy that monastic tranquillity that appears to reign here."

"I am sorry for it," returned Father Ambrose; "but believe me, son, if your mind is disturbed, this retirement is most suited to restore your peace: However, I hope you intend to pass this night here. From what distance did you come?"—Ferdinand named the village, and as he had previously disposed the Count not to be uneasy if he should be absent for the night, he very readily accepted the Father's invitation; for the walk being no small fatigue from the difficulties that impeded his passage, he was not sorry to have a place of rest.

The conversations that took place in the course of the day is not necessary to be related. Nothing was left *unsaid* that could give Ferdinand a favourable opinion of their society, or hold out inducements to fix a wavering mind in a situation so replete with tranquillity and comfort. He heard them with attention and complaisance, but longed earnestly for bed-time, in the hope of holding some converse with Father Joseph, to whom he had found an opportunity of conveying his wishes, which had been answered by a significant nod: Nor was this hope disappointed, in less than an hour after he had retired, the good Father softly opened the door, and appeared before him. Ferdinand took his hand with reverence: "My worthy friend, this is kind indeed!"—"My dear son, I thank *your* kindness in remembering *me*, and am glad my business has procured us the pleasure of seeing you."

"Ah!" said the former, "strange events have happened since I saw you last; but I feel too much interest for you to be prolix on other matters. Tell me, my good Father, have you connexions in the world, attachments of any kind in which I can serve you?"

"None," replied the other, "I stand a solitary being, not more cut off from the world than from connexions. I will tell you my story in a few words:

"My father was a man of family; my mother expired two years after my birth: I was, until six years of age, the darling of my surviving parent, and his chief amusement. About that time he conceived a strong affection for a haughty, dissipated woman, of high birth, but no fortune; this Lady he married: I was sent to a Jesuit's College for education; twice a year I came to see my father, but, alas! how changed, how cold the reception I experienced from the tender endearments I had been accustomed to!—Young as I was, I soon perceived the marked alteration. His Lady looked on me with an invidious eye, and the short periods I was permitted to spend at home, soon became irksome and disagreeable. When I was about fourteen, my tutor one day gave me to understand that it was my father's will that I should dedicate myself to the church.

"I was thunderstruck at this intelligence, for I had other views; my mind was active, my body strong and robust, for my age; I had long entertained a wish to be instructed in military exercises; I wished to go into the army; my father was a man of fortune; he had no children by his Lady; why then was I to be condemned to an unsocial sedentary life I had no propensities to? I reasoned with my tutor; he bid me talk to my father on the subject, and the first time, after this conversation, that I saw him, he soon afforded me the opportunity, by a communication that I little expected. My mother-in-law, after being married nine years, without having any children, was now pregnant. I was not then enough acquainted with the world to practise hypocrisy, or affect a pleasure I could not feel. He observed my silence and my countenance: 'This news does not please you, young man (said he) and you are selfish enough I see to grieve at an event likely to be productive of so much joy to me: I am glad I understand your disposition so well.'

" 'Do not, Sir,' I replied, 'form a conclusion so unfavourable to me, Heaven knows I shall share in every joy of your's; but pardon me, my dear father (added I) if, when I reflect on the coldness which I have ever experienced from my Lady, and the information I have lately received from my tutor, pardon me if I fear the affection you once honoured me with is already greatly weakened, and that the event you allude to will, perhaps, entirely drive me from your heart; that consideration alone, not sordid interest, affects me.'

" 'Boy,' cried he (interrupting me) 'you have at least learned to talk well; but you cannot command your features, those speak an unequivocal language, which I perfectly comprehend: however, you know my pleasure, I design you for the church, it is the proper situation for young men *like you*.' He left me almost petrified with astonishment, there was a something altogether so strange and inexplicable in his words and looks, that I retired to my chamber overcome by a variety of painful emotions: I saw plainly that I had lost a father, and young as I was, I foresaw the consequences to myself. The few hours that I remained buried in reflection gave me months of understanding, but I resolved to make one effort more. I wrote a letter to my father in the most respectful terms, tending to remove every prejudice he had conceived against me, at the same time acknowledging my predilection for the army, and besought his permission to attend in future to military exercises.

"The answer I received was short.—'Return to the College, attend to your duties there, and I shall hereafter consider on the propriety of your request.'—I obeyed without hesitation; and to please my father paid the strictest attention to my tutor, not without observing, that all his lessons were calculated to inspire a dislike of the world, and to display the superior happiness of a monastic life. In due time my mother-in-law was brought to bed of a son, which was announced to me with great exultation: I heard it with a palpitating heart, as the downfal of all my hopes from parental affection.

"I continued two years longer at the College, during which time I saw my father only thrice, and had but little cause to value myself on his tenderness. I was now in my eighteenth year when I received a summons to attend him: I flew with eager expectation, his looks chilled me. "Tis high time, Louis (said he) that you should enter upon your professional duties; I have before now told you I intend you for the Church, my resolution still holds."

" 'Ah! Sir (I exclaimed) why must I be the sacrifice?'

" 'Stop (cried he) and learn who you are, and that you have *no claims* to sacrifice. I never was married to your mother: She was a Bourgeoise, I could not marry her, yet I loved and respected her; whilst she lived I resided in the country, to avoid disagreeable circumstances to her. This truth I was obliged to acknowledge to my wife before she would accept of my hand, having an idea that I had degraded myself; you cannot wonder therefore that she did not treat you with respect, although she has always behaved civilly. I have now a son who must inherit my fortunes. To spare you painful reflections, I wish you to choose the Church, all circumstances may then remain known only to ourselves, and you shall find I will not forget that you are the son of a woman I once loved. It becomes you to preserve her reputation by submitting to my orders.' I heard this long development in a kind of stupid distraction. I replied not a word. He mistook the nature of my feelings for sullenness.

" 'Sir! (said he, raising his voice) I see my *kindness* is thrown away; hear then my *commands*, and my fixed determination: If you comply, and return to the Church, I will endeavour to get you a proper situation; if you refuse, and chalk out a path for yourself, I will give you five hundred Louis-d'ors; leave France, and see me no more." These last words roused me in an instant; pride, grief and indignation, took possession of my soul.—'Since I no longer have claims upon your affection, Sir, since I am to live an alien from you, I may at least be permitted to choose for myself; I will therefore accept of the money you offer me, and learn to forget that I have a father, since he disdains to acknowledge me; but have I no connexions in a humbler line of life? Had my unhappy mother no relations? Or was she too reprobated by all?'

" 'Your mother (answered my father) was an orphan when I first knew her; she resided with a brother, a shopkeeper; he died a short time before her, and I know not that you have any relations in the world. Had you chosen the Church, in me you would have found a parent; but as neither my wishes or commands are attended to, in giving you a sum sufficient, with prudence and economy, to settle you in a line of your own choice. I conceive I have done my duty as to every claim you can have upon me.

" 'There, Sir (added he, rising, and opening his cabinet) there are drafts for £500, Louis d'ors, may they be successfully employed, and gratify your own expectations.' I received the papers with such emotions of mingled pride, indignation and love, that I was incapable of speaking. At the door I turned to take a last look, tears gushed from my eyes: 'Heavens bless you!' was all I uttered, and I saw him turn with his handkerchief to his face.

"Thus was I thrown upon the world without any friends or connexions, a degraded, solitary being. I retired to an auberge in the skirts of the town, and began to consider on my situation. Without rank, fortune, or even a name, how could I think of entering into the army? My pride suggested a thousand insupportable slights I might encounter in a public line of life, and those very circumstances attending the late discovery, so humiliating, served only to render my temper more irritable and haughty.—Without being able to fix on any plan, I resolved immediately to quit France, which I did the following day, and travelled through Germany.

"Strange to say, in one so young as I was at that time, I grew morose and splenetic; I thought every man happier than myself, and I envied and hated all mankind! In this disposition I came into this neighbourhood; its wild romantic hills and vallies charmed me; in the adjacent village I resided some time, and spent my days in rambling in the woods. At length I met with a solitary hut, which seemed to have been not long uninhabited, on the side of a hill. In this spot I fixed my residence for near two years. It has been observed, 'That a person must be either a God, or a brute, who can be able to live alone.' Providence certainly designed us for a social state, and a misanthrope lives a burthen to himself, and dead to every pleasure in life.

"A very severe cold, which I caught in one of my rambles, and which produced a fever that confined me near a week, and precluded me from getting even the necessaries to preserve my existence, first brought me to a sense of my extreme folly in living thus unknowing and unknown. Had my illness continued a few days longer I must have perished from actual want; but it pleased Heaven to restore me to some degree of strength; with difficulty I crawled to this Monastery, as it was much nearer than the village. A worthy Friar, long since dead, relieved my necessities, and by his kindness unlocked my heart. He sympathized with me when he heard my tale, and that sympathy gave an energy to every office of humanity that endeared him to me, and rendered his conversation a balm to heal those wounds long rankling within, and which had been productive of the most hateful passions.

"In a very short time I felt no happiness but in his society, and mistaking the nature of my emotions, I conceived that in this retirement, to which I had once such an insuperable aversion, I should find that peace and comfort the world had denied to me.—I made application here, and was soon admitted, for I had still upwards of three hundred Louis-d'ors, which spoke volumes in my favour in the most persuasive language that can be addressed to Monasteries. The novelty of every thing about me (for there is no judging of the interior management in those places by exterior appearances, even if educated in Convents) the kindness and attention I received from the Fathers, and the pomp and solemnity which accompanied our religious duties, for a time afforded me real transport, and I hourly condemned myself for resisting my father's will. In this frame of mind I wrote to him, but received no answer, and whether it reached his hands, or whether he was living or dead, I know not.

"Within six months after my entrance here my good friend died; we

had a new Superieure, and things wore a different aspect. I had lost my
friend and comforter, that loss could not be supplied. I had acquired a relish for society, and my heart felt a vacuity which I looked round in vain to
have filled up; no one appeared interested for me, and I was permitted to
wander about unheeded with the rest of the brethren. It was now that I
felt how mistaken I had been in the nature of my emotions; without the
converse of my friend, the performance of my duties grew cold, languid,
and tiresome: I regretted my seclusion from the world, and languished to
be at liberty, that I might again enjoy the blessings of society which I had
so rashly renounced. In this frame of mind I continued some months, and
the agitations I endured produced a long and tedious nervous fever. On
the verge of the grave I was brought to a sense of my duty; a revolution
took place in my heart; I soon recovered, and from that period have, with
humble submission, conformed to my situation.

"Thus, my son, I have run over my short history, and from thence you
may learn this important truth, 'Man was not intended for a solitary being,' and be warned never to let the disappointments of life prey upon your
mind, so as to produce a temporary disgust to the world, that may, in a fit of
despair, throw you into situations productive of repentance and unavailing
regret."

CHAPTER VII.

FATHER JOSEPH, having concluded his story, was informed by Ferdinand of
the motives which had brought him to the Monastery, and that having been
successful in his commission he might possibly accompany the Lady, if
within a short time she was capable of the undertaking: "After what I have
said to you," returned the good Father, "I hope you will inform yourself
thoroughly of the Lady's motives for secluding herself from the world,
and advise her to commune with her own heart deliberately and seriously,
and not from a temporary disgust seek to find peace and happiness in a
Convent; the mind should have shaken off worldly considerations, and have
no objects to regret before it is fitted to devote *all* its faculties to religious
duties. For yourself, you have dear connexions, *you* are a father, you have
no right to quit the station in which Providence has placed you, and I hope
are determined by active duties to *deserve*, if you cannot *obtain*, happiness.
The one is in your own power, and if you are disappointed in your wishes
and expectations, be assured it is for wise and good reasons calculated
for your real benefit, though short-sighted mortals judging only of the

present, ungratefully repine in those moments when they ought to be most thankful."

"My good Father," said Ferdinand, with a sigh, "I bow to the justice of your observations; but the human heart is refractory, and often errs against reason and conviction: I promise you, however, that I will no longer indulge my wishes for retirement, and that if I ramble a short time in search of novelty to amuse my thoughts, I will endeavour so far to profit by your advice as to determine on reassuming my station in the army when the campaign opens; and in that field for action I may either obtain a comparative degree of peace, or lose the remembrance of my sorrows altogether."—He added, that the Father might depend upon his observance of the kind cautions he had given respecting the Lady.—They now parted with mutual blessings and good wishes, as they had no hope of holding any farther conversation in the morning.

At a very early hour Ferdinand arose, and appeared in the room where the Friars were assembled after their first matins. Father Ambrose received him with much complacency, and again renewed his promise of introducing the Lady to the neighbouring sisterhood, who he was certain "would make no objections, as she had *sufficient property* to answer the necessary expences her admission would draw upon the house." Ferdinand took leave, and though he cast a longing, lingering look towards the Convent, yet, convinced that of himself he could obtain no satisfactory information, and that all his hopes must rest upon Eugenia, he vented a few anxious sighs, and proceeded with all haste to the Castle.

His arrival was welcomed with much pleasure by all parties, for the intermediate time of his absence had been spent in fruitless endeavours by the Count and Eugenia to suppress their own feelings, and to reconcile and console each other; but each saw the painful emotions neither could disguise, and Eugenia had occasion for abundant resolution and fortitude to withstand the silent grief of the Count, the tenderness of her own heart, and to exert that apparent firmness in her determination as might effectually annihilate every hope, that they could be weakened by affection or arguments; their situation was therefore so distressing, that the company of a third person, particularly Ferdinand's, was a most desirable relief. He entered upon the success of his commission, and failed not to repeat, in the strongest terms, the advice and admonitions of Father Joseph. The Count fixed his eyes on Eugenia with a look that penetrated to her soul. She was greatly agitated for a moment, but struggling for composure, "I thank the good Father, and you, my amiable friend; but I have no doubts of my own resolution, no fear of future regrets: Only *one* object can claim a share in my thoughts with the Deity, to whose service I mean to dedicate the remaining days of my existence; and every remembrance of that too dearly beloved object will more strongly enforce the necessity for pursuing my present plan, by reminding me of my errors, and pointing out the strict observance of my religious duties, as the only means of procuring pardon from Heaven, and of obtaining future tranquillity to myself."

"To a mind resolved like your's, Madam (replied Ferdinand) I have no more to urge, and shall most readily attend you to the destined place when it shall appear convenient to you."—She bowed, and looking on the Count with a tearful eye, rose and retired.

"Come, my friend (said Ferdinand to the Count, perceiving that he was fixed in a profound reverie, with all the marks of extreme sorrow on his features) come, assert that fortitude so becoming in a noble mind, and which for many years has supported you: How delighted would you have felt under the pressure of your sufferings had life and liberty been offered to you on the single condition of the Lady Eugenia's retiring from the world: Would the alternative have admitted of the least hesitation? Certainly not: And can you now repine that she has the power of her own election, and in her own words, 'only prefers her duty to Heaven to her earthly happiness with you?' Let us both unite as fellow sufferers to comfort each other."

"I accept your offer (said the Count, hastily interrupting him.) From this hour you are my friend and brother; we will together seek the path to glory, and in the din of arms forget our private sorrows!"—His eyes sparkled as he spoke, and every feature grew animated; he seemed as if suddenly informed by a new soul, and from that moment struggled to subdue his grief, and assume an appearance of resignation and content.

Several days passed with cheerfulness, tho' not entirely free from anxiety by either party, for the return of their several messengers:—The first that arrived was Ferdinand's, with a letter from Count Rhodophil, and another from the good old Ernest: Respect superceded affection and curiosity. He opened the Count's letter first; it was not a long one.

"He was glad to hear from his brother, whose strange whim of rambling among unfrequented paths on foot had exposed him to so many dangers: He approved of his design of returning to the army, and repeated his readiness to furnish him with money upon all emergencies—congratulated him upon the welfare of his son, without making a single observation on the late occurrences at the Castle, or once mentioning Claudina. He added, that his health not being very good he had some thoughts of travelling, as the spring advanced, therefore might possibly not be so regular in his correspondence, but earnestly requested, that his brother would inform him when it was his intention to join his quarters at Vienna."

This letter was so cold, so uncircumstantial, and in some respects so inconsistent, that Ferdinand, after looking it twice over, felt a dissatisfaction that he could hardly account for.—"He does not press my return (said he) nor lament my absence; it is true, had he done so, I should not have acceded to his wishes; yet methinks he ought to have done it; but perhaps I expect too much, for I have no absolute claims either upon his affection or fortune; the first I can perceive is much weakened, and I may have already intruded too far on the latter; yet why should I think so, when he still makes me such liberal offers? The stile in which those offers are made is what hurts me. Alas! few men that confer obligations have the graceful art of making the obliged person satisfied with the favours he receives; 'tis the manner, more than the act, that strikes a mind of sensibility."

Musing in this manner, with the letter in his hand, he had forgotten, for a few minutes, that there lay another, from which he might hope to derive more information, and greater gratification. Turning his eyes from the letter to the table, he hastily caught up the one written by Ernest: "Ah! (cried he) here at least I shall read the dictates of the heart, of pure affection without reserve."—He broke it open with precipitation, and read what follows:

"HONOURED SIR,

"How my heart rejoiced at the sight of your well-known hand! Ah! my dear young master, hard is your lot to wander about in search of peace; sad, sad doings to be sure: But your dear son, master Charles, is well, and my nephew doats upon him, he is so good, and so clever; he will live, I hope, to be a blessing to you.—You ask, Sir, about Madam Claudina; she is as well *as she can be*, but desires to be forgotten by all the world. At a proper age your daughter will be restored to you, till then I beseech you, Sir, to make no farther inquiries. Madam Claudina is *dead to you*.

"The Count, my master, seems oppressed with melancholy: He has also received some unknown caution, advice, or reproof, from the same voice which astonished you; for a few days ago, after being about an hour in bed, the servants were alarmed by the ringing of his bell; all flew to his room, I among the rest; we found him in the anti-chamber in his shirt, terror in every feature. He asked wildly if any one had been in the chamber or closet? All replied, No.—Had any one heard any groans, or a voice? No, was the answer. He walked the room very fast, regardless of his situation. At length he dismissed all but his valet, who was ordered to stay by him the remainder of the night, and since that a bed has been put up in the anti-chamber for him to sleep close to the Count. These are strange things, my dear Master. I see and hear a great deal, but it does not become me to repeat

more than is necessary. Yesterday Peter told me that his Master was court-
ing the Lady once offered to you, the daughter of Count Benhorff.—You
know, Sir, the Count died some time ago, and left the Lady a great fortune.
Peter said, that after you had refused the Lady, your father offered Count
Rhodophil, but the young Countess would not hear of him, and has continued unmarried ever since.—Your brother used to visit there sometimes,
and since your departure has been to see the Lady every day, and Peter
thinks that she likes him, and that it will be a match at last. So much the
worse for the Lady.

"As to the Count's love for you, Sir, you know what I think; what he has
done, and what he offers to do, is more for fear of the world's blame for his
being unnatural, than from any affection: I am sure of it, and I must speak
my mind, though I dare not speak *all* my mind; but I hope I shall live to see
you happy, my dear Master; if I die, I have taken care to leave such things
in my nephew's hands as will explain every thing. As you are in a friend's
house I wish you would stay there, and not go to the wars; indeed I can't
bear to think you should be driven to that, although any place is better,
aye and *safer* too, than Renaud Castle. Do pray, Sir, write often to your old
servant under cover to my nephew, and fear not for Master Charles or your
interest, whilst I live I will watch over both. God bless you, Sir; may you be
happy, and live to triumph over your enemies, prays,

Your faithful servant,

ERNEST."

This letter from the old steward occasioned various emotions in the
mind of Ferdinand, several expressions were to him inexplicable, and in-
fused suspicions, though unable to fix on the nature of them. That voice,
which still continued its supernatural admonitions, filled him with equal
terror and wonder.—Those secrets, which Ernest dared not to reveal, perplexed and astonished him, and his expressions concerning Claudina were
equally extraordinary. The latter part of the letter seemed to imply a doubt
of his being safe under his brother's roof: He then reverted back to the
conversation Ernest had told him past between the Count and Peter; a conversation which his brother's subsequent conduct and seeming kindness
had almost obliterated from his memory, though he had felt hurt at the
indifference of his behaviour when they parted; those circumstances now
returned with double force, and seemed strengthened by the coldness of
the letter just received.

Distracted with doubt, curiosity and anxiety, he communicated his
sentiments, and the letters to Count M***, who had been some days be-

fore acquainted with his story. The Count perused the letters, and heard his comments, and being pressed to give his judgment, replied, "There undoubtedly hangs a mystery over every circumstance relative to your brother, that without a clue it is impossible to unravel; but I have no doubt in my mind to pronounce that he is not the friend he would appear to be; and I am also convinced, that, however improbable it may appear to you, your wife has been unfaithful to you; whether your brother is acquainted with the circumstance cannot be known, I should rather think he is not, otherwise his affection, or delicacy, would not have prevented him from disclosing it: But since you have now given me a fair opening, I have two proposals to make, which I have been revolving in my mind to submit on the first opportunity to your consideration.

"To you, under Heaven, I am indebted for liberty and life, and for the preservation of Eugenia's, much dearer to me than my own: For some days past I have struggled with my affection and regret; reason, or perhaps despair, has, in some degree, tranquillized my mind to bear the idea of being separated for ever from the only object I ever did, or ever can love. I have no near or dear connexions, perhaps scarcely an acquaintance that may remember me. My fortune is not inconsiderable, and however my estates may be disposed of from a supposition of my death, they must be restored to me: Condescend then, my dear friend, to complete the work of your generous hand, restore my mind, my peace, as you have liberated my body. If I must live in the world, do you make that world estimable in my eyes, by the value of your company: Let us never be separated, mutually unfortunate, let us console each other, reject the paltry assistance offered by an ungenerous brother, and share the fortune of a faithful friend."

Seeing Ferdinand was going to speak, he continued, "Hear my proposals: If retirement is your choice, go with me to Suabia; if you prefer an active life, I will either accompany you to the army, or I will travel with you wherever you please; the instant I hear how my affairs stand, you shall be independent, and then your home shall be mine, and your choice of situation shall meet my approbation, whatever it may be: Thus you will make my life valuable if you consent; but your refusal will cloud my hopes and prospects for ever. I leave you to reflection; a single Yes, or No, is all I will hear on the subject, and on those two monosyllables rest my future happiness."

The Count rose to leave the room.—Ferdinand caught his hand: "Stop, generous friend, no consideration is necessary, I can distinguish between favours coldly offered, and the effusions of benevolence and friendship; the proud heart that would refuse the latter feels not a generous enthusiasm.—I accept with transport your offers, because I know you feel a delight, a gratification superior, even to mine, in the pleasure of bestowing favours.—Yes (added he, embracing the Count) we will indeed console each other; with such a companion I will travel through the painful journey of life with patience and resignation, and to you be indebted for every comfort without feeling myself degraded by the acceptance." The Count was delighted, and withdrew to acquaint Eugenia with the acquisition he had fortunately obtained of a friend and a companion for his future days; whilst Ferdinand retired to reflect on his letters, and the generosity of the friend, so infinitely superior to the obligations frigidly bestowed by a brother.

CHAPTER VIII.

Two days passed away without any material occurrence, the third brought visitors to the Castle. Baron Reiberg and his son, the nearest relations and heirs to the late Baron S***, arrived about the middle of the day at this Solitary Mansion. The Baron had for some years enjoyed the revenues of the estate by the courtesy of the Emperor; every inquiry had been set on foot to discover the existence of the Baron, and all proving fruitless, it seemed so unaccountable, that a person of his rank and fortune should so suddenly disappear, and his fate be unknown, that at length some person in the neighbourhood, who had heard a vague report of his being married to a Lady who had run away the same day to a Convent, conjectured that he had gone a volunteer to the wars under a borrowed name, and had fallen undistinguished among the slain.

This idea soon got abroad, and was generally credited, so that the present Baron found but little difficulty in prevailing upon the Emperor to allow him the possession of the estates, to which he was the legal heir, on the demise of Baron S***. The express sent by Count M***, addressed to the steward, or possessor of the estate, had infinitely surprised him; but as it brought a confirmation of his relation's death, it relieved him from a doubt which had often given him pain, lest he should be dispossessed of his fortune. Curiosity induced him to take the journey, accompanied by his son, and no time was lost in putting his design into execution.

Count M*** received them with politeness, and without reserve related every event which had taken place at the Castle. The astonishment of the two Gentlemen may be easily conceived; they detested the cruelty of the late Baron, and reprobated his conduct in the strongest terms: They could offer no reparation to the Count, who was superior to pecuniary favours; but Baron Reiberg earnestly entreated the Lady Eugenia would accept of that income to which she would have been entitled as the late Baron's widow by the marriage settlement, particularly as the Baron possessed her father's fortune.—This offer she strenuously refused; much generous altercation took place between them, at length a compromise was agreed on. As Eugenia could have no just expectations to any part of the Baron's fortune, neither had she power to claim any share of her father's property bequeathed unconditionally to him; yet, as the Baron, who now possessed all, was so extremely desirous of making some restitution to her, she reluctantly acquiesced with his wishes, to accept from him a sum of money sufficient to insure her a most welcome reception when she retired to the Convent.

This plan met with great opposition from Count M***, who could not support the idea that *his* Eugenia should owe any pecuniary favours to a stranger, and a relation of their cruel persecutor; but the urgent entreaties of the Baron, and the remonstrances of the Lady, who considered the obligation forced upon her, more as a generous *resignation* of a small part of that property to which she had once undoubted claims, than as a *gift* from an indifferent person not benefitted by her family; as a very inconsiderable share of what she had a natural right to have expected, she consented to gratify the Baron's feelings by her acceptance of, and so greatly did he feel interested in her melancholy story, that her acquiescence was considered as a high obligation to himself.

One great difficulty equally affected all parties; it was essential to the Baron, that the death of his relation should be publicly announced, that all doubts should be removed, and his possession of the estates be unquestionably his right. How this matter could be elucidated, without involving the names and story of Count M*** and Eugenia, puzzled them all. Several plans and stories were suggested, but all liable to objections, until Ferdinand being requested to give his opinion, proposed that the account should be as simple as possible, and that *his* name only should be brought forward, in the following manner:—"Having lost the road, he was conducted by chance to this Castle, where he was admitted by the late Baron, who acquainted him with his retirement from the world in consequence of his wife's leaving him on the day of marriage, and flying to a Convent; that unable to discover her retreat, and conscious of her utter dislike to him, he had grown weary and disgusted with mankind, and rented this Solitary Mansion of Count M***, having only one domestic with him. That a few days after Ferdinand's residence with him he was seized with an apoplectic fit, which deprived him of life, in consequence of which Ferdinand had sent off expresses to his estate, and to Count M***, whose abode he had been informed of by the Baron.

This story, corroborated by Francis, he presumed to think, would effectually satisfy any curious persons, if such there were, who felt any concern about the deceased, and the Lady Eugenia might enter into the Convent as his widow, or not as she pleased."

This arrangement was immediately adopted, except that Eugenia utterly disclaimed an intention of assuming a name to which she had no right, and which indeed was odious to her, and as her marriage with Count M*** was a secret to all but the present party, she had determined to take upon herself the name of Madam of Valse, which had been a name in her mother's family; "and carrying with me (added she) all such requisites as may ensure a welcome, and give me consequence in the eyes of the Nuns, I apprehend any investigation of my family must be a matter of indifference to them."

Those difficulties, which had perplexed the Baron and Count, being now got over, the Baron dispatched expresses to his family, conformable to the plan decided on, and ordered all things to be prepared for the funeral, as he thought it an incumbent duty upon him to have the body of his relation deposited in the vault with his ancestors; all requisite preparations were made for that purpose, and within two days the procession was to set off for Bavaria.

That day and the following passed agreeably to all; the Baron and his son were so exceedingly interested for the Count, and so delighted with the placid manners, the unassumed good sense, and good nature of Ferdinand, that the idea of a separation, even on so short an acquaintance, was painful to them; the Baron therefore seized an opportunity, in the course of the evening, to express his wishes that his new friends would accompany him to Bavaria. He urged a number of inducements, backed by so many persuasions, that, had not the Count thought it essential to his interest to visit his own estate, and settle all his long accounts there, he could not have resisted an invitation so warm and pressing: Both Ferdinand and himself promised to pay him a speedy visit when they had executed their present unavoidable business. With this promise the Gentlemen were obliged to be contented, and when the hour arrived for their departure, they took leave with many expressions of esteem and gratitude;—of the Lady Eugenia, with respect and consideration, such as her misfortunes, and present laudable resolution, had a claim to.

Those remaining in the Castle, though they were much pleased with the Gentlemen, could scarcely regret their absence, as it relieved them from all concerns relative to the late Baron, the removal of whose body seemed to take from them a heavy pressure, and a painful inquietude.

Count M*** began to feel some uneasiness, that the messenger he had dispatched to his estate did not return by the time expected, and blamed himself for sending him, as his own appearance would have answered every purpose: Eugenia was very desirous of entering on her new plan, but she could not take Ferdinand from the Count in his present frame of mind, nor did she wish that the latter should accompany her. The following day all their anxiety was done away by the arrival of the expected messenger, and with him the Count's faithful old steward, who had resisted every attempt, persuasion and temptation, of those persons who, being next in succession to the Count, had long since been desirous to profit by his absence, and, under a supposition of his death, to take possession of the estates.

This honest servant produced the orders of his Lord, to hold the management of his fortune until his return to Suabia. He was ready to submit his accounts to their inspection, but he would not resign a trust delegated to him by his master, until convinced *that* master no longer existed. Apprehensive at length that some sinister means would be used against him, he was compelled to appeal to the Duke of Wirtemberg, who, on hearing both sides of the question, decreed that the management of the estates should remain in the steward's hands for seven years longer, subject to the inspection of the heir; after which period, if the Count did not appear to claim his rights, the property should pass into the hands of his heirs.

Eight months only of this limitted seven years remained unexpired, and Mr. Duclos, the steward, had given himself up to despair, when the arrival of the Count's messenger transported him with joy; his eager desire to behold his master would not permit him to wait his return; but sending for a relation, in whom he could confide to remain with the housekeeper, he accompanied the man to the Castle, and seemed ready to expire with delight when admitted to the Count's presence.

Eugenia was not in the room, nor would she be seen by this man, who knew her when she resided with her father. She considered not the alteration which time and affliction had wrought in her face and form, which was such that the steward never would have recollected her; but as this could not in delicacy be urged to her by the Count, he made no objections to her wish of being absent. Ferdinand leaving Mr. Duclos and his master together, repaired to the apartment of Eugenia, whom he found in a flood of tears. He apologized for his intrusion, and was about to withdraw, when she earnestly called on him to return.

"Dear Sir," said she, when she had prevailed upon him to be seated, "you come most opportunely to my relief; I must leave this house to-morrow, indeed I must; the arrival of that good old man has recalled to my mind past scenes that overwhelm me with distress; I shall relapse into sorrow or madness if haunted with recollections that pain me to my very soul; a fugitive daughter, whose conduct perhaps hastened a parent's death, who died without blessing or forgiving me; he might be arbitrary, prejudiced and cruel, but he was my father, to whose goodness I owed every comfort in life, and to whose tenderness, to whose parental care of me in my infancy, I was indebted for my very existence: What sacrifices had not such a parent a right to demand? And what has been the consequences of my resistance to his will?"

Here she wept aloud. This was a subject that wrung the heart of Ferdinand, every word had sunk into his soul, and painful retrospections darted into his mind—Observing his silence, Eugenia resumed her discourse:— "The state you see me in cannot surprise you, but you have the power to tranquillize my spirits: I cannot support a parting interview—I cannot take leave of the Count—I have endeavoured to acquire fortitude, but the heart in such a moment cannot be trusted; let us go then, Sir, to-morrow at an early hour, I will leave a letter, and my clothes can be sent after me. Do not hesitate (pursued she) consider my peace, my *reason* may depend upon your compliance."

"Then, Madam," replied Ferdinand—"assure yourself of my obedience to your wishes; to-morrow I will attend you: I only fear that you will find the way more fatiguing than you are aware of, and that arriving at such a place on foot may excite curiosity, and give rise to unfavourable conjectures."

"Well," answered she, hastily, "make what arrangements you please, but let me go to-morrow, and go without taking leave of the——" "*Count,*" she would have said, but the word died on her tongue, her voice faltered, and she turned from Ferdinand as he arose to leave her. He was greatly affected, and withdrew to consider on the best manner of obliging her. After much deliberation he conceived that he could not accomplish his wishes without communicating their intention to the Count, whose good sense, he trusted, would enable him to coincide with Eugenia's plan, and spare both *her* feelings and *his* own.

In this he was not mistaken, for when he had repeated the late conversation he had held with that Lady, the Count, though evidently much distressed, made no objection: "Her resolution being fixed (said he) I own to you that I think the sooner every thing can be settled the better, for her peace and mine. It is a hard struggle, my friend, to resign the woman we love, for ever, yet, as it is to be, delay can only increase the difficulty, and prolong sorrow.—To-morrow morning I will take Duclos to the village, or, if I cannot walk so far, into the Forest. Let Francis accompany you, and take such things as he can carry; there are now two horses in the stables."

"That is sufficient," exclaimed Ferdinand; "I will walk by the side of Eugenia's, and you may depend upon my care to see her safe into the Convent. We may possibly not return for the night; should it be so, entertain no apprehensions for our safety."

"And must I see Eugenia no more?" asked the Count, with a melancholy air.

"If you wish it, and think it right to indulge yourself with another interview," answered Ferdinand, "an interview that, under the present circumstances, must be painful to both, you certainly may go to her apartment: I presume not to advise, you must be the best judge of the consequences."

"Well then," said the other, with a deep sigh, "I submit to reason, nor will I wound her feelings for the gratification of a moment, which must be equally afflictive to both.—May Heaven restore her peace, and then I cannot be wholly miserable!" He left Ferdinand at those words, whose sympathizing heart felt deeply for this unfortunate pair, and was not sorry they had resolution enough to avoid a last distressing interview. The following day every thing was arranged for the departure of Eugenia; she seemed to have collected all her fortitude for the occasion, and in the hurry of the moment to have forgotten the sacrifice she had made.

On their arrival at the Monastery, Ferdinand seized a moment to recommend Claudina and his child to her notice, and to request that, as she had promised to write *one* letter, under cover to him, a week after her residence in the Convent, she would afford him all the information she could gain relative to those dear objects. Father Ambrose being informed of the Lady's arrival soon made his appearance, and, at Eugenia's request, proceeded with her to the Convent, where she was expected. The parting between her and Ferdinand was very affecting: He bowed upon her hand; "Adieu, my amiable friend," was all he could utter.

"May Heaven bless you," replied she, "remember our common friend, and may peace and happiness be the portion of both!"

When the gates of the Convent opened, grating on their hinges, and the Porteress appeared, Ferdinand's heart beat tumultuously: "What (thought he) have I a wife, a child, within those walls, and cannot I be permitted to have one look?" At the instant, when he was about to speak, to supplicate the Porteress for permission to see his child, the gates closed, and he remained alone. Throwing a reproaching melancholy look at the building as the grave of his affections, he returned to the Monastery, and obtained an interview with Father Joseph: That good man sought to tranquillize his mind, and promised to enter into a correspondence with him when a place should be fixed on for the conveyance of their letters.

In less than an hour Father Ambrose returned, and said he left the Lady apparently much satisfied with her reception and situation. Ferdinand having nothing to detain him, and the time allowing of their return by day-light, he took leave of the Fathers, and to the no small joy of Francis returned to the Castle, where they arrived safely and unexpectedly to the Count, whose anxiety was greatly relieved by the presence of Ferdinand.

The letter which Eugenia left for the Count, it is unnecessary to repeat, as it was only expressive of those sentiments before mentioned, calculated to inspire him with resignation and fortitude.

Mr. Duclos was very urgent with his master to accompany him back, as it would be requisite that he should appear to silence the claims of his relations, and give a sanction to the future proceedings of Duclos, that he might remain unmolested. Ferdinand was of the same opinion, and, after various consultations, it was settled that the Solitary Castle and Estate should be let, if a tenant could be found for it; that the Count and Ferdinand should return with the steward, and after the former had surveyed his estate, and finished his business with Duclos and the tenants, the two Gentlemen should proceed to Vienna, and attend the opening of the campaign. Mean time workmen were hired to repair the Castle, and render it more habitable. They were under some difficulties respecting Francis; he was too far advanced in life to bear the fatigue of travelling, and if they sent him to the village with a comfortable provision, the natural garrulity of age would lead him to talk of the strange events he had seen and heard of, which, among illiterate and superstitious people, might occasion such fears, and such exaggerations, as would very possibly prove injurious to the disposal of the estate, and the reputation of its owner. Frequent consultations were held upon the subject, and at length Francis was admitted to counsel, and asked how he wished to dispose of himself for the remainder of his days, when secured from future want?

"Ah!" replied he, "I am old and helpless, I have no relations living that I know of, nor any place to go to, except to the village, and I don't care much for any body there. I wish, methinks, I could lie at your Lordship's house with that there Gentleman (pointing to Duclos) he looks so good-humoured, and speaks so kindly; but I must go where your Honours please."

This answer of Francis's pleased the Count. "Well, my friend (said he) you shall then go with us; we will go slowly on the journey to accommodate you; a day or two on the road makes no great difference." Francis was profuse in his thanks, and tears bespoke his gratitude. He assured them of his silence respecting the recent events at the Castle; and now that his own destination was determined on, he exerted all his strength and abilities to assist the persons employed in the repairs.—Within a few days after this, a respectable farmer offered to lease the estate; terms were soon concluded upon between them, and immediate possession was to be given; they only waited to hear from Eugenia, and at the promised time her letter came.

The contents gave pleasure, surprise and pain; it breathed a spirit of serenity and contentment. She had entered upon the strict observance of the Convent rules; they grew easy and delightful; her mind was more tranquil, her soul superior to earthly considerations, farther than her wishes for the happiness of her friends, of which the Count was the dearest. She had already met with two Ladies who had kindred souls, in whose society she looked forward to much comfort and pleasure. Her friend Ferdinand would not be *surprised to hear* that one of these Ladies was the person he had requested to see; but she believed he would be *astonished* to be told *that* Lady *was not* Claudina; a coincidence of circumstances had led to a false conjecture on both sides, for the Lady had also been deceived; but it was a certain fact this Lady's name was Theodosia; that she was a stranger to this country, under the most melancholy circumstances from unparalleled ill-treatment, and the child with her was only six months old.—This was all she was allowed to say on the subject, but Ferdinand might be assured, as a solemn truth, that Claudina was not in that Convent, nor ever had been. She then recommended to him an endeavour to banish from his memory a woman he must be assured was unworthy of his regard; nor to waste his time, and ruin his health, in a fruitless pursuit of developing a mystery which could afford him no pleasure: She besought him to attach himself to her dear Count, and in the reciprocal delights of mutual friendship, find that peace and happiness which she daily implored Heaven to bestow on them.

This was nearly the contents of her letter. The Count had generosity enough to rejoice in her tranquillity, though it cost him dear; but the surprise and anxiety of Ferdinand cannot be described. He had established it in his mind for a certainty, that Claudina resided in that Convent, and from thence adduced pleasure to himself when Eugenia had readily agreed to go there, from the expectation of obtaining some intelligence of the former through her; astonished indeed he was, and lost in conjecture. He knew Eugenia too well to believe she would attempt an imposition, or be capable of any duplicity under her present frame of mind; yet it was so extraordinary that the message he sent, and the answer returned, should coincide so exactly with his situation, that the more he reflected, the greater was his surprise, and the more severe his disappointment.

The Count found himself obliged to smother his own feelings, that he might administer consolation to his friend, who, although he could not hope to receive any pleasing intelligence, had Claudina actually been in the Convent, yet felt additional disquietude from being again in a state of ignorance as to her residence. He now determined to see Ernest, to visit his brother for a few days whilst the Count was settling his affairs at his Castle. This design he communicated to him, and could not be persuaded to relinquish.

Both Gentlemen having written to Eugenia, and the tenant being ready to take possession of the Solitary Castle, within a few days they took leave of a place where the Count had known so much misery. His heart felt comparatively light as he quitted it, and but for the painful separation from his dear and much-regretted companion, he would have left that part of the country with transport. Mr. Duclos, Old Francis, and one servant, attended them; they travelled slowly, for the Count was still weak, and Francis very infirm.

When they arrived at a part of the country where the road separated, one direction to the East towards Stutgard, and the other in a direct line to Renaud Castle, a little to the South West of Baden, the Gentlemen halted; the Count once more earnestly pressed his friend to accompany him: "For a few days only shall we be separated," said Ferdinand; "I am mortified that I cannot ask you to my brother's Castle, but an unexpected, perhaps an unwelcome guest, myself, I dare not run the hazard of your reception: If *I* find a welcome, I will immediately dispatch a messenger to you; if on the contrary I meet neither a brother or a friend, within eight days I will insure to myself the possession of the *latter* by joining *you*. Whatever may be my reception, you may depend upon me to accompany you on the earliest notice." Satisfied with this assurance, the Count only requested that the servant might attend him, as he would then have a proper person either to send to him, or to wait upon Ferdinand, when he gave him the pleasure of his company. This friendly desire being complied with, they parted reluctantly, both agitated and occupied by unpleasant reflections.

That same evening, at the close of day, Ferdinand reached his brother's mansion.—He rang at the gate, and when the servant appeared, asked, in the same moment as he dismounted, if Count Rhodophil was at home? The man instantly recollected his voice, and drew near to him: "Heavens bless you, Sir!" exclaimed he, in an accent of joy, "how glad I am to see you returned! No, Sir, my master is not at home, but Mr. Ernest is, and he will be joyful indeed." Ferdinand recommended the servant with him, whose name was Anthony, to his care, and took his way to the steward's apartment. Knocking at the door, the old Gentleman bid him "come in."

"An unexpected friend salutes you," said Ferdinand, as he opened the door. The voice announced him, and in a moment he caught the good Ernest in his arms.—Wonder and joy precluded speech, and the large drops run down his cheeks as he pressed the former to his breast.—"My dear, dear master!" he exclaimed.

"My worthy friend!" returned Ferdinand, "you are doubtless surprised to see me; but I seized a favourable opportunity to see my dear boy, and express my thanks to you." He had taken a seat as he spoke, and requested Ernest to resume his: "I have a thousand things to say, and many questions to ask; but tell me, I conjure you, how affairs stand in this Castle; I find my brother is away from home."

"Yes," replied Ernest, "I believe he is on his daily visit to the Lady Bonhorff."

"But," said Ferdinand, "he wrote to me that he was very low spirited, and had some thoughts of travelling; the former you confirmed."

"True," returned Ernest, "and he is still at times seemingly much oppressed, yet I have reason to believe his design of marrying is in a speedy way of being concluded, from the alterations and preparations ordered, and making in the house."

"Most cordially I wish him happiness," said Ferdinand, adding, with a sigh, "May his union prove a more fortunate one than mine has been; at least he will have no act of disobedience to reflect upon, nor be a weight upon his spirits."

"Ah! Sir," cried Ernest, "there are more causes for being unhappy than one, every man has his share of troubles; but, my dear master, you told me you had found a friend, thank Heaven for that." Ferdinand then briefly mentioned his ramble to the Count's Castle, whom he described as a Gentleman retired from society on account of great misfortunes; but that his arrival had made a change in the Count's sentiments, and they were now going to Vienna to attend the opening of the campaign, and he hoped a friendly intercourse would tend to lighten their mutual misfortunes: "You, my good friend (added he) have it much in your power to alleviate *mine*, if *you choose to do so*."—"Pray, Sir," cried Ernest, "don't break my heart by such a reflection; what I have sworn to I must fulfil; and do your faithful servant the justice to believe, that, could I communicate one word of comfort or pleasure, I would not with-hold it a moment; for Heaven's sake therefore cease to think on what is past. Let me tell you that master Charles is all you can wish, and that a day will come when every thing concerning Madam Claudina will be cleared up, although *you never* will *see her* more."

"Good Heavens!" exclaimed Ferdinand, "what a torture is suspense! Tell me, however, is she in a Convent?"

"At present," replied he, "*she is not*; but in a situation equally dead to the world, and to you: But now, Sir, how do you mean to meet your brother?"

"That depends upon him," answered the other; "I come not to ask favours of him, I have a noble friend, who is more than a brother already; but the voice you mentioned as having alarmed him, that strange unaccountable circumstance, has it disturbed any other part of the family?"

"*Never*," replied Ernest. "Our master's questions, the night he was frightened, gave some strange suspicions to the servants, which were strengthened by a recollection of the odd occurrences about Madam Claudina; but I endeavoured to dispel their apprehensions by several arguments between jest and earnest, and if they still entertain any doubts or fears, they do not express them openly. Last week, my dear master, I gave a sealed packet into the hands of my nephew, directed for you, with a strict charge never to let it pass his hands until my death, without my consent should be first obtained.

"I mention this for your guide whenever the event takes place that closes all my earthly concerns, and I conjure you, Sir, not to let my nephew be ignorant of your residence wherever you go."

This request Ferdinand assured him he would observe. They then entered into a detail of family occurrences, until the bell at the gate announced his brother's return. Ferdinand hastened to the parlour, and there waited the Count's approach, as he supposed the servant would mention his arrival.

CHAPTER IX.

In a few minutes Count Rhodophil entered the room, and with an exclamation of joy embraced his brother, which was as cordially returned. For a moment Ferdinand forgot all past events, and his brother's coolness on former occasions; the seeming sincerity, and warm reception he so little expected, vibrated to his heart, and he felt a true fraternal affection. The Count, after many expressions of joy to see his beloved Ferdinand returned, inquired what had happened to procure him a pleasure so little hoped, though so much wished for? Ferdinand, who had recovered from the momentary transport, was very limitted in his confidence, nor gave the smallest hint relative to the story of Count M***; he avowed his intention of returning to the army accompanied by that Nobleman, and that the visit, which affection and gratitude demanded at Renaud Castle, was chiefly owing to the design his brother had intimated of travelling, in consequence of indifferent health and bad spirits; he was agreeably surprised (he added) to observe in the Count's appearance no traits of either the one or the other.

"I am indeed much better," answered the Count, "and (smiling) have some thoughts of making a different arrangement in my household, which will at least *suspend*, if not entirely supersede any necessity for a journey. In short (added he) I am going to be married, and what will perhaps surprise you, to the very Lady once offered to you, the Lady Amelia Bonhorff! What say you to this, brother?"

"That I most sincerely wish you happy," replied Ferdinand.

"Permit me to observe," said Rhodophil, hastily, "that you shall not be injured by my marriage; I will still be your banker, and answer all your demands, as *I know you are very moderate.*"

"I am much obliged to you," returned Ferdinand; "but one motive which brought me here is, to thank you for all past favours, and to acquaint you that henceforth I shall make no farther demands on your generosity."

"What do you mean?" asked the other.

"I mean that I have accepted an offer to *share* the fortune of *a friend*, not as a dependant, for his soul disdains the idea of *conferring favours*; but he has given me a title to an *independence*, that we may be on an equality, and considers himself as the obliged person by my acceptance."

"A rare instance of generosity indeed," cried the Count, much disconcerted; "you are wonderfully fortunate in acquiring such a friend: But, my dear brother, are you well acquainted with the character of Count M***, for I suppose he is the man? Are you sure no injurious or unworthy design lurks under the *semblance* of generosity? He binds you in chains by this free-will offering stronger and heavier far than a state of dependance, which you can at any time reject without reproach; know your man well therefore before you decline the kindness of a brother, and fix yourself the slave of a stranger."

"I thank you for your caution," answered Ferdinand, coolly; "but *I do know* the man, and can read his heart, where there is neither guile nor duplicity. There are some minds that are superior to falsehood or reserve, such are open to every intelligent person; *his* is enveloped by no dark schemes, he has no points to carry, no errors to disguise, under a *semblance* of friendship."

"Well, well," cried the Count, greatly confused, which he sought to hide by a haughty air of contempt, "enough of your faultless man, I wish he may prove a disinterested friend. How long pray may I flatter myself you propose to stay in the Castle?"

"Three days," answered Ferdinand, "if you will permit me to do so."

"Most certainly, if you can spare me so much of your company: I am sorry you will not remain here long enough to witness my nuptials, which will take place within three weeks."

"O, Rhodophil!"—cried Ferdinand, wounded to the soul by a painful recollection, "O, Rhodophil! may *your* marriage be fortunate and happy; blind, inconsiderate and rash, I have dearly suffered for the impetuosity of *my* passions. You speak not, you ask not after Claudina, yet surely her strange conduct, her sudden disappearance, must sometimes have a place in your thoughts.—Did you never in my absence make any inquiries concerning her?"

"Why should I?" answered he, in a quick tone, "What expectations could *I* form, that, if she absented herself from *you*, any information would be granted to *me?*—In short, brother, I wish you to forget an ungrateful woman, and therefore I never shall revive the subject." Supper being then announced precluded farther conversation, and Ferdinand retired early to his apartment.

He retired, but not to sleep; a thousand bitter thoughts obtruded to agonize his mind; he had carefully examined Rhodophil; he saw confusion, restlessness and perturbation, in every word and look; there was a mystery hung about him that he could not penetrate; yet he saw enough to convince him there existed no brotherly affection in the Count, and that he was not a little pleased to get rid of one he considered as a tax upon his honour and generosity. He next reverted to Claudina, then to the *voice*, which, though he was not credulous in the belief of supernatural missions, yet was it wholly unaccountable in any other light. He passed the night without rest, and when day-light appeared, gladly left his bed, and repaired to that part of the Castle inhabited by Ernest.

The good old man had just opened his window shutters, and was surprised to see Ferdinand thus early, who entered without ceremony, where he could insure to himself a welcome. They had a long conversation, as the Count was no early riser. Ernest mentioned the shepherdess and her father, with whom Ferdinand had passed a night in the cottage under the hanging rocks: The steward had provided them with a safer and a more comfortable habitation, and they blessed the day which brought the strange Gentleman to the side of the rivulet. Ferdinand declared his intention of going after breakfast to see his son, and of leaving the Castle the following day.

"Will not the Count be displeased that you shorten the time you first purposed to stay?" asked Ernest.

"I believe not," replied Ferdinand; "my preference can give neither pleasure nor information; if he is not sincere in his professions of affection, he will be glad to be relieved from the irksomeness of dissembling, and of beholding a man whose penetration he may fear; if on the contrary, I do him injustice, he can set no value on my company, when he knows I have preferred a stranger, by declining all pecuniary favours, and have consented to owe obligations to another;—thus, every way, he can derive no satisfaction from my being here, and he has sufficient employment in his new prospects to engross all his attention." Ernest subscribed to the justice of this opinion, and Ferdinand soon after attended his brother.

A very general and uninteresting conversation took place at table; both seemed equally desirous of avoiding particular subjects, and when breakfast was over Ferdinand ordered his horse, and set off to see his little boy. The meeting was truly affecting; poor Charles hung about his dear father, and repeatedly cried, "My poor mamma is dead, Yes, indeed, my poor mamma is dead!"—Stung to the heart by the infantine tone of sorrow which accompanied these words, and the reflection that his child was deprived of all those maternal cares so necessary at his early age. Ferdinand could not repress his emotions, but pressed his boy to his bosom, whilst the big drops fell on his face.

Mr. Dunloff, the nephew of Ernest, now entered the room, and relieved both. To him the anxious father recommended his little Charles in the most moving terms, beseeching him to be a father to his child, and to watch over the first dawning of reason, that, as his mind expanded, his ideas might be properly directed to the practice of truth, humanity, and a proper pride to disdain a mean or unworthy action. "Pardon me, my dear Sir (added he) for presuming to dictate to you, but I am well convinced, that were children accustomed from the earliest dawn of reason to a strict observance of truth, humanity, and generosity; if the virtues were inculcated with the same care, which is generally bestowed to teach them *different* languages before they are capable of understanding their *own* properly; if the *morals* of children were more attended to as the foundation for *future* improvements, we should see wiser and happier men than are generally met with; but unhappily, in most seminaries for education, the useful is neglected, because the shining, or rather superficial part, is supposed to reflect most credit on the master."

Mr. Dunloff received those remarks of Ferdinand with much complacency, and assured him, that whilst *he* presided over the child, it should be his unremitting study to do his duty in the strictest sense of the word, by forming the *mind*, as well as the manners, of his young pupil, as his reason appeared to expand. "I shall teach him to *love me* (added Mr. Dunloff) and when I have obtained his affection my work will be very easy, for he will fear to offend."

Ferdinand was perfectly satisfied with this Mr. Dunloff: "Ah! (thought he) here is the counterpart of our good Ernest; my boy, under his care, will prove a worthy man." After spending a few hours with little Charles and his master, Ferdinand tore himself from the caresses of the former, and returned, oppressed with melancholy, to his brother's house.

In the evening at supper Ferdinand announced his intention of pursuing his route to the Castle of his friend on the following day. Rhodophil made some faint efforts to detain him, but his *manner* wanted that cordiality which might have been expected from a brother, and therefore the other found no difficulty in persevering. He arose at a very early hour the next morning, that he might have an hour's conversation with Ernest.—The good old man deeply regretted the necessity which obliged him to leave the mansion of his forefathers, but in the present state of things he could not urge his stay. The conversation that ensued it is unnecessary to repeat, as it afforded no information to Ferdinand, and consisted chiefly of assurances on the part of Ernest to watch over his interests, and to pay a fatherly attention to his little son.

When the brothers met to take leave, Rhodophil assumed an air of affection and concern, which Ferdinand really felt. He had been for many years accustomed to consider Rhodophil as a brother and a generous friend. The late strange occurrences had deprived him of every comfort, the coldness of Rhodophil, and a suspicion of his duplicity, completed his misfortunes, and obliged him to turn his eyes towards a stranger for every future expectation of peace and support; but the natural and habitual affection he had so long indulged could not be eradicated entirely, and when Rhodophil embraced him his heart glowed with tenderness. "I leave you, Rhodophil, and perhaps for ever; if I die, remember *my child*; the prospect that now awaits you, may in a short time inform you, what the feelings of a parent are. May you never experience the agonizing pangs I have suffered; but when you become a *husband* and a *father*, think of, and pity *me*."

His emotions became too powerful to proceed; his brother was still more agitated; with difficulty he pronounced a "farewell," and turned quickly into another apartment. "What! (thought Ferdinand) is he *really* grieved? Then have I wronged my brother!" That moment Ernest, who had been a distant witness of this scene, observing the looks of Ferdinand, and guessing at his sentiments, drew near to him: "Heavens bless you, my honoured Sir, doubt not of its protection;" adding, in a low voice, "be not deceived by appearances, pursue your plan."—This roused Ferdinand from a momentary self-reproach, and shaking the friendly hand that was humbly extended: "I thank you, my good friend, and will endeavour to deserve your good wishes;" then lowering his voice, "I will remember your admonitions." No more passed; Ferdinand, attended by the servant who had accompanied him, pursued his route to the Castle of Count M***, which was about thirty miles to the East of Baden, between that and Stutgard, the capital of Suabia.

The wind was high, and the cold very piercing, which retarded his speed a good deal, and finding it would be impossible to reach the end of his journey that night, they hastened to a small village about twelve miles short of it, and arrived, just as the day closed in, at a mean looking inn, at the extremity of a few scattered houses, and, as they were informed, the only house of accommodation in the village. Here, to Ferdinand's great mortification, he found *already accommodated* Mr. D'Alenberg, a German Nobleman, his daughter, and several servants; in short, there were already many more persons than could be conveniently lodged in that place, and they were consulting in what manner to dispose of their company, when the arrival of Ferdinand and his servant threw them into fresh difficulties.

The master of the house came out to inform them they could have no room there. A violent drift of snow came suddenly on, the night was dark, and they had a wood to pass through; these circumstances made it impossible to proceed.—"At least (cried Ferdinand) permit me to sit by your kitchen fire; I can be contented without a bed, but to go on a journey of some miles now, you must see, cannot be thought of."

"I am sorry it cannot be thought about (answered the man) but I know it must be done; for, indeed master, neither in kitchen or cellar have I room for man or beast, be the weather what it will." The fall of snow increasing, Ferdinand again applied both to his humanity and interest, and to the latter he spoke so *forcibly*, that at length he cried, "Well, well, Gentlemen, you must come in, if you insist upon it, the house is too full already, some must turn out somewhere, and you may take your chance with the rest."

Ferdinand hardly attended to the end of this speech, for hastily dismounting he desired the man to take care of his servant and the horses, whilst he made his way to the kitchen, as they called a very miserable small room, already, as the landlord had declared, filled with servants, and two or three other passengers. He had suffered too much from the weather to be fastidious either as to the company or accommodations, and some of the servants observing his situation, and struck by his appearance, drew back, and made way for his advance to the fire.

"I beg," said Ferdinand, in a courteous manner, "that I may displace no one, I only wish for a covering from this dreadful weather, and not to incommode any person."—This address procured him more room, every one seemed ready to give way to a Gentleman so considerate; so true it is, that gentle and complaisant manners, and a conduct free from pretensions and arrogance, are sure to be allowed much more consequence than they give up; for the mind of man, in every situation, naturally revolts against the demands of pride and insolence, but willingly shew respect where the *manners* prove their claim to it, and not the look or tone of assumption.

One of the servants *felt* the *rights* of Ferdinand, and immediately went to the apartment occupied by his master and young Lady, with a report so much in favour of the Gentleman in the kitchen, that it procured him an invitation from Mr. D'Alenberg to "partake of his fire-side and ordinary supper."

Ferdinand saw by the pleasure with which this message was delivered to him, that he was indebted for it to the favourable report of the servant; he therefore accepted the invitation without hesitating, and requested that he would permit his servant to occupy some corner of the room with the present company. This desire was readily accorded to, and he was leaving the kitchen preceded by the servant, when he beheld the figure of an aged man in one corner, whose head was supported by a female, but whether old or young could not be discerned, as she was wrapped up in a large cloak, and her head dress was drawn quite over her face.

Ferdinand stopped:—"Is the man ill?" asked he.

"Very ill indeed," was answered in a low, tremulous voice; "but I believe *all* will soon be over."

"Good God!" returned he, "is he so reduced as to give room for such a supposition, and is there no bed he can be put into?" At that moment the landlord came up:—"You see (said he, addressing the woman) my rooms are so crowded, that I cannot possibly let you stay here; I have no room for sick folks." The woman raised her head:—"What would you have me do, he cannot move?"

"Do!" cried he, "why let somebody help to take him into the out-house, he can't die here."

Ferdinand turned full upon him, and was going to speak, when a sudden groan from the woman, who fell towards him senseless, and dropped the head she had supported, stopped him from speaking. He caught her in his arms, as the servant did the old man, who, to his great terror, proved to be lifeless. All present crowded round those moving objects; Ferdinand conveyed the woman to a seat, and supported her until, by the assistance of water thrown in her face, and forced into her mouth, she began to shew signs of life. In doing this they were obliged to remove her head dress, and open her cloak.—Greatly was every one astonished to behold a young and lovely female, whose complexion, hands and arms, exhibited a delicacy but little suited to her garb or situation.

There is something attractive in beauty, even to the most vulgar souls, and though I would hope the humanity of every man would be excited towards objects in so deplorable a state, yet it is most certain, that when the young woman's face was discovered, all eagerly flew to administer relief, and the buz of pity was general through the room, except with the land-lord, who was rubbing his face with vexation, and exclaimed—"A pretty piece of business this! Here is a dead man, no hole to put him in, nor any one to bury him: Come, come, carry him to the stable for the present."

The unfortunate girl, for she appeared to be not more than nineteen, had just recovered sufficient recollection to hear those words.—She sprang from the encircling arm of Ferdinand, threw herself on the body, and ex-claimed, in a wild, piercing tone:—"To the stable! Great God! the stable! Never, never shall *my* father be so degraded. O! that I could but expire with him; for me, for me, he died!"

Her heart-wounding shrieks brought out Mr. D'Alenberg and his daughter, who stood shocked at the scene before them; she had sunk on the floor, and dragged the lifeless body on her lap. On their entrance she looked up with such an expression of woe and horror, that both involuntarily start-ed back; but suddenly the young Lady exclaimed,—"Good Heavens! Do I not see Louisa Hautweitzer?"

"Yes," said the other, in a tone of voice which touched every one pres-ent, "Yes, I *was* called Louisa Hautweitzer, but *now* I am *nobody*; *there* (put-ting her hand to her father's cheek) there is the author of *my being*, he exists no more, and *I* am a wretch without a name, a home, or a parent. Pray, pray, afford us one small spot of earth, bury us together!" She threw her head down on the face of the deceased, with sighs that seemed to burst her heart-strings.

Miss D'Alenberg took her hand, and addressing her father, "My dear Sir, this young Lady is an old school-fellow of mine, good, amiable, and of genteel birth, save her, pray save her from despair and death!"

The old Gentleman wanted no persuasions to serve the unhappy; he ordered his attendants to carry her into his apartment, but she clung to the body, screaming, "No one should carry her father to a stable;" that he was compelled to have the body taken there also. Ferdinand attended, and Mr. D'Alenberg ordered the priest of the village to be sent for, that he might, through his means, procure a place for the deceased to be carried to, and give some assistance to the unfortunate young woman.

On their entrance into the room the body was placed on two chairs, and Miss D'Alenberg administered wine and drops, which fortunately she had in her pocket, with the most soothing expressions of tenderness to Louisa.

The poor afflicted at length shed a torrent of tears, which greatly relieved her; kissing the hand of the young Lady, "I feel your kindness, but I am undeserving of it; my imprudence, my credulity, has destroyed my father, and made me miserable for ever!" Before any reply could be made the priest appeared, and being informed of this strange event, and assured by Mr. D'Alenberg that *he* would be answerable for every expence, the priest readily consented to receive the body at his house, and to take care of the young woman for the present: Understanding also how greatly they were crowded, he offered to accommodate Miss D'Alenberg with a bed, and as his house was but a few yards distance, and the hostess could lend her cloaks, with the permission of her father, she readily accompanied the unhappy Louisa, who seemed mechanically to follow the body of her father without being at all curious, or even heeding the conversation that had passed. Ferdinand requested leave to attend them with the servants to the house, and taking leave of them at the door, returned, as desired, to Mr. D'Alenberg.

The old Gentleman saluted him with much complacency: "This is a melancholy business," said he; "my daughter seems much interested for her young acquaintance, and indeed the poor girl's situation is very pitiable. I am sorry that a particular engagement will oblige us to leave this place tomorrow: I know not what can be done for this young woman, as her circumstances are unknown to us."

"It is most probable, Sir," answered the other, "that your daughter will gain every information that may be necessary; if she is distressed by pecuniary wants, I will most gladly contribute my share towards her relief; the heart-felt blow she has sustained, time and reason only can reconcile her to bear with patience and resignation."

Mr. D'Alenberg paid Ferdinand a compliment on his humanity, and having learned which road he was taking, seemed not a little pleased that they were going the same way. "My house (said he) is about twenty miles the other side of Stutgard; I have concluded a very advantageous marriage for my daughter, during a visit that I have been making to a friend, and am now hastening home to forward the necessary preparations: I shall, however, borrow a few hours in the morning to see what can be done for the peace and comfort of this poor orphan." Ferdinand had made the same resolution, and after partaking of a very poor supper, he retired to take possession of the bed intended for the young Lady.

He arose at an early hour, and was just drinking his coffee when he was joined by Mr. D'Alenberg. They quickly finished their breakfast, and proceeded to the priest's house, where they met the young Lady with every mark of sorrow on her countenance.

"Ah! Sir," cried she to her father, "poor Louisa is extremely ill: A physician was called in about an hour ago by the good father here, and he pronounces her to be in a violent and dangerous fever; I cannot leave her in this situation, without either a relation or a friend; I knew her, I esteemed her, in happier days, it would be inhuman to forsake her now."

"Indeed it would," answered the good Mr. D'Alenberg; "we will see what can be done to reduce this fever, and then get her removed to our house; if she is only unfortunate, we will protect her; if her conduct has been faulty, she shall be placed out of temptation, and means afforded her to atone for past errors."

"My dear, my generous father!" cried the young Lady, in a tone of exultation, "you know not how happy this kind intention of yours makes your Theresa!"

Ferdinand, who had scarcely looked at Miss D'Alenberg the preceding evening during his concern for Louisa, and who was on his entrance engaged in speaking to the priest, found his attention suddenly engaged by the animated voice behind him; he turned quick round, and met a countenance so interesting, so illumined by a glow of humanity and tenderness, that his eyes were fixed on the young Lady's face, until her blushes, and the confusion with which she turned aside from his eager gaze, made him sensible of his rudeness. It was the enthusiasm of the moment, for the sweet accents of pity and humanity vibrated to the heart of Ferdinand. Mr. D'Alenberg declared he would freely retard his journey for that day, until some information relative to the health and situation of the young woman could be rendered satisfactory to his daughter, and Ferdinand, who was not limitted for a day or two, readily offered to remain there also, as he was equally desirous, to the utmost of his abilities, to share in the pleasure of assisting the unfortunate. The priest, who happily was a man of a good and humane heart, voluntarily made an offer of his humble accommodations to their utmost extent. His sister, an ancient maiden, resided with him, and was equally good and charitable as her brother. Mr. D'Alenberg desired to be at the expence of the burial of poor Louisa's father, and Ferdinand hastily requested the physician might attend at his expence. Miss D'Alenberg was permitted to remain there, and the two Gentlemen took a walk round the village until their return to the miserable inn, where they had ordered dinner. As the Castle of Count M*** lay in the route of his companion, and the landlord was ill prepared to receive or entertain so many persons, Ferdinand sent off his servant with a cursory mention to the Count of the cause that detained him on the road for a day or two, when he should have the advantage of a large escort within a mile of his house.

Towards the evening a message from Miss D'Alenberg carried both Gentlemen to the priest's. They found her in extreme agitation; Louisa had been delirious for several hours, but by copious bleedings, and other applications, now lay more composed: "But, my dear father," added the young Lady, "you will not wonder at my emotions, when I inform you that in the height of her delirium she continually called on Count Wolfran, and in such terms as imply a degree of intimacy very incompatible with his professions to another."

"You indeed surprise me," answered the old Gentleman; "but be not too credulous, my dear Theresa, nor judge rashly on slight presumptions; I hope this young creature will get better, mean time I wish to be informed who she is, and what you know of her."

"My dear Sir," said she, "very soon after I was placed at Ausburgh, Louisa Hautweitzer came there as a boarder; her father was an officer in the Imperial service; she made a very genteel appearance, and was much esteemed throughout the Convent.—As I was her elder by at least three years, she paid me great respect and attention, which I returned by a very sincere attachment.—Four years we continued together. About that time her father came to fetch her from the Convent: I had understood her mother died when she was a child, and she appeared surprised and sorry to leave us, as she was not more than sixteen, and rather too young to conduct her father's family. We parted with regret, and she desired to correspond with me; but from that day I never heard of her, although many of the boarders made inquiries among their friends, which all proved fruitless, as we knew not where her father resided.

"I left the Convent about six months after, and frequently, when I wrote to my companions, inquired if any information had been gained of Louisa; but no one had obtained the least intelligence, and I have often thought it was a very singular circumstance. It is now near three years since I saw her, and it is certain some uncommon misfortunes must have reduced her father to that poverty which is apparent in the dress of Louisa, and the situation in which we met with them. Last night, when I accompanied her to her room, she kissed my hand with an energy that surprised me.— 'Dear Miss D'Alenberg, I deserve not the honour of your attention; I am an unfortunate wretch, a victim to my own credulity, and the baseness of a perjured man; my follies, for sure they were not crimes, yet why should I seek to soften those errors that have eventually destroyed my dear unhappy father! There, there,' cried she, in extreme agitation, 'is the climax of my miseries!'

"She fell into violent hysterics, and recovered only to experience a temporary madness which brought on a terrible fever for many hours. During this suspension of reason she raved on Count Wolfran, called him the 'destroyer of *her* peace, and the murderer of her father.' Then again she exclaimed, 'Heaven was a witness of our union; *I am, I am,* your wife!' In short, Sir, I cannot repeat every expression, nor is it necessary, enough was said to convince me that she has been very ill treated, and to determine on being perfectly acquainted with every circumstance relative to her intimacy with the Count, previous to any preparations for an event, which possibly may never take place."

"I cannot blame your resolution," answered Mr. D'Alenberg; "I am equally anxious with yourself to have this affair elucidated; if, indeed, we are deceived in the Count's character, no prospects of rank, or fortune, shall induce me to entrust him with the happiness of my Theresa." The entrance of Mrs. Dolnitz, the priest's sister, changed the subject; the Gentlemen paid her many compliments on the humanity of her brother, and her kindness to Louisa. She was a woman of plain sense, with a very good heart, and appeared to be much gratified that she had the power of being useful to a fellow creature. "This poor village (said she) affords no accommodations but in our house and the inn; you must experience great inconvenience there I have no doubt, as very few persons lodge in it but from necessity.—I am sorry we can only entertain Miss, and the sick young woman; but our power is more limitted than our wishes and good-will, for my brother is one of the best men in the world, he is truly the father of all his flock. I beg your pardon for saying so much, but when I speak of my brother I could talk for ever."

"I honour you, Madam, for your feelings," said Mr. D'Alenberg; "a good man is a theme that must please every honest mind, and you cannot give us a better eulogium on your *own* character, than by your praises of a worthy brother. Heaven has conducted us to this spot, I trust, for our mutual advantage."——Ferdinand *spoke* little, but his eyes said a great deal, and his heart sympathized in every word of Mr. D'Alenberg's. Mr. Dolnitz and the physician soon after joined them; the latter had found his patient more calm, and the extreme violence of the fever abated. They consulted on proper measures for the interment of the deceased, when Louisa was more composed to speak on the subject. Mr. D'Alenberg drew the physician aside, Miss Theresa returned to the sick chamber: Ferdinand there-

fore entered into a conversation with Mr. Dolnitz, whose modest and unreserved manners, charity without ostentation, and beneficence without
a hope of reward, from a very moderate income, denoted real piety and
goodness of heart. When the others joined them, Theresa's father drawing a purse from his pocket, put it into the hands of Mr. Dolnitz, saying at
the same time, "My worthy Sir, you must permit me to share with you in
your charitable attentions. Be not offended, if, knowing that your income
is very inadequate to the benevolence of your disposition, I entreat you to
disburse this money in whatever manner you please for the advantage of
those persons now in your house, or any others deserving or wanting your
donations."

"I will not decline the office of your almoner, Sir," replied Mr. Dolnitz,
respectfully; "but you must permit me to be accountable to you for the
disbursements; on no other condition can I receive the trust."

"It *must* be as you please," answered the other. The physician, who
lived about two miles from the village, finding the strangers were persons
of consequence, offered the two Gentlemen beds at his house, but they
declined the civility; for although their accommodations were extremely
indifferent, yet, as they were permitted to consider themselves at home in
the house of Mr. Dolnitz, they were very well reconciled to sleep at the
inn.

Ferdinand, indeed, began to consider himself as a useless person; the
generosity of Mr. D'Alenberg left but little for him to do, and having no
other interests but those of humanity towards the unfortunate Louisa, and
as it appeared very probable that the others would be personally concerned
in the events of her story, he was fearful it would betray rather an unwarrantable curiosity, than a concern for the melancholy objects that had at
first engaged his attention, if he remained at the village. He was revolving this in his mind, and consequently looked very thoughtful, which Mr.
D'Alenberg observing, said, "Are you not well, Sir, or has any thing particularly occurred to give you pain?" The other recovering from his reverie by
this address, frankly confessed what had been his ideas, and given him that
momentary thoughtfulness.

Pleased with his ingenuousness, the old Gentleman said, "I know not
the nature of your engagements, or whether you are at liberty to spare us
your company. If a day or two will not break in upon other plans, I do assure you, Sir, that you will make me very particularly happy, by obliging me
with your conversation and residence here for the *short time I hope*, that I
shall find it requisite to remain."

"You do me honour, Sir," replied he, "by the request, which will be a gratification to myself I have not the resolution to decline, and must trust to the kindness of a friend to allow me." They refused an invitation to supper, and returned to the inn, where Ferdinand gave a slight account of himself, as the brother of Count Rhodophil, and an officer in the Imperial service, now going to a friend, who was also about to join the army.

Mr. D'Alenberg said, he was a widower with this only daughter, and a fortune sufficient for all *their* moderate demands, with a surplus for the service of the unfortunate.—"My daughter (said he) has chiefly resided in a Convent, until I thought her age and understanding were mature enough to preside at my table with ease and dignity to herself, and satisfaction to me. I have reason to be perfectly satisfied, and I must think very highly of the man to whom I would entrust the happiness of such a daughter; you have heard enough to understand, that in Count Wolfran I thought such a man had met my wishes. I cannot easily relinquish my hope; his external appearance was decidedly in his favour. The friend, at whose house we met, gave him the highest character, and on his judgment and word, I think, I can place implicit confidence. The exclamations uttered by this young woman in her delirium certainly give rise to unfavourable conjectures, and if on an investigation I discover such circumstances as must impede his marriage with Theresa, I confess to you that it will give me an infinite deal of sorrow, not only because it is an advantageous settlement, but for the honour of human nature I shall regret, that such an exterior, so much understanding, and so many plausible, and apparently, so many *good* qualities should cover a depraved heart."

"Justice demands an impartial and an unprejudiced hearing on both sides," replied Ferdinand, "before we should venture to condemn any person. If Louisa recovers sufficiently to disclose her situation, you will then, in some measure, be enabled to judge what degree of credit may be allowed to her, and give the Count an opportunity to vindicate his own character, if unjustly accused. Miss D'Alenberg appears to be a treasure no common mind can deserve; her beauty, which I believe is superior to most of her sex, I have scarcely remarked, for the heavenly goodness, and animated compassion, she has displayed towards a distressed and unfortunate young woman proves the excellence of her disposition, and intitles her to equal admiration and respect. Heaven forbid that such a mind should not meet with its kindred heart when united for life!"

The old Gentleman, charmed with the energy of Ferdinand's expressions, and delighted with the delicate praise bestowed on his child, felt a lively interest in his behalf, and ventured to inquire more minutely into his situation and prospects. Among other things he said, with a smile, "I do not suppose *you* are married." Ferdinand started; his whole frame was agitated; he attempted to answer, but his faltering tongue was incapable of uttering a word. Mr. D'Alenberg was surprised and concerned: "I beg your pardon (said he) if my impertinent curiosity has given you pain; be assured that I meant no offence, you will therefore confer an obligation on me, by obliterating from your memory the question I incautiously asked."

Ferdinand sensibly felt the politeness of Mr. D'Alenberg, and gladly availed himself of it for the present. The supposition had recalled many painful ideas, which he endeavoured to repress, and with a half-smothered sigh, that did not pass unobserved, he bowed, saying, "You are very obliging, Sir; there are certain questions which sometimes cannot be answered satisfactorily, and particular situations which cannot be explained, without entering into details tedious and uninteresting to a stranger. As a parent of such a daughter you must doubtless be exceedingly uneasy, until the expressions that fell from Louisa are explained to your satisfaction.—A short time, I hope, will elucidate them, for, if she is an ingenuous character, the generous humanity of Miss D'Alenberg will unlock her heart to repose a confidence in that young Lady, otherwise my conjectures will be less favourable of her than they now are."

"My opinion coincides with yours," answered the other, "and tomorrow, I think, will put an end to a suspense that I own gives me an infinity of concern." The evening passed in conversing on a variety of subjects, and when they separated for the night, each Gentleman retired with an increased good opinion of the other, and each internally was desirous of a more intimate acquaintance.

The morning came, and they had scarcely exchanged the customary salutations before a message came from Miss D'Alenberg, requesting the presence of her father, and from the messenger they learned that Louisa was much recovered.

As Ferdinand was not, nor indeed expected to be, included in the invitation to Mr. D'Alenberg, he was preparing to leave the room, after desiring his respects to the young Lady.

"How!" said the old Gentleman, "will you not accompany me?"

"Undoubtedly, Sir, if you wish me to do so. I am only apprehensive of being an intruder."

"No, no," replied the other, "by no means, we have no secrets; if Count Wolfran is worthy of my daughter, it is for his honour that you should know it; if on the contrary he proves to be a worthless character, it is equally proper that he should be exposed; therefore I beg you will go with me." Ferdinand readily assented; they quickly dispatched their breakfast, and set off for the house of Mr. Dolnitz.

They were received by the good Lady of the house with kindness and complacency.—She gave a very favourable account of her patient, the violence of her disorder was abated, and there was less turbulence in her expressions of grief.—"The consolatory attentions of Miss your daughter," said Mrs. Dolnitz to the old Gentleman, "has greatly aided the doctor's prescriptions, perhaps has been of more real service, as it appears the disorder of the body was occasioned by the emotions of the mind."

The entrance of the young Lady interrupted Mrs. Dolnitz, and she immediately withdrew. Miss D'Alenberg seemed a little embarrassed at the presence of Ferdinand, which he observed, and politely rose to leave the room.—"Stay one moment," cried Mr. D'Alenberg. "Tell me, Theresa, in two words, what am I to think of Count Wolfran?"

"As of a man unworthy of your notice, whose crimes disgrace his rank and character. I speak on good grounds, my dear Sir (added she;) Providence has preserved your daughter from infamy and wretchedness."

"Good Heavens!" exclaimed the Father, "can such an exterior, such an apparently polished mind, cover a depraved heart!"

"Yes," replied she, with some emotion, "his person and accomplishments are the superficial covering to veil the blackest designs, the most abandoned and selfish passions. The poor Louisa is a melancholy victim to his baseness, nor is she the only one; but I am writing down her story, which may be perused at leisure. What I have now to request is, that you will send off a servant with a few lines to Count Wolfran, just to say, 'that your daughter, having thoroughly investigated his character, declines, in the most decided manner, the favour he intended her of a *hand*, without a *heart*, or a *name*, to bestow.' Do not add another word, my dear father, his conscience will speak all the rest that may be necessary."

"I will comply with your wishes," answered Mr. D'Alenberg; "my dear Theresa, you are a heroine."

"No," said she, with a faint smile, "it requires no heroism to give up a man one despises. Count Wolfran is not the man a sensible mind can regret. When once the object we had been taught to esteem through false lights, is proved to be a man capable of the vilest duplicity, and most atrocious wickedness, our detestation and contempt must rise in proportion to the deception of our senses, and the heart can endure but little pain in shutting out such an object for ever."

She instantly changed the subject, seeing both Gentlemen were preparing to speak in admiration of her sentiments. She understood the expression of their eyes, therefore assuming a supplicating air, "My dear Sir," said she, "as my obligations to the unfortunate Louisa are infinite, as she is deprived of every friend, and in want of every necessary, though legally entitled to rank and fortune, I trust, you will not refuse to permit your Theresa to be her comforter and friend, to offer her an asylum in your house from the machinations of a base enemy."

"Undoubtedly, my dear girl, you are at liberty to make what offers you please, both for me and yourself; I will confirm them all, and shall look up with gratitude to Heaven for this signal preservation of my child from dishonour and misery."

Mr. Dolnitz now joined them, and was happy to hear of the favourable change in Louisa's fever. "Violent attacks (said he) have generally a speedy termination, and I rejoice that the event has turned in her favour." "I flatter myself," said Miss D'Alenberg, "that our joint attentions will quickly restore her, and that in a day or two we shall be able to take her in a carriage by easy stages to my father's house." After spending three hours in the house of the good priest, the Gentlemen returned to the inn: Here Ferdinand appeared to be under some degree of inquietude, which the old Gentleman remarked, and asked the cause of.

"I confess to you, Sir," answered the other, "that I feel the warmest admiration at the conduct of your daughter, and I am greatly interested for the unhappy Louisa. I am sensible of the honour and pleasure of your conversation; but I am under engagements to meet a friend, whose mind, from some untoward incidents, is but little calculated to bear disappointment, or to be left to its own reflections: Mortified as I am for the necessity which obliges me to leave you, I should not, however, forgive myself if I gave pain to my friend."

"Then you must leave me?" asked Mr. D'Alenberg.

"Indeed I must," replied Ferdinand,—"because it appears you will unavoidably remain here two or three days, and as I dare not intrude so long on the kindness of a friend, the sooner I leave you the better, as my regret to part from you must hourly increase."

"You are a worthy young man," returned Mr. D'Alenberg, "and it is no compliment to say, that I shall part from you with very great reluctance.

"After the deception I have lately met with, you could not wonder if I shut the door of my heart, afraid of entertaining another delusive guest; but I trust that I have not lost my charity, though my confidence may be more guarded. A countenance like your's is a letter of recommendation, and I do assure you, that you will do me a very particular pleasure, if you continue in this country, by bringing your friend in your hand, and insure to him a welcome reception at my house, on your account."

Ferdinand was not backward in his acknowledgments for this kindness, and having now broken the ice, gave orders for his departure immediately after dinner. At Mr. D'Alenberg's request he promised to write to him before his departure for Vienna, if he could not pay him a visit; and the former assured Ferdinand, that if the story of Louisa was of a fit nature to be communicated, he should certainly receive a transcript of it from him. "My daughter (added he) will be surprised and disappointed, when informed of your departure without taking leave."

"Be so good, Sir," said Ferdinand, "to make my best respects to Miss D'Alenberg; I have had so little opportunity of recommending myself to her notice, that I am not vain enough to believe my departure can for a moment engage her attention; but of *her* I shall ever think, with pleasure, admiration and respect. My best wishes also attend the unfortunate young Lady, she so humanely protects; to offer any pecuniary assistance would be an insult to her goodness, and your benevolence; but if on any future occasion either my purse, or personal services, can be useful, command me as freely, Sir, as you would do your own son."

"By Heaven!" exclaimed Mr. D'Alenberg, "I wish you *was my son*; but———."

"You do me infinite honour, Sir," said Ferdinand, interrupting him; "I hope you will find a man *deserving* of the appellation, and whoever he is, his destiny will be enviable, because he will be the happiest of mankind;" then rising from his seat, he inquired if his horse was ready? and being informed it waited for him at the door, he took a hasty, but an affectionate, leave of Mr. D'Alenberg, and followed by his good wishes, set off full speed for the Castle of Count M***.

CHAPTER X.

HE arrived at the Castle without any accident, and was joyfully received by his friend. "I began to complain of you," said the Count; "I am a selfish mortal it is true, for, as I heard from the servant you kindly sent forward, that you were engaged in an affair of distress and sickness, knowing the benevolence and sympathy of your heart, I ought not to have desired to monopolize such a disposition to myself."

"Indeed," replied Ferdinand, "you do me more credit than I deserve: I was merely a spectator of the benevolence of others, without even presuming to offer my mite when I left the unfortunate young woman you have been told of. I left her, indeed, in much better hands, and feeling myself useless, when I understood she was out of danger, I hastened away; though

I confess to you that I left hearts so congenial to my own, and I will say, to yours also, that I lamented the distance which seems placed between us."

At the Count's request he related the scenes already described, and mentioned the characters with esteem and respect.—"It is a singular affair," observed the Count, when he had finished his narration, "and a most providential meeting between the D'Alenberg family and Louisa. I have heard often of Count Wolfran before my seclusion from the world, he was then a very young and a very gay man, he can be but little turned of thirty now. I remember I once saw him, and thought him a most elegant figure."

"So much the worse," said Ferdinand, warmly, "since it is beyond a doubt that he is a villain, and would, most probably, but for this fortunate discovery, have ruined the happiness of a most lovely and amiable young Lady. I hope *I* shall never see him; but come, my dear Count (added he, in a quick tone) tell me in what manner you have been received coming from death to life, and in what way you found all your affairs?"

The Count told him he had found but little difficulty in being acknowledged by his friends, whom he had amused with an account that he had been travelling, under a borrowed name, to avoid trouble, and had resided both in London and Paris as a private man, until he was tired of the frolic.

This story, he said, had gained credit, and, as it was supposed he did not live without a companion, he had been rallied on his English and Parisian Ladies, which he bore tolerably well, and had therefore silenced curiosity by giving way to their own conjectures.

As to his estates, he found them in perfect good order, and was so well satisfied with his good old steward, Mr. Duclos, that he had presented him with a pretty little estate, and made him independent for life. "I have still enough (said he) I trust, to satisfy the demands of gratitude and friendship, and sufficient in my own power to make the man I esteem superior to receiving the narrow bounty of selfish, contracted hearts, who are incapable of doing justice to virtues they know not how to estimate, because no such inhabits their own bosoms.

"The variety of occupations in which I have been engaged," continued he, "since my arrival here, has given a diversity to my thoughts, very favourable towards recovering that tranquillized state of mind I wish for. Happiness is fled like a vision of the brain; but when I remember what I *have* been, and what I am *now*, I should be ungrateful to Providence if I was not thankful for the good, and submit to bear the evil with patience and resignation."

Ferdinand was delighted with the rationality of the Count's sentiments, and presaged much future contentment to a mind capable of such proper discrimination. His friend told him, "that having many accounts to settle, and leases to renew, he apprehended it would be at least a week or ten days before he could conveniently leave the country. Mean time (added he) command here as myself, the carriage, horses and servants, are your's. Do not confine yourself, but make a circuit round the environs of the Castle, you will find amusement and information.—Follow my example, engage your ideas in a continual variety that you may get out of yourself, and avoid a train of unpleasant reflections."

Ferdinand followed the Count's advice, and for three or four days, when the other was engaged with his steward and tenants, he was continually on horseback; but, alas! happiness is not dependant on exterior or local circumstances; whilst his eyes wandered over hills and dales, mountains and glens, his *mind's* eye had other objects in view, and he found it a vain attempt to turn his thoughts on the beauties of nature, whilst the barbed arrow still rankled in his bosom, and the remembrance of past events, of Claudina, his brother, and other recent occurrences, obtruded on his memory. On the contrary, without society, and at liberty to "indulge meditation even to madness," he returned always fatigued in body, and distressed in mind.

The fifth day the weather was bad, and he could not take his accustomed rides; the morning, his friend being busy, he passed in the library, but his temper took its colouring from the weather, and when he entered the dining parlour, the Count was extremely concerned to see his features clouded with melancholy, and all the marks of a deep dejection. "Are you not well," said he, hastily.

"I am certainly not ill," replied Ferdinand; "that is, I have no bodily complaints; but I feel a weight on my spirits which I cannot shake off."

"Ah! my friend," returned the Count, "this inactive life ill agrees with a discontented mind. I am sensible that the present composure of mine is but temporary: I can easily allow for *your* feelings, and am provoked that my haste to finish all my affairs here, compels me to leave you so much alone. In our present state of mind (added he, with a faint smile) we are not fit to be trusted alone; company and active employments suit us much better than solitude."

Ferdinand was about to reply, when a servant entered with a packet for him; being a stranger to the hand, he opened it hastily, and saw the name of D'Alenberg. "Ah!" cried he, "here is a large packet from Mr. D'Alenberg; from its bulk I dare say it contains the history of the poor Louisa."

"You will then have something to amuse, or at least to engage your attention (said the Count) and I am glad of it, as I am obliged to meet two persons for an hour or two after dinner." Ferdinand's impatience, and this friend's engagement, caused them to make a hasty meal, which, when finished, the former retired to the library, and perused the following letter:

MR. D'ALENBERG TO MR. FERDINAND RENAUD.

"I do not forget, my young friend, that you seemed to feel an interest in the late occurrences that fell under your eye; and you impressed me with too favourable an opinion of your heart to doubt of your being anxious for an explanation of such circumstances relative to Louisa, as materially concerned the peace of my Theresa and her father. I have full leave to acquaint you with every particular of the villainous treatment the much-injured young woman has experienced from the most abandoned of men: Crimes like his cannot go unpunished, and it shall not be my fault if the world does not brand him as a villain. I bow with reverence to that Being, whose benign hand conducted us to the spot where the late unfortunate Mr. Hautweitzer breathed his last sigh; had it pleased Heaven to have prolonged his existence to this hour, that he might have seen his child under my protection, the last pang of nature had been stripped of half its terrors; but to regret is useless, it is our duty to think *all is as it should be*. To-morrow we propose to leave this place; our poor invalid thinks she is capable of taking the journey. This morning her worthy father was consigned to the grave; I trust he exists in happier regions.

"The good Dolnitz shall not be forgotten; he and his sister have *hearts*, and good ones too; it is the duty of those that have *power* to enable such persons to gratify their generous humane feelings. You know my address; I again repeat my wishes to see you and your friend; if this lays not in the chapter of possibilities *at present*, I request to hear from you.

"Remember, young man, that you have opened a fresh account; once more I feel an esteem, and place a confidence on a slender knowledge: Old age ought to be wary and circumspect, particularly when deception has so lately wounded an unsuspecting heart; but I have not learned the ungenerous maxims of the world, nor, because I have unfortunately been deceived by a worthless wretch, suspect each man to be a villain.—*You*, I hope, will justify my candour, and when I tell you that you possess my regards, will, by your subsequent conduct, give me credit with myself for my discernment.

"To see you will give me pleasure. To hear you are well and happy is the next best satisfaction you can convey to me; for well *I see*, and *grieve* to see, that you are now *unhappy*: But if the cause originates from no vice or folly of your own, take comfort, *all* may yet be well. My respects to your friend, I know him only by *name*, that speaks in his favour; I should be glad to know more of him. My daughter desires her compliments: Louisa scarcely remembers having seen you, but she is grateful for your attentions. Adieu, my young friend, remember my claims upon you.

C. D'ALENBERG."

This letter was very gratifying to Ferdinand; but he looked it hastily over, being impatient to read the story of Louisa, which was thus prefaced:

"By permission of her friend, and at the request of her father, Miss D'Alenberg sends this transcript of Louisa's misfortunes, in her own words, to Mr. Ferdinand Renaud."

END OF VOLUME II.

The Mysterious Warning

Volume III

MYSTERIOUS WARNING.

CHAPTER I.

MY father was descended from a younger branch of a Noble family: He lost his parents before he attained the age of manhood, and found his commission all his patrimony, and his sword his only friend. He conducted himself so properly in the management of both, that a Captain's commission was his reward at the age of two and twenty.

During the suspension of the next campaign, he went to Strasburg to visit a very distant relation, who had thought proper to recognize him when he was in a situation to provide for himself. With this old gentleman he staid some time, and unfortunately lost his heart to a very amiable young woman, who had every claim to admiration but *one*. That *trifling* deficiency in my *father's* eye, though of great magnitude in the estimation of wiser and more prudent men, was the want of fortune. My father, who had been bred up in the school of liberality, who had no selfish considerations, and paid but little attention to prudential maxims, no sooner discovered that his heart was irrevocably fixed, and that the lady's character justified his pretensions, than he openly avowed his partiality, and sought to gain her favour. In vain his relation remonstrated, soothed, allured, and threatened. He was master of himself—of his own affections—despised such paltry objections as the want of money; persisted in his endeavours to gain the lady—was successful—was transported at his promised *eternal happiness*, and laid up for himself a *"load of cares."*

Reprobated by his mercenary relation, he married, and carried his wife to the quarters where his duty called him. For a time, he was as happy as a man could be, who, in possessing a darling object, hourly expected to be torn from her. It happened, before that dreaded period arrived, peace was concluded on between the contending powers; and he had the supreme delight of remaining with the object of his affections—of looking forward to an increase of family, but had forgot, in the hour of exultation, that he was now reduced to half-pay.

The first moment this blow struck on his heart, was when some preparations were thought necessary for the accommodation of his wife. Alas! then, and not 'till then, did it occur to him, how insufficient the poor pittance he possessed would be to support the unavoidable expences coming upon him. What he could retrench from his own little accustomed indulgencies, he did, and provided, as well as it was possible, for the hour which brought me into the world, and eventually proved the death of a parent I have ever revered, though I never beheld her.

From the day which gave me birth, although she seemed to recover as well as most women do in the like situation, and at the expiration of a proper time, resumed her family employments: whether she caught cold, had any inward complaints or uneasiness of mind; whatever was the cause, I know not, but she fell into a rapid decline, and her pure spirit fled to Heaven five months after she had given me life.

'Tis needless to repeat my father's sufferings; a feeling heart may conceive them; when time and necessity compelled him to struggle with his grief, and remember the pledge his darling wife had left him, he resolved to retire into a distant part of the country, that he might devote his whole time to the care of his child. With this dear father I past my life, until near twelve years of age; and to his unwearied care, I owe *more* than life, in the good and virtuous principles he instilled into my mind. Unhappily he was but little acquainted with mankind;—bred up in the school of adversity, with a narrow income, and few connexions, his spirit had kept him from engaging in habits of company and expence, which he knew his small income could not support; and therefore he had avoided society, and mixed but very seldom among young men of his age and rank, consequently knew but little of their vices, or general profligacy.

I had nearly completed my twelfth year, when my father one day told me, that tho' it would be almost death to him to part with me; yet it was his duty to prefer my interest to his own satisfaction. He had lived in obscurity, and, with the most rigid economy, that he might save a sum sufficient to pay for my pension in a convent for two or three years, that my education might be completed. "The time is now come," said he, "when my intention must take place; I am again called upon in the service of my country; I have inquired for a situation where I can entrust the only treasure Heaven has given me; and where you will acquire such accomplishments and female knowledge, as must be necessary for your future provision."

I shall not dwell on the sorrow which pervaded our bosoms, when the hour came that annihilated all my happiness for ever.—Our little humble dwelling was disposed of; my good old nurse, who had been our only domestic, my father got received into a hospital; and I accompanied him to that convent, where I most fortunately was distinguished by the friendship of Miss D'Alenberg.

I pass over the years I resided in the convent, as nothing material took place in my affairs, until I was one day suddenly called from the refectory, and informed my father waited for me in the parlour. Surprise and joy almost overcame my senses; I flew to my dear parent, and shed tears of unbounded transport; his eyes also overflowed. After the first expressions of joy were a little abated, he told me, he had quitted the army, was arrived to take me from the convent, and desired I would be prepared to quit it the following morning, when he should call and settle for my pension.

I cannot even now forget, nor yet account for, the universal tremor which seized me when I heard of my father's intention: I had many agreeable companions; I loved Miss D'Alenberg, and was honoured with her friendship, except which, I had nothing to regret: And surely my affection for her bore no proportion to the duty and love I owed to my father: Strange, therefore, that I should be shocked—should feel a repugnance, and even horror, at the thoughts of quitting the convent with a parent so dear to me. Alas! it was too sure a presentiment of all the evils that awaited me, and the moment when I left that peaceful abode, was the last of my tranquillity. When I gave my last embrace to my loved Theresa, and the gates closed between us, I gave a faint shriek, and threw myself back in the chaise more than half dead.

My kind, my considerate father, gave way to the first emotions of my grief, and soothed me with so much tenderness, praising the sensibility of my heart. (Ah! he knew not then how dearly we should pay for, how bitterly we should deplore, that fatal sensibility) that I grew ashamed of indulging a sorrow that reproached me with ingratitude to so good a parent. This consideration assisted me in the recovery of more composure, and at length enabled me to recollect our situation, and to ask, where we were going to reside? My dear father heaved a deep sigh.

"I will not attempt to deceive you, my dear Louisa; I can no longer afford to pay for your pension; an unfortunate circumstance has compelled me to leave the service of the Emperor, and obliges me to seek a situation in the army of another Prince; I might have left you ignorant of this compulsatory arrangement; I might have suffered your pension to have run on for another year; but my dear girl, your father cannot stoop to even a negative imposition, and in the incertitude of the success my present plan may lead to, I could not subject you to receive obligations, to be indebted for your support, whilst I had a doubt upon my mind that I might possibly fail in the power of making the just returns due for your maintenance.

"I grieve only for you, my child; but I trust Heaven will give you strength of mind to encounter with the evils of poverty, when unaccompanied with guilt or remorse. I have sought for a retirement where you may not be absolutely excluded from society, but where you may live unknown, and free from observation, without the danger of being subjected to the triumph of insolent prosperity over indigent merit. Louisa, you was nursed in obscurity; to that obscurity you must return. I had flattered myself with far better hopes for you; but those are no more, and we must submit to the fate that controuls us: All that remains is, to bear adverse fortune with patience and fortitude, than we are superior to the evils that befal us.

"You are young, my child, to hear and profit by a lesson so painful to practise as adversity; but you have good sense; you are the daughter of a soldier, and a *man of honour.*" My father pronounced these last words with a peculiar emphasis, and with an animated countenance, that surprised and interested me; but I expressed no curiosity, and contented myself with assuring him, that "my mind should be directed by his precepts, and my conduct deserve his approbation." My answer pleased him, and he endeavoured to rally his spirits, by giving a cheerful turn to our conversation.

We arrived at length to our place of destination, a very small village in the vicinity of Heilbron, romantically and beautifully situated. At the extremity of a few scattered houses, was the residence of a good priest, inhabited by himself, his mother, and a peasant girl as a servant: We were expected, and therefore received with kindness. To one accustomed from childhood to retirement, this solitude had nothing in it so frightful as to create terror or disgust. I was charmed with the mildness, the placid content that pervaded the countenance of my new friends, and not only strove to *appear* pleased, but really *felt* a degree of pleasure in my mind, that I might hope to have cheerful companions. My father watched my looks with visible anxiety; and when he saw me enter into conversation with a lively unembarrassed air, I observed the instantaneous effect it had upon him: Every feature was illumined with satisfaction; he seemed as if a weight had been removed, which had before heavily oppressed his spirits, and from which he had scarcely an expectation of being freed.

In the evening, when we were for a few minutes alone, he asked me, "if I could reconcile myself to reside with the Abbe Bouville and his mother?" I answered in the affirmative, without the least hesitation. He affectionately embraced me:—"Then, my dearest girl, more than half of my sorrows are done away, and I will no longer conceal my situation from you. A general officer, whose arrogance far exceeded his rank, and whose fortune enabled him to support an appearance, that threw every one else at a distance from him by the superiority he assumed. This meanly proud man affected to treat his inferiors in rank and fortune with a supercilious contempt that was insupportable. It happened, that on a particular service, I was subjected to his command; I did my duty, but scorned to flatter his pride by mean flatteries or condescensions unbecoming my character. Provoked, I believe, by my conduct, yet unable to complain of any deficiencies in the services he commanded, he one day gave me three contradictory orders, before I had time to perform either, and consequently I was obliged to apply to him in person, for an explanation of the orders delivered to me.

"The moment I appealed to him, he flew into a violent rage, and accused me of disobeying command. Irritated as I was, I yet suppressed my feelings, and respectfully, though firmly, represented the impossibility of obeying orders which had been in the same instant contradicted by others entirely opposite. He threw himself into a paroxism of rage, and insulted me in a manner beyond all endurance: My indignation, hardly repressed, now burst forth—I defended my conduct, as became a man of spirit, and retorted upon him for his frivolous and indeterminate proceedings. In short, he bore hard upon me—threw me off my guard—and I vented some menacing expressions, which were instantly caught hold of. I was ordered into custody; shortly afterwards brought to a court-martial, and dismissed from the service for 'disobedience of orders, and insulting my commanding officer.'

"I heard the sentence with a disdainful silence. But as soon as I had obtained my liberty, I sent a challenge to my ungenerous enemy. I have no doubt but that he expected it; for on the breaking up of the court, he had set off to other quarters, to 'confer,' as he gave out with other general officers respecting a secret expedition. I was persuaded, by the whole corps, to present a petition to the Emperor; but my spirit rose repugnant to the idea of a *petition.* I therefore wrote a plain narrative of facts, which I sent to my royal master, and quitted the army immediately.

"Alas! my child, when the hurry of tumultuous and indignant passions had subsided, your image swam across my sight; and how was my Louisa to be supported? The first idea that occurred to my reason. What my feelings were, I will not describe. Providence graciously recalled to my mind the Abbe Bouville, whom I had known in early days, and on whose benevolence and wisdom I thought I might repose confidence. I knew his residence, although I had not visited him in his retirement; nor indeed was then certain of his existence, but to seek him, was my only resource; most fortunately I found him; the man my heart could be laid open to, and from whose piety and goodness I could derive comfort. The result of our conference was my journey to the convent; the rest you know; and now, my dear child, here you may reside in safety, whilst I seek in another service that fame, and that recompense, of which I have been unjustly deprived."

CHAPTER II.

THUS my father finished the painful recital of his injuries, and I assured him of my perfect sensibility of his affectionate cares for me, and my resolution to improve my small talents, that I might be enabled to provide for my own maintenance, without being a burthen on so good a father. It would be tiresome to repeat our conversations that evening when he gave me to the care of his good friends. As he had not determined what Prince he should apply to, his journey was undertaken without being able to point out for us any channel of information, until we could hear from himself. The hour of separation was dreadful; but I sought to acquire fortitude, that my father might not have my sufferings to contend with, added to his own.

The next day he left us. It was three weeks before we heard from him, and learnt, he was in the service of the King of Poland. Four months past in a quiet uniform manner, that had tranquillized my mind; and as we had heard several times from my father, whose spirits appeared to return with a ray of hope, from the nature of his employment, my mind naturally partook of the complexion of his, and I grew cheerful and easy, in proportion as his letters breathed content and returning vivacity.

It was about this period when I had been near five months with the good Bouvilles, when we heard that a small hunting seat, situated in a most beautiful park about two miles from the village, was repairing for the reception of a young nobleman, just returning from his travels. This information seemed perfectly immaterial to me; nor had I the least curiosity respecting our neighbour, when told of his arrival.

One morning, coming out of my little apartment, which was in the garden, and entering the parlour, I saw a very genteel young man talking to the Abbe with earnestness; I retired in confusion, muttering some trifling apology; but before I had got three steps from the door, the stranger was at my side; taking my hand respectfully, he entreated my return, protesting he would leave the house instantly, if his presence had driven me from the room. I was so extremely confused, that unable to utter a word, I suffered him to lead me quietly back, and seat me in a chair, before I could recollect myself to make any return to a hundred polite things, that he addressed to me with an astonishing rapidity. After some time, however, I recovered, and on the entrance of Madame Bouville, ventured to join in the conversation. I was soon informed this gentleman was the young Count Wolfran, our neighbour. He made an extreme long visit, and departed with visible reluctance.

The effect that his figure, his compliments, and extreme attention, had upon a young and susceptible heart like mine, need not to be described. A thousand new ideas broke in upon my mind; I passed the night sleepless, and arose without that cheerfulness natural to my disposition. When we met at breakfast, the conversation turned upon our neighbour. The Abbe informed me, that in a hunting party the day before the Count's visit, some of his domestics had greatly injured a small enclosure belonging to the good father, of which he had sent notice to the Count, and which had brought him the preceding day to the house, with a view of persuading the Abbe to part with this field, as it lay contiguous to his grounds. This requisition the other had resisted, and they were growing warm in the argument, when I unhappily broke in upon them, and not another word was said on the subject.

I apologized for interrupting them; my friend said he was much obliged to me; for, added he, smiling, as I had just given my negative in a very decided manner, and he neither renewed the proposition, nor appeared to be displeased when he took leave. I hope I shall hear no more of it. The second day after this, the Count made his appearance, attended by a servant with some game, which he entreated Madame Bouville's acceptance of in terms so friendly and persuasive, that she was obliged, however reluctantly, to receive his presents, and of course to pay him attention and respect.

From that day, he never neglected a single one of making us a visit; and his extreme politeness to me grew so very marked, that the good Abbe thought it requisite to have some conversation with me relative to his attentions. And here let me, with confusion, acknowledge my own weakness and folly. I had suffered my eye to forerun my judgment; was already greatly prejudiced in favour of the Count; and I believe had but too plainly discovered these favourable sentiments towards him, by my unguarded looks and behaviour. The good Abbe soon discovered the secret of my heart, which afforded him no satisfaction, because he was apprehensive of the consequences. He explained the nature of his sentiments to me very freely, but with great delicacy. Alas! how unequal was the dictates of prudence, or the cautious advice of age, to combat with a growing partiality in a young mind, a stranger to the world, and entangled by the dangerous superficial advantages of person, and that softness, that insinuating tenderness, which so easily makes its way into an unsuspecting bosom.

I heard my friend, indeed, with respect, but not with conviction, and the first moment that I saw the Count again, one look, one tender expression, overthrew all the poor Abbe's arguments, and confirmed the seducer's power over my heart. My prudent guardians saw too plainly the danger of my situation, and despairing of gaining any ascendancy over me, they one day took an opportunity of an early visit, when I was not in the way to talk to *him*, in a manner they conceived to be their duty, and to request that he would refrain from any future visits.

He was too closely prest to allow of any disguise or subterfuge, and was at length driven to own his attachment to me in very unequivocal terms. He said, "that he had a small independency from his father securely settled. He had also great expectations from a relation, exceeding old, whose death might daily be expected, besides what he must enjoy hereafter as his paternal fortune; but that he was sensible his father must, and would, disapprove of his marriage with so young a person as Miss Hautweitzer, who, however beautiful and accomplished, was deficient in those requisites which parents too generally looked upon as absolutely essential in a union for life. His own sentiments were far more liberal: Convinced that he should possess a very handsome fortune in his own right, he was perfectly indifferent to the want of it in a person from whom he was to derive his future happiness, which could not be dependent on money. He besought the Abbe's interest with me; said, that he would immediately write to his father of his intentions, and ask his consent, a compliment certainly due to him, but from which he frankly owned he expected nothing agreeable to his wishes, knowing too well the disposition of his father in such matters. However, be the event what it might, it should make no alteration in his sentiments; his present income would be sufficient for competency and happiness; his paternal fortune could not be alienated from him."

All this, and much more, he urged to the Abbe and Madam Bouville; and though their judgment disapproved of a further intimacy, without the sanction of our parents, yet so seducive were his persuasions, so irresistible his solicitations, that if not convinced, they were at least *overborne* by his eloquence, and at length gave a tacit permission to his visits, because they had not resolution to deny him.

This great point gained: He forgot not to make his advantages with me on the open and candid declarations he had made to my friends; whilst I, young and unsuspecting, gloried in the affection of a man so amiable and so disinterested, and gave up my heart without reserve, to the indulgence of passion, for an object so worthy. The Abbe, however, was not quite easy; he felt himself responsible to his friend for the honour and happiness of the child committed to his care; and although the prospect was fascinating, and such as he conceived must be for my interest; yet knowing my father's high notions of honour, he was very doubtful that his approbation to our union would not be obtained, if the Count's father refused his consent. He therefore wrote to my beloved parent on the subject; unhappily this letter never reached him, as he had been ordered on duty to a different part of the country.

Mean time, the Count continued his assiduities to me, and daily insinuated himself more into the favourable opinion of my friends. At this period, the good Madame Bouville caught a violent cold, by being out too late one evening in her garden, when the damps arose imperceptibly round her; the consequence was, a violent rheumatic and inflammatory fever, which in nine days terminated a life that had been uniformly good, pious and charitable.

The poor Abbe felt this stroke most severely; he had lost a parent and a friend,—his own health had been always delicate, and subject to frequent asthmatic spasms; he was of a remarkable studious and retired disposition, but ill calculated to struggle with the common affairs of life in a domestic way, in which he was as unknowing as a child.—My situation with him was another subject of distress, without a companion or an adviser, no female acquaintance to countenance me, alone in the house with him, visited by a young man of fashion avowedly my lover.—What an improper, a dangerous situation!—When the last duties were paid to the respectable woman we had lost, he wrote again to my father, and ventured to hint to me before the Count, that as there certainly was an impropriety in my residence there, he conceived it would be most for my advantage in every sense of the word, to retire into a convent, until some arrangement should be concluded upon by my father.

This opinion was a thunder stroke to us both; so infatuated was I by my fatal passion, that it superseded every sense of decorum and propriety, and I considered only the pangs I must feel in being separated from my lover. After a few moments silence, the Count requested the Abbe to walk with him into the garden: They were absent near an hour: I was almost sick with suspense and apprehension what this conference could mean. At length they returned: Joy shone in the eyes of the Count: he flew towards me; and kissing my hand with transport,—"My love—my Louisa!" exclaimed he, "the dear Abbe has consented to our union."—"Conditionally, only," said the latter, with an embarrassed air; "and I expect you do not interrupt me, Sir, whilst I speak my whole mind to my dear ward."

He then told me, that the Count had urged him to unite us immediately, as the only way to secure my happiness and reputation: That, should his father refuse to gratify his wishes, all he would desire was, that our marriage might be concealed until he had either softened him, or obtained the sanction of his relation, whose fortune would amply support us; whose tender regard for him he had little doubt would incline him to use his influence with his father. In short, every argument love and ingenuity could suggest, he had assailed the Abbe with, and he fairly repeated them all. "Now," added he, "attend, Louisa, to my objections; let reason and dispassionate judgment direct you. I have, I own, very reluctantly, been compelled by an eloquence I could neither silence nor resist, to promise an acquiescence with your determination. Consider well, therefore, before you give your final answer, in which my peace and *your own* is so deeply involved."

He then represented the disgrace and attendant disagreeable consequences to me, which must inevitably wait on a private marriage; the pain which must follow the disapprobation of our friends—the possible repentance and coldness of my husband, when passion subsided; and he found himself an alien from his family, and reflected on the sacrifices he had made to love. In fine, the Abbe said enough to have convinced the reason of a prudent young woman, and to make even a thoughtless one deliberate on the rash step suggested to her by the impetuous passion of a very young man. But alas! with the most painful conviction of my imprudence, I candidly own, I heard him only with impatience, and attended to nothing but the flattering idea of being married to the Count, and being inseparably united to a man, who, I *was persuaded*, would love me for *life with unabating affection*. Childish, romantic expectation! how bitterly have I been convinced of its fallacy, since the very concession I made in his favour, and submitting to the humiliation of a private marriage, must of itself lessen his esteem, when he reflected on my want both of prudence and delicacy. Rarely, indeed, I believe are such marriages happy, as need concealment, or are unsanctioned by the approbation of our parents; but I was to be convinced of this truth by experience; for I refused to listen to the voice of prudence.

When, therefore, the Abbe had exhausted himself, and borne hard upon the patience of the Count, without, to my shame be it confessed, having made the least impression upon me, by all the arguments he adduced against a private marriage. I replied to him with a courage that I saw surprised and hurt him; "that I was very sensible of his regard for my interest and happiness; but that, as the Count had honoured me with an offer of his hand, situated as I was, and with the esteem I felt for him, I could neither be so ungrateful to him, nor so much an enemy to my own happiness, as to decline the offer, which it was impossible my father could disapprove, when declared publicly; and when that time arrived, all apprehensions of the old Count's disapprobation must be done away." My lover threw himself in raptures at my feet, to thank me, and in the same breath, claimed the Abbe's promise. He heaved a deep sigh. "I own," said he, "that I am disappointed, and thought I might trust to the gentle and delicate mind of Louisa for a more proper regard to circumstances: But since my own confidence in her has misled me, and I see that you have acquired an unbounded influence over her heart, I shall no longer oppose your union, because I am now convinced all opposition would be fruitless. Heaven grant that I may have no cause to regret the hour that you first saw each other, and that your marriage may be productive of mutual happiness." We were both too happy to attend much to the evident chagrin of the good Abbe; the Count only replied to what was pleasing to himself, and entered into a consultation in what manner we should live together, without betraying our secret to the world, until it was convenient for our interest to make it known.

After much deliberation, and several schemes formed, and rejected as inexpedient, it was concluded upon, that, as I was scarce known in that neighbourhood, and the Count still less; that he should give up his hunting seat, discharge his servants, all but his valet, in whose secrecy he could depend, and take a small house in a neighbouring hamlet, where, as Mr. and Mrs. Sultsbach, we might live unknown and unobserved, until the Count had softened his family into a compliance with his wishes. His letters to be all addressed to and from the Abbe's house, which, being only four miles from the house proposed for our residence, would quickly afford us every intelligence.

This scheme being adopted, the Count lost no time in putting it into execution; his valet took the house, which, belonging to an officer in the army, whose wife had died in his absence, was let ready furnished, and was very suitable for us. Two maid servants were hired in the hamlet, which, with the valet, was to be all our domestics. Every arrangement was completed in about ten days; and on the morning when we were to take possession of our house, the good Abbe joined our hands before Heaven in his parish church. After the ceremony, when returned to his house, the servant of the Count being the only witness to our union, he seized an opportunity to draw me, for a few moments, into his little study. Taking my hand, the large drops falling from his eyes—"My amiable friend," said he, "I have this day done an act my better judgment condemns; but such are the existing circumstances, that I saw evidently there was no alternative to pursue. The great error I have committed, was admitting the Count as a visitor into my house. All other subsequent events was the result of my weakness in that point; Heaven grant that you may, as now, ever consider it as a fortunate hour for *your* happiness; and that I may never upbraid myself for my conduct, I hope soon to hear from your father; and if he does not disapprove of your union, as you hope, I shall then be better reconciled to myself than I now am. Here is a paper I have drawn up, and signed as a certificate of your marriage, and I entreat you carefully to preserve it." He embraced me with great tenderness, and blessed me with much fervency, promising to be a frequent visitor.

Elated with my marriage, anticipating future scenes of happiness and independence, and enjoying the pleasure my father must feel, when acquainted with a settlement so advantageous to me, not one gloomy idea presented itself in the chapter of possibilities that could for a moment cloud my prospects of felicity. Poor, wretched deluded creature; how soon was thy vain and high raised expectations tumbled into the dust! A month past away on eagle's wings; for every moment brought with it fresh instances of my husband's affection. No letters had as yet arrived from either of our fathers; but both being in the army, though in the service of different princes, we knew they could not always command their time, or be in the route to receive letters; therefore we patiently waited, without feeling any disappointment, as the days past by us.

I had been married nearly five weeks, when one morning, at breakfast, we were surprised by seeing a man on horseback ring at the gate, and presently a message was delivered from the Abbe, who then lay in his bed hopeless of recovery, from the return of his dreadful spasms. He requested to see us without delay. This moment was the first since I had left him that I felt pain, and I prepared instantly to attend him, the Count equally desirous with myself to see our mutual friend. We were not long before we arrived at his house, and beheld him upraised in his bed, struggling for breath, and so amazingly changed in the course of a week's illness, that I was more shocked than ever I had been in my whole life. He ordered the servant to withdraw, and then with extreme difficulty, agonized by the spasms in his side, he addressed us in these words:—"I believe my days, I may say hours of existence, now draw towards a period. I have little to regret but my *neglect* of duties, which, however, I hope I have not *violated*, and trust in a merciful God to pardon all my omissions.

"My dear children, you are now happy in each other; let me entreat you to attend to the duties of your situations, and you will continue so. Count, remember I joined you to my dear charge; her happiness, her honour, are a deposit in your hands, which you are accountable for to the Supreme Being, and to her respectable father. To *your* honour and generosity I bequeath her.

And you, my once dear Louisa, now the wife of a noble gentleman, who has proved his affection for you by disregarding all selfish considerations: Do *you* give *him* credit for his judgment, and prove, by your amiable conduct through life, how much superior virtue and native goodness are to the boasted advantages of riches and titles.—May the Almighty bless you both, and may your union often occasion you to recollect a man to whom, in his last moments, your happiness was his only concern."

With a faltering voice, and infinite labour, the poor Abbe pronounced this affectionate farewell. A relation of his had been sent for, the heir to his small possessions, who entered the house just as he became speechless, and our attendance was no longer necessary.

We returned home oppressed with melancholy: The Count was thoughtful; and I felt more poignant sorrow than I had ever before experienced. My spirits sunk, and a heavy gloom seemed to hang over me, which I could not shake off—too sure a presage that my happiest days were flown to return no more. At supper, I tried to appear cheerful; 'twas an attempt only; for sighs surcharged my bosom in spite of my endeavours to repress them. The Count saw my emotions, and made an effort to be talkative:—At length he said, "We both feel sorrow for our good father, but you know, my love, he often suffered such misery, as his real friends cannot be sorry that he is released from——Most fortunately for us, he lived long enough to give you a husband and a protector. Had he died before that period, how much more cause would you have had for sorrow, without a friend in the world near you." There was something in this speech that displeased me, and I was considering what answer to make, when he added; "except our Frank, there remains no witness now of our union."

"Yes," I replied with some earnestness; "I have one material one, a certificate drawn up, and signed by the good Abbe."—"Have you, indeed?" answered he with surprise, strongly marked in his countenance,—"I am rejoiced to hear it; I hope you take great care of it." "Most certainly," I returned, "I keep it in my little ivory cabinet, presented to me at the convent, and lock that safely in my escrutoire."—"That's right, my love, we may one day find it necessary to produce so unequivocal a proof of our marriage." He then changed the subject, and sought to amuse me by repeating some entertaining anecdotes, that he remarked in his travels. Two days after this event, a messenger came from the late Abbe's, with a letter to the Count, which he had left orders should be forwarded to *him* for his friend the Count; as we still retained the name of Sultsbach.

I trembled at the sight of this letter, and absolutely gasped for breath whilst he perused it. I watched the turn of his countenance, and saw it promised no good to me.—"Tell me," I cried, "what answer has your father given to your request?"—"One that surprises me as much as it hurts me," he replied. "He refuses his consent to our marriage, not merely because you are portionless, but because you are the daughter of a man he hates; one whose insolence obliged him to complain against him, and to have dismissed from the army."—"Good Heavens!" I exclaimed; "is it possible Count Wolfran was that destroyer of my father's happiness! Oh! my dear father, why, why did you not name your cruel enemy to me!" "You mistake the matter," said my husband, very coolly: "It appears that the *insolence* of *Mr. Hautweitzer* drew upon himself the just indignation of *Count Wolfran.*"

The tone in which he pronounced these words, had more in it than the words themselves: It pierced my heart, and I burst into tears. He seemed affected—besought me not to be uneasy; time might do much for us.—The mutual hatred between our fathers was certainly an unlucky business; but as he found that the Count *his* father would soon return to his estate, no endeavours on his side should be wanting to do away the prejudice conceived against me. I endeavoured to be content with this assurance; but from that fatal hour, thought I could perceive a change in his disposition; he grew thoughtful, capricious, and often left me for hours alone, without apologizing or accounting for his frequent absences. No letters arrived from my father, nor did I know where to direct to him. The house of the late Abbe was now occupied by a stranger, and it was a million to one if any letters would ever reach us. This reflection gave me great pain, and I often requested the Count to set an inquiry on foot relative to the Polish army, that I might obtain some intelligence of my father's destination. This, he assured me, he had done without effect.

One day he told me, that as his father might soon return, he thought it would be most expedient for him to visit the relation on whose fortune he had such great expectancies, and prevail on him to interest himself in his behalf. "*He* also," said he, "will doubtless be displeased with me; but I know my influence over him; his anger will be but momentary, and I shall easily persuade him to coincide with my wishes." This proposal from my husband appeared wise and plausible; I had nothing to object to it, but being left alone. This fear and reluctance of being separated for a week or two, he treated as childish, until, ashamed of my folly, I gave into the plan, and a short day was fixed on to begin his journey, which I learnt was at least a hundred and fifty miles distance; but he promised me a letter from every post town.

The day came; I saw him depart with a sad foreboding that some untoward circumstance would intervene between us. I suffered unutterable anguish, and retired to my apartment overwhelmed with grief. After giving way to my sorrow for some time, I tried to shake off the despondency that oppressed me; and having begun some time before to embroider a sword knot for him, I drew out my work to employ myself. I wanted some silver thread, and recollected a parcel of it was in a drawer of my small ivory cabinet, which had been presented to me by my dear Miss D'Alenberg.

I opened the escrutoire, where this cabinet was deposited, and easily found the thread.—A sudden inclination seized me to peruse the certificate of my marriage. I opened the private drawer, and found it empty. Astonishment, for a moment, overpowered me; but recollecting myself, I conceived I had mistaken the drawer. I hastily explored every part of it; but the object of my search could not be found. What my feelings were, I cannot describe; nor can I recollect the anguish of that moment without horror.—What was become of my treasure, or on whom could my suspicions fall? was the first questions that presented themselves to my mind, and caused an universal trembling through my whole frame.

I had some little ornaments of value,—those were all safe; the locks of the trunk and cabinet I found in good order, yet it was a fatal truth that the certificate, which not many days previous to this I had seen in the drawer, was lost, and must have been taken by some one who knew of its importance to me. "Good Heavens!" I exclaimed—"Surely the Count——."—The words died on my tongue; the idea was horrible; the extent of misery which that thought might lead to, overcame my senses, and for a moment rendered me insensible. When my reason returned, in a state little short of distraction, I again renewed my search, but in vain; the fatal certainty of my loss was confirmed, and a thousand dreadful images rushed upon my mind at the same time.

With difficulty I descended to my apartment: I had never entrusted my keys with either of the servants; nor could it be probable they would have taken a paper of no consequence to them, and have left several valuable baubles, which, as I did not wear them, might not have been presently missed. There was but one person that I could suspect; and what his motives could have been, to rob me of a paper he had allowed to be very essential to me, after the death of the good Abbe, was a doubt, the solution of which tortured me almost to madness. Yet so fervent was my affection—so perfect my confidence in the love and honour of my husband, that I strove even against conviction to believe I wronged him by my suspicions, and endeavoured to support my spirits until the following day, when, as I expected to hear from him, so I intended to write, and inform him of this extraordinary event.

CHAPTER III.

THE next day came, and my agitations every hour in the hope of a letter, cannot be expressed. Alas! every succeeding hour, both on that day and the next, brought with it disappointment and sorrow. I grew almost frantic; my servants were astonished at my emotions, which, however, I sought to suppress, were but too visible, as I could neither eat nor sleep. In this state of wretchedness and suspense, I past five days; the sixth put an end to the last, and completed the first. I had scarcely left my pillow, where my wearied head had in vain sought repose, before I was informed a man on horseback at the door had brought a packet for me. I snatched it with trembling eagerness. It was the Count's writing: Even now I sicken at the recollection of what my feelings were, when I perused the contents. Indeed, I could not get through the whole, before I lost my senses, having just time to pull the bell, as I found myself sinking from my chair.

Let me briefly hurry over this part of my story, so dreadful even at this distance of time, that I wonder my life or reason had not been the sacrifice to such inhuman baseness. The letter informed me—

"That his father, having in the most peremptory manner *forbidden our marriage*, in consequence of an engagement he had entered into with another family, and also because of the insuperable aversion he entertained for Mr. Hautweitzer; he (the Count) was inexpressibly grieved to acquaint me, that in obedience to the author of his being, he was compelled, though with extreme reluctance, to relinquish the *hopes* he had indulged of passing his life with a *lady* he so truly loved and esteemed; but the sacred commands he had received, with the insurmountable difficulties that impeded such a union from *ever taking place*, obliged him to take *this method* of conveying to me the information, in compassion to both our feelings. As he must ever be interested in my happiness, he had taken care to leave four hundred crowns in his writing desk, which he hoped would be a sum sufficient to convey me to my father, or support me in the hamlet until his arrival."

Such were the cruel contents of this horrid letter, so deeply imprinted in my memory, never to be erased. The moment I regained my senses, I called for the messenger. No such person was to be found.—While the servant came to me, he had taken the opportunity to disappear. My cruel destiny now unfolded itself at once. I had no witness to my marriage; my certificate had been basely stolen by the most inhuman of mankind: I had assumed a fictitious name, which, when known, must at best give me a questionable and doubtful character, and I had no one being interested enough for me to assert my rights, or chastise the author of my wrongs.

Continual faintings brought me into such a state of weakness by the following day, that my servants thought it necessary to call in a physician, with which I was much displeased; for I most earnestly wished for death; but it pleased Heaven to restore me to health, or at least a comparative health, that I might endure yet greater miseries, if possible, the consequences of my credulity and folly. What bitter self-reproach have I not suffered, and must ever feel to the end of my existence.

As soon as I was able to leave my bed, I determined to pursue my cruel husband, and try, by gentleness, to restore him to a sense of his duty to me; but that, if he still persisted in refusing to acknowledge me as his wife, I would then boldly assert my claims upon him, and publish his baseness to all the world. I knew not where to find my father; but even if I had known, I shrunk from the idea of meeting him under my present humiliating circumstances. When I grew collected enough to form my plan, passion and resentment contributed to give me unusual courage; and from the timid lovesick Louisa, I became the haughty injured wife of Count Wolfran, and assumed a character very unlike my former self.

As he had, in the early days of our marriage, mentioned the residence of his relation, I did not hesitate a moment in forming a resolution to follow him there. I therefore hired a carriage for my journey, dismissed my servants, gave up the house, and prevailed on the relation of my late worthy friend, the Abbe, who resided in the village to take charge of my trunks and other effects. Despair gave me spirits, fortitude, and perseverance, astonishing even to myself, and enabled me, within a very few days, to set off for Ulm, the residence of Baron Nolker, the worthy uncle of a most unworthy man.—Happily, I met with no interruptions or accidents, but arrived safe at a capital inn in the city of Ulm.

It was not difficult to gain information of the Baron's house, or his character; the first was not far from the city, and the landlady of the inn spoke warmly in praise of the latter. I was now to reflect on a proper mode of introducing myself, whether to send for the Count, or go boldly to the house.—Whilst I was deliberating, turning my eyes involuntarily towards the street, I saw him pass with a lady and a gentleman. My whole soul seemed in tumults, racked by love and indignation. I hastily rung the bell, and sent a servant after him, to say that a *gentleman*, an old friend, wished to speak with him immediately: He, knowing the natural timidity of my character, had not, at the moment, the smallest suspicion of my having undertaken such a journey. He turned back, and was in an instant before me.

Never shall I forget the guilt and confusion pourtrayed in his countenance; he started, and was about to retire without uttering a word, scarcely, I believe, knowing his own intentions; but I was too quick, for laying hold of his arm.—"Stop, Count," I cried, endeavouring to repress my emotions.—"Stop, my dear Count, do you not know your Louisa.—Be not offended; I am here unknown, without you choose to acknowledge me." More astonished, if possible, by this address, than even by my presence, he led me in silence to a chair, doubtless considering in what manner to impose on my credulity, or bring me over to his wishes.—"Louisa," said he at length, in a voice soft and agitated, "Louisa, I am surprised and concerned to see you here. You have taken a very wrong step, which may materially injure *me* and *yourself.*" "I hope not," I replied with quickness; "for certainly what affects *you* must concern *me*. Man and wife can have but one interest; but I felt a necessity for coming here, that you might disavow a vile forgery in your name, calculated, no doubt, to make me miserable. I have too firm a reliance on your love, honour, and integrity, to be for a moment imposed upon by an attempt so impudent and so improbable. Here, my love," added I, drawing out the letter I had received; "read this horrid scroll, and then you will not be surprised that your Louisa determined to afford you an opportunity to vindicate your honour, and trace the infamous hand which sought to destroy our happiness."

He took the letter; his hand trembled, and every feature in his face betrayed the agitation of his mind.—"You ought," said he, falteringly, "to have written to me, if there was a necessity for so doing: You must be sensible, that, in the present state of things, your journey here was highly impolitic, to say no worse of it."—"Ah!" cried I, "could you think it possible for me to be composed, when thus convinced that we have some unknown enemy, who, having gone such lengths as to assume your name, and imitate your hand, will surely hesitate at nothing to make us wretched, and may possibly try to practise on *your judgment*, as he designed to do on *my* credulity."

At the moment, when tracing this scene, I am astonished at the fortitude and dissimulation I had the power to acquire over my feelings, and never, I believe, was a man so truly perplexed and confused as the Count. My behaviour was so unexpected, that he was entirely at a loss what answer to frame; whether to own or deny the letter, which he still held without opening it. I saw the workings of his mind, and exulted in the propriety of my plan.—"Why do you not read that detestable scroll?" I asked.—"My dear Louisa," said he, "I have not time now to attend to that or to you; a particular engagement obliges me to leave you, but I will return in the evening, and explain every thing to your satisfaction."—"Well, my love," I replied, "I wish not to *intrude* on your time or engagements: You will find me perfectly obedient to all your wishes;—now that I see you forgive this apparent rash step, and are convinced that the necessity justified my proceeding." He made me some vague and trifling answer; again promised to see me in the evening, and requested I would keep myself concealed.

CHAPTER IV.

When he had left me, I gave a free indulgence to my tears, and those emotions I had so hardly repressed. I saw too plainly the duplicity of his character, and that I was to be the most unfortunate of women. Yet the conduct I had adopted appeared to be the only mode I could pursue. Reproaches would avail nothing, and only harden a depraved mind; whilst, by discrediting the authenticity of the letter, I gave him time for reflection, and an opportunity to disavow it, should honour or tenderness soften him to do me justice.

In a thousand reflections of this kind, I passed the intervening time of his absence; and when I heard his voice at the door speaking to a servant, my heart fluttered almost from its enclosure. He entered the room with an air of haughtiness, mixed with complacency, rather assumed than natural, and bespoke different feelings from those I had observed when he left me. I had time for those remarks, as he deliberately shut the door, took off his hat, and drew a chair close to mine.

"Louisa," said he, in a firm tone, "I come not now to indulge in foolish expressions of a romantic passion, which your own understanding must inform you cannot long exist. I do not pretend to exculpate myself from blame, by pleading the violence of love as an excuse for duplicity; now that the veil is withdrawn, when passion has subsided, I can see and acknowledge my errors. I have misled you. I have imposed upon your reason, and for *my own* gratification, have sacrificed *your* peace; yet I hope it will prove only a temporary suspension." He stopt.—I felt almost choaked with indignation:—However, I commanded myself, and said, "Go on, Sir, as yet I do not comprehend you."

"To be brief, then," resumed he hastily, "for the subject cannot be expatiated upon; My father commands me to marry a young lady of fortune and connexions, to whom my uncle is guardian. I dare not refuse him." Here I started and exclaimed, "How! *dare not?*" "No," answered he, "I dare not: I deceived you as to *my* fortune; I have a very small independence;—my father can dispose of his property as he pleases: My uncle assures me his, only on condition that I comply with my father's commands. Thus I am compelled to obey; for I have no possibility of maintaining you or myself, if I brave their requisitions, and must be for ever reprobated, if I indulge my own desires by a further connexion with a lady, who, however dear to *me*, is the daughter of a man hateful to my father, and obnoxious to my family.

"The compulsatory acquiescence I have been drawn into, has given me an infinite deal of pain; the letter you have given to me I *must acknowledge* (at this moment I was absolutely speechless). Let me add, that on yourself depends your future happiness.—*Your* father is unacquainted with what has past between us. I have not had the temerity to mention any particulars to mine.—You *must* know, that you can *produce* no claims upon me, if I chuse to disavow them. Therefore, both for your honour and interest, you must relinquish all idea of making such claims as you cannot justify: By so doing, you will retain my friendship, and a handsome allowance, which I will settle on you for life. If, on the contrary, you persist in your present plan, to expose yourself, and compel me publicly to throw you off, you will make an irreconcileable enemy of me. Your father will hear the reputation of his daughter for ever destroyed, and the hatred of *my* father will find gratification in the dishonour attached to a family he dislikes.—Consider deliberately on all the arguments I have adduced, for the preservation of *your* character and future independence."

Here the base deceiver stopt, after having completely unmasked his character, and developed his dark designs. The latter part of this long speech had driven all foolish tenderness from my heart. Conscious innocence, pride, and indignation, raised me to a spirit above all fond complainings.—I viewed the man before me with a contempt that superseded affection: For when once an ingenuous mind feels the object of its tenderness in a despicable point of view, as void of integrity or honour, it is not difficult to change the nature of its sentiments, since true love must be founded upon *esteem*; and when *that* is annihilated, the other ceases to exist in a well informed mind. The errors, the imprudence I had been guilty of, in forming this too hasty connexion, perhaps deserved a punishment, but not from him. His behaviour had lifted me above myself, and conveyed more knowledge to my understanding in one hour, than from my little experience I had acquired in years. But to return.

I saw he impatiently and anxiously waited for my answer, as he took a turn or two about the room; whilst I was endeavouring to acquire composure, and some degree of dignity, which might cover him with confusion.—This at length was my reply, with as much calmness as I could assume.

"When I undertook this journey, Sir, it was with a faint hope that some *one* spark of virtue might inhabit your bosom, and that recollection had before now been my friend, to give you a just sense of your duty to me. I therefore gave you an opportunity to recall yourself to honour, and to do me justice.—No such spark of virtue lay dormant: I see all is treachery, deceit, and sordid interest.—Unhappily my weak mind and unguarded heart was captivated by an exterior too fascinating, and a *semblance* of honour I had not the penetration to discover from a reality.—But those days of weakness are no more.—I will preserve the *honour* of my *father*, whatever is the consequence to myself. I have been weak and imprudent, but never will I consent to appear a guilty creature in *his* eyes, for any worldly advantages offered as a compensation for lost innocence.—No, Sir—*my* fame, *my* character, *shall* be justified."

"And pray," said he, interrupting me, "*who* is to justify it? Have you any witnesses to prove it; any testimonies to produce?" "The *last*, Sir, *you know*, you have basely robbed me of; my best friend is indeed no more:—But your servant"——"is a stranger to every thing between us," answered he with a sneer.—"More than that, *you* left the Abbe, and resided with me under a false name. You will find, upon inquiry, *his* knowledge extends no farther."—"'Tis well, Sir," said I, rising.—"I comprehend all your schemes perfectly; I have no more to say to you: Leave me, Sir, and see me no more."

"Louisa," cried he, much agitated, "consider well what you are about; I will not have *my* future happiness destroyed by a rash unthinking girl; do not therefore oblige me to take such measures as must inevitably hurt your peace, and make your father miserable." "Do what you please," I returned; "as *your wife*, I must obey you: And though I utterly despise you, I *never* will forego my claims." He looked at me with a contemptuous smile. "And pray what is the plan you intend to pursue?" "That I shall deliberate upon, and you will doubtless know the result soon." He took up his hat—"You have decided your own fate, Louisa, and must abide the consequence." I made no reply, and he left the room.

No sooner was the door shut, than my spirits sunk; and though I no longer loved the base betrayer, yet the difficulties, the prejudices I had to encounter with; the malevolence of the world, and above all, the hatred of the old Count, who would doubtless shut his ears against conviction, to gratify his malice. All these considerations arose to my view; overpowered the little resolution I had laboured to support, and threw me into the most pitiable state of distress. I determined, however, to see the Baron the following morning, and disclose every circumstance that had passed between his nephew and myself.

I was now alone at an inn, a stranger, without a companion or a servant. The kind of doubtful appearance that I must make to the people, now first occurred; and when I desired to be conducted to my bed-room, I thought the hostess threw a scornful and scrutinizing look at me. Confused and mortified, I hastened to the apartment alloted for me, which was through a short enclosed gallery or passage, that served for a dressing-room, the inner apartment being small. I sent away the servant, locked the bed-room door, and threw myself down in my clothes, so truly miserable, that I had neither inclination or power to take them off.

Towards the morning, I fell into a short slumber, from which I was awakened by a knocking at the door. I hastily opened it. The servant said, a gentleman waited for me below: I could not mistake the person, and my first intention was to refuse seeing him; but presently I conceived the idea that it was *possible* he might repent of his unjust behaviour, and wished to acknowledge it. After a moment's hesitation, therefore, I said, I would attend him, and very soon followed her down stairs. When I entered the room, the Count met me, and seizing my reluctant hand—"Louisa, you have conquered: I have ventured to hazard my best hopes for your happiness.—Success, beyond my expectations, has attended me. My uncle forgives me, and has promised to be my advocate with my father. He even consents to receive *you*, and his carriage will soon be here to fetch you. Forgive my past conduct, which has wrung *my* heart as much as it has wounded *yours*."

This address, so unexpected, penetrated to my heart. Joy, hope, fear, and doubt, by turns assailed me.—*Love* had but a small share in my emotions; for *that* had received too rude a shock; but my fame, my character, was of far too much consequence to reject the possibility of its being established.—Yet still I involuntarily hesitated. He saw the conflict in my mind.— "I do not blame your want of confidence," said he; "I have deserved it; but respect yourself, if you no longer esteem me." Those words were like a talisman. My dear father recurred to my mind, softened my heart, and I burst into tears, yielding up my, 'till then, repulsive hand to him, with a look, that I saw covered him with confusion, and which I then thought was the effusion of a self-convicted mind.—He desired to breakfast with me. I readily complied, but very little conversation ensued. I was afraid of saying too much on my present prospects, lest it should be a tacit reproach on past transactions. His silence, doubtless, proceeded from other ideas, but he was extremely attentive and tender in his manners.

A carriage at length was announced:—"'Tis my uncle's," said he in a quick tone. "Hasten, my dear Louisa, to be received as you may wish for."

My preparations were few, as I had brought but a small trunk with me. He discharged the expences at the house, and with trembling limbs, and a beating heart, I seated myself in the carriage. As it drove off, he asked me, for the first time, to whom I had entrusted the management of my house, and who were acquainted with my journey. The first I told him, was given up; my effects in the house of our old friend, and the cause of my journey, a secret to every one. He praised my conduct and prudence; adding, that he hoped *that day* would see a termination to all my doubts and fears. I thanked him with fervor, and began to make a thousand excuses in my mind for his past unjustifiable behaviour, trying to restore to him my love and confidence.

When suddenly awaking from a deep reverie, I remarked, we were in a narrow gloomy road.—"I thought," said I, "that your uncle's house was not a mile from the town?" "His town house is not," replied he, "but another house to which he set off this morning, is about two miles further on." A sudden chill seized on my heart; but checking a rising apprehension, I remained silent, until we entered a narrow road through a thick wood, and I saw the spires of a large building through the trees.—"Is that the house?" asked I.—"No; my uncle's is about half a mile further; but he talked of calling here, to take up a young lady, a relation, as a companion for you." I, blind and credulous, ready to believe what I wished for to be a truth, simply congratulated myself on his uncle's kind consideration. We soon stopt at the outside of a large building with a pair of iron gates.—"Bless me!" said I, "surely this is a convent."—"Yes, you are right; it is in this convent your future companion resides. I will step out and inquire if my uncle *has* been, or is here." He jumped out of the carriage; was wanting about ten minutes, which I thought an age, when coming up to the door of the chaise, with a smiling countenance—"Step out into the parlour, my dear Louisa; Miss Nolker will attend you instantly. We are before my uncle."

Where was my reason and prudence at that moment, when a duplicity so obvious, a scheme so ill contrived, never struck me as a fallacy. I readily gave my hand to the base betrayer; entered the gates, and in a moment was in the great Court, surrounded by eight or ten nuns, and my companion gone. For the instant I put my foot inside the outer gate, and turned towards the parlour. He dropt my hand; the other gate opened, and the nuns appeared. The whole was so quick, that I scarcely missed his hand before I lost sight of his person.

I looked on the nuns.—"Where am I going, and where is Miss Nolker?" I turned, as if going back to the parlour.—"This way, Miss," said one of the mothers; "this way, if you please." Surrounding me, and urging me forwards—"What is it you mean?" I exclaimed, turning on every side. "What is become of the Count? Where is Miss Nolker?" One of the nuns took my hand.—"Do not distress yourself, by inquiries which cannot be answered to your satisfaction. Accompany us to the Abbess; you will there have every thing explained." I no longer resisted their entreaties. Conviction struck me at once of the vile treachery that had made me it's victim. I saw I was trepanned into a convent to be confined. It was useless to complain to the sisterhood.—I followed them in silence to the apartment where the Abbess was seated in state.

"My dear child," said she, in a soothing voice; "my dear child, you are welcome.—I hope you will find here every thing that can contribute to your peace and tranquillity." Without taking any notice of this *"hope,"* I requested to speak with her alone. She nodded her head, and the nuns retired. I then briefly told her who, and what I was; related the cruelty and imposition of my husband; the crime he meditated of marrying another; and warned her to beware how she became a partner in an action so atrocious, as she might assure herself I had friends who would move Heaven and earth to trace me out, and bring my persecutors to justice.

When I stopt—"Bless me," said she, "This is a very extraordinary story, and totally foreign to the representation I have from Baron Nolker."—"How, Madam!" cried I: "From Baron Nolker?" "Yes, my child," replied she; "'tis by his orders I receive you here. He is a good man, and he will pay your pension here to preserve you from evil, and the deceits of the world." "If this be true," I exclaimed, "then is he imposed upon by the basest of mankind; but I rather think his name has been used without his permission. What, Madam is the information you have received concerning me?" "Excuse me, my dear child, I am not at liberty to answer your question.—Make yourself easy; here you will find friends, and meet with good treatment. If your own story is true, time will elucidate every thing to your advantage. At present, opposition will be in vain. I am amenable for your safety, and if you behave with prudence, in me you shall find a friend."

This speech of her's convinced me at once, that indeed all "opposition would be in vain," and that the plot was laid too deeply, though hastily conceived, for me to countermine at that time. I therefore contented myself with again warning her of the consequences, when my confinement should be known to my friends, and hastily left her presence. I came so quick into the outer room, that I discovered some of the nuns in the act of listening through the cracks of the wainscot. How erroneous is the opinion generally entertained, that those persons detached from the world, and shut up in cloisters, are dead to all the passions which agitate the human frame.

On the contrary, all the little *mean* passions, such as envy, malice, curiosity, and selfishness, are to be found inhabiting the bosoms of too many who have apparently retired from all worldly concerns. The good mothers were confused; but as I addressed them civilly, they soon recovered, and paid me much attention.

When I had been about three weeks in the convent, I was one day much surprised by the information, that my trunks of clothes had been brought that morning, and left without any message or inquiries. On examining them, I found all was perfectly right; my ivory cabinet was also in one of the trunks; but not a single paper of any kind remained. Convinced now that I was to be confined for life, without some miracles should effect my deliverance, my spirits no longer supported me. I fell into a low nervous fever, that reduced me extremely, both in body and mind. One of the lay sisters, who occasionally attended me, appeared to compassionate my situation. She shrugged her shoulders, shook her head, and calling me poor child, gave such indications of pity, that I ventured one day to complain of the cruel deception that had brought me there.

"Have you any friends," asked she, in a low voice, as if fearful of being heard.—"I believe," I replied, "that I have a father, but I know not in what place he resides."—"That's bad, indeed," said she.—"If, however, you can write to any friend, I will find means to get your letter conveyed; the porteress is my aunt; she will not refuse to pass a letter of mine to a relation in the city, and she shall forward one for you." It instantly occurred to me to write to the relation of the Abbe, give her an account of my being forced into a convent, and enclose a letter of information to my father. As it was most probable he would either write or come there, when he had the power of being absent from his duty. I eagerly accepted her good offices, and promised to have my letter ready the following day. In the small trunk that I had brought with me to Ulm, I had packt up my writing box; and most fortunately, when the nuns, as is customary, examined the trunk, they had not deprived me of this treasure; whether from complaisance, or because they were fearful of doing it, I know not, but now this box was to me of inestimable value.

I lost no time in writing, and anxious to exculpate myself from the charge of guilt in the eyes of my father, I gave him a very circumstantial account of every occurrence that had befallen me since our separation, without, at that time, considering what might be the consequences of such information to a man of honour and a parent. The lay sister performed her promise; my spirits revived, and gay hope once more shed her illusive smiles over my mind. But this temporary ease was of short duration. Week after week rolled away, and brought no change in my situation: Continual expectations wore me to a shadow; 'till months passing by, and no letters or intelligence respecting my father, I all at once entertained an idea of his death.

Despondency then took fast hold of me.—I was a prisoner for life, sacrificed by the basest and most avaricious of mankind. Madness and despair worked me to a kind of frenzy; and one day, after a fit of gloomy recollection, I rose in a hurry, flew to the apartment of the Abbess, and insisted, in very peremptory terms, upon being liberated;—bid her, at her peril, detain a wife forced into confinement, and the daughter of an officer who would soon demand me from her hands. She appeared terrified at the state of my mind, tried to sooth, to reason with me; but finding I grew quite outrageous, she called for assistance: I fought like a tyger with three of the nuns; but being overpowered by numbers, I was carried speechless and senseless to an apartment used as a prison, when any of the boarders deserved punishment.

Here I was left alone upon a miserable bed, with some bread and water for my support. Being exhausted by the violence of my passions, and the resistance I had made to the nuns, the turbulence of my emotions subsided, and I fell into a paroxysm of tears, that in all probability preserved me from a state of insanity, so much apprehended by the nuns. After this relief to the oppression of my heart, I dropt asleep, and having some hours rest, waked to a more composed state both of body and mind. I remained alone the remainder of the day, and all night. I was terrified at my situation; the melancholy place where I lay was indeed sufficiently gloomy to inspire terror. Convinced that I should gain nothing by menaces or force, I resolved to adopt a different line of conduct, to subdue my resentment and impatience, if possible, and try the effects of a more conciliatory manner, as if I grew reconciled to what I could not overcome.

Never was the approach of day more welcome than it appeared to me. I had passed such a night of weak, and indeed foolish apprehension, that I am confident the fear of continuing there would have deranged my intellects. When the nuns came to me, and observed the alteration in my temper, they retired, to make, as they said, a favourable report, and obtain my liberty, which, through their interposition, was effected by the dinner hour, when I appeared vexed and mortified, and with a heart throbbing with grief and disappointment. I endured a short lecture from the Abbess (who persisted always in calling me *Miss*) with a sort of restrained pride, that sat very ill, I believe on my features; as she gently cautioned me against indulging improper notions or visionary expectations. I made no reply, but from that hour, gave myself up as a lost creature, disclaimed or forgotten by all my connexions.

Once or twice after this, when I was upon tolerable terms with the Abbess, I ventured to question her, whether Baron Nolker, or his nephew the Count, was still at Ulm.—She assured me they were not; that they had quitted the country within a month after my residence in the convent. She knew not where they were gone to, as she had received a twelvemonth's pension in advance for me. Indeed, I have no doubt but that she had received a handsome douceur besides. This information gave the finish to all my hopes of a release, unless some very unforeseen event should take place. I had forgot to mention, that in my cabinet, among my trinkets, I found the money which the Count mentioned in his letter; for which, indeed, I could have no use, unless hereafter to purchase necessaries.

CHAPTER V.

AND now, my dear Miss D'Alenberg, I am coming to the most melancholy part of my story, which indeed I dread to enter upon. Excuse the prolixity of my recital; the conclusion I shall endeavour to hasten over, as too painful to dwell upon.

I had resided in the convent near eighteen months, without any alteration having taken place in my circumstances. Twice, during that time, I had again written to my father, almost without hope, and as I thought, without effect. One day, about noon, a paper was delivered to the Abbess, brought by a stranger at the grate. She opened and read it, with surprise and confusion strongly marked in her countenance. She withdrew immediately. Very soon after she had left the room, I was desired to attend her. My heart fluttered strangely. Good Heavens! thought I, can that paper relate to me. What now is to become of me? I flew, rather than walked, to her apartment. She still held the paper in her hand.—"Miss," said she, "I have here an order to deliver you up to a gentleman, who calls himself Hautweitzer and——" "My father," I exclaimed, and sunk to the ground.

By the assistance of an attending nun, I was soon recovered.—"Oh! let me fly; let me go to my father," I cried, the moment speech was lent me.—"Stop, Miss," said the Abbess, "you shall be properly conducted: your emotions convince me the claim is just, and that *I have been imposed upon.*" By the bye, I never gave credit to that *assertion*, because she was deaf and callous to every thing I had urged, tending to convince her of the duplicity practised against me. This was no time, however, for words; I was requested to hasten in packing my trunks, as a person waited for me in the parlour. I had no doubt but that this was my father, and my agitations scarcely permitted me to waste a moment. One of the mothers assisted me; I took a hasty and incoherent leave of the community; slid a remembrance into the hand of the lay sister, and, with trembling impatience, run to the parlour, where I beheld—not my father, but a stranger.

I gave a scream, and sunk back in a chair, gasping with terror at my disappointment, uttering something about my father.—"Here, Madam," said the stranger, giving me a slip of paper: "this will satisfy you as to my commission." I snatched the paper, and glancing my eyes over it, saw it was the writing of my father, with only these words: "Come to me, my dearest Louisa, I am at Ulm. My friend will conduct you to the arms of your father."

I no longer hesitated, but giving my hand to the stranger, incapable then of speaking, was by him placed in a carriage. Recovering, in a short time, from my first agitations, I asked some questions relative to my father's situation, and why he had not come for me himself. The gentleman viewed me with an air of compassion, I thought, and seemed embarrassed what answer to give me; but at length said, "he was sorry it fell to his lot to give an explanation of circumstances that must distress me, but that my father had requested him to prepare me for the disagreeable intelligence which must be communicated. Let me, however, assure you," said he, "that Mr. Hautweitzer is entirely out of danger, in a state of convalescence that will soon restore him to perfect health."

Without attending to an exclamation I uttered, he went on—"Your father, Madam, some time since, fought a duel; he was dangerously wounded, but happily not mortally so. He lay long in a doubtful state. I have the pleasure to assure you, all apprehensions of his life are done away. Do not therefore alarm yourself," added he, observing my terror, and the emotions which affected my mind. "My friend wished you to be a little prepared, that the surprise might not too greatly distress you." "Ah! Sir," I exclaimed, "if indeed my father is out of danger, I return thanks to Heaven: But who, pray tell me, was his opponent? My heart already divines."

"It was Count Wolfran."—"The father or the son?" asked I, gasping for breath.—"The father," replied he, "who was the aggressor in every sense of the word."——"And does he live," said I.—"No, he survived but three days." This answer was like a bolt of ice; it threw me into a fit of trembling. Cold damps bedewed my limbs, and I thought my last hour was at hand.— My companion was extremely shocked;—but being a medical man, he had luckily some drops in his pocket, which revived me. He besought me to be composed. The event had turned out favourably for my father, who had been exculpated by the Count's own confession. This, indeed, was some ease to my mind; but the reflection that my folly and imprudent marriage had brought on such shocking events, wounded my very soul, and I was scarcely able to support myself when the carriage stopt at the gentleman's house.

He gave me drops and wine to restore my spirits, and I accompanied him to the apartment, where I found my dear parent supported by pillows in his bed. Our meeting cannot be described; it was most truly distressing to both. He neither blamed or upbraided me, but soothed me by his kindness, which was a thousand times more painful to a self-convicted mind, than the most bitter reproaches could have been. He saw what I felt. "Forgive yourself, my Louisa, for you are exculpated in my eyes. An ingenuous unsuspecting heart was no match for the dark designing arts of an accomplished villain. You erred, 'tis true, but you was young, in love, and a stranger to the world.—*Your* faults were venial ones, even in the eyes of prudence; for you preserved your virtue, and knew not that the man in whom you confided would prove a monster, a disgrace to human nature."

He then told me, that the army in Poland, being sent into winter quarters, he had repaired with all diligence to the house of the good Abbe, not having received either of his letters, or any intimation of his death. He was therefore excessively shocked at the news that awaited him, and my letters were put into his hands. 'Tis not possible to conceive the rage, indignation, and sorrow, which he experienced on reading them; he took his measures instantly, and departed for the house of Count Wolfran. On his arrival, he was informed that the old Count was gone on a visit to his *son* and *daughter*, at their estate near Ulm. Boiling with increased rage at this information, he pursued his journey, and came there when the whole family was rejoicing at the christening of an heir to the estate and title, the young Countess Theodosia having been brought to bed near six weeks.

My father requested to see the old Count on particular business, and was shown into an apartment to wait for him. In a few moments he appeared, and started on seeing the person before him, who, endeavouring to calm his passions, desired he would wave all former animosity, and hear him on an affair which concerned their mutual honour. The other, with a mixture of surprise and haughtiness, requested he would be seated, and hasten what he had to say, as he was particularly engaged with company. My father then drew out my first circumstantial letter, and gave it to him, saying, "read that, Sir, with candour, and give no answer until you have gone through it.—Although we are not friends, yet I trust you are a man of honour."

The Count looked hastily over the letter, several times smiling with an air of disdain and triumph, which the other could ill brook. At length, returning it to my father—"I am sorry the wild chimeras of your daughter should have engaged you in such a fruitless journey. Be assured, she never was the wife of my son, although it is very natural a young lady should wish to throw a veil over her own frailty." My father instantly took fire.—"How dare you," cried he, "insinuate the smallest reflection on the character of my child; her only act of frailty was in supposing truth or honour could inhabit the bosom of a son of your's; but her honour is unblemished, without any stain, but what must follow in being the wife of a villain."

He had raised his voice to a pitch of fury. The other, equally exasperated, exclaimed, "Your daughter was preserved from want and infamy, by my son. Yes," added he, "after having prostituted herself to him, he placed her in a convent, to preserve her from the vilest degradation." My unhappy father, raised almost to a state of madness, forgot every thing at that moment, sprung forwards, and struck the Count.—"Slanderous villain," he cried, "I will choak those words in their birth." That instant the young Count, the Countess, and some others, burst into the room. My father was seized, foaming with rage, whilst some ran to the old Count, whose nose and mouth bled profusely. The son demanded the cause of this outrage, little suspecting who the person was before him. My father exclaimed, "I came here to demand justice, to oblige the son of that man to acknowledge his legal wife. Yes, *my* daughter is *the wife* of Count Wolfran."

A faint shriek from the Countess caught the attention of her husband. He attempted to lead her from the room. "Stop," she cried; "if this man asserts a falsity, let it be proved such. I will abide the decision; I will not leave the room, when an assertion of such consequence to my fame and happiness has been publicly declared." The old Count now advanced.—"You have dared to *degrade me*; you have calumniated *my son.*—Though you are inferior in birth, in rank to me; yet, as having borne arms, I wave my privileges, and challenge you to meet me to-morrow at eight o'clock, in a field at the west end of the city. Your blood only can atone for this outrage."—"I accept the offer," replied my father. Then turning to the Countess—"I feel for you, Madam;—and nothing less than the justice I owe to my child could compel me to give you pain.—Read that letter, Madam, and judge for yourself." He gave my letter into her hands:—The Count exclaimed, "an impudent forgery," and attempted to take it from her.—"No, my Lord," said she—"no, I *will* read it; but strong indeed must be the proofs, e'er I can credit any thing to the disadvantage of *your honour.*"

"Go," cried the old Count arrogantly—"go, Sir, after having interrupted the happiness of this family, to preserve the fame of a worthless daughter; leave it, whilst I can command myself; to-morrow, at eight, I shall expect you." Without deigning any other reply, but "I shall attend you, Sir," my father quitted the house.

He employed the intermediate time in writing to me; lamented his inability to provide for me, and advised me, rather than submit to be confined as a pensioner of the Count's, "to take the veil, if it might be allowed to me under my own name, or the one I bore in the convent." This letter he carried in his pocket to the field of action the next morning, and was very soon joined by the Count and a surgeon, the gentleman who had kindly taken me from the place of my confinement. This gentleman he was astonished to see. He had formerly been a surgeon to a regiment in which my father had a company. On recognizing my father, he advanced, and expressed his regret at being called to attend in such an affair between two gentlemen he respected, and inquired, with some earnestness, if the dispute could not be amicably settled.

My father replied in the negative—"His own honour, and the peace and honour of his daughter, had been irreparably injured." "One favour, Sir," added he, "I will request, because in your power to serve me in. If I fall, in my pocket you will find a letter addressed to my child, under the name of Miss Sultsbach; promise me to convey that letter into her hands, under whatsoever name she may now bear. She is in the convent a few miles from the city;—but until I can do her character justice, I wish not to see her. Perhaps that blessing may be for ever denied to me." The friendly surgeon engaged to observe his request, and the two gentlemen presently engaged.

They fought desperately; several wounds were given and received on both sides, 'till at length each sheathed his sword in the body of his antagonist; both fell, to all appearance, lifeless. Two servants of the Count's had attended at some distance; to those the surgeon made a signal; and as they advanced, two peasants happened to pass through the field, and were likewise called upon to lend their assistance. My father the surgeon most humanely ordered to his own house, and the Count was conveyed to his son's. The blood had been stanched before their removal, and another skilful man was called in to attend upon my father, the surgeon being previously engaged by the Count.

The wounds of both were apprehended at first to be mortal. The Count's verified their fears; for on the third day, all hopes were over. Being informed of his situation, he sent for both surgeons, and the two servants who had carried him home; before them all, he declared he had wronged Mr. Hautweitzer, and had provoked his fate.—He was then sensible that he had injured him in his fame and in his fortune; and he bitterly regretted that his *son's marriage* put it out of his power to do Miss Hautweitzer justice.

After this, he had some serious conversation with his son; but there is every reason to believe, *that son,* so devoid of truth and honour, even in that awful hour, persisted in denying his marriage with me, to his father.

The Count's death was concealed from my father; and though he anxiously wished to see me, yet he would not consent that I should be acquainted with his situation.—The young Count and his family left Ulm on the same day the father died. It was above ten days after this event, before an application was made to the Bishop, for an order to the Abbess to liberate me, which was easily obtained; for the Bishop was nearly related to the Wolfran family, and wished to have the affair as little known or talked of as possible. Therefore the duel was generally supposed to have originated from a military quarrel, and the son's name not mentioned in the business.

This was the information that I received from my beloved parent. Alas! bitter were my self-reproaches; he was wounded both in mind and body; his situation afforded him no means of providing for himself or me; I could adduce no proofs of my marriage, and my assertions would but little avail against the power of an opulent family, who were all interested in preserving the character and honour of their worthless relation. The surgeon, to whom my father related my whole story, sympathized in our distresses. He saw no prospect of good to us in prosecuting my claims. The Count was married in the face of the world; had now a son and heir; no inducements, therefore, of honour or justice, would have any probability of success, where every thing militated against us. "My dear friends," added he, "to Heaven you must leave this unworthy man: Doubt not, but in it's own good time, providence will revenge your wrongs, and punish him. At this moment his feelings are not to be envied.—He must be callous, indeed, if the crimes he has committed, and the death of his father, who fell a victim to his deceptions, does not fill him with horror and hourly regret."

My dear father recovered very slowly;—and we held frequent consultations in what manner we should provide for our mutual support. I believe the anxiety of his mind retarded his recovery, and certainly undermined his constitution, which had long been delicate, from the difficulties and misfortunes he had to struggle with. For myself, a retrospection on the past, and the prospect of the future, was so dark, so afflictive, and so humiliating, that 'tis a miracle how I supported my health, or preserved my reason.

I had resided with my father near a month; he was yet unable to leave his bed, when I was one day informed a lady requested to see me. The message surprised me; but I went down to the apartment, and saw a very elegant woman in deep mourning, who rose at my approach. "Do I see Miss Hautweitzer?" said she, in a very plaintive voice. I answered in the affirmative, and requested she would be seated. She took a letter from her pocket—"Forgive me, Madam, for thus recalling to you such distressing events, but permit me to ask if this letter is of your writing?" I saw it was the letter I had written to my father, and immediately judged the lady before me was the Count's wife. I trembled excessively, and replied, in a faltering voice, "Yes, Madam, it was written by me, and the contents are a solemn truth."

"I do not doubt it," said she, tenderly; "your appearance sufficiently convinces me of it. I am, Madam, equally unfortunate, and equally innocent with yourself; but never will I stand between you and justice.—The cruelty of an unprincipled man cannot annihilate *your* rights. I have *none*— nor have I parents or relations. Fortunately I have still a large income in my own possession sufficient for my ill-star'd child, without any claims on his worthless father. I have quitted the Count, Madam, for ever.—Wretch as he is, he knows we cannot expose him without entailing disgrace on ourselves. You, for want of proofs, and myself on account of my child. To the justice of Heaven, therefore, we must leave him.

"My visit to you was to a sister in affliction; permit me the privileges of one.—I have made very minute inquiries into your character and circumstances; pardon the liberty. Fortune, I hear, has dealt unkindly by Mr. Hautweitzer, and unjust to his merit. From Count Wolfran, I am sure, you will accept no assistance, unless by repentance he restores you to your rights. Deign, then, to make me happy, by permitting me the inexpressible pleasure of preserving you from further distress. Accept an annuity that will place you above want, without having the weight of an obligation to cold unfeeling minds." She rose, embraced me, and burst into tears.

I was so astonished, so penetrated with wonder and admiration, at a generosity and greatness of mind so uncommon, that unable to move or speak, I mingled my tears with her's, and prest her to my bosom with an ardor that spoke my whole soul. She understood the expression of my heart. "Compose yourself," said she, "my amiable friend. Tell me how your worthy father does?"—When speech was lent me, I was not backward in delineating the feelings of admiration with which she had inspired me, and related to her, without reserve, my dear father's situation. She desired to see him; I flew to acquaint him of the dear lady's visit, and the scene that ensued between us, beggars all description. Long my father resisted her generous offers; but at length her irresistible tenderness conquered. She then proposed our living at Stutgard. She had a small estate on the skirts of the city, with a neat house on it: *That*, and a moderate income, for my father would only accept a *very* moderate one, she declared should be ours, for our joint lives; and whenever I should have the misfortune to lose my father, she would claim me as a sister, and as an inmate of her dwelling, wheresoever it was.—"At present," added she, "I design to retire into the convent you have quitted, until I have deliberately fixed on my future plan of life. I am sorry to say, Baron Nolker, who is a worthy man, is yet so prepossessed in favour of his nephew, that your story is entirely discredited, and I am accused of injustice and caprice in separating myself from the Count. 'Tis impossible to argue against prejudice, or to open the eyes of the blind. I submit, therefore to the censures and opinions I cannot controvert; but I will judge for myself; and if I had ever entertained any doubts, your appearance, Madam, must instantly remove them."

I cannot repeat to you a tenth part of the kind and polite attentions we received from this noble-minded lady. My father was affected even to tears, and besought her to add additional value to her favours, by residing with us. She expressed herself obliged to our wishes, but said, the convent was for the present her preferable choice; that it was not unlikely but that hereafter she might pay us a visit; but even that depended on circumstances. "You are not the only one unhappy," said she, taking my hand kindly; "and you have a blessing I never enjoyed, a worthy father." Then rising and taking leave, she said, I should hear from her the following week, and she promised to herself much pleasure in my correspondence. When this dear generous lady had left me, I felt ready to have resigned my claims, to have submitted to bear the ignominy the Count wished to throw on me, rather than be the cause of distressing such a mind as her's.—Yet, on a retrospection of every thing, I could not perceive that sorrow or affection had any share in her regrets for the *necessity* she conceived that had obliged her to leave the Count, I was thoroughly persuaded her love for him never could have equalled mine, from the composure with which she mentioned him; and that idea afforded me no small consolation.

The next week, a gentleman came to us from our generous benefactress, and settled every thing relative to our taking possession of her gift at Stutgard, with a handsome sum for our present wants. This last I declined; for having still by me the money which the Count had left to me, and which was sent with my clothes; I resolved to make use of that without any scruple. My dear father had been so extremely reduced by loss of blood, and anxiety of mind, that his recovery was long, tedious, and fluctuating. Near three months we remained at the surgeon's, during which, I received three letters from the Countess. She had altered her intention of *fixing* in the convent near Ulm, by the persuasions of an old friend, who had professed in a convent not many miles from Baden; and from that situation, I had last the pleasure of hearing from her.

At length my father thought himself able to bear the fatigue of travelling. We took leave of the friendly gentleman to whose care and skill we had been so much indebted, and set off on our journey; but on the second day, it proved more than his strength could support; he was taken ill on the road, and was confined six weeks at an inn before we could proceed. Once more we continued our route, and by easy stages, had reached the skirts of the wood within two miles of this village, when suddenly we were attacked by five or six banditti, who rifled the carriage, took from us our portmanteau and money, cut the traces of the horses, and then bid us walk to the place of our destination, as we had now no baggage to encumber us.

There was no alternative; night was drawing on; and we were compelled to walk; for the horses being loosened, they run away through the wood, and the post boy went in pursuit of them. With infinite difficulty, my poor father crept to the inn, where his troubles in this life were to have an end. A very miserable bed was allowed for him, and I watched by the side of it in inexpressible agonies. The next morning the landlord told us, "we must turn out; he had no bed to spare for sick folkes." I sought to reason with him, and assured him I should soon have money amply to reward him, if he would accommodate my dying father: But in vain I *tried* to reason with a selfish brute. He insisted upon our departure before night; and though he assisted me in getting him down from the hovel which he called a bed-chamber, and saw that he was too weak even to stand alone, nothing could soften his obduracy. The rest you know. My dear, my suffering father, whose life had been a series of misery, was at length, by the folly and fond credulity of his imprudent daughter, cruelly destroyed. That fatal duel, the effects falling on a broken constitution and a wounded spirit, with fatigue and anxiety, at last terminated a life marked out with continual sorrows, from the day of his marriage.

Those sorrows, my misconduct, and the baseness of another, greatly aggravated, and must entail remorse upon my mind to the last day of my existence.

Thus concludes the narrative of the unfortunate Louisa, which she communicated at different periods, as her weakness permitted, and which Miss D'Alenberg was allowed to commit to paper, for the perusal of her father and his friend.

CHAPTER VI.

WHEN Ferdinand had gone through this long story with an indignation and pity natural to a feeling and well-disposed mind, there were some circumstances that struck him in the perusal of it, which led him to believe the lady in the convent where Eugenia was, whom he had supposed to be Claudina, was the Countess of Wolfran, and that she had mistaken him from a coincidence in particular points, for the Count. He was charmed with the character of this lady, and lamented her destiny little less than he grieved for the ill-treated Louisa. Yet it appeared very unaccountable to him that the Count should think of paying his address to another lady, when his recent marriage at Ulm could not be forgotten; and when his uncle was so well acquainted with all those circumstances, was it not natural to suppose that Mr. D'Alenberg would take care to be well informed of the character and connexions of a man with whom he entrusted the happiness of his daughter, previous to the marriage; and if he had made any investigation, by what means had the Count escaped detection, or how could any man expect that he should go unpunished, or not be exposed by those he had already deceived?

In short, the conduct and character of the Count was strange and inexplicable to him; the more he sought to penetrate into either, the more he was puzzled to account for his baseness and folly. Reflecting deliberately on the story of Louisa, he traced the misfortunes of her father to an imprudent marriage in early life, and the subsequent distress of his daughter to the same source. Reverting then to his own perplexities, he could not but acknowledge, that, in forming a union for life with prudence, on the approbation of friends, as well as the mutual affection of the parties concerned, eventually depended the happiness of themselves and all their connexions.

"Yes," said he, with a sigh; "I am now sensible, that out of a thousand instances of wretchedness in a marriage state, there is scarcely one that does not originate from the imprudence of youth, in forming connexions contrary to the advice and inclination of their parents and friends. Parents may *sometimes* be selfish, arbitrary, and unfeeling; but youth is *too generally* impetuous, obstinate, and inconsiderate. They permit their passions to lord it over their reason, and are only convinced, by sad experience and painful consequences, of their own too hasty determinations in such points, as must decide their future happiness or misery."

Whilst he sat ruminating on past occurrences, the Count, having finished his business, entered the library, and rouzed him from his reverie. "Happily," said he, "I have now concluded all my engagements with my tenantry, and in two days shall be at liberty to attend you wherever you please."—"Indeed," cried Ferdinand, "it will be necessary to enter upon some field of action that may change the present current of my thoughts; for an indulgence of them would, in a short time, I believe, turn me into a complete misanthrope." "Nay," returned the Count, "if you are inclined to turn hermit, I am ready to concur in the design. I promise you the world holds forth no allurements to me; and it is only with a wish to forget *myself*, that I propose going into a public situation, if therefore you incline to solitude."

"No, no," said Ferdinand, rising hastily. "Solitude is only the nurse of discontent.—I am equally desirous with yourself to forget that 'such things have been;' and in the busy din of arms, to seek that diversity of thought which may tend to lessen my present vexations. That you may not wonder at the captious manner in which I spoke just now, I entreat you to look over that manuscript I have just finished reading of, whilst I take a walk in the park, and harmonize my mind by a view of the sun, now breaking through the clouds, and shining on the verdant lawn, which refreshed by the passing showers; by its additional enlivening verdure, captivates the eye, and tranquillizes the human breast."

Quitting the library, he strolled through the gardens and park, until the first dinner-bell warned him to return and adjust his dress. At table, he met the Count, who, with an honest energy, and a warmth of heart, which did him honour, expressed his indignation against the villany of Count Wolfran, and equal astonishment, that in so short a period, in the same country, and in the hazard of continual detection, he should have the effrontery to pay his addresses to Miss D'Alenberg. "'Tis a temerity, indeed a mystery," cried Ferdinand, "which I cannot develop. He is neither a madman nor a fool, and yet his rashness would tempt one to believe his senses must have deserted him, or his strong attachment to the sex has thrown him into situations he has not the fortitude, I may say honesty, to decline making an advantage of." "He is a worthless wretch," replied the Count, "and will doubtless meet with a severe retribution; but I am enchanted with the unfortunate lady who bears his name.—Her conduct is so generous, so noble, and so becoming a truly great mind, that I cannot enough admire her. How few women in her situation would have sought out the unhappy Louisa, after having her happiness broken in upon, her own claims let aside, and her child stigmatized, by her connexion with an infamous seducer."

"But what is still more admirable," returned Ferdinand, "is her voluntary secession from the Count, when her rights were indisputable; her marriage witnessed—allowed of; and when, by so doing, she threw up her child's claim to his inheritance, which Louisa never could have contested, from want of proof. Such heroism, such delicacy and disinterestedness, is certainly very uncommon." "True," answered the Count, "her whole conduct evinces a greatness of soul superior to any woman I ever heard of. A mind like her's never could be contented with a doubtful title, or respect a man whose honour was at least equivocal. And what a wretch must he be, who, losing such an angel, could so soon pay court to another."

"Miss D'Alenberg," said Ferdinand, "by the little I have seen of her, is both in person and mind beautiful and captivating; such as might well warrant the warmest passion; and he must be a *thousand* times a villain that would seek to entangle such a woman in the black catalogue of those who have suffered by his artifices. But," added he, "you see what are the wishes of Mr. D'Alenberg. Have you any curiosity; do you feel interest enough for those worthy persons, to step out of the way, and pay them a visit?" "With all my soul," replied his friend;—"we are not circumscribed as to time, and I shall be happy to see such characters as may put one in good humour with human nature."—This point settled, on the second day after, the Count, having taken leave of his tenantry, and recommended them to the kind offices of his steward, whose integrity was beyond all doubt, and whose attachment to his interest had stood the test of time and temptation. He readily accorded with what he saw was the inclination of Ferdinand, and they took the route towards the mansion of Mr. D'Alenberg.

Their presence was equally welcome as unexpected; they were no sooner announced, than the good old gentleman hastened to meet them with a cordiality that was truly gratifying to his visitors. "You have agreeably surprised me," said he to Ferdinand, after saluting the Count.—"My wishes were stronger than my hopes, and I am pleased to find that you gave due credit to my sincerity. You have enhanced the obligation of this visit, by affording me an opportunity of paying my respects to Count M***." Neither of the gentlemen were deficient in proper acknowledgments for the kindness of this reception, and, after a little desultory conversation, Mr. D'Alenberg introduced them to the ladies. Surprise and pleasure were strongly blended in the features of his daughter; nor did the melancholy Louisa appear less gratified, though the languor which hung over her whole frame, gave her less animation. Mr. D'Alenberg, in a cheerful voice, bid them "rally their spirits; and now that he had been fortunate enough to take two gallant knights prisoners, he expected the ladies of the Castle would do *their* best to make their chains easy, and their captivity light."

Theresa answered her father in his own style; and in a short time, the conversation became animated and entertaining. Even Louisa sometimes joined in it when applied to, though it was pretty evident that the effort was painful, and that she had a mind but ill at ease.

In the evening, after the ladies had retired, Mr. D'Alenberg of himself reverted to Louisa's story, and observed that he had to congratulate himself on the discovery of Count Wolfran's baseness, and also, that the heart of his daughter was much less attached to him than might have been expected from his handsome person and insinuating manners. "She has even told me," said he, "that her predilection was never decidedly strong in his favour; but that, having no attachment to another, no reasonable objection could be made against him. On the contrary, all appearances being to his advantage, and seeing that his addresses met with my approbation, she thought herself happy in complying with my wishes, where there was every prospect of future happiness to herself.—What a fortunate escape has my dear child experienced," added he.

"But my dear Sir," cried Ferdinand, "will you pardon me for observing, that it appears rather extraordinary you should not have well informed yourself of the Count's character and circumstances, previous to your consent for addressing Miss D'Alenberg." "You cannot suppose, my young friend," answered he, "that I neglected a duty so important to a parent. I actually did make inquiries, the gentleman at whose house we met with him, told me, that he was a widower; that he had married some time ago a ward of his uncle's, who died soon after she was brought to bed. His father, he said, had been killed in a duel by an officer, on account of an old regimental quarrel;—and that he had the misfortune to lose his worthy uncle very shortly after, for whom he then wore mourning. In short, my friend represented him as a worthy young man, who had met with great distresses from the premature death of his connexions, and congratulated me on the power of restoring him to happiness, by giving him the hand of my daughter.

"I have not the smallest doubt but that my friend implicitly believed every syllable he told me. Louisa's story was known to none but such whose interest it was to keep it secret. The Countess, or more properly speaking, the lady he had married, withdrawing herself and child, declaredly to him, for ever. The death of his uncle soon after that of his father, to whom only he was accountable for his actions, left him at liberty to promulgate what stories he pleased. None were interested either to doubt or to investigate them.—From our earliest acquaintance, I had understood he was going to make a tour to England; and when he had obtained my permission to address Theresa, he warmly solicited us both to join in his intended plan, which coinciding with our inclinations.—When you met with me at the village, I was returning to this house, with the double purpose of making preparations for the wedding, and at least a twelvemonth's absence. The Count and my friend were to join us in a week, when the marriage was to be completed, and we were directly to have set off on our tour. Thus you see he run no risk of an immediate detection, and doubtless would have remained abroad some time, or have changed his usual residence.

"But providence often defeats the deep-laid schemes of villany, and unmasks the contriver to the world. I have written a circumstantial account to my friend, and besought him to treat the base betrayer with the contempt and ignominy he deserves, nor as he values *my* friendship to engage in any personal resentment with a wretch so unworthy of his sword, but to let disgrace mark his steps, and his character fly before him. To the Count I disdained to write. Louisa and my daughter have both written to the Countess; the former, at our request, gratefully declining the generous settlement designed for her father and herself; my daughter, in terms of the warmest admiration of her noble conduct, relating to her the late occurrences, and earnestly entreating her to pay us a visit. Should she do us that favour, there will be a singular trio, two wives, and one intended to make a third."

"Upon my word," said Count M***, "I know not which to admire most, the temerity, or the villany of the man. Such unprecedented baseness in the same province, among his own acquaintance, where so many doubtful circumstances must have appeared against him, had any particular inquiry been set on foot, is truly astonishing." "It would have been more so," observed Ferdinand, "had not many points coincided in his favour. Mr. Hautweitzer's assertions before the old Count and the company, bore no proofs of the marriage which the young one disclaimed. He represented Louisa as his mistress; his father and uncle doubtless believed her to be such. She could adduce no evidence to prove the contrary. Therefore, though his connexion with her was reprehensible, even from his own acknowledgment, yet it bore not the marks of guilt attending a double marriage; nor had his lady sufficient conviction to authorize her withdrawing herself and child from him, had he persisted in his claims. But her honour and delicacy could not be satisfied with a disputed title; and from the Count's subsequent conduct, there is but too much reason to believe, that in possession of her fortune, and weary of being confined to one object, and to a dissembled regularity of life, inconsistent with his libertine principles, he made use of no endeavours to reconcile her doubts, or establish her claims, but left her to her own painful conjectures, the termination of which was in all probability little less satisfactory to him than to herself, as it left him at liberty to form fresh projects, and seek for new objects."

"Upon my word," returned Mr. D'Alenberg, "I believe you have represented the affair in its true point of view; and as a man, without honour or principle, governed by the most sensual and selfish passions, his conduct wants no further explanation; nor can we wonder he should succeed with the ladies, when setting aside his personal attractions, he certainly has the most insinuating address, the most plausible manners I ever beheld; so much so, that you would scarce feel an inclination to make inquiries that you must consider as equally an insult to him, and to your own discernment. But enough of this disgrace to society; let him no more be remembered among us."

Two days past away in this hospitable mansion with such celerity, from the delightful suavity and uncommon cheerfulness which Mr. D'Alenberg exerted to entertain his guests, and the more refined and elegant conversation of the ladies; that, on the third day, which the gentlemen had fixed upon for their departure, they felt infinite reluctance to give up the charms of such society, and relinquish domestic happiness for the clangor of arms, and destructive war. A sigh of heart-felt regret, and painful retrospection, escaped from both, when they met at the breakfast table, prepared for their journey.

"How," said Mr. D'Alenberg; "do you mean to throw a cloud over our little party, by deserting us? Did you come here with the ill-natured purpose of engaging our esteem, of giving us a relish for those pleasures arising from entertaining and improving conversation, and then suddenly leave us to regret and disappointment? In truth, my good friends, this is not well done of you;—and I expect you will give up your intention and your boots together, unless you will escort the ladies in an airing this morning."—"I hope, Sir," replied Ferdinand, with a look of earnestness, and in a tone of dejection; "I hope, Sir, you will believe there needs no persuasion to induce us to comply with your kind wishes, which so well accords with our own inclinations; but there are particular circumstances—motives of honour and delicacy—*feelings* which impel us to give up the happiness we have found in this society, and to follow that plan we have chalked out for ourselves, from whence we expect to derive neither profit nor pleasure, but, in the tumult of a camp, to lose the remembrance of ourselves."

"Far be it from me, to pry impertinently into your motives," returned Mr. D'Alenberg, "or urge you to favour us with your company one moment longer than is consistent with your inclinations and engagements. I must regret that *both* will not allow you to oblige me, but you must be masters of your own time and actions." The Count made suitable acknowledgments to the old gentleman, and lamented the necessity which forced them to relinquish their present happiness.

The ladies spoke not a word; a general dejection pervaded at the table with a silence of some minutes. Mr. D'Alenberg was the first to recover. "Plague on it," said he, affecting a gay tone, "that we cannot always command our wishes, though perhaps they may be sometimes extravagant, and militate against the interests of our friends. Aye, aye, we are not the *best* judges of the fit, and the unfit, I believe, and so must try to reconcile ourselves to present mortifications, looking forward to more pleasing expectations hereafter; and this hope, my friends, I will not relinquish, that we shall one day meet again, when the joy of meeting will amply recompense us for this temporary separation." They all joined cordially in "this hope;" and the moment breakfast was ended, Miss D'Alenberg arose. "I have an utter aversion," said she, with a faint smile, "to formal taking leave. You have my best wishes, gentlemen, for your health and happiness. I flatter myself you will sometimes remember us." With those words hastily pronounced, she quitted the room, followed by Louisa, who made them a similar compliment, without waiting for an answer.

"The girls are sorry to lose their beaus," said the old gentleman: "Their pleasure has been very transient; and if I have any skill in physiognomy, this parting accords as little with your feelings as with ours; and yet *it must be*, I suppose?"

"Dear Sir," cried Ferdinand, "how kindly is that question put, and what justice do you allow to our sentiments. Yes, we *must go*," added he, rising. "May every good angel guard you and your family, and uninterrupted happiness attend your lovely daughter and her suffering friend."

"I thank you most cordially—I thank you," replied Mr. D'Alenberg; "health and success will, I hope, be your's. We may one day meet again."

No more was said; they proceeded down the avenue which led to a gate, where their horses and servants were in waiting. The Count shook the old gentleman's hand, and vaulted into the saddle. As Ferdinand prepared to do the same, he whispered in the other's ear,

"Pity two unfortunate men, both *married*, and *unhappy*. You will do justice to the motives which hastens our departure."

He sprung upon the horse, and waving his hand, they were out of sight in a moment.—Mr. D'Alenberg stood all astonishment, looking after them, his lips half unclosed—words trembling on his tongue; but they were gone; he turned towards the house, deeply musing on Ferdinand's last words, and with a sigh of pity that two such men should be "married and unhappy."

Count M*** and his friend pursued their route for some miles without stopping or speaking, absorbed each in his own painful reflections; the other was unheeded; until, coming out of a wood, and ascending a rising ground a little to the left, Ferdinand saw the hills on which the city of Baden was situated, and instantly recollected his little Charles. Ah! thought he, shall I not once more fold him in my arms; the dear, unhappy, forsaken boy, perhaps soon to be an orphan, without a father or a friend. He stopt his horse, and turning, saw the Count galloping towards him, who, observing his agitation, eagerly inquired if any accident had befallen him.

"No," replied Ferdinand, "but do you not see those distant hills? A little beyond, you know, stands Baden: I have a son."——

"I understand you," said the Count;—"and guess what passes in your heart. But my good friend, you have lately seen him; you know he is in safe and honourable hands.—Why then would you seek a renewal of sorrow to yourself, without conveying a single benefit to him?"

"Enough," returned Ferdinand, pulling his hat over his eyes. "You have convinced me I ought not to seek a selfish gratification, which can only tend to harrow up my soul, and unman my resolutions; no, I will not go."

He spurred on his horse, and was again silent, until they arrived at a small village, where they were obliged to halt, and refresh the poor animals, almost dead with fatigue.

Each being desirous of amusing the other, they soon fell into a cheerful conversation, and sought to forget the *past*, by talking of their *future* plans. The war, which was now to be carried on with great vigour against the Turks; the marriage which the Emperor had projected for his daughter, afterwards so famous in history, as Queen of Hungary; and many other common topics, that carried them out of themselves.

Thus they spent some hours, until they resumed their journey, purposing to sleep at a small town about twelve miles further; but the roads were so bad, and they were so much impeded in their progress, that they were constrained to halt at a wretched inn on the skirts of a small hamlet, and pass a sleepless night, without any tolerable accommodations; but they were going to the *army*, and therefore disdained to complain of hardships, though they paid the price of luxuries.

The dawn of the morning saw them on horseback; and as they rode on, new scenes, and brighter prospects, gave a relief to their minds, and cheered their conversation. The remainder of their journey grew more pleasant; was passed without any accidents, and in due time they arrived in safety at Vienna.

CHAPTER VII.

HERE the busy preparations for the recruiting of the army, the Court of the Emperor, and the multitude of strangers resident there at that time, could not fail of attracting attention, and inspiring ardor in the bosoms of two brave men who wished to distinguish themselves in a cause against their common enemy. Count M*** was introduced to the Emperor, Charles the Sixth, who, having just received an account of the death of that brave and successful General, Prince Eugene, without knowing any one deserving, or capable of undertaking the command of his army, was at that time greatly perplexed, and gratefully acknowledged the volunteer services offered by the Count.—Ferdinand had heretofore been honoured with his approbation, and both gentlemen had abundant cause to be satisfied with their reception.

They passed some weeks at Vienna, in the usual amusements of the city, before the army was ready to take the field; during which time, they had received letters from their friends that had helped to tranquillize their minds. Ferdinand heard from Mr. Dunloff, that his son, and the good old Ernest, were in health; and he had also a letter from his brother, informing him, "that he was married to the Lady Amelia Bonhorff; but at the same time assuring him, that his present engagements did not weaken his regard for Ferdinand, who, whenever he was disposed to prefer services from a brother, to *pecuniary obligations from a stranger*, would always find his arms and purse open to his wishes."

This letter, the tenor of which seemed so affectionate, was nevertheless worded with a stiffness and a sort of haughty upbraiding, an air of superiority that alarmed the pride of Ferdinand, and again recalled to his mind the scene which passed immediately following the death of his father, when he was told, "that he was to be an equal sharer" in that fortune, solely bequeathed to Count Rhodophil, and the servants were ordered to remember they had *two masters.*——Ah! thought Ferdinand, in that moment, sorrow had softened his heart to the ties of nature, and a resolution to make me some reparation for the disappointment he supposed I must feel; but power and prosperity soon changed his sentiments, and chased the tender affections from his heart. He soon exulted in his superiority, and found gratification in ostentatiously bestowing as *favors*, those attentions, and that assistance, which at first he had taught me to expect as my *right*. Alas! how difficult is it for us to know our own hearts. Poor Rhodophil!

that brother disposed to love and honour you. You have, by an ill-judged pride, by a duplicity unworthy of yourself and me—you have alienated from those ties that bound us, and compelled him to prefer that "stranger," whose generosity and spirit disdains the idea of an obligation, where his own nobleness of heart is abundantly gratified in making another happy. A stranger! No—Count M*** is *my brother*; we have congenial souls, superior to the ties of blood.

This idea instantly cheered the mind of Ferdinand, and Count Rhodophil, with all his wealth and boasted happiness, neither excited his envy nor regret. His son and old Ernest were the only objects entitled to share his heart in Baden; not a word was mentioned relative to Claudina; and although a tender and sorrowful remembrance of a woman he once adored, frequently obtruded, yet he had ceased to think of her with those pangs, and that agonized affection, that had wholly occupied his mind previous to his connexion with the Count; and the silence observed by all parties concerning her, was sufficient evidence, that she wished to be forgotten: A sigh followed the conviction, but he endeavoured to divert his attention, by throwing his thoughts on other subjects.

Count M*** had also received a letter from Eugenia: The contents breathed a spirit of piety and cheerfulness; her situation grew daily more pleasant and desirable; peace had once more returned to her bosom, and the performance of religious duties had composed her mind, and she trusted, would atone for her errors. One only regret had power to give her a moment's pain, the union between the Count and herself, which precluded his happiness in that state with a more deserving object: But even *this only* interruption to her perfect content, she did not despair of removing at some future period. Her health, she added, was perfectly restored, and she had acquired a friend whose nobleness of mind was a pattern for her constant imitation.

The Count, who had, from the moment of their separation, exerted all his fortitude and resolution, to bear the decided plan Eugenia had fixed upon, who well knew her perseverance and courage, and saw all future expectations of enjoying her society would be equally vain and fruitless; whose passions, by sufferings, had been weakened and brought under control; though he was wounded to the soul by her determination to forsake him, no sooner found the event had taken place, and that no power or persuasion would avail to make any change in her plan, than he sought to call reason and resolution to his aid, to seek in an active life, and in a diversity of occupation, that variety of ideas which might preclude them from dwelling on one object; and this, with the friendship of Ferdinand, whose similarity of misfortunes, gentleness of manners, and goodness of heart, had gained his warm esteem, assisted him in subduing his sorrows, and restoring his mind to a comparative degree of ease.

The two friends having made a mutual communication of their letters, found, in a reciprocity of sentiment, mutual consolation; they had little doubt but that the lady mentioned in such high terms by Eugenia, was the Countess of Wolfran; nor could they forbear execrating the wretch who had poisoned the happiness of such a woman, by degrading her to a connexion with himself.

In a short time, the Emperor was ready to take the field; the friends were in one Regiment, and determined to share one fate:—They proceeded on their march, and soon came within view of the enemy's lines.—Here the Emperor halted; a council was convened, and the plan of attack settled, which was to take place the following day at sun-rise. The intermediate time the Count and Ferdinand employed in sealing their papers, writing to their friends; and the former generously erased all anxiety from the mind of the latter respecting his little Charles, by a bequest of a handsome provision for him, and constituting Mr. D'Alenberg the protector of his fortune and person; to which trust Ferdinand gladly added his acquiescence and signature; embracing his noble friend in a silent transport, much more expressive than a flow of words.

This necessary arrangement being completed, the Count wrote a tender adieu to his beloved Eugenia.—He had, from her first entrance into the convent, secured *her* future establishment.—Nothing, therefore, remained upon his mind to be performed.—She was already as dead to him; and he left no relatives to mourn his loss, should the chance of war deprive him of life. Their letters and papers were all deposited with the Emperor's private secretary, who was not unknown to the Count, and then they retired each to themselves for a few hours preparatory to the dreadful business of the following day.

At the first dawn of day, the drums and shrill sounding trumpets gave the alarm, and called them to the field.—The friends embraced, and hastened to their posts. The Turkish army was a numerous host; ashamed and enraged at their former defeats, they seemed now resolved to conquer or die on the spot; to retrieve their former blasted laurels, or return no more to meet the fury of their monarch, or bend the neck to the fatal and ignominious bow-string. Their opponents, equally emulous of glory, and desirous to rid themselves of a troublesome enemy, advanced to meet them with eagerness and resolution. A hard fought battle ensued; dreadful was the carnage on both sides; but the multitude prevailed. The Turks poured in on all the ranks of the Imperialists with such velocity, that they were unable to sustain their posts; were compelled to retreat; were pursued, and a horrid slaughter marked their sanguinary fury.

The Count and Ferdinand did all that men could do; they fought like lions; they were beat back several times: Again they rallied and returned to the charge; but though well supported, all availed not; the numbers were too powerful, and the friends fell desperately wounded among the dying and the dead.—The Imperialists were obliged to fly, and the honour of the day rested with the Turks.—By a piece of singular good fortune, the two wounded friends were discovered by a Turkish commander, who perceived they still breathed, though life seemed hovering on their lips, and their wounds pouring forth torrents of blood. The officer who observed their situation, was not deficient in the feelings of humanity; he exerted himself, and called in assistance to stop the bleeding, and bind up their wounds. They were carried to his tent, and properly attended. Insensible alike to his cares or their own danger, they remained for several days with very little signs of life, and with still less hopes of recovery.

During this period, a truce had been agreed upon between the two armies, and the Emperor appeared to be very much inclined to make peace on the terms he had before rejected. The face of things was now changed; Prince Eugene, whose name alone carried with it terror to his enemies, no longer existed.—The Turks had recovered from their panic; their courage returned with their numbers: Charles had many interior enemies, whom it behoved him to guard against. The first wish of his heart was the establishment of the pragmatic sanction, in favour of his daughter Maria Theresa, afterwards Queen of Hungary. To carry this favourite point into execution, he was willing to give up some secondary ones, and finding the Turks were at that time too powerful for him to subdue, he readily was persuaded to make overtures for a truce preparatory to proposals for a peace.

The Turks, though now victorious, had been so harassed, and exhausted in their treasures by former wars, that they made but a show of objections to the Emperor's advances; a truce was therefore speedily agreed upon for six months, and both armies withdrew from the field to their own homes. An exchange of prisoners was also settled, but unfortunately an officer, who had fought by the side of Ferdinand and the Count; seeing them both fall, to all appearance lifeless, reported their death in the army, and the bodies not being found, did not seem extraordinary, as few persons could be distinguished among the slain. The Turkish cavalry, in their pursuit of the vanquished, had rode over, and defaced most of the unhappy victims who lay in heaps upon the plain.

So great was the slaughter on that day, and so many brave men and officers had the Emperor lost, that the news of Count M*** and Ferdinand being fallen with the rest, was only included in the general regret. The gentlemen entrusted with their letters to Mr. D'Alenberg, the Count's steward, and Mr. Dunloff, the good Ernest's nephew, sent them off with the melancholy account that those brave men no longer existed.

Whilst those letters were on their way to cause a mortal affliction to their friends, the Count and Ferdinand were carried in a litter to the house of their preserver in Adrianople. This Turkish commander, as we have observed, had some traits of humanity in his composition, and following the impulse of the moment, had administered relief to the dying friends from compassion alone; but after they had been conveyed to his tent, the blood washed from their persons; the contents of their pockets examined, in which were memorandums that denoted their being men of some condition, the predominant passion of self-interest was a greater stimulative than tenderness towards affording them that unremitted attention which most certainly conduced to the preservation of their lives.

Ferdinand was the first restored to his senses, and a recollection of past events. He saw only Turks around him, and an elderly woman who officiated as a nurse. His reason returned for two or three days before he had strength to speak. He therefore made his silent observations, and was very soon sensible that he was a prisoner. His regret was greatly lessened, when he saw that his friend the Count was also alive, and in a similar situation, from which he derived a hope that they might be companions, and useful to each other. Within a very few days, both gentlemen were enabled faintly to express their gratitude to their preserver, and rejoice in the safety of each other.

To their being together in one room, and capable of conversing now and then with each other, may doubtless be attributed their speedy recovery from a state so very dangerous, and even after the return of their senses, so very often fluctuating from the extreme weakness and debility occasioned by the great loss of blood.

One morning, when Ismael, the Turkish commander, paid them a visit, after they had enjoyed a good night's rest, and found their spirits greatly revived, they entered into a conversation with him relative to the truce which he had informed them was agreed upon between the two powers. He spoke both the German and French languages tolerable well, and they found no difficulty in making him comprehend they were men of family and fortune, and were desirous of returning into Germany as soon as possible.—They besought him, therefore, to let letters be conveyed to their friends, and to let information of their existence be expedited to the Emperor, that they might hope soon to be included in an exchange of prisoners.

This Ismael promised with much seeming sincerity, to undertake for; and assured them, he would exhibit his power and influence to procure for them a speedy release from captivity; giving them to understand, that their rank was known, and that he was answerable for their persons. Far different was the truth; their death had been generally credited in the Imperial army; the little inquiry that had been made relative to their bodies, had been unsatisfactory, and 'twas supposed they had been trampled upon undistinguished in the day of battle, and had been thrown with the multitude of dead bodies beyond all power of discrimination.

When carried to his tent, he perceived, from their military uniform, that they were of some rank in the army; he had therefore craftily destroyed their clothes, and from their wounds, their persons had but few traits left that could answer any description given of them. He had taken care to place no one near them that understood their language;—and by these artful manœuvres, had them securely in his power.

As they advanced in a state of convalescence, he began to reflect, that in Adrianople, it would be impossible to retain them from the hazard of being known, or of finding an opportunity to give information of their existence, if they were permitted to be at liberty, which he could not well refuse when they had recovered strength sufficient to walk.

To perfect his schemes, it was necessary to take them further into the country, where their dependence must rest solely on him, nor any knowledge of affairs reach them but through his hands. This determined on, he came to their apartment one morning with an air of haste and distraction. He told them, a commotion had begun in the city; that the troops, dissatisfied with the commanders for agreeing to a truce, instead of pursuing their victories, had risen in large bodies, both in Constantinople and in that city also; and, as it was impossible to judge of the event, or how far the rage of the soldiery might proceed, their only safety depended on flight. Fortunately he had a country house in the neighbourhood of Philippo, where they would be secure against violence or disaffection. To this house they should be immediately conveyed in a litter, to preserve them from the fury of the mob, which might possibly know no bounds, if they were discovered to be Germans.

This plausible tale, fabricated to impose on the unsuspicious friends, were by them credited without reserve, and they felt the warmest gratitude towards Ismael for his kind solicitude to save and serve them.—Within a few hours, every thing was arranged and they were on the road to Philippo,

Ismael assuring them of his attention to their interests, and that he would
either quickly join them, or if the insurrection was subdued, send orders for
their speedy return.

Their state of health would not admit of travelling fast; therefore the
slow proceeding of the litter was to them a convenience; and in the open
roads they were permitted to be uncovered, and have the benefit of the air.
The small villages they stopt at afforded but indifferent accommodations;
nor did they meet with a single being who understood their language.

On the second day, they halted at a tolerable large hamlet, at one end
of which were the remains of a miserable fort, inhabited by a few soldiers.
The person who commanded them held some conversation with their con-
ductors; presently after which, they made signs for them to alight. Two
of them took hold of the Count to assist him. Ferdinand was preparing
to follow, when instantly two men with drawn scimitars jumped into the
litter, seized his arms. The curtains were closed, and they moved forwards,
regardless of the struggles and exclamations of Ferdinand, and the cries of
the Count, which died away upon his ear as they proceeded.

Too late convinced that some treachery was intended, distracted at
being separated from his friend, and equally incapable of making any resistance, or obtaining any compassion from his guards, without money
to bribe, or language to persuade, he resigned himself to despair; and the
most heartfelt sighs, and pathetic gestures, portrayed the anguish of his
mind. Totally insensible to his distress, and mindful only of their charge,
they conversed with the utmost insensibility, eying *him* continually with
glances of disdain and suspicion.

It was the third day before they arrived at the end of their journey. For
some miles they had travelled through a barren and mountainous country:
At length they descended into a plain, which was extensive, and terminated
with a view of another mountain, on which stood a castle, with several
small fortresses on the declivities, all of which were surrounded with high
walls, that reached a considerable way on the plain. At some distances from
each other, thinly scattered on the skirts of the plain, and a rising hill on one
side, stood a few houses; but the general appearance of the country seemed
desolate and uncultivated.

Ferdinand was permitted to take a view of this cheerless prospect, as
they crossed the plain towards a large pair of gates fixed in the wall at the
foot of a scraggy part of the mountain, and at one end of the wide extended plain. Here a paper was delivered to the sentinel at the gates, which,
having read, they were opened, and proceeding round the mountain, they
came to a similar pair of gates, where the same ceremony was observed,

and on their entrance, an easy winding path-way led them to the Castle, passing several small forts, guarded by savage and half-starved looking men, who scouled under their bushy eye-brows, and, by their haggard ferocious countenance, inspired terror and despair.

At the Castle, Ferdinand was assisted to alight. He was so far exhausted by weakness, fatigue, and distress of mind, that they were obliged to carry him into an apartment, and give him some sherbet to prevent him from fainting. He laid himself down on a sofa, indifferent to life, and overwhelmed with misery. He was now a prisoner in a dreary and uncomfortable place, deprived of society, lost to his child, his friends, and his dear Count. This last stroke of being separated from him, was the completion of his misfortunes; and in the bitterness of his grief, he cursed the barbarians, whose callous hearts had divided them.

At night, he was shewn into a small room about eight feet square, with a couch to sleep on, the only furniture it contained. Some cakes made of rice, a few grapes and sherbet had been put ready for him, of which he partook very sparingly, and retired to rest upon a mattress, covering himself with a quilt, as is the custom of the Turks in all places.

For several hours, Ferdinand lay a prey to the utmost inquietude, and the most distressing recollections. Why Ismael had deceived them, what purpose it was to answer, or wherefore he had cruelly separated him from the Count, were the questions that agitated his mind, and precluded sleep.

Wearied out at length with uncertain conjectures, and his spirits fatigued for want of rest, towards morning, he dropt into an unrefreshing slumber, from which he was awakened by a Turk, who stood beside him with a bason of coffee. He started up, and receiving the bason with an inclination of his head, and a few words in thanks, which, though not understood by the man, yet the tone and courteous look that accompanied them seemed to please him, and a *little* relaxed the unbending severity of his countenance. He stayed until the coffee was drank, then making a sign for the other to follow, he led him into a larger apartment, that overlooked the opposite side of the Castle from that which he had entered at, and appeared to terminate in a wood or grove at some distance beyond the walls. At the right, he observed the ruins of several noble edifices, and farther off a building in a circular form, resembling an amphitheatre.—To the left, were some extensive fields, but uncultivated, there he saw some goats bounding about from thence to the sides of the hills, at the foot of which run a small rivulet of water, clear as crystal.

Such was the prospect that presented itself on all sides, dreary and uncomfortable, without a hope of any thing more animating to gratify the eye, or indulge the search of curiosity; for he judged most rightly, that the walls which enclosed the Castle would be the boundary of his liberty.

For the rest, he had not much to complain of; he was served with fruits generally dried, milk, sherbet, and rice, and with some little show of civility; but he had no one to converse with; no books to amuse him; no friend to partake either of his distresses or comforts; and his own recollections of the past, any more than his expectations of the future, were not calculated to afford him any amusement, or even to indulge a visionary hope of relief.

Yet strange to say, under all this anxiety, with little rest, and less appetite, his weakness decreased: he found himself in three or four days considerably better in health, and with amended strength, which he attributed solely to the salubrity of the air. His solicitude for the safety and health of the Count contributed not a little to augment his uneasiness; and the incertitude whether his letters from Adrianople had been sent to his friends, which, from subsequent transactions, he entertained some doubts of, gave him the most poignant concern.

Entirely precluded from conversation, by his ignorance of the Turkish language, he resolved, if possible, to attain some knowledge of it. The person who commanded at the Castle, now and then visited him.—Policy, as well as good breeding, induced him to behave with politeness. To the man who attended him, he showed a complacency and thankfulness, which appeared to be gratifying. He began, therefore, to make both understand, by his signs, that he wished to comprehend them. He repeated their words, and retained the names of things brought to him, and of such as he pointed out from the windows.

The Turks appeared pleased with his attentions, and desire of knowledge; and in about a week after his residence there, the commander was constant in his visits; delighted in making him understand the names of every thing he wanted; taught him several common and useful expressions; and, as their language is much more comprehensive than our's; as Ferdinand had nothing to divert his thoughts, and was determined to profit by his master's instructions, it is not at all extraordinary, that, in the space of two months, he had acquired as *much* knowledge, if not more, than in the ordinary course of things he might have learnt in six or eight.

During his progression in the language, he had obtained information, that Ismael was nearly related to this gentleman who commanded the Castle; that he had received instructions to be extremely careful of Ferdinand, as a prisoner of his, for whom he expected a considerable ransom. By no means to permit him to emigrate beyond the Castle walls; but at the same time to treat him with civility, that his captivity might not injure his health, and deprive him of the sums he expected for *him*, and also another prisoner, whom he had ordered to be confined elsewhere.

This intelligence unravelled the whole plot to Ferdinand. He saw that liberty was not to be hoped for in the usual way of an exchange, and doubted not but that their letters had been suppressed to prevent the application of their friends. Though he detested the duplicity and avarice of Ismael, yet he was rejoiced to find a clue to account for his conduct, which held out a remote hope, that the Count and himself might be liberated, since he was well assured that any demand he should think proper to make, their friends would readily comply with, however undeserving he might be of their generosity.

This information, in a great degree, contributed to restore both his health and spirits; he made many attempts to find out the name of the place where the Count and he were separated; but Heli, which was the name of the commander, protested his entire ignorance. Whether he was sincere or not, could not be known, and Ferdinand was obliged to be contented with the limited confidence he had obtained, and amuse the tediousness of his captivity, by studying the language with unremitted diligence, and conciliating the esteem of Heli.

He made no attempts to subvert the fidelity which the commander had pledged to Ismael; for in the first place, he held a trust committed and engaged for in a sacred light: And *could* he have satisfied his scruples in that point, he risked every thing; the loss of every indulgence, if he attempted, and was repulsed. By this prudent conduct, he engaged the regard of Heli, who begun to unbend from that frigid reserve and taciturnity which characterize the Turks, and to be pleased with the diligence and progress of his pupil. One morning, when the weather was uncommonly fine, he entered Ferdinand's apartment, who was standing at the window, just then in a very pensive mood.

"Are you not well?" demanded he.

"I cannot say I am ill," answered Ferdinand; "but I am weak enough to be affected by a dream, which I have had, and have risen quite unrefreshed from my couch, with a great depression of spirits."

The Turks are extremely superstitious.—Heli viewed him for a few minutes in silence; at length—"I am sorry you are afflicted," said he; "and it shall not be my fault if you do not shake off this dejection. I am come to a resolution to enlarge your liberty. This morning I have heard from my kinsman Ismael; he is gone to Constantinople. He charges me to be careful of you; but hopes soon to ease me of the trouble, as he expects daily to hear from your friends. Believe me, Christian, I shall rejoice at your enlargement from your captivity, though I shall lose a companion, which, in this solitary place, must be a cause of regret. I come, however, to prove my regard and confidence, to invite you to a walk. Have you no curiosity to stroll beyond these walls?"

"Doubt it not," replied Ferdinand, agreeably surprised.—"I have frequently wished to view those buildings, and that amphitheatre which appears to be mouldering into ruins; but I had too much respect for you to ask any thing you did not seem inclined to offer, or to express a desire to pass beyond the bounds limited for my residence."

"I am not insensible of your moderation," returned he; "and 'tis in that consideration, I am tempted to extend your liberty. Come then, if you can walk. The morning is truly inviting." Ferdinand wanted no further invitation, but with much pleasure, followed his gentle jailer to the gates, which, having passed, they walked on down the declivities into the plain.

They crossed a considerable extent of ground before they came to the ruins of several noble buildings.

"Here," said Heli, "once stood the superb edifices of many Roman senators. In those adjoining fields was fought the memorable battle between Marc Anthony, Augustus Cæsar, Brutus, and Cassius. By tradition, every step you take here is sacred, either from the battles of heroes, or the residence of noble Romans, with whose names or actions I am but little acquainted; but you Christians, who possess an insatiable curiosity, to you every object here must be of consequence."

"Of consequence, indeed," cried Ferdinand, whose heart glowed with the idea that he had the power of contemplating the ground so renowned in story, and reviving the remembrance of those heroes, once law-givers to the world; but how quick the transition from admiration to wonder and regret. "Where now was that mighty universal empire, which delegated her authority over all the known nations of the world? Whose heroes were as invincible in war as they were superior in peace: Whose principles were incorruptible; whose integrity was unquestionable. Are these mouldering ruins; these decayed mansions, all that remain here to mark the conquerors of the world? Melancholy idea.

"Whilst brave, great, and virtuous, Rome was invincible; but when luxury and corruption crept into the state; when senators became venal, and heroes selfish and ambitious, Rome fell from her ancient glory:—Degenerated from her great forefathers—plunged into licentiousness; sunk into a supine weakness.—She turned her arms against herself; destroyed her own powers, and no longer revered as the virtuous republic, giving laws to mankind. Her glory gradually diminished, 'till she fell, to rise no more.

"What a warning to nations! what a lesson to the princes of the present day!—Rome fell by corruption and licentiousness; by civil wars, and internal commotions;—by ambitious and self interested statesmen;—by the *tribunes*; by the *men of the people*, who, loudly crying for *liberty*, and, by factious intrigues, distracting the state, and interrupting the course of justice; by pretending patriotism, and by sowing sedition among the lower classes of men, ever ripe to trample upon all order, and assemble in tumultuous meetings. By such wicked and imprudent measures was *Rome* destroyed.

"Whilst virtuous and united, she was *invulnerable*; but 'a kingdom divided against itself cannot stand,' and in the general decay, *all* share the common ruin: There can be no discrimination; for who shall say to a misguided tumultuous people, *'Thus far* shalt thou go, and *no farther.'* Alas! a turbulent spirit, once raised, it is difficult to subdue; and measures never once intended, are often times pursued to the confusion and ruin of its first projectors."

CHAPTER VIII.

Lost in these, and such like reflections, Ferdinand wandered over the broken monuments of ancient glory, every pillar of which raised an enthusiastic spirit, and a concomitant sorrow. Heli, unmoved, walked among the ruins without either reflection or reverence; but observing that his companion looked fatigued, as well as thoughtful, "I think," said he, "your walk has been sufficiently extensive for the present.—To-morrow you shall take a view of the amphitheatre and the grove. Yet, if it has no other effect than to increase your dejection, we might as well remain in the Castle."

"Do not mistake the nature of my feelings," replied Ferdinand.—"'Tis impossible to view these fragments of ancient grandeur, without ruminating on the causes which tumbled them into ruin. But I assure you, that I am much obliged and gratified by your indulgence; and could the mind of man divest itself from the selfishness inherent to our nature, we should have but little reason to murmur at our own losses and misfortunes, when we reflect on the entire downfall of a nation once so great and mighty as the Romans."

"I cannot say," returned Heli, "that looking on these ruinous palaces, at all lessens my regret for the want of fortune, or comforts me for being doomed to live in this solitary place."

"I am not more abstracted than yourself," said Ferdinand, "since I do not scruple to confess, that I am at this moment *not* the *less* sensible of my own unpleasant situation, less *unmindful* of local attachments, nor *less* anxious for the fate of my friend, when contemplating the fall of empires; but it proves to a thinking mind, that sorrow is the lot of man, in some stage or other of his life: And if he loves his country, he must dread, that the same vices, luxury, ambition, licentiousness, and discontent, too prevalent in most countries, must at length terminate in the destruction of that nation, where their growth is encouraged by faction, and nursed by the countenance of superior abilities."

Heli nodded his head, but whether in approbation of the justice of those observations, or because he did not comprehend them, and could make no reply, cannot be determined; but he had received so little pleasure from the walk, that he stretched his inclination to make the utmost speed back, that the gravity of the Turkish movements would allow of.

Ferdinand, whose mind had found much relief from the novelty of the morning's ramble, after his return, seemed to have recruited both his strength and spirits, and conversed with more cheerfulness than usual.

"I have frequently," said he to Heli, "had an inclination to ask you one question, but I was fearful you would be displeased at my curiosity."

"And what is that," returned the other. "Speak freely; the *answer* depends upon myself."

"Have you no women in this Castle?—Near two months that I have been here, I have seen nor heard of any: Yet can hardly persuade myself that you reside in this solitary place without some companions to soften your melancholy hours."

"And have you not made this inquiry before of the man who attends you?" asked Heli.

"Never," replied Ferdinand.—"I have always forborne the meanness of interrogating a servant relative to his master's concerns."

"I admire your discretion," returned he. "You deserve confidence. I *have* women here, in a distant part of the Castle from this, where they are shut up, and have only a garden to amuse themselves in, which is as much liberty as the laws of our prophet, and the custom of the country, allows them.—You Christians make *your* women infamous by toleration of their vices, and giving the reins to their natural depraved inclinations."

"As I make it an invariable rule," answered Ferdinand, "never to enter into any controversies against declared and established prejudices, I shall make no other reply to your observation, than to assure you, that in the European countries, we generally find an undue restraint, a severity of conduct, either from a parent or a husband, almost always is productive of those errors and vices we are so sedulous to guard them from.

"The English repose an unlimited confidence in *their* women; and though doubtless there may be, and I dare say are, very many who disgrace themselves and their families, yet both, from reading and information, I am led to believe that the number of vicious women bears a much less proportion than in Spain, in some parts of Italy, or even in Turkey, where their whole study, and all their ingenuity, is employed to deceive and betray their husbands, whom they look upon rather as severe masters or jailors, than as the partners of their hearts.

"However, as I before observed, I never interfere in established customs; I am obliged to you for your confidence, and am glad to find that you have such objects with you, as may sooth your solitary hours in a place which appears so distant from all social converse."

"I thank you," returned Heli; "but I have at least as much plague as pleasure with them; and had our prophet exterminated them from the world, mankind would have been no losers."

"And yet," replied Ferdinand, "your prophet has made your chief happiness in paradise to consist of beautiful virgins."

"Yes," said Heli; "but those virgins will be *always* beautiful, *always* young, and never unfaithful."

"Then," returned the other, "you may well bear with their follies and decay here, since their comparative defects must enhance the delights of your promised happiness hereafter."

"Fine talking," cried Heli; "if you had two or three hundred women to rule, who, shut up together, are perpetually quarrelling, envious, jealous, and revengeful; all of whom you must reconcile, please, and caress. I believe you would scarcely think expected pleasures a sufficient recompense to make you patiently endure such a slavery. Thank Heaven, I have *but eight*, and trouble enough *they* give me."

Ferdinand smiled.—"And is not the trouble of your own making. Why increase your plagues; why have *eight* women?—Can you not select one from the number to make you happy, and dismiss the others?"

"One!" exclaimed Heli; "be confined to *one* woman! Great happiness indeed I should find then. And that *one*, what would become of her, without companions.—Shut up from all social converse—nothing to amuse her—nothing to animate or agitate her mind; what a dull insipid mass of clay should I meet, when I condescend to unbend and divert myself."

"I had indeed forgotten *her* situation," returned Ferdinand, "and must acknowledge, if the severity of your customs oblige women to solitude and confinement, *one* could not exist long without a companion; but she might have slaves, attendants to converse with."

"It would never do," said Heli.—"Too much consequence and power thrown into the hands of one woman, would make her insolent and rebellious. By dividing our attentions, we reduce them to an equality that prevents intrigues, discontents, and insolence; makes them emulous to please, and cautious to offend. But they are so capricious and so envious, that among themselves they are perpetually disagreeing, and I am often called upon to decide quarrels, and to compel them to keep good order: Yet, were it not for the variety and spirit this diffuses among them, they could neither entertain me, nor amuse themselves. Therefore, though sometimes I am fatigued and angry at their disputes, upon the whole it is less disagreeable than a stupid sameness, which would be disgusting."

"You have accounted very well," said Ferdinand, "for the necessity that compels you to have many women; and whilst your customs respecting the sex subject them so much to your power, and deny them those rights which our divine legislator bestowed on all mankind without discrimination, that of *liberty* and *free will*. Whilst both their minds and bodies are in captivity, *one* unfortunate female, as you observed, can neither be happy in herself, or make another so."—Heli grew thoughtful, and made no reply.—The subject dropt; and for the remainder of the day, Ferdinand applied himself closely to his studies.

The following day, Heli waited not to be asked, but voluntarily offered to accompany Ferdinand in a walk to the amphitheatre.—The other gladly accepted the civility, and they directed their steps to this noble building. Great part of the circular wall remained entire. Many superb pillars supported different parts of the structure. Nearly one half of the inside was in ruins; but in some places there were regular seats rising over one another to an immense height.

The whole exhibited a sullen state of grandeur sinking to decay. Half broken pillars of marble, of granite, lay scattered in large fragments on a kind of Mosaic pavement. Several fine pieces of sculpture, maimed statues, and decayed paintings, that at the touch crumbled into dust, lay in heaps at different parts of the building. In fine, all was great, admirable, and gratifying;—but at the same time mortifying, depressive, and humiliating, to the pride of human nature.

For who that beheld those stupendous buildings, those superb monuments of antiquity, once adorned by the most virtuous and bravest of mankind, now trampled under foot, decayed, mutilated, and sinking into ruin; but must shrink into nothing, on a comparative view of his own littleness, of the modern architecture of the present day, and feel, that soon the one will be no more, lost and forgotten; levelled to the earth, without a stone remaining to engage either veneration or regret: Whilst on this hallowed ground ages hence, mankind will tread with reverence, and recall to their minds those heroes who once were the saviours of their country, and to the latest posterity will be the envy and admiration of mankind.

Ferdinand eagerly gazed on every part of this immense building. His enthusiastic spirit seemed raised above himself. He glowed with delightful recollections, and traced in his mind's eye, those mighty armies command-ed by the first of men, now marching to the adjoining fields, to decide, in one day, the fate of Rome, then mistress of the world.

But his feelings cannot be described; nor can this weak pen delineate a hundredth part of the admirable remains of this once incomparable structure; in the examining of which, he had spent more than four hours, without going half over the buildings. Heli, whose complaisance was at its utmost stretch, and who had exhibited several marks of impatience; for what was statues or pillars to him, broken and destroyed by time, and the depredations of vulgar uninformed souls. Fragments like these were to him contemptuous ruins; and he admired, at the ignorance and superstition of Ferdinand, in making them objects of such consequence.

"Well," said he, he a tone of fretfulness, "do you design to pass the day here; or are you inclined to walk in the grove?"

The other perfectly comprehended the spirit of the question, and re-plied very complaisantly, "that he was ready to attend him."—To the grove they turned, which, though thick and impervious to the eye, was by no means so extensive as Ferdinand had expected, and seemed to have been the work of modern times; for the trees bore not the marks of centuries. This he remarked.

"I believe you are right," returned Heli. "I have heard this plantation was made by some hermits, who chose this spot to build their cells in, one of which only now remains, and is inhabited by Father Abdalla."

"How!" cried Ferdinand, "does any one reside here?"

"Yes," replied Heli; "one holy man has here devoted his life to serve Allah and his prophet."

They now penetrated through a thick underwood, darkened by some lofty trees, and descending a slope, came to a small rivulet, on the opposite side of which he saw among the trees the moss covered cell of the hermit, who was reclining on a little bank, raised about a foot above the earth, reading the alcoran. They had crossed a small wooden bridge, and, as they approached, he raised his head, and viewed them steadily, but without any marks of surprise; then threw his eyes down towards his book.

Heli saluted him, by laying his right hand on his breast. "Abdalla," said he, "holy man, thou art a true servant to the Most High. Praise be to him, and his prophet Mahomet."

The old man arose, and saluted them courteously. He invited them into his cell, where he set before them some dried fruits, and water clear as crystal.

Ferdinand was charmed with the sweet and placid countenance of this hermit—so different from the frigid austere looks of the Turks in general. His voice was mild, his eye soft, though penetrating; and he invited them to the simple repast, with a cordiality that denoted a beneficent mind.

"'Tis long since I have seen thee brother," said he to Heli.

"True," replied he, "I have had a companion, whom thou seest, a Christian captive, under my care; who has acquired our language tolerably, and deported himself so as to deserve my favour."

"As a captive, I pity him," said Abdalla. "As a Christian, I will pray for him, that our holy prophet may convert him from his errors, as he has enlightened his understanding."

"I thank you, holy father," answered Ferdinand.—"Though a Christian, I reverence true piety, and honour good men of every religion. The prayers of an upright heart I shall ever be grateful for. But pardon me if I ask how long you have resided in this grove?"

"Upwards of fifty years," replied he.—"I was near thirty when I first came here. When young I was bred to arms. I fought under our last great Sultan. He thought I deserved well; he promoted me. This raised me many enemies; I fell under the displeasure of the Grand Visier; that was sufficient to mark my ruin. My death was resolved on; a faithful slave gave me notice of my danger, at the hazard of his own life. We fled together, and after encountering a thousand perils, we arrived at this grove, by a different road than the one to the Castle.—In this cell dwelt a holy man; he received and cherished us. In a few moons after, I lost my faithful Sadi. My grief was unspeakable. That event, and the unjust treatment I had met with, gave me a disgust to the world.

"Here I found a friend, a protector, and an instructive monitor. Our holy prophet sanctified his labours. I renounced the world and all its deadly passions, love, hatred, ambition, and envy. Twenty years I possessed a friend, who was the chosen of Allah, and a true son of the prophet. He purified my heart, and fashioned it like his own.—His translation to paradise is the only cloud that has, for a moment, shadowed my content since the death of Sadi.

"I possess health, and every wish of my heart. I expect soon to enjoy the blessings of Mahomet, the joys of paradise: My days are numbered, and draw to an end: I always keep a week's provision in my cell, lest, for a short time, I should be unable to quit it. Allah be praised; I wait his appointed time, which cannot be far off."

This simple recital inspired Ferdinand with admiration and respect. He bowed involuntarily before the good man, whose animated countenance corresponded with the purity of his heart. "Holy father," said he, "let me entreat your blessing. I am a man of sorrows: Captivity is the least of them: Let me have your prayers, that my latter days may be as tranquil as yours."

"*Hope*, my son—*hope*," replied Abdalla. "Trust in the Most High; so shall thy troubles fly from thee like a passing cloud: Thine enemies be cut down, and thy latter days be peace."

Heli, who grew impatient at this scene, abruptly reminded Ferdinand it was time to return. He turned to the good father.—"You have cheered my spirits," said he. "You have communicated to my heart faith and hope.—If I am permitted, I will see you again. Holy father, remember me in your prayers."

The hermit, with a look of dignified complaisance, bowed his head.— "The blessing of Allah be upon thee, my son, and upon you, my brother."

Heli and Ferdinand left the grove, and returned to the Castle, the former thoughtful and fatigued; for the Turks are extremely indolent; seldom walk for pleasure; and it was no small effort he had made to emerge from the supine indulgence so habitual to him, as to walk two following days. The other, delighted by new scenes, charmed with what he had seen, and looking with admiration and reverence on every spot so celebrated and so sacred, felt an uncommon flow of spirits, and as well as he could, in a language but new to him, expressed to Heli a thousand obligations for his kindness, and spoke of the pleasure he received in the most lively, and, to the other, enthusiastic terms; which was heard with a frigid coldness, and a more than usual reserve.

Ferdinand, at length struck with the silence of Heli, apologized for his loquacity, and restrained his raptures. On arriving at their apartments, Heli threw himself on the sofa, and complained of immense fatigue, though the whole of their walk had not exceeded three miles; but that was a journey to the Turk, who sometimes had been accustomed to visit the hermit, but through a different road; for on the other side of the Castle was a very short way to it; but then they must pass a few scattered houses, which, being inhabited, Heli did not chuse to take Ferdinand near them; nor was he informed that any such places were in the neighbourhood. On the contrary, he supposed Heli's family, and the few soldiers who guarded the small fortresses, he saw on coming to the Castle, were all the people that dwelt in that neglected and deserted spot.

All that day, Heli persevered in an unusual silence. Not that indolent taciturnity natural to the Turks, but a thoughtful gloom seemed to hang upon him, as if revolving, in his mind, some affair of importance.

Ferdinand observed and trembled.—"Some event, productive, I fear, of no good to me, is in contemplation." He passed a night of painful inquietude. The following morning afforded no relief to his anxiety. Heli did not appear at the usual hour.—The noon came, but no Heli. Unable any longer to restrain his impatience, when the slave attended with his coffee—"Is not the governor well?" demanded he.

The man bowed his head, put his finger to his lips, and withdrew. The day passed heavily: He endeavoured to recollect if he had given any offence to Heli; his memory charged him with no fault or imprudence in their several conversations. To what then was owing this sudden and unaccountable revolution in his behaviour?

A second night, and the first part of the second day, passed in the same uneasy conjectures. Towards the close of the day, the door of his apartment opened; Heli appeared, followed by——Judge the transports of Ferdinand—followed by the Count! Yes, his friend Count M***. They flew to embrace each other, regardless of all but the joy of this unexpected meeting; as unlooked for by the Count, as unhoped for by Ferdinand, whose mind, having been wound up to expect some horrid design against him, was so overcome by a rush of sudden joy, that unable to speak, he sunk almost motionless on the sofa.

The effect was momentary; for he soon exclaimed, "My friend! my dear Count.—Dear—generous Heli."

The Count was not less transported, nor less grateful in his expressions to their benefactor. Heli approached them—"I leave you together; an hour hence I shall return, and communicate important news."

He withdrew. The friends had a thousand things to say—a thousand questions to ask. It appeared, that after they had been separated, the Count was carefully guarded. He met with no ill treatment, but he obtained no companion like Heli. His days past heavily, without any employment, and his mind oppressed with sorrow and despair; a situation, he observed, which must very shortly have overpowered his constitution.

The preceding day, Heli accompanied his guard into his miserable apartment. He made him a sign to follow Heli; he knew resistance would be in vain, and was indifferent as to consequences. He was placed in a covered carriage; they travelled all night, and for some hours on this morning.—"When we arrived at this Castle," proceeded the Count, "I supposed I had only changed one prison for another still more dreadful; and when, by signs, I was ordered to accompany Heli to the door of this apartment, I prepared to enter it as the grave of all my hopes, and the closing scene of my life.

"Good Heavens! what a transition from absolute despair to exquisite joy. How little did I hope ever to see my friend again. Yet let me not be too sanguine; perhaps we are prisoners for life; yet if they will permit us to be together, I am careless of future circumstances."

"What is intended by bringing us together," said Ferdinand, "I am as ignorant of as yourself: For when I once questioned Heli as to the place of your confinement, he protested he was ignorant of it. In this, 'tis plain, he practised deception: Therefore I cannot pretend to judge what may be his future views.

"I have experienced civilities from him which call for confidence; and if I am deceived, I would rather suffer for my candor, than wrong him by unjust suspicions."

The Count seemed to derive hope from Ferdinand's account of Heli. They both execrated the treachery of Ismael; judging that, from such a man, they had every thing to dread, should his expectations, or demands of a large ransom, by any unforeseen means, be fruitless.

By the time appointed, Heli entered, and carefully shutting the door, seated himself by Ferdinand.—"I am now going to prove my confidence in you," said he.—"Five days ago, I received intelligence, that my kinsman Ismael was imprisoned, by the machinations of his enemies. This event nearly concerned me; yet I hoped his relations and interest at Constantinople would preserve him. The contrary has happened; the last morning that I walked out with you to the grove, I was informed of his death, the confiscation of his effects, and the determined ruin of all his family.

"I debated in my mind, whether I should fly the approaching storm, and leave you to preserve yourself as you could.—Other thoughts suggested themselves: This government, not being very important, might not be immediately thought of. If I left you, you might indeed regain your liberty, but you might run a thousand hazards.—Your friend would have but little chance of an escape for a long time to come, if ever, as he could not give information to *his* friends, and the persons who had the care of him, were of an inferior order of people.

"Considering all this, I fixed my plan immediately. I set off for the confinement of this gentleman, and demanded him in the Grand Seigneur's name; I was well known; and though I produced no signet, they presumed not to disobey me: By this step I have obliged you both; and if you will solemnly subscribe to the conditions I propose, I will not only give you your liberty, but open to you a way of returning to your own country, without ransom or difficulty. You may possibly entertain some doubts of my sincerity, because I denied the knowledge of your friend's residence, but it was a *trust reposed* in me, and I think myself entitled to the *more* credit, for preserving my faith; you may judge as you please."

"I assure you," replied Ferdinand, who had listened to him very attentively, that he might perfectly understand him, "I honour you for your integrity; name your conditions, therefore, without reserve; they must be hard ones indeed, if we hesitate a moment to fulfil them."

"This then is my plan," returned Heli. "I now acknowledge to you, that within this last moon, peace has been concluded upon between our great Sultan and your Emperor. All officers remaining in Turkey are declared free, and may return to their homes. Nevertheless, many of them, secured as *you* have been, will find great difficulties. It must be in every governor's power to retard their freedom, without he is *interested* to liberate them. You understand me.—And in the next place, the natural aversion the Turks have to you Christians, might subject them to many insults, without they have a proper guard.

"Now, if you will swear to take me with you, and to protect *me*, and *one* person more, in *your* country; I will attend you through the country to the first sea port, as the safest way of going in the habit of a Janizary, and as a guard deputed to see you on your way to the port. The other person I speak of is a woman, once a Christian, but now a true disciple of Mahomet—I cannot leave her behind. She must travel as your wife; but she must be sacred from your touch; for I swear by Allah, if in any one point you disappoint or deceive me, both shall instantly suffer death, though I were sure to die a thousand times."

"I will answer both for my friend and for myself," replied Ferdinand; "that we will sacredly keep our faith with you; that we will amply provide both for you and the woman, and enable you to spend the remainder of your days in comfort."

"Enough," replied Heli; "in two days we will be on the road; but fear not that I shall be a burthen to you; I am not destitute of riches, though hitherto they have been useless to me, because I dared not spend beyond my income. Subject to so many jealous eyes, we must have the 'wisdom of the serpent' to escape our enemies."

Heli departed with a countenance so changed from the gloom and anxiety which had for some time pervaded his features, that even Ferdinand was surprised at the alteration, and the Count viewed him with wonder and curiosity. When he had left the apartment, Ferdinand quickly informed his friend of their agreeable prospects, from the proposals of Heli. The Count was not less pleased than himself, but could not help observing, that they were more indebted to the *selfish* gratifications of the proposer, than to his generosity.

"This man's conduct," said he, "confirms the opinion I have early been taught to hold of the Turks, that in their dealings with us, they are selfish, deceitful, and avaricious. Was it not Heli's interest to escape from this country, I believe we should owe him no obligations, either for our liberty or lives, if the sacrifice of either, or both, were essential to his own views."

"We must not search too nicely into the motives which influences men's actions," returned Ferdinand.—"There are so many hidden springs, so many latent causes.——Sometimes scarcely known to ourselves, from which originate our best purposes, and guide our designs, that I fear few could stand the scrutiny, without the imputation of selfishness."

"I shall not now dispute that point with you," answered the Count, "though I am inclined to think more favourably of human nature than you do."

"Do not mistake my general observation for an invariable rule," said Ferdinand hastily. "There are minds of a superior mould, doubtless; but they are comparatively few. And as for this Turk, as we could have no *right* to *expect* his services, I am willing to accept them upon his own terms."

In the afternoon Heli attended them, and after a long conversation, their plan and route was settled, and he bid them prepare to set off by the eleventh hour next day, when he and the woman would join them.

"The lady, I suppose," said Ferdinand, "must be silent, otherwise her language will betray her."

"Not so," returned he.—"I told you she had been a Christian; nay, more, she is your countrywoman, a German."

"And you can be contented with *one* woman?" asked he, smiling.

"I *cannot* be contented without *this* woman," replied Heli.—"That's all I can answer for at present."

The friends passed a night of impatience, and not entirely free from apprehension.—Should any discovery of Heli take place, they might, as accomplices, be involved in very disagreeable situations. If they discovered *themselves* as German officers, entitled to their liberty, he might, in revenge, accuse them of some crimes which would draw on them unpleasant consequences.—And to irritate, displease, or disappoint a Turk, is seldom done with impunity, they are in general so furious and revengeful.

Therefore, after much consultation, and revolving all circumstances together, they thought it best to submit with a good grace, and trust to the ingenuity and diligence of Heli to extricate them from impending difficulties.

The hour at length came, appointed for their departure. Heli appeared in his usual garb alone; their hearts misgave them.—"Follow me," said he, "and fear nothing."

He led them across a court, and through a small postern door, which opened upon a ragged and unfrequented part of the hill;—and it was with some difficulty they kept their feet steady in going down the declivity. At the bottom was a thick underwood, through which they easily penetrated to a small decayed building: Entering a few steps, they perceived a soldier with a drawn scimitar.—They started back, and supposed themselves betrayed, casting a look of reproach on Heli.—He saw their thoughts in that look.—"This is a friend," said he;—and going forward, he returned with a bundle, that contained the dress of a soldier, and in which he quickly arrayed himself, throwing his other clothes under some large stones and rubbish.

"We have now the day before us," said he, "and no time to lose before we reach a place of safety. I have given out in the Castle, that I shall pass the day with you at the hermit's. No suspicion, therefore, will be entertained 'till night, nor any thoughts of a pursuit 'till morning, because no one has a right to command or leave his post, consequently much time will elapse before that is determined upon."

"But the woman," said Ferdinand.

"Will be safe with us," answered Heli, smiling, and pointing to the soldier, who was so perfectly disguised by her dress and mustaches, that they had not the least suspicion of her sex.

"Will she not be missed?" asked the Count.

"No," replied Heli.—"Yesterday she was impertinent—we quarrelled—I ordered her into confinement, and, in a feigned passion, swore she should remain there three days, sending to her room some dried figs and water. I locked the door, and secured the key.

"This morning I pretended to regret my oath, and said, I would go and consult the holy hermit, how far I dared to remit her punishment. Thus you see neither will be sought after, as I had forbidden any one to approach the door of her apartment; and I am so well beloved by the men, and so little suspected of having any cause to absent myself, as they are ignorant of Ismael's fate, which involves his kindred, that unless an order should arrive to arrest me, I dare say they will not think of my flight, or pursue me 'till after tomorrow, if then; and before that, I trust we shall be in safety."

They could not but acknowledge that he had taken every prudent precaution to preserve them from danger; and without any further conversation, they pursued their way across the plain to the next town, which was a few miles distance. Here they easily procured a carriage, under the pretence that the Count and Ferdinand were prisoners, whom the soldiers had in custody.

The Turkish soldiers are in general so formidable to the common ignorant people, that few would presume to dispute their commands. The same pretence carried them through several small towns and villages without interruption or accident, tho' not without much fatigue, as they proceeded with great speed.

It is not necessary to trace them through their journey, as they had neither time or inclination to make observations. Therefore I shall only say, that they reached the river Danube in safety, which they crossed, and after several days travelling, arrived at Belgrade. Here they rested, and were enabled to breathe, after their fatigues, both of body and mind.

Having stayed two days, they proceeded on to Vienna, and, to the great joy of the whole party, at length entered that Imperial city in perfect safety, just sixteen weeks from the day when the battle took place, and they were carried off by Ismael.

CHAPTER IX.

THE Count and Ferdinand soon made themselves known to some of their acquaintance, and were received with as much surprise as if they had risen from the dead; so firmly was it credited, that they had perished in battle. Proper clothes were soon procured for themselves, Heli and the woman both readily conforming to wear the German dress, though both persevered in their own tenets of religion, and the worship of the prophet Mahomet.

Heli now displayed a great many valuable jewels, worth five or six thousand pounds at least. How he had acquired them, he never thought proper to divulge; nor had they any right to inquire. He had sufficient to live on, in a moderate independence, and proposed retiring into the country, to reside free from observation. The gentlemen sent off letters to their friends immediately on their arrival, as they were very doubtful that their former ones had never gone forward from Adrianople. They purposed waiting on the Emperor, and as there was now no occasion for their active services, to obtain his permission for returning into Suabia.

The morning following, after all their clothes were brought home, Heli entered their apartment, and asked leave to introduce his Fatima in her proper habit. They readily accorded to his request, being desirous of seeing a woman whom he had preferred to all others, and who had changed her own form of worship for that of the man she loved.

He quickly returned, leading in a very beautiful woman, whom he no sooner introduced to Ferdinand, than the latter recoiled a few paces back, with all the marks of strong surprise, and even terror, in his countenance. Heli, observing his emotions, was instantly seized with a jealous fit. He changed colour, and pulled down her veil, drawing her on one side, as if to leave the room.

"Be not offended or hurt, my friend," said Ferdinand, recovering himself, "nor leave the room, I beseech you.—To account for my emotions, I must tell you that this lady bears the strongest resemblance to my late dear and honoured father, that ever I beheld in two persons of different ages and sex. Very striking it must be, to have such an effect on my mind. Let me entreat you, Heli, to uncloud that face, and permit me to ask your lady a few questions."

Heli complied, but it was with an ill grace, his looks betraying suspicion and vexation.

"You say, Madam," said Ferdinand, "that you are a German.—Have the goodness to inform me who, and what you are;—for I am strongly persuaded you are somehow connected with my father's family.—Do not hesitate," added he, seeing she appeared in great confusion.—"Whoever you are, in me you will find a friend ready to promote your happiness with Heli, since he is the man of your choice."

Those words he repeated in the Turkish language to him, to quiet a little the turbulence of his agitations. After some little hesitation, Fatima began the following little narrative:—

"I have heard my mother say, that I was born in Baden; that my father was a nobleman, who had an estate near that city, and seduced her, at an early part of her life, under a promise of being faithful to her, and never marrying, as the difference in their rank precluded him from giving his hand to her."

"Did she never mention his name to you?" asked Ferdinand eagerly.

"She did," resumed Fatima; "it was Count Renaud."

Ferdinand struck his breast, greatly agitated, but requested she would proceed without attending to him.

"My mother informed me, that after my birth, he grew fonder of her every hour; but at length his father compelled him to marry a lady of rank and fortune, under the penalty of being disinherited, if he refused. This caused equal grief to both; and it was long before my mother could be reconciled to see him, or receive his visits; but her dependence on him, and affection for me, at length prevailed, and she had every reason to be convinced that all his real love was confined to her. Under this conviction, she submitted to her situation.

"After some time, she perceived a coldness in his attentions, and a profound melancholy in his looks, for which he assigned no cause, and pretended it was her fancy only; but being convinced, she said, that his dejection must spring from a new attachment, as he was daily more negligent towards her.—She had him carefully watched, and at length discovered that he was passionately in love with a young lady, on a visit to his wife, who, being of family, and virtuous, repulsed him, though it was believed she was equally attached.

"My mother, made desperate by this discovery, gave his wife information of the attachment, and driven to despair, in a fit of madness and jealousy, she accepted the protection of a German officer, who had long persecuted her with his addresses, and accompanied by me and my nurse, quitted Baden for ever, without deigning to see or to reproach him.

"With this officer she resided some years; and although she had a daughter by him, she loved me most affectionately, and has often said I was a perfect resemblance of her once beloved Count. We lived very happily, until I was about twelve years old, my sister only ten, when my mother's protector died, leaving his property divided between her and his daughter, with a small legacy to me. My sister and her fortune was left in the care of my mother, and the latter always assured me, *her* share should be mine at her death; which unfortunately happened in less than a twelvemonth after, and so suddenly, that she had not time to make a will; and as she had lived very retired, and her situation had prevented her from having proper acquaintance, whose honour and integrity might have been useful to us, we were left solely in the care of my old nurse, and a man who had been a kind of humble friend and dependant on the Colonel.

"How they managed I know not; but in less than four years we were informed our fortunes were spent, and that we must seek some employment for our support. Within the last twelvemonth, I had been noticed and followed by a nobleman, who was very amiable, and held high rank in the army.—Want of birth was an invincible obstacle to our marriage, and I had rejected, with disdain, every other overture; but when my nurse explained our situation, I confess, with shame, I no longer kept him at that distance which I ought to have done, and gave him but too much encouragement.

"One morning my nurse came into my room; said she, 'we will sell the furniture, turn everything into money, and leave this place. I have been making inquiries; your father still lives; we will go to Baden; I will find some way of making you known to him, without alarming his family, and oblige him to provide for you, which either fear or affection will make him do. Your sister has also an uncle in Suabia—I will find him out; 'tis fit those relations should maintain you.'

"This proposal of Dupree's.—"

"Dupree!" exclaimed Ferdinand;——"Great God! what do I hear—but go on."

"This proposal," resumed Fatima, "did not please me. I was not willing to run the risk of being rejected as a burthen, or treated with contempt, when I had the alternative of independence, pleasure, and an agreeable lover. I therefore accepted the nobleman's proposals, put myself under his protection, and one evening quitted the house to reside in a more elegant one. In a few days, Dupree found me out, and made such an uproar, and behaved so clamorous, that my protector was compelled to give her a handsome sum to hold her tongue, which perfectly contented her.

"My lover was obliged to join the army. I accompanied him. The General was compelled to give battle; he was victorious, and the Turks defeated; but unhappily a party of them, headed by Heli, had, in the mean time, surrounded the tents, where the women and officers' baggage remained, pillaged them, beat off the guards, and carried me and several other women off in triumph.

"At first I was in despair, and expected death. We were put into a covered wagon, and carried to Adrianople, where I remained in close confinement upwards of two months, and had well nigh fretted myself to death; but the arrival of Heli saved my life; his generosity and affection won my heart;—'tis true, the recluse life I was compelled to lead suited very little with my inclinations; but there was no remedy; and after giving myself up some time to sorrow and regret, which availed nothing, I got the better of my trouble, and resigned myself to my fate.

"When Heli was appointed to the government of Philippo, I gladly accompanied him.—I have had no reason to repent; and thank Heaven, I am once more unexpectedly restored to my own country. What is become of my sister, Dupree, and Keilheim, her friend, I know not. Thus, Sir, I have related my story, and now you know whether I am any ways related to your family or not."

When Fatima ceased speaking, Ferdinand was for a few moments silent, he found but little cause to congratulate himself on the discovery of a relation so nearly connected by blood; whose conduct, even by her own acknowledgment, had been so faulty and reprehensible; but when he viewed that face, whose every look reminded him of his dear and much regretted father, a rush of tenderness sprung to his heart, that obliterated her errors, and rising hastily, he was about to embrace her, forgetful of Heli's presence and uneasy conjectures; he who had needfully observed his emotions during Fatima's relation, and had watched him with an eye of suspicion, furiously rushed between them, darting a look of vengeance at Ferdinand, and muttering curses on her, roughly pulling her from her seat.

"Stop, Heli," cried Ferdinand; "judge not rashly from appearances.—— Fatima is—*my sister!*"

The last word seemed unwillingly pronounced, and to Heli rather the effect of a sudden duplicity, than a serious truth; but Fatima sunk back, evidently shocked and confused repeating the word sister, sister.—"Oh! if that is true, you must despise and hate me."

She burst into tears, and drew down her veil. Heli stood suspended between passion and curiosity. Ferdinand took his hand.

"My friend, compose yourself; I will relate every circumstance to you that indisputably proves *your* Fatima to be my half sister. Strange, indeed, are the events which have brought us to the knowledge of each other; but her features stamp the credibility of her story; and though the situation in which I find her must be wounding to the feelings of a brother, yet, as I can claim no right to control her inclinations, you have nothing to fear from me; she is free to act as she pleases."

Those words, in some degree, calmed the turbulent passions of Heli; he reseated himself without speaking, visibly impatient for the promised explanation. This Ferdinand entered upon; and at the conclusion, addressing Fatima, he said—"If necessity, and not *choice*, is now the tye that binds you to Heli, I think it my duty to offer to you a more eligible situation; from preceding circumstances, delicacy, and honour, equally militate against a hope of an honourable connexion with any other man; but I have the power to procure for you either a residence in the country with some worthy retired family, or to place you in a convent, where I will pay for your pension.

"In providing thus for you, I secure to you the liberty of chusing your own destiny. I pretend to no rights over you beyond what you are willing to allow me. If you voluntarily throw yourself on my protection, your interest shall be as dear to me as my own.—Decide, therefore, for yourself."

"I am very sensible of your kindness," replied Fatima, "but my choice *is* made.—In Turkey, perhaps the desire of liberty might have guided me to embrace your offers with transport; but I am now free; and whilst Heli behaves well, gratitude for his preference of me to all my companions, and for the affection he has displayed towards me during our late dangerous undertaking, induces me to declare, that I will partake of his destiny."

"Yes, Heli," added she in the Turkish language, giving him her hand, "with you I will remain, and trust that I shall never repent refusing my brother's offers to live with you."

The Turk appeared to be transported;—his doubts and suspicions were instantly dispelled, and he thanked her with an air of tenderness and gratitude. Ferdinand was concerned, but not surprised; the libertine life in which she had been engaged by her own confession, gave but small hopes that she could be reconciled to a retired and regular mode of conduct; and from several little traits that escaped her unguardedly, he conceived she had much natural levity that would ill brook restraint: What he could not controul, therefore, he was resigned to; but assuming some degree of freedom, from his connexion with Fatima, he asked Heli in what manner he intended to regulate his future conduct.

"I design," answered he, "to live quietly in the country, not ostentatiously, to avoid observation: To regard Fatima as my wife, and mistress of the other women. I pretend not to have a seraglio here; but as I am unknown, I shall have no visitors, nor will Fatima be exposed to the eyes of men."

Ferdinand accidentally turned *his eyes* on Fatima at those words, and observed a suppressed smile playing on her lips, and an archness in her looks, that but ill accorded with the plan Heli had designed, nor at all correspondent to the mortified and afflicted air she had assumed, when he first discovered himself to her as a brother. This observation tended to confirm his first suspicions, that she had a light mind, and was capable of much duplicity.

He was mortified, by the conviction from the affinity between them, but he had no power to controul her inclinations, nor influence to effect a change in habits she had long since ceased to think vicious or blamable: Therefore, after a long conversation, in which she avowed her partiality for Heli, and a decided preference for his tenets of religion, Ferdinand left them to their own determinations, recommending to both constancy in their attachment, and the practise of good actions towards others. He added a few words of advice to Fatima in German, and concluded with assuring her, that if she should ever want a friend, the daughter of a respected father should always claim his attention and assistance.

When retired to his apartment, he was painfully affected by the recollection of such circumstances in the story of Fatima, as convinced him that his wife Claudina must have been that sister she mentioned, and the daughter of the officer by a woman his father had once been connected with. He

THE MYSTERIOUS WARNING

269

shuddered at the idea. Yet surely, he thought, there cannot be that degree of consanguinity between us, which should raise the dead;—to bid me "fly from *her* arms as I would avoid *sin* and *death*." Or why, if our union was sinful, why was the warning so late.

"Ah!" cried he, "if my father knew her, ought he not to have discovered the secret? But no, it was impossible; had he known she was the child of a woman he once fondly loved, surely he would have made inquiries after her and his own child, nor have left even Claudina in indigence; no, he could not have known this painful mystery, and my fatal impetuous passion blindly led *me* to credit any tale that the wretch Dupree might invent, and to unite myself to the daughter of an infamous woman, who has blighted all my prospects of happiness for ever. Yes, that woman, that mother, if from the grave she can behold the misery that has developed on me, will rejoice, perhaps, that her wrongs from the father are retaliated with bitterness on the son, and that her own offspring has revenged *her* injuries."

This idea led him into a train of unpleasant reflections, that concluded with lamenting his youthful rashness, and an ungovernable passion, of which he was the victim; nor could he help reverting to his father's connexion with the mother of Fatima and Claudina.

Could the libertine, or to speak in the softened term which fashion has established, could the *man* of *gallantry* look forward to the consequences of his errors; did he see the unfortunate innocents born of vicious parents; brought into the world under the stigma of criminality; subject to the eye of scorn;—nourished in vice; corrupted by example;—grow up lovely to the eye, but with minds depraved.—Subject to temptations, they have neither fortitude nor inclination to resist;—sink into a vortex of misery, guilty, hardened, despised, forsaken; and to close the climax, see those unfortunate children of guilty parents abandoned by the world; and when youth and beauty is no more, left to die in wretchedness, without relief, without pity, and without a friend to close their eyes, or speak one word of consolation in that awful moment, when the retrospection of a mispent life, fills them with unutterable sorrow and despair.

"Surely," thought Ferdinand, on reviewing this melancholy picture, which his misfortunes delineated to his mind's eye in the most gloomy colouring; "surely, if the sins of the fathers are visited upon their children, I am marked out as an object for retribution and vengeance. How far my marriage with Claudina may be criminal, I know not.——That union, so rashly entered into, and followed by a father's curses, wants not the aggravation of criminality to add to my wretchedness; and if she *is* a lost, a guilty creature, the sins of the mother have fallen upon us both."

These, and such like reflections, threw him into a profound reverie, from which he was rouzed by the entrance of the Count.

"I left you, for a few moments, my dear Ferdinand," said he, "because I thought you would wish to recover from the surprise and vexation that visibly affected you during the relation Fatima gave of herself; her subsequent choice of attaching herself to Heli, I think ought *not* to afflict you; for perhaps *had* she given him up, you would have found it a very unpleasant task to regulate a young woman like her, accustomed to a gay desultory kind of life."

"Your observation is undoubtedly just," replied he.—"I am convinced she is a stranger to all principles of decorum, and would ill brook that regularity I should naturally have expected. I am mortified, I confess, to find a person who owes her existence to *my* father, under such reprehensible circumstances; but *that* is not the only cause of the surprise and concern you remarked; I am still more *nearly* concerned in her story." He then acquainted the Count with every particular relative to Claudina, and severely condemned his own impetuous passion, which wildly pursued its object, regardless of such information as is generally found essential to confidence, if not absolutely necessary to happiness, that of knowing the family, character, and connexions of those with whom we form a union for life.

"Unquestionably," said the Count; "a prudent man would consider such knowledge highly requisite: But my dear friend, I fear, whilst all-powerful love had such an absolute dominion in your breast—had you really been informed that Claudina was born of worthless or vicious parents, passion would have suggested a thousand alleviating circumstances in her favour, and under the flattering guise of compassion for an unfortunate and innocent young woman, you would have deemed it a meritorious act to rescue her from ruin."

"Perhaps so," answered Ferdinand;—"for the heart, by its pleadings for a beloved object, is generally too hard for the frigid lessons of prudence; and I have given sufficient proofs of my weakness to warrant the severest conclusions against my understanding."

"We will drop the subject, if you please," said the Count, "as it can lead to no pleasurable reflections; and as we propose taking leave of this city in a few days, let us make some visits to diversify our ideas."

Ferdinand very readily consented to a proposal, calculated to draw him from a train of painful retrospections.

In the course of a week, no material incidents happened to the friends. They accompanied Heli in several little excursions round the environs of Vienna, to discover some pleasant retirement that might coincide with his wishes of living unknown and unobserved.

One morning, taking their usual ride, they passed a carriage, which was driving very quick; two gentlemen were in it; and from the transient view they had, Ferdinand thought he had some knowledge of them, but could not ascertain who, or what they were. Presently, however, a servant overtook them, and requested to know if Count M*** was one of the company? The Count, though surprised, readily announced himself, when the man respectfully presented the compliments of Baron Reiberg and his son, who, he said, were waiting in their carriage, to know if their conjectures were right, and hoped the gentlemen would return, if fortunately he was not mistaken.

The Count and Ferdinand readily accompanied the servant back, and were recognized with great pleasure by the Baron, who congratulated himself upon this desired and little expected meeting.

He, with many others, had heard the report of their deaths; but struck with their appearance, as they passed on the road, had stopt his carriage, and dispatched a servant to know whether the resemblance that surprised him was the illusion of his senses or not.

He told them he had a house at Vienna, to which he hoped they would accompany him and his son, and give them the pleasure of considering it as their own, whilst business or amusement induced them to remain in that city. They made proper acknowledgments for this politeness; told him, their stay would be short, and that they had friends with them.

"If your friends will accept of the same accommodations I can offer *you*, gentlemen," said the Baron, "they are heartily at their service; and I feel so much interest and curiosity to know by what means you preserved your lives, when your death was generally credited, that I really cannot relinquish my earnest wish to have you inmates of my mansion. Come, come," added he, seeing they hesitated, and looked at each other, "you know I am in possession of your promise to pay me a visit, and I now claim the performance of it."

This obliging earnestness was irresistible, and they readily accorded with the request, assuring him, that they would wait of him in the evening. Taking the Baron's address with his invitation to their friends, they parted with him for the present, and returned with speed to Heli. Before they rejoined him, Ferdinand observed, "that he could not think of introducing Fatima to the Baron's house, nor did he suppose it would be at all agreeable to Heli. I hope, therefore," said he, "the little estate he is now in view of will answer his wishes."

As he spoke, they saw Heli slowly returning back to meet them.

The Count told him of their meeting with a friend, and took notice the other seemed very thoughtful, which, on demanding the cause, he said he longed for retirement; that the increase of their acquaintance was painful to him, and their self-denial, in giving up so much of their time to his accommodation, was too great a tax upon their kindness.—He had therefore come to a resolution to take the small solitary cottage they had seen the day before; and as it was furnished, he could have immediate possession.

To this plan no objection was made.—They called on the owner of the cottage, and presently concluded the bargain. The house, and a small farm belonging to it, lay extremely retired, on the side of a rising wood, which afforded shelter from the sharp air of the north; and on the south was a delightful garden, with grounds attached to it for their cattle, and other necessaries of life, whilst a small but beautiful rivulet run almost round the house, and fertilized the earth.

Heli, having made the purchase, was impatient to take possession; and on their return to Fatima, bid her prepare for her removal the following morning. It was easy to see she received this mandate with dissatisfaction; nor did a description of her future residence at all tend to lessen her chagrin.—The gay multitudes, which she saw from her windows, were far more gratifying to her than woods or gardens, where she was not likely to see the "human face divine."

Ferdinand easily penetrated into the workings of her mind, and saw but little prospect of happiness to Heli, if it was dependant on the constancy of Fatima. For the present she was silent, because the alternative he had offered to her was also retirement; and therefore, of the two evils, she submitted to accompany Heli, but without ever pretending to a satisfaction she did not feel.

In the evening, the Count and his friend took leave of Heli and his lady. To the latter, Ferdinand ventured a few serious admonitions, but they were heard with a look of careless contempt, and a silent bow.—Heli requested they would sometimes visit him, as themselves would be the only persons he should receive. This they readily promised, and parted with mutual good wishes.

The Baron welcomed them with much cordiality; the young Baron with equal attention; but he had not that pleasant frankness of manners which seemed to characterize his father. On the contrary, it was obvious to both gentlemen, that something oppressive lay upon his spirits, and that tho' he behaved with much complacency and politeness; yet it appeared an effort upon his natural disposition, more inclined to reserve and taciturnity.

The father, who was a man of the world, had travelled a good deal, and profited by his observations on men and manners, exerted himself to entertain his guests; and, by his endeavours, they passed a very pleasant evening.

When the Count and Ferdinand met in the morning, the former took notice of the young Baron's want of spirits, and a disposition so entirely opposite to his father's.

"I made the same observation at the time they passed with us in the solitary Castle," replied Ferdinand—"He then spoke little, and rather avoided than courted society.—But as some characters do not open themselves at once, as we were strangers, and every circumstance there unpleasant, and indeed melancholy, I allowed much for his reserve, and supposed it might be rather accidental than habitual; but I was mistaken I see now; for certainly he has a natural tendency towards an unsocial disposition, and 'tis on the father we must draw for our entertainment here."

They were soon after joined by the Baron. He introduced them to several of his friends; was sedulous to shew his esteem, by every gratification he could procure to them.—Sought every possible mode of entertainment, and delicately avoided any reference to the former unhappy situation of the Count, or his irreparable loss of the lady Eugenia.

Once only that day they saw the young Baron; but they found by the conversation, when he appeared at the dinner table, that he spent his hours chiefly in the library. They remarked his father's extreme solicitude to draw him out, and to amuse him; but the few marks of cheerfulness, which now and then broke off, were evidently forced, and the effects of complaisance only.—After the dinner hour, they saw no more of him.

On the second day of their residence with the Baron, when his son had withdrawn from the table, turning to his guests with a suppressed sigh—"Although you are too polite my friends, to express any curiosity, yet 'tis impossible but that you must observe the peculiar disposition of my son; that unsociability, that dejection of spirits so very visible to every eye, is the only thing that disturbs the tranquillity of my life. Poor unfortunate boy, an early and a strong attachment has embittered every hour of his life for upwards of two years past. Hopeless as it is, he cannot drive the fatal passion from his heart.—All my efforts to restore his spirits are fruitless.

"I flattered myself your conversation would tend to lighten the anguish of his mind, and your example animate him to rise superior over unavoidable and irremediable evils; but I see no change, and therefore feel it necessary to apologize to you for his conduct, by explaining the cause of it."

"I feel deeply interested for the unfortunate young gentleman," replied Ferdinand; "and being a fellow-sufferer, can sympathize with him. As I am nearly of his own age, and know his situation, if you will allow me, I shall use all my endeavours to obtain his notice; and if I succeed, I may, by sharing his confidence, divert the current of his thoughts from dwelling always on one object. That a communication of grief, which hangs heavy on the heart, certainly tends to lighten it, I know by experience."

"You kindly anticipate my wishes," said the Baron.—"If you will condescend to fall in with his humour, and attach yourself to him, 'tis the only chance I can see likely to succeed in drawing him from himself."

This plan being agreed upon, the Baron and Count ordered their horses to ride; and after their departure, Ferdinand ventured to dispatch a servant with his compliments to the young Baron, requesting the honour of his company to take a walk.—Or if that was disagreeable to him, would he permit him to join him in the library. He had waited but a few moments for the return of his message before Reiberg appeared. He politely, tho' distantly, apologized for not making a tender of his services, as he thought his father had taken that office upon himself.

"I have indeed a hundred obligations to the Baron for his attentions," replied Ferdinand; "but my spirits are not always calculated to give or receive pleasure from a mixed society: I often prefer a solitary ramble, or the company of a serious rational companion, to mixing with the great world."

"An uncommon turn of mind in so young a man," observed Reiberg, eying him with a more complacent look; "and what is altogether as singular, I am very much of your opinion: Therefore, Sir, I am at your command, either for a walk, or for the library."

"At present," said Ferdinand, "I prefer the former; let us visit some of the gardens in the suburbs."

The other readily complied. They took a long walk, being absent near three hours; and, on coming back, met the Baron and Count just returned.

"Ah!" said the former, "like minds will mingle.—How natural for youth to court the society of each other."

"And yet I have my doubts," replied Reiberg, "whether the entertainments of these youths have not been of a much graver cast than what you may have engaged in."

"Not unlikely," answered the Count—"My friend is of a sedentary turn, and the amusements he seeks are generally of that complexion."

Reiberg viewed his companion with an air of graciousness, that seldom had pervaded his features, and, in the course of the evening, attached himself to Ferdinand with evident satisfaction.

From that day, the young friends were much together; and in the course of conversation, had both thrown out hints of mutual unhappiness, but each was too delicate to express a desire of prying into the secrets of the other. One morning it had been agreed upon between the Count and Ferdinand, that they would visit Heli and Fatima. They set off at an early hour, and soon reached the cottage.

At the door, reclining on a kind of sofa, lay Heli; the noise of the horses made him start: Discerning who they were, he hastened to meet them.

"Ah!" cried he, "never more wished for, nor more welcome. The prophet has sent you to my wishes, or this night I should have sent for you."

"Have you then particularly wanted us?" asked Ferdinand.

"Yes," replied Heli.—"Strange things have happened; but come into this little room, and I will unfold the whole to you."

As they dismounted and entered, the Count asked for Fatima.

"Ah! the ingrate," cried he; "she is but too well, I believe."

This reply induced them to suppose she had behaved ill, if not deserted him; but they waited a farther explanation from him; and when they were seated, he thus began, addressing Ferdinand, as the Count was not so well acquainted with the language.

"From the first day that we came here, the ungrateful Fatima was sullen and discontented.—I did my best to amuse her; we had only two women slaves, or servants; they attended the business of the house, and to please her, I took no notice of them."

"Two nights ago, at midnight, I was alarmed by a loud knocking at the door; I opened the window, and demanded the cause. I was not understood; but hearing a voice, a woman spoke in a tone of terror and supplication. Without disturbing Fatima in the next room, I took my lamp, and went down, opening the door: A young woman rushed in, and directly swooned at my feet.

"I was then obliged to call for assistance; the women soon came about me; the poor creature was helped, and recovered.—I saw she was very pretty, though pale and thin.—Fatima did her best to revive and console her.

"When she was able to speak, she said she had escaped from a small house in the wood, where she had reason to fear it was intended to murder her. We did not ask many questions; but she was put to bed, and yesterday morning I was told she appeared to be a good deal revived; that she earnestly requested, should any person make inquiry after her, we would deny our knowledge of her. I began to think the prophet had thrown this young woman in my way, to be a solace to me, and a companion for Fatima, so I let them be together.

"About noon, two horsemen, like a gentleman and his servant, appeared at the door.—They asked me had I seen a young woman; I kept her secret.—Whilst they were talking, Fatima came out.—I was very much displeased, and commanded her, pretty roughly, to retire.—She refused, and said some words to the stranger I did not understand.—He smiled, and answered her with great quickness. Highly provoked, I pushed her in, and shut the door.—The traitress opened the window above, and talked again. Enraged to madness, I flew in, dragged her from the window, and gave her a little chastisement, though not what she deserved.

"Her cries brought in the men, who, forcing the door, came up, and snatched her from my hands.—She directly run down stairs.—One of the horsemen took her before him, and they galloped off, regardless of my cries or imprecations.—'Twas in vain to pursue them; I had no horse, and was unacquainted with the turnings in the roads, if I had.

"Whilst I was tearing my beard, and cursing the vile ungrateful wretch, one of the servants came in, and said the young woman was in fits; so here was another plague upon me.—However, I had not lost my charity, so I ascended to help her, but she did not recover 'till night, and has continued very ill ever since; hardly speaks at all, but sighs from the bottom of her heart.—It seems 'twas the voices and bustle those vile Christians made, which occasioned her fits.—This is the state of things here; I am almost mad, and your treacherous wicked sister has basely deserted me; me who preserved her life, and gave her liberty at the hazard of my own!"

"I am more concerned than surprised," said Ferdinand; "for I had no dependence upon her constancy, as she evidently wanted principle.—Retirement suited not with her disposition, and I think you have little cause to regret the loss of such a woman. The young person you speak of may want friends and assistance; if we can be of use to her, I am sure the Count will readily join in offering his services."

"You Christians," answered Heli, "are like the knights in romance, in your wishes to serve women.—Was you more discreet, and less complaisant, they would behave better; but women, having no souls, can practise no virtues, and only subjection and confinement can keep them within bounds."

"Why then accuse Fatima of ingratitude or levity?" said Ferdinand.—"If she has no soul, she may give unbounded loose to her inclinations; and where there exists no virtues, vice and folly only can be expected.—Gratitude is a virtue that flourishes in a noble mind; the produce of the soul, that feels a conscious sense of benefits concerned. If the freedom you procured for Fatima was solely to gratify yourself, she owes you no obligation; nor can you claim any merit from the deed."

"'Tis well," returned Heli, with a lowering brow; "I see what kindness I may expect from you; I have been a tool to all.—Oh! prophet," cried he, with a furious menacing air——

"Stop, Heli," said Ferdinand.—"Spare your appeal to Mahomet; I am more your friend that you are willing to believe; I despise and detest Fatima; she is a worthless woman; you may rejoice to get rid of one who would have proved a constant source of trouble to you; I vindicate her not; nor do I desire ever to hear of her more, because I am convinced she is incorrigible; but any services we can render you, command us, and you shall see that Christians know how to be grateful and hospitable to strangers."

Heli was affected by the earnest tone in which the other addressed him.—He unbent his angry brow, and lowering his voice—

"I believe I may judge too rashly; if so, may our holy prophet, and you, forgive me. I feel that I loved Fatima, but I will try to despise her: If this young woman lives—but I fear she will not; we cannot understand each other.—The few things I know in your language I have said to comfort her; but either she does not, or will not understand me."

"I would ask to see her," said Ferdinand, "and learn who and what she is, if it is agreeable to you."

"Yes," answered Heli, after a little hesitation—"Yes, you *shall* see her; but remember I already design *her* to supply the place of Fatima."

"Fear me not," replied Ferdinand; "I will deserve your confidence."

Heli then preceded them, to announce to her a visit from two of her countrymen.—Ferdinand followed him.—The sick person, who lay fronting the door, at his entrance gave a sudden shriek, and fainted. They advanced hastily to assist her, and in the same moment both recognized the unfortunate young woman, notwithstanding the alteration of her person, and the improbability of her being near Vienna, and both exclaimed, "Louisa! Good Heavens! Louisa!"

"How," said Heli, "do you know *her too?*"

They were too busy in getting water and other things to restore her, immediately to attend to him; but when she began to shew signs of returning life, Ferdinand turned to him—"We do indeed know this lady, one of the most unfortunate of her sex. We left her a few months back under the protection of a worthy family, far from hence. How, or by whom she was brought here, is very extraordinary."

Louisa, for her it was, opened her eyes.—"The shadows are gone," said she, faintly, "or was it the phantom of my brain?"

The Count instantly recollected that it was possible she might have heard of their deaths. Therefore, without advancing, he said, "fear nothing, Madam; two friends of your's are yet alive, and eager to serve you."

"This is happiness indeed!" she exclaimed.—"Where are you?"

Both drew near the sofa, and bowed before her.—Pleasure danced in her eyes, but for a moment she had not the power of speech.

"Take comfort, Madam," said Ferdinand, "you are in safe hands—Mr. and Miss D'Alenberg——."

"Ah!" cried she, much affected, "I have been torn from them; they are on the road."

"What! to Vienna?" asked he.

"I believe so—I left them at Ens; there I was discovered—That villain the Count—he—he got me into his power to destroy me."

She had not strength to proceed, and they requested she would not exhaust herself by the attempt; and turning to Heli, (who was pacing the room, and cursing his malicious stars, and his own folly, for introducing them into the room) "it will be necessary to send a physician to this lady."

The Count offered to fetch one, and immediately set off for that purpose, though Louisa tried to oppose the design. Ferdinand, who was eagerly desirous of hearing some intelligence of the D'Alenberg family, remained with Heli in the apartment.

The latter, greatly agitated, had thrown himself upon a sofa. Louisa looked at him with evident terror, and appeared to shrink from his menacing aspect.

"My evil genius seems to predominate," said he to Ferdinand.—"I am to be robbed of this young woman too by Christian artifices."

"Heli," replied the latter, "do not repine that you are made the instrument to rescue an unfortunate lady from villany. She is of birth and character; has powerful friends, and is married.—She is under the protection of a family I respect, and who will feel the warmest gratitude for her preservation, and can be nothing more to me, or any man, than an object of reverence and admiration.

"You cannot suppose, my good Heli, that every lady, who may eventually be thrown in your way, must be subservient to you; a thousand causes may impede any attentions of your's in a particular light; but for your humanity and kindness, you will ever experience a grateful return."

Heli heard him, but answered not.—A sullen silence denoted a mind but ill satisfied. The remembrance of Fatima's charms, and her elopement, sat heavy at his heart; for he had now no companion that he could converse with, or who even understood his language.

The Count was not long before he returned with a physician, who confirmed Louisa's own judgment, that terror and surprise had caused the great agitation of her spirits, and a shock to her constitution, which was

extremely delicate and languid, but that no immediate danger need be apprehended.—He ordered her some light cordials, and had no doubt but that
she would soon be better.

This opinion of the doctor's was gratifying to all parties; but Ferdinand felt some perplexity on the score of leaving Louisa under the care
of Heli.—He asked, could she be removed? the physician thought there
would be no danger in a proper conveyance.——Where she could be carried to, was the next question. The medical gentleman, finding that they
were strangers on a visit in the city, and that the lady was a person of fashion, and had powerful friends, very humanely offered an apartment in his
own house, an offer most readily accepted, and he hastened off to send a
carriage, and an aunt, who resided with him, to attend on the lady, whilst
he prepared for her reception.

No sooner was this plan communicated to Heli, than he grew quite
furious; upbraided the gentlemen in the most opprobrious words passion
could suggest; but finding that they were resolute, and not to be intimidated, his fury fell upon himself; he cursed his own folly, in preserving two
Christian wretches, whose acquaintance had been the ruin of his peace;
ungenerously ascribing Fatima's desertion from him as originating from
the offers Ferdinand had made of providing for her.

The Count, who was apprehensive of some revengeful stroke from the
mad passion of Heli, kept a steady eye upon all his actions; while Ferdinand
endeavoured, by reason, to calm his transports; and among other things
observed to him, that as there were many Turks in Vienna, he might easily find such as would be useful to him in his domestic arrangements, and
plenty of women who would accept of his protection.

This last argument seemed to have some weight with him; he grew less
agitated; and before the carriage came for Louisa, told them he would take
their advice; and having now *nobody to guard*, he would come into the city
the next day, to seek out some of his countrymen, and *purchase* two or three
beautiful women, that he might no longer think of the unfaithful woman
who had abandoned him.

This resolved on, he assisted in carrying Louisa to the carriage.—A
middle aged respectable lady waited to receive her; cushions were placed
for her to recline on; and moving very slowly, she was safely conveyed to
the physician's house, under whose care the gentlemen left her for the remainder of the day, that quiet might help to restore her;—and although
both were dying with curiosity, yet they suppressed all appearance of it, in
consideration of her weakness.

CHAPTER X.

ON their return to the Baron's house, they found him under a good deal of surprise at their long absence; for so much had their minds been occupied, that they had entirely forgotten the necessary compliment of accounting to the Baron. They apologized for their neglect, by a relation of the cause, and described Louisa as a much injured deserving young woman.

Young Reiberg appeared greatly interested; there was a novelty in the case, which, added to his natural humanity, rouzed him from the apathy that generally predominated over his conduct, and induced him to be particularly anxious in his inquiries, and offers of assisting them to discover, and punish, if possible, the offenders.

Ferdinand was pleased with the warmth he expressed, but not conceiving himself at liberty to disclose the story of Louisa, he only observed, that until she was in a state to elucidate facts, and give them full information, no steps could be taken to do her justice.—"I have *my* suspicions," added he, "as to the person, but do not think it fair to communicate them, lest I should be wrong."

Reiberg seemed pleased with the discretion of Ferdinand, and attached himself to him with an appearance of regard, very flattering to the other, and highly pleasing to the Baron, who presaged the happiest consequences to the peace of his son, should he conceive a friendly regard for Ferdinand, and unlock his bosom to the sympathizing attentions, and disinterested advice of a friend.

Early the following morning, they sent to inquire into the state of Louisa's health, and had the satisfaction to hear she had rested tolerably, was better, and would be happy to see her preservers in the course of the day. This pleasing account diffused general content to the gentlemen, and gave promise that their curiosity might be gratified.

Mean time, Ferdinand felt a good deal of vexation at Fatima's conduct. His reverence to the memory of his father would have led him any lengths to have preserved his child from infamy; but it was too evident that her heart was debased by the way of life she had chosen for herself, and that the loose principles of the parent had descended to the children. Again he sighed at the truth painful experience had taught him, "that the principles and character of parents is an essential consideration, when about to form a union with a young person for life; since *example*, as well as *precept*, must influence the disposition and actions of young and ductile minds, and lay the foundation for progressive virtue or vice."

At a proper hour, the two gentlemen repaired to the house of Dr. Renau, and were introduced to Louisa.—She was seated in an arm chair, and accompanied by Madam Blomfielde, the physician's aunt, who rose at their entrance, and after a few compliments, left the room. They congratulated the invalid on her appearance, so much for the better.

"I am indeed," said she, "under infinite obligations to you, gentlemen, and to the good Doctor; and feeling myself in safety from the power and machinations of the most profligate of men, has restored a comparative peace to my mind, which has its influence on my general state of health. Permit me also to felicitate myself and you, on *your* preservation from death, an event so unquestionably believed by all your friends, that seeing you, Sir (addressing Ferdinand) follow the Turk into the room, occasioned the faintings I was seized with, the weakened state of my head at that moment leading me to suppose it was your spirit emerged from the grave. Forgive me, therefore, if I am desirous of knowing why the report of your death was circulated, and why you have concealed yourselves from your friends."

Ferdinand, without entering into a particular detail, briefly mentioned their captivity, and recent return into Germany; adding, that they had sent off letters to all those whom they supposed might be interested in their fate, and hourly expected letters.—"You may be certain," said he, "we did not omit writing to Mr. D'Alenberg."

"Ah!" cried Louisa, "had those letters reached him before we quitted Suabia, 'tis more than probable we should not have undertaken this journey, and my dear friends would have been spared much sorrow and anxiety. If you will allow for the pauses my weakness may occasion, I will give you a short account of the events which have thus, fortunately for me, procured us a meeting.

"For some time after your departure, my friend Theresa exerted herself to heal the wounds of my mind, and administer to the recovery of my health. I was grateful for her kindness, though it had not its deserved success. Unhappily she caught the contagion of melancholy, and from a disposition of the most enchanting vivacity, changed to a despondency, a kind of habitual gloom in every word and action, that alarmed us inexpressibly. The distress and despair of Mr. D'Alenberg cannot be expressed. She resisted every persuasion, even prayers and tears, to draw from her the cause of such an alarming change, always protesting she could not account for it; that she had no disquietudes, nor any thing that afflicted her mind, but that she had taken an inclination for a monastic life. This inclination her worthy father opposed, and besought her, in the most moving terms, not to desert him, and render his future days wretched.

"With some difficulty she was brought to relinquish her design, and promised she would struggle against the malady that oppressed her.

"I reproached myself incessantly as the cause of her disorder; I would have left the house which I had infected with melancholy, but she protested violently against my design, and I was compelled to submit. Mr. D'Alenberg could assign no other probable idea for her distress of mind, than that she had deceived herself, and was actually warmly attached to the unworthy Count Wolfran."

"Impossible," exclaimed Ferdinand, warmly.—"A mind pure and exalted as her's, could not, for a moment, entertain a preference for such a wretch."

"The event," resumed Louisa, "justifies your assertion. As I felt conscious that her unhappiness, from whatever cause it proceeded, must originate from me, I tried to assume a new character, to stifle my own feelings, and to cover a breaking heart under the mask of cheerfulness. Every effort of mine was exerted to amuse her. We went to Stutgard, compelled her to go into company, to mix sometimes in the entertainments of the city. She refused no request of her father's, but no change appeared in her disposition.

"One day Mr. D'Alenberg received a letter from his friend, who had introduced Count Wolfran to his notice. He lamented that he had not the power to punish a villain who had so basely deceived him, but that, after the most minute inquiries, he had reason to believe the Count had left the kingdom, to avoid the disgrace and shame attendant on a conviction of such vile actions as he had been guilty of.

"This letter the good gentleman read to his daughter in my presence, both of us carefully watching its effects on her. No change appeared in her countenance.—'Poor wretch,' said she, 'what a mind must he possess, conscious of his base duplicity!'

" 'How, my dear!' exclaimed Mr. D'Alenberg, 'do you *pity* him?'

" 'I *do*, Sir,' answered she.—'When we can despise the man, and know he has failed in his pursuits, that he has had no power to injure us, and must be covered with confusion and guilt, charity may induce us to pity one so completely mean and detestable.'

"Those words, delivered without any emotion either in her person or voice, convinced us that Count Wolfran had no share in the disorder of her mind. A thousand different conjectures we then hazarded to each other, but in three days after, the whole was elucidated at once. Mr. D'Alenberg received some intelligence that grieved him, and too hastily communicated it to his daughter:—Its effects were instantaneous; she fell into violent and repeated fits, that ended in a delirium, and discovered the secret so tenaciously observed, so strictly guarded, that I was equally surprised with her father."

"Ah!" said Ferdinand, "may we presume to ask——?"

"Pardon me for interrupting you," returned Louisa; "I would not hear a question that should make me doubt of your delicacy or prudence; all that I can, in honour confide, you, gentlemen, have an undoubted claim to be informed of; but a secret retained with so much perseverance by my friend, can never be at my discretion to reveal."

"Amiable Louisa," exclaimed Ferdinand, "I stand corrected, and take shame to myself, but do justice to the purity of my motives."

"I do," replied she; "I know they were friendly ones, and I saw the same question trembling on the lips of the Count."

"I own it," said he; "and you must allow it was a *natural* question, if not a discreet one, and the impulse of the moment; but, pardon our impatience and interruption."

"This secret discovered," resumed she, "gave the severest affliction to Mr. D'Alenberg.—He had not the power to relieve her distress, or procure happiness to his child.—There were certain circumstances that impeded every hope of restoring her to a cheerful turn of mind, and his despair on the conviction was little less terrifying than the dreadful state in which my charming friend continued for six days.

"At the expiration of that period, Heaven heard the prayers of this worthy father, and restored her to reason. It was near a fortnight before she could leave her bed; and then how affecting was the figure she presented! A delicate skin thrown over a skeleton, a look of dignified sorrow, that wounded every eye, and a struggle for that composure so necessary to her father's peace, which now seemed the only object she had in view. So shadowy was her frame, that we almost feared to breathe, lest it should dissolve into air; and when she spoke, so faint, so sweet was her voice, that it penetrated to the very soul.

"Judge what a father must feel; for I see you are affected. Not to dwell, therefore, on a situation so painful, the fortitude she sought to acquire, and her consideration for her father, which still rendered life valuable to a duteous mind like her's, uniting with youth and a good constitution, restored her to comparative health.—The physicians advised travelling, that change of air, and a variety of objects, might dispel that gloom which seemed to impede her natural cheerfulness, and undermine her strength.

"In compliance with this advice, for near two months past we have lived a desultory kind of life, without any fixed plan, but moving from place to place, as fancy or inclination directed. By this management, we have succeeded in amusing Miss D'Alenberg; and though that playful gaiety, and animating vivacity she once possessed, appears to be entirely lost, yet there is a soft complacency, an earnest desire to *look* contented in every word and action, that highly gratifies her father, and inspires hope, that time and effort may restore her tranquillity.

"About ten days ago, we arrived at Ens, in which city lived a relation of Mr. D'Alenberg, who received us with great kindness. The next evening I accompanied my friend in a walk by the side of the river, not far from our residence. We strolled sometime on the banks; the evening was delightful.—Several boats were passing; the moon was rising in majestic splendor; its beams playing on the smooth surface, and conveying unspeakable tranquillity to the mind. We stood for some time in fixed admiration of the scene, forgetful of the hour, 'till a servant came to remind us of the time we had been absent.

"We were so enchanted with our evening's walk, that we resolved to repeat it the following night, and declined having a servant to attend us, because we apprehended no danger, and wished to be unobserved.

"Unfortunately we were indulged in our request, and we extended our walk, thoughtless of the distance, until no more boats passing, we recollected that it grew late; we turned to quicken our pace home, when suddenly a boat drew towards the shore, and three ordinary looking men jumped out and followed us. Fear lent us wings, though we knew not that they meant any ill. Miss D'Alenberg was more nimble than myself; hastening after her, my foot struck against something, and I fell. Two men instantly seized me; I screamed.

" 'Stop her mouth,' cried one of them, 'and bear her off; the other has got the start of us.'

"I heard no more, but found myself carried to a boat, which rowed off with great swiftness. A large cloak was thrown over me, and between terror and affright, I was scarcely in my senses.

"How long we continued on the water, I know not; I was carried out still wrapped up, and incapable of making any resistance. At length I was uncovered; some bread and wine was given to me, which I refused. I saw only strange faces, and demanded to know why I was thus dragged from my friends?

"No answer was given; and in a short time after, a handkerchief was tied across my mouth. I was again tight wrapped in a cloak, and put into a carriage.—When in the high road, I was uncovered—and high time it was, for I was nearly suffocated, and had suffered great agony. We came within sight of a town; I was then obliged to undergo the same misery again, until we had stopt, changed post horses, and were once more on the road.

"Not to tire you with more particulars, in this manner we proceeded, without stopping to sleep on the road, and only taking some bread and wine from the post-houses. At length we entered a wood: No longer able to preserve silence, I cried out, 'Ah! my God, what is now to become of me!'

"Being so frequently muffled up, and having only once taken any refreshment, both my spirits and strength were exhausted, which, with the terror I felt on entering a thick wood at the close of day, entirely overcame me, and I fainted. How long I continued in this situation, I know not; but on my recovery, I found myself in a very decent apartment, with two men and an elderly woman.

"The former perceiving that my senses were returned, ordered the woman to retire; she obeyed, and after a short whisper, one of the men followed her.

"The other having shut the door, advanced close to me, and, to my infinite astonishment, taking off a false covering of hair, and removing a pair of black eye-brows, discovered to me the features of Count Wolfran. I shrieked with the wildest affright.

" 'Once more,' said he, 'I have you in my power.—You, who have destroyed my happiest prospects, and blasted all my hopes; who have injured my character, and procured for yourself protectors at my expence. What have you to offer as an atonement for the mischief you have done; what reparation can you make for the ruin and disgrace you have brought upon me?'

"I was speechless at this address: The effrontery, and the well-known villany of the man, filled me with the most dreadful apprehensions, and impeded any attempt at articulation; he saw, and enjoyed my terror.

" 'I see,' said the wretch, 'conscious guilt ties your tongue: Know then, that I have taken my measures too securely for you to entertain any hope of an escape from my power. I have two proposals to make, *one* of which you must chuse—*Death* or *marriage*. I should suppose the alternative will not be difficult to decide on.'

"Indignation restored my speech.—'Marriage,' I exclaimed.—'You well know that I am your wife.'

" 'Aye,' said he, 'there is the point on which we differ: That is the assertion which I deny.—You were once indeed a kind obliging girl, and chose to patch up your reputation at the expence of mine. But to have done with this foolery,' said he with a stern look, observing my agitation, 'know, that you are either to marry my servant, your old acquaintance, or this house is your grave.

" 'Understand me—I do not want your murder to hang upon my spirits, but I am determined to secure you from doing me further mischief. My valet *shall* marry you, and in justice to him, I shall indulge him with a few days to amuse his pretty wife;—after which, by his authority, you will be placed in a situation that will effectually secure me from any more discoveries of yours.

" 'I now leave you.—To-morrow, at an early hour, we shall conclude the business.'

"He then opened the door, and retired.—I heard it locked and bolted on the other side.

"For some moments, I remained fixed in astonishment and terror. I knew him too well to doubt of his resolution, and I saw no means of escaping from his power.—Furious and malignant, he was capable of the most atrocious actions, and I had every evil to apprehend.

"The alternative of *death* would have been my preferable choice, but *that* was only thrown out to alarm me.—*Murder* was not *his* choice.—For some hours I sat almost stupified with horror: I found, that during the deprivation of my senses, my pockets had been emptied of their contents. I looked round the apartment; it was a decent room, but without a bed; a sofa, a few chairs, and a table, composed all the furniture.

"One window very high from the ground, with a chintz window curtain: No light was left with me, but fortunately the moon shone sufficiently through the window for me to discriminate every object.

"Rousing at length from the stupor of terror, I placed a chair on the table, and looked through the window; a large garden was under it, and beyond the wood. The distance from the ground was so great, that to reach it, appeared almost impossible; but what will not despair attempt, and ingenuity contrive.

"With some difficulty I got off the window curtain, and with my teeth affected different breaks, by which means I tore it into six parts; but the fear of being heard, obliged me to be long and cautious in doing it.—At length I effected my design; I tied each part together in repeated strong knots; I opened the window softly, and letting it down, saw that it reached the ground.

"There was a chance indeed that it might break, or that my hands might slip; yet as death was far preferable to the evils that impended over me, I was not terrified by the apparent danger. I fastened the end of the curtain to the iron across the window, and with a courage desperation only could inspire, ventured from it, holding firmly by the kind of rope I had made.

"My weight carried me quick down to the first knot: Here my hands were stopt, and it was with the utmost hazard I freed them;—but, by the time I reached the second knot, they were too feeble to support me, and I fell from a great height, but most providentially on a bed of earth, fresh turned up;—and though stunned with the fall, I soon found I had broken no limbs, and in a short time got on my feet, and made towards a door that led into the wood. I had here another difficulty to encounter, to get over the wall, but it was not very high, and I accomplished it, though not without some injury to my person.

"I was now in the wood, unacquainted with any path-way, and exposed to a thousand dangers; but all weighed light in comparison of those I had escaped from: I therefore pierced through the trees, and walked with all the swiftness my strength would permit, though often obliged to sit a few minutes and rest.

"I believe I must have walked upwards of four hours, when I observed a path to the right, which I entered upon, and in a short time came to a descent, from whence I thought I could discern the top of a house.—The idea gave me spirits; I hastened down the declivity, and arrived at that house where most fortunately I met with you.

"That it was the Count who came next morning, I have no doubt: Nor am I surprised that he should take the lady; but as doubtless she betrayed me, I am greatly astonished that he did not return, and force me from thence.

"Thus, gentlemen, I have accounted to you for my appearance.— Heaven, doubtless, sent you for my preservation; but I feel most poignantly for the affliction I know my amiable friend and her benevolent father must suffer, from the incertitude of my fate."

Louisa having concluded her story, Ferdinand proposed setting off immediately for Ens, to relieve the inquietude of her friends. She gratefully thanked him, but said, she had many reasons to prefer sending a messenger, as it was not unlikely that Mr. D'Alenberg might have left Ens, and the journey prove fruitless; but if he would have the goodness to procure a courier, she would endeavour to write both to him and the gentleman they had visited, and by that means should certainly gain intelligence of their route, if they had quitted the city. This method was adopted, and a proper person soon obtained, who was dispatched with the letter.

Mean time, Ferdinand and the Count expressed a good deal of anxiety that they had no return to the letters they had written.—For five or six days past, they had daily expected them, and the disappointment grew very painful.

To divert their attention, they asked the young Count Reiberg to ride with them to the Turk's cottage, as they wished to know if he had gained any information relative to Fatima.

On arriving at the house, they were surprised to see all the window shutters fastened. The Count advanced to the door, and knocking with his whip, found the door was on a jar. They alighted, and repeated the knock; but no one appearing, and fancying they heard a noise something like the moan of a person in pain, they pushed open the door, and ventured in. There was no one below, but an appearance of disorder in the room, the closet open, and things scattered about, that gave them an idea some ruffians had broken in and plundered the house.

They had no fire arms with them, and therefore went cautiously up stairs.—The same disorder was apparent in the first room they entered; but on going through to an inner apartment, how greatly were they astonished and shocked, to behold a gentleman on the floor dead or dying, and Heli also on the floor, with very little appearance of life, though he feebly moved one of his hands, as they hastened towards him.

The blood was running from a wound in his neck; this they quickly staunched with their handkerchiefs, bound up the wound, and raised him upon the sofa; whilst the Count and Baron were attending to him.—Ferdinand had examined the gentleman, who seemed to be dangerously wounded, and scarcely alive. His wound was in the side, and, as they supposed, proceeded from a pistol; therefore, not knowing where the bullet might be lodged they could form no judgment of his danger; however, they stopt the blood, washed his face with cold water, and, by the help of drops, he soon began to show signs of life. He opened his eyes, and making a great effort to speak,

"Your help is in vain—I am dying."

"Do not despair, Sir," said Reiberg.—And pouring some drops into water, he got a little down his throat.—Again trying to speak, he said, "'Tis in vain!"—Not, however, discouraged, they raised him upon a sofa likewise, and Reiberg got upon his horse, and flew towards the city for a surgeon.

On his return with one in a very short space of time, he found they were both alive, Heli in a much better state than the other;—but he preserved a sullen silence; the gentleman was incapable of speaking. The surgeon having examined their wounds, pronounced Heli's not dangerous, but the other's very doubtful, as he could not then extract the ball. After he had dressed them, and given them some cordials to restore their spirits, the gentleman seemed to acquire some strength.

"I must die," said he to the surgeon; "I know I must; flatter me not."

"I fear indeed," answered he; "if you have friends, or any thing to do, no time should be lost."

"*This* then is the end," exclaimed the other feebly, and paused for a few moments; then turning to the gentlemen, "*this* is the conclusion of a life short as to years—but an eternity in vice and wickedness.

"I am Count Wolfran—Louisa Hautweitzer is my lawful wife—she must inherit. I die by the hand of a vile Turk, cut off when projecting the death of others. *This* is retribution.—Women—passion, vile principles, have destroyed me.—I have a house, servants, wretches in the——."

Here his articulation failed; he struggled violently to speak, which occasioned his wounds to bleed afresh, and carried him off in a few moments.

Heli viewed this scene with a gloomy ferocity, but spoke not. Ferdinand and his friends were equally shocked and surprised.

"Unhappy man," cried the Count, "this is indeed a terrible conclusion of an ill-spent life."

"Do you then know the gentleman?" asked the surgeon; "I understood he was a stranger."

"*Personally* so," returned Count M***, "his *name*, I know, has too often been disgraced by bad actions—but *here* they rest."

Turning to Heli—"Perhaps he can give some solution of this strange business.—My friend," said he to Ferdinand, "will you inquire."

The surgeon here interposed.—"I think, gentlemen, you had best defer 'till to-morrow any examination; the sudden and fatal effects which attend the agitation of the spirits, we have just seen; and if I can translate that man's looks, he is not likely to be very placid."

They subscribed to this opinion; and therefore Ferdinand addressed him in very soothing terms, to which the other made no reply.

The body was removed to another room, and the surgeon undertook to send a proper person to attend on Heli.

"But what," cried the Count, "is become of the women servants?"

This question was again asked of Heli.

"The devil has them," answered he, sulkily.

They then proceeded to search the house. No person was to be found; the trunks and closets were all open and stript.

"The house is robbed," said Ferdinand to Heli.

"By your cursed sister," returned he in German.

The surgeon and Reiberg stared.—Ferdinand was extremely confused; but recovering himself—"If the woman you call my sister," answered he in the same language, "has robbed you, you can blame only yourself; I disclaim all knowledge or affinity to her."

Heli did not perfectly understand him, but again furiously and maliciously repeated, "your sister, the cursed Fatima."

Provoked and much hurt, he said to the surgeon, "I entreat of you, Sir, to inquire out for an interpreter for this man; he knows not what he means; let him have a proper person to explain what he says, that he may not be misunderstood."

The surgeon, whose curiosity was evidently much excited, promised instantly to comply with his request; upon which they left him there with one of Count Reiberg's servants, another having been sent away for the surgeon's assistant, on whose arrival he promised to set off and procure an interpreter.

The gentlemen, particularly Ferdinand, left the house under much perturbation. The latter bitterly lamented his folly, in making himself known to Fatima; for as he supposed her capable of any excesses, should the Turk promulgate the report of his consanguinity to her, it would reflect infinite disgrace on his name, and render him an object of curiosity to the inhabitants of the city.

Perplexed and uneasy, he returned to the Baron's, and saw no method to do away the prejudice with which Heli's story and malicious expressions might possibly fill young Reiberg's mind to his disadvantage, than by a brief recital of the adventure which had brought him to the knowledge of Fatima, to the truth of which his friend the Count could bear testimony.

He therefore seized the first opportunity, when the dinner was over, and the servants withdrawn, candidly to repeat every circumstance; and concluded with saying, that from Fatima's elopement, and the presence of Count Wolfran at Heli's, he had little doubt but that they had contrived some dark plot, in the execution of which the Count had fallen a victim; but by whom the house was robbed, or the preceding circumstances, could only be learnt from Heli, whose sullen taciturnity for the present afforded no lights to guide their search.

When Ferdinand had concluded the little narrative, which he thought requisite to do himself justice, he could not avoid remarking an uncommon spirit and animation in the appearance of Reiberg; his looks, his voice, his whole form, seemed to possess a new soul; involved in perplexity on his own affairs, 'till this moment the alteration had escaped his notice.

The other, observing that both the Count and Ferdinand looked at him with surprise, caught the hand of the latter—"My dear Sir, I can translate your thoughts; know then, the events of this morning nearly concern me; they hold out a dawn of hope, a possibility of happiness, which I thought for ever extinguished: Count Wolfran was my mortal enemy; he robbed me of the woman I adored; his relations were her guardians, they compelled her to give him her hand;—*he is dead*, and *she is free.*—Heaven is just—and I may hope."

The Count and Ferdinand were astonished at this development, and more so to find that he was unacquainted with the circumstances that had occasioned a separation between the Count and his lady.

"Where does the Countess reside?" asked Ferdinand.

"I believe in a convent," answered Reiberg.—"I have only once heard from her since her fatal marriage. She wrote to me, that, by mutual consent, she was separated from her husband, and intended to retire from the world; conjured me, as I valued her future happiness, if chance should ever throw me in the way of Count Wolfran, whatever reports might reach my ears, as probably many false stories might be promulgated, never to lift my hand against his, or embitter her days, by hazarding my *own* life: Entreated me to consider her as dead to the world, and to form another connexion, which she knew was most anxiously wished for by my friends.

"The first part of her request I resolved strictly to observe: I sought not Count Wolfran—I desired not to meet him, since his death, by *my* hands, would have placed an insuperable bar to any hopes from Theodosia; but the passion she had inspired was interwoven with my existence, impossible to be eradicated, and being hopeless, produced an entire change in my disposition. I found myself insensibly growing morose, unsociable, and unpleasant to my friends; my temper seemed to be utterly ruined; but the events of this morning has occasioned an entire revolution in my feelings; the possibility of hope has restored me to myself.

"A few words the Count uttered, as he was dying, surprises and confounds me.—He said, '*Louisa:*' The tumult of my spirits, at the moment, has lost the recollection of the other name; but he said, 'Louisa is my wife—she must inherit.'

"What could be meant; had he *two wives*, or is my Theodosia dead? The idea chills me; for I know not the name of the convent she retired to.—'Till this doubt is removed, I cannot give myself up to joy, tho' my heart feels light, and presages happiness. The Count, I know, has an estate near Ulm, and I believe relations there: We must dispatch a courier to them, and then my destiny will be decided."

Count M*** and Ferdinand, having listened with much satisfaction to the volubility of Reiberg, who had spoken more words in a few moments than he had uttered in several days, felt infinite pleasure that they could do away some part of his apprehensions, by assuring him that Theodosia still existed, and even named to him the convent she resided at; but their confidence was limited; for her situation, in respect to the Count, being very delicate, they held themselves bound to conceal that part of her story, and even prevailed with the Baron to delay sending off a messenger until the next morning, under the pretence of gaining further information from Heli; but in reality they wanted to inform Louisa of this event, and consult with her the proper steps necessary to assert her rights.

By advice of the Count, Ferdinand set out to see her, whilst the former, with Reiberg, went to visit Heli.

CHAPTER XI.

WHEN Ferdinand arrived at Dr. Renau's, he heard that Louisa was very much recovered, and on being introduced to her, was charmed to see her more easy, and apparently in better health than he could have expected. After a few compliments, and a little preparatory chat, he bid her prepare to hear news interesting and pleasing, and then entered upon the scenes which they had witnessed at Heli's cottage.

Louisa was both surprised and affected.—She shed many tears for the dreadful fate of a man she once tenderly loved; thus cut off in the high career of vice, when he was planning new schemes of mischief. After she grew a little composed, he repeated the story of Count Reiberg, and concluded with asking what directions she would give him or her friends to prosecute her claims to a share of the late Count's property, as his widow; his last words before witnesses would corroborate the circumstances she could bring forth.—After pausing for some time, she delivered her sentiments in these words:

"There was a time, when, to be acknowledged the wife of Count Wolfran, would have been my pride, my happiness; that time is no more. To be justified in the opinion of my generous friends and protectors, is now the only gratification his confession can afford me.

"I never will make any public claims;—my story is unknown, but among my few friends; there let it rest.—The generous, noble-minded Theodosia, was married in the face of the world; she has a child; that child is his lawful heir; nor for millions would I deprive it of its rights, or occasion confusion to its amiable mother, by the ill natured observations of little minds, who will judge superficially of the deception practised against her.

"This then is my determination: I will not appear in the business; Theodosia is Countess of Wolfran; send an express to her; let her emerge from her solitude, and act for her child, as heir to the Count; her claims are incontestible—mine, *were* I inclined to assert them, might subject me to trouble from his relations; but I have no such inclinations; a thousand reasons of delicacy, honour, and gratitude, determine me to resign all my pretensions."

"But," said Ferdinand, "how shall we account for the last words of the Count, spoken before Reiberg and the surgeon? of which the former has taken notice."

"As the delirium of the moment," answered she.—"The surgeon cannot be interested to investigate it: The Countess will be recognized by all his friends and her's, and Reiberg may be led to believe it was some transient attachment he had lately formed. The words of a dying man, situated as he was, may easily be overlooked."

"Well," said Ferdinand, "I admire your resolution exceedingly; I trust we shall, in a few hours, have the benefit of Mr. D'Alenberg's advice; for I think they will not delay their journey, when they know your situation."

"I believe so," replied Louisa, "and shall rejoice to see them; but my determination is fixed, as to resigning all claims on the deceased or his property.—On that head, I have made up my mind; nor will any advice or persuasions prevail upon me to alter it; and indeed there is less generosity than justice in this resolve, because I have no one that can be benefited by the Count's fortune; and his child is, and ought to be, his heir; therefore, dear Sir, have no doubts on the business; send off to the Countess without delay; I will prepare a letter to go by the same courier."

As Ferdinand observed that she appeared fatigued with talking, and saw she was truly decided, he forebore intruding on her by farther conversation, and retired to procure a messenger; also to fabricate some plausible story to account for the last words of Count Wolfran.

When he returned, he found his friend the Count, and young Reiberg, were still absent; he waited on the Baron, and consulted him about the disposal of the Count's body, until the pleasure of his lady should be made known. The Baron readily undertook to manage that business, and to send a proper person with a shell to remove it from Heli's.

They began to be extremely surprised at the long absence of the others; night came on, and they did not appear, when suddenly a loud knocking revived their spirits; presently they heard a bustle, when four armed men rushed in, and produced their authority to arrest Ferdinand for robbery and murder!

Inconceivably astonished, the Baron and he gazed on each other for a few seconds in silence; but the former first recovering, cried out, "This is a false and malicious charge; I know this gentleman; I can answer for his honour and innocence."

"Very possibly, Sir," replied the principal of them; "but that must be proved; we can do nothing about it; we must obey the warrant; and if the gentleman is innocent, he will soon be at liberty; he must, however, go with us." Ferdinand had by this time recovered from his surprise; turning to the Baron—"Be not disconcerted, Sir, the business will soon take another turn; the man is right; I must comply with the mandate, and appeal elsewhere." At that moment entered the Count and young Reiberg.

"How! What is the meaning of all this?" cried the latter.

His father briefly informed him of the charge and arrest.

"That cursed revengeful Turk," exclaimed the Count; "but he shall not be carried to a prison."

"I beseech you, my good friends," said Ferdinand, "not to oppose the authority issued against me. Innocence is best proved by a quiet submission to the laws, and a proper appeal to higher powers. I am ready to attend you," said he, turning to the man.

"Sir," returned the man, who had spoken before, "you are a gentleman and an honourable one too.—I am certain—I am sorry I am ordered on such an affair; but I hope you will soon have your liberty."

"I thank you, my good fellow," replied he.

Then embracing his friends, after they had inquired where he was to be carried to, they parted.

No sooner had Ferdinand been taken off, than young Reiberg gave the following relation to his father:

"When we arrived at the cottage, we were extremely surprised to be seized upon by five or six men, on our entrance into Heli's apartment. My first idea was, that they were banditti, but I was soon convinced of my mistake. Heli was reclined on the sofa, as we had left him; a man, who we found was an interpreter, standing by his side.

"On seeing us, he spoke with an appearance of chagrin to the other: He asked where the other gentleman was that had been there in the morning? I replied we had left him in the city, and demanded to know the reason we were thus seized upon. The interpreter made the following reply:

" 'I was sent here this morning by a surgeon; just as I arrived, came these men also, with orders to arrest this Turk for the murder of Count Wolfran, information of which had been given to a magistrate.—I explained to Heli their business; he grew outrageous, and denied the fact: Meantime, two of the men had searched the house, had found the dead body, and some empty pistols.

" 'This corroborated the charge, and they were on the point of dragging him away wounded as he is.—When he understood this, he declared, that a gentleman, who called himself Count Ferdinand, but who he believed to be a rogue and a sharper, with his sister, calling herself Fatima, had concerted with the late Count to enter his house, and plunder him of some jewels, which the two former knew he had with him.

" 'That the Count, Fatima, and a strange man, assaulted him; he made resistance;—upon which the woman had stabbed him in the neck, and he directly caught up a pistol, and fired on the Count: That seeing him fall, and Heli faint with the blood that flowed from his wound, also falling, they had proceeded to plunder the house, had carried off his casket of jewels, and fled, leaving him and the Count to all appearance dying; and then the former confessed Ferdinand had persuaded his sister to get possession of those jewels.

" 'In the morning, he said Ferdinand, with two gentlemen, came to the house, the former, no doubt, expecting to find him dead, and seemed much surprised and confused when he saw both alive. The Count dying soon after, Ferdinand went into the rooms, and then returned, crying out, the house was plundered; upon which he (Heli) accused his infamous sister: That Ferdinand spoke to him in the Turkish language, desiring he would not expose him, by calling Fatima his sister; but he disdained any other reply than the same accusation in German; upon which the other, greatly confounded, pretended to show much compassion for him, but made off as soon as he could; and he supposed some of his confederates had charged him with the murder of the Count, to get rid of him; but he now charged Ferdinand, his sister, and other accomplices, with an intent to murder and rob him.

" 'This,' continued the interpreter, 'was the account delivered to the men. Some circumstances seemed improbable; yet there were others not unlikely, because it was plain he had been robbed, by the disorder in the house. Two men were left to guard him, whilst three went away to repeat this story to the magistrate.

" 'They soon returned; we were ordered to wait here, and seize who ever should come to Heli. Mean time, an order was given to arrest this Ferdinand at the house of Baron Reiberg, according to Heli's directions;—and now, gentlemen, this is all I know of the business; the Turk persists in his story, and the affair must be investigated by those in power.'

"When the man concluded his account," said Reiberg, "I asked to speak with Heli, but I was refused; we then demanded to be conducted to the magistrate, which was complied with; and on coming before him, and declaring our names, he permitted us to depart at liberty, as no particular charge had appeared against the Count or myself. All this business occasioned our late return, but we little thought the order for Ferdinand's arrest had been so speedily issued and executed; and now, dear Sir, what can be done?"

"Nothing can be done this night," replied the Baron.—"Early in the morning I will attend the magistrate myself.—At any rate, the Count's testimony and mine will procure his liberty, on our parole of honour, I should suppose."

"That villainous Turk can only be actuated by malice," said the Count; "for he well knows the innocence of my friend.—What share Fatima had in the business, I know not; but I believe that Count Wolfran came there to seek for the lady, and not to rob the house.—I only fear it will be difficult to investigate the truth, for want of evidence; but to-morrow I shall most certainly apply to the Emperor himself to prove the rank of Ferdinand, and then I hope we shall soon confound his accusers."

Ferdinand was conducted to a prison; but he was treated with gentleness, and had (for a prison) tolerable accommodations. He was not without very unpleasant reflections; no letters had arrived from his friends, which involved him in doubts and anxiety for his son, Claudina, and his brother.— By his imprudence, in acknowledging his connexion with the worthless Fatima, he had brought on himself his present disagreeable situation: Then he considered, that if the affair was prosecuted on Heli's testimony against him, he should be compelled to make his father's weakness known, and the attendant circumstances.

He then reverted to the story of Louisa. Miss D'Alenberg's situation gave him the most poignant concern; a young woman so respectable, so charming, a victim to a hopeless passion; who could the object be? that her heart was free, when she consented to marry Count Wolfran, was a certainty avowed by herself. He then recollected every little circumstance of her behaviour, when Count M*** and himself were on a visit to her father. Her politeness and attention *then* appeared to be equally divided, but *now*, on a review of every thing, Ferdinand remembered the Count had much the greater share of her notice. She talked mostly to him; she leant on *his* arm in the garden;—and on the day of their departure, he had observed in taking leave, she fixed her eyes on the Count as she spoke.

"Yes," said he, on recapitulating those trifling circumstances.—"Yes, I am convinced the Count has been so happy to touch that heart so good, so amiable; he is unconscious of the distress he has given birth to, and his situation will, from honour and delicacy, ever preclude him the unspeakable delight of restoring her mind to peace."

What a fatality, thought he, that so lovely a woman should have placed

her affections so unhappily; never shall I forgive myself for that unfortunate introduction to her acquaintance. The more he reflected, the more he
was convinced the Count was the object that had produced the lamentable
change in this amiable young lady.

Our confession at parting, that we were *"married,* and unfortunate,"
her father doubtless repeated, and from thence originated the melancholy
that oppressed the daughter. He sighed heavily for her disappointment, and
scarcely thought life worth preserving, when subject to such various events,
productive of certain misery.

"Did not my child exist," exclaimed he in a fit of despondency; "did
I not feel, that I owe to him a duty I cannot delegate to another, that of
superintending his conduct, and directing his mind as he advances in years;
instructing him to guard against the impetuosity of youthful passions; a too
easy confidence in the seeming integrity of plausible appearances, and from
the example of his unhappy father, see those precepts *illustrated;* example,
which speaks more forcibly to an inexperienced mind than the most elabo-
rate reasoning adduced from theory only. Yes, for *his* sake, I must endeavour
to retain my existence, that my follies may not spread wider in the conduct
of my child."

Under the oppressive recollection of former scenes, and doubtful anxiety for the future, poor Ferdinand passed a wretched night; nor were his
friends much easier.—Count M***, whose affection for him was truly fraternal, lamented, that it was in consequence of his advice they had remained
in Vienna 'till the return of their letters.——Whatever unpleasant consequences might have attended their sudden appearance, they could not have
been productive of such vexatious circumstances as had now happened,
he thought. Yet, then, what might have become of the poor Louisa? How
would young Reiberg have acquired that promise of returning tranquillity,
if the events that had taken place at Heli's had remained unknown? Those
questions again reconciled him to a degree of comparative ease, to think
less of the blame he had attached to himself, and to trust in Heaven for the
protection of his friend, and their deliverance from the malicious accusations of Heli.

The next morning, at the instant when the Count, Baron Reiberg and
his son, were preparing to wait on the magistrate, and from thence, if they
found it necessary, to address the Emperor; the long-expected letters arrived from Suabia. The Count received one from his steward, very much
to his satisfaction; the good Duclos being overjoyed at the restoration of
his master from death to life, particularly as he had applied to the Duke of
Wirtemberg, and obtained leave to keep possession of the estates for six

months, or until a certainty of his master's fate within that period should arrive. This prudent proceeding had saved much trouble.

The next letter was from Eugenia, and written in a style of such content, and calm resignation, that although she expressed an infinity of satisfaction from the receipt of his letter, yet that satisfaction seemed more like the affectionate joy of a sister, than the transports of a wife: Her expressions were kind, but guarded; her congratulations were warm, but not rapturous; in short, it was such a letter as a sister might write to a beloved brother; not one word reverted to past scenes; not a line of regret for their separation. She told him, "she was *more* than tranquil; she was happy: That the tender interest she must ever feel for the state of his mind, was the only cloud that hung over her, otherwise, perfect content; and as she had but little doubt of the good effects of time, of the cares of friendship, and of the advantages resulting from employment and amusements, she hoped that cloud would soon be brushed away to their mutual satisfaction."

The perusal of this letter at first rather displeased Count M***; but at the second reading, he was more just; it was selfish to feel discontent, because religion and good sense had tranquillized her mind, and that the situation she had chosen from the purest motives should have realized her expectations and wishes: Did he not wish her happy, after the years of misery she had struggled with; and was not her conduct truly laudable and praise-worthy? Those reflections recalled him from his temporary displeasure, and rendered the sentiment she expressed more estimable in his eyes, from the very circumstances that first offended him.

She did not mention the Countess in her letter, and therefore it was uncertain if she remained in that convent, or had changed her residence.

The Count, having examined the contents of his own letters, saw there were two also for Ferdinand, one with a black seal. As he was not acquainted with the writing, he could not have an idea from what quarter it came. At first he proposed taking the letters to him; but after a little deliberation, it was settled that young Reiberg should visit him with the letters, whilst the Count and the Baron pursued their first intention of exerting all their joint interest to procure an order for the release of Ferdinand.

END OF VOLUME III.

The Mysterious Warning

Volume IV

MYSTERIOUS WARNING.

CHAPTER I.

THE young Baron Reiberg was admitted without any difficulty to see Ferdinand, but he was excessively shocked on entering the wretched hole of his confinement, though informed it was one of the best rooms in the prison. "One of the best" could not reconcile it to his feelings, and when he embraced the prisoner, his emotions were very visible.

"I thank you most cordially (said the latter) for this kindness; but, my good friend, do not throw your eyes around thus, with such a revolting kind of horror in your features. A prison is not a desirable place I grant ye, but is disarmed of all its terrors when conscious innocence brightens the gloom. *You* know I have no cause for apprehension, this temporary confinement, therefore, is only a little variety in the chequered work of life."

"I am rejoiced (said Reiberg) to find your mind is cheerful in this horrid place; in similar circumstances I am sensible that I should possess neither your resignation or fortitude: However, I think your confinement will be of short duration. My father and the Count are gone earnestly to work, and I am certain will not give over until they have obtained your enlargement. I came here, I hope, to bring you some consolation, to bring you letters from your friends, that you have so much wished for."

Ferdinand eagerly took the letters, looking on the superscription, and then on the seal. "This black herald (said he) forebodes no good news I fear; but the worst *must* be known, and no place so proper as a prison to bear sorrow, or teach patience under unavoidable evils."

He had turned the letter two or three times whilst speaking, irresolute how to open it.—Reiberg observed his embarrassment: "Do you wish to be alone? (said he.) Speak, I will retire, and come to you by and bye."

"No (replied Ferdinand) for my own sake I do not wish it; but perhaps———."

"Say no more (interrupted Reiberg) peruse your letters, I have a book in my pocket." The other obeyed, and with a trembling hand broke the seal.

"It is from Mr. Dunloff (exclaimed he) the guardian of my son! Ah! what am I to hear? Thank Heaven, my child is well."—Reading further on, he again cried out,—"How, Claudina dead! Poor, poor Claudina! then I have indeed lost thee for ever!" He continued to read, his emotions increased, the big drops fell on his face, he turned from the Baron, and leaning against the wall,—"Excuse me (said he, falteringly) I have lost a wife, once dear to my heart!"

Attempting to read on, but being too greatly affected at the moment, "My dear Baron (said he) I avail myself of your considerate kindness. An hour or two hence I shall be better enabled to thank you for this visit."—Reiberg immediately withdrew, trusting on his return to bring an order for his enlargement. Ferdinand, at liberty to indulge the sorrow that oppressed him, read the following letter from Mr. Dunloff:

"Let not the black wax too much alarm you, Sir, your son, my amiable pupil, is well: My good old uncle is also well as a man can be, who is ready to expire with joy, on receiving intelligence so little hoped for and unexpected; but——your Lady, Madam Claudina, who had retired from the world, who was before dead to her friends, is now released from all her cares, and is happy, I trust, in Heaven!

"This event ought not, Sir, to afflict you. My uncle and myself attended her; with him she was some time alone, but before *both* she confessed herself unworthy of your affection, that she had deceived and injured you. She lamented most bitterly your supposed death, the report of which I believe accelerated her's, because she accused herself as the primary cause of all your misfortunes. Not to dwell on this melancholy subject, she died a true penitent, entreating mercy for her offences, and imploring blessings on her dear child, who had long before mourned the loss of his mamma, and was therefore spared any further concern.

"My uncle, who is confined to his bed with the gout, orders me to express his transports of joy for your health and safety.—The letters which conveyed the intelligence of *your* death had nearly deprived *him* of *life*, and brought on that disorder which has hung upon him ever since. He hopes you will condescend to write to him once more before your return, that he may know *where to attend you*. He has not seen the Count, his master, since your letters arrived, but hears they have caused more *surprise* than *pleasure*; of that you will have a circumstantial account hereafter."

Mr. Dunloff concluded his letters with "praises of his young pupil, whose docility and good disposition gave promise of much future satisfaction to his father. His little daughter, whose delicate health would be most considerately attended to by his uncle and himself, was placed with a very worthy woman within a few doors of his own residence, and was visited by him daily. He conjured Ferdinand to divest himself of all anxiety for the health and safety of his children, and rely on his watchful care for the preservation of both."

When Ferdinand had recovered from the first shock naturally felt on hearing a woman he once adored was no more, when he had acquired composure sufficient to peruse the letter through, indignation kept pace with sorrow.

Claudina's last confession had confirmed the implied guilt frequently insinuated, but of which he never could have thought her capable; he resolved in his mind the whole tenor of her conduct; he saw nothing wrong, nothing reprehensible, in word or action, before their removal to Renaud Castle: *There* then she must have met with the object that seduced her from her duty to him and herself; but among all his brother's visitors, there was no particular man to whose artifices he could attribute the misfortune that so deeply wounded him. Lost in conjecture, he saw only that the fact was certain, and from Ernest only he could hope to have the mystery elucidated. He grieved for the unhappy Claudina, and from his soul forgave a crime which her subsequent conduct proved she deeply and sincerely repented of.

"This then (said he) is the termination of an union formed in disobedience, pursued with rashness, which entailed upon me the curses of a parent, brought misery and guilt on her, sorrow, shame, and unavailing repentance, on the wretched Ferdinand!"

He remained for near three hours overwhelmed with the most painful reflections, and entirely forgetful of the other letter which he had put into his pocket. At length the remembrance of his brother made him start from his reverie, recollect the letter, and hastily search for it. The superscription was Count Rhodophil's. He tore it open; it was not a long one.

The Count expressed more surprise than Ferdinand thought needful; the *joy* was more reserved: He said, "that he was delighted to lay aside his mourning, and rejoice in the restoration of a brother;" but he wrote it as if he did not *feel* it; there was an air of constraint; the expressions seemed not the genuine feelings of the heart, but the laboured sentiments of a man fearful he should not say *enough*, and therefore ran into the contrary extreme, and said *too much*; at least so it appeared to Ferdinand.

"Ah! (thought he) all this eloquence breathes not the air of sincerity, which glows in the simple words of nature, uttered by Ernest through his nephew's pen." The farther he read the more he was dissatisfied, and when he had finished the letter he was thoroughly disgusted, and yet knew not well of what to complain.

"Whether it is ill-humour, prejudice, or the effects of a distempered mind, I know not (said he) but certainly this letter does not please me. He mentions the death of Claudina too so slightly, and with such little concern, that it is not decent, and of his own Lady he is entirely silent."

Revolving on those things which appeared so strange and unnatural, he had fallen into a deep dejection, from which he was roused by the entrance of the Baron, and his friend Count M***, who warmly embraced and congratulated him on his liberty.

"Liberty!" repeated Ferdinand, surprised.

"Yes," said the Baron, "we have succeeded in obtaining your freedom on our parole of honour. The accusation of an insignificant person like Heli, without he can adduce proofs to substantiate his charge, is not sufficient to weigh against a man of your birth and merit; but as all accusations claim attention from justice, though your innocence is not questioned, yet, for the due observance of form, we were obliged to be answerable for your appearance."

Ferdinand warmly thanked his generous friends, and preparing to leave the prison, asked after the young Baron.

"He is gone to Heli's (answered the Count) as we wish to know what is transacting there, and whether he still persists in the false story he has promulgated."

They saw the dejection that clouded the countenance of Ferdinand, but avoided appearing to notice it, and exerted themselves to amuse his mind in the way to the Baron's house, where, on their arrival, he was left alone with the Count, who gave him an account of their proceedings, and also the contents of the two letters he had received. Ferdinand was equally as communicative, and in the Count's friendly sympathy found some alleviation to his sorrows.

The late occurrences had rendered them forgetful of Louisa, and they proposed calling on her in the evening. Young Reiberg was not yet returned, and they began to grow uneasy at his absence, when the Baron was informed a Gentleman requested to speak with him; his name D'Alenberg.

They started with joy, the Baron hastened to the library where the servant had conducted him, and very soon returned, introducing him to the Count and Ferdinand.—They flew to welcome him.

"I am at a loss for words (said the friendly Gentleman) to express the unexpected pleasure of this meeting: I came here under the most painful inquietude; two words from this Gentleman (pointing to the Baron) has almost intoxicated me with joy."

The two friends congratulated themselves on this agreeable meeting; the Count eagerly inquired after Miss D'Alenberg.

"Poor Theresa (answered he) has suffered much, a disorder on her spirits, a nervous affection the doctors term it. The strange adventures which befel Louisa did not tend to lessen it; but the letters we received from her and you gave a sudden and uncommon turn, a flow of spirits, such as I could scarcely have expected.

"We lost no time in setting off for Vienna, and arrived safely this morning; but had hardly time to embrace our young friend, when the doctor entered with a story that threw my poor invalids into a very terrible situation, no other than that Count M*** and Count Ferdinand had been accused of robbery and murder, were taken up, and confined in a prison. This relation, of which the doctor could not foresee the sad effects, gave me more exquisite pain than any I had ever experienced: The anxiety I have felt for some hours cannot be described; I came here under the apprehension of hearing the fatal certainty of the doctor's report. How little did I expect to see you both!"

"Indeed, Sir (said Ferdinand) we are much indebted to you for the kind solicitude you express, but there has been but too much truth in the story you heard."

"Well, well (cried Mr. D'Alenberg) I have not time to hear the explanation at present; it is sufficient that I see you safe; I must fly back to remove the anxiety of my daughter and Louisa."

"May we not be permitted to wait upon the Ladies?" asked the Count.

"Not this evening (answered he;) the journey has fatigued Theresa, and she has been thrown into great agitations on *your* account. Early in the morning I will see you again." The Baron invited him to breakfast, and he promised to attend them.

The friends were exceedingly pleased at the arrival of Mr. D'Alenberg, and promised to themselves a speedy termination of an affair so injurious to Ferdinand, from the concurrent testimony of him and Louisa, in his favour; as her account would develop the design of Count Wolfran in forcing his way into Heli's house, and the elopement of Fatima the preceding day with the Count, naturally accounted for the fatal effects that followed his intrusion; for the rest, conceiving that he had lost Louisa through her knowledge of Ferdinand, and feeling himself deceived and abandoned by the person he had acknowledged as a sister, Heli had, from mere malice and revenge, accused Ferdinand of crimes he could not for a moment think him really guilty of. As to the robbery, their suspicions fell on the attendants of

the Count, as the two Barons could prove Ferdinand was in their house during the whole transaction.

On a review of these circumstances they concluded the false accusations would be unquestionably proved, and Heli, if he lived, meet the
punishment his baseness truly deserved. The Baron was just beginning to
express some anxiety for the safety of his son, when he entered the room.

"Your looks are full of importance," said the Baron.

"They are a transcript of my mind then (answered he) for I promise
you that I have not been idle since my departure from you this morning; I
shall therefore wave my congratulations to Ferdinand, and relate to you my
proceedings.

"I repaired without delay to Heli's cottage, most fortunately I met one
of our servants, and took him with me. When arrived there I was admitted
by one of the men who guarded Heli, who told me that he was so much
better, they intended to remove him to the prison.

"I went up to him; he preserved the same sullen silence, and as I could
not make him understand me, I desired the interpreter to inform him, 'that
his malice had proved ineffectual to hurt Ferdinand, whose innocence of his
charges had been satisfactorily proved by my father and his friends; but that
the murder of the Count would bear hard upon *him*, as not a single person
knew *him*, or could he adduce any circumstances in his favour that would
tend to invalidate the proofs against him, for no one would credit a story
so absurd, as that *Count Wolfran* intended to rob his house, whatever were
the motives that brought him there.'—The interpreter repeated my words;
he answered him with fury in his looks, and a kind of desperation in his
air that shocked me. The answer was explained to me thus: That he cursed
Ferdinand, Fatima, and the Count, and to the former attributed all his misfortunes; for Fatima would have been faithful, had she never known him as
a brother, and the other woman (meaning Louisa) might have consoled him
for *her* loss, had not that 'Christian dog' forced himself into her company,
and contrived to get her away; for *all* which he never would forgive him, nor
cease to pray that his prophet Mahomet might destroy him.

"As for himself, he despised all threats, and laughed at their menaces,
for they could not hurt him.

"He was then told, 'that he was to be conveyed to a prison, and that his
trial would prove the innocence of Ferdinand, as Louisa could declare in his
favour by an account of the circumstances of the preceding day, when he
had insulted Count Wolfran, and Fatima voluntarily eloped with him.'

"This intelligence threw him into a violent rage: 'I have lost my jewels,
lost the woman I loved, another torn from me, am wounded, and insulted;

to serve those Christian dogs I have suffered all this! and shall I have no revenge? Great Prophet, avenge thy servant! Shall *I* prove the innocence of Ferdinand? No, he and his sister have been my ruin!'

"He gnashed his teeth with fury, and doubtless had any weapon been at hand he would have destroyed himself; but at this instant was heard a knocking at the door; it was opened; a man entered, who seemed confused at seeing so many persons, and inclined to retreat; but Heli immediately exclaimed, "That is one of the villains," and the interpreter seized him.

"My servant exclaimed, 'How, Sancho!'

" 'Sir (said he to me) this man I well remember; he was discharged from my late master's service for some dishonest practices, and enlisted himself in the army; It is now four years since he left Vienna as a soldier.'

" 'What is your business here?' demanded I, pretty sternly.

" 'Sir (said he) I will to you make a free confession of some very particular circumstances, if you will pledge your honour to save me from punishment; without that assurance I am dumb for ever.'

" 'Being dumb, as you term it, will but little avail when this man proves you entered his house to rob and murder him; but if you are just in your confession, and repent of your crimes, by giving up your accomplices, I will exert my interest to procure you pardon, and you may depend upon my protection.'

"He was then freed, and entered on the following detail. After the last battle with the Turks, the regiment he belonged to being disbanded, he sought to enter again into the service of some Nobleman, but his character was too well known at Vienna; he went therefore to Ratisbon, as he was related to a man who kept an inn there, and who, he thought, might possibly procure him a place.

"At this inn he met with, and was hired by, Count Wolfran, who had only a confidential valet with him. The Count was very fond of the Ladies, and had two or three mistresses in the city. They lived there for some weeks, when the valet one day told him, they should soon go to a small hunting seat, which his master had near Vienna, and as the summer advanced they should travel.

"A few days after this information the valet received a letter, which, he said, would be joyful news to his master. They had several private conferences, and one evening he received orders to pack up the baggage, as they were to leave Ratisbon the following morning. They did so, and arrived at a small village about two miles from the city of Ens; here he was told on no account to mention the name of his master, as they had some private business to transact.

"The same evening the Count sent for him, and, after some conversation, promised him a handsome reward if he would assist in securing and carrying off two Ladies who had greatly injured him. The bribe was too considerable to be refused, and he was ordered to watch in a particular part of the city for the arrival of some company at a Gentleman's house.

"In less than a week, a Gentleman, two Ladies and servants, were seen to alight at the house, which information he conveyed to the Count. He believed the first intention was to attend to their motions, to follow them, and if they could not secure the Ladies whilst they remained in the city, to surround and seize upon them in their road to Vienna.

"The Count never walked in the city, only sailed about the river. The day after the arrival of Mr. D'Alenberg, as he was in a boat, he saw the Ladies alone walking on the banks. This suggested to him a possibility of carrying them off by water. He immediately ordered his carriage to be in waiting every evening at a certain distance; the valet, himself and the Count, disguised, were in a boat with two men he had also bribed for his purpose.

"He little expected to succeed so soon, as the whole scheme depended on seeing the Ladies alone, and no boats on the river to observe him, which might possibly be some time before such an opportunity happened; but, contrary to his expectations, the very next evening they appeared on the banks alone, and walked a considerable way; it grew late, the air was rather cool, and the boats drew off sooner than was customary.

"He lost no time, but made towards the shore and landed; the Ladies seemed frightened, and ran back; they pursued them; one had considerably the start of the other; the one behind fell; she was secured; in that moment, when they could soon have overtaken the other, a boat appeared at a distance coming down the river; they were compelled to retreat with only half of their expected prize.

"She was carried to the boat, and soon conveyed to the carriage, after which, by cross roads, they arrived at the Count's hunting seat. He understood this Lady was an old mistress of the Count's, who had injured him with another whom he loved. He was highly provoked at not getting the other, but swore to be revenged on this.

"What the design was he could not say; the Lady was confined for that night, and they were ordered to be in readiness to travel again: But the next morning all was confusion, the Lady had escaped out of window by a very extraordinary contrivance; the Count was almost raving mad; he ordered the valet and himself to take horses, and attend him through the wood and adjacent villages, and promised a hundred crowns to the person who discovered her.

"They stopped at a small house, at the end of the wood, to make inquiries. A Turk came out; it was with difficulty they understood each other. Whilst they were speaking a very beautiful woman came out, and asked, 'If they were gallant Gentlemen, who would release a Lady from Turks and Infidels?'—The Count told her, he would die in her service.—The Turk compelled her to go in, and presently they heard her scream, upon which they burst into the house, gave the Turk a drubbing, the Lady ran out, the Count took her on his horse, and they rode with her to his house in the wood.

"This Lady pleased him so much that he staid at home with her, only sending the others to make inquiries after the run-away Lady, and he believed might have forgot her, had he not been desirous of revenge, and fearful she would get to her friends.

"He understood from the valet, that when the Lady with them found it was not love that induced the Count to seek her, she owned that the person he sought for, was in the Turk's house, and very ill; upon which it was resolved that they should break into his house, confine him and the women servants, and carry off the Lady.

"Before this scheme was to be executed, they had prepared every thing for leaving the house in the wood, to embark as soon as possible for Turkey, where they intended to leave the Lady in a strange country, without money or friends, to make her way as she could, and all this trouble was taken to satisfy the Count's revenge.—'He believed (he said) there was more plots intended than he was informed of, because the Count and the valet were always conferring together.'

"However, they all set out two nights after for Heli's, the Turk's Lady waiting at some little distance in the carriage. On breaking into the house, the two women escaped by a back door into the wood. Heli told them the Lady was taken away, but they would not believe him, and proceeded to search the house; he taking up pistols foolishly, threatened them, upon which the valet fired and wounded him; in the same moment *he* fired, and the Count fell, crying he was a dead man.

"The valet then said both would die, and they must provide for their own escape; but first he would have some of the Turk's riches. They opened the drawers and closets. He saw the valet take a small box, which he said belonged to the Lady, and he secured it for her. They found gold and many valuables, which they took, and then hastened to the Lady, telling her what had happened.

"She seemed to be much frightened, and asked what they could do? He whispered to her, and then said, 'It would be better to return to the

house for that night, and dismiss the carriage.'—The other thought this
very strange; but presently the valet told the post-boy to bring the carriage
next morning, as his master had met with a friend, and would not go on
his journey that night. They entered the house, only one woman servant
was there, who supposed them gone, and was surprised at their return. The
valet told her the same story he had before said to the post-boy, and then
proposed to the other going immediately into the city, hiring a carriage, and
to bring it at the first dawning of day to a place in the wood, where they
would join him, make the best of their way to the water, get on board a
trading vessel, and sail into Turkey.

"He, frightened with apprehensions of being discovered, staid not to
consider about this strange wild plan; but instantly left them, though on
the road his heart misgave him that some way they intended to deceive
him; but he went on, called up the people at an inn, and ordered a carriage
directly to be ready, resolved to go back in it to the house.

"It was some time, however, before he could execute his purpose, and
the day began to appear as they drove through the wood.—He went to
the appointed spot, no one was there, and he proceeded to the house. The
doors were fastened, he knocked, and at length the servant came down
and let him in. He asked if the Lady and Mr. Bissot were ready?—She had
not seen them.—He went up stairs, knocked at the Lady's door, no one
answered, he opened it, and found the Lady was gone.

"He searched the other apartments, neither of them were in the house,
the back door was on the latch, and he supposed they had gone that way.
He directly got into the carriage, and returned into the wood, every part
of it he searched; where the horses could not penetrate he alighted, and
explored every recess, but all was fruitless; he wasted the whole day in examining the wood and its environs, and at length was compelled to dismiss
the carriage, and return to the house.

"He now thought they had contrived to escape, and leave him to suffer; yet where they could be hid was very extraordinary.—He resolved to go
the next morning to all the post-houses, and, describing their persons, find
if they had, by any means, got a carriage. This he had done all that morning; and at length it came into his head to call at the Turk's, and by some
pretence learn whether the Count and the master of the house were dead
or not."

CHAPTER II.

"S‌uch was the relation," continued the young Baron, "which the fellow gave me. Providence, doubtless, conducted him to the house to clear up the strange mystery of the Count's death, otherwise one would have thought the man mad to come there.

"This account certainly tended to exculpate Heli from the murder, as it was evident he had been wounded first by persons who broke into his house, and every man, in a situation like his, had an indubitable right to defend himself. I ordered the interpreter to explain the man's confession to him, and told him, that, as he could now clearly understand Ferdinand was entirely unacquainted and unconnected with the persons who had injured him; he must be convinced that he ought to make the humblest concessions to that gentleman and his friends for the insult offered to him, by imprisoning his person, and aspersing his character; that if he was disposed to behave properly, I would very readily exert *my* interest to serve *him*.

"At first, I believe, from the looks that accompanied his words, he was stubborn and very ungracious; but after some conversation, the interpreter told me, he was very sensible of my kindness, and sorry for the injury and trouble he had brought on Mr. Ferdinand. The man who had so fortunately dropped in upon us, I left in custody, assuring him that his confinement should be short, and that I would perform all my promises in his favour.

"I left the house at length, and went to the prison; there I had the pleasure to hear our friend had just been liberated; from thence I proceeded to the magistrate's, related to him the odd story I have been repeating to you, and requested the man might be brought before him to-morrow. Also, that some inquiry might be set on foot through the city, to discover, if possible, the wretches who have robbed Heli."

"Ah! my dear Baron," exclaimed Ferdinand, "in that point I cannot wish you success; consider one of them is but too nearly connected with me by blood. Would to Heaven I could recompense Heli for what he has lost."

"That would be a Quixote generosity," said the Count, "which his malice to you can by no means deserve: If, however, he is stript, I have no objection to join in securing to him a support, that may enable him to spend his days with comfort; this our own feelings may be gratified in doing; at the same time that I am persuaded, had he not conceived our company and connexions were necessary for his own convenience, we might have remained in Philippo, and got free how we could."

"I believe you are right in your conclusion," replied Ferdinand; "but through him we *did obtain* our liberty—and I also owe him obligations for civil treatment and many indulgencies; he therefore shall not *want* in a strange country, while I have the means of preventing it.

"Count Wolfran's character and proceedings is, I think, the strangest medley of follies and inconsistencies I ever heard of; for he was open to detection in every scheme he pursued; and that he carried any plan into execution, appears to me the effect of chance and accident; for there was neither regularity nor decision in any thing he undertook. He is said to have been a very handsome and plausible young man; but surely the most inconsiderate that ever existed, and at an early age, has fallen a sacrifice to his own vices and follies."

"Thank Heaven!" said the Count, "that Miss D'Alenberg escaped his villainous designs, and that Louisa was saved from the destruction he threatened to her."

"Again," thought Ferdinand, "I see how it is.—With what earnestness did he inquire of Mr. D'Alenberg for his daughter, and now, with what animation he thanks Heaven in her behalf: The Count is most certainly the object of *her* attachment; and without much penetration, I can see that she has superseded Eugenia in his heart. Yet surely, if I am not greatly mistaken in my judgment, her delicacy will always impede a union with him in his present circumstances.—How unfortunate for both, that such an obstacle should intervene, where both honour and justice must revolt against a single wish to remove it."

As Ferdinand appeared lost in thought, his friends endeavoured to rouse his attention, by talking of the pleasure Louisa must experience in being restored to her friends; and Reiberg naturally reverted to the ill-treatment his adored Countess had experienced from a man of such loose principles and absurd conduct.

"Do not think me selfish and ungenerous," said he, "if I bless the hand of Providence that has recalled from the world a man whose exterior advantages were made the passport to the vilest profligacy, and whose heart was so depraved, that a union with an angel could not ensure his constancy."

The Count and Ferdinand looked at each other, and read their reciprocal sentiments.

"Little does he think of the base duplicity to which his admired Theodosia was the sacrifice, and the unfortunate Louisa a willing victim."

Fatigued with the various occurrences of the day, they all retired early to their apartments, and Ferdinand was at liberty to indulge that sorrow which prest heavily upon his spirits.

Claudina returned to his mind's eye with all that innocence, beauty, and tenderness, which adorned her, when struggling under poverty and affliction. How difficult to believe, that she who had borne every evil with fortitude, who had preserved her honour, when poor and subject to temptation, should, when fortune smiled, when every want and wish was supplied, should fail in the trial, when blest with ease and affluence.

"My absence," said he, "was her ruin; some artful wretch took the advantage of an unguarded moment to destroy her honour and happiness, and to plant thorns in my bosom, which must rankle there for ever."

He more earnestly than ever wished to return into Suabia, and meet with Ernest, Claudina now no more. Surely there could no longer exist reasons for concealing those secrets, known only to that faithful old man, and which had so long tortured him. These uneasy reflections were not the only ones that tormented him: He dreaded the discovery of Fatima, whose association and flight with the late Count's valet, too plainly spoke her guilt, and laid her open to punishment, should they be found; the consequence of which must give him the most painful concern, both as relative to herself, and the disgrace that an illiberal world might attach to his father's memory, and his own name.

"A too hasty discovery of our connexion, by my imprudence," thought he, "has involved me in this additional labyrinth of vexation: Would to Heaven I could leave Vienna; but I cannot separate from the Count, and I fear he will not be prevailed upon to quit the city, now that Mr. D'Alenberg and his charming daughter reside in it."

Under this variety of inquietude, Ferdinand past the night; and when morning dawned, quitted his bed, languid and unrefreshed: He went down and amused himself in the garden, until the servants were up, and then strolled away towards the suburbs, which were infinitely more pleasant than the city itself. Heedless of time or distance, unmindful of his friends, who would naturally feel anxiety at his absence, he proceeded on 'till the connexion of the houses were broken, and a few scattered ones of mean appearance, first led him to recollect the extent of ground he had gone over: He looked at his watch, and, to his surprise, saw that he had exceeded the breakfast hour already, of course could not return in any time for that refreshment, which, until that moment, he had never thought of.

He drew near to the last house; a woman appeared; he asked could he have any thing to eat; she told him bread and milk he was welcome to; this he accepted, and entered a poor little room to rest. Throwing himself upon a window seat, he accidentally cast his eyes upon the floor, and under a small stool opposite to him, thought there lay something like a seal; he rose, and picked it up: To his infinite astonishment, he beheld a gold seal, with a device upon a white cornelian, which he well remembered Heli had purchased for Fatima a day or two after their arrival at Vienna.—He called to the mistress of the house, and asked if that trinket was hers.

"No, indeed, Sir," said she; "I have no such fine things belongs to me, or Anthony either."

"I found it here," returned Ferdinand.

"Dear me, then it surely must have fell out of the pocket of the lady or gentleman that was here yesterday."

"Very possibly," said Ferdinand.—"Pray who were they?"

"I don't know, indeed, Sir,—it was a very tall lady and a short gentleman, that came here, as you have done. Yesterday morning they had some milk, as you be going to have—then they walked away, and in the afternoon camed again—stayed here some time eating bread and fruit; then payed me well—and I have seed no more of them."

The "very *tall* lady" did not answer the figure of Fatima, who, though elegantly formed, was not above the middle size; yet he was confident the seal had been her's.—He asked several questions of the good woman, but could obtain no satisfactory answers.

"Do you think," said he, "that they are in this neighbourhood; for then this trinket might be returned to them?"

"No, indeed," replied she, eying the seal with a look that implied a wish to retain such a pretty bauble; "but perhaps they may come again; for I heard something about 'Pratt's-Grove;' and so likely they be going there to-day, and will call here again, when I shall be sure to give it to them."

"As you please," said Ferdinand, delivering it to her: "'Tis certainly your property, without you see them, or they send for it.—But pray where is 'Pratt's-Grove?'"

"Why, in the Little Island, Sir, where all the gentry goes to make merry, and walk about."

"And can I go to it from hence?"

"O yes, a little below, to the river's side. You will see a boat, that will take you over."

"Then I will go," resolved Ferdinand, swallowing his milk in haste.

With many courtesies and blessings from the good woman, who was well satisfied with his liberality and her golden toy, he left the house, and followed her direction, which brought him to the banks of the river, where a boat lay conveniently for his purpose. He was soon carried over to the Island, which was indeed a little paradise; the most enchanting walks among groves of fine tall spreading trees, that in some places were almost impervious; then suddenly breaking through small openings, long narrow vistas terminated with some beautiful romantic views, that astonished and delighted the observer.

He wandered about here a considerable time, before he began to reflect that this was the most unlikely place in the world for persons to come who wished to be unnoticed, because it was the resort of much company in fine weather. He began likewise to feel himself fatigued, and incapable of making a tour through all the walks that were cut in this beautiful grove. What then shall I do, thought he; go into one of the buildings to rest myself, or return back? He felt ashamed of the impulse that had brought him to the Island, without considering that its situation, and the number of persons who made it a place of entertainment, must effectually preclude any concealment.

"Well then," said he, "I will walk to the next building, repose myself for half an hour, and then return.—Some future day, when my mind is more calculated to admire and enjoy the beauties of this delightful spot, I shall be glad to devote more time to it."

He was now close to the building, and about to enter it, when he thought he heard voices as if disputing; he stopt.

"If you can find the means to get off undiscovered, and will go to England, I will accompany you; but I hate the thoughts of going into Turkey—nor will I go. To remain here many days longer, cannot be done. Had you taken my advice, we had been safe."

"What! to murder the man:—No—I'll have no murder on my conscience.—As to robbing the Turk, I hold it no sin; for they are all a parcel of free-booters and unbelievers; yet I may be hanged for it;—therefore I say, no place so safe as Turkey, where we may live in some snug place like a King and a Queen."

"How ridiculous you are! I tell you again, that there you will be plundered by the Turks.—If you are seen to live without employment, they will suppose you rich;—you will be informed against; your head will be off, and your house destroyed in an hour. I have heard enough of their tricks and rogueries—therefore to England I *will* go: If you don't chuse it, let us divide, and do each as we like."

"No, I shan't part with you so; but I am afraid to leave Vienna, because I dare say there's an information against us before now."

"*Against us!* Pray what have I to do with it—*I* stole nothing; this casket of jewels is my own property."

"The devil it is: Pray how would you have come at it, after running away with the Count?"

At this moment, two gentlemen were seen coming down a vista; a man and a woman darted out from the building, so close upon Ferdinand, that they almost threw him backwards. They were staggered, and retreated; for he stood in a narrow path way; the gentlemen were advancing in front; he stept in after them, and instantly saw that Fatima was in a man's dress, and the man wrapped in a loose robe of her's, with a long cloke and woman's head dress.

She as quickly knew him, and gave a violent scream.

"Be silent," said Ferdinand, "or you are undone; you are traced and discovered; if you attend to me, I will preserve you from punishment; but first return to me the casket of jewels which belongs to Heli, who is alive, and out of danger.—The man you seduced to join in the theft, and then deceived, is in my custody; he had discovered all the Count's designs, and your baseness."

The valet, with the weakness that generally attends little minds, when convicted of guilt, fell at Ferdinand's feet.

"Preserve my life, Sir, and I will give up every——."

"Poor despicable wretch!" exclaimed Fatima, "*Thy* life is not worth saving! You may do with *me*, Sir, as you please; you are *my brother*; it will be honourable for you to deliver *your sister* into the hands of justice; but be assured, whilst I have life, I will retain my jewels; jewels which Heli plundered me of, when he basely broke into the women's tents, rifled our baggage, and carried me off; these jewels were my property, and I will sware to it."

Ferdinand stood thunder-struck at her unparalleled effrontery; she saw her advantage, and pursued it.

"There are persons coming," said she;—"take your choice: Suffer me to leave you instantly, without discovery or pursuit; or if you insult, detain, or give me up, I will immediately declare my affinity to you, claim the late Count Renaud as my father, protest he was married to my mother, commence a process against you for his fortune, and accuse *you* as an accomplice in urging me to regain my own diamonds."

The gentlemen were now pretty near to them; she turned to Ferdinand—"One word of discovery, and you are ruined."—She walked out; the gentlemen past, and she followed them pretty closely. The valet was silent, though dreadfully agitated. Ferdinand kept his eyes fixed on her as long as she remained in sight, with so much mute surprise, such horror and astonishment, that it took from him all power of speech or motion for some minutes.

Recovering at length, when she was lost to his view—"Good Heavens!" he exclaimed, "is it possible that *woman*, so soft, so lovely, so interesting in her gentleness, can, by vice and profligacy of manners, attain to such a degree of boldness and impudent bravery, as would shame the most hardened of mankind!

"For you," said he, turning to the trembling valet—"you who have profited nothing by your crimes, I know not that your conviction could afford any satisfaction to Heli, without the recovery of his property; tho' guilty of many base actions, you scrupled at murder, which I heard that wretch who has left us upbraid you for; and I am even tempted to think the robbery was more the impulse of the moment, from the existing circumstances, which you could not foresee, than a premeditated design.

"If you can repent, perhaps you may find friends; follow me, however, I must dodge that woman."

The man obeyed, and gathering up his robes, looked with conscious shame on his dress, now that he was discovered: They walked quick, and soon came in sight of Fatima, who was then walking with her two beaus towards one part of the Island, where lay a small pleasure-boat;—to Ferdinand's infinite astonishment, one of the gentlemen *handed her* in.

"How," cried he, "has she confessed her sex; or have they penetrated through the disguise?"

The boat put off, and he remained fixed to the spot.

"Well," said he, resuming his recollection, "had this woman's conduct been represented to me by another, I should either have believed it fabulous, or very greatly exaggerated: What a strange adventure have I made of my morning's ramble?"

He then turned, deeply musing, and so entirely forgetful of the valet, that had the man been possessed of a weapon, or any evil designs, he might have had cause to have repented of his carelessness.

But fortunately weapon he had none, and therefore had no temptation to commit an injury, which we know not, desperate as his situation seemed to be, whether he might have had the fortitude or conscience to resist.—For how many are the follies and crimes mankind are drawn into by *opportunity*, to gratify a prevailing passion, which, free from the temptation of the moment, they do not even dream of.

Ferdinand walked slowly back the same way that he came; went into the boat, still followed by the lady valet, whom he very uncourteously left, to seat himself as he liked, to the no small amusement of the boatmen, who concluded the gentleman and lady had been falling out.

When he was landed, he began to quicken his pace, and in much less time than when he set off in the morning, he arrived at the Baron's house. Great had been the solicitude of his friends; the dejection that marked his countenance, when he retired for the night, his early rising, and unaccountable long absence, were circumstances that gave rise to the most painful conjectures: Mr. D'Alenberg had attended the breakfast table, an invitation that had escaped Ferdinand's recollection, and seemed to be extremely surprised when he found the other did not appear; nor could any reason be assigned by his friends, for an omission that carried with it an air of rudeness and neglect.

The Count saw the dissatisfaction of Mr. D'Alenberg, and in justice to his friend, at length mentioned the account he had recently received of his wife's death, which he said deeply affected him.

"How!" said Mr. D'Alenberg, "is his wife *dead?*"

"She is," replied the Count; "and although, for certain family reasons, they were separated, yet Ferdinand dearly loved her, and tenderly regrets her for the present.—When reason and judgment resume their empire over the heart, I hope he will be sensible of the duties he owes to his child and his friends, nor by unavailing grief, hurt his own peace and wound theirs."

"He has a child, then?"

"Yes, a son placed at an academy in Baden."

"He is a very young father," observed the Baron.—"He married very young, a love match—but not a happy one."

"I understand," said Mr. D'Alenberg—"Poor young man; 'tis natural enough that he should feel sorrow on such an event; but I earnestly hope he will not injure his health, nor meet with any accident this morning.—I shall look in upon you again by and bye, after paying a few visits, and shall be glad to see him returned."

He did call in again, and was greatly surprised to see the anxiety of his friend's increased; the Count had intended to pay his devoirs to the two ladies; but he was so extremely uneasy concerning Ferdinand, that he felt no inclination to dress or visit.

Baron Reiberg had just determined to send his servants in quest of Ferdinand, when he appeared, followed, as they thought, by a lady, who stopt short at the door, looking down exceedingly confused. The Count had flown to embrace Ferdinand, reproaching him at the same time for giving them so much concern; but he had hardly spoken, when the lady, standing so awkwardly, struck him; he left his friend, and hastily offered his hand to lead her into the room; an offer which, to his great astonishment, she declined, by a low bow.

Ferdinand, who was about to apologize to the Baron, that moment turned his head, and seeing the surprise of one, and the confusion of the other, with the attitudes of both, tho' he was far from being cheerful, yet the ridiculous situation of the valet, caused him to burst out in a violent laugh, which still more disconcerted the Count, who, bowing to the lady again, came up to Ferdinand.

"For Heaven's sake, what does this mean; who is that—woman?"

"That *woman*," answered he, "has a long story to tell, and is accountable for great part of the time I have been absent.—Suspend your curiosity, however, for a few minutes, and we will return to satisfy it."

He then withdrew, followed still by the lady; the Count and Baron looked at each other for a minute, when the latter exclaimed, laughing heartily,

"Upon my soul, I believe 'tis a fellow disguised."

"A man!" cried the Count; "then indeed, I have made myself ridiculous enough; and now that you have started the idea, I own that I thought she was an odd figure."

"Yet how gallant you was," returned the other: "I wish Reiberg had been here, to have shared your politeness."

"Pray be sparing of your jeers," said the Count; "they may be premature.—You are not certain that your conjectures are right."

The Baron, having once entertained the idea, seemed to be every moment more strongly confirmed in his judgment, and rallied the Count most unmercifully on his politeness to the *fair sex.*

In a short time, Ferdinand returned, having equipped the man with an old suit of clothes, that fitted him tolerably.

"Now," said he, smiling, "allow me to introduce the metamorphosed lady as the late Count Wolfran's valet."

"Is it possible," they both cried; "for Heaven's sake, how have you been so fortunate as to meet with him?"

"I know not," replied Ferdinand very gravely, "whether I can deem it as any piece of *good* fortune; for the meeting has been productive of strange scenes, and I am in a very perplexing predicament; but I will repeat the circumstances to you, and you will be the more competent to advise me. Mean time, permit this man to retire into your kitchen; when his presence is necessary, I will call him.—Go," said he to the valet, "keep your own secret, and wait my orders."

The man bowed, and withdrew.

"What!" cried the Baron, "do you permit him to be at liberty?"

"Keep your surprise for my story," answered he, "and then judge according to the circumstances that will appear before you."

He then entered upon all the events of the day; described Fatima's extraordinary assurance and menaces, and the astonishment that overcame him, and impeded him from making any efforts to stop or to pursue her.

"Her wickedness," added he, "is so complete, that I am confident there is nothing she would leave undone, no perjuries she would scruple at, to be revenged on those who interfere to the prejudice of her schemes. Where, or with whom she is gone, I know not, or whether I ought to inform Heli of the particulars I have related to you. Have you heard of him to-day; has the Baron produced the servant who made the discoveries?"

"Yes," replied the Count; "the man was carried this morning before the magistrate, and, as his story was partly corroborated by Heli, and many particulars confirmed by Louisa, on whom the magistrate waited to take her information, orders were given to discharge the men who kept Heli in custody: Your innocence was declared, and fresh orders sent forth to search for Fatima and the valet, on account of the robbery.—How they have contrived to hide themselves, and yet venture at a place so public as the pleasurable little Island of Pratt, I can't conceive; but I think it very probable Fatima will be discovered."

"Though she justly deserves punishment," returned Ferdinand, "I must hope she will elude the search.—I am sorry, indeed, she is possest of the jewels; but she is so profligate a creature, that I am persuaded she will derive but little benefit from the possession.—Mean time, what is to be done with this valet of the Count's: If he is discovered, we shall not be able to serve him, because his guilt is clearly proved; yet I think he deserves consideration, for the fellow seems penitent; followed me without reluctance, and certainly proved, by their conversation, that he had some principle—a conscience that resisted the idea, and was proof against the persuasion of committing a murder."

"What you say is very true," said the Count; "and I have other reasons for wishing he may escape punishment; the story of Count Wolfran will not bear an investigation." Ferdinand took the hint: This fellow had been present at the marriage of Louisa; had entered into all his master's schemes against her; the whole would therefore come before the public; himself and his friends exposed; the deceit and indignity put upon the Countess would be brought forward, to the mortification of her and young Reiberg. In short, he saw the most painful consequences would ensue, *should* this man be taken up; and how to aid his escape now, seemed a very difficult affair, without risque or reflection to themselves.

"I think," said the Baron, after a little pause, "I can manage this matter.—The description of his person, with the particular orders for seizing him, can hardly take place 'till to-morrow; I want to send an express to my steward in Bavaria: If he sets off immediately this night with credentials from me, he will precede the orders for his arrest, which are not likely to extend far beyond the city. I will give orders to my steward to employ him upon my estate, to use him well, but to keep a watchful eye upon him 'till my return; what think you of this scheme?"

"Let us hear him," said Ferdinand, and called for *his* servant.—He appeared with a confused and mortified air.—Ferdinand told him of the orders given for his apprehension; explained to him the magnitude of his guilt in the bad actions he had been guilty of, and privy to, for his late master; and then repeated the Baron's noble and generous offer to preserve him from shame and death:—"An offer," said he, "so inconsistent with prudence, in trusting to a reformation of your life, that it must appear wonderful to you, and for which you are indebted solely to a few words I heard you say to Fatima, which makes us hope you are not quite abandoned; and if we can save a guilty being to atone for his past offences, and by penitence and good behaviour, to deserve forgiveness from Heaven, we are willing to run the chance in your favour—What say you?"

"My Lords," said the man, throwing himself at their feet, "I humbly thank your goodness: I have been a very wicked wretch; I had a very bad master; and I was too ready to obey him, and join in bad actions; but if your Lordships will please to trust me, in return for a life saved, I will devote it to you, and as faithfully obey a good master, as I too well served a wicked one."

"Rise," said the Baron; "your words please me, and I *will* trust you; within two hours you shall set off; I am only apprehensive the servants may recollect his person."

"My Lord," said he, "fearful that I might be known, I have had my handkerchief to my face, complaining of a violent tooth-ache, and only two servants have seen me at all."

"That's well," returned the Baron; "retire to the antichamber, until all is ready."—The Baron bid his servants instantly to get a horse at the door, as he was going to send Mr. Ferdinand's new servant off with an express.—Mean time, among them, they contrived a small parcel of linen; got him boots and a great coat, and being furnished with money for the journey, and letters from the Baron, he was soon on horseback, and lost no time in pursuing his journey; doubtless no less anxious to get beyond the environs of Vienna, than they were to have him.

This whole business, from the return of Ferdinand, had been planned and executed in about three hours, and he felt great relief to his mind, and a heavy weight taken from his spirits, when the man was gone.

CHAPTER III.

"Now, then," said Ferdinand, "I begin to breathe; and unless Fatima should be apprehended, the preceding circumstances may as well remain untold to Heli."

His friends were of the same opinion, and then mentioned to him the little resentment Mr. D'Alenberg had exprest, and his subsequent uneasiness.

"I expect him every moment," said the Baron; "for I would not send him word of your return, whilst we had so much business in hand; but I am persuaded his anxiety for your safety will bring him here very shortly."

The Baron was right; for in less than a quarter of an hour afterwards, Mr. D'Alenberg was announced. On entering the room, the first object that met his eyes was Ferdinand, who rose to receive him.

"What a truant you are," exclaimed he, embracing him.—"I hope you can well account for your absence, or I know not what punishment you do not deserve, for giving so much uneasiness to your friends."

"A consciousness of *that*," replied Ferdinand, "would be as severe a one as you can wish, since I never yet gave a pain to the bosom of a friend, that did not tenfold wound my own."

"I believe you" returned the other;—"and therefore, without being impertinently inquisitive, or arrogating to myself the power of punishing you, for depriving us of a comfortable breakfast, I shall only say that I am glad to see you returned in safety."

"Most cordially, Sir, I thank you; but I should ill deserve your indulgence, if I held any reserves to you."

He then briefly recapitulated the events which had happened, down to the conclusion of them, just before Mr. D'Alenberg had entered the house.

"*This* has indeed been a busy day," said that gentleman; "for the young Baron has had an infinity of perplexities on his hands to procure Heli's freedom, and the grant of an indulgence to the man who made a confession.

"He is under a gentle restraint at present; and if, at the expiration of three weeks, Fatima and the Count's valet cannot be found, he is to have his liberty, when the Baron has promised to provide for him; though, for my own part," continued Mr. D'Alenberg, "I think it is shewing too much indulgence to vice, to set them on a footing with honest men."

"Not if they *repent*, my dear Sir," said Ferdinand; "you will allow it possible, I hope, that a wicked person *may*, from conviction, *repent* of his crimes; and if the world is merciless, if no good humane man holds out a hand to help the humble and contrite spirit; if they are shunned, reprobated, and despised, where can they seek for shelter, from the sting of conscience, and the scorn of the world? Desperate, wretched and undone; renounced by the *good*, they are driven—they are compelled to return to the society of the *wicked*.—Hopeless, enraged, and disappointed, a hundred to one but they grow more wicked, more abandoned, than in their first career; and are lost, perhaps, body and soul, because the too fastidious, or uncharitable *good* man, conceives it an abomination to shew mercy to the sinner, or stretch forth his hand to drag him from the vortex of vice, into which he is sinking."

"You are right my young monitor," said Mr. D'Alenberg; "I acknowledge my error; *your* system is consistent with humanity and our *duty*; and whether our endeavours to reform the wicked succeed or not, the consciousness of having performed *that duty*, is a sufficient recompense to us, and over-pays all our trouble. You see I am *your* convert at least, and will remember your short lesson as long as I live.

"But to return to ourselves, I must inform you, two fair ladies think themselves extremely neglected, and I fancy you will find it difficult to exculpate a gallant young man who has proved so very *un*-gallant as not to pay his devoirs to a young lady that has come post here to see her friends."

"If *I have* been deficient in those duties, I, Sir, am the sufferer; and the circumstances that has impeded my attendance on the ladies, will, I hope, acquit me in your eyes. Doubtless, my friend, the Count has made *his* peace there, and *then my* presence or absence can be of little consequence."

The moment these words escaped from the lips of Ferdinand, he would have given the world to have recalled them, apprehensive that he had betrayed the Count's secret, and the confidence of Louisa.

Mr. D'Alenberg looked at him with a keen and penetrating eye; the Count, with much surprise, and was for a moment silent.

"I take shame to myself," said he at last, "that I have *not* performed a duty gratitude, respect, and esteem, claimed from me; but in truth, the business of the day, your unexpected elopement this morning, and a variety of perplexing thoughts, totally unqualified me for paying visits. You see, therefore, that you have not only been guilty of omissions yourself, but are the cause of other people's deficiencies."

The Count spoke the last words with a gay air, that a little reconciled Ferdinand to himself for the petulancy of his answer to Mr. D'Alenberg, which he sought to cover by saying, "To-morrow, Sir, I hope we shall have the honour of waiting upon the ladies, and apologizing for our *seeming* neglect."

"Very well," replied he, "I shall so report it, that you may receive a tolerable welcome; and now that I see you safe, I bid you good evening; remember to come early, as I wish to confer with you respecting Louisa's affairs."

Mr. D'Alenberg having left them, the Baron expressed some surprise at the absence of his son.—He had scarcely spoken before he entered, and was rejoiced to see Ferdinand.—He said that he had been with Heli, who was in a very gloomy way for the loss of his riches: Fortunately they had not script his person; he had a snuff-box of value, a watch, and two rings, that were in his pocket; the whole might be worth about eight hundred Louis d'ors; but this, he said, was a trifle; what could he do with a sum like that.

"I then," continued Reiberg, "told him of the generous intentions the Count and Ferdinand had adopted.—I saw he was by no means grateful; and the interpreter told me, that he peremptorily declined all favours from them.—I did not urge the point, from an idea, that when he is in better health, his temper may lose its present ferocity. The women servants had called there, under some apprehensions at having concealed themselves in a small cottage on one side of the wood, and two days being elapsed, they prevailed upon a man and woman to accompany them back.

"The poor creatures were rejoiced to find their little property untouched; one of these he discharged; the other, with the interpreter, remains; I have promised to send an honest jeweller to him tomorrow; for he is resolved to dispose of his property, and lodge the money in safe hands; and when he is well, he intends to give up the cottage, and lodge with the interpreter. So much for Heli." The gentlemen retired at an early hour, with a strict injunction to Ferdinand, not to steal away at day-break again.

The next morning, when they met at breakfast, all seemed to have recovered their spirits, except Ferdinand; *his* looks denoted a mind ill at ease; he eat little, and soon left them to write letters, previous to their purposed visit to Mr. D'Alenberg.

He wrote to Mr. Dunloff, to Ernest, and a short epistle to his brother; he mentioned, that he hoped, in a fortnight or three weeks, he should revisit Suabia; that however earnestly he wished to be at Baden, and see his dear children, the painful remembrance of past scenes, made him dread an interview that must renew all his sorrows.

Having a little relieved his mind by communicating his thoughts, he rejoined his friends, and prepared to accompany them.

They soon arrived at the Doctor's, who had kindly accommodated them all.—Mr. D'Alenberg was ready to introduce them;—the two Barons, as strangers, were first announced; but when the Count and Ferdinand approached Miss D'Alenberg, the latter observed her emotions; she blushed, turned pale, trembled, and, with difficulty, replied to the compliment the Count made her; he, guessing at the situation of her heart, felt extremely for her and the Count; to relieve both, he advanced, and paid his respects;—congratulated himself on the happiness of seeing her; and then turning to Louisa, "I rejoice, my amiable friend, to see you so perfectly recovered."

"I am, indeed," said she, "much better in health, and cannot be otherwise than happy, when blest with the society of my friends and benefactors."

The two Barons were charmed with the ladies, and Mr. D'Alenberg, studious to avoid any retrospection to unpleasant scenes, entered into a spirited conversation on Germanic affairs; the peace concluded with the Turks, the Emperor's schemes in favour of his daughter, Maria Theresa, and such themes as carried them out of their own concerns.

But on talking more fully about the late war, Louisa cried out, "will you forgive me, gentlemen, for interrupting your politics, I long to hear the story of our friends' captivity, and how they amused themselves in Turkey."

"Our amusements, Madam," said the Count, "were very limited; but Ferdinand had certainly the advantage of *me*, and therefore is best qualified to gratify your curiosity."

"Will you have the goodness to indulge us, Sir," asked Miss D'Alenberg, in a voice so low and tremulous, that it touched Ferdinand, who passed the momentary thought, "What an amazing alteration between Miss D'Alenberg and Louisa! the ladies seem to have changed characters."

Then addressing himself to her—"There is so little to entertain you, Madam, in the relation, that it is soon made; for no great variety could be thrown into a life of confinement;" he very readily obeyed her, however, and gave a brief recital of particulars, which have been already noticed.

When he had concluded, the ladies thanked him; Louisa observed archly, "You were peculiarly unfortunate, in not being noticed by some Turkish beauty, who might have broken your chains, and become a partner in your flight.—What a pretty romantic tale is here spoiled for want of a lady to embellish it."

"You will recollect, Madam," answered he, "that I never was permitted to walk, but when Heli was with me; and the side where the ladies resided, was far distant from the apartments I inhabited; therefore I cannot, with any plausibility, violate truth, by boasting of *ladies'* favours; indeed I have no obligations of *that kind*."

"How!" returned she; "are you so vain as to consider *our* friendship and good opinion so entirely your due, that it confers neither favour nor obligation?" "Pardon me, Madam, to *deserve* the *friendship* of two such ladies, would be my highest ambition; and to *obtain* it, I must consider as an honour that will gratify my vainest wishes."

"You have *extorted* a compliment, my dear Louisa," said Miss D'Alenberg, "and now I hope are satisfied."

Ferdinand ought to have replied to this "extorted," but he was out of spirits, and gladly availed himself of some trivial observation of young Reiberg's, to change the subject. This evasion passed not unobserved, which, with the melancholy air of his countenance, made them feel great compassion for him.

For his part, he was not sorry when the visit ended; Mr. D'Alenberg was requested by the Baron to accompany them back to dinner, as the ladies were engaged in making preparations for their appearance in public the next day, Louisa's health being much restored, and company and amusement being indeed indispensables towards removing the dejection of Miss D'Alenberg's spirits.

In their walk home, Ferdinand and the Count being together, the former remarked how thin and pale Miss D'Alenberg was grown.

"She is much altered," added he; "yet I think her more captivating than ever:—There is something so interesting in the softness of her looks, and the melody of her voice."

"You are partial to melancholy beauties," said the Count, smiling.—"I remember you admired Louisa much when she was sorrowful, and apparently declining into her grave; now, that the goddess, health, deigns to revisit, she seems to have lost her estimation with you."

"Not so," quickly replied Ferdinand, apprehensive that his friend was jealous of his attention to Miss D'Alenberg; "I am rejoiced to see her so unexpectedly recovered, and admire her as greatly as ever I did; her pleasing vivacity will, I hope, be of service to her friend.—Yet you must allow, the Count's death so recent, a man whom she so passionately loved, 'tis rather extraordinary that she appears to be so *little* affected."

"Not at all," answered the Count; "she had long ceased to esteem him; his conduct merited her scorn; and his late attempt against her must have eradicated every trait of affection; nor could she think herself safe from his machinations whilst he had existed. Her behaviour, therefore, is very natural;—she is freed from a villain, who had cruelly used her, and relieved from that fear and anxiety which must have embittered every hour in his life time. I applaud her for not pretending to a regret or sorrow, it was impossible she should feel."

"Do you suppose, then," said Ferdinand, "'tis so easy a matter to teach the heart to resign its affections; can the unworthiness of a beloved object so soon eradicate all tenderness from a bosom accustomed to love?"

"I know at *least, that it ought to be so*," replied the Count; "because love ought to be grafted on esteem; and the loss of *one* should be the death of the other."

"*Should be*," repeated Ferdinand with a sigh.—"Alas! how seldom is the refractory heart under the guidance of reason."

Being joined by their friends, the conversation became general, and they walked together to the Baron's house.

They had hardly dined, when a servant entered and said, a man on horseback had a letter for Count Ferdinand, which he refused to deliver to any but himself.—Surprised, he hastily run to the door; the man respectfully gave him the letter "from my master, Count Rhodophil Renaud." Ferdinand, with a trembling hand, broke the seal:—The contents were these:

"*My Dear Brother*,

"Life is ebbing fast; all hopes are over; if you ever wish to see me more, lose no time; set off directly; I have things of consequence to impart, for your interest; if you ever loved me, hasten to the dying

"RHODOPHIL."

"Good God!" exclaimed Ferdinand, "how long has my brother been ill?"

"He has been drooping some time," answered the servant; "but 'tis only a week since the doctor told him his danger, and the Countess is half distracted; for I have heard that day and night he wishes to see you."

"Go to the next inn," said Ferdinand; "refresh yourself; order post horses from the post house; I will be ready in two hours to accompany you."

Excessively agitated, he returned to his friends, produced the letter, and announced his intention of quitting Vienna immediately.

This design produced a general concern; every face was clouded.

"I will go with you," said the Count.

"Indeed you will not," replied Ferdinand; "it was your intention to stay some time longer; the business we have been engaged in may require your presence here; I cannot ask you to my brother's castle; a short time may decide how I am at liberty to act; I shall write the moment I get home."

"Indeed," said Mr. D'Alenberg, "this is very unlucky, and will shorten our stay in Vienna."

"Perhaps, then," said the Baron, "we may all soon follow you; for I have business that calls me into Bavaria, though I postponed it until the time for your departure was fixed, and which indeed I concluded would not happen for some time."

"I wish," said the Count, "you would permit me to go with you; I feel as if I *ought* to go."

"Not a word on the subject," returned Ferdinand; "I leave you here to answer for me to Miss D'Alenberg, to her friend, and all other claims upon me; have the kindness to acquaint the ladies of the necessity which tears me from them for the present, though I hope it will not be long before we meet again."

"I hope the same," said Mr. D'Alenberg; "for you possess my warmest esteem and best wishes."

Ferdinand felt the kindness of his friends, and withdrew, to hide his emotions, and prepare for his journey.

"You will excuse me," said Mr. D'Alenberg, "if I leave you; I like not the parting minute, and have an unpleasant task to perform, in preparing my young folks to receive you in the evening without your friend. I shall expect you, however; we will mingle our regrets."

He left them; the Count repaired to Ferdinand's apartment; again urged his wish to accompany him; but the other as firmly refused it.

"Stay here," said he, "'till you hear from me, and then perhaps I shall solicit, as the first wish of my heart, what I now refuse, the company of my friend."

The Count was silenced, though not satisfied, and assisted very reluctantly in settling things for their separation. The moment arrived; the post horses were at the door, and they parted with equal regret on all sides. Ferdinand determined to take no rest until he arrived at Lintz, but merely changed horses, and proceeded with the greatest expedition. The servant informed him he had business of consequence to do for Madam, the Countess, at Lintz, but which would not detain him many hours.

Here then Ferdinand thought he might rest, and to Lintz they at length arrived, excessively fatigued with long and hard riding. When Ferdinand had ordered some refreshment, the servant left him, and he seized five minutes to write a few lines to Count M***; the man was not long absent; they retired for a few hours to sleep, and then rose to pursue their journey with fresh spirits.

They had got near five miles from Lintz, and had ascended a steep hill, which was covered with trees.—On one side, you saw the plain through which the road lay; on the other side was a craggy mountain, at the foot of which run the river: The path-way was narrow; one horse only could with safety proceed at a time: Ferdinand was turning his horse round a clump of trees, when he received a shot, that brought him tumbling on the earth, and in the same moment, before he had recovered any recollection, he was precipitated down the broken mountain, and fell into the river, so bruised and senseless, that when he recovered his reason, he could scarcely recollect what had befallen him, nor the smallest idea from what hand he had received the injury.

Providentially, in rolling into the river, one of his hands got entangled in some low bushes, that grew on the edge of the water, that he was suspended from sinking, as he might otherwise have done, and the chill of the water restored his senses, but he saw the water was coloured with his blood, and felt that he was growing very faint; he therefore made an effort, by clinging fast to the wood and weeds, to drag himself out, and with some difficulty succeeded.

He found the shot had gone through the fleshy part of his right arm, and slightly wounded his side. With no small labour he got his coat off; for he had many bruises which began to grow painful; he tore his shirt, and with that and his handkerchief, bound up the wound as well as pain would enable him to do; but the effort, loss of blood, and the soreness of his limbs, rendered him extremely faint, and he had just time to drag himself farther on the bank, when he again felt his senses leaving him, and supposed death was at hand.

He returned a second time to life, but so enfeebled, and in so much pain, that he found it impossible to rise, and saw no prospect of relief: He looked round to see if the servant was in a similar situation, but no object met his view, and he had much reason to fear that he was killed upon the spot, and thrown into the river, where he sunk; for he had no doubt upon his mind but that he received the wound from some banditti, and even seemed to have an idea of seeing some objects among the trees just as he was wounded; and he supposed, by falling from the horse, he had *accidentally* rolled down the mountain, as their intention was doubtless to plunder him. Having settled the matter in his own mind, he pitied the fate of the servant, and lamented the distress his brother and friends would feel, when hearing no intelligence of him.

Hopeless of assistance, he thought his struggles for life, had only protracted his fate a few short hours, when he must inevitably perish; his only chance of help was the passing of a boat, and that hope was a very feeble one.

He happened to have two small biscuits, which he had put into his pocket at one of their last stages, but which he found broken in pieces by his fall; for the present he wanted no refreshment; his faintness arose from pain, and the sickness occasioned by rolling down such a tremendous height, which, when he raised his eyes to view it, he considered it as next to a miracle that he had not been dashed to pieces.

For some hours, he remained comfortless and despairing on the bank, when suddenly he saw a figure issue from a cavity in one of the hanging fragments of the rock, that appeared like something human, though bent almost double with age; a blanket wrapped round him, with holes to let out his arms, and tied round the middle with a cord; a long beard, and feeble steps, proclaimed his age and weakness. As this object approached nearer, Ferdinand saw his head was uncovered, exposed to the weather, his venerable silver locks flowing round his shoulders.

He was so struck with wonder and admiration, that he had no power to cry out; and, as he lay, the weeds and wild shrubs almost hid him from being seen. The old man was passing on slowly, and seemingly deeply meditating, when the other exerted himself to say, "Stop! Oh! stop!"

The man started.—"From whence comes that voice?" said he, advancing, and presently discovered Ferdinand.

"Gracious Father!" exclaimed he, "who are you, and how came you here, my son?"

"I fell from the brow of the hill into the river."

"Wonderful Providence! What, unhurt?"

"I cannot say that," replied he; "I am very much bruised, I believe, besides being wounded by a pistol in my arm and side, which occasioned my falling."

"Alas! my son, how shall I help you;—you cannot rise."

"Indeed I cannot; but perhaps I may endeavour to crawl a small distance, if there is any place to receive me."

"Try, then, my child; for I have a comfortable cell, if 'tis possible for you to reach it."

Ferdinand, suddenly inspired with hope, and fresh desires for life, exerted himself with uncommon resolution, and though he felt agonies of pain, he bore it without a groan, so anxious was he to obtain rest and help.

Such is the natural fondness for life implanted in the mind of man, that when sickness and despair has annihilated hope, and taught the suffering wretch to look forward to the close of his existence, as his only refuge from misery, if some unlooked for crisis changes the nature of his disorder, or a dawn of better prospects is presented to his view—he no longer courts death as the end of his troubles, but with new desires, new hopes, he struggles to retain and preserve life, though sure of encountering future ills, and of going through the same sad scene again.

So was it with Ferdinand, to whom an existence for many months, nay, even for years, had been an evil, he thought, he should have felt grateful to be released from, but the near prospect of death had taught him a different lesson; he found he had still some ties on earth that clung to his heart, and whom he shuddered to think of parting with for ever.

Eager, therefore, to profit by the old man's offer, he so successfully laboured, that he got to the part of the rock from whence he saw him emerge; but it was a work of extreme difficulty, and with all the assistance that old age was capable of lending, that he crawled up the broken fragments, and at length crept through the cavity into a spacious cell. The moment he entered, the spirit that had supported him failed, and he fainted.

The venerable man poured water upon him, and when he perceived returning life, forced a little wine down his throat, that revived him.—He next examined his bruises, and anointed them with some oil, the only thing he had that could do good, and having shook up his mattrass of straw, he covered it with a blanket, and laid Ferdinand upon it. In a very short time, overcome with fatigue and weakness, he dropped asleep, and enjoyed comfortable rest for more than six hours.

When he awoke, though stiff and sore, yet his spirits and strength seemed much recruited; the good man gave him some bread and wine, and with a few simple herbs and oil, prepared to dress his wound and bruises.—Luckily the ball passed quite through his arm, and wounded his side, without lodging in it; therefore his venerable host gave him hopes no ill consequences would ensue from that; the bruises would be more troublesome than the wound; but as he observed, 'twas a miracle that every bone had not been broken.

Ferdinand mentioned to him the accident as well as he could recollect; for the whole was so momentary, that he was hardly sensible how it happened. The old man paused, and considered.

"Possibly," said he, "there *may be* banditti in the neighbouring hills and woods, but I never heard of any accident there; 'tis a strange business; but thank Heaven, my son, whatever was their evil intent, you have escaped with life; and if in a few days you are able to walk, there is a castle not far off, where you will be better taken care of than by me."

Ferdinand thanked the venerable man, and was grateful to Heaven, who had so wonderfully preserved him. The simple remedies applied to his hurts, agreed perfectly well with them; and in the course of two days he began to feel considerably better.

CHAPTER IV.

DURING this time he had inquired of his host "how long he had lived in that rock?"

"Many years (replied he;) I had once a place at Court, was esteemed by the late Emperor, and not a small favourite with a Lady he loved. I often attended him when he visited her privately, and I happened to be young and pleased her fancy: I do not pretend to defend my conduct, I ought to have remembered the Emperor was my master and benefactor; but the seducive arts of women it is difficult to withstand, and perhaps I made no efforts for the purpose; be that as it may, the intrigue was discovered, the Lady was disgraced and confined; a criminal accusation, certainly without the least foundation, was set on foot against me; I fled to save my life, for a price was set on my head.

"In a boat I got landed on this side of the river, and strolled to these mountains, resolved to hide myself in a cave till the search was over, and then leave Germany for ever. Climbing the different rocks I at length discovered this cavity, and took courage to enter it: I found it such as you see, whether made by the hand of nature, or the work of some unhappy proscribed man, I know not. This I made my resting place; water and a few herbs, that grew wild here, was all I had for three days, and I found life could not long be supported in that way.

"The fourth day I followed the course of the river a good way, and saw one of the packet-boats, that goes between Ulm and Lintz, with passengers, going by: I called to them, and they drew near; I entreated some provisions; they offered to take me on board; that I declined, telling them peculiar misfortunes had made society hateful to me, and that I had resolved to live in an uninhabited place. The people I believe supposed me to be deranged, but very humanely supplied me. I had not fled without money, which, in the situation I had chosen, was likely to last me a great while; I bargained therefore with the master of the packet-boat regularly to call near that spot, and relieve my necessities, for which I would pay him liberally. This he never failed doing, and though doubtless I ran some risque from the variety of passengers who saw me, yet, whether want of curiosity, indolence, or compassion, saved me I know not; but I suppose the Emperor's wrath abated, and I was totally forgotten.

"I had resided here near two months without venturing to climb the hills, or explore the country beyond the spot I inhabited; but the failure of the regular packet, from what cause I know not, had exhausted my provisions, and gave me a prospect of approaching death if I was not relieved. I saw several boats pass, but at too great a distance to make myself heard. The weather set in cold and dreary, and I was almost in a state of despair, which at length conquered my fears of being discovered, and I resolved to ascend the hills, and penetrate through the woods.

"One morning I set off, but from want of food was too feeble to proceed with any expedition; however I persevered, and with much labour got round the side of these rocky hills to a most beautiful wood of chesnuts, about three miles from hence, and in the midst of the grove saw a Castle. Overcome with fatigue, without hesitation, I advanced and rung at the gate; a man appeared, to whom I mentioned my necessities. I was courteously invited in, had some food given me, and questioned how far I was travelling? Without any disguise I freely told my place of abode, and that hunger had driven me to make application there.

"This story was related to the Lord of the Castle, and I was ordered to attend him. He was a venerable old man, two youths, his sons, were with him. Without telling my name, or assigning my motives, I briefly said, misfortunes had deprived me of my fortune, and driven me from my country.

"The old Lord blamed me for seeking an abode among the mountains, told me that a young and active mind ought not to indulge in solitude and idleness, that there were other countries, and many situations, in which a young man might be useful to society, and creditable to himself.—He was certainly right, but I felt no inclination to seek my fortune, without a name I dared avow, or recommendations to give me consequence.

"I liked the solitary rambling life I had led for some time, an habitual indolence, perhaps an unsocial temper, and I acknowledge, not the smallest inclination for a military life, had altogether received strength from the silence and obscurity of my present dwelling; I therefore declined all his kind advice, and indeed offers, evaded his inquiries, and persisted in my resolution of living among the mountains, woods and glens, so that I could find sufficient sustenance.

"When he found my determination was fixed, I thought he eyed me with contempt: 'A young man to live secluded from society, and from choice lead such an inactive desultory kind of life (said he) can have but a very weak mind, an ignoble soul, or must have deserved to be proscribed by mankind: However, as a fellow creature, you claim relief, therefore I will order for you a few necessaries that may make your cave comfortable, and twice a week my steward shall have orders to relieve your wants. I am going to leave this country in a few days; but will take care you shall not want the means to support your existence.'

"He turned from me and I felt severely humbled. Two servants were sent with me loaded with blankets, a mattress, and several little conveniences. I was something amused by the mixture of curiosity and fear those fellows expressed when they saw my habitation, they assisted me in disposing of the things, and seemed extremely glad when I dismissed them.

"From that hour to this *my* life has been uniformly the same. My dislike of society gained ground daily, and accustoming myself to live upon little, and finding many palatable herbs round the mountains, I have been no great tax upon the bounty of the Castle.—The old Lord I never saw more; one of his sons married and resided in the Castle, but I have understood, from little hints thrown out by the present steward, that he was unhappy, and now lives at some distant part of the country.

"As my clothes wore out I refused others, determined to appear as I lived, like a hermit detached from the world. I take fish here sometimes, and still have what I please from the Castle, which has been long deserted by the family, and only inhabited by the steward, his wife, and two men, who look after the ground and cattle."

Here the hermit stopped; Ferdinand had been very attentive to him, and had decided in his own mind, that he had glossed over his conduct by only a slight account of his falseness and ingratitude to his Prince: He concluded his errors had been of no common magnitude, and such as deserved the severest punishment, or he would never have given up the world. This conclusion was strengthened as he proceeded in the story, and though he felt himself indebted for his assistance, yet the contempt that naturally arose in his mind for a character so unamiable, lessened his sense of gratitude.

He had continual occasions to observe an unequal and unpleasant temper in the hermit. He had a few books, with which he was supplied from the Castle, pens, ink and paper, neither of which seemed to afford him amusement. He was always rambling about, as if weary of his existence, and though he affected the language, as well as the manners, of a hermit, yet he paid but little attention to the duties of religion; his devotions were by fits and starts, and seemed not to proceed from a regular and habitual course.

From all these observations Ferdinand could not respect his host, and therefore was very impatient to get well enough to leave him; but more than a week passed without having strength to walk, his bruises being infinitely more painful than the wound.

During this time the hermit had not been at the Castle, for he had received his usual supply of bread, meat and wine, the very day that Ferdinand was so wonderfully saved from a dreadful death, and having caught a good deal of fish, they had not felt any want of provisions; but now the stock being exhausted, he signified his intention of going to the Castle.—"I should think (said Ferdinand) that blanket covering must be very troublesome to walk any distance with."

"No (replied the other) it is as commodious as a coat, and, were it otherwise, custom would render it easy."

The hermit set off for his walk; Ferdinand, just able to creep about, came out of the cave to enjoy the sun and fresh air; looking round him, he observed on one side a smaller opening nearer to the ground; curiosity led him to this, and stooping almost to the earth, he saw that it widened, and appeared to have light within. This discovery engaged him to crawl into it; at first he found some difficulty, the passage was dark, and the faint light seemed farther off; still he persisted to crawl on, when on a sudden it opened into a large cave, with a rill of water running through it, and dropping from the sides.

A ray of light, which proceeded from a small chasm at the top, served to discover the most beautiful sight that imagination can form: the waters petrified round looked like so many diamonds, hanging in long spars, and twisted into a variety of shapes, glittering so as to dazzle the eye; several large pieces of rock-work hung over the top; many of those shining spars suspended from them, which, with the rill of water, and the solemn stillness of the place, had a most wonderful effect upon the mind of Ferdinand; he was never tired of admiring the beauties of this enchanting cavern.

"How comes it (said he) that the hermit never mentioned this sweet place? What an insensible blockhead he must be; he is fit indeed to live alone, since neither society, nor the beauties of nature have any charms for him, he merely vegetates: What a horrid life! The wild and foolish scheme of rambling that once possessed me, though I am now convinced of its absurdity, yet was ordered by Providence to prove beneficial to others; but this man can have no opportunity of doing good, unless another is thrown over the mountain, or cast up from the river, and even his assistance is given with an apathy that is disgusting."

These ideas passed in his mind whilst he admired the dazzling petrifactions; but feeling himself very chilly, he wisely crept back to the entrance, and remained on the Beach till the old man appeared tolerably loaded.— "Here (said he) is some provisions, and I have related your accident to the steward; he will come here tomorrow, and you may be taken to the Castle if you like."

"Most certainly I shall like it (said Ferdinand) for many reasons." He then told him where he had been, and expressed his surprise, that he had not mentioned a place so replete with natural curiosities.

"To you indeed (answered he) I might have thought it would be interesting; but after once seeing it, I never went a second time, so it slipped my memory: I dare say there are a hundred such places about, but I never sought for any of them."

"What a lifeless, inanimate lump!—(thought Ferdinand:) Yes, indeed, I shall be mighty glad to quit such a being, who has no more soul than the rock he inhabits."

The next day a well-looking, middle aged man appeared at the opening of the rock, and being invited, entered within it. He congratulated Ferdinand with kindness and respect on his miraculous escape from death, or at least broken limbs, and invited him to come and spend a few days at the Castle until he was able to travel.

Ferdinand accepted the offer, but was fearful he could not get there. "With my assistance, a good firm stick, and a little resting, I do not despair (said the steward) and the sooner you make the trial the better."—Ferdinand wanted but very few persuasions to a thing so agreeable to his inclinations as leaving his insensible companion; therefore, after returning his thanks, they parted with equal indifference, and taking the steward's arm he turned his back on the rock.

The distance to the Castle was about three miles, but it was through the woods on the side of the hills, and not very easy walking, which, with the weakness of Ferdinand, made it full three hours before they arrived at it. A bed was ordered to be got ready, and, as it was a luxury he had not enjoyed for some time, he soon fell asleep, and forgot all his cares. Whilst he enjoys a comfortable repose we will look back on his friends at Vienna.

CHAPTER V.

Mr. D'Alenberg, after leaving the Baron's, returned to his daughter, whom he found in tears, her head reclining on the shoulder of Louisa.—"My dear Theresa (said this tender father) have some compassion upon me; must the remnant of my days be embittered by seeing my child unhappy. I have already told you there exists a possibility that every wish of your heart may be gratified."

"No, my dear father, No (said she, raising her head) my happiness is beyond the reach of *possibilities*; but I trust despair will have the same effects of making me composed and resigned, as if I *could* indulge a visionary hope.

These tears will be the last you shall see me shed, not one sigh more shall give you pain; I have given too much indulgence to a fatal weakness which stole upon me insensibly, but now I throw it from my heart for ever. *Your* daughter never shall live to blush for her attachment to an insensible object; but she will admire the constancy of an unfortunate man, and imitate a character that rises upon her every hour. Yes, *his* fortitude, *his* discretion, *his* strict adherence to honour and rectitude of conduct, shall inspire me with equal courage, to bear the misfortunes of life without sinking under them, and teach me to respect *your* feelings by suppressing my *own*."

She rose, and kissing her father's hand.—"Do not look at me (said she) with such tender surprise; this is not a false heroism; you shall see what resolution and a sense of duty will enable me to perform."

Mr. D'Alenberg was charmed with the behaviour of his daughter; but taking an opportunity, on her leaving him, of speaking to Louisa, she followed her friend to another apartment.

In the evening the Count and the two Barons paid a visit to the Ladies; every one expressed their regret at the sudden mandate which had taken their friend from Vienna, and every tongue was lavish in his praise. The Count seemed but half himself without Ferdinand, and could not reconcile it to his own feelings, that he submitted to let him go alone with only his brother's messenger.

Two days after the departure of Ferdinand, a messenger came to the Baron's from Mr. D'Alenberg, acquainting him with the arrival of the Countess Wolfran, and requested to see the Count immediately. He obeyed the summons. On being introduced to an apartment where that Gentleman waited to receive him, after saluting him, "I have been a witness (said he) to one of the most interesting scenes you can possibly conceive, between two amiable and noble minded women. The indiscretion of Louisa, in marrying Count Wolfran without her parent's sanction, she has amply atoned for, not only by her subsequent sufferings, but by a generosity of conduct that highly exalts her.

"You know the subject of the letter she wrote to the Countess, and her fixed determination never to avail herself of the Count's last declaration in her favour. The Countess, on the receipt of her letters, without communicating the contents to any one, set off post for Vienna, leaving her child to the care of a friend in the Convent.

"She came directly to this house; the meeting was truly affecting, and the self-denying arguments on both sides, such as did honour to the goodness of their hearts.—Louisa held one that I thought was incontrovertible. 'In resigning those rights (said she) which you wish me to assume, I forfeit nothing; claims which were never publicly made, nor at any time allowed, from which I could derive but a trifling pecuniary advantage to myself *only*, which must subject me to the talk of the country, and drag me into public notice as an object of compassion for past injuries, and of curiosity for the claims and circumstances so mortifying, which I must adduce to prove my rights; advantages attained under all these considerations would be to me more humiliating than indigence if unnoticed.

" 'Had the Count acknowledged me in the life time of my father, my duty, and regard for *his* honour, would certainly have made me act very differently, and then, my dear Countess, I should not have known the superior nobleness of your mind, so different from the jealousy and hatred a narrow and contracted heart would have felt towards an object who had, however innocently, interrupted her happiness.

" 'Never, were I to live a thousand years, shall I forget your kind visit, and subsequent generosity: And will you deny the poor Louisa the heart-felt satisfaction of imitating, as well as she can, so bright an example?—But to do away every idea of any obligation to me, I own to you, my dear friends, that was I a parent, had I a child to inherit from the claims I might bring forward, *then*, I should feel it a duty to assert them; but to wrong the Countess, married in the face of the world, to disinherit a *lawful* heir, for such is your son; to throw the estates and titles into a very distant branch of the family, to the prejudice of his own child, merely for a temporary advantage to myself—never, never, can I think of it! And after all, what merit is there in giving up claims which the uncertainty of the law might long with-hold, and, perhaps, deny me at last for want of sufficient proofs.'

"Those arguments of Louisa, which I think I have pretty exactly repeated," continued Mr. D'Alenberg, "seemed unanswerable; the Countess had only to oppose what she termed justice and equity; the matter was at length referred to me, and both parties pledged themselves to abide by my determination; without hesitation I pronounced Louisa's conduct both just and proper, and that the Countess ought, without scruple, to act for her son according to the rights allowed her by the world.

"My opinion was decisive, and concluded the debate. Louisa has drawn up a short declaration in these words, to which myself and daughter have signed as witnesses, and to which you also are requested to put your signature.

"Louisa, the daughter of Claude Hautweitzer, thus publicly acknowledges Theodosia—to be the true and lawful wife of Frederic Count Wolfran; and as such entitled to all his estates and effects in right of her son, heir to the late Count Wolfran.—This declaration made before, and witnessed by, &c. &c."

"This paper (pursued Mr. D'Alenberg) she has written herself for the farther satisfaction of the Countess, not that I think there will ever exist any cause that shall make it necessary to produce it, only that there were some persons in the room when Mr. Hautweitzer claimed the Count as *his* daughter's husband; but as the affair fell to the ground, and that claim has never been renewed, there is no great chance that it will be noticed; if it should, this paper will be conclusive, and, Louisa being almost entirely unknown, has consented to adopt our name, and to reconcile the Countess to herself, agrees to accept a very handsome independent settlement.

"Thus all parties are satisfied at last, and all this business has been begun and ended in little more than three hours."

Mr. D'Alenberg having concluded, introduced the Count to the Ladies. He was much struck with the fine person and noble air of the young Countess, and with admiration gazed on three such women, as it would have been extremely difficult to produce their equals.

He earnestly inquired after Eugenia.—"I have a letter for you, Sir," said the Countess, "from my amiable friend. Thank Heaven, her health is amazingly restored, though the fatigues and fasts she voluntarily inflicts upon herself are great trials to a delicate constitution. I have left my child to her tender care, and shall feel inconceivable regret to part from that Lady, and attend to the necessary cares my friends have heaped upon me for the advantage of my son. All my objections are over-ruled and silenced, Sir, but I shall never feel half satisfied with myself."

The Count joined heartily in the opinion before given, and then mentioned the civilities for which he was indebted to Baron Reiberg and his son. The Countess blushed at the name; but with a noble frankness she said, "I doubt not, Sir, from the expression of your countenance, but that you have heard of the early attachment the young Baron honoured me with. My dear father was pleased to consign both my person and fortune to the care of Baron Nolker, and made *his* consent absolutely necessary to my marriage with any man, at the same time recommending Count Wolfran for my husband, if he desired my hand.

"The Baron, though a good man, availed himself of this authority in favour of his nephew, whom *he* certainly thought a good character; my preference of the Baron was reprobated, the acquaintance broken off, and in obedience to the will of my father I consented to sacrifice myself rather than wound my character and delicacy, by forfeiting my fortune to indulge what might have been deemed a juvenile attachment in a giddy young woman.

"I owe the Baron much respect, and many obligations for his strict adherence to my wishes and entreaties. He respected my peace, and I had too much regard for *his*, ever to inform him of the cruel duplicity of Count Wolfran; I rather wished him to believe our separation was my own work, and the effects of my own weak and discontented spirit."

"And your secret, Madam," said the Count, "has never transpired; the Baron feared you was unhappy, suspected the Count did not behave well; but he had no grounds to form his opinion from, as upon inquiry he was told the Count opposed your retirement; and grieved at your absence."

"I am glad the Baron was so informed," returned she; "but the hypocrite never regretted me; the possession of my estates easily consoled him for my absence."

As the Countess was now compelled to appear as the widow of the late Count Wolfran, she was obliged to confine herself till after the funeral, which was ordered to be at the burial-place of his family near Ulm, and every preparation was set on foot to forward the procession in a day or two.

It was singular enough to the company to see two widows, both of whom disdained to assume any appearance of sorrow for a man they equally despised, whose interests, one would suppose, must have been incompatible with each other, linked in the firmest bands of friendship, and each feeling the highest admiration for the merits of her friend.

The fortunate escape of Louisa being talked of, naturally led to the situation of Heli, and she avowed much pain that the poor Turk should have been so great a sufferer by affording her an asylum in his house. "I think it a duty upon me," said she, "to reimburse his losses in some degree, and the Countess having made me so handsome a provision, infinitely beyond my wants, I shall certainly appropriate a part of it for his use, since it is through him ultimately that I am indebted for the blessings I at present enjoy."

This generous intention was only opposed in part, the Count insisting both for himself and Ferdinand, that they should participate in the benefits she proposed for Heli. This claim was at length allowed, and he was commissioned to get a settlement drawn up for the advantage of the Turk.

The day following Mr. D'Alenberg and his daughter was to be presented at Court; she would gladly have declined a fatiguing, and to her little pleasing, ceremony; but as her father appeared desirous of it, she submitted to his wishes. The Count, the two Barons, and the Lady of the first Minister, were to be of the party.

The day came, and Miss D'Alenberg went through the ceremony, was graciously received, and very much admired. One Nobleman of high rank and fortune, was particularly charmed with her, fixed himself in her party, and paid her the most marked attention.

In the evening, when all the friends met at Mr. D'Alenberg's lodgings, the Count gave an account of his commission to Heli, which he had executed that morning, and at length prevailed upon him to accept the settlement; but he declared he would not relax in his endeavours to trace Fatima, and should he recover his jewels, or such part of them as would enable him to live, he would throw up his obligations to Christians, and enjoy the pleasure of revenge upon an ungrateful, abandoned woman.

After the Count had repeated his negociation with Heli, the Gentlemen all rallied Miss D'Alenberg on the conquest she had made that morning at Court.—"I have no doubt," said Baron Reiberg, "but that Mr. D'Alenberg will receive a visit from Count Dusseldoff."

"It will be an unnecessary piece of politeness," said the young Lady, hastily; "for I hope in a few days we shall leave Vienna, and return home. Our appearance this morning I thought a work of supererogation, as our stay here will be so very short."

"Indeed, Madam," returned the Baron, "few young Ladies would think so lightly of such a conquest. Count Dusseldoff is a very worthy young Nobleman, highly in favour with his Royal Master, a very handsome fortune in possession, and his reversionary ones."——

"Dear Sir," exclaimed she, "neither his possessions, or reversions, can be any thing to me. I hope and believe you mistake the nature of his attentions, which certainly extended no farther than common politeness. I beg," continued she, very seriously, seeing the Baron smile, and going to speak, "I entreat you, Sir, to choose some other subject for your observations. Your present ideas are very visionary ones."

"I beg your pardon, Madam," said he, "and have done."

The Countess gladly availed herself of the privilege allowed her as a widow to retire from company, and therefore avoided being seen by the young Baron; but he was changed into a new man, life and animation informed his whole person, and the hope, though a distant one, that a day would arrive when he might be permitted to see his adored Theodosia, and resume his former claims upon her heart, made him submit with a tolerable grace to the rules of decorum.

The next morning the Baron's predictions were verified; Count Dusseldoff sent in his name to Mr. D'Alenberg, his daughter was not present, and he received a visit he considered as an honour. After a very little prefatory discourse, the Count frankly avowed his admiration of Miss D'Alenberg, and requested permission to visit her.

Her father most respectfully acknowledged the honour intended to her, told him that he had long since resigned all parental authority to dictate to her choice, having reason to be perfectly satisfied with her prudence, and assured that she would never form an imprudent attachment; that his Lordship being but little acquainted with her person, and not at all with her disposition, or understanding, he hoped he might be excused for saying, "it was rather a premature declaration."

The Count said, "that it became his character to be candid towards Mr. D'Alenberg; but to the young Lady he should be more reserved, and only requested, for the present, permission to pay him and his daughter that attention, which, as strangers, they were entitled to." This politeness could not be refused, and on that footing the Count was permitted to pay his respects to them in the evening.

He had scarcely left the house before Count M*** was announced, who with great joy produced a few lines he had received from Ferdinand, the same he had written at Lintz. The Ladies were soon informed of the letter, which conveyed his best respects to them, and the whole party seemed rejoiced to hear of his safe arrival there: But this pleasure was short-lived, when Mr. D'Alenberg mentioned the visit he had received, and the permission he had granted.

For a few minutes his daughter seemed in great agitation; she stole several looks at the Count; his countenance said nothing. She soon recovered, and only replied, "her father had a right to see whom he pleased, although *she* could not see the necessity of adding to their acquaintance for the very short time they should stay in that city."—No answer was made to this observation, and the Count receiving an invitation for himself and his friends, they separated soon after.

As he walked back he recollected the secret attachment which Louisa had hinted at as the cause of her friend's disorder upon her spirits, and revolving every occurrence as they rose to his mind, he began to entertain an idea, that either Ferdinand or himself was the object of it. He was many years older than his friend, and he thought very inferior to him in every personal endowment; yet he had remarked she generally addressed herself to him, and the particular looks she had eyed him with when her father spoke of the Count's visit, had not passed unobserved then, and now, from several corroborating circumstances, seemed to proceed from no common cause.

There is no man, at any time of life, but has some latent spark of vanity, which may be raised by accidental and concurring incidents. Count M*** had still such advantages of person, as might well warrant more than a bare supposition that he was not deficient in attraction, and from the *idea* once obtruding on his mind, many little trifling instances were recollected, that fixed it there, and he concluded Miss D'Alenberg had certainly entertained a decided partiality for him.

He was too noble and generous not to lament that he was so distinguished, because he still retained a warm affection for Eugenia, and *had* that
affection been cooled, yet his honour and feelings never would suggest him
to pay particular attention to any woman whilst she existed; he therefore
concluded it would be most prudent and proper for him to relax in his visits, and, if possible, to avoid being a companion in their journey when they
should return into Suabia.

Count Dusseldoff made his visit, and was still more charmed with Miss
D'Alenberg than at first. The little she did say, and that was as little as was
consistent with politeness, gave him the highest opinion of her understanding and cultivated mind. She was above assuming any consequence from his
partiality to her, and being perfectly indifferent to him, she treated him as
a Gentleman chance had thrown in her way, and whom possibly she might
never see again; for she took an opportunity of saying they should *soon*
leave Vienna, and that she was so devoid of fashion, as to prefer the country
to all the amusements a gay and crowded city could hold out to her.

In the course of a week his visits were several times repeated, and at
length he took courage to avow his admiration in very explicit terms. Her
answer was short, but decided: "I am truly sensible of the honour of your
good opinion; but, my Lord, there are insuperable obstacles to any union
between us. My father has the goodness to permit me in this important
business to decide for myself; therefore I am not accountable to any other
person. My Lord, I *never can* be your's: I respect you, I am grateful, but I can
entertain no other sentiments for you, and I beg that I may never more hear
a word on this subject."

The Count, mortified and disappointed, appealed to the father, he absolutely declined any interference, though he acknowledged the Count's
proposals were highly honourable both to himself and daughter; but he
was convinced her resolution was unalterable.—Thus ended the hopes of
Count Dusseldoff, and he ceased to importune her farther.

Whilst this affair was pending Count M*** very seldom called, and
when he did his visits were short, his behaviour cool. The Ladies noticed
this alteration, but supposed it was occasioned by his uneasiness in not
hearing from Ferdinand; indeed *all* grew impatient at his silence, as they
only waited to hear of his arrival and situation to fix on a day for following
him.

Baron Reiberg had received a letter from his steward that the valet was
safe with him, and appeared to be a very *good sort of a man*. This indefinite
term was not misapplied to him, for he had a few good traits in his character, which, if he had belonged to a better master, might have made him a

valuable servant; for he was strictly faithful to him, and made his inclinations and conscience subservient to what he thought was his duty to his employer; unfortunately he had not understanding, or strength of mind, to distinguish between *that* duty, and what he owed to himself and society, the consequence of that slavery and vassallage, which the German Lords exact from their poor tenantry and servants.

Ferdinand had been gone now ten days, no news was received, and they were extremely uneasy; when one day an express arrived to Baron Reiberg from Count Rhodophil, requesting to know "if any servant of his had appeared at the Baron's house to attend on his brother, he had dispatched a messenger more than a fortnight since to implore Ferdinand's return, as he supposed himself then at the point of death; that although much recovered, he was still in a weak state, and very unhappy from not seeing or hearing of his brother, or whether the messenger had reached Vienna or not."

Never was consternation greater than what the Baron and his friends felt on the receipt of this letter; from the date Ferdinand ought to have been there several days preceding it. This, with his silence to them, gave unspeakable apprehensions to the whole party, and accelerated their resolution to quit Vienna. The messenger was sent back with an account of Ferdinand's arrival at Lintz on his way to Baden, since which they had heard nothing of him.

Mr. D'Alenberg declined acquainting the Ladies of the cause which hastened their journey, and Miss D'Alenberg was so desirous of returning, that she readily fell in with her father's opinion, that it was unnecessary to wait for letters from Ferdinand, as they were going to him, and letters could be dispatched after them. Louisa had no will but her friends, and the Countess was anxious to see her son, and had much business to go through at Ulm. Thus the whole party made up their mind for the journey, and the second day after the next was fixed upon for their departure. Here then we leave them to follow Ferdinand.

CHAPTER VI.

THE comforts of a bed, and the prospect of being soon able to pursue his journey, gave him some hours of quiet rest at the castle of Danhaet; he awoke refreshed, and in spirits.—The steward and his wife were worthy people; advanced rather above the middle age, plain in their language and habits, but with excellent hearts, and an honest frankness that engaged confidence.

Ferdinand was extremely desirous to write to his brother and friends; the steward furnished him with materials for writing, and advised his taking a passage in one of the boats that took passengers between Lintz and Ulm. This advice the other readily agreed to follow, as the most easy way of proceeding for a person whose limbs had not yet recovered their strength and pliability. The steward told him they were about seven miles from a post town, but he would get his letters conveyed thither, and also inquire about his passage.

Ferdinand was charmed with the situation of this castle; it was built on the side of a hanging wood, which rose gradually to the top of a high hill, and sheltered it from the keen blasts of the north.—Large plantations of chesnuts seemed to surround it, among which were cut several beautiful walks and narrow vistas, terminated by some picturesque views. In front was a hanging garden of large extent, from whence there was a declivity down to the banks of the river. The castle itself was old and out of repair, but the apartments were noble, and the furniture, though faded and decayed, yet perfectly clean and commodious.

Talking with the steward, he observed the situation was so romantic, and the environs so beautiful, that he was astonished his lord never came to it.

"Why, Sir," answered he, "it is the general opinion of the country, that the left wing of the castle, or rather a detached pavilion, which you see is almost enveloped by the trees, is haunted; and the reason is this; a state prisoner was once confined there, and, as the story goes, was murdered; one of my lord's ancestors had the care of him; 'tis an old and a foolish story, I think—but so it is, our old lord never permitted any one to live in it, and they do say that the present lord was once much frightened, for he and his lady disagreed, and he confined her for a time in that place, only going to her by day himself; how it was, I don't know, but he was frightened, as they say; so he took her away, and put her into a convent, and since that time never returned here."

"A strange story," said Ferdinand; "but did you ever hear or see any thing to terrify you."

"Why, Sir," replied he, "I never go there, because 'tis shut up; but some of the peasants, who have come here of a night, or early in a morning, sware that they have heard strange noises.—For my part, I had no concern in the business, whatever it was; I do no harm to any one, and therefore I live here very quietly; and if there are ghosts there, why I never disturb them, nor they me; I have often wished that strange old man of the rock to live here with us, because the more the merrier; but whether he is afraid of ghosts, or likes his hole in the rock better than a good chamber, I can't tell, but here he won't live, because he says he likes to be alone.

"Here is a fine library—I offer him what books he likes; but two or three will serve him for months; he likes nothing but fishing, and lives upon very little."

"He is a strange worthless being, I think," said Ferdinand, "and altogether such a character as I had no idea of; for he is not a religious man, a man of knowledge, or in any shape desirous of obtaining useful information; a poor pusillanimous idle creature, that crawls upon the earth, insensible to every thing.

"However, if *he* has *no* curiosity, *I have*, and should like of all things, to examine this pavilion."

"You may walk to it, if you can, with all my heart," said the man; "'tis but a little way detached from the building you see;—there is a private communication below stairs, but that has long been nailed up.

"By day, Sir, I am sure you may go, because I often pass it, and never heard any thing in my life."

"Well, then," said Ferdinand, "I will take an opportunity to look at it; you have the keys, I suppose."

"I have, Sir; but the doors have never been opened for more than twelve, aye, more than fourteen years, I believe; therefore I don't suppose the keys will turn now; they hang in the hall, with a ticket to them."

"I shall try them to-morrow," said Ferdinand.

"As you please, Sir," answered he.

But the wife was not quite so easy; she besought him not to go; told several strange stories; declared she had heard odd noises sometimes, when down stairs near the communication passage, and though she trusted in Heaven, and injured no one, yet she would not go into the pavilion for any money.

Ferdinand, who had no fears of supernatural beings, and much curiosity, waited impatiently for the next day; and taking the keys, which the steward had cleaned a little from the rust, he walked to the pavilion;—he was yet but feeble, and when he came to a flight of steps, which led up to the apartments, he seated himself to take breath.

This sequestered spot was surrounded by high trees, at the foot of which were a profusion of shrubs and wild flowers; it seemed formed for retirement and contemplation;—but being long and totally neglected, the outside was decaying; the weeds almost obscured the lower apartments; the glass, in many places, was broken; and in short, the whole bore the marks of desolation.

After having rested for some time, Ferdinand prepared to view the inside of this forlorn place; he tried his keys, but found it impossible to turn them.—Vexed and disconcerted, he descended, and walked round among the weeds, when he discovered another small door with a padlock to it, but he had no key that looked likely to open that; he drew near to it, and taking up the lock in his hand with a sort of quick pull, the staple fell out, and directly he heard the sound of a bell, and saw a string was fastened to the staple.—Surprised, he waited a few moments, to see if any consequence followed the sound of the bell, but all remained still.

This is very singular, thought Ferdinand; and looking round, he observed the weeds seemed to be more broken, as if trodden down; he turned to pull open the door, which resisted his endeavour, and he found must be fastened inside.—He took up the staple, and pulling the string, the bell sounded a second time, and presently a hollow voice was heard, that muttered some inarticulate words, and then groaned.—Though extremely startled at the moment, yet he was convinced the voice was human; that some mystery was attached to the building, and that something more substantial than ghosts or shadowy forms resided there; else why the bell to alarm, and inside fastenings.

Revolving these circumstances in his mind, he made no reply for the present, but determined to watch near that place in the evening. He returned to the steward, repeated the strange account, and his own conjectures; but he found it impossible to encourage him in the idea of its being inhabited by living persons; and instead of deriving any help from him to elucidate the mystery, he had only strengthened the steward's apprehensions, and confirmed the report which he had often been inclined to doubt, and think proceeded from the superstition and credulity of the peasants.

No persuasions, therefore, could induce him to accompany Ferdinand in the evening to hide among the trees and make observations; he then applied to the two men who looked after the grounds and cattle, but they were still more terrified.—One of them declared, that oftentimes he had heard groans, and had seen smoke ascending among the weeds, which, however, were never burnt, and therefore it must come from *"the old one's"* house under-ground, where he would take good care never to disturb him.

It was in vain to combat against ignorance and cowardice; therefore Ferdinand saw he must make his own discoveries; and his strength not admitting of much exertion to force his way, or even to escape, if such a step should be necessary, he felt extremely perplexed how to proceed.

After several schemes formed and rejected, it suddenly darted into his mind, to wrap himself up in a sheet, outside of which he would throw the steward's great coat, and having a dark lanthorn with him, he could conceal himself among the trees, and if in danger of being discovered, by throwing off the coat, and presenting himself with the light, he had little doubt but that he might frighten those who had endeavoured to terrify others. This plan he prepared to put in execution, heedless and deaf to the prayers and remonstrances of his host and hostess, who gave him up for lost.

Towards the close of the evening, Ferdinand, properly habited with a tinder box and a dark lanthorn, placed himself among the trees, opposite to this small door, where he could see every transaction without being observed.

Night came on; every thing was still and silent; he began to grow weary of his situation; the castle clock had gone eleven, when suddenly he espied the figures of four people coming through the trees; he could not distinguish their persons, there being no moon. It must be observed, that Ferdinand had replaced the staple and padlock; they made towards the door; he saw them stand, and heard a faint sound of the bell, and in a moment he lost sight of them, and was convinced they were let in through the door.

"Now, then," said he, "the whole is discovered; this is a retreat for robbers, and we shall soon clear the haunted pavilion."

He returned to the castle, to the no small joy of his friends, but he found it impossible to convince them that the persons he described were living ones; they grew more strongly assured that they were wicked spirits, but that Mr. Ferdinand being good, they had no power to hurt him. He, provoked at their incredulity, at length asked the steward if it was possible to open the door of communication, which he said led underneath to the pavilion: The other hesitated a long time; but on being urged, said,

"Perhaps it might, as it was nailed up on this side, supposing that the ghosts had not fastened it on the other, as they did the padlock door."

"But," said the woman, "it would be better to go in the day-time, and force open the front door of the pavilion."

Ferdinand hesitated and considered.—"If, as I suppose," said he, "some part of the gang are always in the house, they are doubtless prepared for resistance, and will sell their lives dearly; in forcing the door, some of us may be killed; no, let us discover, if possible, who and what they are, and then we can take measures to surprise them, perhaps without danger."

The woman shook her head.

"Ah!" said she, "they are no living folks, I dare say; and it would be better to go by day, when they do not appear."

"But," replied Ferdinand, "that won't do; I wish to see them *appear*."

He then went down to the passage, which was like the colonade of a cloyster, and saw the door: By the help of an instrument, he drew the screws from the hinges, and with very little noise, opened the door, which discovered a similar passage to the one he was in, but quite dark; he procured his dark lanthorn, and proceeded softly through the passage; lamps were hung on one side, which no doubt were formerly lighted, but all was extremely gloomy and damp.

He came at length to a flight of steps, and hesitated a few minutes whether he should venture to proceed, yet it would be folly to go back so unsatisfied; he had just ascended the first stair, when he heard a loud laughing, as if of two or three persons: He listened—the sound seemed to come from no great distance, and he heard voices as if extremely merry.

He continued to ascend with great caution, and entered a sort of lobby, from whence he heard the voices more distinctly; to go forwards alone, he thought would be madness, as he must expect instant death, if discovered. He was now sufficiently assured of what mind the inhabitants were, and proper steps might be taken to secure them through this passage.

He turned, therefore, to make good his retreat; he heard the noise of feet directly over his head, and stept forwards as quick and softly as possible, blaming his own rashness for advancing so far; he looked for the stairs, in his confusion he had past them; for this lobby went the whole length of the building. Sensible of his error, he was going back, when he heard some one coming down stairs, and the glimmering of a light approaching, he could not advance, but turned his lanthorn and retreated on one side, giving himself up for lost.

A man appeared with a light, and passed so close to Ferdinand, that it was impossible to avoid seeing him; he just snatched a look at him as he started, and, with a groan, fell on the floor.—Though infinitely surprised, he had no time to lose, as the fall and groan must alarm the others; he therefore quickly trod back through the lobby, found the stairs, and, with all the strength he could exert, run through the passage, which, having gained, he ventured not to close the door, but in a moment got up to the stair-case of the castle apartments, and appeared before the steward and his wife so out of breath and agitated, that they both concluded he had seen the ghosts.

When he could speak, he informed them of what he had heard and seen; and so far, said he, are the persons there from being shadowy beings, that I have no doubt, from the fellow's fright, but that he took me for one; at least I hope he did, as then my progress through the passages will not be discovered.

"And if it is," said the woman, "then for a certain we shall all be murdered."

Ferdinand was not perfectly free from the same idea; yet still he thought no time should be lost, to get proper persons to secure those men, who were evidently a gang of banditti.

The steward was persuaded to take a horse, and ride immediately to the next post-town, declare what had happened, and bring a party as private as possible, to seize upon them at night—much against the opinion of the wife, who was for letting them rest quiet, whoever they were, alive or dead, rather than bring themselves into trouble; but at length Ferdinand prevailed, by saying what a great reward they would obtain by taking them.—This consideration a little reconciled her to the absence of her husband; therefore, at day-break, he got his horse, and set off with all haste.

He had been gone about three hours, when there was a knocking at the door; Ferdinand was gone to lay down on a sofa in the library; the good woman was alone, the men being about the grounds, and she was afraid to open the door without some one with her; she came to him in the library, and entreated he would have the goodness to come out, and then she would speak from the window, which she did, and asked the person what he wanted; he wished to speak with her husband; he was not at home; could he come in and wait for him, as he had business of consequence to tell him.—Without answering, she drew in her head to ask Ferdinand's opinion; he advanced to the window, and just as he was in view of the man, the fellow started, screamed, attempted to run, but fell on the ground.

Ferdinand hastened out, spoke, and took the man's arm to assist him; he turned, and looking up, discovered the very face of the servant his brother had sent to attend him back to Baden.

Both were thunderstruck, and for a moment speechless.—The man exclaimed,

"Alive! is it possible—alive!"

"Yes, my good friend," replied the other, "most wonderfully preserved from death, and I rejoice to see *you*; for I have often felt much concern for the uncertainty of your fate."

"Concern for me! Good God! but I see Providence will always bring wicked deeds to light.—Pray, Sir, tell me. Did I see you last night in the lobby of yonder pavilion?"

"I was certainly there," answered Ferdinand, "and frightened a man, I believe—could that be you?"

"It was, Sir; and from that fright, you will now know all; for though I find it was no ghost, as I thought, yet, as I said before, Providence discovers all things, and I will make a free confession."

"Come in then," said Ferdinand, "and whatever you have to confess, speak freely, and assure yourself of my pardon, if you have done me any wrong."

He then entered into a long story, which, as the substance of it will be detailed hereafter, it is not necessary to give now; but it concluded with avowing, that he had orders to destroy Ferdinand on the most convenient spot, to avoid a discovery; that he had engaged others to assist him, who were in waiting in the grove at the top of the hill, one of which fired at him, and he being dismounted, as he fell, rolled him over the hill, supposing he must be dead.

That he hastened to his employer, received the sum agreed for, and only yesterday joined his friends; that having among them got a great deal of money and jewels, they proposed to leave off that trade, go over to England, set up for gentlemen, and take to the gaming-table.

This scheme they had intended to execute in about ten days time; there were six of them concerned, two of whom always remained in the pavilion; the other four occasionally drest as gentlemen; found out when any travellers of consequence were going on the roads, and then came back, disguised themselves, and plundered where they expected a good booty. Some of his comrades had inhabited that pavilion many years, but he had only joined them lately.

Returning yesterday with his money, which he should not have done, but that he knew his share of their stock was considerably greater than what he possessed, and sure between them of making more money when they pleased, of his employer; he said, they had a feast, and were extremely merry last night, and he was sent down to the cellar for some particular fine wine; going through the lobby, he saw something stand against the wall; going nearer, he saw, as he thought, the ghost of Mr. Ferdinand; terror instantly seized him, and he fell into a fit.

The noise he made brought down the others; and when he recovered, so much had conscience overpowered his senses, that he still insisted that he saw him before his eyes, wherever he turned: Some of his friends ridiculed him, but one or two seemed as much terrified as himself.

In short, he went to bed, but could not stay alone; and when he reflected upon all his wickedness, he thought he would go to the castle, and confess the whole; only he did not intend to say he threw the murdered gentleman over the hill, and, as he did not fire at him, he hoped, by impeaching the rest, he should obtain pardon.

Following this resolution, when the other four went out before daybreak, and left him and another in bed; he took the advantage of the other, and stole off; came to the castle, but again seeing Ferdinand, concluded the

ghost haunted him, and intended to run away, when his fright threw him
down.

This story and discovery so shocked Ferdinand, that he could hardly
keep himself from fainting, but he assured the man of his protection, if he
would repent of his past life.—This he faithfully promised; but his fears of
the ghost having subsided, and his terrors of murder being done away, he already regretted the confession which horror and the fright of the moment
had drawn from him.

Ferdinand told him by what means he entered the lobby, and the steps
they intended to take that night, to surprise the whole gang, when at table.
It was fortunate for him, perhaps, that the two men of the house now entered, and were a check upon the villain, who was inwardly cursing his stars
for making him such a terrified coward.

He told Ferdinand they assembled together earlier than usual the last
evening, to celebrate his return, but would hardly meet 'till one or two in
the morning on this night; that he thought it best for himself to return, as
he could account for his absence, and then he would take care to put aside
all instruments of destruction against their appearing, to prevent any harm
to Ferdinand and his party.

The unsuspecting Ferdinand praised the man's humanity, and advised
him to depart immediately, and expect him about one o'clock. Away he
went, cured of his fears, and like a true rogue, finding it most for his interest, he would make a merit of being true to his accomplices, and establish
an opinion of his own courage and integrity.

The steward returned, properly accompanied for their intended expedition, and was astonished when informed of the visitor they had in his
absence, and not sorry that they should have a friend to prevent mischief.

At the appointed hour, they silently proceeded through the passages, and ascending the stairs, reached the lobby; all was still;—not a voice
heard.—This appeared extraordinary; however, two resolute men went before up the stairs to the apartment where Ferdinand had heard them the
preceding evening; the door was open; the room empty; chairs, tables, and
trunks, all in disorder.—They looked at each other.

"What can this mean?" cried Ferdinand

They run from room to room, on that floor which was the lower one;
then ascended, searched the house through; it was entirely empty, not only
of its inhabitants, but of the vast riches the man had boasted of.

"The villain has betrayed us," said Ferdinand; "they are all off."

They descended to the cellars, and there found the little door wide
open, and all clear. 'Twas now plain they had all taken their flight; and to

have discovered and irritated such a band of ruffians, was a very serious business. The steward lamented his interference; he had no doubt but that they would return, and murder every one at the castle.

Ferdinand was not quite easy, though he seemed to make light of the fears of others, and they returned extremely disconcerted.

That the robbers could not be at any great distance was certain; but there were so many caves and subterranean passages in the hills and rocks adjacent, that it was judged both fruitless and dangerous to trace them, even if they had any clue to guide their search.—They had taken their riches with them; the informer had said, they intended to leave the place, therefore they were now reduced to hope they never might return.

Ferdinand bore all the vexation and mortification of this disappointment, since, had he not been too credulous, he never would have permitted the man to return back, but have retained him as a necessary evidence. He accused his own imprudence, and execrated the wretch whose feigned penitence had deceived him.

CHAPTER VII.

THAT night was past without rest by any part of the family at the Castle. Every breath of wind, the least motion of the trees, was magnified into the sound of feet, and murmuring of voices. Day-light at last came, and their terrors began a little to subside; they met dejected and unrefreshed; Ferdinand, ashamed of his credulity, tortured by the recollection of the man's information, and grieved at the painful situation his imprudence had thrown the family into, who had so kindly attended to him, with many other additional causes of inquietude, appeared with a countenance so truly dejected, an air of such anxious concern for them, that instead of affording them any comfort, he more completely alarmed their fears.

He found it impossible to raise his own spirits, or recall to his friends that cheerfulness his folly had deprived them of. On that day or the next, the passage boat was expected; but could he leave them in such a perilous situation, forsake them in the prospect of danger they incurred by complying with his wishes? Impossible, neither honour nor humanity would permit it.

He had written to his friends at Vienna, he had little doubt but that some of them would come to him, at any rate he must remain where he was a few days, and share the danger, or, if contrary to their apprehensions, the robbers should have fled the country, he would then have the satisfaction of leaving them as happy as he found them.

Waving therefore all considerations of self-interest, and repelling the extreme solicitude he felt for returning into Suabia, he frankly told the steward, "he would not leave them until he saw the event of what they so much dreaded. A day or two (said he) will, I hope, do away all your fears; there is nothing in this Castle to tempt their avarice, and surely they will scarcely neglect their own safety, and hazard a discovery, solely from a desire of revenge." They heard him, and were pleased at the moment; but when fear has taken absolute possession of the mind, hope is but a temporary guest, and is soon clouded with redoubled terrors at the slightest circumstance that justifies their first emotions.

Thus it happened to them, for soon after he had succeeded in raising them from their dismal apprehensions of death and murder, one of the men came in with a small box he had found in the wood just behind the Castle. This box was opened, and, to their infinite surprise, contained a gold watch, three diamond rings, of no very great value, a purse with thirty Louis-d'ors, and two embroidered handkerchiefs.

"This box was certainly dropped by the robbers," exclaimed the steward; "they are hid in the wood, and when they have secured all their property they will come and be revenged on us." His wife instantly caught the alarm; she cried, and wrung her hands, "lamented the day that ever they had indulged people's curiosity to be their own destruction."

Ferdinand was obliged to give way to the torrent, and remained silent till the turbulence of grief and passion had exhausted itself; then he told them, "he had no doubt but that the gang had dropped the box; at the same time he still believed they were gone from that neighbourhood without any intention of returning, and advised sending the two men at the different post towns to gain intelligence."

But their fears would not let them part with the men beyond sight of the house, and they passed that day and the succeeding night under the same horrors, and with as little rest as the former ones. When the *second* morning came, it brought a return of spirits, and a glimmering of hope, which Ferdinand encouraged, as indeed his own apprehensions were now done away, and therefore the serenity of his aspect gave weight to his words, and had the desired effect of restoring some degree of tranquillity to their minds.

In the course of the day the steward's wife was capable of admiring the contents of the box, and asked, with some *little* earnestness, what was to be done with them, and to whom they must belong?

"To *you*, undoubtedly," said Ferdinand; "it is impossible to guess at, or to find the owner, as they may have been years in the robber's possession;

nor is the value of that magnitude to make them of any mighty consequence to a person, such as we may suppose the owner to have been. The
watch and rings you will keep; should any inquiry be made, you can restore
them; but the money you may use without scruple."

This opinion of Ferdinand's so exactly corresponded with her's, that in
a moment her countenance cleared, and if she had any fears, the loss of her
riches was the most predominant one. A tolerable quiet night succeeded,
and the third day restored them all to so much composure, that the good
woman now praised Ferdinand for his courage in "routing the robbers, and
convincing the neighbourhood that no ghosts had lived there."

She was one of those very prudent persons, who, feeling their own interest concerned, chuse always to judge by the event of things in their own
favour, without considering the *causes* of the fit, or the unfit.

Matters being thus returned into the accustomed channel with the
steward and his family, Ferdinand was impatient to leave them, particularly
as he had no letters from Vienna. He wrote a second time to the Count,
declaring his intention of going immediately to Baden, and to remain in the
house of Mr. Dunloff, until apprised of the Count's and Mr. D'Alenberg's
arrival at their seats.——That same evening he had the satisfaction to hear,
he might embark the next morning for Ulm. He took leave of his hospitable
friends with much kindness, and requested to hear from them, should they
gain any information of the robbers.

With an eager desire to return, but with the most tormenting ideas
and suspicions, that wrung his very soul with sorrow, he entered that boat
which was to convey him to his own country, where he was to investigate
such events as must realize those suspicions, or involve him in a cloud of
doubt for the remainder of his days.

So many, and so various, were the causes that produced sorrow and
misery to Ferdinand, that there existed no possibility of future comfort, or
any cure for those wounds severally inflicted by those he had loved.

The weather was favourable, and he was soon landed at Ulm, where,
on application to a Gentleman who knew his family, he was furnished with
money to pay his passage, and carry him on his journey.

Without meeting any accident on the road, he at length arrived at
Baden; but as he drew near to the spot inhabited by his brother, once in
the possession of a beloved and revered father, he turned his head from the
Castle of Renaud, shrunk with horror from the ideas that crowded on his
mind, and, as if blasted by the view, almost flew on to the city, and arrived
at the house of Mr. Dunloff sick and breathless.

The good man flew out to receive him: "Heaven be praised!" said he, and seeing his situation he conducted him to a room, making him drink a bumper of wine, which a little restored him.

"Oh! Sir," cried Mr. Dunloff, "Heaven has sent you in a critical minute, Providence often permits the wicked man to triumph for a time, only to make its justice more conspicuous in the punishment of the offender."

"What do you mean?" said Ferdinand:—"Tell me, how are my dear children?"

"Do not grieve to be told, Sir, that your little daughter is in Heaven. Master Charles is well, and every thing the fondest father can wish him to be. Your little girl has been recalled to its native skies about a fortnight since, no care was wanting, but a weak constitution sunk under the malady of the measles, and—she is at rest."

Seeing Ferdinand was affected, he went on to divert his ideas into another source.—"You must prepare your mind, Sir, for a shocking and interesting discovery, my uncle——"

"The good Ernest?" cried Ferdinand.—"I am ungrateful not to have asked for him." "He is wonderfully recovered, Heaven has heard his prayers, and prolonged his life to see the completion of his wishes. Ah! Sir, your brother"—"What of him?" said Ferdinand, starting at the name—"is in a state of distraction; for this week past he raves incessantly; he has deeply injured you, and now all is discovered."

"Has he then confessed, is it possible it can be true, that he hired a villain to murder me? But before I hear more (said he) let me see my poor Charles." Mr. Dunloff, who stood in an attitude of wild amazement, started, and rung the bell. The lovely boy soon appeared, and flew into the arms of his father. His features were too like the deceased Claudina's not to make Ferdinand's heart bleed at the recollection; he pressed him to his bosom, and for a few moments the tender feelings of nature precluded speech.

Dunloff, who was impatient to explain every thing of so much importance, besought him to let Charles retire for the present.—The other consented in silence, when the tutor said, "Your last words, Sir, overpowered me! Is it possible the Count can have proceeded to such terrible lengths as your question seemed to imply?"

"I hope not (said Ferdinand) for gladly would I believe the villain wronged him."—"Before I request a more explicit account of this alarming business, let me send to my uncle, and rejoice him with the news of your safe arrival."

"I understood," said Ferdinand, "that he had quitted my brother——."

"Yes, Sir, but the Countess sent for him again when the Count was seized with this dreadful disorder of his senses."

Mr. Dunloff being returned into the room, after he had dispatched a messenger, respectfully entreated Ferdinand to explain those words which had so greatly shocked him.—He very readily took up his story from the arrival of his brother's messenger to the present hour, repeating the particulars which the assassin had told him in his momentary fit of penitence.

During this recital Mr. Dunloff expressed the utmost surprise and horror.—"How true is the observation (exclaimed he) that one crime leads to a thousand others, and that when a man has made his mind familiar with guilt, he proceeds on to the most detestable actions, and plunges headlong into the blackest enormities! Gracious Heaven! that jealousy and avarice should gradually tend to robbery and murder!

"I would prepare you, Sir, for the scenes you must witness, and the shocking discovery that will wound every feeling of your heart; but I know not where or how to begin, the packet must speak for itself."

"What packet?" demanded Ferdinand.

"It was written and delivered by Madam Claudina to my uncle, with a strict charge not to deliver it to you till after her death, and then you was to have it without delay.

"This packet my uncle entrusted, sealed up, to me for you, lest death should suddenly cut him off, and his papers fall under the inspection of his master. When Madam Claudina was seized with her last illness, the consequence of the general report, and belief of your death, for it threw her into fits that at last occasioned the termination of her existence. She wrote a letter to Count Rhodophil, conjuring my uncle to deliver it himself, and at the same time permitted him to open the packet entrusted for you, to read it, and keep the bond enclosed for the benefit of her son.

"She expired in true penitence for her sins, and I humbly hope the Almighty will extend his mercy towards her. My uncle, borne down with sorrow for your supposed death, though he would sometimes indulge a hope against all apparent probability, was so overcome with the sad scene of her last hour, that he fell ill, and could not attend on the Count; I was commissioned to do it, and accordingly waited upon him: I found him in high spirits, the Countess in the room.

"I had only sent in my name: I took the letter from my pocket, which had been superscribed by my uncle, and delivered it. He broke the seal, and opened it; instantly his colour changed, his hands trembled, and his whole frame was agitated.

" 'Bless me, Sir (said the Countess) what ails you?' The hypocrite struggled to recover himself; he falteringly told her, 'it was a letter that announced the death of an old friend, whom he was grieved to lose.'

" 'I thank you, Sir (said he to me;) be so good to tell your uncle I shall call at his apartment, and ask how he does by and bye.'

"To give you an idea of his confusion and tremulous voice is impossible. The Countess looked extremely surprised: I gave him a penetrating glance, and withdrew.

"The next morning he saw my uncle; he first soothed him, and tried to get the packet Claudina had given him; but in vain were persuasions and threats, for he at length told him it was not in his possession. This highly irritated him; many words passed, which ended in his bidding my uncle to leave his house.—Nothing could be more impolitic, knowing how much he was in his power; but he trusted to the honour of a man he treated ill, and soon repented of his behaviour.

"That night my uncle was removed to this house; the Count heard of it, and met him as he was carrying out. He pressed him to turn back.

" 'No, Sir,' said he, 'an old and faithful servant can be turned out but *once*.—You fear me, and therefore you hate me; but I never shall disturb the peace of your family.' My uncle continued a long time in a fluctuating way, which at last turned to a fit of the gout, and held him many weeks.

"During this time your letter came, I could scarcely credit my senses when I saw the address, and prepared my uncle well as I could; but indeed he almost expired with joy when I presented it to him. The next day, Peter, the Count's man, called 'to ask after Mr. Ernest,' he said; but I believe to observe whether we had received a letter, which was made no secret of.—'This will be bad news to somebody,' said he, and withdrew not much pleased I thought.

"A few days after he called again; the Count, he said, was very low spirited, eat nothing, and he believed was going fast. 'He talks of sending for his brother to make his peace with him before he dies.'—'Indeed! (said my uncle) well, then I shall think he *does* repent; my poor master *must know all*, for I pledged myself to deliver Madam Claudina's letter after her death.'—Peter said it would be better not, it would only make Mr. Ferdinand unhappy. Away he went, and a day or two after we heard you were sent for.

"About a week ago Peter came again in a violent hurry; his master was desperately ill in a bad fever, seized the day before, just after writing a letter to Vienna to Mr. Ferdinand's friends, to know why he did not come as he expected. That night the fever grew worse, he was light-headed, and talked at random, often called for his brother and Ernest, therefore the Countess begged my uncle would come to the Castle. He was but poorly, yet thought it his duty to go, and has remained there from that time.

"Your brother still continues in a deplorable way, sometimes furious, at other times melancholy, and has made such discoveries of his crimes, as though they must prove beneficial to you, yet, will, I am sure, give you infinite deal of pain, I mean with respect to the will he destroyed, and which your father, the late Count Renaud, made a few days before his death."

"Is it possible," cried Ferdinand, "and was *I* remembered in that will?"

"Yes, Sir, he gave you his blessing, and pardoned all your undutiful conduct, and persevering obstinacy, and left a handsome fortune to your children."

Before Ferdinand could reply, so greatly was he agitated, the messenger returned from Ernest, and Ferdinand was desired to hasten to the Castle. He obeyed the summons, and was first conducted to the Countess; they met with a little confusion on both sides; she was greatly affected.

"Your unhappy brother (said she) has, within the last two hours, been restored to his reason; the physicians say it is the last effort of nature, and bespeaks approaching death: He has been informed of your arrival; much caution was used to break it to him, but he bore it without any great emotion. He said he wished to be private with Ernest, and I withdrew. Now I will inform him you are here."

Ferdinand was so inexpressibly shocked, and so reluctant to see a man in the agonies of death, whose life had been so culpable, that when the Countess returned in tears, and besought him to hasten into the room, his legs trembled under him, and with great difficulty he tottered into the apartment, where a sight met him sufficiently dreadful to appal the stoutest resolution.

Rhodophil was supported by pillows, his face long, pale, and distorted, his eyes wildly rolling then on Ernest, who supported him on one side, as Peter did on the other, and then throwing them upwards with an earnest supplicating stare. Ferdinand stopped a moment irresolute whether to proceed or not.—Rhodophil's eye dropping, fixed on him, "Save me! save me! (he cried) he comes to strike daggers to my soul!"

"Compose yourself, Sir" (said Ernest.)—Ferdinand advanced to the bed, the scene before him, the horrors of his brother's mind penetrated to his heart. He threw himself on his knees, "I beseech you, Rhodophil, to be composed, to *forgive yourself;* Heaven is my witness, that of whatsoever nature, and however great, are the injuries you have done me, I forgive you, and most earnestly pray that Heaven may extend its mercy towards you."

"You know not what you say (cried he, looking wildly on his brother;) my crimes are beyond pardon, cannot be forgiven, here or hereafter."

"And who shall dare to limit the mercy of Heaven?" said Ferdinand; "the magnitude of your crimes may deserve punishment, but what can exceed the torments you now feel?"

"O, it is horror indeed!" cried the wretched man: "Let the guilty look on me and tremble, foul deeds will come to light; see, see, there is Claudina calling on me, imprecating curses on my head, me, the seducer of innocence, the destroyer of my brother's honour."

"Gracious Heaven!" cried Ferdinand, and sunk on the floor. This sight threw Rhodophil into ravings: "Now, now, I have murdered him again! See! how the blood streams, it covers me, hide, hide me, from his blood!" During this dreadful paroxysm they had recovered Ferdinand, and placed him in a chair by the bedside. He viewed the guilty Rhodophil with averted looks of mingled horror and compassion.

He again recovered a temporary interval of reason on seeing his brother raised from the floor: "Ferdinand (said he) I have been a most atrocious villain—I have ever deceived and betrayed you; my father's spirit, for I have heard *his voice* more than once, has warned, has upbraided me, for my crimes: Hark! hark! I hear him now. O, pardon! pardon!" Again he fell into ravings, till again exhausted, by the use of cordials, reason weakly returned. At this moment Ernest fell on his knees: "Do you, Sir, pardon *me*, and compose your spirits—it was *my voice* that has occasionally alarmed you."

"How!" cried Ferdinand, "was it *your* voice that addressed itself to me?"

"I confess it, Sir," said Ernest, "I had many suspicions, and some proofs that you were most unfairly dealt with; excluded from my good master's sight long before he died, by misrepresentations, I could gain no access to him either in person or by letter. I had heard much, but not enough to found proofs upon, nor would *my* single testimony avail. I saw your misery and despair when cut off from all hope of a last forgiveness. I concealed myself in a closet, and in the agony of the moment, the words I pronounced, you thought proceeded from the dead body of your father. Heaven forgive me, if I did wrong; but it tranquillized *your* mind, and that was my only object.

"Twice afterwards I made use of the same device; the last time, the deceit was surely meritorious, for *then* I was master of a secret that froze me with horror; but to spare *you*, I had recourse to that method of warning you from——."

"O, Heavens!" said Ferdinand, "what a black scene of iniquity opens before me! Unhappy man!" cried he, violently agitated; "What indeed must be the torture of your mind!" Rhodophil gasped for breath, every feature seemed convulsed, he struggled for speech.

"Pray for me, pray for the wretch who cannot pray for himself."—More cordials were administered, and a temporary strength returned: "Now, now,

I can speak; I always hated you," said he, hastily addressing Ferdinand; "I sought to warp our father's mind against you, and pretended love to wound more deeply.

"I saw and loved Claudina; I tried to buy her of Dupree through an agent; she loved you; my offers were rejected. In revenge I persuaded you to marry, knowing *that* would ruin you with your father. *I* informed him of it. He disbelieved it. He sent for you; all was discovered, and drove you from the house.

"*I* intercepted every letter, and represented you careless of his affection, and deficient both in love and duty, yet I pleaded with him to forgive you when I had worked him to a pitch of fury that made him outrageous.

"*I* kept Ernest from his confidence, by assuring him he had encouraged you. Under these impressions, one day, in a great fury, he made a will in my favour; but I believe grief, for your supposed neglect of him, preyed upon his mind, he fell into a swift decay.

"I told him you knew of his illness, but never inquired for him; once or twice Ernest petitioned for you, but he disregarded him.

"A week before his death he one day called me to his bed—'Tell the ungrateful Ferdinand (said he) that on my death-bed I forgive him: I revoke a curse that has preyed upon *my* spirits; may Heaven forgive his unnatural behaviour, *as I do.*'

"The next day he sent for his lawyer; I was alarmed; the lawyer was from home, the clerk came; he would make a new will, he did so: I pretended to rejoice at it. He left your children his estate in Bavaria, and you a thousand crowns a year, with the small farm on the skirts of the Forest; also an annuity to Ernest of two hundred crowns.

"Those bequests were not much in comparison to what I became heir to, but it made you independent, and that was death to me.

"I sounded the clerk; I found him fit for my purpose; he was friendless and venal. The will was destroyed. I kept every one from the room till my father expired; the rest you know.

"Then to complete my revenge I had you at the Castle.

"I poisoned the mind of Claudina; I told a thousand falsehoods; you assisted my designs by going to the army; I made her believe you repented of your marriage, which occasioned your melancholy; in short I succeeded, I corrupted her mind, and dishonoured her person.

"Revenge was complete—she was pregnant—you returning—I sought to persuade her to destroy the child—she was taken ill—miscarried—and all we thought was well.

"You returned; *the voice,* which *she* thought supernatural, threw her into horrors. She sent for Ernest, confessed she had wronged you, and, having sworn *him* to secrecy, got him to procure her escape.

"I had reason to fear Ernest, therefore did not dare to discharge him. My mind was always distracted, terror and guilt my constant companions, for I always dreaded a discovery.

"The clerk who had made the will went into Austria—he spent the money in dissipation—joined with a set of gamblers—frequently made demands upon me for money, accompanied with threats.

"At length news arrived of your death; then I thought my misery at an end, and my fears all done away. One only trouble remained: I had married solely that you nor your children should be benefitted after my death: My wife seemed not likely to have children; your boy must inherit, that distracted me; I could not come at him, he was too well taken care of, and I was still in the power of Ernest during the life of Claudina.

"Happily, as I thought, she died soon after; but her letter spoke daggers to my soul, and made me fearful of my own shadow.

"Whilst I was struggling with this imbecility of mind, came an account of your being still in existence which rendered me desperate, and resolve on your death as the only chance of escaping shame and punishment, Claudina having informed me that she had left a packet for you, confessing all her crimes.

"I wrote to the man who had before but too well served me, and held out such advantages, promised such a sum as I knew he would not resist, and when he had completed your destruction, he was to meet me at Ulm, and receive his reward.

"I made an excuse of business to go there, and wait the event. He came, assured me that you was murdered, and thrown into the river; and added, that being associated with a set of men, who were both gamblers and robbers, it was their intention on his return to leave the country with their booty, and go into England, and as banditti were known to infest those mountains, it would be generally believed both you and him had been plundered and murdered.

"I hugged myself in security, gave him the promised reward, returned home, and pretended to be uneasy that you did not arrive: I believed myself safe from a discovery, when the avenging hand of Heaven was uplifted to overwhelm me with the punishment due to my crimes.

"Eternal justice preserved *you*, and the day of retribution is at hand; a life of deceit, crimes and falsehoods, will soon be terminated *here*, and my soul trembles for its doom *hereafter*."

CHAPTER VIII.

THUS ended the confession of the wretched guilty Rhodophil, which was not made without many breaks, pauses, and frequent refreshments, to enable him to proceed in the dreadful story; but we would not notice them to interrupt the narrative.

Ferdinand sat fixed in the chair; his eyes rivetted on his brother, or occasionally thrown up to Heaven; he shuddered with horror, but spoke not a single word.

When the story was concluded, and the miserable object before him lay gasping for breath, he clasped his hands, tears streaming down his cheeks.

"Gracious father!" said he, "extend *thy* mercy to this unhappy man; may the long torment conscious guilt has inflicted—may the unspeakable terrors of a distracted mind plead in mitigation of his crimes; and may his sufferings obtain the same forgiveness from Heaven, which, with my whole soul, I accord to him here."

To this fervent address, Ernest pronounced an amen.—The wretched man seemed inwardly to join in prayer; he lay exhausted and speechless; the effort he had made during the confession of his crimes, reduced him to the last extremity; nor could he utter a single word for some time.

At length he wished to be alone with Ernest: Ferdinand, with tottering steps, reached the antichamber, and sunk on a sofa, overpowered by the recollection of what he had heard, and hardly believing it possible human nature could be debased by such deliberate malice and unheard of wickedness.

He remained for three hours alone; for he could not see any one, but was at length again summoned to the sick chamber; Rhodophil had again recovered speech, and besought him once more to pronounce him forgiven, and to join Ernest in prayers for him to Heaven.

Poor—poor Rhodophil! On the bed of death, with all the horrors of a guilty conscience, who can describe thy feelings; what lethean draught can silence the inward monitor, than now shrinks trembling from the view of futurity!!!

Most fervent were the prayers they offered to the throne of mercy; he seemed to have a temporary calmness, and at last dropped into a slumber. Ferdinand was persuaded to withdraw; the Countess had ordered a bed for him; he gladly retired to it for a few hours, to recover his spirits.

The night passed without any change;—Rhodophil dozed, started, and often waked in great horror, but his senses were not much deranged. In the morning Ferdinand entered the room just as he had desired to see his Countess; they met at his bedside; he spoke very inwardly, and with much difficulty of respiration, he entreated her pardon for many acts of unkindness and inattention; owned his motives for marrying her were her large fortune, and the hope of an heir to prevent Ferdinand or his son from succeeding him.

He praised and blessed her.—Then taking Ferdinand's hand, he feebly prest it,

"Be her friend," said he.—"May Heaven bless you, and pardon me.—See the end of guilt and duplicity.—Truth and innocence only can make a death-bed easy.—The virtuous man looks forward with hope; the guilty one with fear and trembling—Heaven have mercy on me!!!"

Those were the last words he spoke.—Violent convulsive hiccups soon came on, which drove the Countess and Ferdinand to their respective apartments, unable to support the last struggle of nature; and in less than a quarter of an hour, the latter was informed the dreadful scene had closed!!!

Thus then expired the unhappy Rhodophil, only seven and twenty years of age.—Ferdinand requested Ernest and Mr. Dunloff to take the management of every thing upon themselves, for he was incapable of giving directions; he entreated them to let the confession of the wretched Rhodophil rest in their own bosoms, and, if possible, never to hint a word relative to the story, on any occasion whatever. This they faithfully promised; and at his request, Mr. Dunloff undertook to write for him to Count M*** and his friends, directing them at the Count's castle; and if he was not arrived, to have them forwarded to Vienna.

We will now look back on the friends of Ferdinand, who were suffering the most painful inquietude on his account. The day preceding the one appointed by them to leave Vienna, the Count called on Heli at the interpreter's, and, to his surprise, found him preparing to leave Germany in a few days.

"I was coming to you," said he; "a great revolution has taken place in my affairs;—the Grand Seigneur is dead; his successor was the friend of our family; my uncle is appointed to a place of much eminence, and I shall return to my own country without fear, and sure of preferment.

"Your bounty to me, therefore, I intended to resign, and only request a sufficient sum to carry me safe into Constantinople.—I go with joy, for I like neither your country or customs; and the women I detest.

"The ungrateful Fatima will have cause to repent her desertion of me, now I might have placed her at the head of a hundred women, perhaps; but no matter, I shall soon find others to please and console me."

The Count was not sorry to hear of this change in Heli's hopes and circumstances;—he assured him of their ready concurrence to his wishes, and took leave of him to get the business immediately settled. They also procured the liberty of the man who had been detained as a witness against Fatima, as after a fruitless search, they had given up any farther inquiry.

On the following day, Mr. D'Alenberg, his daughter, Louisa, the Countess of Wolfran, the two Barons, and the Count M***, accompanied by their servants, left Vienna, determined to proceed through Lintz, and make some inquiries after Ferdinand. The ladies were entirely unacquainted with their apprehensions for his safety, and supposed him with his brother.

As they stopt at the same inn Ferdinand had rested in, they were quickly informed of his leaving Lintz on the very day he had written to them, and, in their course of inquiries, learnt that a band of robbers sometimes infested the neighbouring hills and woods, which made it extremely hazardous for passengers, and therefore the landlord persuaded the company to go the lower road, as having less woods to travel through.

This account made them excessively apprehensive that Ferdinand had unhappily fallen in with the gang, and had been murdered. The Count accused himself incessantly, and protested, that, should any accident have befallen his friend, he never should enjoy peace more, or forgive himself, for not insisting upon going with him.—The Barons were extremely concerned; Mr. D'Alenberg overpowered with sorrow.

His extreme dejection, and the inquietude not to be concealed, which pervaded the countenance of Count M***, alarmed the ladies, and Miss D'Alenberg earnestly inquired of her father the cause of so visible a disorder.—He tried to evade her curiosity, but only augmented it, because perfectly assured he *was* uneasy, his endeavours to hide it from her, proved it was a matter of some consequence; she therefore caught the infection of her father's looks, and though she ceased to importune him, she saw there was some affliction preparing for her, which he was unwilling to communicate.

The Countess and Louisa were not more composed; each thought the painful secret must concern herself, and were equally unhappy.

A general air of concern pervaded through the whole party, and every one seemed to avoid particular conversation, though the Count, impressed with the idea that Miss D'Alenberg viewed him with some degree of preference, which indeed was justified by her behaviour to him; exerted all his endeavours to assume a tranquillity far distant from his heart, that he might not communicate his uneasiness to her: But the disguise was too flimsy to succeed, and only the more strongly convinced her that something lay hid, that would not bear investigation.

Mr. D'Alenberg had a small estate at Augsburg; he proposed to his friends going there, and sending off an express to Count Rhodophil, also, another to Mr. Dunloff.—This proposal met their approbation; the Barons could not resolve to separate themselves from the party, until some intelligence was gained to remove or confirm their present conjectures.

The ladies made no opposition; they frankly avowed to each other the painful suspense which tortured their imaginations, and anxiously sought for some clue to elucidate the mystery, but it was plain they must wait for the discovery.

They proceeded on to Augsburg, a very unsocial party, and arrived there without any accident: Being unexpected, they were not presently, or comfortably accommodated, but they were not fastidious, and bore inconveniencies without repining.

The same night of their arrival, two messengers were procured; letters written and sent off: One of them was ordered to proceed on to the Count's estate, if he obtained no satisfactory answer from Mr. Dunloff.—The gentlemen took a walk in the garden after this business had been expedited. There was a small pavilion of two rooms, each opening into, and fronting different walks, with a communication door between them.

The gentlemen entered one of these rooms and sat down.

"I am convinced," said the Count, as if continuing a conversation—"I am convinced, that if we do not gain satisfactory information from the return of the expresses, it will be impossible to impose longer on the sagacity of the ladies, already so much alarmed; we cannot dissemble our inquietude, and the dreadful certainty of what we fear, if unhappily it proves such, *must* be known to them at last."

"True," answered Mr. D'Alenberg;—"but whilst there exists a possibility that Ferdinand lives, I would not wound them by our——."

He had not time to finish the sentence;—an exclamation of "Help, help," from the adjoining room, caused them to pull open the door, where they beheld Miss D'Alenberg on the floor, the Countess and Louisa endeavouring to raise her.

They flew to her assistance; she was cold and senseless; what a sight for a father!—Poor Mr. D'Alenberg was in agonies: The young Baron, more collected, had hastened to the house, and returned with drops and water, which, on applying, she shewed signs of returning life, and was raised and placed on two chairs, Louisa supporting her in her arms.

She opened her eyes, and saw the whole group standing round her, her father holding her hand between his trembling ones.

"Ah!" said she, "Ferdinand is then dead!"

"Not so, I hope, my dear Theresa," replied he tenderly.

"Dying, if not dead," returned she, "the dreadful certainty will soon arrive—A *second time* to feel this blow—alas! 'tis too, too much to bear."

Mr. D'Alenberg and the ladies besought her to retire into the house; she submitted in silence to their wishes, and was supported through the garden; the Count remained rooted to the spot, inconceivably astonished at a discovery so little expected.

"What an unfortunate adventure," said Baron Reiberg, "that we should be overheard; I had not the smallest idea of Miss D'Alenberg's attachment to our friend."

"Nor *I*, I promise you," returned the Count, trying to recover from his surprise; "nor I am sure had Ferdinand."

"But if he lives," said the Baron, "as he is now a disengaged man, I hope the young lady will be happy; for she is a most charming young woman."

"Indeed she is," replied the Count;—"Heaven grant my friend may be alive; the rest we must leave to Providence."

They returned to the house, not a little disconcerted that accident had revealed what they had so industriously sought to conceal.

Mean time, Mr. D'Alenberg found it requisite, for the peace of his daughter, to enter into a full explanation of their hopes and fears; disguise would no longer avail to impose upon her, and he candidly laid every thing before her.

When he had concluded, and again mentioned *hope*,

"My dear Sir," said she, interrupting him, with a solemnity of look and accent, that penetrated to his heart—"my dear Sir, do not attempt to delude me with *hope*; rather seek to strengthen my mind, and fortify it to expect the worst. I always told you, because I always felt, that the preference I entertained for that unfortunate young man would terminate unhappily.

"It was the soft melancholy of his air, the tuneful accents of his voice, and the effusions of a bright understanding and pleasing vivacity, which now and then broke through the cloud that seemed to overcast his mind: It was those affecting appearances that stole insensibly into my heart, and to see Ferdinand was to pity him; pity soon ripened into esteem and affection, and now there is an end of all."

"Do not decide so peremptorily," said her father; "*hope* may still exist."

"You once before told me so, Sir," returned she; "but I have never listened to the flatterer; yet I had brought my mind to a comparative degree of content, when he was so unexpectedly restored to us; not that I could ever flatter myself with his esteem, nor circumstanced as he was, ought I to have wished for it."

"Dear Theresa," said Mr. D'Alenberg, "those circumstances are changed; he has lately lost his wife, from whom he was parted."

"Why would you tell me so, to enhance my distress? Oh! my dear father, my Louisa, assist me to derive courage from the extent of my misfortunes; teach me to submit to the dispensations of Providence, that I may not cloud the last days of a beloved parent with sorrow, by an imprudent attachment."

Her father embraced her with streaming eyes, entreating her not to give way to despair, though he could hardly bid her to indulge hope. He retired and left her with the ladies, and in the evening she appeared at supper with them.

The gentlemen were agreeably surprised; she tried to eat, though she could not swallow three mouthfuls; she endeavoured to speak, to smile, but it was a smile of woe that shocked every one present; but her efforts were astonishing to her father, and convinced him of the dignity of her mind, and what struggles she was capable of, to afford him peace.

Four days of painful suspense they had endured, in which the delicate frame of Miss D'Alenberg seemed to be falling a sacrifice to the strength of her mind, and the assumption of a fortitude her spirits but ill supplied. They were sitting at the dinner table when the return of a messenger was announced; she turned faint and sick.

"I will retire, if you please," said she to her father, and accompanied by her two friends, tottered out of the room.

With difficulty, they preserved her from fainting.

"I shall soon know the *worst*," said she, "and that is some degree of ease from this dreadful uncertainty. If he lives, I am indifferent as to *myself*; for where there is no expectation, there can be no disappointment."

Her trembling frame spoke the agitations of her heart, when suddenly the door opened, and Mr. D'Alenberg appeared with an animated countenance.

"*He lives*," she exclaimed; and leaning her head on the bosom of Louisa, burst into a flood of tears, the first she had shed for three days.

"*He does*, my dear Theresa; a letter from Mr. Dunloff has restored us all to happiness.

"He lives, indeed, wonderfully preserved, and arrived only two days before the messenger.—His brother had expired that day, and therefore both men went to Dunloff's, who quickly sent one back with intelligence so much desired; the other is gone on to Count M***'s, to give notice of his return."

Mr. D'Alenberg might have proceeded for an hour; his beloved daughter heard nothing, thought of nothing, but "Ferdinand is alive; yes, that amiable and unfortunate young man is the care of Heaven; his life is preserved!!!"

"Will you not come down, my Theresa, and hear read, or read yourself, this charming letter? We shall pursue our journey tomorrow, if you are capable of bearing the fatigue."

"Yes," said she, starting up; "let me hear the letter, dear Sir—how good you are."

She descended to the parlour, where Mr. Dunloff's letter was presented to her; she devoured the contents with great avidity, and joined, with astonishing composure, in the mutual congratulations they made each other, for the completion of their wishes.

The next morning they left Augsburg.—The two Barons resolved to attend them to Ulm, as they made that in their route to drop the Countess, who engaged, the moment she had settled her affairs, to bring her son with her, and spend some weeks at Mr. D'Alenberg's. The Barons took leave of her there; but young Reiberg so earnestly inportuned his father, that he might be permitted to accompany his friend the Count, that the old gentleman consented, and also engaged to join them very soon.

They all proceeded to the Count's mansion, as being nearest to Ferdinand; arrived there without any accident, and immediately sent a servant, with letters to Castle Renaud.

Those letters reached Ferdinand just as he returned from the funeral of his brother.—What delightful sensations sprung to his heart, when he found his friends were so near to him; he thought his obligations to them superseded the cold forms of decorum in circumstances like his, therefore, sending for his faithful old Ernest, he requested Mr. Dunloff and his son would come to the castle, and remain with him during his absence.

He had entreated the Countess to remain there, and command, as usual; but she declined the offer, and the day preceding the funeral, had removed to the house of a friend, until one of her own was ready to receive her. She had a good estate of her own, and a very handsome settlement from Rhodophil.

Ferdinand detained the messenger, that he might accompany him, and agreeably surprise his friends.—When he was announced, they could hardly credit the information;—all started up, and, in a moment, he received the embraces of his three friends: The ladies were present; Miss D'Alenberg behaved like a heroine; she said little, but that little was extremely proper.

At length he was quietly seated; they asked him a hundred questions in a breath.

"Spare me at present," said he; "I wish not to remember unpleasant scenes now, when I am so perfectly happy."

He certainly thought himself so at that moment; but soon after, when in conversation, he beheld Miss D'Alenberg speaking with some attention to the Count—Ah! thought he, how unfortunate, that such a charming young woman should encourage a hopeless passion.—Then the numberless little incidents in which he had admired her, came to his recollection; he watched her attentively; thought her more beautiful than ever, and again sighed that the Count was precluded from rendering her happy.

He was so lost in thought, and absorbed in attention towards them, that Mr. D'Alenberg was obliged to remind him that he had not once asked for the lovely Countess.

"Forgive me," said he: "I have the highest respect for that estimable woman, but I have my excuse before me. When looking at those ladies, is it possible to recollect any others.—I hope, however, you left that amiable lady well."

"Perfectly so," said Reiberg; "and 'tis only in this company that I can pardon your omission."

Ferdinand had always so carefully avoided saying even a gallant thing to a lady, that the little compliment he uttered caught the attention of Miss D'Alenberg; she looked at him; he withdrew his eyes, and fixed them on Louisa, to whom he addressed some trifling question, that called the blood from the cheeks of the other, and she again turned towards the Count.

He was a minute observer of the scene, and instantly thought he understood the recesses of Ferdinand's heart better than he did himself. Nor was the Count mistaken.

The very first day Ferdinand had seen Miss D'Alenberg, he was charmed with her humanity, and generous compassion for Louisa. The sentiments she uttered were so congenial to his own feelings, that her character was instantly decided in his breast to be a worthy one. He felt exceedingly for the base duplicity of Count Wolfran's conduct, and rejoiced that such a woman had not fallen a victim to it.

When at her father's house, she seemed still more worthy of admiration; the study, the chief pleasure of her life, was to obey and contribute to his amusement.—She was sensible without affectation; cheerful without levity; attentive to every part of domestic management, without the least ostentation: Added to which, her polite kindness to Louisa denoted a mind above the idea of *conferring* favours, but was herself the obliged person, in being permitted to offer them.

Such was the character of Miss D'Alenberg.—He admired, he revered her; but at that time, the recent unaccountable troubles that hung over him; his affection for Claudina, which, though weakened, was not extinguished, and his peculiar situation, impeded every thought of Miss D'Alenberg, otherwise than as a most estimable young woman.

But when the Count and himself had so fortunately met with Louisa, the story she related of her friend's melancholy and secret attachment, the dormant admiration of her person and mind, again blazed forth; he felt the sincerest concern for her situation, not entirely unmixed with envy, for the man who was the object of her preferable regard.—This object, his sagacity at length discovered to be Count M***, and he also was convinced the unfortunate partiality was a mutual one. Here then he sighed in silence, as he thought in pity to them, and in that pity stifled his own regrets.

When he received an account of Claudina's death, he was greatly affected; her ill conduct, though plainly avowed, had not effaced her image from his heart, or eradicated the tenderness which was once reciprocal.— He lamented her death; he grieved for her depravity; but his sorrow was not of that deep heart-felt kind, which he must have felt in other circumstances, because reason whispered to his mind that she had proved unworthy.

When Mr. D'Alenberg and his daughter arrived at Vienna, and he waited upon them, he saw, as he judged, a confirmation of his suspicions of the unfortunate preference that young lady entertained for the Count, and without being sensible of it himself, he certainly exhibited some little petulance in his conversation, which did not pass unobserved.

He was then sent for to his brother, and his agitations on that account superseded all other ideas. The subsequent events pretty much engrossed his mind; and it was not until his present arrival at the Count's, when he saw Miss D'Alenberg with circumstances so much altered in his own favour, that the sentiments he had long suppressed, and was scarcely conscious of, now burst full upon him, mingled with the painful regret that his friend possessed that invaluable heart he thought above all price; and from his unfortunate situation, was precluded from even a wish to profit by the preference he was honoured with, and of course both must be unhappy.

Thus have we accounted for the workings of Ferdinand's mind, and for those sentiments which now, for the first time, were no longer concealed from himself.

Louisa made her own observations in silence.—Her friend, who saw the direction of Ferdinand's eyes, and felt the little compliment that had escaped him, immediately gave Louisa the credit of it.

"Yes," said she, mentally, "I see the attraction, and now there exists, on either side, no obstacles to impede their union.—Well, then, I will teach my heart to rejoice in their happiness, and henceforth draw only on my dear father for my future tranquillity." Impressed with this idea, she turned her eyes tenderly towards her father, and saw an expression of joy in his, that greatly surprised her, but which she immediately attributed to the pleasure of seeing his friend.

In the evening, the company walked into the gardens, and strolling through the shrubbery, they accidentally fell into small parties.—Louisa designedly led her friend from the company, and seemed to be in very uncommon spirits; Miss D'Alenberg thought it was not *quite so decorous*; but she allowed for the human heart; and a conquest, such as Ferdinand, justified the little breach of delicacy towards a friend.

"You are more than usually cheerful, my dear Louisa?"

"Indeed I am; the arrival of our friend has gratified my warmest wishes."

"May every wish of your heart be realized; you may suppose *I* do not feel less pleasure, though his presence is not of that immediate consequence to me, as to my dear Louisa."

"Indeed," cried the other, at once penetrating into the nature of her feelings, "indeed, have you then changed your favourable opinion of Ferdinand, since he is become a *widower* and a *Count?*"

"No," said Miss D'Alenberg, a little piqued; "but I hope I have fortitude and generosity sufficient to change the nature of my sentiments in favour of my friends."

"I see," returned Louisa, "that you suspect the new Count has a partiality for me."

"It *was a suspicion,*" said the other; "but his behaviour this day amounts to a confirmation; and believe me, my dear Louisa, weak as you have seen me in many instances, I have acquired that command over my feelings, now that I see him alive and happy; that I am enabled to partake in your mutual felicity, though, for a time, perhaps I should not chuse to be an *eye-witness* of it."

"Generous friend," exclaimed Louisa, kissing her hand, "I know the sincerity of your heart, and doubt not but that the nobleness of your mind would support you under the most *painful* disappointment, if productive of happiness to those you love: But undeceive yourself, my beloved Theresa, Ferdinand respects me as the *friend* of Miss D'Alenberg; but my amiable Theresa is the sole possessor of his *heart.*"

"Impossible," cried she, "impossible, dear Louisa; you must be mistaken."

"Indeed I am not," returned she; "an attentive observer can translate the looks of a lover, and is not often mistaken; at least suspend your conclusion against him for a day or two.—I will be answerable for the events."

"Against him!" repeated Miss D'Alenberg; "his supposed preference of you does credit to his judgment."

"I shall not dispute *that* point with you," answered she, smiling, "because it gratifies my self-love; but here they come, and I only beseech you to open your eyes, and disperse the mist that clouds *your judgment*."

The gentlemen, who had joined in different walks, now approached the ladies, the eyes of Ferdinand meeting those of Miss D'Alenberg's. She blushed excessively, from thinking of the preceding conversation; she turned to Louisa, the archness of whose looks more greatly disconcerted her; her disorder was very visible, which, when Louisa remarked, she drew the attention off from her friend by a sprightly sally, that brought Mr. D'Alenberg upon *her*: He rallied her upon her gaiety, for which he was indebted, he said, to the company of their beaus. This passed off the confusion of his daughter, and she recovered her spirits.

CHAPTER IX.

THE next morning Mr. D'Alenberg and Ferdinand happened to meet in the avenue before the house, where the latter was strolling apparently lost in thought.—"My good friend," said the old Gentleman, "I have scarce had an opportunity to speak my perfect satisfaction at the termination of your troubles: I know not indeed all your story, but I know enough to interest me warmly in your happiness."

"You do me great honour, Sir," replied Ferdinand; "but though the veil is withdrawn from the mystery, which so long rendered me wretched, yet the disclosure has been attended with the knowledge of so many painful circumstances, that *at times* I feel my spirits sink under the recollection of them."

"Time, and a variety of objects," said Mr. D'Alenberg, "will, I hope, by and bye, have its usual effects, and blunt the remembrance of former sorrows. I thank Heaven, there is much alteration in the disorder that affected my daughter's spirits, from the very remedy I prescribe for you; do you not think her complexion and cheerfulness are returning?"

"I hope so," replied Ferdinand, "most fervently I hope it; every one must feel interested for a young lady so *truly* excellent, that the beauty of her person is her least perfection."

"I thank you for the warmth of your sentiments," said Mr. D'Alenberg, "which encourages me to speak freely to you; there is only one man in the world that I am desirous of calling son, *that man is a friend of your's.*"

"A friend of mine!" repeated Ferdinand, starting in great confusion, adding, in a tremulous voice, "any man must be highly honoured by such a distinction; but I am at a loss to guess who you mean."

"The Count's unfortunate situation sets *him* entirely out of the question," interrupted Mr. D'Alenberg.—"Indeed, Sir! the young Baron's predilection in favour of the Countess is not unknown to you."

"No," returned he, "that's a point settled. The Gentleman I mean has *now*, I believe, neither a prior engagement or attachment, he is one who engaged *my esteem* the first day I saw him, from particular traits of humanity and honour that I observed in him, and from the conversations, short as they were, that gave me a perfect good opinion of his head and his heart. Unfortunate circumstances at that time stepped between me and my wishes, which are now, I believe, all done away. Are you at a loss *now* to know *my man?*"

During this speech Ferdinand had been violently agitated; at the conclusion he caught the hand of Mr. D'Alenberg: "Ah! Sir, how flattering is your kindness; I will not affect to misunderstand you, but can that happy distinguished man presume to hope Miss D'Alenberg views him with the partial eyes of her father? No, he cannot, he dares not, flatter himself with an idea, his own observation convinces him would be erroneous."

"*You* would not then *decline* the connexion, should Theresa be more discerning than you are so ready to suppose?"

"*Decline!* dear Sir! to call *you* father; to contribute to the happiness of your lovely daughter, would indeed be to ensure my own, and render me the most enviable of mankind. Your kindness has dragged a secret forth from the inmost recesses of my heart, and by its palpitation convinces me, *that heart* is entirely engrossed by Miss D'Alenberg."

"Well," said the old Gentleman, infinitely delighted, "you shall not at any rate bear the torture of suspense, you shall speak to her this day, if she sees with her father's eyes, you have nothing to fear. If I am mistaken, and her inclination is not in your favour, I shall be sorry and disappointed; but—you shall ever be the son of my affection."

Ferdinand was so entirely overcome by this kindness, that words were denied to him, and, confused at his emotions, he turned abruptly from him.

The party assembled at breakfast, all seemed gay and happy except the two lovers. After the repast Mr. D'Alenberg asked the Ladies and Ferdinand to view a small pavilion the Count's steward had lately erected in a beautiful shrubbery.—The name of a pavilion caused his daughter to shudder.—She remembered a conversation which had passed in a similar place that had given her the most poignant grief; but no objection being made, they readily accompanied him, and were highly pleased with the steward's taste.

"There is another spot, not far off," said Mr. D'Alenberg, "where a small building may be erected to an advantage. Come hither, Louisa, I will have *your* opinion *first.*" She started up, took his arm, and they were out of sight in a moment.

Miss D'Alenberg was rooted to her seat in breathless terror; Ferdinand was little less discomposed, but recovering himself—"I know not, Madam, whether you will have the goodness to pardon my temerity in seizing this opportunity of opening to you my whole heart, a heart long tortured by the most painful events.

"Ever since I had the honour of knowing Miss D'Alenberg I have considered her as the most amiable of women, and respected her accordingly. My unhappy situation precluded every selfish wish, and *her* happiness was my first concern, independent of my own.

"That situation is now changed, and though perhaps I may err against the common rules of decorum, yet I hope Miss D'Alenberg will not condemn me if I am solicitous to know whether my future destiny is to be happy or wretched; if my kind stars ordain the former, then my anxiety is removed; if on the contrary *I am* to be unfortunate, the sooner I fly from hence the better.

"Need I add, Madam, that *you* are the arbitress of that destiny, that on *you* must rest all my hopes of future bliss? If you will deign to admit me a candidate for your favour, if no happier man has superseded me, and rendered all my hopes of felicity successless, if you will permit me to dedicate *my* future life to the delightful study of rendering *your's* happy, then indeed I may congratulate myself on being the most fortunate of mankind; the wounds which have been given by the hands of those I loved and trusted, and which yet rankle in my bosom, *you* only can heal, and from you I would derive that peace which the world has hitherto denied to me."

Whilst Ferdinand was speaking with an earnestness and solemnity in his manner that was truly touching, Miss D'Alenberg had time to recall her fleeting spirits, and compose her mind sufficiently to answer him, tho' not without some emotion.

"This address, Sir, is so unexpected, so opposite to the idea that I had entertained of your sentiments, that surprise has no small share in my too visible emotions; the love of candour, and a strict adherence to truth, were the first lessons I received from the best of mothers: Her precepts and example have governed every action of my life, I will therefore frankly confess."—She stopped.

"Ah! Madam, speak, go on, keep me not in suspense."

"I scarce know what I ought to say, yet I *will* confess, such is my esteem for your character, that I am persuaded, if I have really the power of contributing to *your* happiness, I cannot fail of insuring *my own*."

The moment she had pronounced the last words, Ferdinand threw himself on his knee, and kissed her hand:—"Forgive me," was all he could utter. She raised him, and for a moment both were silent.

"Your generous frankness, my dear Miss D'Alenberg, has overwhelmed me with rapture; my future life must speak my gratitude; joy is not eloquent when so complete as mine."

She arose—"If you please we will seek my father."—He took her hand, and obeyed in silence. They saw Mr. D'Alenberg and Louisa advancing.

"Heyday!" said the latter, "what are you both speechless? Have you exhausted all your stock of ideas, that not a single word is left to ask our opinion of the intended plan for building?"

"You are malicious, Louisa," returned her friend, blushing.

"Sorrow, my dear Madam," answered Ferdinand, "often makes people plaintive, and the overcharged heart sometimes finds relief in complaining; but joy is a miser, and I feel at present too happy to be communicative."

"Extremely well explained, I must own," said Louisa, "a few words has done the business. Come, my silent friend, *you* shall give me *your* opinion of our judgment!"—Saying this she drew Miss D'Alenberg away, leaving her father and Ferdinand together. The latter instantly embraced Mr. D'Alenberg. "I am the happiest of men!"

"*One* only of *the happiest*," replied he, returning the embrace, "for I share with you."

The party did not meet together till the dinner hour, but Mr. D'Alenberg had seized an opportunity to inform Count M*** and the young Baron of the completion of his wishes, and they very sincerely rejoiced in the promised happiness of Ferdinand.

At table Louisa was the most talkative of the company.—"I cannot help remarking, with an infinity of pleasure," said the Count, "on the agreeable change there is in your health and spirits, Madam."

"I am sure," answered she, "the intention of your remark is friendly, but not at all calculated to increase my cheerfulness, by reminding me of the alteration. Retrospections are not always pleasing, and I owe much of my health and spirits to a resolution henceforth to look forwards."

"I beg your pardon, my dear Madam," returned he, very seriously, "your reproof is very just, and I take shame to myself for the rudeness of my observation, which I entreat you to believe arose entirely from the real delight I felt in the charms of your conversation."

"It must be owned," said she, with a returning smile, "that you know how to extricate yourself from an error extremely well, and my self-love accepts of the apology."

They had scarcely dined when an express came from Ernest with letters to Ferdinand. He retired to read them, and was surprised to find one from the steward of the Castle of Danhaet, with information, that "two days after his departure, the hermit had called there for his customary allowance, and informed him, that he had been alarmed the preceding day by seeing some men come out of one of the caves in the rock; he was not discovered himself, but he supposed they were some proscribed persons, or banditti.

"This intelligence," continued the steward, "I instantly conveyed to the Magistrates, who sent a party of men that same night to the rocks, and they remained concealed in the hermit's cave to make their observations.

"About midnight a boat was seen advancing to the Beach; two men landed, and were presently out of sight, but in less than half an hour returned with four others, all well loaded. As they proceeded towards the boat, the guards silently issued from the cave, and were upon them before they were discerned. They threw down their booty, and attempted to fly; one fired a pistol; the fire was returned; in the same moment two fell, and they were surrounded, taken, and conveyed to Lintz.

"The two wounded were not in much danger. One of them, who was most hurt, proved to be the villain, who had imposed upon Ferdinand.

"Several robberies and frauds were proved against them, and they had property to a great amount. Amongst the rest, a casket of jewels, which they had defrauded a Lady of, and seduced her from Vienna, where they oftentimes went as Gentlemen, to obtain a knowledge of what travellers were going on the road.

"They had formerly dwelt in the caves under the hills; but hearing the foolish story that the pavilion was haunted; they availed themselves of it, to get possession there, and securing all the doors and windows so as to prevent a surprise, fixing a bell at the little area door, that, should any one attempt it, the persons below by groans might frighten, and impose on the credulity of the peasants, as the gang only came there at night, and had a watch word.

"This confession was made by the same villain who had before applied at the Castle, and the same cowardly spirit, generally attendant on roguery, had now induced him to make a complete discovery to save his life.

"He was not of the party when they took the jewels from the Lady, but had heard she had brought them from Turkey. What became of her after they had stripped her on the mountains, none of them could tell."

The steward concluded, by saying, that "there was little doubt but that they would all suffer for their crimes; the property remained in the hands of the Magistrates to be claimed."

This letter gave Ferdinand further occasion to admire at the justice of Providence, which sooner or later brings villany to its deserved punishment; for

> "Foul deeds will rise,
> Tho' all the earth o'erwhelms them, to men's eyes."

He had not the smallest doubt but that Fatima was the Lady from whom they had taken the jewels, and the two Gentlemen, with whom she embarked from Pratt's-Grove at Vienna, two of this abandoned gang of ruffians, though he lamented the depravity of her heart, and detested the baseness of her character, he saw a severe retribution had overtaken her, and therefore felt an anxiety, mixed with compassion, for the uncertain fate of one who claimed her being from his, more than ever, revered father.

He could not bear to reflect on the conduct of Rhodophil; a regular course of duplicity, instigated by the vilest passions, had pervaded through his whole life, and when he considered how greatly his own senses and reason had been imposed upon by his artful management, when he found that even his father had been the dupe of a profound dissimulation, difficult to be conceived in the heart of man. He sighed for the late unhappy Claudina, who had fallen a victim to the same complicated baseness.

Nursed in vice and dissipation, the seeds of virtue were never nourished in her bosom, and the wretch, to whose care she had fallen at an early age, had doubtless taught her but one lesson, "to make the most of her beauty," yet it is certain (thought he) that she loved me; that she bore adversity with sweetness and patience, and but for the insidious arts of a cruel spoiler, the dormant passions, which accelerated her ruin, for gaiety and dress, might have been buried in the duties of a wife and mother:

But a weak mind, and the taint of early dissipation, aided the work of a cruel enemy; and the progressive vice that marked *his* conduct, led him at last to the commission of the most horrid crimes.

From those dreadful objects he turned his eyes to contemplate and admire the exemplary conduct of his amiable friends, and most fervently offered his prayers to Heaven, that they might enjoy the happiness their virtues so well deserved; to those friends he returned, and communicated the contents of the letter he had received.

No one could be sorry that such a nest of villains were on the point of being extirminated; but Ferdinand could never prevail upon himself to charge his brother with the assassination he met with, nor the heinous crime which had led to it; those two particular atrocities he forbore to mention even to his best friends; he left them always to suppose he was only attacked in common with other passengers.

A week was spent at the Count's in all the delights of love and friendship, in which time the Ladies heard from the Countess, that "she had found no difficulty in having her affairs settled, no one had doubted her rights, nor any other claim seemed to be remembered; she hoped therefore, in less than a month, to join them at Mr. D'Alenberg's mansion."

The party now prepared to separate; the Baron to his father's Castle for a short time, having received an invitation to meet his beloved Countess; Mr. D'Alenberg, with his daughter and Louisa, to their own house; and the Count returning with Ferdinand, his affairs requiring his presence at Castle Renaud.

He found it extremely difficult to tear himself from his charming Theresa, but she pleaded delicacy and decorum. The recent death of his wife and brother, though separated from the one, and ill-treated by the other, had some claims to observance.

"I am far," said she, "from being a slave to forms, but the good opinion of the world is always worth preserving, and the sacrifice of one's inclinations for a short time, will be much less painful, than a consciousness of having forfeited that opinion by an appearance of *indecorum*; therefore, until our friends join us, you must not be offended if you are excluded from being an inmate of our house."

Ferdinand turned to Louisa, "Hasten the journey of your sweet Countess, my dear friend; the Baron will feel the attraction, and my time of probation will be shortened."—She nodded an assenting smile; but the remainder of the day passed not like the former ones; they knew they were to separate, and the idea threw a cloud over every countenance.

The next morning they parted different ways, for Miss D'Alenberg would not permit the Gentlemen to accompany them a step out of their road:—"Why should we prolong the pain we feel in separating?" said she; "Let the moment be short and decided; one adieu conveys the same meaning as a thousand." They submitted reluctantly to her wishes, and left the house immediately.

The Count had not heard from Eugenia since his return; he was uneasy at it, and had written to her the preceding day. Francis, their old attendant at the Solitary Castle, lived happy and contented under the protection of Mr. Duclos, the Count's steward, and blessed the day that brought Ferdinand to that desolate mansion.

The two friends arrived in safety at Castle Renaud, where the good and faithful Ernest was ready to receive them, accompanied by his nephew and little Charles. The Count was charmed with the sweet boy, and when he admired his features, thought Ferdinand perfectly acquitted for his strong attachment to his mother.

They had been three days at the Castle, when one evening Ferdinand was informed that a woman, of a very ordinary appearance, wished to speak with him; the Count would have withdrawn:—"By no means," said Ferdinand, and ordered her admittance.—She entered, wrapped in a long cloak, and her head so covered that no part of her face was visible but her eyes.

"What is your business?" demanded he.

"Justice!" replied she, fiercely, and throwing off her hood, discovered Fatima.

"Fatima!" exclaimed he.

"No longer Fatima," said she, "but Charlotte, daughter to the late Count Renaud, and as such entitled to be provided for by his heir."

Her astonishing assurance for a moment disconcerted both Gentlemen; but Ferdinand recovering, and looking on her with some indignation:

"The provision you so rudely demand was once *offered*, when I was less able to serve you, myself *then* supported by the bounty of a friend; but you will remember it was offered to you *conditionally*. Your birth does *not entitle* you to make any *demands* upon me; but the respect I owe to the memory of my father will incline me to do it, if you deserve it."

"I scorn the idea of an obligation," said she, "I come to claim my *right*, and to tell you, that secure as you think yourself of the title and estates you have taken possession of, I can annihilate *your* claims in a moment, if you dispute *mine*."

"Charlotte, since that is your name, do not injure yourself by an insolent asperity that ill becomes you: I am inclined to serve you, but it must be in my own manner, nothing shall be extorted from me."

"And I *disdain* a favour," said she:—"*Know then*, your father was *married* to my mother, consequently neither the late Rhodophil or yourself were entitled to inherit."

"This is so wild a chimera," said Ferdinand, "that I know not which to admire most, the impudence or the falsehood of the assertion."

"You shall find," returned she, "that it is a decided truth; I have two witnesses to prove the marriage, and shall immediately enter a process against you, unless you consent to give me a moiety of your fortune."

"And pray," asked Ferdinand, with a disdainful smile, "who, and where are your witnesses?"

"They are in Baden, and without you accede quietly to my proposal, to-morrow shall witness the publication of *my* claims, your father's memory shall be branded as it deserves, and you, *you* shall be known as the child of disgrace, assuming rank and title, to which you have no pretensions."

Never was astonishment equal to the Count's, or perturbation of spirits like Ferdinand's—that this fabricated story was an impudent forgery he had no doubt, and he was well assured could not be maintained; but then she was capable of promulgating the falsehood through the town, his father's memory would be branded by a hundred malicious tongues that delight in a tale of scandal; if in revenge she instituted a suit, he must appear to controvert her assertions, and in the mean time hold only a doubtful title, and a disputed estate.

Whilst he was silently revolving in his mind those perplexities, the Count was considering how to undermine this plot against the interest of his friend.

"I think," said he, mildly, "if this Lady has the proofs she speaks of, it will be much more for your interest and honour to compromise the affair between you, than to enter into a tedious process, that in the end must injure both; I would advise you, my friend, to deal cautiously, hear the witnesses, and, if you cannot disprove their testimony, then settle the business amicably between you.—The Lady can claim neither the title nor family estate, she may injure *you* by *her* claims, and throw both into another branch of the family, but she would be no gainer by that; supposing therefore her story to be just, it is for your mutual interest that it should not transpire beyond ourselves."

Whilst the Count was speaking, Ferdinand looked at him with the utmost surprise, but a turn in his eye undeceived him in a moment; therefore when he ended his observations, the other seemed to be considering, and at length, with an air of reluctance, replied, "Your counsel is difficult to follow, yet you are my only friend, and as such best entitled to advise me."

"Well, then, Madam, bring your witnesses to-morrow morning, I only request that till you have produced your proofs, and have my answer, you will not divulge to any one what you have said here."

"I do promise (said she) and will attend you to-morrow, when you will find it most for your advantage to pay attention to my demands, and the advice of your friend."—She then withdrew.

"This is the most impudent, ill-concerted scheme I ever heard of (said the Count.)—This woman knowing how tenderly you regard the reputation of your late father, has founded her plot upon your weakness: Now let us instantly send to Baden for officers of justice to be here at an early hour, and, my life for it, we shall frighten them into a confession, be the witnesses who they may."

Ferdinand was compelled to adopt this plan, though it did not exactly correspond with his inclination. This woman was the child of his father, as such he could have wished to save her from disgrace, and have made her life comfortable; but she insisted upon rights which his duty to himself and his heirs would not permit him to allow of.

He passed a sleepless night.—"Foolish mortals as we are (said he) when pluming ourselves in a fancied security of happiness! here is a blow, which, if persisted in, must at least interrupt, if not annihilate all my hopes of future felicity with Miss D'Alenberg; for no compromise will I make, or enjoy a doubtful title to which I have no claim.—Ah! (cried he) the sins of the fathers are multiplied upon their children! What a lesson to parents, what a pharos to the gay and dissipated of both sexes, when their crimes and follies are thus extended to their wretched posterity."

The morning came; he arose languid and unhappy; in vain the Count sought to disperse his gloomy ideas; every way he turned his thoughts, they were pregnant with trouble and vexation.

The officers came; they were placed in a closet adjoining to the room in which Ferdinand prepared to receive Fatima, or rather Charlotte. In a short time two women and a man were announced, one of whom proved to be Dupree, the man was unknown.

"How! (exclaimed Ferdinand) Dupree!"

"Yes (said she) Dupree. 'Till lately I knew not that your sister was alive, and therefore, for poor Claudina's sake, I was entirely silent on a subject that must have injured you, without benefitting any one I know; but having accidentally discovered Charlotte, justice now compels me to speak."

"You lived then with Charlotte's mother?" asked the Count; for the sight of Dupree had recalled such a train of unpleasant ideas to Ferdinand, that he could not speak.

"Yes (replied she) before the Count paid his addresses to her. He finding *she was virtuous*, and above all his offers, at length determined to marry her unknown to his father, exactly (said she, addressing Ferdinand) as *you* proceeded with respect to *Claudina*. This Gentleman, Mr. Keilheim and myself, were the witnesses to the marriage, which was private in her own house."

"Who was the priest?" demanded the Count.

"Mr. Reinheim, of Baden, who died soon after Charlotte was born, which gave the Count courage to comply with his father's commands, and marry the mother of Rhodophil. He represented to my poor mistress that a discovery of her marriage would ruin him, as he had no fortune to support her; but that, if she would be content to live as she had done, and permit him to marry, she would always be conscious of her own innocence, always enjoy his love, and he would make ample provision for her children.

"She foolishly consented rather than injure the man she loved. He married a wife he never liked, and was constant in his love to my mistress, 'till unluckily, Ferdinand's mother came a visiting to his house, he then fell in love with her, and basely used both wives.

"My mistress sent for him, and threatened to disclose the marriage. He laughed at her, the priest was dead, she had consented to appear at his mistress, his present wife had powerful friends, and every one would be convinced her claim was only founded on malice and revenge; he therefore defied her power.

"Just at this time a young Nobleman, high in the army, whom I shall name by and bye, who was distractedly in love with my mistress, made her the most liberal proposals of a good settlement. She, in a fit of passion and resentment, accepted his offers, and left Baden with him, though she sent word to the Count she would always hold a rod over him, and some day or other prove the rights of her child.

"With this Nobleman she resided till his death, and Claudina was his daughter. They lived very expensive, and she had no great matter left to support her children, which I believe broke her heart, for she died soon after him, leaving her daughters to the care of Mr. Keilheim and myself.

"We did what we could for them, but found it would be necessary for them to do something to maintain themselves, or that we must apply to their relations.

"We were consulting about coming to Baden, and proving the rights of Charlotte, when she foolishly eloped from us with an officer, and followed him to the camp. A battle followed soon after, he was killed, and we could gain no intelligence of her. Mr. Keilheim went to England with a friend on particular business, and advised me to go to Suabia with Claudina, and make her known to her father's brother, who would doubtless provide for her. I took the journey, and came to the Nobleman's house; to my great vexation he had been gone abroad above three years, and nobody knew if he was alive or dead."

"What was this Nobleman's name?" demanded the Count, much agitated.

"Count M*** (replied she.) I believe *you know him.*"

"Good God! (exclaimed he) but go on."

"Well (said she) after abundance of inquiries, I could hear of no relation likely to be of service to Claudina; I therefore took a small house in the suburbs of Baden, to wait for the return of her uncle, and in the hope that her beauty might get her provided for: I also expected the return of Mr. Keilheim, when I intended making myself known to Count Renaud, and demand of him some provision for keeping his secret.

"In a short time after the Count's sons both fell in love with Claudina. Rhodophil wanted her as a mistress, Ferdinand courted her for a wife, and I learned he was the favourite son; I therefore made no application to the Count on her account; the marriage took place, and Ferdinand was turned out of doors. This vexed me, but I thought time would reconcile the father to his son, so as to provide for him; but he was obstinate, without considering he had done the same thing, and they were reduced to much distress. About this time I heard from Mr. Keilheim that his friend was dead, and had left him some property; that he was ill at Hamburgh, and desired me to come to him. Glad to be no longer a burthen upon Claudina, and willing to save her from the sorrow of parting, I went away without taking leave.

"I contrived, however, to hear of her, and was rejoiced to learn the Count was dead, Ferdinand and she provided for, and living at the Castle, not then believing Charlotte was alive, I thought myself free from the whole business, and troubled my head no more about them. This, Gentlemen, is the whole story."

CHAPTER X.

She had repeated every circumstance with such exactitude, and without the least hesitation, there seemed a degree of probability in the story not easily to be controverted, that both the Count and Ferdinand were staggered and confused.

The Count well remembered, that his elder brother was said to have taken a mistress with him from Baden, and he now was struck with the recollection that when he beheld little Charles, the features seemed familiar to him, his was an exact copy of his mother's face, and he had no doubt but she resembled her father.

Turning to Ferdinand, "Claudina then was my brother's child, and *I* have an interest in your sweet boy."

Ferdinand was deeply engaged in revolving Dupree's story. Quickly recollecting himself, said he, "You say, that you left us suddenly to spare Claudina the pain of parting; but was it necessary to *rob* us, to carry off the few valuables we had, and leave us in distress? Was it consistent with your love for her, never to write, or give any account of yourself?"

"What (said the Count) was you robbed?"

"Yes (answered Ferdinand) on rising one morning we found the door on the latch, and the drawers emptied."

"I know nothing of that (said Dupree) I cannot answer for any person's getting into the house after I left it."

"But you *shall answer for it* (cried the Count, with joy dancing in his eyes.) Within there!" The officers entered, and instantly seized all three. Ferdinand then spoke:—"I charge *you*, Dupree, with robbing me, with entering into a vile conspiracy against me, and these persons as your accomplices."

"You shall instantly go to prison, and remain confined on my charges, till I have discovered the whole of your vile plot, which will not be long first (added the Count.)—There is a Gentleman in Baden, you little think of, who will witness to your frauds."

This last speech threw the man and woman into great confusion, though merely an impromptu of the moment.

"For *you* (said Ferdinand to Fatima)—whatever is your name, base, unprincipled woman, foolish as wicked; by gentleness and contrition for your errors, I may say crimes, you might have obtained from me a comfortable provision for life; by fabricating this compilation of falsehoods, by joining with this worthless pair, whose abandoned principles early sowed the seeds of corruption in *your* mind, you have entirely shut my heart against you, and the robbery you committed on Heli will prove the depravity of your mind.

"The valet of Count Wolfran now lives with a friend of mine. The villains who robbed you of the diamonds which you plundered from your benefactor, they are now in custody, and soon will your story come before the public, as Heli has instituted a criminal process against you.

"*That name* I have been so solicitous to save from the disgrace of giving birth to a wretch like you, can no longer be injured, for such a mother may be supposed to have given many fathers to her children, and any depositions from such infamous persons can only be treated with contempt. Officers take them to prison."

Fatima stood with a sullen intrepidity that both shocked and surprised them. The man changed colour, and was silent, not a syllable had he spoken; but when the officer led Dupree to the door, that cowardice generally attendant on a conviction of crimes, at once took from her all the courage she had assumed. "Stop, stop," she cried, and falling on her knees, "Save me from a prison, preserve me from punishment, and I will confess all."

That moment Fatima, who stood near her, snatched a dagger from her side, and quick as thought stabbed Dupree, and then plunged it into her own bosom; both fell. The action was so sudden, so unexpected, that no one was in time to prevent her.

Ferdinand was inexpressibly alarmed; he ran to her, as the Count did to Dupree:—"Rash, unhappy Fatima! what have you done? Let some one fly for a surgeon."

"*He is at hand*," said she, faintly, "death will soon preserve me from the shame of detection and punishment; that abandoned wretch is the cause of this, she suggested the scheme to ruin you. I lived long enough in Turkey to learn the use of a dagger."

"Wretched girl!" said Ferdinand, agonized by this scene, "why did you doubt my mercy, or generosity?"

"Because I scorned to humble myself, or sue for favours.

"Heli, you, and all are revenged, and I am beyond your power."—These were the last words she spoke; in a few minutes all was over!

Ferdinand, agitated in the most dreadful manner, accused himself for rashly irritating such a mind as her's, and was exceedingly shocked at so dreadful a catastrophe to the life of an unprincipled woman.

Dupree's wound did not appear to be so dangerous, the blood was stopped, and she was taken to another room; the man was detained in custody in the house for the present. The surgeon came, and examined the wound; it was a doubtful case, he said, and could not as yet be decided upon. After it was dressed, she desired to see Ferdinand and the Count.

"I may now (said she) confess the truth; the story of the marriage *was false*. My mistress left a good sum of money behind her. Keilheim is my brother: We lived upon it while it lasted, but he gambled a good deal, and it soon went. I had intended to make a good price of Charlotte, but she disposed of herself, and I had only a trifle; then I determined to apply to Count M***, who really is uncle, by the father, to your late wife; but he was abroad.

"Keilheim went as a valet de chambre to an English Gentleman, and left me what he could. I settled at Baden, and had an intention of applying to Count Renaud, and passing Claudina upon *him* as *his daughter*, by saying she was older than she was; but then I feared he might take her from me to provide for her, and I should only get a trifle, as I know he never liked me; therefore I thought the only way was to sell her for a good price. You fell in love with her; I had other offers which I wanted her to accept; but she loved you, thought as you would marry her she might one day have a title, and a fortune; the rest you know.

"I heard from my brother; his master was dead, and he had *secured* to himself all his effects. He was returned to Ratisbon, and proposed I should come and live with him, as he had opened a gambling-house. *I did* take from you—all I could, and went to him.

"One day, going through the streets, a short time since, I passed a young woman, who seemed to look earnestly at me, and presently pronounced my name; I turned, it was Charlotte.

"Overjoyed at meeting, I took her home. She there told me her whole story of being carried to Turkey, meeting with you, returning to Vienna, and being carried off from the Turk by a Count, who was killed by Heli; upon which she fled from him with a box of jewels the *Count had given* to her.—She intended to go to England, but crossing some mountains she was set upon by ruffians, and robbed of all her property, and had travelled on to Ratisbon, by the little trifle left in her pocket. In this city she that day arrived with a design to make the most of her beauty, with an Englishman if possible, and then leave Germany.

"Keilheim had been unlucky at play; we were something distressed; the kindness you had shewn to Charlotte made me believe it easy to impose upon you. We set an inquiry on foot about you, heard that Claudina and your brother were dead; we then formed this scheme, which has turned out so fatal to Charlotte, and, I fear, to myself."

This confession was made at intervals, as she had power to speak, and amazed the Gentlemen at such a regular system of vice as those wretches had long pursued; but Providence had at length overtaken them, nor would suffer the innocent to be a victim to such abominable duplicity.

In vain may the wicked hope to deceive the virtuous and unsuspecting mind, unobserved and undiscovered; there is a watchful and unerring eye, to whom all their black and artful schemes are laid open, and who, in its own good time, defeats the machinations of the wicked, and brings the offenders to the punishment they deserve.

The wretched Dupree languished three days, and then expired of a mortification.—Keilheim was taken to prison, and being convicted of entering into a conspiracy to injure Ferdinand, was condemned to perpetual imprisonment, which happily prevented *him* from extending his crimes in future.

This strange and tumultuous business exceedingly deranged and hurried Ferdinand; the Count had written a detail of it to Mr. D'Alenberg, who was greatly concerned for the anxiety it must have given to his friend; nor was his lovely daughter less affected; she added a postscript to her father's letter that more effectually calmed his spirits, and restored his serenity, than a hundred arguments from the Count on the folly of indulging regret for such a character as Charlotte's.

"I must ever pity her fate (said Ferdinand) deprived by her birth of the precepts and example of a *virtuous* parent, her mind was contaminated before she was of an age to acquire any fixed principles. No father to own, or support her, left, deserted by every connexion, and consigned to the trust of such depraved wretches: Ah! my friend, who can wonder at the excesses that followed, and the ruin that befel two unfortunate young women!

"Let the seducer of innocence but reflect one moment on the crimes he propagates, the destruction he meditates, and the dreadful consequences of his success; let him but reflect on the accumulated sins which may be multiplied on his head by the unfortunate beings he may give existence to; let him but extend his views beyond his own selfish gratifications, and he will shrink with horror from the seduction of innocence, and be himself the guardian of that honour, on which depends the happiness or misery of those unborn!"

The Count most readily subscribed to the truth of those observations, but to change the immediate subject that distressed him, he congratulated himself on the connexion he claimed with little Charles.

"When you marry (said he) I claim him as my companion, nor must you deny me; Mr. Dunloff shall reside with him; we shall, I trust, often enjoy each other's society, and you will judge whether I perform my duty or not."—Ferdinand could not, without wounding the feelings of his friend, refuse a request so generous and affectionate; he therefore accepted it in the warmest terms of acknowledgment: "He shall have two fathers (said he) and hold a divided affection that will gratify us both.

"It is time now (added he) that I should perform a duty that both affection and gratitude demand. I know it was the intention of my late dear father to have provided handsomely for my worthy Ernest; that trust happily devolves on me: Souls like his are above pecuniary reward, nor does he want it, farther than to have the power of enlarging his benevolent purposes; therefore I must add other gratifications to prove my sense of his worth." He then rang the bell, and requested to speak with Mr. Ernest. The good old man came in, pleasure dancing in every feature to attend the commands of his loved master.

Ferdinand desired he would be seated.—Ernest looked at the Count. He translated the look: "My good friend, pray be seated." He immediately complied. "My dear Ernest (said Ferdinand) the packet Mr. Dunloff delivered to me, after the death of my brother, contained little more than he himself acquainted me with, and when I had perused the contents I committed it to the flames, and with it all resentment for past injuries.

"I have forborne from that time to enter on the subject. This Gentleman you know to be the unfortunate Claudina's uncle, I therefore speak freely before him; it can be attended with no ill consequences now, if I ask you where she resided? where she died?"

"In a small house, Sir, on the skirts of the Forest, with a worthy man and woman, who had known better days; but were reduced to be pensioners to your good father, the late Lord; it was one of the things that gave me a suspicion against that will, that no mention was made of this worthy pair: I had recollected the sending for the lawyer, and the clerk's being shut up, and my heart presaged that a will, dictated by resentment, would be cancelled or altered.

"The will produced therefore surprised me, because I knew it was the hasty work of a moment. After the funeral I inquired for this clerk; he had left his master. This confirmed me in my suspicions, but they availed nothing. I once or twice dropped a hint to the late Count, which I saw alarmed him; I believe he feared and hated me.—Pardon my prolixity, Sir.

"This worthy couple that I was speaking of, were strangers to every one in the Castle but myself. When Madam Claudina opened her mind to me, and resolved to quit the house, I went there, said it was an unfortunate sick Lady and her child, who wished to remain entirely unknown and unseen. They received her with pleasure; there she lived repentant, and her health soon fell a sacrifice to the remembrance of her errors. The news of your death closed the scene."

"And where is this worthy pair at present?" asked Ferdinand.

"In the same house, Sir."

"Who supports them?"

"Their *wants* are *very few*; their little garden and a cow supply the *chief* of them."

"And *you the rest*, good and respectable man! (cried Ferdinand) what a heart is yours! Kings might envy *your* feelings, for justice and charity preside over them."

At that moment dinner was announced. Ernest arose: "Stop, my *friend* (said Ferdinand) this day ends *all other* distinctions between us; *my* heart swells to imitate your's; henceforth be always near me; teach me by your example to be loved in my youth, and revered in my decline of life, *like you.* Yes, *you* are the *father* of my affections, the friend of *my* friend," putting his hand into the Count's, who pressed it with both of his; "no longer my steward, but my companion and benefactor."

Ernest, overcome by emotions that swelled to his throat, and almost burst his bosom, had just strength to pull open a button or two, and sunk into a chair:—"Too much (said he, sobbing) it is too much, this graciousness!" A friendly shower of tears fell down his venerable face, and relieved the oppressed heart; neither of them had dry eyes for the moment.

"Come (said Ferdinand, trying to recover himself) come, the dinner waits, we dine together," taking Ernest by the arm.

"Excuse me, Sir, good Sir excuse me, not to-day, I cannot; give me time to recover myself; I cannot *obey* you now."

"Dear Ernest, obedience and command exists no longer between us; I will oblige you now, but from this day we have no separate tables. Within an hour I hope you will join us to drink a health to all our friends."

"I will, I will attend you, Sir (cried he, still sobbing) but spare me for the present." The friends withdrew.

"I honour you, my dear friend (said the Count) for the deserved kindness you have shewn that good man. Would to Heaven that such instances were more frequent, that virtue, and goodness of heart, should be the only distinguishing mark to exact respect and attention; hereditary honours, when disgraced by improper and disorderly conduct, ought, in my opinion, to be classed far beneath the poorest upright man, whilst principles, and a mind like Ernest's would grace a diadem."

That evening the Count received a letter from Eugenia, who continued in tolerable health and spirits. She much regretted the loss of her friend, the Countess; but loved her too well not to rejoice in *her* opening prospects of happiness, though she was the sufferer.

Two days after Mr. D'Alenberg wrote to them that the Countess was arrived, and that the family party wanted their agreeable society, of which due notice had been sent to Baron Reiberg.

The friends wanted no further persuasions to a visit so gratifying to their wishes; Ernest no longer the steward, but friend of Ferdinand, undertook all necessary arrangements for the reception of a Lady, whose society was to constitute the happiness of his beloved *master,* a name ever dear to his heart.

Ferdinand paid a visit to his sister-in-law, the Countess, entreated her friendship in very sincere terms, saying, "he hoped shortly to bring home a Lady who would feel happy to cultivate her acquaintance."—Her reply was equally affectionate and polite.

He commissioned Ernest to make that family comfortable, who had given an asylum to Claudina. He wrote to the steward of Danfelt Castle, offering him the same situation in his family, if he still was desirous of a change, sending him a handsome present, which, if he preferred remaining at the Castle, he would remit to him annually.

Thus, having settled all the demands of gratitude and civility, with a light heart, and a thousand transporting hopes, he accompanied the Count to Mr. D'Alenberg's.

It is needless to say their arrival was announced to the general satisfaction of the family, and Ferdinand thanked the old Gentleman, with the warmest gratitude, for shortening the time of his probation, and permitting him the happy opportunity of cultivating that esteem his lovely daughter had so generously avowed. In less than a week the young Baron made an addition to their society. Two months was spent by this agreeable party in all the delights that love and friendship could bestow; and, at the expiration of that time, Mr. D'Alenberg prevailed on his daughter and the Countess to make their lovers happy.—"Enough has been sacrificed to decorum (said he) it is now time to satisfy the demands of a tender attachment; life is short, and I wish to enjoy what remains of it, in the contemplation of my children's felicity."

The plea was unanswerable, and Miss D'Alenberg resigned her hand without the smallest reluctance to the happy Ferdinand. On the same day the Baron and the Countess were also united.

Previous to which, that Lady insisted upon disclosing to him the story of Louisa, and her own situation.—"I could not feel happy (said she) to know there was a transaction of such consequence in my life, a secret to my husband, where mutual confidence must be the basis for mutual happiness; it would also be a treason against Louisa, which I could never forgive myself, not to do justice to a nobleness of mind that has few examples." The Baron was indeed surprised, but having heard the precedent the Countess had set Louisa, when the latter was distressed and unhappy; he said, his admiration was so equally divided between both Ladies, that it was difficult to pronounce where the preference lay.

Ferdinand before his marriage heard from the steward of Danfelt Castle, who gratefully thanked him for his goodness; but said a great alteration had taken place there; his master was reconciled to his Lady after a separation of fifteen years, it being found out by the confession of a servant that the Lady was innocent, and accused only out of revenge; he was therefore now preparing the Castle for their reception. He added, that the robbers, having been convicted by the evidence of several persons, had all suffered death, and the box of jewels was claimed by a Gentleman of Vienna to remit into Turkey.—Thus ended all future concern, either for Heli, or the robbers.

Peter, who had been valet to Rhodophil, who had been privy to most of his bad actions, yet had always felt *gratitude* to Ernest for preserving his life, and to whose information Ernest was often obliged, *him* Ferdinand could not retain in his family, but in the hope that a *grateful* mind could not be ultimately a *bad* one, he settled on him an annuity sufficient to maintain him with comfort, for so long as his conduct should deserve it.

The Gentlemen and their Ladies resided one month with Mr. D'Alenberg after their marriage, and then separated, with a promise of paying each other an annual visit. Louisa, at her own request, remained with Mr. D'Alenberg to supply the place of his daughter.

The Count accompanied Ferdinand and his Lady to Castle Renaud, where the worthy Ernest was presented to the Countess in such flattering terms, that the good creature almost expired with joy.—"Now (cried he, tears stealing down his face) *now* I have lived to see my master happy; I have lived long enough for *myself*; the remainder of my days must be devoted to the service of *that Master*, whose gracious Providence has defeated the schemes of the wicked, and having punished *one error* in early youth, which was productive of so many evils, has at length purified him to a fulness of joy!"

Ferdinand, from the day of his marriage with the charming Theresa, had nothing wherewith to reproach himself, or to interrupt their mutual happiness; he found, in the sweets of that union, that perfect felicity, which must result from a connexion formed on the principles of reason and virtue; whilst, generally speaking, those marriages, contracted contrary to the wishes of parents, influenced chiefly by transient personal charms, and hurried on by rash tumultuous passions, seldom fail to be productive of sorrow, regret and reproach—perhaps of punishment and shame.—We have only to add, that in less than three years after the marriage of Ferdinand, the once unfortunate, but then happy Eugenia, was translated from a state of resignation and piety, to a life of blessed immortality:—From *her* melancholy story may be deduced two observations of equal importance to society; when a parent exercises an undue authority over his child, and compels her to give a reluctant hand without a heart; by giving his sanction in the outset to deception and perjury; he has little to expect but that the consequences will be fatal to her honour and happiness.

A parent has an undoubted right to a negative voice, to *persuade*, to *reason*, and *direct* a young and unexperienced mind; but to force a child to the altar, from motives of ambition, interest, or to gratify any selfish passions, too generally lays the foundation for that indifference, and neglect of the domestic duties, which terminates in folly, vice, and the ruin of all social happiness.

In the conduct of Baron S***, may be traced the fatal effects of indulging that gloomy misanthropy, which feeds a proud spirit and a callosity of heart, insensible to every feeling but its own gratification, which, when opposed, may lead to the most determined cruelty and revenge.

Count M*** was greatly affected at the death of Eugenia; but by their separation he had been long weaned from that excess of passion he had felt in early life, and which had been productive of so much sorrow to both; his grief had less poignancy than he must otherwise have known, and the society of his friends contributed to restore his peace, though he ever preserved a tender remembrance of his first love.

In less than a twelvemonth after her decease, he offered himself to, and was accepted by, the amiable Louisa. They had no children, and Charles, the son of Ferdinand, was the worthy successor to the Count's fortune.

The compulsive marriage of Count Renaud, from which originated all the misfortunes that attended himself and his family, and the very rash and imprudent one which Ferdinand contracted, hold out lessons of equal importance to the consideration of parents and children.

But our hero, having been severely punished for the impetuosity and folly which marked his first attachment, found, in his union with Theresa, that unclouded happiness so seldom the lot of mortals.

Sensible of the blessings he received, it was his unremitting endeavour, by rectitude of conduct, by generosity to the deserving, and by benevolence to the unfortunate, to communicate an equal portion of felicity to all within the circle of his acquaintance.

From the characters of Rhodophil and Fatima, we may trace the progression of vice, and its fatal termination!

> "Vice to be hated,
> Needs but to be seen."

FINIS.

NOTES

Rhodophil (p. 7)—Eliza Parsons appears to have borrowed the name Rhodo-phil from one of the characters in John Dryden's 1672 comedy, *Marriage à la Mode*.

Suabia (p. 77)—Suabia, now Schwaben, was originally a Dukedom in South Western Germany. It is now in Switzerland.

Somnus (p. 86)—The Roman god of sleep.

Aaron's rod (p. 134)—A remarkable rod owned by the high priest Aaron, brother of Moses, which, in addition to performing miraculous feats during the Exodus of the Israelites from Egypt, also swallowed up the rods owned by Pharaoh's magicians.

mother-in-law (p. 152)—That is, step-mother. The term is often used at this time, and is quite logical:—the woman who marries one's father is, in law, one's mother.

louis d'or (p. 154)—The louis-d'or was a gold coin, replaced during the French Revolution by the franc.

auberge (p. 154)—A tavern.

Sultsbach (p. 207)—Sultzbach is in Alsace, but Eliza Parsons may have got the name from the Duke of Sultsbach in *Foxe's Book of Martyrs* (1563).

sword knot (p. 211)—An ornamental lanyard, a decorative tassel for the hilt of a sword.

douceur (p. 223)—"Softener": a bribe.

Queen of Hungary (p. 239)—This is the daughter of Karl (Charles) VI, Holy Roman Emperor between 1711 and 1740. Maria Theresa of Austria, (1717-1780) was Queen of Hungary and Bohemia after her father's death but as he had no male heirs, her accession to the Habsburg throne led to the War of the Austrian Succession. Upon the death in 1745 of Karl VI, who had claimed the throne, in 1745, Maria Theresa's husband Francis I became Holy Roman Emperor and she his consort, though this seems to have been a technicality, she having ruled as Holy Roman Empress since the death of her father. The mention of the projected marriage dates the setting of the text to around 1736. There were numerous wars involving Austria and Turkey, among other states and nations, in this period.

Prince Eugene (p. 240)—Prince Eugene of Savoy, instrumental in the estab-lishment of the Austrian-Hungarian Empire, died in 1736, once again dating the setting of this text.

Adrianople (p. 244)—Now Edirne, in Thrace.

Philippo (p. 245)—Philippi in Macedonia.

alcoran (p. 255)—The Qur'an.

Janizary (p. 260)—A Turkish infantryman.

Pratt's-Grove (p. 314)—Here there is a strange mélange of the exotic and the
   local. Though Eliza Parsons has thus far provided an authentic geog-
   raphy for her characters, Pratt's Grove is, or was, in Chelsfield, Orp-
   ington, Kent.

Danhaet (p. 344)—I have retained this spelling wherever it appears thus,
   though later in the text, the name is rendered as "Danfelt." I think it
   likely it is a misreading of Eliza Parsons's handwriting of "Danfelt."

the old one's house under-ground (p. 347)—That is, the Devil.

lethean (p. 363)—The waters of the river Lethe in Hades induce forgetful-
   ness.

The Northanger Abbey Horrid Novels

CLERMONT
Regina Maria Roche
Edited by Natalie Schroeder

CASTLE OF WOLFENBACH
Eliza Parsons
Edited by Diane Long Hoeveler

THE NECROMANCER; OR, THE TALE OF THE BLACK FOREST
"Peter Teuthold"
Edited by Jeffrey Cass

THE MIDNIGHT BELL
Francis Lathom
Introduction by David Punter

THE MYSTERIOUS WARNING
Eliza Parsons
Edited by Karen Morton

Forthcoming

HORRID MYSTERIES
Karl Grosse

THE ORPHAN OF THE RHINE
Eleanor Sleath

Visit www.valancourtbooks.com to order or for more information.

CPSIA information can be obtained at www.ICGtesting.com
Printed in the USA
BVOW041051241011

274391BV00018B/133/A

9 781934 555347